THE GATES OF HELL

Also by Harrison E. Salisbury:

Harrison E. Salisbury

THE GATES
OF
HELL

RANDOM HOUSE

A Bernard Geis Associates Book

NEW YORK

Copyright © 1975 by Harrison E. Salisbury
All rights reserved under International and Pan-
American Copyright Conventions. Published in the
United States by Random House, Inc., New York,
and simultaneously in Canada by Random House
Canada Limited, Toronto

Library of Congress Cataloging in Publication Data

Salisbury, Harrison Evans, 1908-
The gates of hell.

"A Bernard Geis Associates book."
I. Title.
PZ4.S168Gat   [PS3569.A4596]   813'.5'4   75-10291
ISBN 0-394-49953-0

Manufactured in the United States of America
2 3 4 5 6 7 8 9   9 8 7 6 5 4 3 2   2 4 6 8 9 7 5 3
First Edition

For my Russian friends,
living and dead,
in Russia and out

THE GATES OF HELL

Chapter 1

ANDROPOV glanced at his watch, The sweep second hand was just coming up to ten o'clock. Two hours to go. Two hours to the meeting. He stared a moment at the watch with its sweep hand, decimals of a second, stop-plunger, inset dials for one minute and one hour, day-and-date calendar. Really, it was almost a chronometer. The Clara Zetkin factory had just begun to turn them out—the Strela, or the Arrow, as they called the watch—and the factory director had sent one to Andropov in a red box with a gray silk cushion, and a note expressing hope that it might lighten his work. "Time," wrote the director, "is money—so the Americans say." Andropov was not yet accustomed to the watch on his wrist. He smiled slightly when he recalled the director's note. Of course, he was just trying to curry favor, but in a sense it was quite appropriate, for, after all, whether the director knew it or not, it was one of Andropov's men who had brought back the Swiss model from which the Strela had been so pedantically copied.

* * *

Ten o'clock of a Sunday morning, the eighteenth of June. Andropov was a bit tired and more nervous than he hoped he showed. From the broad plate-glass window that formed almost one wall of his office he could see the sun pouring down into Dzerzhinskaya Square. The window was hung with heavy taupe silk curtains, but he had drawn them back a little and stood there for a moment watching the trolley buses, emerging like a queue of mechanical elephants in random order from Kirov Street, moving to the right around the weathered brown granite of the flower-planted island in the middle of the square where stood the statue of the first chief of Soviet Security, Felix Dzerzhinsky, and passing almost below his very window. The curtains were open only a few inches—the sun flooding through their translucence—but if anyone entered to talk with him, Andropov would certainly have drawn them completely to prevent detection of his conversation by laser-monitoring of the plate-glass vibrations. His own security specialists felt certain that the use of the heavy bullet-proof plate glass made vibration detection impossible. But who could tell? Perhaps, in the West some new breakthrough had been accomplished. Better to draw the curtains than expose the intimate secrets of the Minister of State Security.

Ten o'clock. Andropov could see from his third-floor window up toward the Polytechnic Institute and almost but not quite to the point on the oblong mall where Novaya Ploshchad turned into Staraya Ploshchad, site of Central Committee Headquarters, the place where the meeting would convene at noon. He could, if he wished, watch the cars of his colleagues as they moved up Lubyanka Hill from Theater Place—Karl Marx Square, as he reminded himself they now called it—and swung to the right and along the Novaya Ploshchad to Staraya Ploshchad. But he had no intention of whiling away the two hours in such a fashion. He had much to do. Most important, he must analyze with the greatest accuracy the exact situation which would prevail when Comrade Brezhnev called the meeting to order at twelve o'clock. Andropov had been up at seven and in his office by eight on this Sunday in violation of the convention against Sunday work. But there was no remedy for it. The situation was delicate at best, critical at worst, so critical that it had been 3 A.M. before he sank into sleep in his town house on the lip of the Sparrow Hills.

Ten o'clock. *Voz-18*, Sunday, the eighteenth, his watch said. The Morgans should be through customs now. The Pan Am flight was scheduled to depart at 10 A.M., but the takeoff would be delayed a few minutes by the attentions being given the American writer and his photographer-wife as their baggage was inspected.

Andropov did not feel comfortable about this search and even less, for that matter, over the one last night at the National Hotel, but he saw no alternative. The whole Morgan episode had been, in a sense, a failure, a faux pas, he supposed, although he would argue that it was a calculated gamble, one worth risking. It had not worked. He had recognized that it might not when he approved the issuance of the visas. The Morgans had applied ostensibly so that Helga could take some new photographs for an updated edition of their book on Russia. They also wanted to meet with "Russian colleagues," artists and writers, leaders of the Writers Union, their old friends, the poets Yevtushenko and Voznesensky, and to be present for the premiere of Morgan's play *Adam and Eve*, which Lyubimov was putting on at the Taganka Theater in a version adapted, or rather concocted, by Yevtushenko.

But of course Andropov knew that their real purpose was to meet with Andrei Sokolov and try to persuade him to leave the Soviet Union and come to the West. Since Andropov himself personally and privately had decided, for a complicated series of reasons, that this would on balance provide the most favorable option for solution of the Sokolov affair, he had approved the request for visas. This he did, although there had been, as might be expected, adverse recommendations from the Secretariat of the Writers' Union, from the Foreign Ministry and, as a matter of fact, from the operational level of his own ministry.

Andropov slowly and carefully pulled each finger of his right hand with the thumb and first two fingers of his left, feeling with satisfaction the slight snap of the cartilage of his middle joints. Then he did the same with the fingers of his left hand. He was double-jointed, and in moments of boredom or tension he was apt to snap his fingers. He was aware that this habit betrayed tension, and refrained from exercising it in the presence of his comrades. He knew that he carefully (but he hoped unnoticeably) scrutinized each of them for such telltale signs: for example, the slightly warmer, more liquid tone of Brezhnev's voice, solicitously inquiring after your health before imparting a bit of bad news; or the soft hesitant cough with which Kosygin prefaced any really sharp negative point, as though to slip it in so quietly that only hours later would his victim realize that he had been stabbed to the heart. Andropov had made a whole catalogue of such habits, and he presumed his colleagues were equally prescient—otherwise how could they have become and remained members of the Politburo?

He glanced at his watch again. Five after ten. At almost any moment he could expect the telephone to ring with a report from his agent at airport customs. Not that he really expected anything. And as for the affair of last night at the National Hotel—well, he might as well face it. It had been an out-and-out scandal. A disaster. One that was going to make headlines around the world, which was why he, himself, in violation of all precedent and, some might say, in violation of security itself, had gone to the hotel after Gorbunov called to report what had happened. Andropov was no fool. He realized perfectly well the fuss that the international press would make as soon as the author and his wife reached Paris, their first stop outside the Soviet Union, and reported that the Soviet secret police had entered their suite at the National. It did have to be the Lenin suite of all places, the suite where Lenin had lived in those first hectic weeks when the Bolshevik government fled Petrograd in 1918—the corner rooms with their unparalleled view across Menazhny Square and over the pink Kremlin walls and right up into the Red Square.

And, of course, it had been no ordinary search. They had carried out ordinary searches of the suite each day in the absence of the Morgans, and especially after each visit the author and his wife paid to the dacha at Peredelkino where Andrei Sokolov had been staying with the composer, Aram Aryutinyan. What they were looking for, Andropov himself could not say with certainty. But it had to be something in writing—an indictment or, perhaps, an appeal. Who could say? Some kind of a revelation or another—an even more damaging novel than *Taishet 303* perhaps. They did know that Sokolov had been working for a long time on a magnum opus, no glimpse of which Andropov's men had managed to snatch. There had to be something. If Sokolov was not prepared to leave Russia, he was equally not prepared to sit quietly, devoting himself to philosophical contemplation of the future. If he was not prepared to go into exile he had something else afoot.

The devil was that what they were looking for could be as small as a packet of matches or even smaller, a microdot, perhaps, although he did not honestly believe that Sokolov had the capability of reducing his manuscript to a microdot. But microfilm—that was a different matter. Even if neither Sokolov nor his friends knew microfilming, a manuscript could be photographed with ease with any 35-mm camera, and, of course, Helga Morgan had not one but five of the most expensive 35-mm's in existence and all of the lenses and attachments for such work.

If Sokolov had—as Andropov had hoped—yielded to the argument that the internal climate in the Soviet Union had become too hostile, and had he therefore applied for permission to leave the country, that would have been one thing. Then, let him go and good riddance. Let him make his propaganda in the West if he wanted. It would be simple to destroy his reputation in Russia and that was what counted. He could be called a turncoat, a traitor, a dollar-chaser, a hypocrite, a cat's paw of the capitalists, a running dog of the imperialists—the whole old bag of clichés.

Andropov knew it by heart and despised it. But only secretly, just as he despised the game he was now playing. But never mind what he really thought or what his colleagues really thought—the fact that, if truth were told, he believed that Sokolov's work should be published in the Soviet Union, that his indictment of the Stalinist terror and prison camps was not only just and true but in the best interests of the country; that if he, Andropov, had his way not only would censorship be abolished, but so would most of the internal functions of his own ministry. All of these facts only made it the more imperative that he leave no stone unturned in the handling of this case. To be sure, not one of his colleagues even suspected that he harbored such thoughts —or did they? He could not but recall the emphasis with which Shelest had said only last week: "I am confident that Comrade Andropov will handle this matter with all his customary zeal." There had been just a shade of emphasis on the word "customary," just a nuance. Indeed, he had hardly noted it when Shelest spoke except to feel instinctively that there was a false note there. And it was only much later as he ran over the evening's events before going to sleep that he heard in his inner ear Shelest's voice. No, he could not be mistaken. The implication was there. When Shelest said "customary" he was implying not zeal but lack of zeal. And if the implication was clear to Andropov, it was clear to others; indeed, Shelest would not have spoken had he not been fully confident that there were others who understood his meaning.

*   *   *

Ten after ten. The call should be coming through. There had better be no repeat of last night's scandal. It was not that his men had violated their instructions. At least not technically. Petrov, the detail commander, was a reliable, conscientious deputy. Andropov's instructions had been careful and precise. They were to search the National suite before the Morgans returned. They were to search again in the presence of the Morgans shortly after they returned from Sokolov's dacha. And he had authorized a search of their persons as well. But he did not anticipate that the agents would require the writer and his photographer-wife to remain apart, just where they happened to be when the agents entered the door without knocking—Morgan in the bathroom on the toilet and Mrs. Morgan at the writing desk in the living room. (Actually Morgan was eventually moved from the bathroom to the bedroom by the agents, but this did not exactly help matters.) The search was carried out in the Morgans' presence as planned. Nothing was found. The agents had carefully gone through all of the luggage again—Morgan's big pigskin suitcase with the heavy brass-buckled straps, Mrs. Morgan's two personal suitcases and the clutter of her camera equipment, the five Leicas, the worn zippered bag in which she carried her lenses, the brown canvas knapsack in which she deposited her exposed and unexposed film. No sign of anything. They had gone over the suite more carefully than ever before for what good that might do—after all, in years of searching the rooms at the National the agents knew a good bit better than the occupants where it was possible and where it was not possible to hide things.

"We checked the chandelier. We unscrewed every light bulb. We took the bedposts apart," Petrov told him. "We rolled back the big carpet and examined every inch of the parquet. We took up each square that it was possible to loosen. We inspected the stonework of the little balustrade. We flushed and reflushed the toilet, inspected the grease traps. Nothing."

Then they had taken the step which provoked Gorbunov's call to Andropov. They had moved Morgan to the bedroom, where they ordered him to disrobe. When he refused, four agents—Morgan was a large and strongly built man—simply overpowered him, stripped off his clothing, examined every inch of it, particularly, of course, the shoes, and then hand-forced his jaws open, inspected the fillings of his teeth and wound up by inserting a vaselined finger up his anus. Nothing. Simultaneously, two women agents were examining Mrs. Morgan. Unlike her husband, she had offered no physical resistance, thank God, and had instead haughtily and quickly slipped off her dress, her brassiere and underpants. "I suppose," she said coolly, "you follow the same filthy practice as the Nazis in Germany and want to look between my legs. Well, hurry up and have your look and get this charade over with. It's a blessing that I lived under Hitler and am used to pigs like you."

The women agents had done their duty, carried out the body search. Nothing.

It was at that point that Petrov had telephoned Gorbunov to report failure. Then Gorbunov called Andropov and he decided to go personally to the scene. He did not reprimand Petrov for carrying out a skin search, although the idea that the agents would employ this procedure had not entered his mind. He put this question aside for later examination, and although he had gone to the hotel himself he did not expect to find anything. Whatever it was that Sokolov had done, was doing or planned to do, he was not employing the American writer as his instrument.

No. Andropov did not go to the National hoping to make some major discovery which his agents had overlooked. Rather, he had gone for quite other reasons. It seemed to him extraordinarily important to get a personal feeling of the scene, of what the Morgans were like, of what kind of an explosion was to be expected when they got to the West, to satisfy his personal conviction that they were, in fact, a red herring, and, most of all, he now had to admit, he had gone because of Shelest's remark about "customary zeal." He deliberately wished to display zeal, and no matter what kind of a shambles had occurred at the National he proposed to conduct himself in such a way that no one, not even Shelest, could insinuate that he had been guilty of any lack of "zeal."

So he had gone to the hotel. He had met with the Morgans. He had listened to their hysterical accusations, to Morgan's enraged threat "Wait till you see the headlines in *The New York Times*," to Helga Morgan's icy remarks that "even Hitler never looked up my ass—it took the representatives of the workers' state to achieve that peak of culture." He offered apologies—thin, meticulous, correct—and then permitted Petrov quickly to review for him the entire search procedure. For the sake of form he let the men go over the bags again. Of course, nothing turned up. There remained the question of the film. He would swear that nothing would be found there, but at the customs they would inspect again, and alas, it would be necessary without advising Mrs. Morgan to pass the whole baggage through X-ray. That would wash out any undeveloped negatives, micro or otherwise. He was sorry. It would also wash out all the film she had taken in Russia as well as the stock of unused photo material. There would be more complaints about that. But what else could he do? As a matter of fact, he decided as his Zim limousine was taking him home through the empty Moscow streets that he would pass both Morgans through an X-ray exposure as well. If (though he did not for a minute believe this) either had swallowed a film capsule, that too would be blanked. Then let anyone contend that due to lack of zeal or carelessness the Morgans had been able to smuggle Sokolov's materials out of the USSR!

Ten-thirteen. The phone rang. Andropov lifted the receiver from the secure pad on which the instrument was placed. (Once again he asked himself: Was it reasonable to expect an outside tap on the telephone of the Minister of State Security? It was not. His phone was recorded continuously for his own use and his own protection. If there were any other taps they could only be placed by his colleagues.)

It was Petrov, of course, from the airport. They had inspected the Morgans' baggage again. Clean. They had searched their pockets, briefcases and pocketbooks. Clean. They had passed both the baggage and the Morgans through X-ray. They had seized two items. One was a large silver samovar which Sokolov had given to the Morgans. There was no reason to suppose anything could be hidden in it, but just to be on the safe side they held it. Yes, and also an ikon, a rather good ikon. Morgan said that it, too, was a present—from Sokolov. There could be something glued inside it. They seized the ikon on grounds that export of ancient art objects was forbidden. The grounds for seizing the samovar were that it was made of precious metal—silver—and thus forbidden to export. Morgan had made a rather unpleasant fuss. Not any more unpleasant than the one at the National except that he had shouted quite loudly in the customs hall and a good many foreigners had heard him. His language had been extremely defamatory. He called the agents "fascist pigs," "anti-Semitic bastards," "Stalinist sons-of-bitches," "Beria-ites," "Cossacks," "motherfuckers" and several other epithets of American jargon which the agents did not quite catch.

The question was, Should they let them go?

"Have they been permitted to board the plane?" Andropov asked. No, Petrov said. All the other passengers had been boarded. The Morgans were still detained at the customs hall. He awaited orders.

Andropov smiled grimly to himself. Aloud he said to Petrov, "Since you have found nothing, Dmitri Pavlovich, you have no grounds to hold them any longer. Permit them to board the plane and depart."

He replaced the receiver carefully. He was convinced now that his suspicion of Shelest's remark was fully justified. First, there had been the remark about zeal. Then Petrov's own zeal last night in overfulfilling his instructions and conducting the skin search of a world-famous couple, and now, finally, and probably most revealing, Petrov's request for orders before letting the Morgans leave the country. In other words, he, Andropov, must give a *positive* order to permit the couple's departure. The record would now show that they had left the USSR at Andropov's instruction. Very clever. His zeal was, indeed, being put to the test. It was now 10:21. In exactly ninety-nine minutes he would sit down with the comrades to decide Sokolov's fate. Sokolov's fate? Or his own?

Chapter 2

THE butt of the shotgun inside its worn canvas-and-leather case
kicked at the boy's ribs each time he took a step, although he was moving very slowly and with great caution through the reedy marsh that
lay alongside the river. It was four o'clock of a chilly October day, and
the sun already looked thin and yellow in the cloud banks to the west.
Andrei Sokolov had been walking for more than two hours and his
lips were blue. He had shoved his hands inside his jacket, but it was
worn too thin to offer much resistance to the cold, and he had wet his
feet and trouser bottoms in the bog. The reeds grew so tall here that
the boy was almost hidden and only when he pushed his body through
the thick canes did he see that he had arrived at a backwater which
lay beside the river.

As he broke through the thicket Andrei suddenly froze. There on
the surface of the slough rested a half-dozen ducks, their necks green
and shimmering and their bodies mottled brown. He dropped his right
shoulder slightly, letting the gun case slide down into his hand, and
holding his head and body utterly still, slipped out the gun. It was a
double-barreled Berdan shotgun, whose breach was intricately etched
and engraved with a pattern of leaves and flowers and a bird, a *sokol*,
or hawk, all embossed—as Andrei had been told—at his father's order
by the English gunmaker at Rostov (who was not English at all but
an excellent peasant gunsmith whose father before him had also been
a gunsmith and a serf). Andrei had already put two of his three shells
into the chambers, and now he brought it up to his shoulder. Nestling
the clumsy weapon against his thin shoulder, he did not take his eyes off
the ducks. The birds had not moved. He leveled the gun—there, the
nearest duck, a fine drake, not a hundred feet away, was right on
the hairline. His fingers curled around the two triggers, softly and
gently, imperceptibly tightening in the squeeze which his uncle Boris
had taught him. He slowly drew the fingers tighter and then halted.
He could feel perspiration break out on his forehead. It was not *that*.
Not what he had been afraid of. It was something else. He had almost

done the impermissible. He had almost fired upon a duck sitting in the water, a clear target and impossible to miss, but one which by the rules of hunting he must not fire upon. His hand trembled as he lowered the gun.

To be sure, the reason why he had almost fired was that *the other* had suddenly possessed his mind and this realization passed over him like a wave of heat from an open oven. Again he trembled. His hands around the gun felt weak, but he compelled himself to be steady. Of course, he was not hunting properly. He did not have a dog. They had no room for a dog, his mother and himself, in their little room off Sadovaya Street—no room and no money to feed a dog. He knew just what he should be doing now. The dog—perhaps two dogs should be picking their way through the reeds ahead of him, white dogs with deep ochre liver-spots or, perhaps, red dogs with silky hair—dogs named Rover and Jack. (Why was it that all Russian dogs had English names? His uncle had never told him.) The dogs should be up ahead finding the birds, raising them at his signal, and after he had fired, swimming out in the brackish water and bringing them back, gunmetal blue, mottled brown with a green stripe around the neck and a thin sliver of blood coming from between their yellow bills. That was the way it should be. But he had no dog, and as he stood there the ducks began to move on the water, down the draw, away from him. What to do?

Andrei stooped quickly and threw a clod of earth into the water. It landed with a splash near the ducks and they rose with a rush of wings. As they rose, Andrei, his eye down the dull gunmetal barrel, carefully leading the birds, gently squeezed one trigger and then the other so close to simultaneously that the two shots sounded like a single extended roar.

The kick of the gun, powerful enough with one blast and twice as strong with two, rammed into his shoulder and threw him backward almost sprawling to the ground. But he saw the lead duck and one following plummet from the air and he felt an iron band encircle his stomach and bind his chest so tightly he could hardly breathe. He ran forward along the edge of the slough—holding his gun high with one hand—waded in and pulled up the ducks, each dead, each with red staining the water around it.

Andrei dropped the ducks for a moment in the rushes and plunged his cold, bloody hands into the icy water, then shook them fiercely and dried them roughly on his thin jacket. He picked up his gun, broke it quickly, ejecting the two spent shells, and slipped it back in the case. He put the ducks in the small canvas bag tied to his belt, thrust the strap of the gun case over his shoulder and started back home.

The iron band that had constricted his chest was loosening now, but he felt a burning deep inside and the sensation did not vanish even when he started to shiver as the temperature swiftly dropped with the sinking sun. He began a dogtrot to keep warm, running a hundred paces, walking a hundred, then running again. As he ran, the butt of the gun jammed into his ribs at every pace. He tried to pull the case further around his shoulder, but this did not help. Finally he simply jogged along, more and more insensitive to pain, to cold. Even his mind began to numb. But despite the numbness, he felt a kind of coolness, a confidence. He knew that he would never pull a trigger without thinking of *that*, would never see a gun without *that thought* involuntarily entering his mind. It would come. He knew this. But it would not paralyze him. He could command his body, he could command his arms and his hands, and gradually, in time, he would command his mind and thoughts. He would bring the target into sight, and his finger would press down on the trigger and squeeze relentlessly. As he thought about this he again felt his fingers around the triggers, squeezing—he saw the birds at the start of their flight, wings whirring rapidly to gain speed, their flight flat against the surface of the water, and then there was the rock of the explosion, the backward thrust of his body under the kick of the gun, the sight of the birds faltering and falling. Again and again the sequence ran past his eyes like a film stuck in its track.

It was dark now, and Andrei had reached the outskirts of the city—scattered houses, dim lights in the windows, housewives hurrying home with coats clutched against the wind, carrying string bags filled with potatoes, onions, cabbages, a fat loaf of black bread. Now he was passing shops, their windows steamed and yellowed by the light. Trolley cars, sparks flying, clattered across the intersections.

Andrei was cold and tired, and the stubborn drive which had taken him through the afternoon was beginning to wear thin. He began to count the distance to the little flat, the room on the long corridor on the second floor of the old building where his mother was waiting. He knew that he was late and he knew his mother would be worried. Now there were more people in the streets. More lights. Even an occasional sputtering arc lamp at the crossings. The people hurried on, their heads down, pulled into their coats against the cold and the wind, glancing to neither right nor left. Andrei did not look at those who passed him, nor did they look at him.

Presently Andrei rounded a sharp corner, darted into an arched entranceway and pushed through a heavy wooden door into a hall which smelled of cabbage and that odor of mildew and rot permeating the walls of buildings whose drains have leaked for many years. He bounded up the stairs to the second-floor landing and pushed the bell of the flat on the left-hand side. Three short rings. That was his mother's ring and his own. Each room in the flat was occupied by a separate family and each had its own combination of rings. He heard his mother's footsteps hurrying down the hall, and in a moment he was inside the entryway, surrounded by its darkness and familiarity.

"You're so late, Andrei," his mother said as he knew she would.

"I'm sorry, Mama," Andrei replied, slipping down the corridor and into their room. He took off his jacket, deftly slinging the gun in its case onto the hook under his coat. His mother watched his face anxiously in the dusk of the room, lighted only by a dim kerosene lamp.

"I made a bit of soup and there is a piece of bread," she said. "I'll just see if I can warm it."

She left the room with the pot in her hand but was back in a moment. "We'll have to eat it as it is, I'm afraid," she said. "Lydia and Maria are using the stove and wouldn't let me near it. They said I'd had my turn."

Andrei went to his mother and put his arms around her. "Never mind, Mama. Look, I've got something for us."

He reached for his canvas bag and pulled out the ducks. "We'll have a feast."

His mother stared at the birds and then at Andrei. "You've been hunting," she said, her face unbelieving. "You've used your father's gun."

Andrei did not reply immediately. Finally, he raised his head. "Yes, Mama. I went hunting down by the Don in the canebrakes and I took Papa's gun. I've been practicing with it now for a long time. Uncle Boris showed me. He said it was time I learned to shoot, and I thought so, too."

His mother looked at him as though she was seeing the boy for the first time. Suddenly, a sound escaped from her lips—like the cry of a hare, its foot caught in a trap—then she slumped to the floor. Andrei rushed to his mother and lifted her head, cradling it in his arms. He brushed back her hair and passed his hand across her forehead again and again. Presently, she stirred and looked up at her son.

"Andrushka, forgive me," she said. "I could not help it. From the day your father died, I haven't been able to bear the sight of a gun. And you know you promised when you were a little boy, never to shoot, never to fire, never to touch a gun."

"Yes, Mama, I know all that," Andrei said. "But I was a little boy. I didn't understand then. Now I'm growing up. I must be able to use a gun. I know what you feel, but it is time to put ghosts behind us. I know that the gun belonged to Papa and that the gun killed Papa. But we can't live our lives with ghosts, Mama. Papa would not want that. He would want me to learn to shoot and to use a gun—his gun. He was an officer and a soldier who fought for Russia. I think that is what he would like for me and, perhaps, that is what I too would like."

As the boy talked his mother gradually quieted and drew him to her breast. Finally, she sighed. "Yes, Andrei. Your father would want this. I will try not to say more."

She pulled herself up and the two sat down over the pot of cold borscht, their spoons breaking the thin crust of sunflower-seed grease that had congealed on the surface of the soup during the long wait in the cold room.

"Tomorrow night, Mama," Andrei said. "We'll have duck."

His mother laughed softly. "Yes, of course, but only one at a time. I think I'll stay up late tonight until everyone has gone to bed and cook the ducks. I really don't want anyone to know." She sighed. "But be careful, Andrei. Do be careful. What about the gun?"

"I'll take it back to Uncle tomorrow," he said. "There won't be any trouble because he belongs to the Hunters Club."

*   *   *

Andrei was tired and chilled. He climbed into his bed on top of the two trunks as his mother sat beside the flickering lamp. For a while he watched her lined and drawn face. Then he closed his eyes and almost immediately saw again what he had seen in his mind a thousand times—his father's face, smiling and handsome and very young, looking as it did in the picture his mother kept in her locket. His father wore his major's uniform—well, not exactly a uniform. He was wearing his polished black-leather boots, his dark-blue artilleryman's breeches with their thin red line at the seam and his Army blouse. But over it he had thrown an English shooting jacket with shell pockets and leather rub spots on the elbows, and instead of a military cap he wore a plaid hunter's hat with a falcon's feather tucked into the brim. Andrei could see every detail. In fact, the shooting jacket and hat still rested at the bottom of the trunk he was lying on.

Early one sunshiny morning in June, when the air was soft and fragrant, his father had picked up his gun from where it rested against a pillar of the veranda. He checked the shells in their wallets, then strolled out over the meadow and called the two dogs. Soon he vanished out of sight in the deep grass. Later there came the distant roar of a shotgun and then stillness, followed by the faint, fierce howling of the dogs. The howling went on and on and did not halt. Presently, two men came from behind the house. One was an older man, with a long mustache and a white Ukrainian blouse. The other, much younger, was Andrei's uncle. They listened to the dogs for a moment and one of them muttered, "Something wrong." They hurried off over the meadow that rose slowly toward the mountains beyond.

Andrei watched the two men now in his mind, as they went toward the swiftly flowing mountain stream. They were alarmed—alarmed enough to run—and Andrei, too, knew that something was wrong.

His father lay out there beyond the meadow with a shotgun wound in his belly. Even now Andrei could see the blood pumping from the great wound in spurts. He could see his father's face, white as paper, his eyes closed and the two dogs sitting ten feet away, their muzzles pointed to the sky, howling.

And when Andrei reached that point in the story (which he had told himself over and over again) he had to bite his lips so hard that they bled. His father lay there dying of a wound from the gun which that afternoon he, Andrei, had fired. Even the thought always caught him in a clammy grip and he felt it now.

He had tried to reconstruct the story because somehow he knew that it was not the gun which caused his father's death. Sometimes it seemed to him that he was on the verge of discovery, seeing in his mind's eye exactly what happened at the moment when the distant roar of the gun echoed over the meadow. And then, as in a heat wave on the summer steppe, the image would waver and vanish. Finally, he had understood what his grandfather never said, what his uncle kept in silence and what lay at the heart of his mother's fear. He knew that they were not really certain that this was just a hunter's accident. They were not certain that the gun had not been turned against his father—by another's hand or his father's own.

And yet, it seemed to Andrei that logic could provide an answer even if evidence did not. How could it have been an accident? His father was a skilled hunter. He had owned the shotgun for many years and had fired it hundreds of times, thousands. How could he have tripped and fallen over his gun? This was not the answer.

Andrei knew that his father was a brave man, who had been decorated for gallantry in action, for heroism against the Germans—the St. George's Cross—by the Czar's own order. His father was a hero and a patriot and he did not turn the gun against himself. Never would he have done that.

And so, Andrei thought, there was only the third alternative. Someone else had fired the gun. Almost certainly one who knew his father, a close friend, perhaps, someone he trusted. The times had been turbulent. Of course, his father had been on the side of the Revolution. He was a brave, progressive man. But everywhere there were Whites, counterrevolutionaries, bandits. His father must have been murdered by the White Guards. This was Andrei's secret thought, his private conclusion, or his secret hope, for he believed that no one in the family really did know what happened—not his grandfather, not his uncle, not his mother, and least of all himself, to be sure, for he was not born for six long months after the day his father died.

Chapter 3

MARIA Petrovna Sokolov sat motionless beside the smoking kerosene lamp, her eyes lost in shadows. She was hardly aware of Andrei as he swiftly crawled under the coverlet on his makeshift bed. She was living again the black terror of that June day when her husband of a year, her lover of four years, had died. What she remembered most vividly was the scent of the tobacco plants along the fresh-sanded walk that led from the veranda where she stood as her brother and old Feodor appeared at the lower edge of the meadow carrying some heavy burden between them. She stood there in the soft June air, the heavy scent of the nikotina rising to her nostrils and wondered what they were carrying. She was wearing a white dress of muslin with a high waist and bouffant shoulders, and embroidered in soft natural silk. Masha, her old *nanya*, had made it for her. She was very proud of the dress and knew that she looked handsome in it, her chestnut hair, deep brown eyes and dark skin contrasting with the pure white of the gown. She stood on the veranda puzzled and vaguely concerned, but it was not until the two men were halfway across the meadow that she suddenly realized what they were carrying.

Instantly she knew it was Ilya and that he was dead. She knew it as she leaped from the veranda steps and ran toward them. She knew that Ilya, who had fought four years through the war (the year was 1918) without receiving a wound more serious than a scratch, was dead, and that she was to blame, and that nothing that ever was to happen in her life, not even the birth of the child who now lay three months in her womb, would change this.

She ran across the meadow, the long white gown swirling closely around her slender legs and firm body, her mouth open in a frozen gasp of terror, her heart pounding. Ahead she saw the men stumble, almost fall and then sink down, resting their heavy burden on the ground. Reaching them, she threw herself on Ilya's body, crushing her mouth against his, grasping his head in her hands and raising it again and again from the ground in a compulsive gesture, sobbing and quite mad, not perceiving that terribly wounded as he was, Ilya was still breathing. Then she fainted.

She had come awake in the great front bedroom on the second floor of the manor house, the room with the heavy mahogany-framed pier glass, the armoire large enough to house a small pony, and the French windows opening out onto the terrace over the veranda. It was their room, the one her parents had put at the disposal of herself and Ilya. The heavy magenta curtains were drawn and she could not understand why she was in bed. Suddenly her eyes in the darkened room caught sight of her white gown, now stained and torn, lying across a chair and she knew that life had changed irrevocably for her and that nothing which might happen, nothing which could happen, would ever change it back.

Why had he done it? Not for an instant did she suppose that it could have been an accident. Ilya had hunted since he was a child. She had been so proud of his skill with weapons, his fine seat on a horse, his manners, his carriage. He was not a Cossack, but her father had been a bit amusing about that. "Almost as good as a Cossack," he had said. There was no higher praise. But it had all come to ashes, and now she was alone and always would be alone with Ilya's child, which had not yet moved in her womb.

Why had he done it? She could not bear to think. The quarrel had been so sudden, so pointless, so banal. She could not even remember how it had begun. They had been talking of the future. And why not, God knows, now that her son was on the way—she *knew* it would be a son and so did Ilya. Suddenly Ilya was saying, "I don't know how much longer we can go on this way, dearest. Last night my old friend Leonid Borovitsky dropped by. He didn't even get down from his horse. He had a message from Colonel Sazonov." "What sort of message?" Maria had asked. Ilya looked at her guiltily. "He asked me to join them in the regiment they are forming. It's the only way, Maria. You know what the Reds have done at Pavlodar and Mineralnye Vody. And the estates of the Kolobinskys and the Dubroks—burned to the ground. God alone knows what happened to the families. Who will be next? Ourselves?"

Her mind was afire but she said nothing as Ilya went on talking. "I don't want to go," he said. "I don't want to leave my darling. But what can I do? Russia has fallen into anarchy. No one hates the Czar, the Czarina, Rasputin and the whole rotten crowd more than me. After all, I have spoken for reform and even for Revolution."

Ilya strode the room as he talked. At the university he had worshiped the Narodnovoltsi, the romantic young revolutionaries of the 1880's. But look how things had turned out. The Germans in the Ukraine. The Caucasus ablaze. Civil war. Starvation. The cattle slaughtered, the grain fields fired, the manor houses razed. Ilya's heart was in the Don. She had screamed at him: "How can you even think of such a thing with your wife pregnant and carrying your son? You fought with the Army for four years. That is enough!"

She could not bear to think of the other details. She had simply gone crazy. She had slapped Ilya's face. She had broken a mirror. She had spat out angry words like bullets. All night long she had sobbed on the big bed, door locked against Ilya. Let him suffer. Hadn't she suffered when he joined his regiment in 1914? Hadn't she suffered every minute, every hour, every day, never knowing whether he would live or die? Hadn't she died a thousand times? And even after they were married in 1917—on his brief leave—and then back to the front again . . . My God, of what flesh did he think she was made? She was a woman and he was her man and his place was beside her, in her arms, his strong body resting against hers, not running off again with some colonel and his comrades into another war.

Let Russia go. Who needed more strife? So she had said. And at dawn she slept—alone in the big bed. Once she woke briefly. Had she heard a gentle knock? She rushed to the door. No one there. She threw herself down again and slept deeply. When she awoke, the house was silent in that lonely silence that falls when all have arisen, all have breakfasted, all have gone off. She was alone; she could feel it, she could *hear* it. Slowly she dressed, her anger at Ilya returning but muted and somehow gentle and sad. How could he have left her alone all night? Never before had it happened.

Slowly she dressed and as she sat at the dressing table she had a sudden thought. She rose and swiftly opened the armoire and lifted out her white gown—her beautiful white gown. She slipped it over her head and caught a glimpse of herself in the pier glass. Instantly her spirits changed. She could not wait for Ilya to see her. She would dare him to leave her now. Laughing to herself, she skipped down the broad staircase.

The long room, half filled with mahogany and horsehair furniture, was empty. So was the dining room with its low wooden ceiling and its view through the small window of the kitchen garden. She smiled her secret pleasure. Where might Ilya be? Had he gone out on the trail, taking his horse? Idly she wandered back through the living room and onto the veranda, standing there and looking off into the distance when her attention was caught by the figures of two men appearing at the distant edge of the meadow. They were carrying some heavy burden . . . That was how it had happened. And it was she who had killed him, regardless of whose hand had grasped the gun. It was her hand that had aimed the barrel, her finger that had squeezed the trigger just as surely as if she had actually been there. Of course, she could not bear the sight of the gun, any gun. The thought made her shudder. And now Andrei wanted to be a soldier—like his father.

*   *   *

The room was icy. Andrei lay sleeping, breathing evenly. The kerosene in the lamp was almost out. She rose with a shudder and taking the ducks out of her son's canvas bag began methodically to pluck them. If she was fortunate the kitchen would be empty by midnight and she would be able to cook them. She would cook the two together and get it done before the prying eyes of one of the tenants discovered what she was about. She would be up half the night but that was better than a row and the suspicion of the neighbors.

Perhaps, thought Maria, as she plucked the down from the ducks and stuffed it into an old linen pillowcase, she had made a terrible mistake with her life. Perhaps the vow she had given Ilya never to marry again had been wrong. But she did not believe so. What matter that it was a post-mortem promise, that she had sworn it on that incredibly pure, bright day when they had buried Ilya in the far corner of the churchyard where three twisted cedars formed a natural grove? What matter that she made her silent promise to her beautiful young dead husband while he lay there in the pine box onto which her first fistful of red clay earth fell like the rattle of distant machine-gun fire?

She had made the pledge and she had kept it. She had told herself again and again that it was the only atonement she could offer for Ilya's death.

But the price. She had not become some kind of a nun. She had known other men. She would, she was certain, have simply gone mad otherwise. But she always held her feelings on a chain—never let herself go. Turning away from the man, as she had turned from the engineer Vladimir, just at the moment when her whole being urged her to throw herself forward, to suffuse herself in the strong male principle—it was as unnatural and cruel as the strange rites of the *skoptsy,* the cults of castrates which still lurked deep in the Siberian forests, the *skoptsy* who deliberately cut their genitals from their bodies, hurling them bloody and torn into the fire for the greater glory of God.

But what was God's glory in this strange Russian land? She wished that she could be certain, as certain as her sister-in-law, Tetya Sofia, or even as her mother had become in her last years, or her barbarous great bear of a father—so skeptical, so scoffing in her childhood, so shaken, so superstitious in old age. As for herself—did she believe, really believe? Not with the embracing passion of Sofia. It was Tetya Sofia, not she, who had taken Andrei to the great cathedral on Sennaya Square when they had come back to Rostov from Kislovodsk. Andrei was three and he had not been baptized. Of course, neither she nor Ilya had been believers. How could they have been in those brave young days when they were throwing down the challenge to the world of their elders, the world around them, the Orthodox Church with its cant and its ritual and its corrupt and complacent priests who always seemed to be wiping from their lips the greasy remains of a fatted lamb before bestowing the vicar's kiss? But she had believed on the bright June afternoon of Ilya's burial when she had sworn her oath and she believed now. What else was there in which to believe?

The birds were dressed now, cold and slightly slippery under her hands. She had slit their soft bellies, withdrawn the gizzards and entrails, cut off the heads with a sharp knife. It was well after midnight. She took the iron pot, the old *skovoroda*, and rested the birds in it. There was a bit of onion in the cupboard and she rubbed it roughly over the birds. Then, pot in hand, she silently opened the door and silently crept in worn slippers down the long corridor. No light showed from any room. She closed the kitchen door behind her. Please God let them all sleep on for an hour or so till the birds were cooked. Please God let no one come. Let no one see. Let no one ask any questions. Please, no questions.

Chapter 4

ONE afternoon in September of 1928, one of those magnificent autumn days for which the Don was famous—a high blue sky, a hot sun, and almost no wind—Andrei, who was ten, and his best friend Vanya Chernov bounded out of school. The boys were in training, so they told themselves, to be long-distance runners like the famous Finn, Paavo Nurmi. Every day they ran to school. Every day they ran home. The two were inseparable. They sat for hours together over their books—Andrei was better than Vanya in math; Vanya was better than Andrei in language. They dreamed together of the future: Andrei was certain that he would join the Red Army, Vanya was going to be an engineer.

"But if for some reason I don't go into the Red Army," Andrei said, "then I think I'll also be an engineer."

He was, as a matter of fact, greatly attracted to engineering. The air in those times was filled with talk of grandiose construction projects, and Andrei's mother in her eternal quest for work—she was forever being dismissed for one reason or another (actually, of course, because of her nonproletarian antecedents)—had gotten a job in the building of the Rostselmash plant, a big new agricultural machinery works which was rising around the core of an old International Tractor plant. There she had met Vladimir Setlin and his friend, Pavel Turkin, and Pavel's wife, Irena, and the Zolotovs, man and wife, all engineers, all young, all jolly, all endlessly excited by the challenge of building Russia into the twentieth century.

"Look at this," Vladimir Setlin would say to the young people gathered in Maria and Andrei's room. Andrei lay on his trunk-top bed, his eyes feverish with excitement, listening to the talk. "Look at the plan I'm drawing up. I think it's more economical to ship the iron ore of the Magnitogorsk magnetic anomaly to the Kuznetsk coal fields two hundred miles to the east than the other way around."

"Nonsense," Turkin would snap. "You've got your costs all wrong."

The talk would bubble for hours around the battered German silver samovar, the engineers drinking tea, arguing, shouting, laughing, making hasty sketches of their ideas on scraps of paper or simply drawing the designs with broad gestures in the air.

As Andrei listened he saw the panorama of the new Russia which these wonderful young people would build—indeed, already were building. Their cheeks flushed and their voices rose.

"The Volga," Turkin proclaimed. "Take the Volga—what is it now? A dead loss. Oh, we use it to ship grain and a little oil. But why not turn it into a chain of inland seas. Dam it for power. Build locks. Generate electricity. Put old Mother Volga to work for the new Russia."

Zolotov thought this was nonsense. "Don't waste money and energy on water transportation," he insisted. "This is the era of railroads. Russia must go forward, not backward."

How could the engineers not capture Andrei's imagination? They came back from the *taiga* mosquito-bitten and so sunburned they looked like Kazakhs. They told tales of running sight-lines across the wilderness and of new geological finds in the high Pamirs.

"There's no other word for it," Andrei told his friend Vanya. "The engineers are the true heroes of our times."

On this sunny September afternoon Andrei and Vanya did not go directly home. First they headed at a steady dogtrot for the bulletin board at the corner of Sadovaya and Voskresenskaya streets. Here the newspaper *Izvestia* was pasted up each afternoon. Andrei had a passion for reading *Izvestia*. The newspaper was, in fact, the first thing he had ever read. He could remember sitting in his uncle's lap in the big old armchair with its red velour upholstery badly worn, the iron springs coming through, and picking out the headlines with his uncle's patient help. He had learned to read early; in fact, had been reading for nearly three years before he started school.

Now day after day he and Vanya stopped at the *Izvestia* board on the way home, no matter how hot or how cold, even when the icy chill of winter made him hop up and down to keep the circulation going in his feet, beating his mittened hands together and boxing his freezing ears. Andrei would read through the main editorial, though it was filled with words he really didn't understand, and pore over the political commentaries and the bulletins on the great triumphs of Communism.

What was it about *Izvestia* that so fascinated him? He really didn't know, but for some reason it seemed to the rather ragged youngster on the Rostov street that there was concealed in *Izvestia*'s difficult prose a secret he must grasp—a secret which would provide the clue to the incomprehensible life that flowed around him.

"It's like a puzzle," he once explained to Vanya. "I know there is something in those words which I have to find out."

While Andrei and Vanya stood reading the paper, others also

would be poring over *Izvestia*'s reports. One whom they frequently saw and for whom they waited respectfully was old Professor Pavlov of the Agricultural Institute. He seemed tremendously venerable to Andrei with his salt-and-pepper scholar's beard and his puttyish complexion. His worn but strongly brushed black cloth coat had an even more worn velvet collar; his gold spectacles, lodged well down on his nose, were attached by a black silk cord to the lapel of a very old but very well cut tweed suit, obviously made from fine British suitings many years ago by an excellent tailor. Andrei was to carry that image of Professor Pavlov in his mind all his life, as well as the circumstance that in 1932 Pavlov had vanished. He had been arrested and, it was whispered, executed as "an enemy of the people," and a spy for British intelligence. Could it have been his British tweeds which did him in?

Vanya and Andrei jogged through the Rostov streets, lined with acacias, their mottled grayish bark giving them an air of age and dignity. A few droshkies clattered along the street, the horses wearing starched-cloth capets to protect them from the fierce black flies, the drivers lazily flicking their whips across the complacent buttocks of their nags, the passengers drowsing in the rear seats. Here and there a peasant's cart stood in the shadow of the acacias, a heavy bullock immobile in the shafts, the peasant asleep over a bulging burlap bag of grain. No one knew it yet but 1928 was the last year that sleepy peasants would be seen in Rostov with bulging sacks of grain, and unslaughtered bullocks.

The shops had not yet taken down their shutters. All Rostov dozed except for the schoolboys newly released from school. As Andrei and Vanya approached the bulletin board they slowed their pace to a walk and finally to a shuffle. In front of the paling stood Professor Pavlov. He had made one concession to the heat. He was wearing not his velvet-collared overcoat but an equally worn and faded linen duster neatly buttoned to the top button at the collar—the second button, Andrei noted, was missing. The professor was planted before the new *Izvestia* reading with extreme care. Andrei and Vanya politely stood aside, busying themselves for the hundredth time with the notices posted on the other board. For sale—a mahogany wardrobe, a Singer sewing machine, a bolt of woolen goods, a man's sheepskin coat; the employment notices—Siberian Timber Trust seeks workers, TransSib Railroad requires steamfitters, volunteers wanted for construction at Magnitogorsk; a concert at the Workers and Peasants Hall would be given that night, a song-and-dance ensemble of the Railroad Police.

Something unusual had attracted the professor's interest, an article on page one of *Izvestia*. When he had gone through it a third time he suddenly muttered aloud. Andrei and Vanya looked at each other in surprise. What Professor Pavlov had said was: "*Chort vozmi*! Devil take it!" The phrase had exploded out of him from some inner depths. He turned on his heel and shaking his head, walked swiftly down the Sadovaya. There was no trouble spotting the story which had aroused Professor Pavlov's interest. A two-column headline described the "Trial of the Wreckers," the Shakhty trial as it came to be known. Fifty-three engineers working in the great Shakhty coal center seventy-five kilometers north of Rostov—some from the old intelligentsia, trained under the Czarist regime, some not—had, it was said, plotted to wreck Soviet industries. They had acted at the secret instruction of confederates abroad, some connected with the former White regime of Baron Wrangel, some with the British imperialists, some with the Socialist Revolutionaries, the revolutionary party which was the old and forbidden rival of the Communists. Three resident foreigners were involved, too—Germans.

Andrei read the account with excitement. One engineer, it was said, caused the extracting machinery at Coal Mine No. 223 to fail. Another had approved defective locomotive boilers; later, one had exploded, wrecking a goods train and taking seven lives. One engineer had mixed broken glass into sausage. Another ruined a milling lathe by authorizing improper settings. The state prosecutor demanded the death penalty. Andrei read the story from beginning to end, then, like Professor Pavlov, began to read it again.

Vanya interrupted him: "Andrei, what's the idea? Just because the professor read the story three times you don't have to."

"I do," Andrei said firmly.

"Well," Vanya said, "I have to get home. I'm late already."

"Go ahead," Andrei said. "I want to read some more."

Vanya hesitated, then shrugged his shoulders and loped down the street. Andrei carefully read the story again. His excitement mounted. He was seized by a conviction so strong that his body almost shook. He *knew* what Professor Pavlov meant when he said, *"Chort vozmi!"* Professor Pavlov did not believe the story of the engineer-wreckers and neither did Andrei, although in this moment he could not have told why if his life depended on it. Something was wrong. He was sure of it and he was equally certain that sooner or later he would understand what was wrong and why he felt it so strongly.

Every day for six days Andrei could hardly wait to get to the corner of Sadovaya and Voskresenskaya to read the latest report on the trial. Each man was telling his story, proclaiming his guilt. One told how he had deliberately overloaded the smelting mill, knowing that if it ran twenty days at temperatures above capacity, it was certain to break down. There was a passage that Andrei read with great care in which the engineer told of his hopes for his country, his ambitions of realizing the great Russian dream and how this had turned to ashes in his work of sabotage.

To Andrei these words struck a sympathetic chord. This was the kind of talk he had heard in the long nights of conversation of his mother's friends—of their plans for transforming a backward, ignorant, rude country into the most advanced nation in the world.

Each day Andrei found old Professor Pavlov there before him. Each day the professor stalked away down Sadovaya, muttering to himself; each day he was more gray, his eyes behind their gold-rimmed spectacles more sunken; each day his shoulders were more shrunken, his head bowed. Professor Pavlov was shriveling before Andrei's eyes like the old witch in the fairy tale who had been drenched by a pail of water.

One day as Andrei approached the bulletin board he saw another figure just leaving. It was Vladimir Setlin, his mother's friend, the engineer. There was a strange look on Vladimir's face that shocked Andrei, a look he could only interpret as fear, as the look of a trapped man. Vladimir walked straight ahead, passing Andrei at a distance of six feet. He moved like a sleepwalker, his eyes fixed and unseeing, his legs moving mechanically and a little jerkily like a wind-up doll, his shoulders slumped, his head crooked.

Andrei hurried to the board. The headline on the story was black and large. It read simply: "Death of the Wreckers." All had been convicted of high crimes against the state. The twelve-year-old son of one had begged the court to sentence his father to death. Eleven men were sentenced to be shot (later six of these sentences were commuted to life imprisonment); the remainder received long terms in corrective labor camps. The executions of five men had already been carried out by a firing squad.

As if by mutual agreement, Andrei and Vanya did not discuss the trial of the engineers. Vanya was not with Andrei on the day when he saw Vladimir Setlin. The next day, a Saturday, the boys were together again. It was a *subbotnik*, a Saturday of voluntary labor, when all the population of Rostov was mobilized to go to the countryside to help bring in the grain harvest. Andrei and Vanya reported at 6 A.M. at Grade School 89 and marched with their classmates to the nearby Red October State farm. They sang along the way—all kinds of songs, including a favorite they had learned in anti-religious parades, "There Is No God in the Sky." When they were relaxing at lunch-time in the shade of a big truck, Vanya began to talk. "Did you see? The engineer-wreckers were convicted. They have all been punished."

"Yes, five have been shot," Andrei said precisely. There was a pause. Vanya munched silently on a heel of *chorny khleb*, black bread. Then he spoke again. "What do you think, Andrei? How could they do a thing like that?" Andrei hesitated. He was not sure why he had not discussed the case with Vanya. Finally he spoke quietly, almost in an undertone. "They aren't guilty," he said. "It didn't happen that way."

Vanya stopped chewing and stared at Andrei. "What do you mean?"

"Just what I said," Andrei repeated firmly. "They didn't do it."

"Then . . . do you mean *Izvestia* isn't telling the truth?"

"I don't know," Andrei said. "I don't know. I can't believe the engineers are wreckers. They are too much like our engineers, the ones we know. Something else has to be behind this thing."

Vanya continued to gaze at Andrei in astonishment. "What are you going to do?" he finally asked.

When Andrei finally spoke Vanya saw in his eyes a new fire. "I don't know what I'm going to do about it," Andrei said. "But by the time I'm grown up I will know. I'm going to find out what is going wrong. And then I will decide."

At that point a rather skinny classmate with a pimply face and thick, heavy lips blew a brief blast on his bugle—lunch recess was over. As far as the eye could see, the fields were alive with hundreds of people—men and women, school children, university students, factory workers, white-mustached old men, office workers already red with sunburn, old babushkas from the embroidery artels and muscular men from the Rostselmash. There were even Red Army men, bare to the waist or wearing purple-dyed undershirts, tanned and sweating. Andrei's mother was there with her engineer friends and their wives, as were Andrei's schoolteachers.

A Party agitator (some said he was the Party Secretary himself) had mounted a rough-hewn wooden tribune at one end of the field and was shouting slogans through a big megaphone: "All strength to the harvest," "Win the battle of the grain," and "Grain is power." A brass band played martial music and the field was enveloped in dust and noise.

There were red flags on the trucks, and red banners waved on the rostrum. Andrei felt a swell of pride as he and his classmates swept along, tossing the sheaves into circular windrows. At one side of the field a grain harvester sailed across the field, cutting a golden swath and leaving behind the bound sheaves, scattered on the dry earth like bodies fallen under machine-gun fire. Andrei and his comrades moved behind, stacking the sheaves. Far back, much more slowly, moved a long line of women, Andrei's mother among them, loading the yellow sheaves into carts to be carried to the thresher. There the sheaves were fed into the great red-sided machine, black smoke chuffing from a tall funnel and drifting lazily over the field. From a long red spout spurted a stream of flint-hard grain that filled the trucks and carts which moved across to the distant horizon, hauling the grain into the Rostov elevators.

"It's like a battle," Andrei told Vanya. "It's a battle to get the grain in on time, before the weather changes."

"That's right," Vanya said a little solemnly. "We're fighting for the motherland."

Andrei's back ached and his hands were cut and bleeding from the rough straw, but his heart swelled with patriotism and pride that he was part of this great effort—with Vanya, his mother, all the people of Rostov. All over Russia the same battle was going forward. It was one army with a single thought, an invincible army. In his enthusiasm, thoughts of the engineer-wreckers were left far behind. Everything was concentrated on this remarkable feeling of solidarity. So, he knew, his father must have felt when he marched off to war in 1914; so he would feel if new war threatened from the hated capitalists, the French and the English. The sun peeled the skin from his face but Andrei felt happy. His father, he thought, would be proud of him.

The work went on and on. Dusk fell, but they were not finished. The flicker of gasoline and acetylene lamps cut the murk. It was growing so dark that Andrei and his schoolmates began to stumble in the stubble rows as they gathered the sheaves. Finally someone shouted, "Assemble at the platform." Tired, thirsty, every limb aching, faces burning with the long day's sun, the youngsters marched across the field to the platform, where now the band was silent, where the thresher no longer chuffed out smoke and grain (it had broken down at 4 P.M.), but where the Party agitator, his voice so hoarse it hardly sounded human, still croaked away.

Andrei kept an eye out for his mother. She was nowhere to be seen. But he did see one face he recognized. Professor Pavlov was lying outside the Red Cross tent, his head resting on a bundle of his rolled-up clothing, his shirt open and his breath coming in and out of his lungs with a harsh rasp. It was only a glimpse in the flickering glare of the acetylene light, but Andrei suddenly wondered—Had the professor suffered a stroke in the heat and exhaustion? Had he done it deliberately?

Many years later, when Andrei understood much better what was happening in his country he became convinced that, indeed, Professor Pavlov had come out to the harvest *subbotnik* seeking and hoping to find an end to his life. And considering what was about to happen to him (his subsequent arrest and vanishment in the concentration camp system), Andrei could only conclude that this had been a natural, even an intelligent, act on the part of the professor.

*　　*　　*

Maria Sokolov had been tired and worn when she met at 6 A.M. with the engineers' collective. She had spent the evening with Vladimir Setlin and the Zolotovs, and they had talked in cautious but fearful terms concerning the trial of the engineer-wreckers. None of the men involved in the case had come from Rostov—four were from Moscow, three from Kiev, four from Kharkov and the rest from the Donbas. "But,"

Vladimir Setlin said, "I know one of those men. I went to the Institute in Leningrad with him. We worked together in Shakhty until I transferred to the Rostselmash Construction Project." Vladimir respected his friend, knew him to be a hard-working idealistic young man, a man really no different from themselves. Vladimir had worked in the same *Kombinat* with his friend, in the power department, installing and operating the very boilers his friend was now charged with sabotaging. "In fact, we both applied for jobs at Rostselmash," Vladimir said, his voice trembling, "and it is only chance that I got a job, and my friend, Robert, did not."

"So now what?" Vladimir said it with clenched teeth and anger in his voice. "I know Robert was not guilty of sabotage. None whatever. I know it. I know Robert as well as myself. His whole life was dedicated to one thing and one thing only—the building of a new Russia."

"You know, Maria Petrovna," he continued, "there is something wrong here, something terribly wrong. If Robert is guilty then so is our whole class at the Institute. We all felt alike and thought alike."

Maria tried to comfort him. "Dear Vladimir Petrovich," she said, "surely there is some kind of a mistake. Perhaps there is a confusion of identity. Something or someone has gotten mixed up and sooner or later it will all be straightened out."

Vladimir took a deep breath. "Maria Petrovna, I wish you could be right. I wish to God you could be right. But the fact is that Robert has been sentenced to the supreme punishment, and, in fact, he has already been executed. Shot. He is dead. There is no correction that can be made of that."

Maria had gotten little enough sleep in the few hours of night that remained and now she was riding in the back of a bouncing truck which was taking the engineers collective out of the city to the Red October farm. Vladimir put his arm around her shoulder and spoke in a scarcely audible whisper: "I must say this, though I hate to. I should not see you again. It is dangerous for you. They have called a meeting of the Party *aktiv* on Monday. There is going to be trouble and I'm afraid it may be serious trouble."

Maria Petrovna said not a word in reply but her eyes burned an answer to Vladimir. She seemed to be saying "No" with her entire being.

* * *

It was nearly midnight when Maria climbed the stairs to the room on the Sadovaya. She found Andrei there before her, asleep on his trunk bed, his arms flung out—one dangling off the trunk, the other thrown up against the wall. He lay on his back, his mouth open, breathing deeply, his thin body red from the day in the blistering sun. She had just enough strength to bend over and lightly kiss his forehead. Did she have the energy to go to the water tap in the courtyard and splash water over her exhausted body? She hesitated, then went down the steps, splashed herself with water, dragged herself upstairs again, and collapsed on her cot. Her mind was tortured. Must she be on the move like a hunted beast once again, looking for an obscure niche where for a little while she could find work that would bring enough bread to keep them from starvation—some job so obscure no one would bother to ask her any fateful questions?

Chapter 5

ANDROPOV had hardly replaced the receiver after instructing Petrov to let the Morgans depart when he lifted it again and asked that Gorbunov join him. Andropov believed Gorbunov to be his most trustworthy associate. He was not a veteran officer of the KGB but Andropov's own man, his colleague from the Central Committee, whom he had brought, along with a few others, when Andropov had been suddenly shifted to the KGB from his post of liaison with foreign Communist parties in 1967. Andropov understood very well how his role was defined. He was the Party's watchdog over state security just as Shelepin and Semichastny had been before him. His task was not simple. He was to run the KGB and the other security services efficiently and effectively; he was at all times to protect the security of the state, but at the same time, he was to make absolutely certain that the security services did not acquire, as they had under Stalin, a life and authority of their own. He was not only to protect the state by means of an all-powerful, all-knowing security apparatus, he was to protect the Party, and, specifically, the Party oligarchy against the rise of an apparatus which could, by its own efforts or by joining forces with a given political leader or clique, come to dominate the state and, particularly, to displace the ruling and ever-precarious Brezhnev-Kosygin coalition. This, of course, meant among other things that Andropov himself could not create a security empire in his own name which he might use as a stepping stone to power.

It had been no accident that Gorbunov had telephoned on Saturday night to report the fiasco at the National Hotel over the search of the Morgans. Gorbunov was vigilant in watching over Andropov's interests and as quick as Andropov to sense that something unusual was going on, something peculiar, something not exactly within precedent, which, because of its political sensitivity, the Minister should know of immediately.

Gorbunov was a rather heavyset man whose age could not be

guessed from his appearance. It could have been anything from the early thirties to the early sixties. In point of fact, he was forty-three years old, just young enough to have escaped military service in the war but old enough to have the most vivid recollections of being evacuated with his mother—his father, of course, was at the front—to a village in the Urals where they lived for two years in the unheated ground-floor stall of a peasant house. They nearly starved to death, froze in the winter and were constantly bitten by lice in the quarters they shared with two cows and a pig. Like all the other Moscow refugees they were hated by the peasant women and their children (no men whatever remained in the village) and survived these conditions until they were able to make their way back to Moscow.

Gorbunov had joined his fortunes to Andropov nearly ten years before but like any prudent man, he had built up a reserve commitment to the "other side," which in this case meant the career KGB apparatus.

Now Gorbunov responded quickly to Andropov's summons.

Andropov turned instantly as he heard the door of the office open, and with a flick of his hand, he pulled the dun-colored curtains over the window, closing the narrow slit out which he had been staring.

"Oh, Georgi Andreyevich," he said. "Thank you for coming. There's something I want you to look into."

He walked back to his desk, sitting down leisurely and motioning Gorbunov to sit as well. His unhurried manner was meant to convey to Gorbunov not only his customary self-confidence but his lack of nervousness. Manner, Andropov had long understood, was at least as important as the instructions he might give.

"I'm afraid, Georgi Andreyevich, you didn't get your usual beauty rest last night," he remarked with a deliberate smile and a wink designed to display solidarity.

"*Nichevo*, Yuri Vladimirovich," Gorbunov replied. "Sometimes it can't be helped."

"That's a fact," Andropov said. "And I had hoped to get out in the country for some fishing this morning. Oh, well, we'll make up for it another time. But one more thing about those Morgans—miserable people they certainly are. They are off now to the West. Petrov put them through the wringer again at the airport. Another row, I'm afraid. But, of course, he found nothing."

Andropov paused and sighed.

"You know, Yuri Vladimirovich," Gorbunov said, "that's no surprise to me. It would have been a surprise if he had found something. The whole business was too obvious. Like a scene from one of those old spy melodramas by Pogodin—you remember? They were always filled with obvious clues—stolen codes, messages concealed in boot heels, things like that."

"Yes," said Andropov, "I'm inclined to agree. The whole thing was an act from a bad play. Yet, once you start you really must go ahead. And that reminds me—there is one thing still to be checked out. Petrov confiscated two articles from the Morgans—a fine old samovar which Sokolov gave them and an ikon. I don't know how good the ikon is. Probably not a bad one. Now, I don't for a moment suppose either of them contains any clues—but take a look. Petrov has sent them in from the airport. They should be here at any moment. The samovar is the least likely place I can think of to conceal anything, but take it apart. Maybe under the handles. Maybe engraved on the inner surface. Who knows? Maybe something is scratched under the silver plate. And the ikon—well, you know they are often laminated. It could be that a message has been laminated between the layers of wood."

Andropov paused. Gorbunov looked at him with a skeptical smile. "Not much chance," he said dryly.

"I agree," Andropov said. "I certainly agree. But after all the devil we've raised we aren't going to overlook any bets. Anyway. Take them apart and let me know."

He looked at his new chronometer. Twenty-five after ten. "It shouldn't take long," he said. "See if you can get me a report by eleven. I'd like to close this case out."

Gorbunov smiled. *"Slushayu,"* he said. "I'll be right on it."

*   *   *

It was a very short lead time, Andropov knew, but time was short. He wanted that information in hand before he walked out of his office at 11:55 to attend the Politburo meeting. He knew that by giving Gorbunov so short a deadline he was telling him, in effect, that this was a top priority matter. He did not like to expose this fact to Gorbunov but he had no alternative. Besides, he told himself, Gorbunov had undoubtedly deduced already how important the case was.

When he went to the meeting, he must be armed with at least two more weapons. He must know, if possible, what Sokolov actually intended to do and, equally important, he must know what Shelest intended. He had little enough room for maneuver. Without these two facts he might well find that he had no room for maneuver.

As for establishing what Sokolov's plans, strategy and tactics were, he had one, perhaps two, cards to play—sources which might give him a clue or even half a clue. He lifted the phone again and called his other trusted deputy, Abramov. "Step in for a moment, Abram Abramovich." Who could say—maybe luck would be with him. As to the other problem—the overall problem, precisely what ammunition Shelest had, what support he could muster—that, Andropov thought, he probably would have to determine by his own insight and analysis. As he settled back in his chair two things happened simultaneously: the door opened, admitting Abramov, and the telephone rang. Andropov's hand moved instantly to the instrument. That the call had been rung through at the moment Abramov entered meant that one of his Politburo colleagues must be on the line. Andropov's standing instruction was that no calls—except from *there*—were to be put through while he was with a visitor. He raised the telephone to his ear, saying, "*Slushayu*," while signaling Abramov to take a seat.

Chapter 6

ANDREI Sokolov had been asleep on his trunk bed long enough so that as he awakened he thought it must be morning. But it was still dark, and he realized that what had awakened him was the soft sobbing of his mother. He saw her sitting at the table, and beside her, holding her closely with one arm around her shoulders was the engineer Vladimir Setlin.

Andrei closed his eyes. Yet, he could not help hearing the engineer say, "You know how much I hate this. You know I would never say it if I were not thinking of you, Maria Petrovna. But I am afraid of what is going to happen in our engineering collective. We have had three meetings already to discuss the trial of the fifty-three. Perhaps I am too panicky. But I know there is going to be trouble. Bad trouble. If I can—and I really am not at all sure that it's possible—I will get out myself. I applied a week ago to the Timber Trust. They need engineers in Igorka. God knows I don't want to go to the depths of Siberia. But I can see the trouble coming. Actually, it's already here. As for you, dearest Marusha, you are non-Party. You can slip away instantly and quietly. You must not stay and become a sacrifice—to God knows what. You must leave immediately."

His mother continued to sob and Vladimir Setlin tried to comfort her. Presently, Andrei heard his mother whisper, "Oh, Valya. I'm so tired. So worn out. Constantly on the run from one little job to another. I've never done anything wrong. I try my best to do my work and I do it well and work hard and long and yet—this happens, again and again."

She paused and Andrei heard nothing for a while. Then his mother resumed: "You know, Valya, were it not for Andrei, were it not for my boy—I do not think I would go on. It would be so easy to end it. So easy and so peaceful."

Vladimir interrupted her: "No, no, Maria Petrovna. You must not talk like this."

"Oh, I'm not going to do anything to myself. Of course not. And in the morning I'll hand in my resignation. I'll say I can't carry on the work and look after my child as well, and they will accept it quickly. And then I will start the hunt all over again. But I'm so tired, Valya. So tired. You have no idea. And you will be going away. And all my friends will leave again and we will no longer sit around the table, dreaming our dreams, talking about changing the world, talking about building a new Russia . . ."

She sobbed quietly and was still sobbing when Andrei once again dropped off to sleep.

* * *

Andrei's mother did not get another job. She made the rounds but no work was to be had. Andrei remembered those weeks as among the hardest of his childhood.

One evening they had an unexpected visitor—Andrei's uncle Boris. Andrei admired his uncle, almost to the point of hero worship. He saw in him, in some sense, a surrogate of his father. His uncle, like his father, loved hunting and guns and he, too, had been in the Army. His hobby was automobiles. Indeed, as he had often told Andrei, he had owned, in the old days, one of the few Rolls-Royces in Russia. Boris became almost poetic when he talked of it. "You can't imagine how beautiful it was—dark wine-colored coachwork, brass fittings, gleaming black leather upholstery, genuine electric lights—a wonderful improvement over the old acetylene lamps. And would you believe it, I drove it more than 120 kilometers per hour!"

Boris had given the car to the Imperial Army in 1914 and it was used by Grand Duke Nikolai Nikolayevich, Nikolasha, the Czar's uncle, the Commander in Chief.

"When the Revolution came," he said, "the beauty, my Rolls, was reserved for the use of Comrade Lenin. But Comrade Lenin preferred a Packard, I can't imagine why. And so the Rolls was turned over to Comrade Trotsky, but Comrade Trotsky did not think it was appropriate to ride in an automobile built, as he said, for English earls and Russian grand dukes, and so, in the end, the Rolls was given to the Commissariat of Foreign Affairs." There it apparently was felt that the elegant machine shed dignity and status on Commissars Chicherin and Krestinsky in their dealings, necessary and inevitable, with the frock-coated and gray-spatted diplomats of the international bourgeoisie.

Andrei's uncle had described the Rolls so many times that Andrei could see it when he closed his eyes. His uncle had even shown him a rather faded snapshot. "That was taken by a genuine Brownie Kodak, one of the first to come into Russia before the war," Boris said. "And I still have it. But, of course, I can't get film for it." That snapshot showed his uncle at the steering wheel, and beside him, his aunt, wearing a picture hat with flowers to which an ample driving veil was attached. In the rear seat sat Andrei's mother, very young and laughing, also in a wide-brimmed hat. Beside her was the rather blurred figure of a man whose identity Andrei did not know except that it was not his father.

Boris was an excellent mechanic. He knew automobiles and motors inside out. When the Revolution was over and the family fortune (mostly his wife's) largely dispersed, he got a job, first at a truck maintenance center and later as a bus driver. These proletarian occupations stood him in good stead when, as repeatedly occurred, one local Chekist or another launched an inquiry into his bourgeois origins.

What boy would not worship an uncle who was a master of automobiles, a sportsman, a member of the Gun Club and later the Hunters Society, a man who spoke of the world in broad horizon, who told stories of the spas of Germany, Bad Nauheim, Karlsbad, the Riviera, Cannes, Paris, Berlin, St. Petersburg? Furthermore—and this was important to Andrei, especially in his chauvinistic youth—Boris had supported the Revolution, had welcomed its coming and loyally worked, or so he insisted, for its success. Nevertheless, there was something about Uncle Boris that had bothered Andrei as far back as he could remember. What was it? Why, he once asked his mother, did his uncle laugh so loudly, too loudly? "And why, Mama, don't Uncle Boris's eyes change when he smiles? They just go on staring at you."

His mother had no answer to the question. Later it struck Andrei that Boris was the hero of every story Boris told and that whenever anything went wrong in one of these stories—he was arrested, lost money in a business deal, failed to bring down a brace of ducks, missed a shot at a wild boar—it was never the fault of Boris.

On the evening of his uncle's unexpected visit, such negative thoughts were far from Andrei's mind. Maria Petrovna was then deeply despondent. It had been more than a month since she had given up her job with the engineers, and except for a chance to work as a porter or a sidewalk vendor of cigarettes, not a job had she found available. Boris had not been in Rostov for two years, not since he had moved with his wife to Armavir. Now he had dropped from heaven, as it were, bubbling with good spirits, teasing his sister, laughing at her complaints, ridiculing the idea that she couldn't find work, telling one story after another of his adventures (he had had another run-in with the local OGPU, which was why he had taken to his heels and suddenly returned to Rostov), all in a manner so hearty and warm that even his desperate sister found herself responding to his gaiety. Boris then pulled out of a battered leather valise a bottle of excellent Georgian Tsinindali wine, a long piece of fat sausage, three cucumbers, several very large tomatoes and two white onions, which he had bought from peasant women, planted them down on the table and announced, "Come now, Maria. We shall have a real *pir*, a feast."

And they did have a feast. Maria had little to contribute—a box with half a dozen chocolates (the remains of a present from the engineer Vladimir) which she had been hoarding, a jar of salt pickles and half a loaf of black bread. But *pir* it was, and Maria even became gay after the second glass of the Tsinindali. But the wine could not entirely ease her troubled mind; she turned to her brother and said, "You know, Boris, I must find work—otherwise we soon will starve."

Boris thought a moment, then slapped his hand down hard on the table. "I've got it," he said. "If my old friend, Herman Schneider, is still alive the problem is solved."

Herman Schneider, he explained, was a professor who taught stenography—shorthand and typewriting. He gave private lessons.

"There's only one reason you have trouble finding something to do," Boris told Maria. "You are capable enough, but you have no special skills. Now, the Professor is just the man for you. Let him teach you stenography. You can learn it in no time at all—and then see what happens. I guarantee you'll have a job as a skilled secretary in jig time."

To Andrei's amazement, it worked out almost precisely as his uncle said. Boris wrote down on a scrap of paper the Professor's address, Dom 12/15 Ulitsa Engels. The next day when Andrei got home he found his mother excited, joyful, a new woman. "You won't believe it, Andrushka," she said. "I've done it. I went to see Professor Schneider. He's going to give me lessons and I'll soon be a stenographer. I took the old samovar to the pawnshop. That will pay for the lessons."

*   *   *

She threw herself into her studies with the passion of a young girl, quickly became skilled in her new "profession" and found a job —one which took her really by surprise—working in the local militia or police office. The surprise was that a person with her antecedents, the bourgeois origin which had caused so many troubles in the past, should find a post in the militia office, even though, of course, it was not a position of any political sensitivity. Hers was merely the task of jotting down memoranda dealing, most often, with property matters, claims, disputes, reports to be submitted to higher authorities concerning the civil activities of the police, and of typing the endless forms that constituted the links in the paper chain binding the enormous state bureaucracy together.

Her employment, it was quite clear, was strictly a product of her technical proficiency and of the idiosyncratic quirk of the major in charge of the section for civil cases. "This is a workers' state," the major was fond of saying, "and we must have a workers' culture." By this he meant technical training. He had apparently read a good deal about stenography, and as he told Maria, "I am convinced that this skill is essential for proficient police work. It will give us a scientific method of recording data and will provide a record free of the usual human deviations."

For Maria Petrovna, the job was an incredible stroke of luck. It saved her life—literally—and, as Andrei came to realize, it may have saved his as well.

Chapter 7

ANDREI slept not a wink all night. He turned back and forth on his trunk bed. The quilt slipped to the floor. He pulled it back up. It slipped again. He let it lie there. He watched the first rays of light in the sky and heard the roosters crowing in the yard behind the building. He was too excited to sleep, for this morning he was taking the train to Armavir to visit his aunt and uncle. His uncle had talked of the visit when he had come to see Maria and Andrei in Rostov.

As it turned out, Maria could not go, and Andrei would make his first train trip alone. It was June 1929. School had been out for three days, and Andrei was in a fever of anticipation. It seemed to him like a dividing line in his life, an end to his childhood. Even with all the troubles he and his mother had endured, his life seemed to him warm and secure. It seemed so to him even in those days when he and his mother had lived in the cowshed on the outskirts of town which was freezing in winter and wet when it rained. They had just come to Rostov and it was the only place his mother could get—a shed backed up to the rear wall of a peasant hut at the very edge of the city. Andrei shivered when he thought of the peasant woman, the old *babushka* who rented the shed to his mother and who poked her head into the door at any moment, day or night, to snarl, "What are you up to now? Mind you don't burn us all down." She had a deathly fear of fire. When she found Andrei alone she would douse the tiny fire on the crude clay hearth with half a bucket of water and Andrei would shiver until his mother returned.

And there had been worse times, too, which he could not remember—the civil war days of 1919, 1920 and 1921, when he was just a baby—the fighting in Kislovodsk and Mineralnye Vody. But all this seemed to Andrei to have been a time of adventure, of heroes and villains, of Red Army and White—something larger than life, like a thriller at the American movies his mother would sometimes spare the rubles to take him to.

Now, Andrei thought, he was going off by himself into the world. Alone. It was exciting, but it was also frightening.

His mother had packed his father's worn brown leather briefcase with two shirts, a change of underwear, two pairs of socks (all he had), a sweater, a toothbrush and comb, a towel, and three handkerchiefs. There was also a present for his aunt—a cake of Pears' soap which Maria had bought on Sunday at the Sennaya market. God knew from what hoard it had survived. For his uncle, there was a black Parker fountain pen from the same place.

His mother took him to the big poorly whitewashed station with bullet marks and shell-splintered plaster still plainly visible, mementos of the civil war, of the repeated battles fought between Red and White for control of Rostov. They arrived at the station an hour after daybreak. Although the Armavir train was not due to leave until ten, there already was a crowd before the ticket windows, and the station was filled with peasants with their bundles. They had slept there all night on the floor and now they were beginning to stir. Among them were clean-faced young peasant mothers, their heads demurely covered with white scarves, a decent black shawl around their shoulders, and wearing flowered calico skirts, who opened their white blouses of linen or cotton to give suck to their nursing babies from white bulbous breasts, blue-veined and rich with milk—madonnas with blue eyes, open faces, flaxen hair and warm bosoms.

*　　*　　*

In the yard outside there was a long line before the *kipyatok*, the kiosk where boiling water poured from a tap into mugs, canteens, jars and kettles. Most of those in line were men, shirtless in purple or blue undershirts. In one hand they clutched a razor and a bar of soap, in the other a battered white enamel mug. Over their shoulders they draped towels of cheap Osnaburg edged in red or blue. The men filled their mugs with hot water, then moved on to the platform and shaved themselves roughly, using the dusty windows as mirrors. Others in the queue carried small kettles or battered white china teapots. They filled these with boiling water, added a pinch of very black tea and drank the liquid with their breakfast of black bread and a bit of hard sausage—sometimes so hard they soaked it in the tea to soften it.

Along the station platform, peasant women began to appear, some barefoot, some wearing soft leather boots that were dusty from walking two or three hours into the city from the countryside. All of them wore capacious white aprons. Some had small wooden boxes on which to display their wares, others spread out a piece of cotton flour sacking and arranged their goods on the cloth. They sold cucumbers and small half-green tomatoes, piles of radishes, roasted chickens, pots of *smetana* and cottage cheeses, jars of *kvas*, heads of fresh cabbage, red and white. There were also containers of chopped sour cabbage, cups of fermented milk, *tvorg*, hard-boiled eggs, half a dozen kinds of soft cheeses, *pirozhki* stuffed with meat and onions, and also with cheese. Some rather unappetizing-looking blood sausages lay on display, near slabs of lard and hunks of raw bacon, particularly for the Ukrainians who put lard on their bread and ate their bacon raw. For finer palates, there were small paper twists of *malinas* (raspberries) and *klukvi* (strawberries), fresh picked in the fields—all of this spread out to tempt the travelers.

Andrei and his mother made their way through the throng and joined the long queue before the still unopened *kassa* where the tickets were sold. "It's not such a long journey to Armavir," Maria told Andrei. "It only took a few hours in the old days." "Then why, Mama," Andrei asked, "is everybody here so early?"

"Nobody knows in these times," Maria responded, "when the train will leave. Or how long it may take to get to Armavir. It could be six hours or twelve or even twenty-four. So people get to the station very early and queue for their tickets. Nobody knows how many tickets will be sold."

"Was it always like this, Mama?" Andrei asked. "Was it like this when Papa was alive?"

Maria glanced about her. "No, Andrei," she said in a whisper. "It was different in the old days."

Andrei and his mother waited two hours in the ticket queue, then they pushed out onto the platform. On this June morning, possibly because the crowd was not remarkably large by the standards of those times, the black-uniformed railroad police allowed the ticket holders on the platform, and in the crush Maria was able to accompany her son, she holding the precious ticket, he struggling with the bulky portfolio.

Andrei and Maria were in great luck. The train appeared less than two hours late. As it pulled to a halt, Maria embraced Andrei, thrust the ticket into his hands, kissed him, and pushed him forward in the crowd so that he was among the first to scramble up into the hard car. Soon he put his head out the third window, crying, "Goodbye, Mama!"

Maria caught no more glimpses of her son, for he had been shoved ahead in the car and jammed between the long benches on the other side. He was surrounded by people, all pushing and trying to lay claim to one little square of space. In spite of the shoving, the crowding, the jamming, everyone seemed in good spirits. There was even a young man with a *bayan*, a small Russian accordion. Soon he was entertaining the car with an endless recital of *chastushkas*—those long improvised street verses that blended one into the other; one song dealt endlessly with the loves of Marushka, a village girl whose favors were sought (and repeatedly won) by a succession of Ivans, Tolyas, Feofans, Leonids, Zhenyas and Olegs. Some passengers had occupied their wait with vodka, and now they cheerily joined in the singing.

The train had not been long under way before new vodka bottles made their appearance and were passed hand to hand after the owners, with a professional flick of the thumb, had pried off the thin red wax seals and then, with an even more professional jolt of the hand against the bottom of the bottle, started the corks with their ritual covering of tissue paper from the bottles' necks.

Andrei was tremendously excited. Because Armavir was on the direct Caucasus line, he would be retracing his steps toward Kislovodsk and Mineralnye Vody. Mineralnye Vody he could hardly remember, but Kislovodsk was different. His grandfather's house there glowed in his mind like a blood-red ikon lamp. Possibly that was due in part to his mother's stories. "I left my heart in Kislovodsk," she had told Andrei. "That was where your father and I first lived together as man and wife; that was where my father's house was, not actually in the city but in the nearby countryside."

And that was where Andrei's first memories were rooted. He remembered—or so it seemed—the old wooden manor house with its pseudo-Russian façade, the blue-painted wooden crenelations, the balconies, the carved wooden cornices, the many-faceted windows. Most vividly, he could visualize the great glass veranda—warm even in winter—with its blue-and-amber panes set into the lights so that, playing on the floor, he moved from a pool of indigo to one of yellow and when he looked at his hands one was the color of summer sky and the other was like the wine that poured from a dusty green bottle.

He could still see the high mountains with their white caps in the distance . . . the rushing mountain streams (he had been so frightened that he had cried when he was taken to the bridge that crossed over the yellow turbulent stream). Of his grandfather, he remembered most the loud voice and long flowing mustache which smelled of tobacco when he kissed Andrei. His grandmother had been a compact, red-cheeked woman, who wore a high-necked dress, a gold watch pinned to her breast and a smell of violets about her. And he could remember, too, men with red armbands and rifles in their hands running through the streets and a sound like firecrackers going off in the distance.

Andrei surveyed his situation on the train. He was lodged between the last two benches in the car. The benches faced each other and were jammed, three persons on each side. In the space between them, along with Andrei, was a bulging sack, filled with something metallic he could feel when he was shoved up against it. It belonged to a very large, very pregnant peasant woman. The woman and the sack were of almost equal size. She had managed to push the sack between the two benches and had seated herself on it, her haunches spread on either side, her belly bulging out and almost resting on the sack itself. Andrei was wedged in almost upon her. "I'm sorry," he said whenever the swaying of the train threw him half sitting, half reclining onto the sack. The woman looked at him with a kind of angry yellow light in her eyes but said nothing. Andrei's head was at the level of the peasant woman's outspread legs, compelling him to look right up the two marble-veined thighs to the point where her ragged shift half concealed, half exposed her protuberant bushy mound. When he turned his head slightly, he found himself looking across the knees of a small red-whiskered man, sitting on the bench, and obviously—from their constantly whispered and rather nervous conversation—the husband of the woman between whose thighs Andrei found himself thrust.

The aisles were filled completely, some passengers standing, others sitting with heels cocked back on their bundles and boxes. Yet, crowded as the car was, there seemed to be nothing but good spirits. Soon a man in tattered Red Army uniform, one sleeve pinned to his blouse because of a missing arm and hobbling on one leg, the other severed at the knee, and holding in front of him with his one good hand his Red Army cap, slowly joggled his way through the car, shaking his cap before him which rattled with a kind of leaden resonance with the kopek pieces deposited in it. As he made his way along the car, men and women fumbled in their pockets and found torn ruble notes or kopek pieces and deposited them in the cap. "Thank you," the soldier kept saying. "May God bless you."

* * *

It was early morning, about five, when the train halted. A day and night had passed, with Andrei dozing on and off. Now the sudden crash of the train stopping threw him against the bench so hard, his head rang.

Andrei pushed up through the forest of legs surrounding him. The peasant woman was still sprawled on the sack, only half awake. The sweat had run from her pores for hours and now the powerful stench made Andrei giddy. He could see that the train had stopped on the open steppe across which the sun's first rays were edging, cool and monochromatic, exposing the land flat and without shadow. Presently, horsemen came clattering alongside the train—Red Army men. They positioned themselves beside each car and an officer shouted through the open window: "Everybody out! Bring your things and line up alongside the car."

The frightened passengers moved slowly, as in a dream. Women looked at each other unbelieving. They began to shamble through the exits, carrying their string bags, their parcels neatly tied with cord around white linen, their bags, their sacks, their battered boxes and false leather suitcases.

The face of the great peasant woman on the sack had gone white as milk. Her husband was trembling. Their eyes met and then wandered and the woman put both of her hands to her belly as if she was holding in the baby that rested in her womb, trying to quiet it.

Andrei shuffled out with the crowd, leaving them sitting there, paralyzed with fear. He slipped down the train steps and stood beside the car with the other passengers. The sun at the edge of the steppe had risen enough so that it appeared as a great red ball, its rays seeming to follow the curvature of the earth, just high enough to cast a blinding light in the eyes of the huddled passengers. Presently, the car was emptied. Everyone had emerged—everyone but the peasant woman and her trembling husband. An officer dismounted, a tousled-haired blond youngster with a small black Nagan revolver in hand. He motioned to one of his troopers who slipped from his horse, swinging his carbine into his hands. The two mounted the steps, and entered the train. Andrei's eyes followed them. The last thing he noticed was that the trooper's boots were worn-out, the soles had come loose and they slapped the steps as he entered the train.

The passengers stood silently in the thin morning sun, looking at no one, staring into open space. It was as though each was trying to pretend to himself that he was not there, that nothing, in fact, was happening. Andrei listened intently. He heard the officer speak, a halting, rather high-pitched voice. Then the woman, the great peasant woman. He could not hear the words. Her voice sounded like the uncertain whine of the wind in the chimney. Then a sharper word from the officer, possibly a command. Then a shriek, a shriek such as his ears had never heard, and quickly a pop like the sound of a blown-up paper bag burst by a blow of the hand, and a wail that must have come from the woman's soul. Then another pop. Then quiet. Absolute quiet. A moment later the officer appeared at the car door. His face was blank and drained of blood.

"Come, give a hand," he shouted to another trooper. The crowd waited in a stillness so deep Andrei could hear his own breath moving in and out of his windpipe. Somewhere in the distance, very far away, he heard a cock crow, and nearer, up the line of the train, the metallic sound of heavy equipment being moved . . .

Andrei could feel the hair on the back of his neck rising as he stood outside the car, his father's battered briefcase clutched tightly in his hands, as he waited what seemed an endless wait. Then he heard the shuffle of the soldiers' boots. They were carrying something from the train. Andrei saw first the broad back sides of the troopers, bent over and walking backwards, then a heavy burden. It was the great sack on which the big peasant woman had been sitting. They carried it to the side of the train, dropped it with a clatter and then reentered the car.

There was a brief wait, then the troopers' backs emerged again; again they were bent over, but this time it was the peasant woman they carried, her head rolling to one side, blood soaking the front of her cotton blouse, dripping over her still bulging belly, coursing down the heavy thighs to the ground. The sweating troopers carried her from the train and dropped her beside the sack. A murmur rose from the passengers like the rising swell of the surf. The horsemen sat nervously on their seats and some reached toward their carbines. Andrei swallowed and clenched his teeth. He could not really understand that this woman whose thighs had been jammed into his face, whose sweat he had breathed, whose body heat had billowed up from under her skirt and passed over him like waves from an oven door, this woman so powerful, so alive, was lying a few feet away from him lifeless, her blood staining the hard ground.

As Andrei watched, transfixed, the soldiers emerged again. This time their burden was not so heavy. The ragged bearded husband also was covered with blood. His head had rolled back, the whites of his eyes showing. The soldiers dropped him roughly beside the woman, and Andrei saw that the man was not yet dead. His mouth was open and his lungs were drawing in huge gulps of air, like a frightened rabbit held in the hunter's hand.

All along the train now there was a flutter of agitation. Two men on horseback rode up—apparently the commanding officers. They counseled briefly with the unmounted officer. There was another distant pop, then a succession of them up toward the forward part of the train. No one moved. In the distance a woman was screaming. Then a sharp command passed down the line: "Passengers reboard."

Andrei scrambled into the car, automatically going back into the cul de sac he had shared with the peasant woman. The floor of the car was sticky and it was not until much later that he realized this was blood. By this time, jammed as before, the train was moving slowly across the endless fields. But now it moved in silence. No more *chastushkas*. No drinking. No jokes. No alms-gathering soldiers. Occasionally a child would cry or whimper, only to be slapped to silence by its mother. Andrei got up and stood in the narrow space between the wooden seat rows. Through the windows he could see the fields that stretched to the horizon. The train rolled slowly forward across the sea of grain.

What had happened? Why had the woman and her husband been shot? Were they carrying some contraband in the sack? The questions rolled around in Andrei's mind but he had no answers. Perhaps they were Whites. Perhaps the troops were frightened. Who could say? The rails clicked beneath him. The silent car was hot with the wind from the plain. The people took care that their eyes did not meet. It was late afternoon when the train finally pulled into Armavir. Andrei's uncle and aunt were waiting at the station. They had been there for six hours.

"What made the train so late?" Uncle Boris asked. Andrei started to speak, then stopped. Finally he said, "It didn't go very fast. And we had some long stops."

Andrei crawled into bed that night almost too frightened to sleep. Every time he closed his eyes he saw the peasant woman covered with blood. The thin pop of the Nagan sounded again and again in his ears.

He said nothing to his aunt and his uncle. He could not have explained why he kept his silence. Perhaps because he was too terrified. Perhaps because he sensed that they were already frightened and that this would only frighten them more. He knew, as a child knows these things, that his aunt and uncle were tense, angry, uncertain, and that his presence was something less than welcome.

His aunt told him with her customary bluntness when he arose, stiff and thick-headed in the morning, that she and his uncle had decided to leave Armavir and return to Rostov.

"It's impossible to live here," she said. "There's no culture here. No kind of life for your uncle and myself. Armavir is impossible. Everything is impossible."

He never got an explanation from his aunt of what made Armavir so "impossible," but even in his short visit he began to have some idea. Twice he was awakened in the night by a fusillade of shots.

"What was that about?" he asked his Uncle Boris.

Boris stared at him gloomily. "Who knows?" Then he added, "Better not to ask."

When Andrei went with his aunt to the market, he was amazed to find it almost deserted. Most of the stalls were empty. There was not one woman in a white apron selling milk and eggs and cheese. Only here and there he saw a morose peasant, silently smoking *makhorka*, coarse tobacco, in a twist of newspaper, sitting glumly beside a sack of potatoes. The city women walked aimlessly around the building.

"It's impossible to live so!" his aunt exclaimed. "The peasants are bringing nothing to sell. Or maybe they have nothing. They are afraid or angry. Perhaps both. What's to become of us? There's no food in the city."

"Why is this, Auntie?" Andrei asked.

His aunt shot him a dark look. "You know very well why it is. Don't ask me foolish questions."

But Andrei did not know. To be sure, the farms had been collectivized, the kulaks had been repressed, the poor peasants had been given their "rights." He had read all this in *Izvestia*. He read the headlines every day, and every day they proclaimed new victories. He had listened to the speeches in school and gloried in the banners hung up in the streets and the headlines in the newspapers. He was gratified to see the frightened faces of those peasants whom he believed must be the hated kulaks, the rich peasants who were the target of the campaign. It had started in the winter, and as with most events at that time, he felt a surge of patriotic pride. It was a giant leap toward Communism in Our Times. A great crusade. The whole country moving forward. It made him think again of the day in the harvest fields when the whole city of Rostov had moved as one—one for all, all for one.

Of course, Andrei knew that there had been grumbling, he knew there had been sabotage and that the struggle was not easy. Even in Rostov there had been talk of trouble in the countryside. And one afternoon he and Vanya stopped to watch as a long column of prisoners were driven through the Rostov streets. They were peasants from the countryside, many of them barefoot, others wearing *lapta*, shoes of woven bark. The men had gaunt faces, strong, dust-covered bodies. Their eyes roved the sidewalks and some were muttering "*Voda, vodidchka,* water, a little water" under their breaths so that the guards, young tow-headed lads with red armbands and Tommy guns, would not hear.

But it was only in Armavir that it struck Andrei that something had gone seriously wrong. Here in Armavir it was not just talk or rumors. It was the empty stalls in the market. The queues in the food stores. Though Andrei was used to queues, these were a block long, and even after the shop doors clanged shut—the heavy iron partitions put up and the great iron locks as big as his double fist slammed into place—the people still stood there, waiting. What were they waiting for? Andrei did not know, but he understood that it was not a question which he should ask aloud.

Chapter 8

THE voice on the other end of the line was that of Maximov, Brezhnev's personal secretary. "One moment," he said. Andropov glanced at Abramov. Ordinarily he would have asked him to step outside, but this morning he felt it did no harm to have his deputy hear him talking with the Party Secretary.

"Good morning, Yuri Vladimirovich," Andropov heard Brezhnev saying.

"Good morning, Leonid Ilych," he replied.

"I do not want to trouble you," Brezhnev said, "but for the sake of convenience we will meet here at the Kremlin instead of at Staraya Ploshchad. Do you have any objections?"

Andropov answered swiftly. "No, Leonid Ilych," he said. "No objections. Appropriate measures will be taken. It is only that, in general, on Sundays I am convinced that Staraya Ploshchad is to be preferred."

"I understand," Brezhnev replied. "So we will meet at twelve."

Andropov put the telephone down, but instantly picked it up again: "Get me Gorbunov." In a moment Gorbunov came on the line. "The meeting place has been shifted from Staraya Ploshchad to the Kremlin," he said. "Give the appropriate instructions."

As he turned to Abramov several thoughts ran through his mind. It was not just "appropriate" that Brezhnev had called, it was somewhat more than that. The shift of the meeting place was not unusual, but such a message would ordinarily have simply passed between Brezhnev's personal secretariat and Andropov's. On the other hand, since the shooting incident at the Borovitsky Gate in which Brezhnev's chauffeur was killed, Andropov had very strongly laid down the line that meetings of the Politburo at the Kremlin during the daytime hours on weekends did constitute a security risk. The reason was simple. The Borovitsky Gate was used for civilian foot traffic in and out of the Kremlin. On weekends there was certain to be a mass of tourists. Because of the fact that the great Armory building was built flush to the Kremlin street, there was no way to screen incoming motor traffic from foot traffic on the sidewalk a few paces away. The alternative might be to close the Kremlin at those times when the Politburo was meeting or to throw up police barricades which would prevent the public from using the Borovitsky Gate. While either measure could have been justified on security grounds, it was contrary to the political line that sought to contrast the ease and freedom of access to the Kremlin with the locked gates and barred doors of Stalin's era.

Andropov had even toyed with the notion of reopening the long-sealed Tainitskya or "secret" gate to the Kremlin—the one that once had given access to traffic from the Moscow River. He could then quite easily have constructed a completely secure underground tunnel beneath the Kremlin gardens right into the great Kremlin Palace. In fact, the underground passages existed from ancient times and merely needed to be enlarged. But he quickly found that no sentiment for such an undertaking existed among his colleagues, so he simply shelved the idea for a more propitious moment.

For the moment, Andropov put aside any real analysis of the Brezhnev call. He turned to the waiting Abramov. "Abram Abramovich," he said, "I need two things rather quickly, in the next hour or so, as a matter of fact. What is the exact nature of the secret work with which the author Sokolov has been busy during the last year or more? I know we have not been able to lay hands on it. But as I recall, we have an uncashed chit. Should we not invite his friend Krasin to the flat on Gorky Street and see what he can tell us? As you know he owes us one."

"Quite right," Abramov said. "That is why we never pressed charges against him. I'll do it immediately."

"And another thing, Abram Abramovich," said Andropov. "You told me a week ago that Louis was on to something about Sokolov. If it wasn't simply more of his fancy talk, he should be able to deliver."

"Very good," Abramov replied, rising to go.

"Sorry to hurry you," Andropov said, shaking his shoulders. "But you know how it is with these questions. If the answer was simple we wouldn't be asked."

Chapter 9

WHEN Vanya and Andrei stepped out of school one afternoon in the early autumn of 1930, they instantly crinkled their noses. There was a smell of smoke in the air—not strong but persistent, acrid and pervasive.

"What is it?" Vanya asked.

"There must be a big fire someplace," Andrei replied. They looked at the sky for a telltale column of smoke but saw only a vague haze that seemed to hang over the city.

"It smells familiar," Andrei said. "But it's not wood smoke. It can't be the Opera House burning down."

"And it's not coal or kerosene," Vanya added.

The smell was pungent but not unpleasant, as though bread had been left too long in the oven or batter was scorching on a stove top.

Suddenly Andrei had an idea: "Vanya, do you know what I think? I think it is the smell of burning grain. Maybe one of the elevators caught fire."

The boys decided to have a look. They caught the No. 7 tram to the harbor docks, where the grain elevators massed like great concrete citadels. But when they got to the harbor the elevators stood untouched. No fire. Not even any activity. Not even the usual line of trucks and railroad cars discharging their golden flow from the Kuban.

"Maybe," Andrei told Vanya, "the grain is burning in the country depots or in the fields. That would explain the smoke."

Vanya was silent a moment. The same thought ran through the minds of both boys. Finally Vanya whispered, "Perhaps, something bad has happened."

A few days later all Rostov was whispering about the fires that had swept the fields—great storms of fire, like a *burya*, the terrible Siberian blizzard.

"It wasn't an accident," Andrei's Aunt Sofia whispered one night. "The fires were set. Just as in the days of 1905 when the peasants burned the landlords' houses, the red cock was put into the grain fields. They say the shooting has been going on ever since."

Andrei's mother shook her head over the story. "You mustn't say such things, Tetya Sofia," she said. "It's dangerous."

Tetya Sofia snorted. "Everyone's saying it and it's true. There's going to be more suffering this winter. I've got a hundred kilos of potatoes dug into a dry hole in the cellar. We're going to need them before March."

Rostov was a curious city, unlike any other Russian city. It was a great grain-trading center, second port in all Russia for the shipment of grain overseas, and in the terrible famine years the port never stopped work, the outward flow of yellow grain never completely ceased. Andrei himself saw this when he went down to the harbor to look at the ships. He was fascinated by the heavily laden freighters—Greek ships, English ships, French ships—hauling away the grain that funneled from the high elevators lining the piers. Even he, young as he was, found this strange. No food in the shops, but an endless stream of wheat going abroad. There was barbed wire around the elevators and the piers, and the freight trains were surrounded by Red Army men with Tommy guns.

"It's the Jews," Tetya Sofia insisted as Andrei's frightened mother tried to shut her up. "They are selling the grain for gold and we Russians are starving. So it has always been. They drink our blood, our good Russian blood."

"Tetya Sofia," Maria said. "I'm not going to listen to you. Let's talk of something else."

A grim look came over Tetya Sofia's face. "Let me tell you what happened today," she said. "I was coming out of our building when I saw this woman on her hands and knees. Her head was dropped to one side and she was crawling to our doorstep. When I came out she gasped, 'For God's sake, a piece of bread.' I started to brush past her—how can I give bread to every beggar—and she spoke again. 'Don't you know me, Tetya Sofia? I am Valya, the daughter of your friend Polina.'"

Only then had Sofia recognized the woman. She was not a dying old hag—she was Valya, the beautiful seventeen-year-old daughter of her old friend Polina.

"Why, I attended the girl's christening," Tetya Sofia said. "I saw her in her long white embroidered gown. I watched her grow up. She was a fairy child with golden hair and blue eyes. Now she was a bag of bones."

"What did you do?" Maria asked.

"What could I do?" Tetya Sofia said piously. "I got her a crust of bread, I broke it into a saucer of milk and I fed her the pieces. But she couldn't eat. It was too late. Christ gathered her to his bosom.

It was God's will. Just as well, perhaps. Ones like that can't survive in this terrible world of ours."

Later Andrei talked with Vanya. "I don't believe the Jews have anything to do with this," he said. "Tetya Sofia is an old lady and she is filled with all kinds of prejudice from the old days. But something terrible is wrong."

"That's what you thought when the Shakhty engineers were tried," Vanya said. "Do you still think that? What about this new trial that's going on—the Industrial Party trial? Do you think they caused the famine?"

The boys were jogging around the big outdoor track on the island in the Don just off the Rostov embankment. Andrei looked around. No one was in sight.

"I don't know what to say about the Industrial Party trial," he said. He was thinking of the lecture they had been given that week by their teacher, Natalia Sverdlova, a worn, thin-faced woman with rimless pince-nez. She had read the account of the trial in *Pravda* and then the class had discussed it. "They are miserable traitors," a dark-haired girl named Sonya had exclaimed of the defendants. "They are vermin and they must be shot."

Andrei said nothing. Vanya, however, had spoken up, declaring that "in this moment of crisis there can be no faltering in the ranks of the defenders of the world's first proletarian state." Andrei was glad that he had not been called upon. His mind was not clear about the Industrial Party trial. He had read about these men who were supposed to have been secretly opposing the decisions of the five-year plan but it seemed to him he had heard it all before.

"What bothers me about the Industrial Party trial," Andrei said, "is that it sounds just like what we heard in the trial of the engineers."

"You mean you think somebody has made all this up—that the charges are falsified?"

Andrei did not respond. Finally he said, "Vanya, I don't know what to think. But there is something wrong. I felt that before and I feel it now. Why were the peasants burning their grain in the autumn? Why is food so short? I don't think it's the engineers and I don't think it's the industrial managers."

"You know, Andrei," Vanya said. "It's not easy to build socialism. There are a lot of sacrifices and setbacks—and enemies."

Andrei knew it was not a simple thing. It was not just "they" who were to blame, as his aunt kept saying—"they" being Jews or the commissars or the government—that mysterious all-powerful "they" on which generation after generation of Russians had blamed the ills of their lives.

A year later, in 1932, a third big trial was announced—this one of the Mensheviks. Again Andrei read every word of the testimony as published in *Izvestia*. It sounded to him like the Shakhty trial, and the Industrial Party trial—there was something not real, not genuine, something contrived about the case.

Again he told Vanya, "There's something wrong here. Something made up. It did not happen like that."

Andrei did not succeed in convincing Vanya, but Vanya admired the cool logic of Andrei's mind. He was not moved by what Andrei said because, as Andrei himself admitted, he did not really understand the basis of his feeling—it was more visceral than intellectual. Yet, because Vanya was accustomed to deferring to Andrei's opinion, for the first time a small secret dent began to show in his passionately revered image of the Great Leader Stalin, for whom all of the school had by now joined in ritual praise. Andrei had long said of Stalin, "I simply don't trust him."

Hunger and hardship grew in Rostov. Only because Andrei's mother had her stenographer's job in police headquarters were she and Andrei able to survive without severe suffering. Maria's job ensured a skimpy ration even during the worst of times.

Then came another stroke of chance—but a dangerous one. One day the pleasant major who had hired Maria simply vanished. Maria feared that at any moment she might be arrested too, but she was not, simply because she had become a fixture, a convenience that went with the office, a human machine into which you spoke and out came neatly typed lines, recording precisely what you had said.

But when an opportunity came she quietly slipped out of the job at police headquarters into an identical position in the Rostov branch of the State Bank. Again, she worked like a gray mouse, her head bent, leaning closer and closer to the thin tracings of her shorthand as the light faded from the big unwashed window, typing more slowly as her eyes strained to make out the symbols until, finally, when dusk had actually fallen, the head bookkeeper sullenly switched on the single bare electric bulb.

These were years of confusion and of change in Russia and in the lives of Andrei and his mother. Later Andrei would have great difficulty in recalling the sequence of events and understanding what lay behind them. There was, for example, the case of the artist Ryabushkin, who seemed to appear out of nowhere. One evening when Andrei returned to the apartment, he found with his mother, a tall, rather cadaverous man who wore a rakish broad-brimmed velvet hat. When Andrei entered the room Ryabushkin leaped to his feet, grasped the hat—it was deep purple, almost midnight-hued, really quite dashing—and swung it in a broad gesture, sweeping the dusty floor, and bowed deeply.

"Ryabushkin," the man said. "At your service."

His mother seemed a bit flustered. "This is our new friend," she said. "He is an artist from Moscow who has come to live in Rostov."

What wind might have brought this strange creature into his mother's life Andrei was never able to figure out. But for a while, for a few weeks, his mother was gay and happy as a young girl, blushing when Ryabushkin appeared each evening and laughing and smiling at his every remark.

Ryabushkin even made her pose for him and painted her portrait— not a good portrait, as Andrei instantly perceived. His mother had a saucy mouth and a merry one when she was in good spirits. Ryabushkin hadn't grasped that at all. There was a kind of wooden quality about the painting and Andrei was not really able to conceal his feelings.

The Ryabushkin affair was short-lived. One evening Andrei got home late after studying in the library and found his mother pacing the floor, so angry she could hardly speak. Never in his life had he seen her like this. A quick glance told him that the Ryabushkin portrait was missing from the wall.

"What's the matter, Mama?" Andrei asked.

"What's the matter?" she repeated. "I'll tell you what's the matter. I just threw that tramp Ryabushkin out of the house. And that cheap painting along with him."

There had been a fearful row, she told Andrei. "He has been seeing some woman, some bitch," she said. "I took the picture from the wall and threw it after him. 'Take this cheap bric-a-brac and give it to that woman. It will probably suit her taste.'"

"You did just the right thing, Mama," Andrei said, putting his arm around his mother's shoulders, upon which she immediately burst into uncontrollable sobbing. Andrei patted her and stroked her arms, until finally she stopped crying.

"Andrei," she said, "I've been such a fool. Such a fool. I can't think what your father would have said of me."

*　　*　　*

Now a passion began to embrace Andrei which blotted out almost everything else in his life. It no longer made a difference whether he had a crust of bread and a piece of cheese before he went to school in the morning. Nor did he race down to the bulletin board to devour *Izvestia* as he had for years.

Andrei's passion was for mathematics: algebra, higher algebra, geometry, trigonometry, calculus, higher theorems. It was like a rage. While some of his friends began to be crazy about girls, bragging endlessly of kisses, of squeezes, of breasts felt, of thighs caressed and even more, and where others, like Vanya, fell in love with football and clandestinely climbed through a ragged hole in the fence of the Dynamo Stadium—Andrei was transfixed by mathematics. He took great joy in a well-balanced theorem, in the ecstasy of solving a difficult problem in calculus, in watching the components drop into place, one by one, until the answer almost wrote itself.

"You can't understand, Vanya," Andrei told his friend. "There is nothing in life so pure, so exciting as a mathematics problem."

"Well," said Vanya, "it's a very useful science if you are going to be an engineer or a chemist."

"Not to mention the Red Army," said Andrei. "For an artillerist there is nothing like mathematics."

"Is that what you think you will be, Andrei?" Vanya asked.

"Perhaps," said Andrei. "You remember what Napoleon said— God is on the side of the heavy battalions."

Chapter 10

IT was June 1935. The "last good year," as it seemed in retrospect to so many, although that was not how it seemed to Andrei. In fact, when he grew older, he wondered if there had ever been a good year.

June 1935 was examination week. Five days from nine to one. Each day arriving at the school on Chkalov Street, climbing three flights to the big examination room on the third floor. The stale smell of chalk. Of sweat. Of urine from the leaky plumbing. Of moldy plaster. The smell of schools, all schools.

Each day Andrei wrote his responses—in Russian language, in German, in Russian history, in Marxism-Leninism, in mathematics. Each day, the blue examination copybook in hand, he went to his seat, checked the inkwell and filled it from the bottle on the master's desk. He set out his nib pen (and a spare nib in case something went wrong), carefully wiped his pen on an ink-stained muslin rag, laid the copybook before him, and carefully and precisely wrote "Andrei Ilych Sokolov, Class IX," in the left-hand corner. Then—and only then— he turned his eyes to the blackboard, where the questions had been written out by the master in large Cyrillic. Andrei read each question slowly, turning over in his mind the problem it posed and the time that would be required for writing out his answer. After he had read and absorbed each question, he went back to the beginning and ran them through somewhat rapidly, just to be certain there were no hidden pitfalls. Then he made a quick calculation of the total time required: twenty minutes for No. 1, thirty for No. 2; an hour for No. 3 and so on. He added the sum rapidly. He always liked a margin of at least half an hour to provide a cushion if an unexpected problem turned up. Now he dipped his pen in ink. He hesitated a moment to order his thoughts and then, rapidly and precisely, began to write.

This was Andrei's style—fast, careful, exact, almost military. It was the pattern of his mind. First, scout the terrain thoroughly. Take note of every possible difficulty and possible advantage. Measure his resources against the task at hand. Be certain of the perils that lay ahead. Beware of surprises. Be sure that your tools are in good condition, that your mind is clear and has been stocked with the knowledge essential for the task.

Andrei knew his assets well. He had a logical, orderly mind, a retentive memory. Until he was fifteen, he had possessed almost total recall. At first he had assumed this was a normal human trait shared by everyone, but became aware that his was a special quality when he and Vanya were studying together. He could read a page of history, for example, and repeat the contents almost word for word. He could listen to a lecture on Marxism-Leninism and reproduce the philosophical argument and even quote the citations from Marx, complete with source and page number. Vanya, however, had to commit such things to memory by repeated reading and recitation.

Andrei's special memory became even more apparent in his "queen study," as he called it—mathematics. Here the logical bent of his mind and precise memory insured him almost perfect marks. If he came to follow a military career like his father, he was certain that these attributes would powerfully influence his ability to rise to the top of his profession. Not for a moment did he think of serving as a common soldier. If he entered the Red Army it would be in the hope of moving up to the highest rank. And with the rise of danger in the world, Hitler's coming to power in Germany and the growing peril of a European war, Andrei could not help thinking in the most serious terms of a military career.

He was at that age when all things seem possible. He had even thought about writing and literature, although he really did not know what kind of writing it might be. Possibly history. He had a passion for digging things out, for solving puzzles.

*　　*　　*

Now, on this soft June day, Andrei climbed the flight of stairs for the last examination of the year, mathematics, which most of his classmates dreaded but to which he looked forward with a pleasure that was almost a passion. His only concern was that none of the problems would seriously challenge his abilities.

He had arrived a few minutes early and stood in the corridor outside the examination room waiting for the door to open. Vanya had come with him, grim and fearful. Andrei was certain that he would score five in math, the top grade, but Vanya had never done better than a four. Neither was talkative. Each seemed to have drawn back into his mind, preparing for the ordeal. Precisely at nine the door opened and the students entered the room.

Andrei carefully went through the preliminaries and then looked up at the blackboard. The formulae, the equations, the theorems were all laid out. He checked them more quickly than was his custom, almost breathless with anticipation. As he finished, a sense of disappointment swept over him. There was not a single problem that was not familiar to him. He knew the answers to each or knew the formula for finding the answer. Nothing to stretch his mind or show off his special abilities. He felt let down, but like a good soldier he dipped his pen into the inkwell, lowered his head and began carefully and neatly, with exquisite precision, to sketch out his answer to the first problem.

*   *   *

The morning passed with remarkable speed. Andrei heard the noon whistle blow. There was no clock in the room, but the master customarily announced the final hour—"One hour more"—and the last half-hour—"Half an hour more." By twelve-thirty Andrei had finished and turned back to page one to read over his anwers carefully. There were almost no corrections to make. Once he had made a small, obvious transposition, writing an "x" for a "y." He corrected this.

It was not considered good form to leave before the final moment. When the master announced, "All papers within five minutes," Andrei let his eyes move across the room, idling away the last few minutes. Vanya was still scribbling furiously. His whole hand was ink-stained, and he had managed to get ink stains on his forehead and right check where he had brushed away his forelock. Olga Baranova, a blue-eyed, heavy-breasted girl, was sitting back in her chair, her bold glance roving around the room. Her eyes caught Andrei's and she winked. Andrei felt himself blushing and quickly turned away. Across the room his only rival in mathematics, Lev Shapiro, had obviously finished. He was thumbing through his examination booklet, running one hand through his shock of long dark hair.

Andrei felt let down. He knew he had done well, not brilliantly— the conventionality of the mathematics questions had prevented him from showing off. But he was certain of fives in four of his subjects. Possibly he might get a four in Marxism-Leninism. He simply found it difficult to spend as much time as he should on a subject which, to his mind, was largely a matter of mastering by rote, a series of sententious sayings. His attitude did not stem from lack of interest or alienation from Lenin's philosophy. He read Lenin with the deepest interest, founded on respect. But the formulations of Lenin's thought, or that of Marx, for that matter, as presented in the class lectures and textbooks, seemed to lack real content, and already the contrast between what he regarded as the vapidity of Stalin's formulations as compared with Lenin's seemed shocking. He felt the same undefined concern about this that he had felt over the long accounts of the trials in *Izvestia*. He was increasingly struck by the disparity between Lenin's writings and the use to which they were put in polemics and propaganda. The Kirov case in Leningrad—the murder of the Leningrad Party Secretary last December first (which had even been reflected in some arrests in the middle school)—had struck him with special force.

Just as he had been viscerally convinced that the trials of which he had read were somehow contrived, so now his conviction was overwhelming that behind the Kirov case lay the same pudgy hand—the hand of Stalin.

At last the master spoke. "All papers in." One by one, the students deposited the blue folders on the master's desk, filing out into the corridor and trickling down the staircase. At the entrance to the school a knot of students were laughing and joking. "School's out, school's out," one of the girls sang in a falsetto pitch. Olga Baranova was in the center of the group. "How about it, classmates?" she cried. "Shall we have a *gulyanye* tonight? It's a perfect night for it." Others took up the cry. "A *gulyanye*! A *gulyanye*!" A *gulyanye* or "walking out" was really the prerogative of upperclassmen. Andrei had never been on a "walking out." Olga's bold eyes met his. "You'll come, won't you, Andrei—and Vanya too." Andrei was flattered and embarrassed and a little excited. "Of course, we will," he said. "It's agreed," Olga shouted. "Everybody here. Eight o'clock on the school steps."

*   *   *

Andrei was late. He had waited until his mother came home in order to tell her he was going on the *gulyanye* and now he was half trotting, half running, hoping to get to the school steps before his comrades left. He arrived, sweat running down his neck into the open collar of his clean white shirt. Olga greeted him with mock anger. "About time, Andrushka," she said. "You keep your comrades waiting—but not the master."

The youngsters linked arms and, six or eight abreast, moved slowly down the street in ragged ranks. Each girl was wearing a white shirtwaist and dark skirt; the boys, white shirts and dark trousers. They all gleamed with fresh, soapy scrubbing, their cheeks red, their hair damp. In school, the girls' hair hung uniformly in two simple pigtails tied with red ribbon, but now some, including Olga, had done up their hair by winding the braids about the crown of their heads in traditional Russian style. Several boys, but not Andrei, had combed their hair with the typical dangling lock over the forehead, worn by generations of village swains.

It was a fine June evening, warm and light, with the air moving softly. The youngsters began to sing, as they slowly strolled through Rostov's quiet streets, the Sadovaya, the Voskresenskaya and finally into the big square in front of the cathedral. Olga had locked arms with Andrei as they left the school steps. She was on his right. On his left, though Andrei was hardly conscious of her presence, was Rosa Litvin, a rather thin Jewish girl with dark hair. When the students sang sad and melancholy songs of love, Olga turned to Andrei and looked deep into his eyes, her red cheeks glowing.

Sometimes the youngsters walked, holding hands and swinging

them, sometimes they threw their arms over each other's shoulders. When Olga put her arm around Andrei she drew him close, and her full breast pressed softly against his thin ribs. sending a quiver of excitement through him.

The *gulyanye* went on through the dusk of the long June evening. Occasionally, the classmates encountered other bands of strolling youngsters, students of two or three institutes in Rostov, also celebrating the end of the school year, and even students from Rostov University. The youngsters strolled together, sang a few songs, then separated, then came together again.

At mid-evening, all descended on the traditional meeting place, the Morozhenoye Shop, an ice cream parlor in the center of town. They crowded around the tables on the sidewalk and overflowed into the shop.

If they had been university students, celebrating the finish of their four years, they would have ordered champagne, but as middle school students, they ordered *plumberg*, a kind of ice cream sundae decorated with a maraschino cherry and a spoonful of strawberry jam. Olga kept her arm thrust through Andrei's. He felt the warmth of her skin, and as they sat at the little marble-topped table, he felt her thigh against his own, first softly and then more strongly. Almost without a conscious act he felt himself pressing against her. She gave no sign of noticing except to tighten her arm against his. Before midnight they had finished their ice cream and headed again for the cathedral square. There, as the chime in the City Hall struck midnight (the bells in the cathedral had long since been silenced), all the *gulyanies* joined together. They sank the "Internationale," and "Stenka Razin" and a dozen other songs and then slowly began to break up, sometimes in groups of a dozen or more or sometimes in twos or fours.

Andrei found himself walking out of the square and down the Voskresenskaya with Olga. Now she pressed openly against him, her warm breast firm against his chest, her hip tight against his and moving with his hip with each step they took.

"Oh, Andrushka, it is such a beautiful night. It must not end. Let's go and walk by the river."

They walked on, Andrei quiet, his heart pounding with excitement. He had never had his arm around a girl before, but Olga had gently pulled his arm around her waist as they broke off from the group and walked alone under the shadow of the acacias. Now she put her hand on his and softly pulled it up until his hand was encircling her rich breast. Andrei let his hand rest there without moving, but presently she took her free hand and pressed his hand hard against her breast. He could hear the deep intake of her breath.

Now they had reached the grassy embankment, and the broad river lay before them. Here and there tiny lights winked on the opposite shore, but the river itself flowed quietly, like liquid black velvet. In the faint distance they heard the whisper of a song. Some of those in the *gulyanye* were still roaming the city streets, strolling and singing.

"It's so beautiful," Olga said. "Let's sit a minute." As they sank down Olga pressed herself against Andrei and drew his head over to her until their lips met, hers heavy and warm and greedily devouring his. Suddenly her tongue darted between his lips and her body thrust against his own, almost enveloping him. Now they were lying side by side in the long grass, and Olga's hand, fumbling with her blouse, opened it and pulled Andrei's hand against her warm breast. She held her hand over his and he felt the hardness of the nipple under his fingers. A surge of excitement flowed through him. He caressed the breast, and in a moment Olga had opened her other breast to him, whispering huskily, "Kiss me, Andrushka. Kiss me." He put his lips against her breast as her hand pressed his head upon her. "Harder, harder," she murmured.

A moment later Andrei felt Olga's hand grasping at his trousers. "I want to feel you," she said. Her fingers were encircling him, caressing him, and a moment later, exactly how he never knew for all the excitement that boiled in his body, he felt himself atop her, her legs spread and pulled up beneath him and himself thrusting into her so deep and so hard he could not have halted had a militiaman pressed a pistol against his forehead. In a moment there was an explosion of his loins and he collapsed on the broad abdomen and strong thighs of the girl beneath him, shuddering and shaking as though with the fever. He felt himself crying and laughing and covering Olga's face with wet kisses.

He had never made love to a girl before. And ten years later, twenty years later, even in the despair and dark of the Vladimir isolator, even on the edge of the frozen "zone" of Lager 303 in Taishet, even as he thought he lay dying in a dirt-floored *ayul* in Turkmenistan, the memory of Olga would come back to him and his heart would beat a little faster, his blood pressure would rise a few degrees, and adrenaline would flow into his veins.

Olga was whispering to him. "That never happened to you before." It was not a question, but a statement of fact.

"No, never."

"And it never will again," the girl said. "Nothing ever again is like the first time."

They lay without speaking and without movement, so long that Andrei felt Olga must have slipped off into sleep. But finally she spoke. "Come, Andrushka," she said. "We must go. It is late and you must be home."

They scrambled to their feet. "Listen," Olga said. "Don't take me home. I don't want that. Don't come after me. Just remember me."

Before Andrei realized what she was doing, Olga had turned and disappeared into the blackness of the embankment.

*   *   *

Andrei's mother was asleep when he opened the door to their room.
He slipped into bed without awakening her. For hours Andrei did not
sleep. Again and again he felt himself enclosed in the richness of
Olga's body, and his breath quickened. Slowly the excitement began
to leave him and he asked himself how he, always so careful, so logical,
could have been picked up by a tidal wave that he had not even
known existed.

*   *   *

In the morning Andrei's mother looked at him curiously. "You stayed
out very late, Andrei," she said. "I hope you didn't go drinking."

Andrei smiled gravely. "No, Mama. I didn't go drinking."

The next evening he went around to the house where Olga lived.
He rang the bell, and her mother, a big clear-eyed woman, came to
the door. She looked as Olga would look when she was older. No, she
said, Olga wasn't home. She had gone away for the summer to work
on the Magnitogorsk project with some of the other Komsomols.
Andrei thanked the woman and wandered slowly back home. He never
saw Olga again. She did not appear when school started in the fall.
One of the girls said that she had gotten married to one of her comrades, someone working with her at Magnitogorsk.

Chapter 11

WHERE did Brezhnev stand? Andropov stared into space. Could there be anything about Brezhnev that he had not long since understood? Not likely. Nor did thinking about Brezhnev tell him much about what position his other Politburo colleagues would be taking up when they met at noon.

First, there was the question of the meeting itself. Wednesday was the normal meeting day. But Brezhnev had proposed the unusual Sunday meeting because of the double pressure of two foreign guests whose schedules almost overlapped—Pompidou just finishing his visit and Sadat coming only a few hours after Pompidou's departure. Very bad scheduling by Gromyko, but he had been compelled to advance the time for Sadat's visit because Kissinger was flying out to Cairo very early in the week and it was important that the discussion be held with Sadat before the American sat down with him. That being true, Andropov did not feel there was any special significance attached to the fact that the Politburo meeting was being held on Sunday rather than Wednesday.

Of course, Brezhnev was the man who had the most weight in the discussion that would be held, and therefore, in a sense, he was a key to the problem. But he was a key that would not turn until the positions of all the others had been disclosed. Brezhnev did not alone make any decision. Ordinarily he spoke last, and that enabled him to judge the balance very closely. He did not like to appear on the losing side of any question, and certainly he would not appear on the losing side of *this* question. But, thought Andropov, one must try to understand the real balance of Brezhnev's feelings—just where would he delicately tilt the balance so that his supporters would know which way the boss thought the wind should blow?

Andropov thought carefully. In the first place, Brezhnev would prefer to support him, Andropov, the sitting Minister of State Security. After all, he, Andropov, was Brezhnev's nominee, or so he had good reason to suppose. Perhaps his appointment had been a mutual decision by Brezhnev and Kosygin. Their power had been more evenly matched in those days. In any event, Andropov had always clearly shown that he was Brezhnev's man. There had been no disagreements. They had always voted on the same side. That, of course, he could count as an asset.

Going into the issue, so far as he could understand the position, Brezhnev would be leaning toward him. But what would be Brezhnev's view on the delicate issue of the author Sokolov? Would he favor expulsion or repression—arrest, trial and prison? Or would he want to go on, as long as possible, on an equivocal course—not making waves, as Leonid Ilych had once put it? That was certainly the Brezhnev style. Don't create too much of a fuss. And particularly don't create too much fuss when you are in the middle of delicate negotiations with the USA, trying to work out a détente, trying to get the capital funds and the technology to get the Soviet economy moving again, trying to shift Washington over to the Moscow side in case of trouble with China.

That, to be sure, Andropov had understood from the start. And that was why he had tried to move discreetly. He had hoped that Sokolov would tire of the struggle of writing and publishing within Russia and pick up his typewriter, his manuscripts, his wife and his children and go abroad to carry on, say in Paris, or possibly in the United States if the CIA and its puppet publishers (well, maybe they weren't puppets, he conceded, but they played the CIA game) wanted to foot the bill.

Was there any reason why Brezhnev should want to shift away from this centrist, middle-of-the-road position? None so far as Andropov could see. None, that is, unless the balance of the Politburo had switched against Brezhnev on this question. In *that* case—well . . . then it was an entirely different matter. In that case Brezhnev would be certain to shift over so that he was, as usual, at the head of the majority.

And that, to be sure, was the nub of this game, why Andropov had to know, before he went into the meeting, exactly how each of his colleagues was going to vote so that he, too, could be with the majority—not, he hoped, a majority which would put the ax to his neck. And that was why the subtle shadings of the remarks made by Shelest and any hidden implications of Brezhnev's call had to be understood. Otherwise he would go into the meeting half-blind—with only a partial idea of how the wind was blowing—and there could be no more dangerous position, particularly since he would be asked to report on the Sokolov affair before anyone else had spoken. He would have to put his case first, and the way in which he presented it, no matter how many safeguards he built into the presentation, was likely to determine his fate.

And there had been no clue from Brezhnev. No hint from his Secretariat. It was, in fact, rare that Brezhnev gave a supporter more than the faintest hint of his position in advance. He simply assumed you were clever enough to figure it out for yourself—and if you weren't, then you probably weren't clever enough to be in the Politburo in the first place and could suffer the consequences. If the issue was finely tuned, and if Brezhnev didn't want any member of the Politburo to feel that he had suffered even a slight defeat—well, then he was not going to offer any advance tip on how he would like this vote to go. So, Andropov thought to himself, no use wasting time on Brezhnev. There is no clue there except reinforcement of what he already knew—the vote might be close.

Chapter 12

PROBABLY it was the medal that brought it all back. Not a real medal—just a bronze strip on which was imprinted: "Honored Marksman." It was awarded to Andrei late in the summer of 1935, the summer before his last year in middle school. A week or so after the *gulyanye* he and Vanya went with a Komsomol team to help build an irrigation system at the Kuban State Farm. It was hard work, but Andrei enjoyed it: up at five, an hour for calisthenics and a bite to eat, then at six marching out to the construction projects.

In the evening there was volleyball and lectures in Marxist-Leninist theory, talks on the very threatening international situation and on the internal situation—equally threatening, since it was the time of the first purge trials. On Sundays, and occasionally on weekdays after work, there were paramilitary exercises. Both boys and girls engaged in rifle shooting, machine-gun operation and aircraft recognition.

Andrei was an excellent shot, though he had never gone hunting alone again after his boyhood excursion for ducks. His Uncle Boris had decided that there was a risk that someone might spot Andrei shooting and blame Boris for the unauthorized loan of his gun. He did, however, let Andrei occasionally go hunting with him.

Now Andrei swept the field and was rewarded with the small bronze bar that carried the words: "Honored Marksman," and was attached to a cheap ribbon of crimson and gold. He had been given the medal at a rather tawdry ceremony toward the end of summer.

After the ceremony at the Workers Club, Andrei and Vanya slipped outside and walked for a long time in the quiet night. The sky was vivid with stars and they talked more openly than Andrei was accustomed to about their lives, about the future, about the present. They talked about Germany. Andrei had followed Hitler's rise with horrified fascination. He had read every report that *Izvestia* had published on the rise of the Nazis with the same care as he had read about the Kirov case, the Party purge that had followed and the earlier prosecutions. It seemed to both young men that the fate of Europe, the fate of their country was held in the balance by Hitler. Yet, both believed in the strength of the Red Army and Russia's ability to defend her frontiers.

"The only question I wonder about," Andrei said, "is this. Should we wait until we are attacked or should we move in first? If we wait, Hitler will just get stronger and stronger."

Vanya was against immediate action. "Hitler may get stronger," he said, "but look at ourselves. We are going forward by leaps and bounds."

Andrei conceded this was true but confessed his worry. "The Germans are better organizers than we," he said. "I am not sure that they will not move ahead more rapidly than we."

Vanya chuckled. "Just because you got that medal, Andrei, doesn't make you such a great military expert."

When Vanya said "medal," a curious feeling came over Andrei. He was powerfully reminded of something on the edge of consciousness, something that had happened many years ago. He fell silent and the two walked on in the starlit darkness as Andrei struggled to bring the memory to the surface. Suddenly he shuddered. The memory flooded into his mind so powerfully he gasped for breath.

"What's the matter, Andrei?" Vanya asked.

Andrei did not reply immediately, the surge of recall was too powerful. Finally, he mumbled, "Nothing. I just thought of something, that's all. Let's go back to the club."

*   *   *

It had been a raw, chilly Sunday afternoon. He was very, very small and the family had not yet left Kislovodsk. He remembered that his mother seemed pale and nervous. She opened the large iron-bound trunk, the one on which he slept, and began hurriedly to take things out. He stood at her side watching. He could guess how young he had been—he could just see over the edge and peer into the trunk. She drew out the old greatcoat that had belonged to his father, carefully examining it. He could still remember the smell of the mothballs, so strong it made him sneeze. She took out a yellow straw hat and put it aside. When he reached out to touch it she thrust his hand aside roughly, almost fiercely. "Don't interfere, Andrushka," she said. Andrei could still hear the sharp passion in her voice.

Perhaps that was why the incident had rushed so strongly back into his mind. It had not been often that his mother spoke so to him. She pulled article after article out of the trunk—an old ikon in a red plush carrying case, some kind of leather-bound book with brass clasps, a great silver samovar, wrapped in a fold of brown velvet. He had never seen anything so beautiful, and when his mother put the samovar down beside him he turned and put his hand on the velvet. He could still feels its softness, curiously silky, almost flowing under his touch. His mother dug deeper and deeper into the trunk until she found what it was she was looking for—a small black box. She opened it, looked at it closely, and then, her voice very throaty, almost a sob, squatted down beside Andrei. "Andrushka, dearest," she had said. "I want you to see this. It was your father's."

He looked at the open box, about the size and shape of a pack of playing cards. It was lined with soft white silk, and against the silk, as on a tiny cushion, there was a beautiful object, white and gold, in the form of a Maltese cross. He reached out to touch it.

"No, Andrushka," his mother said again sharply. "Don't touch it. Just look at it. This was your father's. He won it for bravery. His country gave it to him. It is a St. George's cross—something to be very proud of and to remember. But it is a secret. Just for you and Mama to know. Promise."

And, of course, he promised. He did not know what the words meant—except the part about his father, who was the bravest man in the world. Somehow he was sure that his father wasn't dead, that Andrei would wake up some morning and he would be standing at his bedside, just as he looked in the picture in the golden locket his mother wore around her neck. He would wake up and his father would say, "Hello there, Andrushka," and he would reach out with very strong arms and seize Andrei by the shoulders and lift him way up over his head . . .

Andrei sighed. It had been a long time since that dream had come to him, but he remembered waking up again and again as a child from the dream of his father's presence. He remembered the thin sense of despair when he opened his eyes and there was no one there—only his mother struggling out of bed, pulling on her skirt and blouse, staring at herself in the cracked mirror and sighing as she began to draw the comb through her hair.

*   *   *

The medal! Of course, he had always known that his father had won the Cross of St. George. It was knowledge that had lain close to his heart through his whole life. He could no more have put it out of his mind than he could put the thought of his father out of his mind. It was one of the strongest sources of his pride in his father. But the memory of this Sunday when his mother had rummaged through the old trunk, hastily shown the medal to him and sworn him to secrecy—that had slipped completely out of his consciousness until now, and he realized that this was no accident.

Never had his mother again referred to the events of that afternoon —and for reasons that were obvious to him as he looked back. His mother had dressed him, bundled him up in his worn white fur coat and his round white fur cap. He still carried a tactile memory of that fur in his fingers and on the palm of his hand—soft, smooth fur, probably rabbit, in places worn down to the hard brittle skin. She had dressed him warmly, although it was early spring. She had dressed herself warmly, too. He seemed to recall her wearing her black broadcloth coat with the gray caracul collar and cuffs and the caracul muff he loved so well. She had with her a string bag, and into the string bag she had put a small tin tobacco box that he could still see perfectly clearly, yellow with red decorations and lettering—Asmolov Tobacco Co., it must have been. The box had stood on a shelf and his mother kept bits of string, a spool or two of thread, a small pair of gold scissors and a golden thimble in it. She had dumped these out into a broken teapot and into the box she put the medal on its cushion, wrapping it in tissue paper. Then she put a white muslin cloth over the tin box, wrapped that in a piece of heavy brown paper, wrapped that, in turn, in newspaper, tied it with string and popped it into her string bag. She took a big metal spoon from the drawer, wrapped it in paper, took a few onions and potatoes from the storage place between the windows, put all of this into the string bag and said, "Come, Andrushka, we're going for a walk."

He did not remember the walk very well except that it was very far and very cold and the wind blew, and when he whimpered, his mother just took him by the hand and said, "Hurry, Andrushka, walk faster and you'll not be cold."

They walked a long way and had gotten to the edge of town when he recognized that they were in the graveyard where his father was buried and where his mother had taken him before. It was deserted on this raw day, and for some reason his mother kept muttering to herself, "*Slava Bogu, Slava Bogu.* Thank God."

They made their way through the monuments and tombstones to the far corner and the twisted pines under which his father lay buried. They walked up to the cross—it was made of stone and his name was carved on it—and his mother knelt and crossed herself. The earth was muddy and Andrei remembered that his feet were wet and cold. His mother glanced around, then hurriedly scraped a small square free of leaves and, reaching into her bag, drew out the big spoon. She quickly began to make a small hole in the earth. "Stand right here, Andrushka," she said. "Keep looking around and tell me if you see anyone."

He stood, twisting and turning, but no one came into view. It seemed only a moment when his mother was back on her feet again, brushing the mud from her knees and kicking leaves and twigs over the hole, until no mark of it remained. She had wrapped up the spoon in newspaper again, and he noticed that the box was no longer in the string bag.

His mother turned, took him by the hand and they began the long walk back to town. That was all he remembered. His mother had never mentioned the day again. And it was only now on this gentle August night as the childish brass plate inscribed "Honored Marksman" glowed dimly on his breast that the episode rushed back into his mind, and with the recollection a realization that on that chilly afternoon his mother had buried his father's St. George's cross. Quite clearly she had been afraid of a midnight knock on the door, of a search by police who would find the medal and see it as evidence that she was a member of the "former people," as the bourgeois were called. He did not believe there had ever been a search of their room. But he remembered that only about two months previously his mother had come home one night tired and more than usually harassed and said, "Andrei, let's look over the books again. Let's be sure there isn't anything on the shelves that might cause trouble."

She did not have to say more. He knew very well what she meant. Indeed, he could remember at least two other times when she had feverishly pawed over their little collection of books and hurriedly put aside a few volumes. One was Bukharin's famous *ABC's of Communism*. He had regretted parting with that, but she had been very firm. She had pulled it to bits. Late that night when everyone was asleep she fed the bits, one by one, into the stove very carefully, and had stirred the ashes three times to be sure that not a scrap was left. Now they looked over the books again. There wasn't much left on the shelf. A volume of the *Short Course History of the Party*. She moved this to the top shelf. She put paperback sets of Stalin's speeches beside it. Also Stalin's *Principles of Leninism*. These were the ikons of the bookshelf. There was a handful of foreign translations—a book of H.G. Wells, two Conan Doyle mysteries, Dickens' *David Copperfield*, Mark Twain's *Huckleberry Finn*, Jack London's *Call of the Wild*, something by Jerome K. Jerome, a volume of Heine, one of Schiller, a collection of Shakespeare's plays.

She picked them up one by one, looking at them nervously.

"Mother," he said, "surely there's nothing wrong with these. Don't be so nervous."

"You just don't know what you're saying, Andrushka," she retorted angrily. "We have to be careful. It only takes one book!"

She reached for the Wells. "I don't think we need this." He had said nothing. Any word would have upset her more. He watched helplessly as she tore out the pages of the book. She tore each page in half and then started burning it leaf by leaf. Slowly. By the open window so the smell of burning paper would not drift through the house. When the pages were burned and a heap of ashes remained in a saucer, she looked at the binding in despair.

"This won't burn," she said.

"Never mind, Mother," he said. "Just give it to me. I'll go for a walk and throw it into a sewer."

Of course, he had always known about his father's receiving the Cross of St. George, but his mother had admonished him again and again not to mention it. "In general, Andrushka," she had said many, many times, "it is best not to talk of our own affairs. These are private. Just between you and me. There is no need for others to know what they don't need to know. These are our secrets, and we don't want to share them with anyone."

Old habits are hard to break. Andrei said nothing to Vanya of the revelation that had surged through his mind even when they came to a halt at the edge of the field beside the new culvert which they had installed. But Vanya raised another delicate subject.

"What do you think, Andrei," Vanya said, "about the plot of the Zinovievists and the Kirov assassination? Do you think there is some connection between them and Hitler?"

Andrei picked a straw from the field and sucked it through his teeth. "I don't think so, Vanya," he said. He hesitated and then continued. "I guess there is no reason why I shouldn't say this. But there seems to me to be a clear line running through all of these trials— from that first one we read about, the engineers at Shakhty, then the Prom Party, the Mensheviks, and now this latest one."

"That's what I thought you might say," Vanya said. "But what I don't understand is how you connect them all. You've always been so suspicious. But exactly what is it that you are suspicious about?"

Andrei sighed. "I wish I could tell you straight out," he said. "I believe in everything that Lenin did, but somehow after his death things have changed."

"But that means Stalin," Vanya said. "Isn't that what you're saying?"

"I guess so," Andrei said. "What I can't see— and I admit this— is how it all fits together. Before Stalin we didn't have these strange plots, these trials in which men who seem to be—certainly most of them—honest, hard-working engineers, or ministers or officials or members of the Party are suddenly charged with the horrible crimes. Then they get up and testify that they are guilty of even worse things."

Vanya shook his head. "Still, Andrei, you know we are surrounded by enemies, Hitler and all that," he said. "Don't you think they are plotting to disrupt the country and weaken us from within?"

"Perhaps," Andrei said. "But we were much weaker in 1920. The country was a shambles. The Whites were nearly as strong as the Reds. The French, the British, the Japanese and even the Americans invaded Russia. We were starving to death—and still we came out on top. Today we are so strong I can't see anyone plotting from within."

"Maybe it's Hitler," Vanya said.

"Maybe it is," Andrei conceded. "But remember this—the plots and conspiracies and trials were going on before anyone heard of Hitler. And they weren't going on in Lenin's day—right?"

Vanya agreed.

"So that's what sticks in my mind," Andrei said. "That and other things. When I read Lenin's works they don't sound the way they do when they are quoted in *Izvestia*. Just look them up. You can read a great deal in Lenin without ever hearing a word about Stalin. But that's not the way it comes out in *Izvestia*."

The boys started back toward the hall. It was hard for Andrei to think of any logical reason why Stalin—if it was Stalin—would concoct such charges and stage such trials. That was the gap in his logic which he could not fill.

As the boys drew nearer to the hall they could hear music. Misha was playing the piano, Mitya his *bayan* and Volodya a rather battered cornet. It was the last night of the Komsomol *komanderovka*, their summer task, and in the morning they would be on their way back to town.

As the boys came up to the building they could see couples dancing. A good many of the girls were dancing together, holding each other closely about the waist, their heavy bosoms swaying and moving against each other. Half of the boys stood around the walls, staring morosely at the girls or, here and there, in little knots, talking and paying little attention to the dancing. Andrei stepped through the door and stood at the edge of the floor.

Suddenly he felt a tug at his arm. It was a dark, thin-shouldered Jewish girl named Rosa. "Come on, Andrei," she said. "Don't let me be an old maid." She looked at him with such a saucy half-comic, half-tragic expression that Andrei grinned and put his arm around her.

"Come on, Rosa," he said. "Of course you'll not be an old maid. Not while I'm around."

They whirled around the floor so fast that Rosa's eyes sparkled and Andrei's head began to swim. He felt her clinging to him more and more strongly, her thin body warm against his own.

As the music stopped they were beside the open door and Andrei, not breaking step, whirled her over the threshold into the starlit darkness.

"Oh, Andrei, what a good dance," Rosa exclaimed, nestling against him.

"Shall we go for a walk?" he whispered, putting his arm around her bony shoulder and pulling her closer to him.

She looked up at him—one moment sparkling and the next moment breaking away. "No, Andrushka. No. Thank you very much." And before he could catch his breath she had disappeared beyond the building, hurrying off toward the women's barracks.

Chapter 13

NEW Year's Eve. The crunch of hard snow. Boots squeaking with each step. Crisp air. Windows embroidered with frost. Laughter. Singing in the distance. Crowds four deep at the shops. Buying the last sugar-coated cake from the shelf, cleaning out the stock of sprats, of herring in wine sauce, of small-grain black caviar, of juicy red, of gray beluga, buying the last loaf of crusty white bread, of heavy moist black loaves, the crimson-paper boxes of chocolates fom the Red October factory and blue-and-white boxes of Belomor cigarettes. Buying vodka, buying wine, buying cognac. Buying, buying, buying.

Where did the money come from? Andrei could not imagine. He waited in the queue and finally made his choice—an orange, a little discolored, a little soft, but a real orange, not a mandarin or tangerine. God alone knew where it had come from. It cost ten rubles and there were only three oranges left. He tucked it carefully into the worn pocket of his jacket and hurried out into the evening. He was filled with anticipation, yet there was a lump in his throat when he thought of his mother. It was the first New Year's Eve he had not spent with her. True, she had company—her old friend, Eugenia Chernov, a widow like herself, with whom she had gone to school at the fashionable Taneev Girls' Gymnasium in the years before World War I.

As far back as Andrei could remember, he had always been with his mother on this night. He remembered their first New Year's in Rostov, living in the hovel, when he was too little really to know about New Year's Eve. His mother had dressed him in a dark-green velvet suit with short trousers and a lace collar. There was a candle on the table and he could even now see her beautiful face in the soft glow, her heavy hair piled high like a crown of burnished chestnut, her eyes sparkling yet soft, a blush of pink in her cheeks. She wore a dress he never saw again—with a low neck and long skirt and very rustling. It must have been silk, a long white dress. On the table stood a small bottle of wine. He hadn't known what wine was then, just that it smelled like a bouquet of flowers with a spicy tang. His mother poured a glass for herself and a thimbleful for him. They knew when midnight came by the sound of bells in the distance (there must have been a church whose bell tower did not yet stand empty like the sagging jaws of a toothless hag) and scattered rifle shots, popping like loud firecrackers, the same noise, he now recalled, he had heard when the train halted on the Don steppe south of Rostov.

His mother raised her glass:

"You raise yours, too, Andrushka," she said. *"Snovem godem, Snovem schastya, dorogoi.* Now say the same to Mama."

And he had raised his glass and repeated in his faltering child's voice: *"Snovem godem, Snovem schastya*—a Happy New Year and all happiness to you!" As he said those words and held his little glass of the wonderfully exotic red liquid, his mother's eyes filled with tears and she hastily swallowed the wine, half choking, holding back a sob and grasping him to her breast, saying, "Oh, Andrushka, Andrushka. I'm so unhappy I just can't help it. I am. I am. And whatever is going to become of us, my dearest, dearest boy." He did not know what to make of his mother's sudden sadness and he began to whimper. She must have missed his father desperately and in her mind would have been the memory of New Year's Eves with him, of gay, festive holidays before World War I and the Revolution, times when all of life was so different Andrei could hardly imagine it.

*   *   *

He hurried down the Sadovaya, crossing over into a narrow *pereulok* that led him to Ulitza Frunze, down Ulitza Frunze to the intersection of the street named for the twenty-six martyred Baku commissars and around the corner to the building where Rosa lived. He had seen Rosa a dozen times in the autumn after coming back from the Komsomol camp. She was not an ordinary girl. They had studied together quite often and the quickness of her mind and her enigmatic quality intrigued him.

Rosa seemed to know things he was only beginning to discover about himself. For example, as he talked about the terrible disaster in World War I which overcame the armies of General Samsonov (in which his father had served) she would interrupt to say, "But, Andrushka, how do you know that Samsonov was betrayed by Rennenkampf? How can you be certain he wasn't simply a silly old fool?" It was, he agreed, an excellent question, and it compelled him to think again, to test his thesis, which was heavily colored by fanatical hero worship of his father. Since his father had fought under Samsonov and had brought back the firm conviction—as Andrei well knew— that Samsonov and his army had been victims of the treachery of Rennenkampf and the German camarilla in St. Petersburg, it was to be expected that Andrei would have absorbed this conviction.

Rosa's cool question drove Andrei to the library to pore over again the old histories of World War I, the old magazines with pictures of the campaign, only to come back to Rosa a few nights later saying, "Rosa, I know now. And my conviction was correct. Samsonov was a good general, probably not a great one. He was old but he was honest, and Rennenkampf did betray him—I'm not certain why. Perhaps he wasn't a German sympathizer. The German name doesn't tell the whole story. Maybe he was just a bad general or an ambitious one. But those are details. What is important is what I said to you in the first place— Samsonov's betrayal, Russia's betrayal of her finest men, a great army, lost by Russian blundering, Russian intrigue, Russian inefficiency and, perhaps, Russian treachery."

Rosa had listened seriously, even solemnly, fixing her gray eyes on him. Then after a moment she said saucily, "I think, Andrushka, that I'm not altogether useless to you. At least I make your mind work." The remark made him somehow feel faintly embarrassed—as though he had just learned a lesson he should long since have learned.

*   *   *

So it had gone. Several times they had been to the theater. Andrei was passionate about the theater but could rarely afford to go. Rosa's uncle was an actor in the Rostov State Drama theater and sometimes she got tickets from him. One evening they saw *Hamlet*. Andrei knew *Hamlet* almost by heart and had acted in it at school, but never before had he seen a professional performance. As the play went on he felt himself on the stage, speaking the lines, declaiming "To be or not to be," moving through each stage of Hamlet's fateful indecision. "That touched you very much," Rosa said as they walked home. "I felt you were no longer beside me."

Andrei laughed. "I wasn't," he said. "I was up there on the stage myself."

Rosa gave him a curious look, put her arm in his and they walked on in silence. A fortnight later they saw Bulgakov's *The Day of the Turbins*. Again Andrei was enormously excited.

"Look, Andrushka," Rosa said as they waited in the queue for the old woman to hand them their coats, "look at what you did to my hand."

She put out her hand and he could see clearly the red marks of his fingernails, five red half-circles imprinted across the palm of her hand. He stared astonished at how carried away he must have been.

They walked out of the theater lobby and into the darkened street. It was an unusually warm evening in November. Earlier snows had melted, and now there were golden days and evenings when the air was sharp but not chilling, and the smoke hung above the houses and fallen leaves from the lime trees rustled underfoot. As they walked back to Rosa's home, Andrei continued under the spell of the play, with its clear picture of life in a family of Whites, the enemies of the Revolution. He had not thought much about the Whites, or rather, he had thought of them only in conventional terms, as the "enemy," villains who had opposed the Revolution, tried to defeat it, struggling to cling to their riches won by oppressing the people.

Andrei had seen for the first time—and the fact that this was a discovery was in itself a shock—that the Whites were ordinary men and women. They were like his aunt and his uncle, his grandfather and grandmother, or even, he hated to admit, his mother and father. He himself could have been a member of such a family. It was only chance, fate, that he was not.

*   *   *

Now Andrei hurried along the cold streets to the New Year's party at Rosa's home, thinking of this bittersweet girl, of her cool gray eyes and the way she looked so straight into his own that it sometimes seemed she could actually see his thoughts forming in his mind. At those moments he could no more keep his tongue from speaking whatever idea was passing through his mind than he could halt his lungs from drawing in a fresh breath of air.

Now he was at the big old graystone building where she lived. He pulled back the heavy wooden door and began climbing the dim staircase to the Litvins' apartment on the second floor. It was protected against the winter cold by a heavy felt-padded door through which Andrei could hear the muffled sound of voices and laughter. He had hardly pressed the button when a blond girl of about his age, one whom he had not seen before, pulled the door back and said elaborately, "Welcome to our castle!" A bit confused, Andrei stepped in and Rosa appeared almost immediately. "This is my cousin, Galya," she said. "Isn't she beautiful? She expects you to fall in love with her immediately." Galya laughed and vanished.

Andrei felt suddenly shy. He slipped off his jacket, pulling the orange from his pocket. It seemed more discolored than it did in the store. Perhaps it was spoiled. He should be giving her something exotic —a pineapple from Hawaii, perhaps, or a bracelet of opals from Ceylon. But it was too late now. "Here's something for you," he said, his voice going flat. "An orange!" Rosa exclaimed. "Andrei, where could you have found it? I didn't know there was another orange in the world." She gave him the lightest of kisses, really just a brush of her lips, and Andrei's heart melted. Perhaps the orange wasn't so discolored after all.

Then Rosa led him into a room filled with people, some young, some old. Andrei saw several classmates, but there were a good many older people he did not know. In fact, he recognized none besides Rosa's mother, dark like her daughter, and her father, a rather reserved man wearing a gray-checked jacket that had a faint air of *ancien régime* about it. He was a doctor and Rosa's mother had been an actress.

Andrei felt uncomfortable. There were too many people he did

not know in the room. There was too much noise. He was not used
to this kind of occasion and he wished he had not come. He found himself at the end of the room, separated from Rosa, who seemed to have
disappeared. Standing beside him was a tall, very handsome, self-
assured man with black hair cut rather long, an aquiline nose and a
certain air, a way of carefully articulating each word, that told you he
was someone important and that when he spoke you were expected to
listen. Indeed, Andrei did begin to listen. Quickly he found himself
entranced. The speaker was Zakharsky, the famous Moscow actor, and
he had come to Rostov not just for a visit or a temporary engagement
with the Rostov theater but to organize his own Institute of Dramatic
Arts. As Andrei listened to Zakharsky's mellifluous voice he grew more
and more excited. It seemed to him that this was no ordinary meeting
but one that had been dictated by fate. It was not for nothing that
the theater had so powerfully attracted him. The theater was to be
his life, and Zakharsky was the *deus ex machina* which would make
this possible. Zakharsky was speaking to a man whom Andrei quickly
recognized as Rosa's uncle, the actor. Andrei found himself unable to
hold back his curiosity and began to ask the questions that burned inside of him. Zakharsky had just arrived. The first classes at the new
school would be admitted at the beginning of the academic year in
September.

Zakharsky said, speaking more to Rosa's uncle than to Andrei,
"This, you understand, will by no means be an institution of provincial
status. We will insist on the very highest of standards. What we do not
need is another fly-by-night school for mediocre provincial actors."

Andrei listened as in a trance.

"Our requirements," Zakharsky was saying, "will be as high as
Moscow's. Perhaps higher. I do not know how many students will be
able to meet them. But better one Yermolova or one Mordvin than a
dozen Chichikovs."

All around there was the bubble and spatter of conversation, but
Andrei heard no one but Zakharsky. He realized he was standing beside
the actor, saying nothing, probably making the worst of impressions.
But his mind was so full of his dream that he was transfixed.

*   *   *

Eventually it occurred to Andrei that Rosa was nowhere in sight.
He was overcome by a desire to find her, to tell her about his new-
found goal. He slipped away from Zakharsky and went down the hall
toward the kitchen, where he found Rosa's mother with two other
woman, apparently relatives, busy preparing food. There was no sign
of Rosa, nor, Andrei now realized, of several of Rosa's friends.

Just beyond the kitchen a door stood ajar and Andrei heard the
murmur of voices. He pushed on the door and went in. The room was
dark and for a moment he thought he had made a mistake. Then he

saw a candle burning on a table and dimly perceived a figure in the darkness beside it. There was a sudden titter and he realized there were more people in the room. As he came closer the seated figure turned, and he saw it was Rosa, her eyes twinkling. Before her was a mirror in which, as he approached, his face was clearly seen. Only then did Andrei understand what was happening. It was, of course, the old Russian custom—fortunetelling on New Year's Eve. A girl would sit before a mirror, a lighted candle on the table, and wait for her beloved's face to appear in the mirror.

"Rosa!" the girls cried. "He's yours. Andrei is your future!"

Rosa looked up at Andrei. There was a seriousness in her face that Andrei had never seen before. "Don't mind us, Andrei," she said. "I know you don't believe in girls' superstitions. It's just our old custom."

"Don't you believe her," one of the girls spoke from the shadows. "It's the real thing. You are Rosa's future. There's no doubt of it. The mirror knows."

Another girl spoke: "Andrushka, don't you want your fortune told? Come on. Let's do the tea leaves."

"Now, girls," Rosa said, "Andrei is very serious. He doesn't want to play these games."

"No," he said. "Let's see what my fate will be."

The light was turned on, and Galya, Rosa's cousin, ran out of the room. "I'll bring the tea," she said and was back in a moment with a teapot, cup and saucer.

"Now, Andrei," she said. "You must pour a cup of tea and drink some of it."

Andrei poured a cup and took a taste.

"No, more, more," Galya said. "There can't be more than a sip left in the cup."

"You don't have to do it, Andrei," Rosa said. "It's just a silly game, you know."

Andrei grinned and gulped most of the tea.

"Fine," Galya said. "Now, turn over the cup and spill the tea into the saucer—all of it, the tea and the tea leaves."

Andrei did as he was told and there was a bob of blond heads as the girls leaned over the saucer.

"What do you see, Galya?" Andrei asked.

"Oh, Andrushka," she cried. "It's so complicated. Everything is going to happen in your life. There is love and adventure and good and bad. You are going to travel. You are going to be disappointed. You are going to love very deeply and you will go very far away. Very far. But I can't tell what that's about. Not just travel, I think. Something else. Maybe you are going to be a soldier. It's just not clear."

She broke off. Andrei was puzzled. He had a feeling Galya saw something in the tea leaves she did not want to tell.

"Is that it, Andrei?" Rosa asked. "You do think about being a soldier sometimes, don't you?"

"Yes," Andrei said hesitantly. "But maybe not. I'm beginning to change my mind."

"Come on, girls," Rosa said. "We've teased Andrei enough. Let's go back to the party." But she put her hand on Andrei's arm and held him back as they walked to the door.

"I'm sorry, Andrushka," she said. "I know you don't like such silly things. Forgive me. Besides it is the old custom on New Year's Eve."

She looked at him in silence a moment. Then the ironic look came back to her face. "It is a terrible fate to be my future, isn't it, Andrei?" Then she whispered, "Don't tell the others. But I'll not let you go— even to the Army."

"But I'm not going into the Army," Andrei burst out. "I'm going into the theater. It's what I've always wanted to do, but only tonight when I talked with Zakharsky did I really understand. Does that just sound crazy, Rosa?"

Rosa's gray eyes searched his face earnestly. She seemed uncertain, but she spoke firmly, decisively: "No, it doesn't sound crazy. I do understand, Andrei, I do understand. I've known that there was something you wanted, something you were searching for."

Rosa continued to peer deep into Andrei's eyes. He felt that her gaze penetrated into his very soul. "Yes, Andrei," she finally said. "The theater. You know my mother was on the stage for a time. It was her whole life, I think. Then I came along and she gave it up."

*   *   *

Andrei did not stay at the party long after midnight. He was worried about his mother. Rosa kissed him lightly on the cheek as he left. "*Snovem godem*, Andrushka," she said. "*Snovem schastya*—my fate!"

*   *   *

The wind had come up. The night had borne out its evil promise. A grainy snow drove into Andrei's face. Here and there on the street were people in clusters, talking loudly, singing. They had been drinking and welcoming the new year. His mother was alone when he came in, sitting beside the light reading. "Oh, Andrushka," she said, "I'm so glad you came back."

"Didn't Eugenia Ivanovna come?" he asked.

"Oh yes," his mother replied, "but we decided it was silly for two old women like us to sit around all evening sipping wine and talking about the past. It would just make us despondent. So I sent her home. But why did you come back so early—didn't you like the party?"

Andrei smiled and put his arms around his mother. "Yes, Mama, it was a nice party, but I decided to come back to you."

"That was very good of you, Andrushka," she said. "You are a good boy, but you needn't have done that. I'm all right. I was just sitting here, reading Chekhov again. Eugenia brought me this book of his stories. I've been reading over *The Woman with the Dog*. I do love it. It always makes me feel so sad—not unhappy—just sad in a warm familiar way, if you can understand."

There was still a bottle of wine standing on the table. Maria poured out two small glasses.

"*Snovem godem, snovem schastya*, Andrushka," she said.

"*Snovem godem, snovem schastya*, Mama," he replied.

Andrei did not sleep for a long time. He saw himself standing before the audience, declaiming his lines. He could see the faces fixed on him, the power of his voice transfixing them. It almost made him dizzy.

But there was the question of getting into the Institute. Could he win admission? He should have been studying for it. Perhaps, he might even have gotten some small tasks at the Rostov theater. Been a stage-hand or a prompter boy. Instead, he had thrown himself into mathematics. Never mind. He would try. He must.

And he was not, after all, entirely an amateur. He had taken part in school plays. At least he knew some fundamentals. If he tried hard enough he would not fail. He was certain of it.

His mind turned to Rosa. There was something about her conduct this evening, something more serious than he had seen before. Was he really her future? Somehow, he liked the idea. There was a quality about Rosa that pulled him to her, an excitement in being with her. Was he falling in love? No. That didn't seem likely—he had no plans for falling in love. Still . . . there was that old Russian saying—the one with whom you spend New Year's Eve you will spend the whole new year with. He smiled to himself.

Chapter 14

ANDROPOV quietly snapped the knuckles of his left hand. The cartilage of his third and fourth fingers gave a satisfactory snap. He did the same with each finger of his other hand. Only the second finger snapped.

The next man to consider was Kosygin. A difficult man to analyze. He seemed, perhaps, more principled, less "political" in his views than Brezhnev; but Andropov was inclined to think this was an illusion deliberately cultivated by Kosygin. He was the only man left in the Politburo who had been repressed by Stalin. The only one—but for Suslov—who had been close to Stalin. The others had died or retired or been removed. Kosygin stayed on. He maintained a vague aura of "liberalism," possibly because of his past persecution, possibly because of principle.

Andropov felt that objectively Kosygin was not a liberal. He was a pragmatist like the rest of the Politburo men, a technician, an efficient executive. He could not abide sloppy bureaucrats, shiftlessness or cant. He was not and never had been an ideologue. He had never gotten on with Suslov. Probably in the West he would have been a successful corporation director—the head of U.S. Steel or Imperial Chemicals. It was not for nothing that he had for so long been a protégé of Mikoyan, of whom it was said as a standing quip (and probably it was Stalin who had said it first) that if he had emigrated to America like so many of his countrymen, he would have wound up a millionaire.

Well, where did all this put Kosygin in the present situation? He would, as always, adopt a no-nonsense attitude. He had never in any way displayed either partiality or hostility toward Andropov. All that mattered to Kosygin was the question of whether Andropov and his men were doing their job effectively or whether they were interfering with that sphere which was Kosygin's prime concern—industry, development of trade, the economic structure of the Soviet Union.

Once, Andropov recalled, Kosygin had complained, not strongly but very precisely, of overzealousness when a detail of undercover men went into action against a prominent West German industrialist, a steel manufacturer who came to Moscow for trade talks. Andropov remembered the case well. The KGB had information—reliable and authentic, not just cheap gossip or an agent's provocation—that this Schmidt or Schultz had close connections with American intelligence. And so, quite naturally, a rather conventional operation was set up. A female operative, attractive and skillful, was assigned as Schmidt's interpreter. As was to be expected, he invited her to dine. She slipped the usual knockout drops into his drink and the customary nude *in flagrante delicto* photographs were made. Schmidt was then delivered to the sobering-up station, where at 6 A.M., extremely angry, somewhat frightened and still quite nauseated, he regained consciousness and hurried off to his Embassy.

There had been hell to pay for Andropov. It wasn't so much the anger of the German Embassy—who couldn't live with that? It was the anger of Kosygin (and the Soviet Oil Trust that had hoped to make a large-scale purchase of difficult-to-obtain gas pipeline materials). The agents' action cost six months in construction time before the oil trust was able to place the order with the Japanese, and as Kosygin had told Andropov personally and privately, the operation had been even more costly. This particular German firm, whatever its connection with the CIA, was a remarkably specialized steel manufacturer, and the Soviet Oil Trust had been anticipating obtaining a number of important steel specialties which, in fact, would have constituted a technological breakthrough. If the CIA was willing to let the German deal with them, why should the KGB oppose it? Kosygin had told this to him quite without passion or anger, not trying to put the blame on Andropov.

"What is done is done, Yuri Vladimirovich," Kosygin had said. "But it is most important, don't you think, that before you take Step A you know where Step B will lead and Step C and Step D and so on?"

"I understand, Alexei Nikolayevich," Andropov had told Kosygin. "Believe me, we will draw the appropriate conclusions."

That had closed the incident. There was not one more word from Kosygin. For himself, Andropov took the occasion to tighten reins on the provocations section. He welcomed the opportunity, since he had been aware for a considerable time of the unreliability of this group and, in fact, the triviality of most of their operations, which often were carried out in a spirit of "atmospherics"—mild terrorization of the foreign colony to inhibit diplomatic desire for contact with Russian nationals. He did not, of course, abolish the section, which would have been his personal inclination. It was too much the favorite of the old guard. To abolish it would simply have put a weapon in their hands against him. Better to constrict, control and observe.

But this incident had its application in the present situation. Within the context of Kosygin's clearly expressed attitudes, what would his views be at the meeting today?

What would concern Kosygin would be economics. Kosygin would ask himself: What is the action least damaging to trade relations and most beneficial for the détente necessary to open up more widely the American technological storehouse to Soviet industry?

In a word, Andropov thought, Kosygin's views are essentially mine. He would oppose the martyrdom of Sokolov, the deliberate creation of a propaganda ikon around which an anti-Soviet anti-détente campaign could be mounted in the United States and throughout the world. He would certainly prefer as Andropov did, the peaceful emigration of Sokolov to the West, there to sink with little or no trace, one hoped, into the quicksands of the capitalist wasteland.

Kosygin, Andropov concluded, was an ally in principle. But would he vote to support these opinions? Ah, this was another question. There had been a time when Andropov could have expected more from Kosygin. But that was several years ago, when Kosygin still thought of himself and was thought of by his Politburo colleagues as a possible alternative to Brezhnev. This had come close to reality on two occasions, the most recent being 1970, when there was a genuine chance that Brezhnev might fall. But then it had gradually become apparent that Brezhnev had an advantage that Kosygin could never enjoy—the support of the big Party guns of the Central Committee, the bosses of Sverdlovsk, of Kharkov, of Novosibirsk, of Omsk, of the Donbas and the Kuzbas, the heavy-handed, broad-shouldered, square-headed Party mechanics who made certain that the planned quotas for rolled steel, for tractors, for cotton and wheat were met. These men put their muscle behind Brezhnev, and gradually his power had risen and Kosygin's had ebbed. But only to a certain level. No one in the Politburo was going to let one man's power exceed that of the whole, of the collective. And so Kosygin was as secure as ever in the Premiership, even more secure, it might be said, as a reminder to Brezhnev by his colleagues that no matter how they supported him they also supported an alternative to him.

Kosygin was a shrewd man. He knew his role was that of a balance to Brezhnev. Only in an extreme circumstance was he a true alternative, and so he held to his quiet businesslike posture.

So, thought Andropov, Kosygin would permit himself a dry and unemotional expression of his views, shrewd and sparse. His tendency would be clearly understood within the Politburo. But—the vote? He would not go against the majority, and by the time he spoke, the majority should be clearly revealed. Thus, Kosygin would play no genuine role in the debate. He was, Andropov was certain, an ally. Kosygin would not be against him. He would be for him, but this circumstance, so far as Andropov could make out, would carry absolutely no weight in the outcome.

Chapter 15

IN the end, Andrei was not admitted to the Drama Institute, and for a reason which, for a long time, he could not think of without a feeling of shame—as if he had been made a fool of or, what was worse, he had made a fool of himself.

It happened in this way. In the spring he applied for admission and took the examinations. He had also applied to Rostov University—it was only common sense, since the Drama Institute would admit but twenty students. He had, he thought, not done badly in the drama examination. The written tests were no problem, and though perhaps he was not the best judge, having listened to the other competitors, he felt he had done all right in the readings. One of his exercises had been the soliloquy from *Hamlet*, "To be or not to be." Rosa insisted that his rendition was not satisfactory, simply because he could not simulate doubt and anguished indecision.

"No, Andrei," she said. "It won't do. No one would believe that you had any trouble making up your mind. You know exactly what you are doing. There is no hesitation. The words speak of doubt but you are completely certain. If you had been Hamlet there could have been no play."

There was something in what she said. But in another recitation, Ryleev's "Who in his heart is Russian," Rosa admitted he did superlatively.

"Andrei," she said, "you are wonderful with Ryleev. So strong. Courage just sparkles in your eyes. You must always play heroes—strong heroes. Never weaklings."

Apparently he had been passable or more than passable in his tests and his acting, but then came the ridiculous part. The candidates had to take a physical examination. And the doctor disqualified Andrei.

"You see, young man," he had said. "To go on the stage you must possess a pair of strong lungs and strong vocal cords. And you have neither. I think that when you were a small child you suffered a light case of tuberculosis."

The doctor was sorry, but he refused to sign a certificate. What to do? Andrei was reluctant to speak to Zakharsky. Though he had encouraged Andrei to apply for admission to the institute, Andrei had a feeling that this had been just politeness. Yet in the end, because Rosa insisted, he did approach the actor.

With mixed feelings Andrei spoke to Zakharsky when he appeared at the Litvin house the next evening. The actor drew himself up a bit and smiled. "It's quite ridiculous," he said. "I'm glad you asked me about this. It is nothing but bureaucratic nonsense. As a matter of fact, when I was your age I had to spend six months in a sanatorium in the Crimea—my health was very frail. But to say that this had interfered with my career as an actor—ridiculous!"

Andrei listened to Zakharsky with rising hope. In his excitement he lost the thread of what Zakharsky was saying, then suddenly he heard: "But, Andrei Ilych, you know my situation. It is, shall we say, a bit delicate. I've just taken over this position. There are certain matters of tact, certain political considerations to which I must pay heed— at least for the moment. Another year it will, I hope, be different."

Zakharsky shrugged his shoulders. "Who knows in these times?" he mused. "Who knows how long I'll be here or where I may be in another year?"

A certain note had come in Zakharsky's voice that Andrei would long remember. It was not a note of pathos, nor of defensiveness. It was that of a man bewildered, a man uncertain of his fate. Instantly, Andrei recalled what he had heard of Zakharsky and what his own common sense had told him must be the case—that Zakharsky had not left the Vakhtangov Theater in Moscow and come to Rostov because of an overwhelming desire to improve the art of the drama in a region remote from the glittering footlights of Moscow. Obviously he was in exile, exile imposed possibly by himself as a substitute for some harsher fate, or possibly officially ordered. A misstep might catapult him further from Moscow's orbit. Whatever Zakharsky might feel, he was not going to change the rules of admission for a callow young man he had seen three or four times and barely knew.

By the time Zakharsky brought his apology to a rather confused halt Andrei understood that it had been foolish to put himself in so stupid a situation. Reasons of health, indeed! Perhaps, even that was not the reason. Perhaps it was something else, something more obscure or more serious. He clenched his jaw and said goodbye to Zakharsky as rapidly as he could. Andrei slipped quietly down the staircase and through the outer door when he heard footsteps behind him. It was Rosa.

"So, Andrei Ilych," she said, "it was 'No.'" When he glanced at her darkly, she hurried on. "I didn't speak to anyone, but I know. I argued for you to speak with him even though I didn't think there was much chance. Well, honestly, perhaps, I didn't think there was *any* chance."

Andrei exploded. "So," he said. "So—you were playing games with me. Putting me to a test! Well, it's the last game you'll play with me!"

He lengthened his stride so that Rosa had to run to keep pace. "Go find some other dog to play Pavlov with. You'll cut no window in my stomach. You can be sure of that."

Andrei half ran, half walked through the center of town and on to the embankment of the river. He walked and walked, finally slowing his pace, and climbing to the very edge of the river, sat there staring out at the island in midstream. He was shivering with rage, with shame, with disappointment. His whole world had crumbled. He had violated every principle on which he based his life—careful planning, caution, analysis of factors pro and con, rational decision-making, understanding himself and understanding those he was dealing with.

To go to Zakharsky had been wrong from every standpoint. But that was a trivial wrong. Far worse was permitting Rosa to persuade him to do it when he knew, felt by instinct and understood in his mind, that it was wrong.

And why had he permitted himself to be persuaded? Because he had wanted so much to enter the Drama Institute, even though logic told him his chances were not good. If he wanted to go on the stage he should have been devoting his life to the theater, not to mathematics, not to the other things that interested him so passionately—history, politics, and writing. Did he think the theater was more important than any of these? Not really. But perhaps it had not been entirely wrong to apply to the institute. What was wrong was that he had permitted his emotions to swamp him. Why had he let himself be persuaded by Rosa? Because of weakness. He had become too fond of her, too close to her, too dependent upon her.

Well, said Andrei to himself. There was, as Rosa was fond of saying, a lesson in this. The lesson was to hold himself under control. Not to permit himself to be overcast by whirlwinds of feeling. Not to be under anyone's influence. He had permitted Rosa to move him off the base of logical reasoning on which his life was founded. No more. That was the lesson he had learned. He would miss her, of course. Even in his anger he understood that. But he had made his choice. No Rosa. No theater.

He rose and began slowly walking along the river. His anger had almost left him and he now felt only a deep sadness and a sense of loss. No doubt, Andrei thought, life will take me many places—strange, even dangerous places—but so long as I am master of myself I know I can overcome the rapids and the whirlpools.

*   *   *

Andrei's mind was back working in familiar channels now. Perhaps this stupid crisis had done some good after all. It had brought him up short and compelled him to see where he was headed. Now he understood he was going to the university to specialize in his beloved mathematics, to work at his writing, to continue to explore history. If he looked long and hard enough into the past he should find the key to the enigma of the present. The key to exactly what and how things went wrong in Russia.

He was convinced he knew the name of the answer. It was Stalin. But knowing the name of the answer was one thing; knowing how to make his case, knowing what to do with it when and if he had it—well, that was all for the future. What he now had to do was to concentrate, develop his faculties, strengthen his will. He thought of the man who had been Lenin's hero—Rakhmatev, hero of Chernyshevsky's novel. Rakhmatev strengthened himself by sleeping on a bed of nails, he deprived himself of women and wine, he slept only four hours a night—nothing diverted him from his objectives. That was carrying it a bit too far. But probably Chernyshevsky simply exaggerated for literary purposes. The basic idea was correct. He must make himself more of a Rakhmatev. Rakhmatev would never have permitted himself to be beguiled either by the thought of going on the stage or by a brilliant girl and powerful personality like Rosa.

When he arrived home, his mind was filled with Rakhmatev and the need to sacrifice and strengthen his will. Though he was hungry, he told his mother he would not eat.

He picked the volume of Chernyshevsky from the small bookshelf and sat down at the table. Only then did he perceive that his mother was upset. The familiar frown of deep worry was back on her forehead and her lips were working.

"What's the matter, Mama?" he asked, putting his hand on hers.

"I don't know, Andrei," she said. "But they say that Gusev has been called up for investigation." Gusev was the chief of the State Bank where she worked.

Andrei sighed. "Well, Mama," he said, "who knows? Maybe it's bad, maybe not. But there's nothing for you to worry about. It's just the big bosses. You know how they come and go."

"I suppose you're right, Andrei," she replied, "but I can't help it. Every time it happens I'm frightened all over again. Suppose they come to me?"

Andrei patted her hand. "They won't, Mother. You know that. They never have. It's just the big fish they are after."

Andrei settled down to read Chernyshevsky, but found himself brooding over his mother's worries. Nothing ever seemed to go smoothly for long in this complicated world. Of course she was right to worry when the chief of the office was arrested. Who could know what that might mean? Was he an embezzler? Did he tuck some rubles in his pocket? Or was it a political arrest? There were so many of them you could hardly follow what the charges were supposed to be—Trotskyite, Bukharinite, Zinovievite, Rightist, Leftist, Deviationist. When he formed the words in his mind there was an instant flash of rejection. There simply could not be all of these traitors in the country. As for her mother's boss—well, who could say? And there was absolutely nothing someone like his mother could do. That was the tragedy of Russia. As the peasants used to say, "Heaven is high and the Czar is far away." Who was there to hear the voice of a lone woman crying in the night?

Chapter 16

IT was June 1941.

Andrei awoke to the absolute stillness of the first hour of dawn. The sun was slanting through the window and painting a patch of brightness on the white plaster beyond the bed. Slowly the angle of the sun's ray widened and began to embrace their bodies, Rosa's and his own. He lay on his side against the wall and she on her back half turned toward him, her mouth slightly open and her breasts gently and rhythmically rising with each breath. Andrei looked at Rosa, her lips full and slightly moistened by her breath, the small beauty of her breasts with their dark aureoles and the reddish points of the nipples, the slender, slender waist and the slender boy's hips, the dark silky brush of hair between her strong slim legs. He could feel the warmth of the sun now on his own body, and he was possessed by excitement, as he always was when he looked at Rosa's body, and an overwhelming sense of well-being, of happiness beyond anything he had imagined possible.

To lie awake in this early hour with the window open, the sun coming through, the city beyond still drugged in the sleep of exhaustion and the world beyond that filled with all of its mysterious and unknowable happenings, alone, yet not alone beside this woman whose fate was joined to his—he had not supposed such happiness existed. In fact, he thought with a smile, he had for a time believed it was not possible. He had renounced her, cast her out of his life, turned his back, decided once and forever that he must make his way alone. How long ago that all seemed today, how distant, how unreal, how childish.

He had avoided Rosa for months, running away from her, until one evening at the library she had marched up to him just as he was leaving, seized his jacket by the lapels and said fiercely, "You are not going to get away, Andrei, until you listen to me and put an end to this foolishness." And to his surprise he found himself walking out of the building with her and talking as though there had never been any interruption in their relationship. She told him why she had insisted that he try by every means to win admission to the drama school so that even if he was not successful, and she did not think he would be, he could never look back in regret and say to himself that had he only spoken to Zakharsky he might have gotten in. And, as she spoke, he realized he had always understood this and he told her that this was true. And he also told her that he had had to test his strength so that he could know that he actually was strong. She had crinkled her nose and looked at him with a wry smile, and said, "I think there is a lesson in this for us, Andrushka, for both you and me." And he had laughed and suddenly put his arms around her and they had kissed right in the middle of the Sadovaya.

And then, two or three evenings later, he and Rosa had strolled along the Sadovaya, arms around each other, in that contentment which comes from the joy of a man and woman in love touching each other, feeling the rhythm of their bodies together, thinking only of each other. Rosa said, "Andrei, let's not leave anything to chance. Let's not ever again let ourselves be separated." And he responded: "Never, my darling. Never." And so, she continued, why don't we go to the registry office and register our marriage—not because we need to be registered but just so that there will be that little barrier around us which keeps us apart from everyone else.

They had not gone the next morning. At first the idea seemed alien to him. Why should any bureaucrat lay his seal on the joy they had in each other, in the private world they had created. But Rosa insisted. Not strongly, but gently, and he understood that this had great meaning for her. So on a morning when neither of them had classes at the university, they slipped away and went, alone, to an office building with flaking yellow paint and double windows, climbed a cold dark staircase to the second floor, opened a dirty brown door and found themselves in a tiny waiting room with a small wicket window which, naturally, as in all Soviet institutions, was closed. A scrawled sign on a piece of gray cardboard said: "Hours of Registration: 11 A.M. to 1 P.M." The clock in the street had said 11:30. Andrei rapped gently at the closed window. Nothing happened, although he could see the shadow of someone beyond the wicket. He rapped again. Nothing happened. He winked at Rosa, and taking a three-ruble bill from his pocket, slid it silently under the wicket, waited a moment and then rapped when the corner of the bill had disappeared. Now the wicket was pulled back swiftly and the head of a gray-haired woman wearing a black dress with a rather dirty white collar appeared, saying in a nasal, irritated voice: "Birth, death or marriage?" Andrei's grin broadened. "Marriage."

The clerk sniffed and pushed out to him a sheet of paper that proved to be the form on which marriages were registered. Andrei and Rosa sat at the small table and filled out the form. It was quite simple—requiring only names, addresses, occupations, names of parents and date of effective registration of marriage.

In five minutes the form had been completed. Andrei looked up. The only decoration of the office was an aging portrait of Stalin, not the kind seen in most government offices but one of the cheap chromos sold in stationery stores for one ruble, fifty kopeks. The wicket was again closed. Andrei knocked gently. Nothing happened. He knocked again. The wicket stayed closed. Finally he said in a low voice, "It's the marriage registration." A moment later the gray-haired clerk opened the wicket and took the form from Andrei, carefully checking each item. She ran through it once, then a second time.

"*Khorosho,*" she said. "Very well. That will cost you ten rubles."

Andrei pulled the note from his pocket and handed it over.

"Is that all?" he asked pleasantly.

"That's all," said the woman and closed the wicket. He turned to Rosa.

"That's all," he said. "That's what she says."

Rosa laughed. "That's what she thinks. It's only the beginning."

She pulled Andrei to her and kissed him full on the lips, Andrei flung his arms around her and lifted her from the floor. At that moment a man and woman, middle-aged, the man in *valenki*, the woman in a white wool peasant scarf came up the staircase.

"What is it?" Rosa said gaily, "Marriage, birth or death?"

The couple shyly cast down their eyes. Rosa strode to the clerk's window and rapped sharply. "Open up," she cried. "A marriage awaits."

*   *   *

How odd life was! His mind wandered back to the present. Today was Sunday, the twenty-first, or was it the twenty-second of June? Within an hour or so, he would wake Rosa, they would get up, meet Vanya and his girl, hire a boat and row up the Don to their favorite island, Peschaniya. And then at nightfall they would row lazily back to the wharf in the warm twilight, singing songs on the water and listening to others singing. And then, and then . . .

Well, in another week he and Rosa would go to Kislovodsk and take up their teaching jobs. It was such good fortune that they had both gotten positions in the same secondary school, he in mathematics, Rosa in history. Great good luck. To be sure, he would have preferred Rostov or Kharkov. But Kislovodsk would do for a year or two. And there should be time enough for his writing. He had gotten more and more excited over the possibility of writing. His correspondence course with the Gorky Institute in Moscow had gone well, and when Rosa and he visited there a month ago Professor Vasilov had been very encouraging. He had particularly liked Andrei's sketch of his father's experiences in the Samsonov campaign. God! There was so much to do. He could not wait to start. He could hardly bear to stay in bed.

Suddenly Andrei realized that Rosa was awake, her clear gray eyes burning into his, her arms reaching out to his shoulders, drawing him to her, imperiously.

Presently, they fell apart, once more quiet. Then Rosa raised herself on her arm, leaned over Andrei, and putting her face very close to his, said, "You do like me, don't you, Andrei?" He grinned. "And I do excite you, don't I?" He smiled. "And you do love me, you really truly love me?" she asked with that urgency Andrei sometimes heard in her voice. "Yes, Rosa," he said. "I love you. I like you. You excite me."

"That's good," she said, crinkling her nose. "I love you, Andrei. That's the whole point of this. And now maybe we'd better get up."

* * *

It was already hot when Andrei and Rosa got to the wharf. The sun was blazing down. The sky was deep blue with no hint of a cloud. Already heat waves shimmered from the great granaries of Rostovport and a smell of creosote rose from the heavy timbers of the wharf. Vanya and his girl, Nina, were waiting for them. Nina was a wide-faced, almost plump blond girl with a trace of a Ukrainian accent. She wore a sheer white blouse through which the heavy pink brassiere confining her large breasts was visible, and a very short pink cotton skirt which did not quite conceal her square-cut black rayon underpants.

Nina sat in the rear of the boat, "for ballast," Vanya insisted. Rosa sat in the bow. "You're the boatswain," Vanya said. "What's a boatswain?" she asked. "Well, I don't know," Vanya confessed. "But that's what you are. We must keep up with nautical niceties."

The two boys took the oars and began to pull upstream. The current of the Don was sluggish here and the boat quickly began to move ahead in sharp spurts. Early as it was, they were by no means the only ones on the river. Presently they were overtaken by the Don River excursion steamer, headed for the upper river islands and crammed with passengers who lined the decks and shouted greetings to the rowers.

The Don was wide and shallow and flowed through fertile black fields, green with wheat. They passed herds of cattle wallowing in the mud, watched over by lazy boys with long wooden poles with which to prod the cattle. It grew hotter and hotter. Andrei and Vanya stripped to the waist. Their skin was white, streaked with red. They pulled stubbornly on the oars and spoke little. Rivulets of sweat trickled down their faces, curled around their necks and soaked into their chests. Once they passed a sailboat becalmed and drifting close to the willow-lined shore. Once two muscular young men in blue-and-red sports jerseys overtook and passed them with flashing oars.

It was ten o'clock before they reached Peschaniya. The girls hopped
out, the boys pulled up the boat, and Andrei in a single gesture ripped
off his trousers and splashed into the water, Vanya after him. Later
they stretched out and refreshed themselves in the shade of the willows.
Andrei lay with his head in Rosa's lap.

"Did you read the Tass communiqué?" Vanya asked Andrei. It was
not a real question, since, of course, everyone in Russia had read the
communiqué. It had been published a week ago and was a denial
of rumors that relations between Russia and Germany had deteriorated
and that the two countries were near the point of war.

"Of course I read it," Andrei said. "What did you make of it?"

Vanya squinted as he had a habit of doing when he couldn't
make up his mind. "Well," he said, "that's really the question I was
asking you. My opinion is that somebody, probably the English, has
been trying to start trouble by spreading rumors that we are getting
ready to attack Hitler. Obviously we aren't."

Rosa spoke up. "That's not Andrei's way of looking at it, is it?"

Andrei frowned. "No. Not exactly. "

"You think there is some basis for the rumors?" Vanya asked. "You
think we might be getting ready to attack the Germans? I don't believe
it."

"No-o," Andrei spoke hesitantly. "Probably not that. But something must be going on. We don't issue statements like that without
very good reason. Maybe it is the other way around. Maybe Hitler is
getting ready to attack us. You know my opinion of the Pact."

Andrei had said from the first that the Nazi-Soviet Pact was a
cynical deal between two swindlers. Of course, he did not say this
publicly, but he long since had ceased to conceal his opinions from
Vanya and he no longer had any secrets from Rosa.

"They are both swindlers," he had told Vanya. "Swindlers. There
is no other word for it. Each is smiling at the other and holding one
hand behind his back. In that hand each holds a knife, and each
knows the other has a knife in his hand. Let one turn his back for an
instant, and the other will be on him like a highwayman."

"But why now, Andrei?" Vanya persisted, "what's happened? Everything is moving along smoothly. The Germans are getting ready to
storm the English Channel. We're sending them all the oil and wheat
they need. Why turn on us? It doesn't make sense."

"I know that," Andrei replied. "I can't explain what's happening.
But I don't trust either of them. Something must be going on. For instance—did you know that the Rostov station was closed for two
days last week? No trains passed through, north or south. Why? Nobody
would say, but one of the railroadmen told a friend who told me that
the lines were tied up with a big military movement, Troops from
the Caucasus moving up to the Ukraine."

Vanya shrugged his shoulders. "Come on, Andrei," he said. "You know there isn't anything unusual about that. Troops are always going through Rostov—down to the Caucasus, back north, off to the Volga, off to the Ukraine."

Rosa interrupted. "That's true," she said. "It may not mean anything at all. Andrei agrees, don't you, that it could be a coincidence? But supposing it's not?"

The four youngsters sat silently for a moment. A small tug pushing a barge filled with stone slowly chugged past. They waved to the tugboat captain. His wife and three small children were standing outside the wheelhouse. The passage of the tug caused a small wake and the waves lapped languidly along the sandy shore.

"How I envy those people," Nina remarked. "What a lovely, peaceful life."

Andrei sighed. "Look," he said. "I know everybody thinks that the Tass communiqué means there won't be any war. Well, I hope that is true. But we all know there is a very complicated game being played. Maybe Big Mustache will play it better than Little Mustache. Maybe it is all Churchill's doing—if so, he is a lot more clever than I think."

"Churchill would do anything to get Russia into the war," Nina interjected.

"Oh, I agree," Andrei said. "Of course he would. But maybe he doesn't have to do anything. If you start from the premise that the two Mustaches entered into a marriage of convenience; that each thought his interests were temporarily—remember that word—*temporarily* served by working together, then it just becomes a matter of timing before one or the other breaks off and goes back to his basic position, which is—"

"Unalterable hatred," Rosa said.

"Yes," Andrei said. "Hatred—well, maybe not hatred. But unalterable rivalry. Each fears and distrusts the other. Each sees war as inevitable. So why wouldn't one or, perhaps both, try to pick the least likely moment when the other has his guard down—to attack?"

"I don't know," Nina said. "It's hard to think of things like that, lying here in the sun, looking at the water. It's too peaceful."

*   *   *

In the silence that followed, the sound of a *bayan* could be heard. Andrei and his friends were not alone on the island. Half a dozen other young people were camped just down the beach and now their young voices were singing—"*Daleko . . . daleko . . .*" the song of a Siberian border guard dying far away from his home and his sweetheart.

"Such a sad song," Nina said. "It almost makes me cry."

Rosa shook her shoulders. "Oh, Andrei, let's put aside all this gloom and enjoy ourselves. It's such a beautiful fine day, the sun is so hot, the river so peaceful.

She leaned down and lightly kissed him on the lips. He smiled up at her. "Yes," he said. "I agree. Let's enjoy ourselves."

They went swimming again, wandered through the oak clusters, looking for berries or mushrooms, found neither, built a small fire, cooked some sausages, and drank a couple of bottles of beer. Then they sat in the thin shade of the willows, content and drowsy. Rosa leaned against Andrei, her arm around him and her head on his shoulder. Suddenly she spoke. "Why don't we go and pick some flowers, Andrei?"

Then she whispered in his ear, "Say yes." "Why not?" he said. They strolled hand in hand through the underbrush toward a grassy spot surrounded by willows that Andrei had seen when they had been looking for berries and mushrooms. They sank down on the grass, arms around each other.

"Oh, Andrei," Rosa said. "I'm so happy with you. If only it can last. If only nothing happens." Andrei nuzzled her ear, saying nothing. The contentment he had felt in the early morning as he lay beside Rosa watching her asleep came back to him. Lazily he pulled her close, putting his hands around her breasts, feeling the small pointed nipples stiffening. They lay in each other's arms languidly, touching each other and feeling the heat of their bodies mingle with the heat of the sun. There was clover in the grass, crushed beneath their bodies, and its strong perfume came over them like a wave. Beside Rosa's head, where her dark hair flowed out in a mane, Andrei saw a golden bumblebee, swaying on a full white clover blossom. As he pressed himself against Rosa, his hands around the smallness of her waist, his lips open against hers, Andrei heard a faint shout. He lifted his head a moment, then lowered his lips again to Rosa. He heard another shout, a bit closer, a bit more clear. It sounded as though someone was calling his name. Rosa's eyes had been closed. They opened suddenly. "Andrei," she said. "It's you. Someone is calling. It must be Vanya." "Oh, the devil," he said. "Let him call." But another shout came, still nearer. He made a face so forlorn and so comic, so like a circus clown, that Rosa could only laugh.

"Oh, Andrei, never mind," she said. "Let's go and see what's the matter. Maybe the boat floated away and we'll have to spend the night— I hope."

They rose and walked hand in hand in the direction of Vanya's cries, perfectly clear now, only a few dozen yards distant. In a moment they came out of the clearing and saw Vanya with Nina at his side. When he saw Andrei and Rosa emerge from the grove, he called, "Come quick. We've got to be going. It's"—his voice stumbled over the words—"it's war, Andrei. It's war. The Germans."

"Oh, no!" Rosa cried.

"The Germans!" Andrei said. "So that was it. The bastards!"

The four ran back to where the boat was pulled up. "The excursion boat came by," Vanya explained. "They had a radio and they heard the announcement. Molotov announced it at noon."

"What happened?" Andrei asked. He was trembling with excitement. Tears streamed from Rosa's eyes as she blindly gathered their things and tossed them into the boat. Nina moved like an automaton, her pleasant face frozen. In a moment the boat was back in the water. Up the shore they could see the boats of the other youngsters putting out in the river.

"I just don't know," Vanya said. "I don't think they knew on the excursion boat. They just shouted that Molotov had announced the attack. That it was war. The Germans started it this morning. Just at dawn."

"At dawn?" Andrei asked.

"Yes, I think so," Vanya replied. "They came across the frontier. And they bombed some cities."

"At dawn," Andrei repeated to himself, his arms pulling his oar strongly through the water. "At dawn. How curious. I woke this morning just after dawn. The sun was coming up."

"Oh, Andrei, how terrible! That was why you woke. I'll always believe that," Rosa cried. "Forgive me for weeping. I can't help it. What are we going to do?"

"Going to do?" Andrei spoke confidently. "Why, what is there to do? We will join the Red Army and beat the fascist bastards. Not that it will be easy. But we will beat them in spite of everything. Hitler will learn the same lesson Napoleon learned. And the Kaiser."

"That's right," Vanya chimed in. "When we get back to the wharf we will go straight to the mobilization point."

Andrei clenched his teeth sharply. "If there is a mobilization point. This is going to be difficult. You understand what it means? It means the Germans caught us off guard. My God! Do you understand what a fool our great leader has been? Issuing communiqués, pretending everything is all right. And at that very moment our honorable ally is massing his forces on our frontiers and preparing to attack. And he did attack. And it was a surprise. It had to be. My God!"

Andrei grew more excited as he talked. It was as if he had suddenly resolved a fiendishly complex mathematical formula.

"Of course," he shouted, pulling his oar so hard he splashed water over the whole boat. "Oh, of course. It is all so clear now. My God! How could we be so childish? You know what the Tass communiqué was about? That wasn't for us. Not for us Russians! That wasn't supposed to reassure us. Not at all. It was to reassure the Germans that everything was all right and to reassure our government, the Boss. To make him feel that everything was going fine—when he knew it wasn't, when the signs all showed something different. Oh, yes, I understand that now. And Hitler understood it too."

"There wasn't any answer from the Germans," Vanya observed.

"Of course not," snapped Andrei. "They didn't have to answer it. They knew what they were doing. They weren't afraid of anything we were doing. They had their armies moved up. They knew when their attack was going to start. Oh—what a stupid game!"

"But," Vanya spoke hesitantly, "don't you think, perhaps, we were playing for time? Getting ourselves ready to—"

"Getting ourselves ready to what?" Andrei interrupted. "You know we aren't ready. What have we been doing? What's it like in our country when we are preparing for something? Where were the campaigns? Where were the crusades? Have we Komsomols been doing anything? You know we haven't. *Chort!* The devil! It was a game of bluff and we've lost and we'll pay for it. And maybe the Mustache, too."

The more he spoke, the angrier Andrei became. He pulled his oar with short, choppy strokes that kept splashing the boat with water.

"Andrushka," Rosa said, laughing. "Maybe you should row more and talk less. Or row less and talk more. You're going to swamp the boat."

Andrei turned and glowered at her.

"Besides," Vanya said. "What happened isn't what counts now. What counts now is what is going to happen."

"That's true," Andrei said more quietly. "What happens now is what we must concern ourselves with. We will have enough on our hands. Thank God we have good tanks and good planes and a big country and we know how to fight. But it is going to be very hard. Now is when we will feel the loss of Tukhachevsky and all the other generals who were executed in 1938. What madness! Tukhachevsky wouldn't have been fooled by this. You can bet your life on that. So old Mustache shot him and all the rest. What a crime! Oh, we're paying for that now."

There was silence as Andrei spoke. Finally Rosa said, "Yes, Andrei, I'm sure you're right. But do be careful. Some things are better not said."

*   *   *

It was late afternoon when they pulled up at the wharf. The sun had grown steadily hotter. It burned down on the Don like a great lens and its rays, striking the water, turned the surface into a reflecting glass so blinding it was impossible to look at with the naked eye. They clambered onto the tarred wharf to find no attendant, no one at all, just the empty quayside street. But from loudspeakers at every corner they heard the blaring sound of military music, interspersed with the sound of an announcer speaking in eloquent tones that reverberated so strongly against the warehouse walls his words could not be understood.

"We'd best go to Komsomol headquarters," Andrei said. The four youngsters, sunburned and red, hurried through the streets. As they

neared the Sadovaya they met more and more people. Trucks with Red
Army men moved along the boulevard and groups of workingmen with
red armbands, some with rifles, marched along the pavement. The
loudspeakers blared Molotov's speech repeatedly. They heard him
speak in flat, unemotional tones about the unpremeditated attack,
"without declaration of war and without any claims being made on
the Soviet Union." The loudspeaker was hung outside Gastronom No.
1, the big grocery store, and the store was jammed with men and
women. One crowd was trying to force its way in, and another crowd,
arms laden with food, was struggling to get out. "Our cause is just,"
they heard Molotov saying. "The enemy will be crushed."

Along the street there was one queue after another. The State
Savings Bank was closed. A knot of old women, white kerchiefs on
their heads, decent black coats over their white shirtwaists, stood outside. One was wailing. "Oh, what will I do? All my money is gone."
Andrei looked at Rosa knowingly. Obviously there had been a run
on the savings banks. At the pawnshop next door the queue extended
half a block down the street. "My God," Andrei said. "It's starting all
over again. Just like 1914. People are buying things. Anything. Anything
at all."

The shoe store was jammed, women coming out with pairs of men's
boots clutched to their bosoms. At the confectionery store a harried
shopgirl was trying to close the door. "There's no more, comrades," she
kept crying. "We haven't any chocolate left. It's all sold."

They had to fight their way into the Komsomol office. It seemed
as though all of the students at the university had gathered there.
"Andrei," one shouted, "I've just volunteered." "We're leaving in the
morning," another said. A thin dark-haired girl stood against the wall
silently crying, tears coursing down her face. Two tow-headed youngsters struggled past her. "Don't cry, *devushka*," one shouted. "We'll
clear the bastards out of the country in no time."

Someone at the back of the room kept shouting, "Comrades, comrades, let there be order. Everything will be done. Please maintain
order." Several young girls with red armbands lettered in gold moved
through the crowd. "Just form lines, comrades," they repeated. "Just
form lines." A high-pitched voice could be heard saying, again and
again: "It's not cultured. It's not cultured." A soprano voice cried,
"I'm here, Petrushka, here. Don't leave me. Don't leave me."

Finally, Andrei managed to reach a desk at the rear of the room
where a serious young man named Pavel Kurbatov, one of the Komsomol secretaries, was trying to answer a dozen questions at once. He
kept repeating hopelessly: "One question at a time, comrades." Finally,
he took notice of Andrei, whom he knew, and permitted himself a thin
smile. "The usual, I suppose," he said. "You want to volunteer?" "Yes,"
Andrei said. "Immediately." "Well, it doesn't go quite that fast,"
Kurbatov replied. "First, you'll have to put your name down. Not here.

But at the next desk. Then, it's a question. What are you doing now?"
Andrei shrugged his shoulders: "As you know, I just graduated. I'm
supposed to go to Kislovodsk this week to report as a middle school
teacher." "We'll have to see about that," Kurbatov said. "I think, for
the present, teachers, doctors and engineers are not to be taken. But
tomorrow we should have exact orders."

*   *   *

An hour later the four young people emerged. The loudspeaker was
blaring Molotov's speech again: "Our cause is just . . . Victory will be
ours . . ." All four had registered for the Red Army. The question of
the girls was uncertain—whether they would be taken for regular
military service or for hospital duties. There was no decision on this.
Vanya was ecstatic—he had been told to report to the military authorities in the morning. He had not yet been assigned to an engineering
job, so he was free to join the Red Army. Andrei was despondent.
"It's ridiculous," he said. "Do they really think that I'm going to teach
mathematics to a bunch of wet-eared middle school students when
Russia is in danger? Even the Czarist government in 1914 showed more
common sense than that."

Rosa looked at Andrei sharply. "Andrei," she said, deadly serious,
"don't say such things! It's wartime."

He looked at her in some surprise, then smiled grimly. "You are
right, as usual," he said. "It's wartime."

The four walked quietly down the bright street. A red-and-yellow
streetcar clanged past, small boys clinging to the outside. A long column
of olive-drab military trucks, heavy tarpaulins covering their freight,
rumbled by.

"Incidentally," Andrei said, "why do you suppose we heard Molotov
today instead of the Mustache? What do you think, Vanya?"

Vanya started to reply when a low whine, rapidly rising to a higher
pitch, filled the air. It rose and fell and rose and fell. The youngsters
looked at each other in amazement. "Air raid!" Andrei cried. "Take
cover."

They glanced along the street. Just ahead was a white-and-black
sign saying "Bomb Shelter," with an arrow pointing down a flight of
stairs beside a building. They started to run. Andrei had an arm around
Rosa as they hurried down the steps. "It is wartime, all right," he said.
"And we'll not forget it. Not for a long, long time."

Chapter 17

FROM the back of the bus they could see the dust rising in their wake, first as a dense cloud, then gradually diffusing over the green fields of wheat like soft brown mist. Rosa and Andrei were sitting at the very end of what was really a truck with tarpaulins to shade them from the sun and long wooden slats on each side to sit on. The truck was filled. People sat not only on the long benches but in the space between, on their suitcases and bundles. Others simply leaned against the legs of the passengers on the sides. Andrei had not even tried to get tickets for the train to Kislovodsk. The Rostov station was simply overwhelmed. There were hundreds, perhaps thousands of people, camped in and around it. The militia had cordoned off the whole area and no passenger trains were moving in or out. All the lines were reserved for military movements and supplies. How long the jam would last no one could guess.

Andrei looked out across the steppe almost unseeing. Rosa squeezed his hand. "Don't feel bad, Andrushka," she said. "You know it will only be a little time." Andrei and Rosa had been ordered by the Komsomol to go to Kislovodsk and report to the school to which they had been assigned. At the same time they would go to the Military Enrollment Office and register. It would then be up to the Kislovodsk authorities as to whether they would be called up and when. That was the rule. For the moment, at any rate, schoolteachers were not permitted to volunteer. Those were instructions from Moscow and there were no exceptions.

Vanya had been accepted for military duty. They had said goodbye to him the night before. He was going to officers training school. That had already been decided. This depressed Andrei even more. He did not smile when Vanya joked: "I'll be a lieutenant before you're a buck private, Andrei. And you'll have to give me the full salute or suffer the consequences of the military code."

Andrei led Vanya to a quiet corner of the room. He began speaking in a low voice which no one else could overhear. He spoke with almost fanatical determination.

"Whatever happens, Vanya," Andrei said, "we must stay in touch. There are two things about this war of which I am certain. The first is that Russia in the end will win as she did against Napoleon. The second is that Mustache must go. Do you remember the Dekabristi, the young officers who rose against Nicholas the First?"

"Of course," said Vanya. "Everyone knows the story of the rising of the Dekabristi."

"Don't forget them," Andrei said, embracing his friend and looking deep in his eyes. "Don't forget them."

"It's so ridiculous," Andrei told Rosa. "I know that it will be just a little time. Maybe only a few days. But why this red tape? Why couldn't I have joined along with Vanya? Maybe we could have gone to training school together, although, of course, I'd rather get into the artillery. My father was in the artillery, you know."

Rosa asked, "Are you worried about your mother? Will she be all right?"

Andrei pondered the question. His mother had told him simply and factually, without a doubt in her voice, that she never expected to see him again. "You might as well know it, Andrei," she said. "We are saying goodbye. War took your father from me. I know that he died after he got home. But it was war that did it. Without that there wouldn't have been"—she had been on the point of saying "the quarrel." But she halted and left the sentence dangling.

"You are too young, Andrei, you don't know what war means," she went on. "It destroyed our life. It destroyed our family. Thank God I had you. There was nothing else, and now, you, too, will go." He tried to comfort her. "That's not what Papa would have said," he said gently.

"No, Andrushka," she said with infinite sadness. "It is not. But I don't always say what he would have said. I'm a woman and I'm your mother. I have seen great suffering in the world and in my life, as well. It's not your fault, Andrushka, I don't blame you. It is just the way the world is. But you must not imagine that life will be better. It won't be."

"But it's not as though I was leaving you all alone," Andrei argued. "At least Tetya Sofia is here, though I know that she is difficult sometimes. And Eugenia Chernov. You won't be entirely alone."

It was true that Tetya Sofia had come to Rostov. She had moved back when Uncle Boris died of a heart attack the year before. She was more crotchety than ever, but underneath, Andrei felt, she was fond of his mother. After all, she had no other living relatives, only his mother and himself.

His mother shrugged her shoulders. "Oh, Sofia and I will get along," she said. "Not that she is a great comfort. We are like two old dogs. We used to snap and snarl at each other, but now we just growl a little and mumble under our breath."

"So," Andrei said. "Perhaps it won't be as bad as you think."

His mother looked hard into his eyes. "No, Andrei, it will be. I know that and you know it, too, but you don't want to admit it because you know how sad I feel," she said. "I don't know what will happen. Somehow, I think that you will come through the war safely. Your father did. But it's what comes after war. That's the dangerous part. That's how his life was lost. And as for myself, well, let's be honest, Andrushka, dear. I'm not young anymore. I've had a long life. You've made me very happy. I guess we must think of that."

They had sat silently for a bit. Then his mother spoke again. "Andrei, you'll think this is very silly of me, I know. And your father would say that I had gone daft, right out of my head. But since Tetya Sofia came back to Rostov we have been going to church together. She was always a great one for church, you know. I never was. Your father and I used to make fun of our parents and their churchy ways when we were young. But that was really very wrong. In any event on Sunday I'm going to the cathedral and light a candle for you. Please don't mind."

They had sat a minute or two beside the table with the kerosene lamp. How many nights he and his mother had sat reading there he could not imagine. Now he fingered the silver watch in his pocket which his Uncle Boris had left him. It had been given to Boris by his father when he graduated from the gymnasium, and when Aunt Sofia had given it to Andrei, she had said, "Boris wanted you to have it." Well, it was big and bulky and sturdy. It still kept good time. On the outside of the silver case was the date 1906. Inside the case was engraved "To B P K from P B K For graduation—May 30, 1906."

Andrei rose and embraced his mother. "Well, Mama," he said. "I'll say goodbye now. You know we will not be so far away. Kislovodsk is not China. Who knows when I'll go to war?"

His mother did not respond. She kept her arms around Andrei. Then she spoke. "No, Andrushka, Kislovodsk is not so far away. In fact, it is where you were born and where your father is buried. Go to the graveyard when you get there, put flowers on the grave and write to me."

*   *   *

"It's very hard to be a woman in war, Andrushka," Rosa was saying as they traveled toward Kislovodsk. "The men are killed and the women go on living, but it's not real life. I don't want to live if you die."

Andrei drew her closer to him. "*Dorogoya, dorogoya,*" he whispered.

"Dear, dear." The bus rattled and bumped on the dusty road. There was hardly a building in sight. Here and there across the open steppe could be seen the whitewashed clusters of machine tractor stations. The area was divided into enormous state farms, some of them twenty and thirty miles square. The grain extended in vast quadrangles, bisected here and there by narrow willow-lined lanes and an occasional irrigation ditch.

It was a long all-day trip to Kislovodsk. Every two or three hours the bus halted to let passengers off or take more aboard and to let the cramped and shaken riders stretch their legs, get a breath of air or empty their bladders and bowels in the ditches and behind low bushes along the road. Most of the passengers were peasants. They talked little while the bus was moving. It jolted too much and they had their mouths and noses covered with kerchiefs to keep out the dust. But at each pause there was talk of the war. An elderly peasant with yellow stained mustache, worn leather boots and a half-length black coat tied back with a piece of rope began talking to Andrei. Despite the heat he still wore his woolen winter cap with flopping earflaps.

"What do you think, young man?" he said. "Our lads will teach old Hitler a lesson, eh? They'll knock him to smithereens, eh?"

Andrei smiled. "Well, grandpa," he said, "we'll teach the Germans a lesson all right. But it won't be so easy, you know."

"No, young man," the peasant said. He spoke with a strong Ukrainian accent. "It won't be so easy. That's certain. The Germans are clever fellows. We had some in the village where I grew up. Yes, indeed. They were clever all right. Worked very hard but not very pleasant. Put on airs, they did."

"Where would that be?" Andrei asked.

"That was in our little village of Vishnopol, young man," the peasant said. "Very good cherries we raised there. Our village was famous for its cherries. And its pretty girls. Everyone talked about them. But, of course, that was a long time ago. Everything is changed now. I haven't been there for a long time."

The driver of the bus sounded his horn, and the passengers scrambled aboard again, resuming their seats. The bouncing and the dust began again. Now the road was rising a bit and a low range of mountains could be seen to the northeast.

Andrei began talking to Rosa in a low voice, whispering into her ear. "That peasant who was talking to me," he said, "is worried. He doesn't come out and say anything directly because that isn't his way. But he will probably ask me some more questions when we stop again. And his instinct is right. It's very difficult to fool a peasant when he relies on his instinct. If he tries to reason—well, he's lost. But their instinct is unerring. And, of course, he's right. Things are going badly already."

"How badly, Andrei?" Rosa asked.

He shook his head. "Very badly, I think," he replied. "You watch. Today is the sixth day of the war. We know that it began unexpectedly. We know we were caught unprepared. And what has happened every day? Well, the communiqués are vague. But they don't claim any victories. And each day the battle is raging at a point further east. Every sign is bad. If we were doing well there would be something to show it in the communiqués."

Andrei thought for a moment and then went on: "You remember on Sunday evening I asked Vanya the question—Why Molotov? Where is the Mustache? Where indeed? Do you realize we have heard nothing from him? Not one word?"

Rosa frowned and Andrei fell silent. For all the freedom with which he mentioned "the Mustache" to Vanya and to Rosa he was perfectly aware that what he was saying was dangerous—supremely dangerous if he should be overheard.

Just after noon the bus rattled over the iron fretwork bridge across the Kuban River and pulled into the public square at Armavir. A sulky girl was selling fruit water by the glass from a curbside stand. Rosa and Andrei drank some of the pink-colored liquid. It was impossible to know what flavor it was. And as Andrei had predicted, the old peasant again fell into conversation with him.

"They say," he said, "that we have a plan for taking the Germans in. That we will lure them on, wait till they are off guard and then smash them. What do you think, young man?"

Andrei frowned and hesitated in order to indicate the seriousness with which he took the question. "Our leaders have a plan for everything," he said solemnly.

"Oh yes," the peasant hurriedly agreed. "So they do. So they do."

"Yes," Andrei continued. "You may be sure they have a plan and a good one, too. You remember, when Napoleon came to Russia in 1812, he thought it was going to be easy going. But he went home with his tail between his legs. Russia was too much for him."

"Indeed, it was," the peasant agreed. "We Russians are pretty clever, too. So you think something like that may happen again?"

Andrei pursed his lips. "Well," he said. "I'll not say either way. I'll just say I think we can all have confidence that we'll teach the fascists a lesson in the end."

The peasant shook his head thoughtfully. "I suppose you're right, young man," he said. Then with a sly note in his voice he continued, "Napoleon . . . hummm. But he got to Moscow. I just wonder—"

It was not possible to know what the peasant was going to "wonder" because Andrei sharply interrupted him to say, "Incidentally, you left Vishnopol some years back?"

"Yes," the peasant nodded.

"When would that be that you left there?" Andrei persisted.

"Some years back, young man," the peasant said, beginning to move away, "some years back."

Rosa had listened quietly to the interchange. As the peasant moved off, she said, "That wasn't fair, Andrei."

Andrei had a stubborn look on his face. "Possibly not, Rosa," he said. "But I really didn't like his questions very much. Especially not that one about Napoleon and Moscow. Very clever. Why should he ask me? Just because he sees that I'm not a peasant? Maybe it was that. Maybe something else. I just thought I'd let him know that two could play this little game. It's pretty clear he had to leave at the time of collectivization. Otherwise he would have answered my question. He's a shrewd one. Probably he was a kulak. God knows what he is now."

* * *

Andrei and Rosa were exhausted when the bus creaked into Kislovodsk at ten o'clock at night. Clouds had come up in the afternoon and they had hardly a glimpse of the great Caucasus chain, rising straight from the floor of the plain. There had been one break in the gray sky, and some of the passengers claimed they had seen snow-clad Elbruz, but Rosa and Andrei, in the back of the bus, saw nothing.

It took them an hour to find a hostel where they could spend the night and they sank into bed, too tired even to try to get a bite to eat. Andrei was depressed about himself, and the more he thought about the situation at the front, the more depressed he felt about his country. They had heard the communiqué from the loudspeaker on the street as they walked through town looking for the hostel. It said that active defense was being carried on in the regions of Dvinsk and Minsk. Baranovichi had been evacuated in heavy fighting. Each day the locale of the fighting was further east.

Andrei fell asleep filled with concern and he awoke with the same gnawing feeling. Moreover, he was ravenously hungry. He and Rosa were in a long barrackslike chamber, filled with double-decker beds. He was sleeping on the top bed, Rosa on the lower. There were probably twenty young people in the common room. He looked down at Rosa. She was awake, looking straight up. She gave him a slow wink with her right eye. For some reason she had great difficulty in winking. She could only wink with the right eye. He smiled, pulled on his trousers and went out to the washroom. When he returned Rosa was up and dressed. Andrei was in a better mood. "I felt terrible," he confessed, "but your wink changed my mood."

After breakfast they spent the morning at business. First, they went to the secondary school and reported to the director, a worn, middle-aged woman with faded blond hair. a shirtwaist pinned with a small pink cameo at the neck and steel-rimmed glasses that rode down on her nose. She was surprised to see them—surprised that they had come and certain they would not stay.

"I never expected to see you," she said. "When we heard the announcement on Sunday I assumed that none of the young teachers would report, that you would all be called up."

She had heard nothing of the Moscow edict that schoolteachers were not to be mobilized for the moment. "I don't think our authorities have heard about that either," she said. "I know that Pavlov, our chemistry teacher, has already gone. And my assistant Semachenko has gone. I imagine that when you report to the Military you will go too."

But that was not the case. Andrei and Rosa registered at the Military Enrollment office and were told the same thing they had heard in Rostov. At least temporarily, teachers were a reserved occupation. They would be notified when and if any change in the regulations was issued. To Andrei's suggestion that he would be of more value to the motherland in the Red Army than standing behind a schoolroom desk the captain with middle-age worry lines eroding his face shrugged his shoulders: "Regulations are regulations, young man. That's the first thing you learn in the Red Army."

Andrei and Rosa wandered out into the filtered sunshine. Haze hung over the mountaintops.

"Well, Rosa," Andrei said, making an effort to throw off his evil mood. "You know this is my birthplace. I think I should show you around."

Rosa smiled. "I would be delighted."

"The trouble is," Andrei said with a wry smile, "I remember very little about it. I was three years old when I left Kislovodsk and I've never been back. The only two things I can recall are my grandfather's house, which was on the edge of the town and my father's grave, which is also on the edge of town and must be in the same general direction."

"Which way is that?" Rosa asked.

Andrei looked puzzled. "Well, I'm not sure. But I think we walked down a long street with mountains rising on both sides."

They began strolling north along a street that seemed to lead out of town. As Andrei walked a curious sensation came over him. "You know, Rosa," he said finally. "I'm almost certain that I walked along this street with my mother one cold Sunday in spring, when I was a very small boy."

"And you remember it?" Rosa asked in surprise.

"No," he responded. "I don't remember it exactly. It's . . . It's . . . hard to describe. It's more like a tactile memory. I feel the distances."

They were approaching a corner in which one lane turned a bit to the northwest, the other northeast. Andrei unhesitatingly took the lane to the northeast. "This is the one," he said. "I know it."

They walked a little further. "The church and the graveyard where Papa is buried are very close now," he said. "In fact, I think we should begin to see the church just beyond the next corner."

As he walked he grew possessed with excitement. He kept stopping —glancing to the right and to the left. He was not quite clear what he was doing but it seemed to him that he was judging respective distances. They came up to the next square—and suddenly he felt lost. Just beyond the corner where he had expected to see the church and graveyard there was a sprawling construction, not yet finished. A crane still stood beside it. There were high brick walls and a great curved bowl. It was unmistakably a new stadium, not quite completed.

Andrei halted.

"Something has gone wrong Rosa," he said. "You saw how I walked up to here. I could almost feel my steps, just as though I were following an old trail. But there's something wrong. The church should be here and the graveyard beyond. But I've made a mistake. It's a new stadium . . . Perhaps we should have taken the other lane."

The remarkable confidence that had brought him to this point had gone, like air from a balloon. Andrei stood uncertain and puzzled.

Rosa was silent, too. But finally she spoke. "Perhaps, Andrei," she said, "you haven't made a mistake. Perhaps someone else has."

Andrei frowned. "What do you mean, Rosa?"

She pointed to the stadium. "They haven't finished building it yet," she said. "Perhaps your church was there and the graveyard, too."

Andrei turned and looked very hard, as if once again getting his bearings. "No harm in asking," he said. He went up to a high wooden gate that had been placed at the entrance to the stadium. There was a small wooden sentry box beside it in which a bored soldier with rifle and bayonet was lazily leaning. He stiffened when Andrei approached.

"Excuse me, comrade," Andrei said. "I seem to have lost my bearings. I'm looking for an old church I thought was just around here. St. Basil's, I think it was called."

The soldier squinted at Andrei.

"There's no church here now," he said rather sullenly.

"I see that," Andrei replied. "But was there a church here?"

"That there was," the soldier said. "There was an old broken-down church right out there." He pointed to his left. "It had been used to store grain for a long time and it was full of rats. You should have seen them run when we toppled it over. Like a pack of wolves they were."

"*You* saw them?" Andrei asked in surprise.

"That I did,'" he said. "We cleared the site, my comrades and I, and we put up the new building. We used every stone in that church for our foundations."

"And was there a graveyard back of the church?" Andrei asked.

The soldier smiled. "That there was. That there was. You should have seen the bones we tumbled in when we were making the foundations. Masses of them. Skulls too."

"What about the gravestones?" Andrei said. "Did anyone move them?"

"The stones?" the soldier asked. "No one took notice of them. Well, maybe a stonecutter did come by and hauled away a few. Said he could use them again. But the rest we just toppled into the foundations along with the bones."

Andrei stood a minute. There was something he wanted to ask but he could not think what it was.

"So there's your church, comrade, and there's your graveyard," the soldier said. "All neat and standing straight and doing some good for the likes of you and me. No longer moldering away."

Andrei turned back to Rosa. His face was drained of blood and his eyes stared at her blankly.

"Rosa," he said. "What a great joke! What a perfect joke. You see that stadium? A very useful thing. A very modern building. And the best part is that when we build the new we find a use for the old. That's St. Basil's church there, you see. Those stones and bricks. And, Rosa, that's my father's gravestone, holding it up. His gravestone and his bones, too. They make a wonderful foundation."

Rosa looked at him wide-eyed.

"You see, Rosa," he went on, "that is the superiority of our new order in Russia. It has the very best of foundations. The bones of the dead and the tombstones of the men who gave their lives for their country. In our new Russia there is no waste. We use everything."

Chapter 18

ANDREI lifted a tangle of harness from the peg on the stable wall and followed Prohar Ivanovich to the paddock. Prohar, a squat heavy-set man with the slow stride and squinting eyes of a peasant born to the steppe, already had a dirty brown gelding standing in the traces of the cart.

"Give it here, lad," he said. "I'll show you again how it goes." Andrei watched as Prohar lifted the heavy wooden collar over the horse's head, deftly inserted the bit, untangled the traces, adjusted a strap here, another there and, miraculously, the horse stood hitched to the cart. Could Andrei learn to do it? He *had* to. He was in the Red Army but what an Army! He was a hostler in a horse transport company.

Three months had gone by. Each week Rosa and he had visited the Military Enrollment Office. Each week the same story. Nothing. Rosa tried to quiet him. But how could he be quiet? Russia was in peril. The Germans were battering at the gates of Leningrad. Kiev had fallen. The drive on Moscow was gaining momentum. And still each week the weary-faced captain shrugged his shoulders. "It's a technicality," he said. "But I don't make the regulations." Andrei even wrote a letter to Voroshilov. He refused to write to Stalin. "How can I?" he asked Rosa. "You know what I think of him. I can't bear to put the name on paper."

Andrei grew more and more tense. He hardly ate. He snapped at Rosa. His face became thinner and more drawn. Somehow he and Rosa taught their classes. They took long walks in the mountains. Every day for a week they got up at dawn and, once, the rosy clouds opened like the curtains of a theater and they saw the lofty peak of the Elbruz in all its majesty. But nothing raised Andrei's spirits.

Nor could he turn his mind away from the destruction of his father's grave. He came back to it again and again in talking with Rosa. He told her the story of his visit to the cemetery as a three-year-old, the burial of the tobacco box containing his father's St. George's cross.

"When the memory of burying the box came back to me," he said, "I knew that someday I would come here and dig up the box. I was sure that I would do so. And when my mother asked me to visit my father's grave I thought to myself that at last I would bring the cross back to her. I knew that the medal might have rusted away. Well, that's a natural thing. Nothing to be upset about. But that his grave would be destroyed—destroyed not only with deliberation but with pride, with the conviction that this was a positive step, that this act would push forward the frontiers of our society. No, that idea was beyond my imagination. My mother asked me to put flowers on the grave. What can I do? I've written her a lie. I said that I had done it."

Rosa tried to calm him, but he would not be calmed.

"It's not just that," he said. "How can Russia respect herself if she destroys her own past, her own history? We are spitting on ourselves. If we spit on our past we spit on our present."

"But, Andrei," Rosa had said, "A revolution is a break with the past. That's what it must be by definition. And we did destroy the past in order to build the new."

Andrei refused to accept her reasoning. "The Revolution did not take place to destroy Russia's past," he insisted. "Russia has a glorious past. The aim of the Revolution was to destroy the rotten parts of the past so that a new and better society could be built. Lenin valued the past. He valued the achievements of the past. He even gave orders that the great cultural, artistic and historic monuments of Russia were to be preserved."

"Yes," Rosa replied. "But he also said that you do not make a Revolution without breaking eggs."

"Broken eggs!" Andrei exploded. "Broken eggs! You call the bones of Russia's heroes broken eggs? And Lenin didn't say that you had to go on breaking eggs year after year and long after the Revolution had come into power. Of course, when you are fighting a battle things get knocked about. But this is different. They had a thousand places to build that stadium. They chose to build it on the church site. They chose to destroy the church and the graves. That was a free decision. No one compelled them to do it. Nor was it an accidental choice. They did this because they wanted to. Because they *believed* in doing it."

Andrei grew more agitated. They were sitting on a ledge at the Koltso Gora, facing Elbruz, which, as usual, had hidden its peak in the clouds.

Rosa put her hand over Andrei's mouth. "Please, Andrei," she begged. "It's not that I disagree with you. I do agree. You know that. But you must not talk this way. Not even to me. You are not an adolescent. You are a responsible man. I love you and I beg you to think of yourself and even to think of me."

Andrei stared silently toward the mountain. When he finally spoke it was in a low, controlled voice but one that vibrated with feeling.

"I will be as careful as I can, Rosa. I assure you of that. But something you must understand. I believe that we will win the war. There will be—there already have been—terrible losses. The Russian people will defeat Hitler just as we defeated Napoleon. And the day will come when the rule of Mustache will end. I don't know how. But then a new day will dawn for Russia. When this war is over a new Dekabristi will succeed."

Andrei fell silent a moment, his eyes fixed on the distant mountains. Then he resumed: "It will happen. It must happen. And I will give my life, if I must, that it may happen."

They sat awhile in silence, then started back. Rosa put her arm around Andrei's waist and he held her closely. Andrei sensed how deeply his words troubled her, and in spite of his confidence in his ultimately optimistic prophecy, he was himself shaken.

As he walked through the streets of Kislovodsk toward the end of the warm afternoon in early September Andrei saw peasant carts slowly moving over the rough pavement, the faces of the peasants like stone; men and women were walking under the poplar trees in the gardens of the mineral water resort, talking quietly, their eyes fixed on some distant point. Under the shade trees were the ambulatory wounded—almost all of them officers—spending several weeks of convalescence before returning to their units. Before the shops, with their empty showcases, stood the usual queues. To Andrei the faces of these people seemed blank, as though they were citizens of another continent, another hemisphere, almost another planet. In fact, they had no real faces, merely plastic masks behind which they concealed their nature, their views, their very persons.

Rosa was right. He could not speak out. No one would listen. No one would believe him. They would walk on without turning their heads. Their ears would close. Nothing would happen. Nothing at all. Most would think him mad. Even the police would think him mad, but as a precaution they would arrest him and send him to Siberia. And Rosa, too.

He and Rosa turned into the whitewashed courtyard of the house where they had rented a room and climbed slowly to the second floor. Tucked into a crack in the door was a coarse gray card—Andrei's call-up notice. He was ordered to report for induction within twenty-four hours.

*   *   *

The next morning Andrei appeared at the call-up center with a hundred or more other recruits—teenage boys, a few middle-aged men, some peasants, stolid and silent—a grab bag, Andrei thought, or even the bottom of a grab bag. He embraced Rosa for the last time. "I will write, darling," he said. "As often as I can. Perhaps I'll keep a diary and send it to you from time to time. So I will never really be far away."

"Love me," Rosa said. "Love me always."

"I love you," Andrei said, kissing her as the sergeant began to hurry the recruits into the long reception room. Andrei looked back, and as long as he could turn his head, he saw Rosa standing frozen, her eyes fixed on him. She wore the severe white shirtwaist and dark skirt that was her teacher's costume. As soon as Andrei vanished from sight, she would, he knew, make her way to her classroom, apologize for being a little late, and take up the task of instructing the ninth form in beginning Russian history, just as, thought Andrei, he would soon be undergoing instruction in the beginning elements of military art.

*   *   *

Andrei could not believe what actually happened at the induction center. Each recruit was checked off a list. Each took, and passed, a perfunctory physical examination. Each was handed a uniform. If it fit him this was sheer chance. Some men traded trousers and jackets and got a little closer to their proper size. For the first time in his life Andrei wound foot cloths around his feet. The boots he pulled on over them were so big they would hardly stay on his feet. Finally, the men were formed up in rough columns. A sergeant counted them off in ranks of fifty. Andrei's column then marched—straggled would have been a better word for it—through the Kislovodsk streets to the freight station. There they were loaded onto a freight car and hauled north through Essentuki and Pyatigorsk, almost to Mineralnye Vody. Here they were dropped off on a siding and marched up a rocky road to the barracks and stables of the 240th Transport Company, a unit that then comprised one hundred peasant carts, forty heavy horse-drawn wagons, ten Zis trucks (only two of which were operative), three hundred and fifty horses and about four hundred men, including the fifty new recruits.

It was nightfall before the men were shoved into their barracks after a hasty supper of kasha gruel into which some sunflower seed oil had been stirred.

Andrei still could not believe it the next morning when the men were turned out at 5 A.M. to clean manure from the stables. At six they were lined up for inspection and given a piece of black bread and tea. Then under the supervision of the sergeants they were set to work harnessing the horses. It would, Andrei thought, have been unbelievably comic, a scene out of Gogol perhaps, had it not been so tragic. They were not even issued weapons. If there was one talent that he could put at the disposal of his country it was his skill as a marksman. He asked the sergeant whether they would be issued rifles. The sergeant looked at him as though he had taken leave of his mind. "What for?"

he asked. "To shoot the horses?" As Andrei wrote Rosa, it made about as much sense to assign him to a horse-drawn transport unit as it did to keep him in a schoolroom trying to din algebra into the heads of unruly teenagers. Less, actually. At least he knew algebra. He had never been closer to a horse in his life than the back seat of a droshky.

On that first day the new men were set down in the dining hall and ordered to make out their *anketas*—the detailed biographies that would follow them throughout their Army career—birthplace, names of parents, names of grandparents, occupation of parents and grand-parents, social origins, nationality, schooling, places of residence, occu-pations, skills, arrests, names of relatives living abroad, every fact that the bureaucracy thought had some pertinence. The more Andrei pon-dered his assignment as a drover, the more he felt that he must try to change it. Finally, as he handed in his *anketa* he asked the sergeant if he might have a word with the captain. The sergeant, taken aback by Andrei's request—or perhaps understanding that a cucumber had somehow been mixed up with the cabbages—escorted Andrei to the captain, a thin-faced, dark-haired Georgian with a narrow black mustache and a pimply complexion.

"Recruit Andrei Ilych Sokolov requests permission to speak to you, Captain sir," said the sergeant, saluting. He then turned smartly and left the room.

The captain looked at Andrei as though he had found a cockroach in his borscht.

"Comrade Captain," Andrei began, "may I—"

He was not permitted to finish his sentence. The captain inter-rupted: "You have not been given permission to speak." He was smoking a *papirosi*, a long tubular Russian cigarette. He sat a moment, then smashed his cigarette in the saucer which served as his ashtray and turned back to the reports he had been reading. Andrei stood immobile. Five minutes passed. The captain did not look up from his papers. Ten minutes. Twenty minutes. The captain suddenly spoke without lifting his eyes from his papers: "Return to your post." Andrei saluted, turned awkwardly and left the room.

The function of the 240th Transport Company was a simple one. It was attached to the 42nd Division, the garrison division for the north Caucasus spas from Mineralnye Vody to Kislovodsk. Its principal duty was to haul supplies—flour, salt, hay, oats, coal, meat, ammuni-tion, potatoes, buckwheat grits, cabbage, axle grease, kerosene—from the junction point at Mineralnye Vody to the barracks and camps of the division.

If the war had touched the operations of the 240th Transport Com-pany, Andrei could not perceive it. Everything was done in a slow, peasant way. Convoys of carts set out one day and returned the next. Two convoys a week for men and horses was the maximum. Although eight of the company's ten trucks were out of service, no effort at repairing them was being made—not that the repairs were difficult, but simply that these were men accustomed to horses, not machines. Prohar Ivanovich explained to him: "With a horse you know where you're at. There's plenty of feed. You don't have to haul gasoline. No parts to get out of order. If he gets distemper—well, you give him a dose and he recovers or he doesn't. If he doesn't you get another horse. It's just as simple as that."

It was not simple for Andrei. He learned quickly enough to harness the horses, but he was not permitted to drive a cart. He was classified as a loader. He hoisted heavy grain sacks and put them on the wagons and carts. He cleaned the manure. He curried the horses. He hauled hay and water and oats. He felt that the captain kept a surly eye on him, but nothing was said, even after Andrei filled out and handed in the appropriate forms requesting permission to be transferred to an artillery training school. Perhaps he was kept on the manure detail as a form of penance but this was hard to prove. The new recruits performed the most menial tasks. Discipline was strict and, often, Andrei felt, without point. Sometimes the captain ordered them out for calisthenics at 4 A.M., before the stable chores were performed. Once they were ordered to calisthenics at eight in the evening and kept at them until after midnight as a punishment. A barrel of lard had disappeared from the mess. No trace of it could be found and the most intimidating interrogation by the security detail turned up no clues.

*   *   *

A month or so after induction Andrei was ordered to ride with Prohar Ivanovich as loader. Prohar Ivanovich was driving one of the heavy four-horse wagons in a convoy hauling ammunition to a battery located on the mountain road near Zheleznovodsk. It was a steep, narrow, stone trail, not much wider than the wagon itself, ascending in a series of switchbacks blasted out of the mountain wall. As the convoy moved around a sharp switchback, the wagon ahead of Prohar's lurched slightly. Possibly a wheel struck a heavy stone and it was shoved toward the edge of the cliff. Possibly the lead horse swerved a bit. It was impossible to tell exactly what had happened, but the right rear wagon wheel slipped to the edge of the stone cliff and then slowly the wagon began to slide into open space, with such excruciating slowness that the driver had time to feel what was happening and frantically to lash his horses. It was too late. The horses lurched powerfully forward, but the heavily laden wagon continued sliding over the edge, dragging the horses after it and almost entangling Prohar's lead horses. In fact, had Prohar not reared in his seat, pulling with all his strength on the reins and bellowing like a bull, his wagon, too, would have tumbled over the mountain wall.

Half the horses in the column reared up in fear, their ears suddenly pointing skyward as the troopers, cursing a whole symphony of the ripest and richest Mother oaths in their ripe and rich vocabulary, pulled them in. The driver of the ill-fated team hurled himself from his seat as he felt the wagon slip into open space, landing on his back on the stone floor of the road where he lay, stunned, as the captain, his brows dark with fury, his face almost purple, dashed back from the head of the column accompanied by two of his sergeants. The driver tried to lift himself to his feet but the captain struck him a savage blow in the face with the flat side of his revolver. Andrei was close enough to hear the bones of the driver's nose and jaw crunch. The soldier again toppled to the stone floor of the trail.

The captain stood a moment, his revolver in hand. He started to lift it, then changed his mind. Shouting to the two sergeants he said: "Beat him!" Without waiting he walked back to the head of the column. One sergeant stepped over to the soldier who lay half-conscious on the road, his face a mass of blood and gave him a vicious kick in the ribs. Again Andrei heard the crack of bones. He started to raise himself from the wagon seat, unable to bear the sight of the torture, when he felt Prohar's great fist encircle his arm with the grip of a bear trap. "*Stoy*," Prohar whispered between his lips. "*Stoy, molodoi chelovek*, Stop, young man." The grip of the peasant drover was so powerful, Andrei could not have moved had he thrown all his strength against it. He turned, appealing, to Prohar. Andrei knew that tears stood in his eyes. He did not care. As he turned he could hear the heavy thud of jackboots and the muffled cries of pain of the soldier. Prohar did not look at him. He stared straight ahead. But through his clenching lips he kept saying: "*Stoy. Stoy.* Stop. Stop. Young man."

The beating was over in three minutes. The two sergeants, their eyes red, their faces burning, puffing a bit, lifted the body of the trooper, bleeding, his limbs crumpled and broken, unconscious but somehow still alive, and hurled it casually on top of the ammunition boxes on Prohar's wagon. They stepped back to the road, their hands on their revolver holsters and slowly looked up at Prohar and Andrei. Prohar stared back, his eyes fixed, his face like granite. Andrei stared too. He knew his face must be chalk-white. But he stared without expression into the eyes of the heavily breathing men. They paused a moment, then moved on up the column, walking slowly and easily, their hands resting on their belts, staring in the faces of the other drivers. The column resumed its course. Andrei looked over the cliff as they rounded the corner. Far below he saw the tangled mass of the wagon and the horses. Fortunately, the ammunition had not exploded.

The soldier lay crumpled on the jolting ammunition cases. He was breathing in quick gulps that rattled fiercely as the air was forced through his broken nose into his broken rib cage.

"Can't we do something, Prohar?" he whispered.

Prohar moved his head slightly. "Nothing, young lad. Nothing," he said. "Not unless you want a sample of that yourself."

The soldier was still alive when they reached the battery half an hour later. As the supply column waited to unload, two security officers came up to the wagon, pulled the soldier off the cases, letting his body fall to the ground; each grasping a leg, they simply hauled it over the rough earth. The last sight Andrei had was of the man's head, bouncing from side to side as the security men dragged the body over the court-yard to the iron-barred prison cell. If the soldier's neck had not been broken before, it clearly was broken now.

On the return trip Andrei sat silently beside Prohar. He knew the peasant did not want to talk about what had happened. But within himself he kept asking, Why? Why? Why? It was not the soldier's fault that the wagon and horses had been lost. Or, even supposing that it was, was this an offense for which a man should give his life? He thought of the dark and angry eyes of the Georgian captain and now this rage. The man was mad. A murderer. And wasn't this not only a crime against man but a crime against the state—for when had the state more need of men than in this hour?

Finally, he could restrain himself no longer.

"Tell me, Prohar," he said. "Does this often happen?"

Prohar remained silent for a long time, his eyes fixed on his horses. At last he spoke in a very low tone, and again he barely moved his lips so that from a distance of a few feet no one would have realized that he was speaking.

"No," he said. "Not often. Once before, we lost a wagon on this trail."

"Did the same thing happen?" Andrei asked.

"No," Prohar said. "No. That time they just tossed the man over the cliff."

*   *   *

Andrei had begun to keep a diary. He wrote on a packet of thin cig-arette papers, in a tiny, exact hand, using a fine nib drawing pen. That evening as he lay in his bunk he made an entry: "In the Czar's time it was considered very humane to prohibit serf owners from imposing capital punishment on their serfs. Only the lash. And in the Czar's Army it was the same. Soldiers could be lashed or beaten with staves. But they could not be executed. If it chanced that after one hundred lashes or two hundred blows of a stave they happened to die, that was their business. Nothing like this happens in our Soviet times. In the Red Army the lash and the stave are forbidden. If a soldier should happen to die because he collides forcibly with the heel of a Nagan or falls heavily on a stone pavement or should chance to topple over a cliff—that is his bad luck. After all, in our progressive times, corporal punishment has been abolished. This is one more achievement of our humane socialist society."

Chapter 19

THERE must, Andrei thought, be a flat wheel on the coach in which he was riding. Or perhaps five days on the hard upper bunk pounded the rhythm of the wheels into his body. His whole life reverberated to the clackety-clack of the wheels. His skull vibrated and his eyes seemed to be bulging from their sockets. How much longer could the ride go on? He was dizzy, his bones ached, his throat was sore and he felt he must be running a fever. Lying on the bunk just under the ceiling he breathed hot stale air filled with the smells of half a hundred bodies. The smells had been seeping into the car for five days and accumulating like sludge in a cesspool.

It was late afternoon or early evening. He looked again at his Uncle Boris's big silver watch. Yes, five o'clock on the fifth day of this endless train ride from the Caucasus. The unexpected—the almost incredible —had happened. Andrei had been ordered to report for training to the artillery officers' school. Up to the last he had feared that in some manner the Georgian captain would spoil things for him, but nothing whatever happened. He was released from duty with the 240th Transport Company and handed his orders for military travel to Moscow to report on arrival at the artillery school. Three days after getting the notice he was on his way.

The night before departure Andrei got a bottle of vodka, actually *samogan*—moonshine—from one of the hostlers who lived in the village of Zheleznovodsk. He shared it with Prohar Ivanovich and two other men with whom he had formed a comradeship—Semyon Semyonovich and Artem Vasiliyevich. All three were peasants, each had grown up on the Don steppes. They were slow, solid, strong and cautious men who expected little from life and were seldom disappointed in their expectations. They knew horses as well as humans, and each had the ingrained peasant habit of survival. They never volunteered for duty, yet never appeared to hang back. They obeyed orders, but never brilliantly and never too quickly. They knew the habits of each sergeant—all were evil men, but some were cowards and others were reckless. They knew whom to flatter, whom to cheat, whom to avoid. They understood the black passions that boiled up inside the Georgian captain and knew how to make themselves scarce when his anger was rising or, if they could not escape his path, how to use the peasant's old trick of demeaning themselves to soften his blows and divert his anger.

Andrei respected them as much as any men he had met, and he now realized that Prohar Ivanovich had literally saved his life when the sergeants were beating the ill-fated driver.

Andrei's comrades drank the vodka swiftly and with little talk. They wiped the mouth of the bottle with their sleeves, threw their heads back and let the vodka pour down their throats. Each wiped his mouth with his sleeve and chewed a piece of black bread as the next man drank. The bottle was passed around only twice.

"Well, good enough, lad," Semyon said. "Keep your head down when the firing starts. A dead soldier is no good to himself or anyone else."

"That I will," Andrei replied.

"Carting may not be very exciting," Semyon added, "but it's healthier than getting shot at."

"True enough," Andrei replied.

"Ah, well, there'll always be some shit for you to shovel here if you change your mind," Artem said in a dry voice. "You'll be going to Moscow. The Germans believe they are going to take our Moscow. But I think that's not so easy to do."

"No," Andrei agreed. "Not so easy. They didn't take it in October. Now it's November. Soon it will be December. I think day by day it gets harder and harder."

"The Germans think we Russians are very stupid," Artem went on. "And God grant it we are. But we are strong when we pull together. That's what the Nazis forgot to take into account."

Prohar picked up the empty bottle, squinted at it, laid it down. "Yes," he said. "You'll be in Moscow soon enough and they'll be putting boards on your shoulders and stars on those boards—that's right?"

"I hope so, Prohar Ivanovich," Andrei replied.

Prohar Ivanovich sighed. "Well, young man," he went on. "One thing I will say. Just remember your old comrades in the horse company after you get those boards. Just don't forget us and our life together as soldiers."

Indeed, Andrei would never forget his first days of Army life with the 240th Company. And now, in the hard car nearing Moscow, a feeling of warmth washed over him at the thought of his farewell with his comrades. He could not have imagined that this memory in later times would return to haunt him, to cause him to look into the very fiber of his being and to examine his conduct as strictly—more strictly —than a priest taking confession.

*   *   *

The train was passing stations at more frequent intervals, now that they were drawing near to Moscow. Andrei pulled out of his breast pocket a postcard, and with a worn pencil wrote—with difficulty, because of the swaying of the train—a note to Vanya, whose training school was in Moscow or nearby. Andrei was uncertain whether Vanya had finished training but he knew that many classes had been sent en masse into active service during the terrible days of September and October. Maybe they could meet, maybe not. He signed it, "Your Faithful Dek-ist." That was the way he and Vanya had been signing their letters. There had been no question from the military censor. If he had been asked, Andrei would have explained that the abbreviation stood for "Deka-brist"—that is, Decembrist. Since the Decembrists were great heroes of the Revolution and revered as patriots before their time, it did not then, or later, occur to him that anyone could find this form improper. Had he been pressed, however, to tell the full truth he would have been compelled to admit that he was using the word in a very special sense— one which Mustache was hardly likely to approve.

Despite his exhaustion from the long trip, Andrei was excited. He had been to Moscow only once, a few days in the past spring with Rosa. Now he was returning at a historic moment. For weeks Moscow had battled with her back to the wall against the Nazi onslaught. The Germans, he knew, had gotten almost to the outskirts of the city. But, strong as was his hatred for Stalin, Andrei felt certain that Stalin's presence in the capital for the November seventh holiday and parade in Red Square was no theatrical gesture. It meant that Stalin believed the capital could and would be held. He was, in this symbolic way, saying as much not only to the Russian people but to the Nazis and to the whole world.

Andrei had one deep regret as the train began to move very slowly into Moscow. He had been unable to see his mother when he passed through Rostov on the way north because he was not permitted to leave the train during its stop there. He was growing anxious at the signs of a German breakthrough into the Donbas just north of Rostov. If the German drive was not swiftly halted, it could easily sweep to the outskirts of Rostov and Andrei was not sanguine about the ability of the Red Army to stop the Nazis there. If what he had seen of the Army of the Caucasus in the 240th Transport Company—and what he had heard from his comrades about the 42nd Division—was a criterion, re-sistance to the Nazis would be feeble indeed.

And he was worried, too, about Rosa. She was now in the Red Army, accepted for service as a nurse. But where she was being sent—or had been sent—and whether she would be attached to the field service or to a base hospital he had no idea. All he had was her military post-box number.

The train moved slowly into the Kursk station and came to a halt.

Andrei dropped down from his bunk, pulled on his greatcoat and battered fur hat with its rabbit ears, slung the knapsack with his few possessions over his back, checked to see that he had his orders in his breast pocket, and patiently waited in the aisle as the passengers slowly shuffled to the door of the car. There were two military police at the car door with Tommy guns over their backs and red armbands. They carefully examined the passports and papers of the passengers, the bulk of them soldiers and officers. Most of the officers were waved on. The soldiers were ordered to stand aside and wait.

When the train had finally been emptied, the military police formed the soldiers into columns of two and escorted them to the station *komandatura,* the military commandant. Here each man's identity papers and orders were again examined, this time with minute care. A number of soldiers were ordered to stand aside. Andrei, however, was passed through and given an address on Frunze street to which he was to report. He pushed his way through the station. It was 8 P.M. Out on the street it was bitter cold. The city was blacked out to total darkness. As he stood a moment in the cold and dark night to let his eyes adjust he heard faint thunder in the distance. Cannon. It was the first time since the start of the war that he had heard gunfire.

*   *   *

On the eighteenth of February 1942, two men were killed by live shell-fire. Like Andrei, they were students at the 12th Artillery Training School, on an old estate about twenty miles west of Moscow. Like Andrei, they were participating in a training exercise, moving forward under the barbed wire from a line of trenches that had been dug by some previous class. The temperature on this day was twenty degrees below zero Fahrenheit and the ground was like iron. Moving half a mile across shell holes to another series of trenches held by the supposed enemy, they were crawling flat on their stomachs, rifle in one hand, wearing snow capes that made them almost invisible at a distance of two or three hundred yards. They had been warned that live shells would be fired over them in a creeping barrage that would reach and then advance beyond the trenches ahead of them. If they broke pace or stood up they would be killed. The men faithfully followed their orders. Unfortunately, a small military accident occurred. There was a shortfall of one shell. It burst fifty feet from the two men and they were instantly killed by shell fragments. Andrei, forty or fifty feet further away, heard the fragments whistle through the air around him and saw the bodies of the two men literally torn to shreds. Two or three bloody fragments hit him, but only later, when he returned to barracks, did he find a rip in his white cape where a splinter had torn it.

No man halted when the accident occurred. The orders were explicit. Move forward at the designated pace regardless of obstacles. Not until the students reached and occupied their objectives did the commanding officer, a lieutenant not more than a year older than Andrei, direct a squad to return, recover the bodies and deliver them to the morgue.

This was the style of training school. Severe. Disciplined. Remorseless. The men were up at 5 A.M. for physical exercises. Indoor classes in the morning. Training maneuvers in the afternoon. Sometimes overnight maneuvers. Always with artillery. Mathematics classes. Range finding. Map reading. Trigonometry. The rules of command. Military discipline. The officers' code. Officers did not eat with their men. Officers did not live with their men. Each officer had his enlisted orderly. No friendship was permitted between officers and enlisted men. Men were not permitted to address officers familiarly, that is, they could not employ the "thou" form; officers were authorized to use the familiar form in addressing men. It was the duty of the officer to maintain discipline inviolate. The officer was not permitted to carry his luggage or parcels—an orderly carried his things. Nor was he permitted to sit in other than orchestra or box seats at the theater.

But this was not a caste system, the instructors insisted. Not at all. This was simply to maintain iron discipline, for without iron discipline the Army could not meet the tasks given it by the Party and the government. The officers' ration was superior to that of his men because his responsibilities were greater. His quarters were better because his duties were greater. Each officer must display unflinching obedience to his superior. The military code permitted no exceptions. The officer presented his opinion to his superior when invited. A command was an order to obey. It was not the duty of the lower officer to question the decision of his superior.

Three men in Andrei's barracks got a bottle of vodka somewhere one Saturday night. The young lieutenant in charge unexpectedly entered the barracks and found them drinking. Within ten minutes the three men had been stripped of their rank as officers in training and ordered to the front to join a *strafny* battalion, a penalty battalion, that was the alternative to death before the firing squad. These battalions were used to form the first assault wave on impregnable positions. Machine-gun squads were placed behind to mow them down if they faltered. They attacked tanks with gasoline grenades or hurled themselves under the treads with loads of dynamite. They walked through—and exploded—enemy mine fields so that the regulars could safely follow the trail of their shattered bodies. They died at gun positions shackled to their guns.

*   *   *

"It is difficult," Andrei wrote Rosa. (She was serving in a field hospital attached to the army that first yielded Rostov and then retook the city a week later. She had seen his mother and wrote Andrei that she had come through the fighting and brief Nazi occupation without harm.)

"The regime is demanding. Heavy. But I am doing well. And at last I am happy. I am learning to be an officer, and I am certain I will serve our country as I hoped."

For the first time Andrei felt at home. He was doing what he had long expected to do, following the footsteps of his father, becoming an artillery officer. At last his technical proficiency in mathematics was being put to valid use. He had slipped easily into the rigid discipline. In a sense it was an extension of his own self-discipline; his logical and exact conduct of his own affairs; his effort to arrange his life with precision, to observe, to analyze, to solve problems, to model himself on Lenin's own literary hero, Rakhmatev. He did not brood over the punishment inflicted on his three comrades sent to the *strafny* battalion. This was war. Andrei not only did the demanding physical exercises imposed by the drill schedule. He did more. His body became lean and muscled.

He and his comrades cheered when the Red Army launched its great December offensive on the Moscow front and drove the Nazis back through the bitter cold to positions fifty and sixty miles outside the city.

"Our first big victory!" he wrote Vanya, who was on active service, a junior lieutenant in an infantry division participating in the Moscow offensive. "I congratulate you and all of the men of the active Red Army. I am confident this is the first victory of a series which will end in Berlin." He signed himself "Your Faithful Dek-ist" and added, "You are all Dek-ists now," making a play on words, since the Moscow victory was won in December.

The failure of the winter offensive of January and February 1942, particularly the offensive that was designed to lift the siege of Leningrad, depressed Andrei, and he made an entry in his diary, one of the infinite number of tiny entries which he jotted down. He found he could put two hundred words on a single piece of cigarette paper. "We can defeat the Nazis—but will we? Big Mustache understands no more than Little Mustache. In the summer Little Mustache tried to win on all fronts. It cost us terribly. But he failed. In the winter Big Mustache tried to push back little Mustache on all fronts. He failed. We will pay a terrible price for the insanity of the Mustaches next summer."

On April 29, on the eve of the May Day celebrations, Andrei was commissioned a junior lieutenant. He was assigned to the 349th Artillery Brigade on the Central Front. On May 1 he swung down from the command car in which he had ridden from Moscow, strode to a newly built log hut, camouflaged by fresh-cut pine boughs, was waved inside by the sentry on duty and drew himself up in a smart salute before a middle-aged major who sat before a rough pine plank table studying a sectional map with a pair of calipers.

"Junior Lieutenant Andrei Ilych Sokolov reporting for duty, Comrade Major."

The major removed the pair of silver-rimmed glasses he was wearing, took a glance at Andrei, apparently saw nothing objectionable in his appearance and said, "Tell the orderly to show you to quarters, then return here as soon as possible. Can you operate range-finding equipment? Yes? Very good. I'll send you up to our observation post as soon as you are ready. We lost a lieutenant there this morning. You can take his place."

* * *

Twenty-one days shy of eleven months after the Nazis had attacked and almost seven months since being inducted into the Red Army, at shortly after 2 P.M. on May 1st, Junior Lieutenant Andrei Sokolov lowered himself into the fixed steel gear of an optical artillery observation post. The position was located in the tottering belfry tower of a badly damaged Orthodox church, some miles east and south of Orel on the southeastern flank of the Moscow front. It had been, Andrei noted as he climbed the crude wooden ladder attached to the shattered wall of the tower, a working church until fairly recently. Looking out from the tower he could see part of the onion dome, its curved space still glowing in faded blue, and here and there the outline of once gilded stars. He wondered how much the peasant congregation had paid for the decoration. The tower itself had been punched with holes many times by Nazi fire and Andrei found it hard to believe it would support his weight.

An enlisted man stood beside him, reading out the coordinates as Andrei carefully zeroed the lenses onto the distant village where, it was known, the Nazis had mounted a battery. At 2:22 P.M., observing a flash of gunfire from the village, he calmly read the coordinates into his cable-connected mouthpiece. "For Russia!" he whispered. Seconds later he saw the flash of a Russian shell explode on target.

At that moment, for the first time in his twenty-two years of life, Andrei felt a completely fulfilled man. Where his father had laid down his sword, Andrei now had lifted up his own.

Chapter 20

ANDROPOV took the slip of very thin paper which Gorbunov handed him and laid it on the brown pad that covered the central portion of his desk. Gorbunov made no attempt to conceal his excitement.

"Your hunch, Yuri Vladimirovich, was really extraordinary," Gorbunov said. "The ikon is a splendid one. At least a couple of hundred years old. Perhaps, more. But the backing is much more modern. Exactly how old I can't say offhand."

"How did you find the note, Georgi Andreyevich?" Andropov asked. He, too, was startled by the circumstance and made no effort to conceal his reaction from his subordinate.

"Well," Gorbunov said. "To start with, I looked at the ikon carefully. Unlike some of them this one is not made of laminated wood. It is a solid piece. But when I turned it over I saw that it had a thin veneer backing that had been daubed with black paint not too long ago. The wood, itself, was attached to the ikon by tiny invisible nails.

"So, I simply took my penknife and inserted the blade under the thin wood, and applying gentle pressure, began to raise the small nails. There was really no trouble about it at all, and in a minute the veneer backing came off in my hand and there was this slip of paper—not attached either to the ikon or the veneer, just resting there. Obviously placed there for concealment."

"Excellent," Andropov said. "Excellent. Now let's see what the message says."

He turned it sideways so the two of them could read it simultaneously.

There was just one line on the paper—printed in small type. It read:

Звенѣть, колокола!

"Hmm," Andropov said. "Ring out the bell."

"Oh, yes," Gorbunov said. "I knew you would think so. It is perfectly obvious. It is a code message. That is, not really a code. It is an instruction to someone abroad."

"To carry out certain previously given orders," Andropov said.

"Obviously," said Gorbunov. "Not a code. A cipher, I suppose you'd call it technically. We have no way of knowing what the order may be which is to be fulfilled. But we do know who was giving the order, and by a process of deduction, we should be able to know its general nature."

"That is quite true," Andropov said, staring very hard at the little slip of paper.

"Sokolov has, as we know, confederates abroad," Gorbunov ran on, unable to stop chattering in his excitement. "By passing this word he is almost certainly telling them to go ahead with some prearranged plan. The symbolism of the message suggests that he is instructing them to make public some document or other."

"That certainly sounds logical," Andropov said. "But it does seem puzzling that he would send a written or, rather, printed, message when all he had to do was to whisper it into the ear of the Morgans."

"That bothered me at the start, too," Gorbunov said. "But then I thought: After all, Sokolov is an extremely careful man. He does not trust anyone—save perhaps two or three persons who were close to him in prison. He might be perfectly prepared to use the Morgans to transmit his message, but entirely unwilling for conspiratorial reasons to give it to them textually."

"I don't follow that exactly," Andropov said.

"Well," Gorbunov explained, "he conceals the message in the ikon. The Morgans don't know it exists. There is no way they can give it away. Even if it is found they are none the wiser. But at the same time, he could tell them. 'Do give my regards to my old friend, Ivan Ivanovich, when you get back to America. By the way, he fancies himself a specialist in ikons—you might show this one to him.' "

"True," Andropov said, but he allowed a certain note of skepticism to enter his voice.

Gorbunov detected it. "Well, Yuri Vladimirovich," he said, "that is a very primitive kind of scenario. But I think you can perceive very well the possibilities that exist."

"Oh, yes," Andropov replied. "I do indeed. I'm not suggesting that something like this wasn't possible. I was merely trying to test the hypothesis."

*　　*　　*

Andropov continued to stare at the curt message, running his finger over the paper. As he did so he noticed that a tiny segment at the end flaked off. He let the paper lie in front of him and stared out into space, pondering the possibilities.

"That was first-class work, Gorbunov," he said. "I didn't really suppose you'd turn up something. But it shows that one must never overlook a single possibility. Which reminds me—what about the samovar? Have you had a chance to look at that?"

Gorbunov smiled.

"We'll probably end up by dissolving it in acid," he laughed. "But as of now I can tell you the following. There are no messages and no signs of any messages scratched or engraved on its surface, neither the inner nor the outer surface. I myself knocked off the handles with a hammer. They are only soldered on. Nothing under them and the joints are obviously very old. The silver plating is old, too, and there is no sign anywhere of any recent silver dip or new plating which could have been applied to cover something engraved on an earlier surface. There remains the inside of the spout. I turned that over to an assistant to cut open with a cold chisel. But I'd bet my career there is nothing there."

"Well," Andropov said, "I'm certainly inclined to agree with you. But we want to cover all possibilities. So let him continue his work with the cold chisel."

"Oh, that he will, I assure you," Gorbunov said. He was growing more and more expansive. "Do you have any further instructions, Yuri Vladimirovich, in the light of our discovery?"

Andropov grimaced inwardly at Gorbunov's use of the term "our discovery." He really was pushing a bit hard on this one. Well, perhaps, that was only natural. He knitted his brows a bit, pretending to consider, before responding to Gorbunov's question.

"We-ll," he drew out the word, "I think not at this very moment, Georgi Andreyevich. There are some other bits and pieces which I want to assemble before drawing firm recommendations."

Gorbunov seemed a bit taken aback. He hesitated, then plunged ahead. "If I might make a suggestion, Yuri Vladimirovich," he said, waiting for Andropov's encouragement.

"Surely, Georgi Andreyevich."

"Well," Gorbunov continued. "I just thought, perhaps, in view of this new evidence you might want to go forward with certain measures, say, with respect to Sokolov. As a matter of fact, anticipating that possibility I took the liberty of ordering a special detail to stand by—just in case there was some urgency . . ." Gorbunov's voice trailed off. Possibly he suspected by Andropov's expression that he was treading on slippery ground.

Andropov made no immediate reply. Again, he seemed to be considering Gorbunov's proposal. Actually, his mind was making some lightning calculations. Perhaps Gorbunov was not so completely reliable as he had thought. Very interesting. He immediately slipped back into his customary tone of close and friendly collaboration. He smiled, tapped the table with his finger a minute, then spoke: "That's extraordinarily thoughtful, Georgi Andreyevich. But let's not move so fast that we miss any threads of this affair. I think for the moment you had better just wait. And, of course, proceed with the study of the samovar."

Gorbunov relaxed. "Very good, Yuri Vladimirovich," he said. "I'll be on instant call."

* * *

As Gorbunov left the room Andropov lowered his head very close to the thin slip of yellowed paper. Yes. As he suspected, he could detect the scent of age, the musty smell of old paper. He very slowly slipped an ordinary sheet of rather soft foolscap under the slip, being careful to preserve the broken-off fragment as well. This was old, brittle paper. Very curious paper for a contemporary conspirator like Sokolov to use to phrase a message. Where would he get it? To be sure, he could use it to deflect suspicion. To an ordinary eye, it would certainly not seem to be part of a plot against the Soviet state. In fact, the more Andropov thought about it, the more he wondered himself. There was something about the note that had thrown him off at the very beginning, but what with Gorbunov's excitement and his own, he had not been able to focus on the element that subliminally had attracted his attention. He studied the note again:

Звенѣть, колокола!

Suddenly he started to chuckle, but hastily suppressed the sound, turning it into a cough. This was no time for chuckles to be recorded on the eavesdropping devices that naturally were implanted in his office. He took the little piece of paper and very carefully placed it in an envelope, including the tiny broken fragment. Then he sealed the envelope and put it in his pocket. For the first time since the miserable Sokolov business had begun, he felt a surge of confidence. He still did not know what was going to happen at the Politburo meeting and he certainly didn't appreciate Gorbunov's "helpful initiative" in assembling a task force to arrest Sokolov. But all of this paled in the light of this odd and valuable piece of paper which he now had in his breast pocket.

Just how long, he wondered, had it been since the last *yat* had vanished from Russian typography? Forty years? Fifty years? A long, long time, that was certain.

Chapter 21

HAD it not been for Peter Vasiliyevich, Andrei would never have made his way back to the command post. Peter Vasiliyevich was the soldier who read the coordinates out to Andrei at the observation tower. There had been little enough action. After the initial exchange, in which Andrei's battery had scored a hit, there had been only desultory shots, every hour or so. "It's by the clock, Lieutenant," the private told Andrei. "We're both firing a round an hour. Just so that each side shows the other that it's still alive." Andrei kept track. The private was correct. The German shots came precisely on the hour: 4 P.M., 5 P.M., 6 P.M., 7 P.M. There was nothing like the Germans for punctuality. The Russian shots were not quite so regular, but they seemed to be timed to the half-hour.

With full darkness Andrei was ordered to return to the command post. His legs were stiff from the hours of sitting at the range-finding apparatus, and he found himself almost sliding down the narrow wooden ladder that connected the belfry with the ground. Darkness was total. The night was overcast. No stars. Not a sound to be heard. Andrei could not even make out the tall frame of Peter Vasiliyevich standing two or three paces from him. Nor had he any idea of directions or how he was to find his way back to the command post. As Andrei stood in bewilderment, Peter Vasiliyevich spoke: "Better give me your arm, Comrade Lieutenant. It's so dark it will be difficult to find our way." Andrei took a step or two and extended a groping hand in the direction of the voice. He was remarkably reassured when he felt the firm, tough shoulder of the straight-figured private.

"Very good, Peter Vasiliyevich," Andrei said. "Let's see how it goes."

The two men moved along, side by side, Peter's strong hand encircling Andrei's slender arm.

"Ah," the soldier said, "it's only too easy to lose your way at night. I was coming back one night from our observation post. Not a very good one, just a small elevation in a patch of woods. I was more or less feeling my way when I heard some voices. Something about them caught my ear. Didn't quite sound like our lads. I stopped and crept forward a few paces—they were the *nemtsi*, the Germans. Somehow I had reversed directions entirely. Another step and I'd have fallen right into their lines."

"That was a close one," Andrei said.

"It was, indeed," the soldier replied. "It doesn't pay to be too hasty at the front. As the old saying goes—haste makes waste. In fact, it can quite take your life away. Just like that."

The men walked a bit in silence, Andrei frequently stumbling on the broken terrain. His eyes could now perceive the faint distinction between sky and earth, but the sky was so dim he could make out no landmarks—even had he known them. He had been so excited when coming up to the observation post earlier in the day that he retained only a vague notion of the terrain. The ruined church was not in the village proper but in an open field a quarter mile away. The path leading to the command post ran across several open fields and then into a forest. The ground was slippery and full of water. Two or three times Andrei would have fallen had it not been for Peter's firm grip.

Andrei heard a distant pop and almost simultaneously saw a sallow light spread flatly over the landscape. It was, he realized, a magnesium flare, and it hung as if suspended a thousand feet over the front lines, casting all objects into shadowless relief. Though Andrei knew what it was and understood that in its light tiny figures like those of himself and Peter Vasiliyevich could not be seen, he felt strangely frightened, as though he had awakened from a nightmare to find himself standing naked in Red Square before a multitude of people.

The soldier's reaction was quite different. "That's a help," he laughed. "They're trying to light our way home."

"Whose flare would that be?" Andrei asked.

"Oh, theirs, I think. We only use them when we are advancing or when we think they are getting ready to attack. But they put them up all the time. Maybe they are nervous. Maybe they want to catch the patrols we have out near their lines. Hard to say what the Germans think."

*   *   *

In the light of the flare, Andrei saw that they were nearing the edge of the forest where the command post and batteries were located. He wondered what had happened to the lieutenant whom he had replaced. Peter Vasiliyevich had made no mention of him, and Andrei, his mind filled with officers' indoctrination, was reluctant to ask such a question. In fact, he had some qualms about Peter's gesture of taking him by the arm—surely this was not allowed under the provisions of the officers' code—yet it was so familiar, so sensible, and so lacking in self-consciousness that Andrei accepted it as an act of comradeship between man and man.

"Have you been long with this unit?" Andrei asked.

"Long enough," the soldier replied. "We came from Siberia in the fall and fought in the Battle of Moscow."

"So you're a *Siberyak?*"

"Not really, Lieutenant. I'm from the Volga. Simbirsk. Our unit just happened to be in Siberia."

"Have you occupied this position very long?"

"We came to this place toward the end of winter, late March it was. Just beginning to get a little warmer. We got here in time for the spring thaw. Once the thaw starts it's not so easy to move the guns."

They had entered the forest now and the darkness was even more impenetrable.

Finally Andrei asked the question that had been on his mind since morning. "What happened to the lieutenant whom I replaced?"

Peter did not reply immediately, and when he did, Andrei could hear the note of peasant caution in his voice. "That, Lieutenant, I can't rightly say. I wasn't at the observation post. He had Gleb Andreyevich with him. What I heard was that there was an accident. Lieutenant Petrov it was, he fell from the ladder and was killed."

"An accident then?"

"So I heard."

Andrei heard a faint mechanical sound. Later he realized it was the click of a rifle bolt. Peter said: "It's the guard post, sir."

They identified themselves and passed through the sandbagged outpost into the headquarters compound.

*   *   *

Andrei found the commanding officer, Major Stromlin, in the mess hut next to the command post. With him were half a dozen officers of the battery, standing about a table, vodka glasses in hand.

"Ah, comrades," the major said as Andrei entered. "Our newest addition, Lieutenant Sokolov. Come, Lieutenant, and join us in a toast to the May first holiday."

A *rumka* of vodka was hastily poured for Andrei. "*Do adna,* bottoms up!" the major cried.

Andrei threw his head back and downed the fiery liquor. He did not like vodka, never drank it by choice. But he knew that the officers' code required him to drink on comradely terms with his fellow officers and particularly his superiors. He sensed that the mood of the officers was quiet and serious—or tired. Though the vodka seemed to relax their nerves a little, they were on guard, ready for action at any moment, but pleased to have a respite. In addition to the vodka, there were some *zakuski*—hors d'oeuvres, a little caviar, a little tinned crab from the Far East, some cheese and black bread, cucumber pickles and pickled tomatoes. A thin, dark-haired mess girl wearing a private's stripes moved in and out of the room unobtrusively, bringing a bottle of vodka, a few more glasses, a loaf of bread. Andrei hardly noticed her, she was so slim and she moved so quickly and quietly about the room.

"Did you come from Moscow this morning, Lieutenant?" the major asked.

"No, Comrade Major," Andrei replied. "I came from outside of Moscow. I haven't been in the city for some weeks."

"My wife is there," the major said. "At least I believe she is. I haven't heard from her since winter. Perhaps she has been sent away, although I have not heard of any evacuations since our offensive pushed back the Germans."

"You participated in the December offensive?" Andrei asked.

"Yes," the major said. "We did. We laid down preparatory fire for the breakthrough on the Volokolamsk *chaussée* and then we followed up as rapidly as we could. As a medium artillery battery we could not move as fast as the tanks and the infantry when the breakthrough came."

One of the lieutenants came up and the major turned away.

"My name is Petroshenko," the lieutenant said. "I know it sounds Ukrainian. But I'm a *Moskvich* born and bred. I hear you come from the Don country."

Andrei hadn't the slightest notion of how Petroshenko might have heard anything about him, but he responded quickly. "Well, not exactly, I come from Rostov. But I'm really a city proletarian, not a Don Cossack."

Petroshenko smiled—a tight hard smile. He was very blond, his bald head was shaven, and Andrei instinctively did not like or trust him.

"What have you heard about your predecessor?" Petroshenko asked.

"Not much," Andrei said. "Do you mean Lieutenant Petrov?"

"That's the one."

"Well, what did happen? I was told he fell off the ladder."

"Who told you that?" snapped Petroshenko suspiciously.

Andrei paused. His dislike of the man was even more strongly stimulated. He should not have made the remark. Still, there it was.

"The private who worked the post with me this afternoon," Andrei said, "told me that was what he had heard."

"What's this private's name?" Petroshenko asked in a tone which reminded Andrei of a prosecutor's.

"I don't know his family name," Andrei said. "Peter Vasiliyevich, I think he is called."

"That's the man," said Petroshenko. "Keep your ears open, and if you hear anything more let me know."

To Andrei's surprise, Petroshenko abruptly left him and walked out of the hut.

A small man on the verge of middle age, his hair closely cropped in almost a Prussian bristle, offered his hand to Andrei. He wore captain's shoulder boards. "Smirnov is my name," the captain said with a smile. "Welcome to our small artillery collective."

They traded toasts.

"You have come to us directly from artillery school, I understand," the captain said. "What devil's wind ever blew you into the artillery school?"

Andrei smiled, "My own wind, I guess," he answered. "It was what I thought I was suited for. I had specialized in mathematics."

"You don't say!" the captain grinned. "Welcome to the club. I, too, am a mathematics specialist, a graduate of Leningrad University faculty."

"And I graduated from Rostov University," Andrei said.

"We are true colleagues," the cheerful captain said. "Mathematics is the queen of science, my old Professor Pokrovsky used to say. And I believe he is correct."

"We share that belief also," Andrei said.

"Perhaps," the captain said, "you might occasionally care to join me in a mathematical game. I'm very fond of mathematical puzzles."

"A pleasure," Andrei responded.

"Tell me," the captain said with an encouraging smile. "I noticed you were talking with Lieutenant Petroshenko."

"Yes," Andrei said. "We were talking about the unfortunate accident of Lieutenant Petrov."

"That's it," said the captain. "I thought as much. Now what, I wonder, did Petroshenko have to say about it?"

Andrei started to answer and then grimaced in puzzlement. "Well, as a matter of fact, he didn't say anything about it. Not really. He kept asking me questions. But, of course, I don't know anything either."

"A sad case, young man." Then, quickly changing the subject, Captain Smirnov said, "Have you been in Moscow these last days? Are there any changes in the city? What do they think there of the summer prospects?"

Andrei admitted that he'd seen little of the city. He had seen the damage on the Arbat where German bombs had destroyed the Vakhtangov Theater and the Praha Restaurant. He had, of course, seen the camouflage paint on Red Square, and the burned-out Nazi tank near Khimki on the city's outskirts. As for the war, there wasn't much to say. "Disappointment, I guess you might say, that we didn't make more progress in the winter but high hopes for the spring and summer."

"Well, yes," the captain agreed. "You would find many here who share that view. More concentration. That's what was needed. Still is. Concentrated blows. For instance, here in the center. We could have pushed the Germans back—maybe another hundred and fifty kilometers. But only if we used all our strength. Don't let anyone tell you the Nazis have lost their strength. Not for a minute. We had them off balance during the winter, but they are going to give us a rough time this summer."

An hour later a slim, dark-haired lieutenant came up to Andrei. Andrei had noticed him for some time because, alone of the men in the room, he was drinking heavily, and unlike the others, stood morosely by himself, exchanging few words. He did not bother to introduce himself, merely extended his *rumka* to Andrei. The two men touched glasses. "*Do adna,*" the unknown lieutenant said. Andrei automatically repeated the ritual words and tossed off his glass, which providentially had only a teaspoonful of liquor in it.

"I saw you talking to that *swolich,* Petroshenko," the lieutenant said.

"Yes, I was talking with Petroshenko."

"What was he talking about?" the lieutenant said almost rudely.

"He was talking about Lieutenant Petrov," Andrei replied.

"That *swolich*! That bastard!" the lieutenant exclaimed. Then catching himself up, he said, "Excuse me. It's not your fault. But I simply can't stand that bastard. And it's even worse having him muck about Petrov. For all the good it can do anyone now."

Andrei was nonplused. "Excuse me," he said. "But what is it about Petroshenko? And what did happen to Petrov?"

The lieutenant frowned, hesitated, then made up his mid. "You seem to be a good sort," he said. "I guess there's no secret about this, really. Everyone here knows at any rate. In the first place, Petroshenko is the security officer. Understand? I don't have to dot any *i*'s or cross any *t*'s—right? In the second place, Petrov was my best friend. My comrade. We went through the Battle of Moscow together, understand? There wasn't a better artillery man in the Red Army. Nor a better comrade. He saved my life. Literally shot a Nazi sergeant in the head as he was about to thrust a bayonet in my back. Incredible!"

The lieutenant fell silent. He stared gloomily into space and toyed with his vodka glass.

"Well," he continued. "What's there to say? That *swolich* Petroshenko had been nosing around my friend. He knew we both hated him. Couldn't abide him. Nor could any of the other comrades. We didn't make any bones about it.

"Then last night Petrov told me Petroshenko had called him in. Told him he would either cooperate with him or he would be arrested as a 'defeatist.' Petrov laughed in his face. Then Petroshenko made a threat about Petrov's wife. I don't know what it was. Petrov wouldn't tell me. In fact, that was all I was able to worm out of him last night. He just sat in the hut with his head in his hands, saying, 'It's all over. I'm finished.' He was still sitting there when I turned in last night. That was the last I saw of him. The next thing I knew was that he had been killed in this so-called accident."

The lieutenant stopped talking and poured himself another *rumka* of vodka.

"So that's why Petroshenko is interested in how Petrov came to die," Andrei said.

"Yes," said the lieutenant, almost spitting out the words. "The murderer is interested in the fate of his victim."

*   *   *

The next morning as Andrei and Peter Vasiliyevich made their way up to the observation post the soldier seemed in a dour mood but said nothing to Andrei.

"You don't seem very cheerful, Peter Vasiliyevich," Andrei finally said as they neared the ruined church.

"That I'm not, Comrade Lieutenant," Peter said. "I'm sorry to say I'm not in very good spirits."

"Is there any special reason?" Andrei asked.

Peter looked around as if to see whether there was anyone within earshot. "Yes," he said. "I was called in for interrogation last night."

"What!" Andrei exclaimed. "By Petroshenko?"

"The very man," Peter replied. "By Comrade Lieutenant Petroshenko."

"What did he want to ask you about?"

"The death of Lieutenant Petrov."

"But you knew nothing of that."

"Yes, thank the Lord, I didn't. But I had a hard time convincing him of that."

"Well," said Andrei. "Anyway, that's over."

Peter shook his head and walked on, the grim look not leaving his face. As they arrived at the base of the ladder he spoke again. "I don't think, Comrade Lieutenant, that it's entirely over. They arrested Gleb Andreyevich this morning and took him away."

Chapter 22

ROSA sat on a wooden chair beside the small table at the doorway of the cement-floored ward. She was so tired that when she looked at the names of the wounded on a long slip of yellow paper thumbtacked to the table, she could not bring the writing into focus. She saw nothing but a grayish blur. It was late evening, but she could not say how many days and nights she had been working without interruption—except for moments like this when she lay her head on the table and dozed for half an hour. A week? Two weeks? There was no longer any way of telling.

In fact, this had been her life since she had come on duty at the field hospital in November. The front was crumbling then. The wounded flooded into the hospital. The hospital itself fell back to Rostov. Hardly had it arrived than it was pulled out, literally in twelve hours, and sent down the railroad in freight cars to Armavir. In the bitter November cold, some of the wounded died. Many were frostbitten. That was when the Nazis captured Rostov. Back again to Rostov in late December after the Nazis had been driven out and then on a few miles north toward Novocherkassk. Never any surcease from care of the wounded; never enough hands to tend to them; never enough doctors to treat the wounds or to operate on mangled bodies; not enough beds; not enough morphine to kill the pain; every night the air filled with the screams of the dying; the stench of the suppurating wounds; the vomit; the feces; the urine; the phlegm; the sweat; the chloroform, the formaldehyde, the ether; the exhaustion.

Why she did not collapse into unconsciousness now, Rosa could not say. Perhaps she had passed the point at which body and mind could relax. She felt attached to consciousness by thin wires of weariness that tugged at every nerve, piercing her body with pain—from lice-bitten scalp to aching feet, stinking in boots that had not been off for a week.

She had had a letter from Andrei a week ago. His enthusiasm at being at the front—over finally serving his country with the best of his talents—bubbled onto the pages of his letter. She was so tired she could hardly read, and she had not had the strength to answer him. Nor the spirit. Not now. In a few days perhaps she would be a little less weary. What could she write? That she had been worn to a bundle of dirty rags and bones, an aching mass of protoplasm, hardly capable of thinking, with no feeling except the unremitting pain of strained muscle? Could she write something cheerful about the war? What was cheerful about it? That the lines in the southeast were beginning to waver again? That every wind blew in the rumor of a new Nazi offensive? That life was not too bad in Rostov—when it was already so much worse than Andrei knew? She had not told him the real truth about his mother. To be sure, she had survived the week or so of the Nazi occupation. But the State Bank building had been destroyed. The director and three top employees had been shot by the Nazis; the breakthrough had come too suddenly for them to get away. Andrei's mother had escaped but she was left without a job. How she was getting along Rosa had no idea.

Nor had Rosa told Andrei about her father. He had, of course, gone into the Army as soon as war broke out, as a military surgeon. Somewhere in the terrible retreat through the Donbas his field unit had been overrun. No one knew what had happened. Had they survived and been taken prisoner? Had they been killed? The stories of the Nazis were so terrible—and she had seen some of those who had been tortured, men with their eyes burned out, their testicles ripped and penises torn off, women with breasts gouged and sticks driven into their vaginas—that she hoped her father was dead rather than in the hands of sadists.

*　　*　　*

Rosa pulled herself up from the chair. Amid the funereal sounds of the ward, her ears detected the faint cry of one of the wounded calling thinly but desperately for help. She pulled herself up and moved into the long dark room so crowded with wounded, lying on beds and on the floor, that she could hardly make her way among them.

Finally, she reached the soldier, and even in the murk she recognized him immediately. He was a very young man with chestnut hair and blue eyes, a young man so beautiful he could have been a girl. She had thought of this when he had been brought in that afternoon. He was unconscious then, white as paste, and even then she had known that he would not survive. She was seldom wrong about that now—who would survive and who would not. This beautiful boy had been like a bluebell picked in a summer meadow on a hot July afternoon. In a few hours he would be gone. Now he was clutching her arm with the bony grasp of the dying. "Nurse," he said, "Nurse, I am freezing to death. Can't you get me something warm?" She could feel his body tremble as he held on to her. She put her hand on his forehead. It was hot and faintly damp. Her hand felt rough and sandy on the soft skin of his forehead.

"Please," the youngster said. "I'm sorry to be a bother. But I can't seem to get warm. I'm freezing to death. I can't even feel my feet."

Rosa felt his body quivering. How could she make him warm? There were no blankets. No hot water. Nothing. "Please," he said. "Please, Nurse. I'm freezing." Nothing. Nothing but herself. She gently lowered her body onto the bed, opening her arms and carefully drawing the dying boy to her, touching him lightly with her lips, letting her warm breath flow over his face, slipping her arms under his frail body, pressing her breasts against his trembling chest and her thin abdomen against his, taking care not to crush the stumps of his legs. "Oh," he whispered. "How nice! Now I'm getting warmer."

Rosa held him close, feeling the tremors slowly diminish. She had thought that her heart could no longer break, but as she held the beautiful young soldier in her arms, sobs rose in her throat so strong she could hardly hold them back. How mad was the world! How terrible was life! Suddenly Rosa awoke with a shudder. She had dropped off for a moment, her arms cradling the dying man. Gently she began to slip away, then more hurriedly, lifting herself off the bed in a single swift movement. She leaned over the boy for the last time, pulling the dirty sheet up over his head. He had no need of her warmth any longer. In the morning his body would be placed in cotton sacking, loaded onto one of the peasant carts that lined up at daybreak and taken to the field beyond the village where, day by day, the rows of graves with their simple wooden markers grew more rapidly than the scrawny furrows of wheat the women and children of the village had managed to sow in the uncertain spring.

Rosa sank down again at her desk. Wearily she drew a line through the young soldier's name, Vladimir Vladimirovich Andreyev, and with the scratchy pen noted the time, 2:30 A.M., and the date, April 22. The war had been going on for ten months. What was there about it, what *could* there be about it, to make Andrei so enthusiastic?

Chapter 23

ANDREI had hung his uncle's big round watch on a nail beside his bunk. Now he reached for it, flipped open the silver case and looked at the time by the flicker of a candle stub. Ten-thirty. At nine, Andrei had dropped off to sleep after writing for an hour in his diary. Now he was being shaken awake by the little mess attendant. "Wake up, Comrade Lieutenant," she said. "Wake up. You must report to the Comrade Major immediately." Andrei found himself staring into her eyes; they were dark and glowed like topaz.

There were four junior lieutenants asleep in the hut. The mess attendant shook each of them awake and left. Andrei knew by the banging of doors, the muffled conversations, the tread of feet and the sound of a jeep motor that the compound was stirring. He and his comrades threw on their clothes, exchanging few words. With a splash of water from the tin basin they rubbed their eyes open and hurried to the command hut. The room was filled with men and with the harsh smoke of *makhorka,* the Red Army's bitter, pungent tobacco, smoked in twists of newspaper—goat's legs, as the soldiers called them.

Major Stromlin called Andrei to his table. "We have emergency orders. We are being transferred to another position. You'll get the details later. But now you must go immediately to the observation post at the belfry tower and retrieve the optical instruments. Get the cable as well if that can be done before our departure hour at two A.M. It will be a close thing. Take Peter Vasiliyevich and a squad of men, and see how rapidly you can get it done."

Andrei found the private just outside the hut, already alerted. "I've four men here, Comrade Lieutenant," Peter said. "And a small cart."

They made their way forward to the church tower. Dark as it was, Peter and his men had no trouble in finding their way. Andrei did not feel he was leading them, rather that they were kindly permitting him to accompany him. Once at the abandoned church a soldier swiftly climbed the ladder, carrying a heavy rope and a pulley. He fashioned a primitive hoist and attached it to the heavy steel apparatus. As his companions eased the gear down, he descended the ladder, carefully guiding the gear to keep the lenses from banging on the bricks and stone.

It was a starlit night and the operation moved smoothly. But recovering the cable was a different matter. The observation post was more than a mile from the command compound. The wire ran across the fields, through marshy spots, here and there tacked to trees, but for the most part just stretched along the ground. They improvised a drum from a log and wound up the wire as best they could.

At a few minutes short of two, Andrei, guided by a gentle suggestion from Peter, went back to the command post and reported that his men—and the wire—were only a few minutes behind.

"Good," the major said. "We're running very close to schedule. Now I've put you in command of the miscellaneous supply train. That is the general supplies—not the artillery, not the ammunition, not the food and forage. In other words, the odds and ends. We are moving to the railhead at Demidovo. Embarkation there begins at six A.M."

Andrei paid a last visit to the sleeping hut. He picked up his father's worn leather briefcase. It held some toilet articles, medicines his mother had forced upon him, chocolates, photographs and his "wartime library"—a volume of Clausewitz, presented to him by Vanya with the inscription "In memory of December 14, 1825" (the date of the Decembrist revolt); a very worn volume of Yesenin, a rare copy of his first collection of verse, *Radunitsa* (presented to him by Rosa with the inscription "For my life and love"); and a volume of Dante that Andrei's mother had unexpectedly sent to him after he had left Rostov—in it she had written: "Never forget. To my beloved son."

There was also Andrei's dictionary, a compact pre-revolutionary edition of Dal printed by Sytin on very thin, excellent paper. In his iron-cornered suitcase were his clothes and several manuscripts, including his essay on the Samsonov campaign. In the forty-eight hours since he joined the battery he had not yet taken the heavy cords off his suitcase. Now he simply picked it up along with his briefcase and went to the compound. Here he found Peter Vasiliyevich waiting for him. "We've completed the task," Peter said.

Andrei gave the soldier his suitcase and ordered him to place it on the cart with the wire and range-finding apparatus.

*   *   *

It was close to three when the column finally began to move from the base. Andrei's convoy brought up the rear—twenty carts and wagons, bulging under dark tarpaulins with God knows what kind of materials. In the darkness the drivers cursed each other, cursed the horses, cursed the Germans—and, no doubt under their breaths, the commanders who had set them off at this ungodly hour.

To Andrei, as well, it made little sense. Why couldn't the orders have come through a few hours earlier? The preparations would have been made in daylight, the columns would have gotten under way at nightfall, and the whole command would have been boarded under cover of darkness with no chance of the Nazis discovering that the chickens had fled the coop.

It could be that a great emergency had arisen, but Andrei got no feeling of this. He did not know where they were going, what the new assignment might be—in fact, he was only vaguely aware of the battery's present assignment on this far southeastern corner of the Central Front—but he had the conviction that what was involved now was lack of foresight, not critical necessity.

As Andrei rode at the head of his mixed convoy with Peter Vasiliye-vich by his side he smiled inwardly. Back again with the horses. It seemed to be his fate. But, at least, having had some experience in the drover's trade, he knew what to expect. His unit, all horse-drawn, was bound to move at a slower pace than the trucks, the tractors and the heavier units ahead.

After half an hour the column halted for no observable reason. Nothing was said and in about fifteen minutes movement was resumed. But not for long. Another halt. Another delay. This time the cheerful Captain Smirnov came riding back in a jeep.

"One of the artillery tractors has broken down," he said. "Unfortunately the ground is too marshy to go around it. We'll just have to wait."

"There's something to be said, after all, for horse transport," Andrei smiled, thinking of his comrades of the Caucasian front.

"Yes," said the captain. "There is also something to be said for issuing orders in a timely fashion, so that they can be carried out with some regard to deadlines."

"But," Andrei said, "this is an emergency—"

"Everything is an emergency, Andrei Ilych," the captain said. "This is an emergency only in the sense that orders were given so late that no one can carry them out within the time allotted for the task."

"You mean we will not meet the six A.M. deadline?"

"Quite impossible. We will not reach the railhead by six A.M. And it is not only our guns. There will be comparable delays among all of the other units."

"Like one domino toppling another," Andrei observed.

"Indeed," said the captain. "So it has been since the start of the war. On the very first day I was serving with a unit near the border. The alert message that war was likely to break out was received by our regiment four hours *after* we had been attacked by Nazi bombing planes. For four hours we had been at war, but we could get no instructions."

The captain fell silent, listening. There was a sound of motors being started in the distance. "Perhaps, we are going to get moving again," he said. "But just remember that first day of war. And another thing I must say," he continued as the jeep began to move away. "Later on it was worse."

*   *   *

It was 8 A.M. and had been full daylight for three hours when Andrei's detachment reached train-side. The guns were already on the flat cars and the last of the ammunition train was being loaded. Andrei noticed that machine guns had been mounted on the cars to protect against low-flying air attacks, but there were no anti-aircraft guns, nor, so far as he could see, were the multipurpose guns mounted so that they could drive off attackers. There was one reassuring circumstance. A low-lying mist still covered most of the fields. Visibility would be poor for another hour, by which time they should be well on their way.

Shortly after the train began to move Captain Smirnov appeared and voiced aloud Andrei's doubts about the wisdom of their movements.

Andrei was alarmed. "Isn't there something we should do?" he asked.

The captain chuckled. "There are so many things we should do that I can't even think how to begin. Moreover, none of the things we should do are permitted to be done because our orders are to proceed with all possible speed by rail from Demidovo to Chernodym, where we will unload and place ourselves at the disposal of the Army. And orders, my dear Andrei Ilych, are orders, in this, as in every army. The first thing is to carry them out. Later on, if our unit is wiped out by Nazi bombing, a court of inquiry can be assembled to determine where the responsibility for the catastrophe should be placed."

"Then," Andrei asked, "we are being shifted to another front?"

"Just so," said the captain. "From the southeasternmost sector of the Central Front to the northwesternmost sector of the Southwestern Front—in other words, we are joining our closest neighbors to the south."

"That means," Andrei said with rising excitement, "that we should be going into action very shortly."

"A reasonable enough conclusion," the captain sighed. "Draw from it such comfort as you may. Now, suppose we turn our minds away from questions which we cannot resolve to questions which with some exercise of our minds we *may* be able to solve."

He pulled a small blue paper-covered book from his breast pocket and said, "It just happens that I have here a brand-new collection of mathematical brain-twisters—would you like to join me in a little intellectual exercise?"

*   *   *

The train clattered along at a slow, steady pace. Andrei calculated that they were running at a little more than twenty and certainly a little less than thirty kilometers an hour. The line had been badly bombed in places, and in these sectors the train slowed to a crawl. Alongside the tracks were shell craters, often ten or twenty feet wide, filled with muddy water. The fields stretched flatly in all directions. It was good black soil, but there were almost no signs of preparation for a new crop—no spring plowing and only here and there some evidence that fields were being hand-sown. Andrei realized that the rail line ran very close and almost parallel to the front, and that some of the ground must have been returned to Russian hands only by the winter offensive.

Absorbed as he was in the captain's mathematical problems, Andrei did not note the passage of time, and it was with surprise that he looked at his watch during a brief halt and saw that it was nearly noon. The mist had long since lifted, but the day continued overcast and cool. Thus far they had sighted no Nazi observation planes.

"This is sheer luck," the captain said, "certainly not good management. Sometimes it happens. At the start of the war, my battalion happened by chance to be on training maneuvers, about sixty miles east of the frontier. The rest of our command was further forward. We should have been there, too, but nobody bothered to issue the order. The result? Our forward command was wiped out in the first two days of border fighting. *Completely.* Not one man got back to our lines so far as I know. My unit had no orders, as I told you. None. We simply joined with some of the other troops in our area and fought a rear-guard action. We were lucky. We never were encircled by the Germans. We fought and fell back. Fought and fell back. All the way to Moscow. To be sure, there weren't many of us left by that time—the major and I are among the few survivors."

"Then this isn't your original battery?" Andrei asked.

"Certainly not. We were reassigned to this battery, which was being brought up from Siberia. We had nothing of our own left. For that matter, there aren't too many Siberians left, either, after going through the Battle of Moscow."

A thought occurred to Andrei. "I've not seen Lieutenant Petroshenko since this movement began," he observed.

The captain, concentrating on a tricky algebraic formulation, gave no sign of hearing. But after a few minutes, having solved the problem, he explained: "He had to go away on an investigation."

"You mean the case of Lieutenant Petrov?"

"Yes. He arrested one of the soldiers and took him off. A lot of nonsense in my opinion. It's perfectly clear that Lieutenant Petrov missed his step, took a header and had the bad luck to break his neck, poor lad."

* * *

The train shuffled along all day. Andrei waited in expectation of a Nazi plane attack, but the skies were empty. One lone plane flew high overhead, but whether Russian or German, it was too high to say.

Late in the day Andrei joined Peter Vasiliyevich. The soldier sat silently smoking a goat's leg that smelled as though the *makhorka* was diluted with cabbage leaves, as undoubtedly it was.

Peter Vasiliyevich carried himself a little proudly, almost formally. He walked and spoke slowly and carefully, as though he first thought over where to place his feet and which word to utter. How old he might be, Andrei found it hard to guess—probably in his fifties—but Peter's fellow soldiers invariably called him "Dedya Petya"—Grandpa Peter—and he accepted this as a natural recognition of his character and experience. He did not readily mix in the horseplay of the younger men and spoke more rarely than they. He possessed a strong sense of responsibility and respect for authority even when he had good reason to know better. Andrei knew that when Dedya Petya was given an order, he would fulfill it, even if it was an order with which he basically disagreed. But if he did disagree, he would almost certainly, in a tactful manner—a manner which by no means challenged the authority of his superior—try to let his superior know where his objections lay or, at least, that he did have another point of view. And Andrei quickly learned—as had his superiors before him—that if Dedya Petya had something to say, it was wise to let him speak and consider very carefully what he said.

Now Andrei had no particular thought on his mind. He simply enjoyed talking with Dedya Petya. He observed that they had been fortunate in avoiding any German bombing and that the weather had been favorable. He also expressed concern that they would not get a hot meal that night. None of these gambits produced a response from the soldier. Finally, Andrei said, "Do you have something on your mind, Peter Vasiliyevich?"

The soldier sighed. "Well, I guess you might say that, Comrade Lieutenant."

"What is it?" Andrei asked.

"They say," Dedya Petya replied, "that we are going down to the Southwest Front and that a big battle will be opening up—a big offensive against the *swolich nemtsi*."

"I don't know for certain," Andrei replied, "but that sounds likely."

"So you see"—Dedya Petya shook his shoulders—"it's something to think about."

Andrei had a sudden insight. "You preferred it where we were," he said.

"Well, yes, Comrade Lieutenant," he said with some reluctance. "Yes. It was quiet there. We had good quarters. No problem about hot meals. A man could relax a little."

"And our new spot won't be so quiet," Andrei observed.

"That it won't," Dedya Petya said, spitting over the side of the flatcar. "That it won't, Comrade Lieutenant, and not all of us are going to find our way home after the battle they are getting ready to fight."

*　　*　　*

Andrei said nothing. His own nerves were tingling over the move to the new front. They had been since Sonya, the slim mess girl, had shaken him awake last night. Everything that had happened since then had a special dimension for him because of the anticipation of the new theater of action; of a battle—a BATTLE, as he called it in his mind, consciously spelling it with capital letters. This was what he had been preparing for. Not just since autumn, but all his life. The battle for Russia. The battle against Russia's foes. He had not thought of it in individual terms, in human terms. He had thought of it in big letters and on an heroic scale. And now he realized that there were other ways of looking at it.

Dedya Petya looked at it in the most simple and human terms of danger, of death and survival, of his own death and the death of his comrades. He, Andrei, saw it as a titanic struggle, hurling the enemy back, and most important, as an opportunity for being heroic under fire. But he did not know battle. He had heard a few cannon shots. A few shells had dropped somewhere too far for him even to know where they fell. In his training under fire, he had been frightened and had clenched his fists until his nails cut into his palms. He knew what it was to be afraid. But he knew, or thought he knew, how to control the signs of fear.

Andrei understood that he *wanted* the battle, now, this minute. He was ready for it.

Night fell. The men chewed at their hard black bread and washed it down with a swig of water from their canteens. The train nosed on through the darkness. It grew colder, and the men huddled closer together in their greatcoats, dozing as the train bumped along in the night. Andrei and the major and the captain, and even the horses in the cattle cars, slept as the train picked its way through the Russian night. It crawled slowly over the land with its fresh scent of black earth, the cold still oozing out of the soil like water from the mountain cliffs; there was no light on the land and no sound other than the wind rippling through the canvas lashings, the wheels grumping over the track joints, a thin trail of soot from the engine's stack and an occasional cluster of sparks like summer fireflies, but no bell, no whistle, nothing but the wind and the click of wheels on rails as the train moved across the dark countryside. Sometimes on the far horizon a glow could be seen against the clouds, dim and mysterious; sometimes, tiny sparkles of fire in the very great distance; sometimes, when the train halted (as it often did) the very distant sound of thunder, which Andrei knew was not thunder but heavy guns. Then slowly with painful groans the engine would begin to move again and, gaining momentum, would continue its nagging progress through the blackness from nowhere to nowhere.

The engineer, Andrei thought in one waking moment, must know where the train is going. He must have his orders. He must know the villages he is passing through; the switchlines he crosses over and the name of his destination. But how could even he be certain? There were no signal lights, no red or emerald or amber lights glowing, only the dark train like a messenger from Mars—or to Mars—slipping silently past. There was no one to see them go. No children peering from courtyard gates, no women glancing from cottage windows, no old men turning to look as they came wearily home from the fields. No one.

The train might take them all the way back to the Urals. Or straight into German territory. Who might know the difference? His thought grew confused. He could not tell whether he was sleeping or waking. Was he going into battle on a train of his dreams or was it a real train dreamily moving toward gunfire, catastrophe and death? The thoughts moved around in his head like chariots on a carousel until suddenly he awoke. It was half-daylight. The train had halted. He was frozen and stiff as a cripple. All around him he could hear the clatter and clink of metal and nearby the neighing of horses. They had arrived—where, he had no notion.

Chapter 24

FOR several days convoys had moved only by night, holding to the shelter of small forests during the day. The whole area was alive with troops, trucks, guns, tanks. The High Command was jockeying its forces into place for attack. It was endlessly nerve-wracking. The Nazis knew that something was up. In fact, Captain Smirnov was convinced they had an operation of their own in preparation since Nazi reconnaissance planes began flying over almost at treetop level. Orders were: Don't fire on them—do nothing to give them a clue to the concentrations that the General Staff was massing for the attack. That was what this was, an attack on Kharkov, as Andrei and his comrades now knew—a double pincers attack to try to regain Kharkov, a trap sprung simultaneously from the northeast, where Andrei's battery had finally been deployed, and from the southeast. The Russians held a stubby bulge into the Nazi line here. The idea was to drive out from the north and south edges and unhinge the Nazi hold on Kharkov.

"It's a classic maneuver," Captain Smirnov said after looking at the field maps. "We have a knife at their throat."

"Then," said Andrei, "we shouldn't have too much trouble plunging in the knife."

"Well," said the captain, "that's the question. The Germans are too good soldiers not to understand the weakness of our position. Our salient is too narrow. I can't help wondering whether they have left this just as bait for a larger trap they are preparing to spring on us."

Andrei had now talked enough with the captain to have a ready grasp of his pessimistic and profoundly alienated attitude toward the Soviet High Command.

"It's not that we don't have good officers," the captain said, reflectively picking his nose. "We do. At least, we did. I think our Central Front Command was as good as any in the Red Army. And they were shot—every last man of them. Certainly it wasn't their fault that we were taken in by the Nazi attack on June twenty-second. It wasn't their fault that the fortifications weren't complete, the guns not installed and the Air Force destroyed on the ground."

"But," Andrei insisted, "they could have taken elementary precautions. The planes could have been camouflaged. The troops could have occupied their forward positions."

For the first time in their brief acquaintance Captain Smirnov bristled. "Precautions, my ass!" he exploded. "We were ordered— *ordered*, mind you—not to take precautions because this might upset the Germans. We weren't permitted to move up to the front positions. It might make the Germans suspicious of us, by God!"

Smirnov ran his hands through his hair. "I'm sorry, Andrei Ilych," he said. "I didn't mean to lose my temper. But you simply don't know what was going on. Or what is still going on, for that matter."

In his indignation the captain began to pace back and forth outside the crude shelter—a few pine branches with a tarpaulin thrown over to keep out the rain—where they were talking. Only the most temporary accommodations had been ordered because the battery was expected at any moment to go into action or be moved further along the line.

"I can't imagine such a thing," Andrei exclaimed.

"Nor can I," the captain again exploded, "but that's what happened. Every effort was expended right up to the night of June 21–22 to convince the Germans how deep our friendship was, how peaceful were our intentions. That's what the Tass communiqué was all about. But that wasn't all. My God, do you know that the Nazis sent observation planes over our lines every day, even deep into the rear, and we had orders not to fire on them? Worse than that—a plane came down one day just outside Minsk. Engine trouble. The pilot climbed out and said they had lost their way! Imagine! Not a cloud in the sky! And the plane filled with cameras and reconnaissance equipment and the pilot's own map with our positions marked in red ink."

"What happened?" Andrei asked.

"What happened?" Captain Smirnov's face was so red, Andrei thought he might blow up. "What happened was that we called Headquarters. They instructed us to give the Nazis a good meal, plenty of vodka, help them repair the plane, gas it up and send it back to Germany."

"And you did?" Andrei inquired.

"We did," the captain replied. "So help me God, we did just that. And if that plane didn't lead the Nazi bombers back to Minsk in the morning of the twenty-second it was only because the bombers already had learned the way themselves on practice runs."

*　　*　　*

Andrei had learned a good deal about Dedya Petya in the days of constant movement. Peter had a wife and three children living on a collective farm near Simbirsk, one of the oldest, most backward

Volga cities, but he had not seen them for ten years. Why? It was hard to say. He had been a river man in his young years, moving up and down the Volga, sometimes as a roustabout on a steamboat, sometimes as a deck hand on the barges. He had itchy feet. He got a job on a barge plying the Kama River and then another with the Timber Trust, ferrying log rafts down the River Ob. He hadn't liked the Siberian rivers as much as the Volga, his first love. He wandered on to other jobs and then, on a whim, joined the Red Army, thinking it would help him to get an education beyond his four years of rural school. "That's not enough, you know," he told Andrei. "A man has to have something in his head these days. Like yourself. You have to know mathematics and something more than simple reading. You have to understand machinery."

That was how Peter had wound up in a Siberian artillery unit. The Red Army didn't give him as much training as he had hoped, but he picked up a good bit of knowledge about trucks. After the war —"If I get through the war," as he carefully qualified his statement —he hoped to get a job as a truck driver. Would he go back to Simbirsk? That depended. He'd cross that bridge when he came to it.

"No use making plans," he said. "There's only a dozen of us left from the old group from Barnaul. And now we've got a new battle to fight."

He wrote his wife's name and address on a scrap of paper and gave it to Andrei. "Just in case, Comrade Lieutenant," he said. "You could drop them a letter." Andrei folded it into his breast-pocket wallet, where he already had the address of Captain Smirnov's wife in Moscow ("At least that's where she was the last I heard") and the address of the girl friend of Sasha Alexiev, the young lieutenant, whose friend Petrov had fallen from the ladder. Andrei had given Rosa's address to Captain Smirnov.

* * *

The region through which Andrei's battery had moved was one of broad rolling fields, broken by small copses and occasional forests which were either the fragmented remnants of the original forest cover or planted stands dating back to Czarist days when the area had been largely held in well-managed medium-sized estates owned by the nobility or the upper bourgeoisie. The lands were now divided into collective farms which, generally speaking, tended to conform to the limits of the old estates.

In earlier times the whole region had been covered by oak forests and formed the boundary between the gray middle soils of Russia and the rich *chernozem*, the black soil, which the Russian peasants thought was the richest in the world. It was in a sense, an in-between region, really beyond the boundaries of the Ukraine (although some

tried to insist that Kharkov was the "modern" capital of the Ukraine),
and north of the lands of the upper Don which imperceptibly opened
into the enormous wheat lands of the South.

Spring was late here, and the fields were just beginning to green.
The tiny buds of the birch were pink but had not yet burst; the willows were shedding their fuzzy gray and in the marshes the first white
and purple paschal flowers had begun to appear. But the nights were
cold and the soldiers wrapped themselves in their greatcoats like
mummies; fires were forbidden lest they give away the rapidly in-
creasing density of the troop concentration.

The houses were no larger than the typical log-cut peasant huts
of northern Russia and generally had roofs of thatch, or more likely
of tin, but now they were more apt to be built of peasant-dried brick
covered with plaster or of laths and willow, smeared with plaster or
baked mud and tinted yellow or rose or green or, occasionally, whitewashed. They had neat wooden picket fences and fruit trees painted
white to a mark four feet from the ground. There were chicken coops
and pigpens beside the houses and, Andrei noticed, women and
children in almost every cottage but rarely a man—only old grandpas
and an occasional teenage boy. The fact that the front line was a few
miles distant seemed to make no difference. Girls hung over the
fences and laughed with the soldiers. Yellow-haired youngsters surrounded the parked tanks. It was a curious blend of the eternal peasant
life of the Russian countryside and the technology of modern war.

*   *   *

It was the evening of the eleventh of May 1942. Dusk was falling
rapidly but Andrei could still see the white kerchiefs of the women
in the half light as they stood around the well, quietly talking, small
children clinging to their skirts. Andrei's battery was camped just
beyond the village in a grove of widely spaced oaks, actually the
common, where once the cows and goats had been pastured. Save for
a goat or two Andrei had seen none of these. Either the women had
locked their cows into their huts for safekeeping, or the animals had
been slaughtered in the fall and winter. Earlier, while some soldiers
were bantering with the women, one bold young man had tried to
embrace a full-bodied peasant girl, but she had shaken him off with
a single move of her hard-muscled body. "You're not man enough
for me," she had taunted. "I'd wear you down to a sheep's ear in half
an hour."

"Come on, *devushka*," the soldier insisted. "Come back in the
woods and learn what a man's iron is like."

"Iron," the girl spat the word. "More like kneaded dough, I'm
thinking." She raised her skirt and flipped it in the soldier's face in
the traditional peasant woman's gesture of contempt, exposing, in the
process, her ample behind with its modest covering of light blue

knitted shorts. The teasing had gone on and on and finally the soldier and the girl did wander off in the direction of the woods.

There was in the late twilight the pleasant scent of smoke from the peasant chimneys. If the troops were permitted no fires and no hot meals, this did not keep the peasant women from cooking as usual for their families and for a few soldiers who had taken advantage of the proximity of the women to improve on their rations.

Andrei's mind, filled with thoughts of the morrow, eagerly turned to these scenes, so simple, so universal, so Russian, so far from the clang, the blood, danger and terror of war. Here life was going on a few hundred yards from the scene where, in the morning, Death would move to center stage. Nor would Death confine its dark shadow to the soldiers, the fighting men. Shells would fall into the villages, huts would be torn apart. Women's bodies would lie shattered on the village streets. Children would cry without answer. Why, he wondered, had the villagers been permitted to stay? The High Command was bending every effort to mask the troop concentration, to prevent the Nazis from getting a sniff of what was about to happen. The villagers could not be evacuated without long cavalcades of women, their children, their possessions and their animals. They would impede the incoming troops and cause endless delay and confusion. Yes, Andrei understood the psychology of the High Command. But was it right? Didn't the Red Army owe it to its own people whom it was defending to get the women and children out of the way—to warn them at least of what was coming? Of course, the women knew a battle was going to be fought, but they did not know what a battle really was. They did not know its dangers, its terror.

They did not understand the reality: that just five or six miles away was the enemy, the Nazis in their tanks, with their great guns, their armored units crawling closer and closer and their soldiers sitting in small groups in dugouts or huts, smelling the same smells of the land, hearing the same sounds and glancing now and then at the same sliver of the moon.

How strange it was to imagine the enemy camp and perhaps an enemy lieutenant, not unlike himself, standing on a village street listening to the dying sounds of dusk. Strange, too, Andrei thought, that he could feel no hatred for the enemy. Perhaps, it was because he had never seen a Nazi soldier, had never been fired upon, had never fired a gun himself at any living thing—except a brace of ducks.

He pulled out his Uncle Boris's watch and flipped open its silver case. It was nine o'clock. He must get back to his encampment, check his units once again, and get a few hours' sleep. In the morning he would not be working as an artillery fire spotter, but would be with Captain Smirnov, second in command of a battery. The attack would begin at 6:30 with one hour's artillery preparation. The troops would move at 7:30.

Chapter 25

SONYA, the mess attendant, touched his shoulder and in her quiet voice said, "It's three o'clock, Comrade Lieutenant. Time to get up."

"*Spasibo*, thank you," Andrei replied, and shook himself awake. He had slept badly, fully clothed, with his greatcoat thrown over him. It was full darkness. Not a light showed and only by straining his ears could he catch the muffled sounds that meant the encampment was beginning to stir.

Before he lay down to sleep Andrei had written two notes, one to Rosa and one to his mother. To Rosa he had written: "My beloved wife, do not grieve. I do not want to die but if I must, I am proud to die for my country, for our Russia. Bless you for loving me. I cannot say how sad I am to leave you. And how much I love you." To his mother he wrote: "Beloved Mother, I say farewell to you as Father must have said so many years ago. How I regret not seeing you again! I worry for you and tenderly embrace you. Your Andrei."

He had folded each note into a little triangle, addressed it, and when he met Captain Smirnov for a glass of tea before going to the battery he handed them to him, uttering the customary phrase "Just in case." Smirnov smiled thinly and took from his breast pocket a similar tricorn, handing it to Andrei and saying, "Please." The two men drank their tea in silence. Andrei refused the vodka which was passed around. He was nervous, of course. He understood why, but hated to admit the reason—that he was afraid that he would panic under fire and would not be able to conceal his fear.

The officers met with Major Stromlin. The formal orders were handed out. The plan of operations was again gone over, briefly and simply. The task of the battery was to lay down a box barrage. The coordinates for each gun had been worked out, the rate of fire, timing. The box barrage would lift and the battery would offer supporting fire at the direction of division headquarters which was being prepared to advance to more forward positions with the movement of troops and tanks. Major Stromlin, too, appeared tired. His eyes were red. Andrei wondered if he had gotten any sleep whatever.

"Our task is clear," Major Stromlin said. "I caution you only to be alert to any sudden and unexpected changes. And particularly to be prepared for rapid movement once our forces begin their advance."

The mess girl circulated with her tea kettle. "Do you care for some more tea, Comrade Lieutenant?" she asked Andrei.

"Thank you," Andrei replied. She lowered her eyes as she poured the tea. Andrei noticed just the slightest tremor in her hand. He thought to himself, Poor girl, she is frightened but we are all pretending that we are not.

*　　*　　*

The first streaks of pearl were showing in the sky as Andrei and Captain Smirnov left the headquarters hut for the battery. The temperature had dropped close to freezing during the night but birds were beginning to sing in the half-light. No other noise broke the stillness of the countryside. Or almost no noise. Andrei thought he heard a faint whisper, the sounds of thousands of men taking quiet steps, speaking in hushed tones, moving with velvet tread, preparing for battle. Perhaps, he thought, it was his imagination, or just the wind.

Smirnov inspected the battery with care, as Andrei watched intently. Each gun was examined—the sighting mechanisms, elevations and calibrations. They tested telephonic communications with the command, checked the supply of shells and their disposition, and also the tractors and transport, placing them close, but not too close, to the guns and ammunition.

Smirnov spoke to each member of the gun crews. His easy good humor had vanished this morning. He was stern and exacting. Finally, he was finished. "We are as ready as we are going to be," he told Andrei. "Now let's check our watches." First, he called Command and coordinated his watch—it was a rather large German wristwatch with a second hand—with headquarters. Then Andrei adjusted his old silver pocket piece to the captain's. The time was 6:14. In the distance Andrei heard a boom. He looked at the captain. "Theirs," Smirnov said. "Too close for ours. Just a casual round. It means nothing." The captain was right. There was no follow-up. The sun was rising now. A nice day, Andrei thought, then caught himself. A nice day?

Andrei stood looking at his watch. The sun was slanting through the still-bare branches of the grove of oaks where the guns were emplaced. The hand slowly moved: 6:25, 6:26, 6:27 (he heard the sound of cannon in the distance; not all watches were coordinated), 6:28 (more guns opened up), 6:29 (still more), 6:30—the three guns of their battery roared; all the guns in the world roared. He could feel the air vibrate. The shells whistled as they passed overhead and at the perimeter of his field of vision Andrei could see yellow and red explosions, clouds of dust rising and, soon, pillars of smoke and flame. The thunder reverberated across the small fields and copses, and almost immediately there was answering fire from the Germans, explosions back and to the left of the emplacement but none very close.

For the moment, thought Andrei, the Germans are firing at random. They have been stunned by the suddenness and the weight of our attack. The battery's guns fired steadily. The men moved like clockwork. The shells fed steadily into the great chambers and roared off through the sky like an aerial express.

Andrei was surprised to see a flock of magpies rising and wheeling over the field, startled out of their morning feeding by the cannonade. Andrei's task was to direct the communications point, relaying messages to and from command center. He got a call now. Headquarters was asking a slight shift in the fire, to concentrate on the distant perimeter of the quadrant assigned to them—apparently a movement of troops or tanks had been spotted. The acid smell of explosives filled Andrei's nostrils. Ammunition parties steadily rolled up new rounds of shells. The gunners methodically readjusted their settings. No counterbattery had come their way. It was, Andrei thought, something like working in an excessively noisy factory, a blast furnace, perhaps, with the constant clang of heavy machinery and the deafening roar of the explosions.

Suddenly Andrei noticed a group of tanks moving off to the right. He had not even heard them. He looked at his watch—forty-five minutes of barrage had already gone by. The tanks were beginning to push out and position themselves to move up to the battered Nazi lines the moment the barrage was lifted. Now he saw troops dismounting from trucks that had come up behind the battery. This was a motorized division and the men let themselves down, quickly forming into long single columns and following after the tanks.

* * *

Headquarters was calling again. New coordinates to be used in a creeping barrage that was to be laid down as soon as the box barrage ended at 7:30. There would be a five-minute interlude, then renewed fire, closely coordinated by headquarters to remain ahead of the troops and quickly to concentrate on any resistance points.

As 7:30 approached, the guns of the front began to diminish their fire. Again it was evident that not all the watches and clocks were coordinated to the minute. The answering German fire became more apparent. It seemed to be concentrating on guns to the left of Andrei's battery, and once the ground rocked with a very heavy explosion and smoke rose over the Russian position. An ammunition depot had been hit.

At 7:30 the battery halted fire. The gun crews were sweating. They took a moment to swig from canteens and wipe themselves with their shirts. Andrei discovered to his surprise that he was sweating too. Captain Smirnov pulled out a small flask of vodka. "Will you join me?" he asked. Andrei hesitated. Smirnov smiled. "Don't think you have to," he said. "Plenty of time later on. We've just begun. Now comes the hard part."

The sounds of battle grew more intense. Tanks up ahead were firing, and German shells began to fall closer to the battery's position. Orders for fire came swiftly now. There was a drone of planes in the sky and suddenly a ripple of flame and a swift bouquet of explosions near a battery located some distance to the left of Andrei's. He did not think the bombs had fallen very close. His nerves, he realized, were tense but he was not conscious of being afraid. It was as though he was surrounded by a great shell of sound, so loud, so dense, so vibrant that it absorbed all danger. It was only in the momentary lulls in firing that Andrei felt the tension rise, only then was there time to wonder whether the next moment would bring down a shell on their position.

Now he passed on instructions to hold fire for further orders. The guns fell silent. The gunners again drank from their gunmetal canteens. Captain Smirnov came to Andrei's side. "I think we will be moving up," he said. "The tanks are well beyond the German perimeter, and from the sound of the guns they have broken through into the open."

Captain Smirnov was right. Twenty minutes later the battery was ordered to move up to the next village. The Nazis were falling back along the sector in disorder. Russian tanks had already penetrated deep in their rear.

It was midafternoon before they entered the village. The first German counterattack had come just as they began to move up. It was violent. The Soviet tanks were heavily engaged. Some infantry units fell back toward the battery. Then Soviet planes appeared and the movement forward resumed. Twice the battery had come under fire as it crawled ahead. Once it was Stukas. The Nazi dive bombers came over the village so low they could not release their bombs. Their machine guns sprayed Andrei's detachment. Two men suffered minor wounds, little more than scratches. But as the guns moved forward again artillery fire began.

"That's the Stukas," Captain Smirnov told Andrei. "They reported back our position, but luckily they did not get it very precisely."

*   *   *

Smoke hung over the village and the moldy smell of burning thatch. Two dead horses, necks twisted and stomachs bloated, lay beside the road. A German soldier, his greatcoat spread wide as a skirt, sprawled beside them, his face a mass of purpled flesh. Everywhere lay paper, tin cans, half-opened packing cases, wads of excelsior. Bits of cotton batting were picked up by the wind like chubby white moths. The broken frame of a gun carriage stood in the middle of the street, a smashed truck smoldering beside it.

It was the first time Andrei had seen the litter of war. It was, he thought, as though a giant had shaken out the pockets of ten thousand men and scattered the contents across the landscape. Everything was dirty and broken. Not a house in the village was undamaged. Most lay in heaps of plaster and mortar, crockery mixed with the bedclothes. At first it seemed there was not a living creature in the village, but as the battery moved in two children, a boy and a girl, each under ten, each thin, faces dirty, wearing dirty *valenki* and wadded jackets, pushed up the wooden door of a potato bin and emerged in the daylight. They watched the Russian troops in a daze.

Andrei spoke to them. They stared back at him like deaf-mutes. For the moment, at least, they were deaf-mutes, their senses shattered by the inferno of the barrage. As Andrei halted beside the children he saw to his surprise a white goose, its feathers bedraggled and dirty, emerge from the same potato cellar. It spread its wings, shook them with a shudder and proceeded to pick its way through the mud, pecking at grain spilled into the street from some broken supply train. There were four more German bodies just beyond the potato cellar. They lay in a cluster, killed by a single burst of machine-gun fire. Beyond them, on the other side of the village street, Andrei saw a woman's feet, white and naked, protruding from the rubble of a cottage.

The battery made its way from one end of the village to the other. Not one living thing appeared—only the deaf-mute children and the dirty goose. At the far edge of the village was the smashed rubble of a barricade and a Nazi machine-gun position. Apparently a rear guard. Here lay the bodies of three Red Army men and around the smashed machine gun several Germans. It was hard to tell how many. The bodies had been mashed to pulp by the treads of a Russian tank. Andrei's nostrils were filled with the smell of war—the acrid smell of the burning thatch, the heavy odor of diesel fuel, the pungent cordite, the raw stink of smashed latrines and the sweet smell of dead animals and dead men.

It was only as the battery moved beyond the village and began to deploy in its new position that the thought came to Andrei: the village, the destruction, the dead—this was his doing, the work of his battery. The village had been within the quadrant of their fire. Their guns and their shells had turned it into rubble and taken scores of lives. He recalled his thoughts of last night. This had been a village much as the one in which he had sauntered—peaceful, the women staring from behind the fences or gathered around the well. And there might have been a buxom young girl flirting with a young Nazi subaltern,

flipping up her skirts. Why not? That was life. And now? That subaltern could be one of the bodies beginning to bloat along the village
street. And the young girl? Possibly those were her feet protruding from
the rubble of the destroyed house.

But he had no time to pursue the thought. There was a tremendous
explosion and a column of black smoke rose in the air just ahead. My
God! Andrei thought. They've got our range. He glanced at Dedya
Petya who was riding beside him. "A mine, Comrade Lieutenant," the
soldier said. "Very dangerous when we move up. The *nemtsi* always
leave them behind. Almost always." The column halted. It was as
Dedya Petya had said. A truck had been blown up. The driver was
killed and two sergeants badly wounded, one with his feet blown off,
the other's abdomen torn open.

Beyond the village the battery moved into another small oak forest
and readied the guns for action. Here, too, Nazis had been before
them. There were sandbagged emplacements, trenches, shelters, almost
intact. These Germans had escaped the bombardment and apparently
had moved out ahead of the Russian attack.

*   *   *

Major Stromlin sent for Andrei almost immediately and ordered
him to take a squad and try to locate a site for an observation post.
Andrei, Peter Vasiliyevich and four men armed with Tommy guns
carefully began moving forward through the oak grove. Like the village, it was filled with the debris of the retreating army—bottles, clothing, tin cans, machinery—but, most of all, paper. Toilet paper in long
festoons around the limbs of trees. Filing papers, newspapers, letters,
all of the scrap paper of the army strewn over the landscape.

The squad stumbled over the body of a young German officer, his
head almost severed at the neck by a piece of shrapnel. The contents
of his map case lay scattered about him—German marks, letters, pictures of his sweetheart, maps of the front-line sector, order papers, three
glossy photographs torn from a magazine of fleshy German nudes, a
tin-backed picture of Christ colored rose and blue.

"That's the way it ends," Peter Vasiliyevich said, nodding toward
the body. "A bag of papers strewn across the ground and a broken
neck. That's the way it ends."

On the far side of the copse, Andrei and his men came out on a
meadow beyond which rose a small elevation, possibly fifty feet high.
The men climbed the hill, carefully wriggling on their bellies. Rolling
country lay before them and the wind brought the heavy scent of burning buildings. They could see black smoke rising in the distance. The
only cover was a sheep pen of mud and willow twigs which lay just
below the brow of the hill, put up to protect the animals from the
winter blizzards. There was a clear view for a mile or a mile and a half

in three directions. What was more important was that there was no other elevation close enough to be worth considering.

The drawback was its openness. Even if they utilized the sheep pen, they could easily be spotted by low-flying aircraft.

"Not very good," Andrei said, half to himself, half to Peter.

"No," Dedya Petya replied, "But there is nothing else in sight."

Andrei took out his field glasses and carefully scanned the horizon. The continuous sound of battle rose and died in an arc that exceeded 180 degrees. There was smoke on the horizon and smoke in the nearer ranges as well. Shells were dropping behind them, quite possibly in the woods where the battery was deploying. Near the left perimeter, Andrei saw a straggling column of men slowly moving southwest in his direction. At first he thought they were Germans, but then concluded they were Russian wounded making their way back from the scene of action.

Andrei once more scanned the entire horizon, then squirmed his way back below the crown of the hill, straightened himself and said to the men, "This is it."

They did not begin running out the communications wire until dusk, and it was well after midnight before the lines were hooked up and the sheep pen turned into some kind of an observation post. They dug a waist-high protective pit, stretched tarpaulins above it on a light frame of willow branches, scattered earth and dry grass over the roof for camouflage and opened up the side of the pen to give themselves an arc for observation. When the post was completed, Andrei and his companions huddled down in their greatcoats and waited for morning. They were exhausted, cold and hungry. They had had nothing to eat except some black bread since dawn. Whether there would be food in the morning was questionable.

*   *   *

Andrei took a last look at the horizon, scanning it with his night glasses. There were fires in the distance, reflected rosy in the sky, and occasional flares, also at a distance. The big guns were silent, but at intervals he heard the faint chatter of a machine gun or a single explosion that might be a grenade. He was almost too tired to think. It had been an exhausting day. Had he been afraid? Yes. And was he still afraid even now with the cloak of darkness to protect him? Yes, he was still afraid. We are all afraid, he thought to himself with some wonder. All of us. We can't help it. But we do not show it except in little, almost hidden ways. He thought of Sonya, the mess girl, and the tremor of her hand. He thought of Captain Smirnov's stern, businesslike mien. Taking out his notebook he wrote in a tiny hand:

"We are all afraid. And anyone who is not afraid is a fool. Death is our master and we wait his invitation like fools who stand beside a roulette table watching for the little ball to spin and bounce into the pocket. Sooner or later the ball will fall into our pocket. Each of ours. Some tonight. Some tomorrow. Some the day after. Some not for years. But sooner or later it comes to all, for in this game there is only one winner: the grand master, Death."

Chapter 26

NOT until the third night in the observation post did Andrei and his men get a hot meal. Each day the fighting became more stubborn. The Red Army clung to the territory it had gained but could not push the Nazis back further. The Germans counterattacked again and again, and the observation post operated under severe difficulties. German shelling cut the telephone line many times. One man was wounded making repairs. The battery itself was intact, or nearly so. The guns, transport and ammunition, now almost exhausted, had escaped direct hits, although shells had fallen all through the woods and there had been a dozen casualties.

At dusk on the third night Sonya appeared with a great pail of meat soup. The five men surrounded the big pail and dipped their tin cups into it like famine victims while Sonya collapsed in exhaustion. The pot had been very heavy. Hardly had the hungry men guzzled the soup than artillery fire sprang up, erratic yet persistent. Andrei listened to the German guns. The fire was not heavy but it was close. The shells were falling in a box pattern, in front of, behind and at both sides of the observation post and also in the wooded copse where the guns were sited.

"Better spend the night here, Comrade," Andrei told the girl. "You can go back at first light."

"But they are expecting me back," the girl said anxiously.

Andrei thought a moment. "Can you find your way back in the dark?"

"I'm afraid not but I'll try."

"No," Andrei said with decision." "We can't spare a guide for you. I'll just tell Command that we'll send you back at first light."

He passed the message back to headquarters by telephone and ordered one of his troopers to improvise a bed for the girl in the corner of the sheep pen. An hour later he turned the telephone over to the soldier who had the night watch and threw himself down on his bedroll. He was wakeful and nervous. The shelling had not entirely ceased. It halted for a while. Sprang up. Halted. Resumed. There seemed to be no pattern except to keep the Russians off balance. He had not experienced this random firing nor had the others, not even the veteran Dedya Petya. Andrei was lying on his back thinking what the shelling might mean when he felt a faint rustle. It was Sonya. She had crawled to his side and now lay beside him, her head beside his.

"Do you mind, Comrade Lieutenant?" she asked. "I can't sleep and somehow it seems so strange here." She fell silent, then continued: "I guess I'm just afraid. I know I shouldn't be."

"Of course I don't mind," Andrei whispered. He put his arm around the girl and drew her to him, feeling her warm breath on his cheek and her soft breasts under the harsh stiffness of her uniform. She sighed. "It is very lonely," she said, "being at war. There are comrades all around and yet I feel so much alone." Andrei brushed his lips lightly across her cool brow. He could feel the trembling of her body.

"Oh, *dorogoya*, dearest," he whispered. "Don't feel bad. Don't be fearful. We are here together. No harm will come to you. I'll see to that." His heart was touched as though by a child's cry, and he felt tears quietly flowing from the girl's eyes.

"Oh," she said. "If you only knew. No one calls me *dorogoya*. It's *devushka* (girl) here, *devushka* there. Or *devka* (slut). Or something harsher. I can't believe I am here. I think I must be dreaming."

For answer there was a whine, and an instant later, a shell exploded not a hundred yards away. The ground shook, and earth and stones rained down on the lookout. The duty soldier quickly called battery. The phone line had not been cut. No harm had been done. Sonya pressed herself closer to Andrei and now he could feel the quick beating of her heart. Again he kissed her forehead and felt her pulling his head down so that her lips met his and greedily returned his kiss.

They lay locked in each other's arms, their bodies slowly moving against each other, not by will or volition, merely by some law of nature, moving gently, trying to annihilate any space, any barrier that separated them. Andrei felt Sonya's tongue darting between his lips. He ran his hand inside her tunic and closed it over her breast, which moved soft and quivering with his touch. He could feel her nipple enlarging, and the sensation sent excitement racing through his body. They struggled against each other, now not speaking, now each breathing more heavily and Andrei felt her drawing up her skirt as he in haste pressed himself against her. "Please," the girl said. "Please. Love me. I want you so much. Please." He thrust at her and she arched her back to meet his thrust. He felt himself drive deep within her as she whispered in a voice that grew more hoarse, more deep: "Love me. Love me. Love me."

Andrei had forgotten everything—the war, the shells, the dugout, his comrades, his love for Rosa, danger, death—everything. His whole being was fused and concentrated in the emotion that boiled, leaped and finally erupted like a volcano. A moment later he had collapsed upon the thin girl's small body, almost inert. As he lay sprawled over her, he heard her whispering in his ear: "Andrusha. I love you. I love you. I knew this would happen the moment I saw you that first night."

"Dear, dear Sonichka," Andrei murmured. "My dear girl. It has never happened like this with me. I just want to lie here with you forever and forever."

They slept. How long Andrei could not say. He awoke to the sharp call of the *dezhurny*: "Comrade Lieutenant, Comrade Lieutenant, the line is out again."

Andrei's arms were empty. Somehow, at some time, Sonya had crawled back to her corner. Andrei shook himself out of the blanket and joined the soldier.

"When did it go out?" he asked.

"Just when I called you," the soldier said. "Well, you know, I've checked at half-hour intervals. According to schedule. The last time was three o'clock. The line was working. So it must be three-thirty."

Andrei pulled out his big silver watch and lit a match. The soldier was correct. Well, what to do? It was still dark. No sense in sending out a work party along the line now. In half an hour or a little more it would be first light and the break could be mended. If Command had any instructions it was their responsibility to send a courier to him, not the other way around, unless, of course, he had important intelligence to transmit, as he did not. The only intelligence, the only thing that had happened, was the sudden incandescence of Sonya and himself.

It had been overpowering, overwhelming, like a gasoline torch. He had not thought of what was happening, of what Sonya meant to him or he to her. He had not thought of his love for Rosa—for he loved Rosa. He had not the slightest doubt of that. But what was Sonya? A solar flare sent out by the sun—bursting out a hundred thousand miles and then vanishing in an eternal void?

*   *   *

Andrei knew of what they called "front marriages," men and women who had wives or husbands in the rear but "front husbands" or "front wives" serving beside them in the Red Army. There was talk of it continuously, and there were examples in this very battery—Major Stromlin, for instance, and Natasha, the chief adjutant of the brigade. These relationships were open and honest and respected by all. Yet he could not think of Sonya as a "front wife."

He pulled back the flap of the tarpaulin and walked out into the open. In the quiet, Andrei thought that he could begin to inhale the greenness of spring. A gentle wind from the northwest had just sprung up. The first signs of dawn appeared, an almost imperceptible change in the quality of the blackness that made it not quite so black.

Andrei reentered the dugout. Dedya Petya had begun to stir.

"The line is out," Andrei said. "First light is coming on. Take a lad and mend the break. And start the mess girl on her way back."

Andrei glanced at the corner where Sonya was curled, still sleeping. He moved over and knelt at her side, putting his head close to hers. "Wake up, little one," he said. Her eyes opened wide in wonder, then a smile broke over her face and with one hand she pulled his face to hers and kissed him.

"I'll be gone in a minute," she said, "but not for long."

Andrei rose swiftly. It was unseemly, he knew, for the commanding officer of the post to display personal emotion before his men. He wondered which of them knew—then quickly put the thought out of his mind. It did not matter. Not so long as he maintained the separation of ranks dictated by his training manual.

He walked a few steps down the rear of the hill with Sonya and Dedya Petya. He squeezed Sonya's hand, and then said, "I'll leave you now in Dedya Petya's hands. He'll point you straight. Safe journey."

Sonya smiled again. "Thank you, Comrade Lieutenant."

* * *

Andrei returned to the post. He looked out through the observation slit. Light was coming on but it was overcast and misty. He found himself edgy about last night's shelling. Curious. And worried about the offensive. They had not made the expected gains after the first day's breakthrough. It had been like beating one's head on a stone wall—almost as though the Germans had expected the attack and had concentrated forces right here to meet it. Curious.

Andrei heard guns to the left. Not artillery fire. Small-arms and machine-gun fire. Concentrated bursts. It sounded as though the Russians had opened up on an attacking party. Possibly night infiltrators. He swept the 180-degree arc of his vision with the glasses but could make out nothing. The light was not good enough to use the optical observation instruments.

A wave of feeling passed over Andrei—a flare-up of the wild explosion he had experienced with Sonya. Simultaneously a shell slammed down almost on the post with a noise like the world ending. The concussion came close to rupturing Andrei's eardrums and he could feel the earth move. The dirt-covered tarpaulin shuddered like a sail bursting in the wind. Shrapnel and shell fragments flew in all directions, slashing through the tarpaulin and landing in the dugout, red-hot and sizzling against the moist earth. None of the men were hurt.

"They can't come any closer than that," one soldier observed.

"They can," another replied, "but you'd not be around to know it."

The shell was followed quickly by another a bit to their rear, and then another and another. It was apparent to Andrei that the German battery was laying down a precise pattern of fire in almost a straight line from the observation post back to the battery. He had instant fear for Dedya Petya and Sonya. The shells were falling one after the other right along the communications line.

He looked at the men. They followed the sounds with unconcealed concern. "Not good," he said shortly.

"Not good," agreed one of the men.

Andrei slithered out the rear of the post and looked back toward the battery. He could see nothing in the uncertain morning light, but as he stood there he heard the German shells continue to feel their way into the woods where they were now falling—possibly amid the battery.

Helpless rage overcame Andrei. What could he do? No phone. He could send out another soldier, but that made no sense. And he did not have a man to spare. He could hardly keep from turning down the hill and wildly running back along the wire. Somehow, he compelled himself to go back to the dugout. He sat beside the phone. There was plenty of action along the front. Russian shelling as well as German. With the improvement of the light, the familiar pattern of fire and smoke on the horizon had reappeared, and when Andrei looked to the rear he could see smoke rising from the grove of woods where the battery was located.

Still his line was dead. Andrei had looked at his watch a dozen times. He pulled it out again. Nearly 6 A.M. He could not wait much longer. If the line could not be restored they must revert to couriers. His mind filled with the gloomiest thoughts. Suddenly he heard the characteristic *burrrr*. The line was working. Battery was calling.

Andrei responded swiftly. They had lost a gun. There had been casualties in the gun crews. Dedya Petya had arrived at battery. The line had been severed in three places and was now repaired. He would return immediately to Post with more spare wire. The soldier who accompanied him had been wounded. A shell fragment had broken his arm. He could not immediately be replaced. What of the mess girl, Andrei asked, had she yet returned? No, the lieutenant at the other end answered, no, she had not returned. Unfortunately, Dedya Petya reported, she had been killed in the same burst that wounded the soldier. Damn shame, the lieutenant added. She was a fine girl. Now, on the day's operations. The Germans were mounting a powerful drive to the south against the adjacent sector. It might be necessary to withdraw in this sector as well. Andrei was to maintain closest communications. A move might be necessary suddenly. Intelligence felt there was very likely to be a German attack. No instructions yet as to the battery's fire. Watch carefully for signs of German battery work and signs of movement. That is all for the present.

Andrei acknowledged the orders, then put the mouthpiece on its stand.

Sonya dead? He could not believe it. His mind could not accept it. He could still feel the press of her body on his, see the smile lighting her face, hear her small voice saying, "But not for long." He could feel the touch of her hands on him, the gentle pressure of her breasts when she softly slipped under his blanket. He could feel himself alive within her living body. He could feel her alive. Alive. Alive. It could not be. He felt the tears from her eyes flowing again on his cheek and he bit his lips until he could taste the warm blood.

Finally he heard one of the soldiers saying, "Comrade Lieutenant, the phone. It's ringing."

Only then did he hear the *burrrr*. He picked it up and said, "*Slushyu.* At your service . . ."

Chapter 27

ABRAMOV was puzzled, and he frankly admitted it to Andropov.

"I will tell you about it, Yuri Vladimirovich, just as Louis put it to us," Abramov said, tugging at his ear. "We were compelled to speak with him on the telephone because of the shortness of time and the fact that he is out in the country at his dacha."

"The dacha we paid for," Andropov said ironically.

"Yes," Abramov smiled. "The dacha that our money bought. Well, in any event he had two things to say. The first was really not important. Or rather, it was simply what we already knew. That the actual object of the Morgans' trip to Moscow was to try to persuade Sokolov to leave and come to New York. As we know, they failed in that. Louis had some details of their conversations. But they add nothing to what we know. The fact is that the Morgans and Sokolov did not get on well together. Too much personality on both sides, I suspect."

"From what I know," Andropov said thoughtfully, "I would agree. Sokolov is very independent. Very egocentric. Altogether not an easy man. And both the Morgans, as we have found, have hot tempers."

"That's certainly been our experience," Abramov agreed. "Now, the other item from Louis is this. And here is where the puzzle comes in. He tells me that he heard—secondhand, to be sure—that Jacques Dumas, the French existentialist writer who was here last month, was told by one of the 'senior dissidents,' as he put it, that there was more in the original 1945 case against Sokolov than met the eye."

Andropov snorted. "What the devil is that supposed to mean?" He was irritated and did not mind showing it. Mysterious hints! The last thing he needed at this point.

"I know, I know, Yuri Vladimirovich," Abramov hastened to say. He was a small man and his head was rather bald and it tended to become rosy when Abramov was excited. And the telltale pink now appeared.

"I know just how you feel," Abramov again assured his chief. Actually he had almost not presented the evidence. It was so cryptic and he knew that Andropov detested Louis on principle and had often asked aloud who benefited most by their partnership—the correspondent with the scandalous reputation and huge expense account or the Ministry of State Security.

"The point is," Abramov went on, "the only 'senior dissident' Dumas met was Perets, the great chemist, and, as I hardly need tell you, Perets is not a man given to gossip."

"True enough," Andropov agreed. "He is not given to gossip but he is given to naïveté. Politics is not his strong point, and he has hardly had any contact with Sokolov except in these last few months."

"I share your judgment so far as Perets' political naïveté is concerned, Yuri Vladimirovich," Abramov continued. "But let's consider another aspect of the affair. Perets would not knowingly repeat a piece of unfounded gossip. He has a rigid code of ethics. If, in fact, he did make this remark to Dumas—and, of course, Dumas, himself, is not necessarily reliable—I do not think that he would make it lightly."

Andropov pondered a moment. "I'd share your judgment on that, Abram Abramovich, but it just seems to me that this is not a moment to be tracking down obscure elements of ancient history."

Abramov smiled. "No, I'm not proposing any detailed historical research. Obviously this is not the time or place. But I did take the occasion to have the Ministry librarian bring me the 1945 file on Sokolov as well as the 1956 Military Rehabilitation Report, and I looked through them to see if there was any clue lying on the surface which might bear on such a remark."

"And . . ." Andropov said, letting the word drag out. Must they dig back almost thirty years into one more of the hundreds of thousands—God, not even hundreds of thousands but millions—of cases which his predecessors had hacked together during the Stalin days?

Abramov sensed Andropov's impatience, yet he felt he must continue.

"I have run back through the case, Yuri Vladimirovich," he said. "I must say that it takes the conventional form. He was arrested at the front, sent back to Moscow for interrogation. The charge was participation in an anti-Soviet organization. After half a year of interrogation the case was closed with his signature on the usual documents, and he was sentenced to nine years of corrective labor. The Military Board examined the file in 1956. Found no basis for the charges. Annulled the original indictment and gave him a full rehabilitation. At that time he was living in Kysel-Khor in Turkmenistan under forced residence. This was, as you know, lifted."

"Well," Andropov said wearily, "to be sure. I know all of that. Good God, the whole world knows all of these details. They have been broadcast and printed in every language of the world except the hundred and eighty-seven dialects contained within the Union of Soviet Socialist Republics. And we know the basis of the whole case, his correspondence with his friend Vanya on the First Ukrainian Front. And we know that his friend was also sentenced to prison camp in the same case. And that the 'anti-Soviet organization' comprised these two young soldiers, writing back and forth between the First Belorussian Front and the First Ukrainian Front."

"Perfectly true," Abramov replied. He was convinced now that he had made an error in bringing the matter up. Andropov was obviously in no mood to ponder this clue—one which Abramov could not help thinking might actually have a good deal of significance.

"And did you discover anything which we did not know?" Andropov asked sharply.

"No-o-o," Abramov replied. "I can't really say that I did. The interrogator's report is missing. This was noted by the Military Commission. Of course, this is not unusual. So many of the reports did disappear or possibly were never written. The Military Commission acted in the absence of the report, utilizing the data available. It's all there—not that there is much of it. Two or three letters which Sokolov sent to this friend and two or three which he received."

Andropov mastered his irritation. There was no need to show it. Bad form. Make Abramov think that the case was more important than he wanted him to think, especially since it *was* more important. After all, the man was trying his best not to overlook anything.

Andropov managed a smile. "Oh, well, Abram Abramovich," he said. "Who knows what it all means? Much—or nothing. Just leave that file with me and I'll have a run through it. Now, what about Sokolov's friend Krasin—are we talking with him?"

Abramov looked at his wristwatch. "At this very minute," he said. "In the flat on Gorky Street. I'll be hearing something shortly. In fact, I'd better get back to my office for the call."

"Thank you, Abram Abramovich," Andropov said with an easy smile. "Maybe we'll have better luck with the next pigeon."

As Abramov closed the door behind him Andropov clasped his hands on the desk before him and fell immediately into deep analytic thought.

Where, after all, did Suslov stand on the Sokolov matter?

Chapter 28

THE voice on the phone—it was that of Lieutenant Alexei, but at first Andrei did not recognize his hoarse screech—he was literally screaming, "Get back here immediately."

"What about the equipment, the wire?" Andrei asked.

"Forget it!" Alexei screamed. "We're pulling out. Not a moment to waste."

Andrei turned to his men: "We're leaving immediately. Guns, bedrolls, knapsacks. Nothing else."

He swept up his bedroll and Tommy gun, hooked his briefcase to his belt, gave his suitcase to a soldier, and they were off.

The noise of firing had grown steadily louder, and now was all around them. As they emerged from the observation post Andrei could see a tank burning in the foreground hardly a mile away. German or Russian he could not tell. The sound of firing to the south was rising in crescendo, and as they hurried back toward the compound they could see smoke rising above it. There was a sound of whistling in the air and the explosion of shells ahead of them. Andrei's mouth was dry, and he could feel the hair on the back of his neck rising. He was frightened, far more than before. What had happened he was not experienced enough to determine, but it seemed clear that a Nazi breakthrough was in progress, if not right at this spot, then somewhere close by, probably in the sector just south of them.

Andrei was leading his men at a jogging pace, but he realized that they could not keep it up and compelled himself to slow down. They were following the communication wire straight back to the battery. They had passed craters both to its right and to its left. Now they came to a wide one, a hit directly on the line. It must have been broken and, in fact, Andrei quickly noted the splices which Dedya Petya had made at either side of the yawning hole.

As they circled the crater a splash of telltale red on the ground made his heart skip a beat. Here was where Sonya had died. It must have been. That must be her blood. For a moment he saw in his mind the scene—the girl sprawled out, her blood flowing into the Russian earth and just beyond her the wounded soldier, his arm crumpled at his side. He could even imagine Dedya Petya moving with his slow and careful pace, first to the girl, kneeling over her, quickly determining that there was no life; turning to the soldier, helping him to his feet, putting a crude sling on his arm; then lifting Sonya's body—he was strong as a great pine tree, was Dedya Petya—putting it across his shoulders, mindless of the blood that flowed down his uniform tunic, giving his hand and shoulder to the wounded soldier and somehow managing to get back to the compound.

That was how it had happened. So it must have been. Andrei felt his stomach churning. The fear that was in him and the emotion for Sonya so rocked him that he even staggered a pace or two. "Take care, Comrade Lieutenant," one of the soldiers said. Andrei took a grip on himself. He realized dimly that his men were concerned for him. They must know, he thought. He pulled himself together, and silently they entered the woods where the battery was deployed—had been deployed. Around them fires blazed in the forest. Caches of supplies touched off before the pullout. But where was the battery? They pushed further and further into the grove.

All around lay the debris of the abandoned position. The guns had been pulled out. The emplacements stood broken and bare. One gun was still on site, its barrel twisted. Had it been a direct hit, Andrei wondered. One of the men reading his mind said, "They blew it up. Probably the transport was destroyed." Of course—Andrei realized. And a bit further along they saw the great gun tractor. It had been smashed by a bomb.

Suddenly Andrei realized that shells were again plowing their way through the scene of complete demolition. They were coming closer. He and his men leaped into one of the German entrenchments. Shell after shell slammned into the ground, the shrapnel keening around them as they cowered in the bottom of the Nazi ditch. The explosions were so close they could almost taste the bitter cordite. Finally the shelling lifted, and they pushed their way through the grove. No one was left. There were dead horses in one of the corrals. Hit by the German bombs. They lay in a random pile, bellies slashed, yellow guts trailing over the black earth.

What could have happened, Andrei wondered? The call to him must have come just as they were pulling out. The order must have been given with extreme suddenness. In fact, thought Andrei, perhaps they were in such a hurry they forgot to call the observation post until a moment before leaving.

Only one thing could have generated such urgency. The Nazis must have broken through. In fact, the Nazis might well be ahead of them already.

They made their way back through the smashed village. There were new shell holes and the remains of the houses were more battered. There was a Russian body just beside the village street. Was it one of the men of the battery? Andrei and his three comrades glanced at it as they went past. They could not tell. The man's face had been blown away. Only the white inner bones and shreds of bloody flesh remained.

Good God, Andrei thought. Please God it wasn't that way with Sonya! Please God! He had another thought. Where was Sonya's body? Had there been time to bury it? Had it simply been left behind in one of the shelters for the Germans to find and mutilate? This seemed the worst to Andrei. The thought struck him like a machine-gun bullet, and he stumbled and fell headlong in the dirty muck of the village street. One of the soldiers picked him up. "Careful there, Comrade Lieutenant," the man said. Andrei was covered with mud from head to toe. Instantly he looked to his submachine gun. Strapped to his back, it had escaped the dirt. Beside the street lay a pile of cotton waste, discarded by some tank sergeant, Russian or German. Andrei took the stuff and managed to get the worst of the dirt off his face and uniform. Andrei told his men: "Well, you see what's happened. The battery had to get away in a hurry. We'll just follow along and with good luck we'll catch up to them. They don't have much of a lead on us."

The men agreed.

"However," Andrei warned, "we must keep a sharp eye about us. The battery pulled out in a devil of a hurry. I'm afraid that means a German breakthrough. They may even be ahead of us. Watch carefully."

He knew this was as obvious to the men as it was to himself, but somehow he felt the men expected him to speak.

They were out of the village now and moving along the road they had taken coming up to the front. There was constant firing, but at some distance. What now worried Andrei was the possibility of Nazi planes. At any moment they might appear overhead and a spray of machine-gun fire would finish them.

"Let's spread out a bit," Andrei said, "so we are not all clumped together on the road. We won't make such a good target for a plane."

He went ahead a hundred yards and took the lead. The others spread out at similar intervals. There was no difficulty in following the line of retreat. It was marked by a litter of discarded blanket rolls, an overturned peasant cart with a broken axle and a load of oats, jettisoned knapsacks, even coats here and there. The men had been moving fast and many were moving on foot. They were discarding burdens that had become too heavy to carry at the rapid pace of their retreat.

Andrei was walking swiftly himself, walking close to the ditch beside the road, ready to jump at the first sound of a plane. Once again to the right he heard the sound of cannonading. Not heavy enough for battery work, he thought. He wished he had had more experience in understanding the sound of the guns. The thought had just entered his mind when he heard the characteristic roar of a plane and instinctively dove for the ditch beside the road. It was a low-flying German fighter-bomber, and it swept up the road spitting bullets as it came. Andrei buried his head in his arms. He was in a ditch just deep enough to protect his body. The plane raced past like a hurricane. Andrei heard the bullets spattering, and almost as quickly as he heard them, realized that he was safe and that the plane had moved on.

Andrei pulled himself out of the ditch, once again covered with mud, and looked back to his men. Only two were clambering from the ditch. The third soldier, the sergeant, lay in the road, arms flung out. Andrei ran back and knelt beside him. He could not have heard the plane in time. Two or possibly three bullets had slammed into his body. There was no pulse. The blood was just beginning to ooze out from under him and spread in a dark pool in the deep rut of the road.

Andrei clenched his hands. Was this his fault? Should he have kept the men together? He could not say. The other men came up beside him.

"Nothing for it," Andrei said grimly. "Help me move him to the field just beyond the ditch."

They carried the heavy body across the road over the ditch and lay it on the black earth of the field.

"Get me a stick," Andrei said. One of the soldiers returned with a piece of wood, possibly a stave from an ammunition box. Andrei hurriedly penciled the sergeant's name—Anton Pavlovich Antonov—the date May 18, 1942. He drove the stake into the ground beside the soldier, hung the man's helmet on it, took from Antonov's bloody jacket pocket a small wallet with identification, checked to see if his family's name and address were there—they were—and turned to his men: "Let's go." He thrust the wallet into his blouse pocket, wiping the blood on his sleeve.

An hour later Andrei and his two companions caught up with the straggling battery. It had paused momentarily while mechanics struggled to get the tractor hauling the one remaining gun to work again. Three trucks were functioning, one carrying the small stock of shells, the others food and five wounded men. The rest of the transport was carts and wagons. About twenty of them, Andrei estimated. Most of the men were marching.

The first man Andrei saw was Captain Smirnov. The captain gave him a weary greeting. "Good to see you," he said. "I was afraid we had left you to the wolves—or worse."

Andrei managed a faint smile.

"You'll find the major up ahead with the gun," Captain Smirnov said. "You'd think we have enough trouble without that."

Andrei pushed up along the column until he found the major. He was overseeing the tractor repairs, and his face appeared even more gaunt and drawn than usual.

"Well, Sokolov," he said as Andrei saluted. "Sorry to give you such short notice. But we had to get away in a hurry. As you can observe."

Andrei nodded his head. "We abandoned all of our equipment," Andrei reported, "except for what we could carry. And I must report that Sergeant Antonov was killed by a Nazi strafing plane just east of the village."

The major nodded. "The same fellow, I presume, who flew over our column. We had several losses." He sighed and ran his hand over his eyes.

"Now," he told Andrei, "we must move as rapidly as we can to the east and then to the northeast. Our position has been badly outflanked by a Nazi breakthrough just south of here. A German panzer unit is moving east very rapidly and parallel to us. At any moment they may swing to the north and we will be virtually encircled. In fact, this may have already have occurred. Our task is to keep the unit intact and move with all possible speed."

"Very good," Andrei replied.

"And, Sokolov. Take charge of the wagon column again. Lieutenant Alexei has been in charge, but he was one of the casualties of that strafing plane."

Andrei went back to the head of the diminished column of carts. Not to his surprise he found Dedya Petya there, driving the first wagon. The soldier silently saluted as Andrei clambered up and sat on the seat beside him. He slung his briefcase under the seat and had his suitcase stowed there too.

Dedya Petya sighed and shook his head. "Difficult times," he said. "Very difficult. And we aren't out of it by any means." Andrei nodded grimly. "That's right, Dedya Petya," he said, staring straight ahead. They sat without talking. Then Andrei came to himself, dismounted and walked back along the column of wagons, counting them and taking a quick survey of their contents. There were nineteen wagons and carts. In each there were wounded, lying or sitting amid heaps of hastily assembled baggage, including considerable grain and forage for the horses.

As Andrei returned to Dedya Petya the column, axles creaking and squealing, began to lumber along. At rough count Andrei believed there were about forty wounded in his train. He sat silently beside Dedya Petya. Again the emotions over Sonya welled up in him—his sorrow, his desolation, his pain, his anger. He could hold back no longer.

"What happened?" he asked Dedya Petya.

The soldier looked at him with a sad, solemn face and shrugged his shoulders. "What is there to say, Lieutenant?" he replied. "We were following the wire back. The girl had gotten a bit ahead of us. We stopped to fix the wire. The shells came slamming down. Vanya and I threw ourselves to the ground. One burst almost on top of us. Thank the Lord it didn't touch me. A fragment caught Vanya in the arm. Broke it. I looked ahead. There was this big hole where the shell had hit."

"But what about the girl?" Andrei broke in. "What happened to her?"

"As I said, Comrade Lieutenant," Dedya Petya resumed patiently, "she was a bit ahead of us and the shell must have come down right on top of her. There was hardly a sign of her left. Just scraps of uniform, you know."

"Just scraps?" Andrei asked unbelievingly.

"Just scraps," Dedya Petya said slowly. "But you might say it was for the best, Comrade Lieutenant. If it is going to happen, then it should happen quickly. Like lightning, you know?"

"Scraps," Andrei muttered. He was sinking into a void that turned every color of his life into gray. What meaning had life, any life, that it could with the snap of a finger be snuffed out? How could only scraps remain of that voice, those thin hands, those soft breasts, that frail body, that tornado of feeling? Andrei was lost in his grief when he heard Dedya Petya's voice continuing, low, slow and exact. The man was fumbling in his pocket.

"There is just this," Dedya Petya said. "I took the liberty of bringing it along. It was in her hand. I found it there."

He handed over to Andrei a worn uniform button, a zinc-and-copper button with the hammer-and-sickle mark on it. Andrei looked at it in the palm of his hand with confusion. This had survived but the girl had not—this tiny ornament, of which millions existed throughout the Red Army. Eight to each tunic, this button had passed through the inferno of the explosion of cordite and steel. It was not touched. But the small woman's body which had within hours become for Andrei as precious as life itself had perished. Scraps . . . scraps . . . He could hardly bear to repeat the word in his mind, but he could not halt its mnemonic repetition again and again and again.

Black anger, black despair, boiled inside him. He was hardly conscious of the fact that the column was moving along as rapidly as the horses could pull. He was not aware when they came to a brief halt and again resumed. He did not hear the guns firing in the distance. He did not notice the military debris along the road, nor smell the smoke of the peasant cottages burning in the large village off to the right. Dedya Petya sat straight and silent, his face drawn tight against any emotion. Andrei rode beside him, his spirit tottering into the abyss.

Presently he felt something in his hand, hard, round and warm from the clutch of his fist. He opened it in wonder. Oh, yes, there it was, the button that Sonya had held in her hand. He did not dare ask how or where Dedya Petya had found it. He could not bear another detail. He held the button so hard he could almost feel the hammer-and-sickle design imprinting itself on his palm.

Andrei rocked in the seat of the wagon oblivious of the ruts, the jolts, the bouncing. His gaze was down, fixed unseeing on his muddy boots. Slowly his eyes wandered up along the dirty orange-and-black stripe that denoted service in the artillery. It followed up his spattered tunic. Odd, he thought—one of his buttons was missing. And then understood that the girl had taken it with her, a memento of their night together—until she could come back.

Chapter 29

THE night was dark, and Andrei thought there was a scent of fear in it. I am frightened, he told himself, and he could feel his pulse racing. The fear was like salt in his mouth. Not only was he frightened, he was bruised, beaten, overwhelmed—most of all, spiritually—by the events of the last twenty-four hours. And he was more tired than he had ever thought it was possible to be. Now he waited dull and leaden with his comrades for the breakthrough. A General Pegov was in charge, a divisional general. Andrei was not certain which division. One of those broken by the German counterattack, or counteroffensive as it seemed to be.

The plan could not have been more simple. The ill-assorted men had been divided into two unequal segments. Major Stromlin's command provided the core of the first—his was the only force that was relatively intact. He still had his cannon, his three trucks and eighteen of the nineteen carts. A small group, not more than twenty men, would be deployed a half-mile to the south. This group would open up with machine guns and grenade launchers until it attracted the Germans' attention. As soon as battle was joined there, the main force would move ahead silently and, hopefully, without notice, until it reached the comparative safety of the Russian lines.

The tactic was possible only because there were no continuous lines, neither Russian or German. They had come up on the flank of a German panzer column. If they could pass this point they should be able to rejoin the Soviet forces about five miles distant. General Pegov had favored abandonment of Stromlin's gun and wagon train. Stromlin insisted that he had kept his force intact thus far and was not going to leave his wounded to the mercy of the Nazis. The general finally yielded with the proviso that if the wagon train or gun at any point endangered the safety of the group, they were to be jettisoned immediately.

"We are going to bring our men out," Stromlin told Andrei. "And it is your responsibility to bring through the wagons. I cannot foresee any circumstance under which they will have to be abandoned—do you understand?"

Andrei saluted. "I understand."

He returned to Dedya Petya and explained the situation. They were gathered in a birch and aspen forest that adjoined an extensive marsh. At the edge of the forest, close to the place where they were huddled, was a small dirt road. The Nazis, they believed, were concentrated to the right beyond the marsh and on both sides of a small stream that flowed out of it. They were moving on a good road that ran roughly parallel to the dirt road which was the Russian escape route. Because of the marsh the panzers had not deployed toward the dirt road. If the column could pass this point without detection they should have only a few miles to go before rejoining the main Russian forces.

"Our task," Andrei told Dedya Petya, "is to keep the column together and keep it moving."

Dedya Petya shook his head. He was obviously doubtful. "The horses are very tired," he said. "Some are not in very good shape. Better have a look at them."

Andrei and Dedya Petya inspected the horses, and it was decided to reduce the wagon train to fifteen, using the best of the horses and throwing out enough supplies to accommodate the wounded. Each wagon axle was carefully greased and each driver was instructed that at the sign of breakdown he was to cut out of the column. If possible the wounded would be transferred to the remaining wagons. But there was to be no halt once the movement began. Success depended on speed and surprise.

* * *

By 3 A.M. the column had assembled along the dirt road. This time the gun and tractor were placed behind the three trucks and the fifteen wagons. The column moved forward about a mile in the darkness. Andrei, afoot, checked each wagon. The axles were running quietly. A suggestion that the horses' hooves be muffled with cloth bandages had been vetoed by Dedya Petya. "They'll just come off and the horses will stumble about," he said. It was a dark night, very cold. Only occasionally did they hear distant shellfire. The men waited nervously. The attack group was to open up at 3:30, but the main column was not to move for fifteen minutes to give the Nazis time to engage. The wait seemed endless. Andrei kept looking at his watch. He could see nothing in the darkness, and lighting a match was forbidden. Then Dedya Petya clutched his sleeve. "There," he said, "it's beginning."

Andrei heard the first burst of fire. In the stillness it sounded as though it was in the next field. The Soviet machine guns chattered. A grenade launcher went into action. Suddenly a German flare appeared off to the right, further away than Andrei had expected. There was the sound of answering machine-gun fire and the echo of a heavier gun. The firing continued, rising and falling on both sides. And to a whispered command passed down the line from rank to rank, Andrei's column began to move. The sound of the machine guns blotted out the inevitable clatter of the horses and the inevitable creak of the wagon frames. It even blotted out the sound of the great tractor chuffing along with the battery's gun.

The column moved carefully and steadily down the small road. Nothing was visible on either side. The first fifteen minutes passed without incident. The wheeled transport and the men on foot moved rapidly ahead. There was no sign of Nazi detection. The sound of firing on the right continued, although a bit more distant now.

The second quarter-hour was the same. The wagons rolled on unimpeded. Andrei could hear the trucks ahead of him. Their engines sounded louder, now that they were farther from the din of the fire fight, and the heavy tractor seemed to roar like a thrashing machine. How could the Germans not hear it? Andrei now understood the general's reluctance to include the gun in the column. It was a hazard, but Major Stromlin himself was riding with it. Andrei did not know, but he had the feeling if worst came to worst the major might simply detach a crew and go down fighting with his gun. Later on, he realized that this was sheer romantics, but at that moment as the hour neared four, with the inevitable first traces of light, almost anything seemed possible.

The sound of the machine guns had almost died away when Andrei heard the *clump, clump* of heavy explosives. Two shells had been fired toward their rear, quite possibly close to the road along which they were moving. Then two more plowed in at the same location, so far as the ear could detect. "Perhaps they are finding our range," Andrei said to Dedya Petya. The soldier pondered the question. Meantime two more came in. "I think not, Comrade Lieutenant," Dedya Petya said. "I think that they are trying to prevent the escape of our rear guard, of the fire party. I think the fight has broken off and our lads are trying to get away. The Nazi devils are trying to cut them off."

Andrei said nothing. He was really too tired to think, but he realized that the shelling was a good sign. The Nazis had not yet detected the escape of the main column.

Nor did the Germans spot the fleeing Russians. At a little before 6 A.M., in broad daylight, the column was fired upon for the first time —by their own Russian comrades who mistook them for an approaching Nazi attack group. Fortunately, the fire of the Soviet machine gun fell short, and before the gun got the range a reconnaissance detachment had made contact with the head of the column and the group reached the shelter of its lines.

The "shelter" of the Russian lines turned out to be shelter in name only. The men hardly had time to wolf down dry rations and fill their canteens with boiled water than the order to continue movement was given.

For the next four days the battery, still hauling its one gun but now reduced to two trucks and twelve wagons, continued to move. It survived Stuka attacks on the highway, a near cutoff by a German motorized division, a machine-gun assault by a Soviet rear-guard unit that, again, did not recognize their comrades and a very brief cannonading by a German tank or gun-carrier (in which two wagons and their personnel, including wounded, were lost). On at least three occasions Major Stromlin was ordered to abandon his gun but managed to talk his superiors out of it.

When they finally reached Voronezh and, to Andrei's astonishment, found that it was beyond the sweep of the German attack, the company was still, technically, a viable fighting body. The major's achievement was nothing short of extraordinary. He had brought his company in through one of the worst disasters to befall the Red Army. Although he had only a handful of officers and men still technically fit for action, he was almost immediately given the battlefield decoration of Order of the Red Star. And Andrei received the Medal of the Patriotic War.

*   *   *

Andrei lay in the grass beside a muddy stream that wandered through the pasture and let the sun flood down on him. He had washed every scrap of clothing he possessed, and it lay scattered about him drying in the hot sunshine. In fact, the whole pasture had turned into a crazy quilt of soldiers' clothing. The company, withdrawn from action, was recuperating, waiting to be reorganized.

By the officers' code Andrei should have ordered a soldier to do his washing, but he could not bring himself to do it. He wanted his clothes to be meticulously clean, and, moreover, he wanted the dull monotony of scrubbing each article, beating it on a stone as the village women did and then setting it out into the sun. And he wanted to scrub himself from head to toe, to rub the harsh soap through his hair and into his skin until it was red and raw. He wanted to get the stink of battle out of his lungs, off his body and out of his clothes. He could not scrub out of his mind the stale smell of fear, the cloying odor of death, the endless stench of fire and destruction. Nor could he erase the pain imprinted there. But, somehow, he felt that by this vigorous washing he had purified his body, and this might be the first step toward purifying his mind.

The night before, he and Captain Smirnov had sat very late, consuming a bottle of vodka, something Andrei had rarely done. But each had much on his mind.

"You must understand," the captain said after the third vodka, "that we have no right to be sitting here in this pleasant little hut. We have no right to be alive."

Andrei had bridled a bit at that. He regarded their escape as something of a miracle, but a miracle that had been accomplished by military skill and determination.

"Not at all," the captain said. "Forgive me for being blunt. We have all been honored for the achievement of bringing our company out intact—right? We emerged as a fighting unit. Few others did— right? A very considerable success that has been marked by the appropriate decorations, and I have no doubt some promotions will be forthcoming as well."

"But don't you think the honors and promotions were earned?" Andrei asked in some surprise.

"I think," the captain said, "they were earned in the worst way— they were earned by jeopardizing the safety of the whole for the satisfaction of one individual's ambition. To put it bluntly, by hanging on to that damn gun of ours, not to mention your carts and wagons, we turned our escape group into a limping rabbit. If the Nazis had noticed us we would have been massacred—all of us. Not a chance of getting away. If we had left the damn gun and the transport and simply slipped down that road in peace and quiet we would have increased our chances of success by—well, you work out the percentage on your slip stick."

"But," Andrei protested, "then we would have left the gun to the Germans and abandoned all our wounded."

"So the gun would be a big gain for the Germans—yes? After capturing God knows how many thousands of our guns in every part of the battlefield. True, we would have left some of the wounded. But we could have gotten many of them away. And how much of a contribution would that have been to the thousands of men who fell into Nazi hands in that terrible battle?"

*   *   *

It was true, Andrei thought. The major's action had been motivated by ambition and some perverse quality of stubbornness. This could be good. It also could have been fatal. But what was far more important to Andrei was what Smirnov had said about the whole battle.

"An incredible blunder," Smirnov raged. "You could say that last June we were surprised by the Nazi attack, and we were, even though we should not have been. But this time—well, we have been at war nearly a year. We know the Germans. We know ourselves. And we deliberately attack them with weaker forces just as they are coming up to peak strength for their own offensive. And we do it in broad daylight —just as able to count noses as they are. And our losses—do you realize that we have lost the entire summer offensive here in these past few days? That we will be fighting on the defensive, and likely at terrible odds, all the rest of the year? That the advantage we gained at Moscow and in those not-too-well-thought-out winter campaigns has just run through our fingers like beer from a splintered barrel? In the last ten days we've lost all we gained. All of it."

Then Smirnov had whispered into Andrei's ear. "Do you know," he said, "how many men the Germans claim in this latest military achievement of our remarkable High Command? No less than two hundred and forty thousand captured. Captured, mind you. How many more dead and wounded? You might guess another two hundred and fifty thousand. Half a million men, not to speak of arms and equipment, guns, tanks and the rest."

Where did the responsibility lie? It was perfectly clear in Andrei's mind. At the top. And by that he meant Stalin. He had hinted at this in talking with Captain Smirnov last night, had almost burst out with it but had restrained himself. He had said enough so that Smirnov understood him and Smirnov had said enough so that Andrei knew that he agreed; that, in fact, Captain Smirnov, perhaps because he had been in the Army since before the start of the war, had gone through the terrible Tukhachevsky purge, had seen desolation cripple the Red Army, had been at the front when the June 22 attack had come, had seen the commanders of the Central Front made scapegoats and shot, had seen all of the self-delusion, the paranoia and worse—because of all this his feelings were stronger, more emotional than Andrei's. But they both, in the end, put the blame in the same place.

Stalin had approved the Kharkov offensive. It was planned and executed by a general whom he approved—Timoshenko. Beside all this the major's conduct in jeopardizing the escape attempt for the sake of his personal ambition seemed trivial to Andrei. At worst the major would have cost the Red Army the loss of three hundred or four hundred men. But Mustache and his generals threw away men by the hundred thousand. If half a million men had been lost at Kharkov, how many million had Russia lost since June 22? And from where would the Russian blood come to replace this terrible drain? His mind raced on and on. He thought of his father and World War I, and he began to compose in his mind the long entry he would place in his diary that evening—on Russian blood and how it had spilled over the earth.

No wonder the rich *chernozem* was so fertile. Its blackness came from the stuff of Russian lives. Had ten million perished in World War I? More likely twenty million all told. Two or three million died in the Revolution and Civil War and another five or ten of famine and disease. Perhaps five million left the country. And how many died in the collectivization? Maybe another ten million. Who could say? No longer did collectivization seem so heroic to him. And the purges—another ten. He reeled off the endless zeros in his mind until they floated across his consciousness like endless puffs of white smoke—million upon million upon million. This was the heart of Russia bleeding, bleeding year by year, generation after generation.

It was for the living to bring to an end this Calvary of the Russian people. It was for men like himself. Like himself and Vanya. Like himself and Smirnov. And there were others, more than anyone could count. They would win this war and they would return to Moscow for the great victory parade, the ceremonial in Red Square. All honor to the brave men who had saved Russia in its hour of peril.

And there in the Red Square with the assemblage of the masses and the leaders enshrined in the Mausoleum they would dedicate themselves to a new Russia, a pure Russia, a Russia purged of evil, purged of the spirit of Mustache—and of Mustache himself. A new Russia would be dedicated to the true spirit of Lenin, to the great ideals of Communism. It would be a Russia true to its own people and to its great history, capable of leading the Russian people—and the people of the world—to a life without cruelty, in which men and women lived freely and openly, working together, without torment and torture. It would be a world in which the just prevailed over the wicked, such a world as the men and women who made 1917 had dreamed of.

*   *   *

These were the ideals of the *new* Dekabristi, Andrei thought, the same as the ideals of the old Dekabristi, of Lenin and his comrades, of the Russian people, until Stalin slyly slipped into power and began to turn the whole thing upside down.

For the first time Andrei thought of Sonya without dark agony. She was, he said to himself, born too soon into the world, too soon and too good. She with the millions of others, the zeros without end, was a victim of the same terrible man. His policies, his errors, his terror, his stupidity and his false shrewdness had led directly from that moment in January 1924 when he swore his famous oath to Lenin to the moment just at dawn on May 18, 1942, when a Nazi shell obliterated a mess girl of the 349th Artillery Brigade whose full name Andrei did not even know at the moment of her death.

Sitting in a comfortable peasant hut, fresh sunshine burning out the stale horror of his mind, Andrei took up his fine-nibbed pen and began to draft a letter to Vanya, setting down his fundamental beliefs.

"We believe," he began, "in a Russia truly Russian and truly Communist." The words seemed to dictate themselves. Within the hour the statement was finished. It was brief, only a page, and was in the form of a new oath to Lenin, to reaffirm Lenin's principles. He thought of Molotov's words on June 22—"Our cause is just, our cause will triumph." It will, he told himself. It must.

Chapter 30

ANDREI'S mother had been dead for nearly six months before he even learned that she had died—through a bare word in a note from Rosa. Not until fifteen years had flowed by would he hear from his Aunt Sofia the circumstances of his mother's last days.

The truth was that after the Kharkov debacle Andrei had lost touch with everyone—with his mother, with Rosa, with Vanya and even for a time, with the war itself. The 349th Artillery Brigade, consisting only of the remnants of Major Stromlin's company, was pulled out of line. The other companies had simply been obliterated, lost without a trace.

Major Stromlin was given a new command—the 73rd Special Artillery Battalion—and was promoted to lieutenant colonel. The new battalion was formed around the surviving cadre of his old company. Captain—now Major—Smirnov was number two in command. Andrei was made a senior lieutenant and placed in charge of an audio reconnaissance company.

To Andrei's astonishment and disgust, Lieutenant Petroshenko had reappeared, vulgar and unctuous, to serve as security officer of the new battalion. He had escaped all the hell of Kharkov, having been off with his prisoner, Private Gleb Andreyevich, the "suspect" in the case of Lieutenant Petrov's death at the church tower. Nonetheless he sported the same new medal as Andrei, and like Andrei, he had been promoted to senior lieutenant. As to what might have become of the ill-fated Gleb Andreyevich, Andrei learned nothing except for dark and portentous hints: "The law is taking its course," "Those who deserve it are being justly punished" and "We in the security forces have our own way of handling affairs."

The new equipment for Andrei's audio unit did not arrive for two months, and Andrei and his company, new men except for a few old hands like Dedya Petya, were given another two months' training to learn how to use it. The weapons companies received new cannon and howitzers, and the whole unit spent six weeks in complicated maneuvers. All of this took place deep in the safe and secure rear, east of Kostroma on the upper Volga, as backward and isolated a region of Russia as Andrei had ever seen. In this province *bast* shoes made of bark could still be seen; the women went barefoot to the fields and some old men wore the old Russian gownlike caftans and carried oaken crooks, as in the time of Ivan the Terrible. The fields were often tilled with wooden plows. In the absence of tractors and horses, women hitched themselves, three to the yoke, and pulled the plows, their backs straining and the harness cutting into their heavy breasts.

In this bear's den the war seemed distant and unreal, but news came that Rostov had fallen again to the Nazis, that the southern and southwest fronts had crumbled. The Germans drove toward Stalingrad and the Volga. Nazi armored columns plunged deep into the Caucasus, heading for the rich oil fields of Baku. Never had the war looked worse. At any moment Andrei expected his new unit to be hurled into the conflagration, but the orders did not come.

*   *   *

At the end of July, Andrei got a letter from his mother, mailed a few days before the second fall of Rostov. Maria Petrovna was not feeling well. Life was difficult. For the moment she was without work. The fact was, Andrei knew, she had had no work since the Russians recaptured Rostov six months earlier. She had received the package of tinned food (Andrei was sending his mother food as often as he could, sometimes from his rations, sometimes purchased from the black market). She had had a letter from Rosa but there was no news in it. Aunt Sofia was well. His mother hoped her next letter would be more interesting. She congratulated him on his medal. "Take care, my dear boy," she said.

A day or two later he had a note from Rosa, written almost simultaneously with that from his mother. Her hospital was going to move again. She hoped to make a brief visit to Rostov and see her mother and his mother. She longed for him. "How long will this war keep us apart, my darling?" No comment on his medal. Probably she had not gotten his letter telling about it.

Vanya simply vanished into the blue. Andrei had seen him soon after getting to Voronezh. They spent a glorious night telling each other about the war, affirming their conviction that Stalin and his generals had committed one colossal blunder after another. Vanya had heard from a friend the story of the Kiev tragedy, how more than a million men were lost to Nazi encirclement because of Stalin's refusal to permit retreat in time to escape the German noose. Andrei told Vanya of the Kharkov disaster and the Russian loss of half a million men. They speculated on the cost of the Leningrad siege. "A million lives—at least," Vanya said. Andrei had heard the total was half again larger. They traded stories about the lack of preparedness at the start of the war and the refusal of Stalin to permit the Red Army to fight back even after the German attack had actually started.

"But don't you see, Vanya," Andrei said in excitement, "these are just details. Granted they are details that loom as high as the Himalayas. But these disasters were certain to occur. They were inevitable under Stalin, just as we have known since the time of Marx that the downfall of capitalism was inevitable. Disaster cannot be escaped under the rule of the Mustache. This is his hallmark. He can do nothing else. He is capable of nothing else. The whole essence of Lenin's teaching has been lost."

"You'll find plenty of support for that among the officers in my regiment," Vanya said. "But don't forget the common soldiers who still go into battle shouting, '*Za Stalinu.*' "

"Oh, I know that," Andrei told his friend. "Stalin is the great symbol. It was the same in the days of the Czar. The peasants used to say, 'If only the Little Father knew,' and they say the same about Mustache. If only Stalin knew . . . But he does know. He knows it all and directs it all, and it has cost how many million lives do you think?"

Vanya shook his head. "Ten million?"

"Chicken feed," Andrei said. "Chicken feed. Twenty-five million. Maybe thirty million. And by the end of the war—who knows—fifty?"

Andrei gave Vanya a copy of his oath to Lenin. Vanya suggested a few changes and they wrote out two new clean copies, one for Vanya, one for Andrei.

"But you know, Vanya," Andrei said, "these are not just Lenin's principles. This is the great Russian tradition. The Decembrists. Pushkin, Herzen and his Bell. I know Lenin turned against the Narodnaya Volya, the People's Will, but that was because he objected to their terrorist tactics, not their goals. Lenin's revolution was the culmination of one hundred years of Russian striving, Russian idealism, dedication to the cause of the people. And now this Georgian cretin, this ignorant seminarian who can't even speak decent Russian, has turned the holy Russian cause against itself."

Andrei raised his *rumka* and touched it to Vanya's. "Ring out the bell, as Herzen said," he toasted. "And as Lenin said *Iz iskra plamya*— let the flame burst from the spark. *Do adna!* Bottoms up!"

The two young men drank. The next morning they parted. Each agreed to find five like-minded men for the cause. No more. Let each of these five find five, Andrei said. And so on.

But numbers, he said, were not important.

"By the time we march in victory through Red Square," he said, "we'll need no allies. We will all be as one."

*   *   *

Shortly after, Andrei and the new "battalion" were shipped off to Kostroma, and, Andrei guessed, Vanya's division was sucked into the Stalingrad campaign. For months Andrei heard nothing from his friend.

It was the fate of his mother that deeply concerned Andrei. Somehow he had confidence in Rosa's ability to survive. But his mother—whether she was living under Nazi occupation in Rostov or had managed to escape the city in one of the evacuation parties—either way he feared for her life.

And rightly so.

"She lost her spirit when the war started and you went away," Aunt Sofia later told him. "I'd known her for thirty years. And I could see it in an instant. 'Maria Petrovna,' I told her, 'don't be so downcast. That boy of yours—he isn't going to get himself killed—particularly with that horse company he's attached to.'"

"But," said his aunt, "she was convinced she would never see you again. She said the first war had taken her husband and the second war would take the rest. And when the Nazis captured Rostov in '41, I don't mind saying to my own nephew in all privacy that I did not think that would be altogether a disaster. Not then. We had suffered enough since 1917. But your mother did not agree. She never did agree with me."

The two women had not gotten away when the Nazis broke into the city. Apparently they quarreled quite harshly over the Germans. This, Andrei could believe. His mother was a real Russian patriot like his father. The arrival of the Germans meant that Maria Petrovna had no work and no chance of getting work. Moreover, she was half-sick, complaining of pains in her stomach. She hardly ate. She grew thinner and thinner. Even after the Nazis were driven out, the situation of the women did not improve. The bank had been blown up. Maria Petrovna's employers had been shot and the bank did not reopen. Food was short. It became harder and harder to survive, Tetya Sofia did some black-marketeering.

"What else was there to do?" she said. She went out to the countryside and looked up some of the peasants she and Boris had once known. She managed to buy eggs and meat, brought them into Rostov and sold them at exorbitant prices. "A fortune," she said proudly. "But, of course, the money was useless. There was nothing to buy."

"I kept Maria Petrovna alive," she told him, "if I say so myself. It wasn't easy. Your mother, Andrei, was not an easy person. I think she had made up her mind to die. That's what I think. In fact, I told her so. I said, 'Maria Petrovna, you are going against the will of God. God has willed that we are to live and endure what life brings to us.

What you are doing is committing slow suicide and that is against the law of the Church.' "

But neither lectures nor threats had any effect. "And in no time the Germans were back, so help me God," his aunt said. "And this time it looked like they were here to stay. God knows they were cruel. I must say that. There were bodies hanging from yardarms in all the squares. And no food in the market. It was worse than ever."

Andrei's mother was seriously ill. She continued to lose weight. She could keep nothing in her stomach.

"Once," Tetya Sofia said, "I even managed to get her a little *koumis,* mare's milk. Everyone knows it is the best thing in the world for stomach disorder. But she couldn't keep it down. I guess I knew then that the end was inevitable."

*   *   *

The two women were living in the room which Andrei knew so well, the one that he and his mother had occupied for most of his life. He could picture the scene. Even discounting his aunt's pious interjections, he knew it must have been extraordinarily difficult. There was only one bed. He had slept until he was married to Rosa on a makeshift bed of trunks. That was where Tetya Sofia slept.

"Your mother lived for her letters from you," she said, "but when the Germans took Rostov, that ended it. She never got another letter."

"What about Rosa?" Andrei interjected. "Didn't Mama hear from her?"

Sofia narrowed her eyes. She did not like Rosa. Hated her, in fact. And made no bones about it. "I can't remember," she finally said. "It's too much to burden an old woman like me with questions like that. Maybe Rosa saw her once, maybe not. I'm not sure. But she certainly was nowhere around at the end. No one was. You weren't there. The rest of the family was dead. The only one there was myself, your old Tetya Sofia. But I never left your mother's side, God in heaven save us. I was there when she gasped her end. I shut her eyes and lighted a candle at her feet and I got the priest to come and we gave her a decent and proper burial, which is more than I am likely to get in these bad times."

Andrei had thanked his aunt again for all she had done. So far as he could understand, his mother had died of general malnutrition. Starvation complicated by stomach ailments, possibly cancer. She certainly had no proper treatment.

"There weren't any doctors," Tetya Sofia said frankly. "They all ran away with the Russians or the Nazis shot them. The pigs. And the German doctors wouldn't lift a finger, not for Russians. The more of us died the better they liked it. When I think of the airs the Germans gave themselves when Boris and I went to Bad Nauheim on our honey-

moon, and when we went to the opera in Berlin. How everyone looked
up to the Germans! The greatest geniuses on earth—Goethe, Heine,
Schiller, Mozart and the rest. So cultured. German music. German art.
German medicine. German universities. *Mein Gott!*"

The old woman interrupted her litany and spat vulgarly and
savagely on the dirt floor of her hovel.

"German *Kultur!*" she said. "They are heathens. Atheist pigs!"

But that, she assured Andrei, had not kept her from making a
personal appeal to the German *Kommandant* for medical help for
Andrei's dying mother. She had even gotten an interview with the
commander.

"At least I made them understand that there was one lady left
in Russia," she said in a haughty voice. She had, she told Andrei,
dressed in her best gown "from the former times," one which Boris had
bought for her in Paris. It was turquoise crepe de Chine with a high
waist, nipped in very snugly under the bosom and flowing freely in
long pleats—almost to the ground—a beautiful gown from Poiret.
She had worn her amber brooch, her long green wool coat with its red
fox collar and a great mauve hat with an ostrich feather. How she had
managed to preserve these relics from her trip to Paris in the spring
of 1913 Andrei could not imagine.

"They knew I was not just another one of the canaille," she said.
Apparently, the young captain at the German headquarters had never
seen anything like Tetya Sofia, who must have given off an immediate
aura of Kaiserin Germany, the rather faded watering places of the petty
nobility. And Andrei knew she spoke in a correct if creaky German,
which apparently convinced the officer that he was confronting a
genuine ghost of Wilhelmian times—the ancient aunt, perhaps, of
some improbable German family which somehow had survived the
terror of 1917 and the horrors of the Bolsheviks.

Tetya Sofia told Andrei she had spoken of her friends, the Prince
and Princess Schwarzenberg, Count Hohenlohe and the Stoessels of
Baden-Baden. The young captain may have been overwhelmed by
nostalgia. In any case, he had ushered her into the presence of his
superior, whose response was somewhat different.

The *Kommandant* asked Sofia if she was a Soviet citizen of Russian
origin. He promptly established that she possessed not a drop of
superior German blood in her veins and that her mission was in behalf
of another Soviet citizen, also of Russian blood.

According to Tetya Sofia's account, he didn't go any further. "What
did you bring this creature here for?" he roared to the captain. "Get
rid of her and fumigate this room. Don't you know an epidemic of
black pox has broken out among the *Untermenschen?*"

"I did not give him the privilege of showing me out," Tetya Sofia
said proudly. "I turned my back on him and swept from the room,
saying, 'And I thought the Bolsheviki were the scum of the earth!'"

Had she said it? Andrei wondered. And, what difference did it make? What his aunt had not understood was that the past was dead. The past of her wealth and extravagance, the Russia of champagne and gypsies and caviar and summers on the Riviera, was gone. And so was the Germany of the petty nobility that proliferated like sparrows in all of the old-fashioned spas, the Germany of the walrus-mustached *Herren Professoren*, the kind who spent four lazy years in Russia teaching Tetya Sofia German, the Germany of *Gemütlichkeit* and fussy water closets, of order, science, art and constipation.

Andrei's mother had survived the Nazi occupation of Rostov, but not for long. The Russians had not finally driven the Germans back over the Don and freed the gateway to the north Caucasus until mid-February of 1943, a month or so after the tremendous victory at Stalingrad.

"She was too far gone by then," Sofia said. "There was not much to do for her. And no one to help even if she could have been helped. The new Commissars couldn't be bothered about the likes of ordinary people. All they were interested in was getting the port operating."

His mother had died in the same room where she and Andrei had lived for so long. In the same bed.

"But I did get her a decent burial," Tetya Sofia said. "In the churchyard at Nakhitchevan on the outskirts of town. It's a nice enough place, but it wasn't easy. It cost me a pair of men's good *valenki* and three bottles of vodka. Don't ask me how I got them, but I had a little nest egg put away."

There had been only three mourners at the funeral: Tetya Sofia and two old women who lived in the apartment.

"The priest was all right," Tetya Sofia said, "but the gravediggers! They hardly bothered to push away the bones in the old grave to put down a new coffin."

His aunt had paid a stoneworker for a gravestone.

"It is a beautiful one, too," she said, her eyes sparkling a bit. "I don't know whose grave he took it from. But he chiseled out the name and carved your mother's on it. Not too expensive. A pound of sugar and an old fur hat I happened to have."

After she had buried his mother, Tetya Sofia said, they had tried to oust her from his mother's room. Finally she had gotten the right to it by giving the housing bureau agent a good piece of fat bacon and a couple of thousand rubles.

"Imagine," his aunt exclaimed. "Trying to throw me on the street. A helpless old woman like me!"

*   *   *

Andrei had received news of his mother's death on the eve of the battle of Kursk-Orel, the greatest battle of the war. He did not yet know that he was about to participate in this remarkable struggle, the largest confrontation of men and armor the world had ever seen. But he did know that the new 73rd Special Artillery Battalion was to have its christening in combat and he was certain that it would give a good account of itself. His acoustical company was his pride and joy. He was like a child with a new toy. The equipment was first-class, the liaison with the guns almost automatic. He could not wait to test it all in battle.

He wrote about this to Rosa in guarded terms. She was no longer in the Army. She had taken leave to help her mother, who had fallen ill, and managed to get her out of Rostov and, by a succession of dangerous adventures across mountains and over deserts, to the safety of Tashkent, in Central Asia. By now Rosa's hospital unit had been captured in the German descent on the Caucasus. She herself was suffering from malaria and the Army gave her a medical discharge.

"Andrei, how I long to see you, my darling," she wrote. "This war has been going on for a hundred years. Please, dearest, please—don't just wait for me as Simonov says in his poem—come to me or bring me to you."

The idea, Andrei admitted, was preposterous, but he made up his mind. If he survived the big battle that was about to open—and somehow he was certain that he would—he would see Rosa. She was, after all, his wife. She had as much right to be with her husband as the "front wives" had to be with their "front husbands." He would do it. He was filled with determination and confidence. The tide of battle had changed. The advantage lay with the Russians. It would not change back again. The victory was a certainty, only a matter of time. And then the day of the new Dekabristi would be at hand.

That night Andrei wrote a long entry in his diary: "Mama died alone, without me. Had I been there she would not have died. She is another victim on the endless list of victims. Can it not be said that a government which no longer is capable of protecting its people, which, in fact, lets their lives be extinguished like those of common flies and with no more concern and no more conscience—can it not be said that such a government has lost the mandate to rule and that the people have just cause to make another? That is the question that haunts my mind and I think there can be but one answer."

Chapter 31

SO, Andropov said to himself, we come to Suslov, and frankly he is a man whom I probably never will understand. The fact was, he thought, that he either knew too much about Suslov or entirely too little. Suslov regarded himself as the last great Marxist of his time, greater than Stalin (he was still a fairly open Stalinist). In Suslov's rare convivial moments, he would explain that he could not really criticize Stalin's ideological philosophy too harshly, since he himself had provided so much of its underpinning in the later years. Andropov did not quite believe that. He knew and could document the fact that Stalin not infrequently borrowed wholesale from others. It was his impression that Suslov merely did donkey work for Stalin, digging up the appropriate quotations from Marx, Engels and Lenin to support whatever policy Stalin was bent on pursuing.

Suslov was a skilled professional ideologist, although whether he was the last "great" ideologist of the day, Andropov was not prepared to say. Suslov was extraordinarily contemptuous of Mao and the Chinese Marxists and by common consent and prior claims he was the leader in the ideological struggle with Peking.

Suslov reminded Andropov a great deal of Molotov in his pedantic and scholastic approach to every question.

Yet, there was another side to Suslov as well. He had a genuine sense of humor, dry but sharp. He could make jokes about himself. He was no stiff professor, despite his steel-rimmed spectacles and dandruff-powdered shoulders. He liked the ladies, although he had permitted himself no real liaisons for many, many years. He liked to dance, although here again he had not indulged since the early years after Stalin's death. He had despised Khrushchev, although rallying to his side during the 1957 anti-Party plot, and it was he who had persuaded Mikoyan to join in the successful plot of 1964 to oust Khrushchev. Without Mikoyan to lull Khrushchev's suspicions the plot might not have succeeded. Suslov probably had convinced himself after Stalin's death that he could be the *éminence grise* behind Khrushchev or that in time he could oust Khrushchev and take his place—indeed, in 1964 he may have planned to first get rid of Khrushchev, then force Brezhnev and Kosygin to stand down for him.

It had not worked out. Suslov possessed that prime talent for a Politburo man—the ability to survive, to come through every crisis with his influence unshaken and his position secure. But life had shown that he could not tip the balance of forces to his own personal advantage. He himself had not been able to win the general secretaryship and never would. Time had passed him by. Yet in a sense this made him more dangerous. He was a bitter and frustrated man.

* * *

Andropov's telephone rang and he gave a little start. Think of the devil! For it was, in fact, Mikhail Andreyevich Suslov on the line.

Andropov hesitated the briefest of seconds—just to get any echo of his thoughts out of his tongue—then spoke: "Good morning, Mikhail Andreyevich."

"Thank you, Yuri Vladimirovich," Suslov replied. "Forgive me for troubling you, but one of my assistants passed on to me a rumor he had picked up somewhere that you have arrested Sokolov or, perhaps, are on the point of arresting him?"

There was no pause in Andropov's response. It whipped back at Suslov like a boxer's glove.

"No, on both counts, Mikhail Andreyevich," Andropov replied. "I wonder where that rumor may have originated."

Suslov apologized. He did not know where the report had come from. Possibly it was the same old BBC, trying to spread misinformation.

"I'm sorry to have troubled you," he told Andropov. "But I wanted to be appropriately prepared if the question was going to arise at the meeting in that sharp form."

Andropov put the receiver down a bit harder than was his custom. Usually, he liked to lay it down so gently that the conversation seemed not to end but just to float off into thin air. A grim look swept his face. BBC misinformation! Fat likelihood! He knew where this juicy tip came from, all right. It came from his own valued, trusted Gorbunov, perhaps not Gorbunov himself, but one of Gorbunov's assistants. No. It could not be an assistant. He heard again Gorbunov's voice assuming just a hint of slyness, or oiliness, as he had told Andropov of summoning an emergency detail to carry out Sokolov's immediate arrest—if desired. It had to be Gorbunov himself. And Gorbunov had no doubt made the telephone call to Suslov even before he came in to report the finding of the message.

The *swolich*! The bastard! Andropov cursed under his breath and then quickly wiped the emotion off his face. No need to indulge himself because, after all, Gorbunov unwittingly had proved most helpful.

Andropov now knew that he was not to be trusted, that he offered a direct-line connection to Suslov. And having a direct-line connection to Suslov was, in a sense, even better than having a reliable assistant—if, in fact, such a paragon existed in this world of double loyalty and paranoia. Knowing something about Suslov which Suslov did not know he knew provided a means of misdirecting Suslov a time or two (Andropov knew that Suslov was too shrewd not to realize after one or two gambits that the Gorbunov connection was not reliable)—it was a priceless asset. He even began to smile. The breaks were beginning to come his way.

Nothing but overeagerness could have inspired the Suslov telephone call. What to conclude? Suslov was playing the Sokolov card *very* hard. He must be hoping to blackmail Brezhnev in some form. Use this as a lever to enhance his own influence. How could that be? Suslov would never play low-level politics. The stakes had to be considerably higher, Suslov must be playing for real power. He, Andropov, had some of it, but he had been scrupulous in abstaining from using it for his own personal ambitions. Certainly there was a power base in the big beefy provincial party organizations and in the huge industrial aggregates, but Andropov could tick them over one by one and count them on Brezhnev's side. They had practically invented Brezhnev.

Where else would one look? There was only one place: the Army. In the Politburo that meant Marshal Grechko. Before settling himself to analyze Grechko, another thought came to Andropov. He got Abramov on the phone. "Abram Abramovich, run a check for me, will you, and see if there has been anything carried by BBC in the last twenty-four hours on Sokolov. Oh, yes. Might as well check the other transmissions while you are at it: VOA, RFE, Radio Liberty, the Deutschlandsender. Anything at all."

Andropov put down the receiver, then quickly raised it again.

"Have one of the girls run down to the library," he told his secretary. "I want to see some copies of Herzen's *Bell*. You know—the magazine he published in London. Originals if we can get them without too much trouble. Half a dozen issues will do."

He smiled with satisfaction. Now—where did Marshal Grechko fit into the puzzle?

Chapter 32

WAR is universal. The battle is particular. War is like an ocean—it washes over continents. It changes nations and peoples, wipes out empires, gives birth to others. The battle acts on a different scale. It destroys a village, kills the last pig, the last goat, the last suckling child. But the next village flourishes, eggs and chickens sell at ten times their worth, silver pieces heap up in the buried pot behind the shed, and the bellies of the women swell fruitfully with the alien seed of the passing Army. War writes a new book in the works of history; the battle a new chapter and, sometimes, only a sentence.

Later on, when Andrei read of the battle of Kursk-Orel, even when he talked with other men who fought in it, he realized that the battle he read about, the battle the others spoke of, was not *his* battle. The terms used were "hurricane of fire," "armadas of tanks," "mountains of bodies," of the earth trembling under heavy explosions and waves of suffocating smoke that shrouded the battlefield. Others spoke of German regiments slaughtered to the last man, the heaps of bodies lying like carcasses after a rabbit hunt.

Andrei was told of men gone deaf from the cannonading and others who ruptured their vocal cords trying to shout above the din. There were some found wandering about the battlefield, unwounded, eyes glazed, mouths drooling, bereft of reason, reduced to idiocy by the horror. The wounded were so numerous that hospitals as far east as Omsk and Novosibirsk were jammed. Officers were flown to Alma-Ata, and Khabarovsk for treatment. It took weeks to bury the dead, and tens of thousands of German prisoners were employed in the grisly task.

The most distant points of the fighting lay two hundred kilometers apart. When it was over, the Russian losses were colossal, but the German losses were fatal. Never again was the Wehrmacht able to mount an offensive in Russia. From that July moment in 1943 the Third Reich was doomed. Every German soldier and every Russian soldier knew it.

But to Andrei and to the 73rd Special Artillery Battalion, Kursk-Orel was not an inferno, a descent into hell. It was, instead, an exquisite exercise in technical precision, a ballet of artillery fire, an island of mathematical perfection surrounded by chaos.

*   *   *

The 73rd Special Artillery Battalion was positioned on the northern perimeter of the battleground. Andrei found everything the opposite of what it had been at Kharkov. Russian planning now was meticulous. Andrei's battalion moved into position nearly a month before the German attack. The Russian command *knew* that the Germans were mounting a powerful armored offensive. They knew *where* the blow would fall. They knew *when* it would come. And they knew how they would defeat it: they would assemble the most powerful armored force the world had even seen behind the most powerful concentration of artillery the world had ever heard. They would back this mighty mass with a million and a half men, calculate every field of fire in advance. Sow the earth with tens of thousands of tank mines and anti-personnel mines. The attacking Germans would be channeled into pre-fixed fire lanes and smashed with high explosives. Once the Nazi momentum had been spent, a mint-new Soviet armored force would attack, attack, attack. It was the tactic Von Kleist had used at Kharkov. This time Zhukov and Rokossovsky would teach the Germans a lesson from their own exercise book.

Andrei watched the preparations with tingling blood. This was his kind of fighting. He knew enough of war now to know good generalship, and he could feel the assured professionalism, the power, the authority of the Red Army as it assembled. The 73rd Special Battalion was outfitted with nothing but new equipment, as was battalion after battalion, artillery unit after artillery unit. Andrei had not believed there were so many guns in the world. (After it was all over, he heard that there were twenty thousand cannon in the northern segment of the battlefield alone.) As for tanks—there were so many there hardly seemed room for them in the wide rolling countryside. Hundreds were semiconcealed, dug in to be used as fixed artillery until the moment of their commitment to battle.

The function of the 73rd had been carefully calculated long before the battle began. It was to offer no fire at all in the first stage, the stage in which the Germans committed themselves, brought out their armor and attempted to pierce the Russian defense line. The Russian defense was constructed of three principal barriers. If the Germans penetrated the first—and it was Russian tactics to assume that this line would be penetrated in hard fighting in which the German armor would be badly hurt—they would find themselves lodged between the first and second lines. The first line would not collapse. It would swing around and, between them, the first and second lines would pulverize the

German tanks and any infantry so ill-fated as to enter the box.

The 73rd was positioned to concentrate on the "box," once it had been filled with Nazi armor. Andrei's audio reconnaissance company was located well forward, perfectly dug in, heavily camouflaged and protected in deep dugouts with excellent vantage points for the audio equipment. There were triangulated pickup points and rapid calculation of the sound waves that enabled Andrei to get an instant and almost precise fix on any German gun, no matter how well camouflaged, no matter whether the firing was at night, under cover of fog, artificial smoke or any other device for confusion the Nazis could invent.

If, contrary to Soviet calculation, the Nazis began to overrun the second echelon of defense, the 73rd Battalion would drop back to a similar position, already prepared, between the second and third lines and there the game of the box would be played out again.

Even Dedya Petya, who, in general, had remained a skeptic of the new audio system ("I'd rather depend on my eyes than my ears when I'm pointing my gun at a wolf"), was filled with admiration for the echeloned Russian battle position. "As the peddler said when the master unexpectedly came home and found him in bed with the mistress, times have changed," he observed. "I think we will show the *nemtsi* a thing or two. I think they will find that we simple Russians are a little more difficult than they had counted on." Nor was Dedya Petya as depressed as he ordinarily was when the moment of combat drew near, and, Andrei observed, this spirit was general among the men.

"It's true," Major Smirnov agreed. "We all feel it. The Battle of Moscow taught us the Germans could be beaten. Stalingrad showed us we could turn the war around. Now, looking at this forest of guns and tanks—we know we are going to crush the Germans, crush Hitler, destroy the Third Reich. We know it."

"We know it *now*," Andrei said.

"True," the major said. "There were some moments when we were falling back in the autumn of 1941 when I was not so certain."

"I have always been certain," Andrei said, "perhaps because I did not know how bad things were in the autumn of 1941. But I think I would have been in any case, because my certainty was based on belief in the country as a whole, in the Russian people as a whole, despite the terrible mistakes that had been made."

"And still can be made," Major Smirnov said grimly.

"The victory parade will change that," Andrei said, smiling. He had long since shared his ideas with the major, had showed him the "oath," had enlisted him as one of his "five." Major Smirnov was not as confident in the future as Andrei, but he did firmly believe that the system was bound to change once the war had been won.

Lowering his voice now and glancing quickly around to make certain the dugout was empty, Smirnov added, "So long as the likes of

Petroshenko are on hand, you can be certain that mistakes are going to be made."

Andrei grimaced. He could not abide the bland hypocrisy of the Security officer and stayed as far away from him as possible. He had learned from Dedya Petya that Private Gleb Andreyevich had been given a twelve-year sentence for "conspiracy to endanger the life of a Soviet officer," the officer being the unfortunate Lieutenant Petrov. Andrei was now certain that Petrov had deliberately killed himself by jumping from the church tower as a result of the threats made against him by Petroshenko. Gleb's only connection with the case was the bad luck to have witnessed the lieutenant's suicide.

Andrei had talked with Major Smirnov of his suspicions. The good-natured major simply shook his head. "You see, Andrei Ilych, there is nothing to be done in a case like this," he had said. "We have our suspicions and they are undoubtedly well based. But neither of us was present at the accident or suicide or whatever it was. Lieutenant Alexei, to whom Lieutenant Petrov told of his conversation with Petroshenko, is dead. The only result of our intervening would be for this miserable miscreant to cook up a case against us, too. To win against these Security men you not only have to catch them red-handed, committing a crime in the presence of reputable witnesses, you must have powerful political influence as well."

*   *   *

As it happened, the battle opened in a rather surprising way, not early in the morning, when it was expected, but at two one afternoon, when good German burghers should have been settling down to a nap after a heavy meal of goose and a bottle or two of Rhine wine. Suddenly the sky exploded. The long-awaited Nazi attack had begun.

In the opening phase Andrei and his men had nothing to do. The German shellfire did not reach into their positions. The Nazi artillery and Stukas concentrated on the forward lines. Soon Nazi tanks began to appear, mechanized elephant caravans lumbering through the tall corn.

Andrei and his men monitored the German guns, just for the exercise, and occasionally through his field glasses he had distant glimpses of German tanks trapped in the Soviet mine fields. But the first day of the battle ended with the 73rd Battalian still on the sidelines. They had not fired a shot and none had fallen in their zone.

The second day was a day of killing. By midmorning dozens of German armored vehicles were caught in the box. And now for the first time the 73rd opened up on the German batteries which were attempting to silence Russian anti-tank guns and Russian T-34 tanks and the Russian tank killer squads.

The 73rd operated like a well-orchestrated symphony. One German gun after another was located, correlated, fired upon and silenced. Andrei kept track with a stubby pencil on a short piece of scratch pad. He could not always be a hundred percent certain, but if a German gun had fired three or four rounds, was then fired upon two or three times by the 73rd and thereafter was silent, he felt it safe to record a kill. In one hour between 5 P.M. and 6 P.M. on July fifth he recorded eight "certain" kills, and four doubtfuls. There was no direct German counterbattery, although occasionally a wave of German shelling would sweep over the mid-battlefield like a summer thunderstorm, doing about as much damage.

The precision of his men's work thrilled Andrei. Now he understood the pride of a good schoolmaster when his pupils offered a perfect declamation. So it was with the audio company. Each man functioned like a vital part in a sensitive piece of machinery; commands were unnecessary. Andrei knew that if a stray bullet hit him the men would carry out their functions without a missed step. There was no tension. No nervousness. Andrei understood perfectly well that an enormous battle was raging all about him but he felt no fear. He felt excitement and an enormous sense of participation. His battery was working for the first time under fire exactly as Andrei had known it would, and if he was not mistaken, this was merely a tiny cross-section of how the great Soviet force assembled here—coordinated, precisioned, tuned to perfect pitch by the conductor, General Rokossovsky—was operating.

Andrei watched for five minutes a new Panther trapped in the steel spiderweb the Russians had spun. First, the Panther hit a land mine which blew off one of its treads. Then it attempted to level its gun to exterminate a nearby Russian tank-killer battery. But the task was hopeless. The tank killers opened up, shells plunging into and around the Panther. At the end of three minutes the Panther was aflame. Andrei saw the hatch open and one man leap like a flaming torch over the steel side. No more men came forth. The flames plumed up red and black for twenty minutes, then died away.

*   *   *

All night the battle continued. Parachute magnesium flares and Very lights threw the landscape into reliefless profile. But Andrei did not need to look out across the field. The headphones and the delicate microinstruments told the story. The guns did not halt. The Germans tried counterbattery work now, trying to protect the battlefield where their tank rescue crews—mechanical teams, protected by squads with flame throwers and machine guns—sought vainly to salvage damaged armored units and help surviving crews to escape. But Russian crews were on the battlefield as well, armed with their own flame throwers. They clambered aboard the helpless behemoths, stuck the nozzle of the flame throwers down the ventilation duct, gave a burst of flame—and that was the end.

This, Andrei thought, was surely the war of the twenty-first century—the eerie light, the clanging of the repair crews, the overhead whistle of shells, the raw searing of the flame throwers. Occasionally a Nazi flame thrower met a Soviet flame thrower and the two squads fused each other in 2,000-degree heat. Only a few hundred meters away, the cool technical work of Andrei's sound crew, their earphones replacing bayonets and ammeters taking the place of ancient catapults, continued without pause. At dawn, the Germans brought up smoke machines and tried to lay a cover over the field to protect a new wave of armor. But a light breeze came with the rising sun and blew the smoke away. Andrei had been at his post all night, but he felt as fresh as at the beginning. The smoke made him chuckle. He could hear right through it!

There was hard fighting on the third day, but Andrei gave his men cat naps of two or three hours. He himself lay down but he got little sleep, too excited by the magnificent performance of his battery and battalion and by the hardening conviction that a German catastrophe was taking place before his eyes.

On the fifth day the Germans began to pull back. In this sector, at least, they had never managed to get further than the "box" between the first and second lines. Now the Russians went over to the attack. The 73rd moved forward in giant leaps, ten kilometers, twenty kilometers, hard pressed to keep in contact with the advancing Soviet armor. Here again, all was according to plan. Never once did they lose contact with their armored neighbors and the motorized supporting infantry. Each time the Germans halted and tried to make a stand, the 73rd (and the other batteries) moved into place and demolished the Nazi rear guard.

*   *   *

It was, Andrei now knew, a classic battle. As the days went by he began to have some appreciation of the losses. He and his men moved between alleys of burned-out tanks, demolished German troop carriers, mounds of bodies. Bodies were everywhere, and they were not always German. The villages were heaps of burned thatch, crumbled plaster and smashed men and women. The 73rd went forward through what seemed like a fire path. For the first time Andrei saw German prisoners, by the thousands—bedraggled men, arms in slings, feet bandaged and bloody, without helmets, faces sun-blistered, silted with dust. They sat on the ground in irregular heaps, heads down, or straggled along the roads, escorted by Russian Tommy gunners, or marched across fields still sown with mines, to collect bodies and booty under guard of Russian security detachments.

Once, as his column moved slowly past a prisoner group, a blond young soldier, his head bandaged, his face white as flour, his lips ulcered, hoarsely shouted: "*Voda*, water, *danke, voda.*" Andrei turned his head, although he had a fresh-filled canteen on his hip. "Let him suffer, the Nazi bastard," he heard someone say. He looked up, and Petroshenko passed by, grin on his lips. A wave of shame passed over Andrei, for the same words had formed unspoken on his lips. "Let him suffer, Nazi bastard." The words would echo through his brain for years to come and each time a blush of shame would come over his face.

The fighting went on for another ten days. The Russians pushed ahead, straightened out the bulges in their lines, pushed the Nazis back from Orel, then settled down to consolidate. There had been fifteen hundred or more Nazi tanks in action, and possibly twice that many Russian armored vehicles. It was a battle that military strategists and historians would still be studying twenty-five years later. It established principles of tank warfare that were accepted by all armies as classic. It doomed an already doomed Hitler to defeat.

Andrei wrote to Vanya: "I don't know whether you participated in the great battle or not. Probably you did. Our unit gave what I think was a classic performance. You know I've always said that artillery is the queen of battle (in this respect I agree with Comrade Stalin). If there was any doubt in my mind, this engagement wiped it out. Even the chessboard analgoy is correct. Artillery is the *queen*.

"How magnificent are our Russian fighting men when they are commanded by brilliant leaders. Rokossovsky, Zhukov—great names."

As usual, he signed himself "Your Dek-ist."

He wrote to Rosa. "Dearest: We will be united very soon. I have a plan. Don't be surprised. The long wait will soon be ended." He added a P.S.: "We have just fought a classic battle. A great victory. I'll tell you about it when I see you."

*　　*　　*

The battalion was given a special citation for its work at Kursk-Orel. Lieutenant Colonel Stromlin was promoted to colonel and was decorated again with the Order of the Red Star. Andrei was promoted to captain and won another medal. Major Smirnov became Lieutenant Colonel Smirnov, and Andrei managed to get Dedya Petya promoted to sergeant, although Dedya Petya strongly protested, "I'd rather just be one of the lads in the ranks, it's more comfortable." When Andrei insisted Dedya Petya took his promotion grudgingly; he felt it a bad omen.

Chapter 33

NOT until after eight in the evening did Rosa get away from the hospital. Once again she was a nurse, this time in the Central City Hospital in Rostov. It was a barren building with little electricity, and the temperature of the wards was almost as low as in the dark and empty streets outside swept by icy winds from the steppe. She had hoped to leave the hospital early enough to stand in the queue for potatoes, but it was too late now. Perhaps her mother had managed to get some during the day.

Rosa hurried down the unlighted street, the wind whipping at her back and sending the gritty snow that had fallen earlier swirling along in angry gusts. Neither streetcars nor buses were running, but fortunately the room she and her mother shared was less than a mile from the hospital.

She was tired, cold, hungry, depressed. It was the third war winter and nothing was easy in Rostov. The work in the hospital crushed her spirit. There was so little she could do. Most of the patients were brought there simply to die. Of dysentery, of tuberculosis, of starvation, and—they tried desperately to keep this secret—of cholera. Rosa worried about her mother, she worried about herself, and most of all, she worried about Andrei. Thank God he was alive. Or at least he had survived up to now. But she had heard nothing from him for a month and it took but an instant to snuff out the life of a man. Working with the ill and wounded she had become acutely conscious of the slender thread by which life hangs suspended.

As she hurried home she knew it would not be much warmer than the street. At best, there would be little to eat. If only there might be some hot tea! The thought possessed her as she stumbled up the dark and icy steps to their second-floor room. Her fingers were so cold she dropped the key three times before she fumbled it into the lock. Inside she found her mother sitting at the table. Facing her in a straight chair sat a sad-faced Red Army sergeant, very up-

right and uncomfortable, his sheepskin hat in his lap, his gray Army
greatcoat tightly buttoned. My God, Rosa thought, Andrei! The
soldier had come to tell her that Andrei was dead. Her heart choked in
her throat. She could not see clearly. Her mother spoke, "He's here
from Andrei."

"Oh, no!" Rosa cried. "Oh, no!"

The soldier was standing now, very ill at ease, and he bowed
formally.

"He's been waiting two hours," she heard her mother saying. "And
he has a message for you."

"For God's sake," Rosa cried, "what happened to him? How did he
die? Tell me, Tell me—"

"Oh, miss, you don't understand," the man said. His voice was low
and melodious. "Nothing has happened to Captain Sokolov. He is
quite all right."

Rosa dropped into a chair. She could not understand. "Then
what?"

"He has a message for you, Rosa," her mother said. "You've got
it all mixed up. He says Andrei is very well."

Rosa put her head down on the table and burst into tears. She
could not help herself. It was too much. The cold, the hospital, the
strain, and then the shock, the fear that Andrei had been killed.
Finally, she raised her head. "I'm sorry. I was sure Andrei was dead."

"Oh, no, miss," the sergeant said. "You see, you can read this for
yourself. It is a message from the captain."

He fumbled in his inner breast pocket and drew out a rather
crumpled envelope that had obviously been in his pocket for some
time.

"Here you are, miss," he said.

Rosa tore open the letter. "Oh, heavens!" she cried. "Heavens! How
wonderful! Do you know what's in this?"

The tall man nodded his head, smiling slightly. "Yes, miss."

Suddenly Rosa leaped up and danced around the table. She gave
her mother a hug. Then she threw her arms around the soldier.

"I'm so happy," she cried. "So happy. And I know who you are—
you're Dedya Petya, aren't you?"

The soldier turned his eyes down bashfully. "Yes, miss, that's what
many of them do call me, all right."

*   *   *

It had taken Andrei a bit longer than he had anticipated to arrange
his reunion with Rosa. The summer had passed, and the autumn. Now
it was December. The battalion had gone into reserve status. It was
resting in pleasant quarters southeast of Mogilev, a circumstance Andrei
regarded with some irony, since Mogilev had been the Czar's headquarters during World War I. After quiet maneuvering, Andrei had

arranged leave for Dedya Petya to visit his family in Simbirsk for a week. He got permission for Dedya Petya to go on to Rostov, bringing with him not only the letter for Rosa but Army travel orders to enable Rosa to accompany Dedya Petya back to the base near Mogilev.

"Never you mind how I managed this," Andrei later told Rosa with a superior smile when she finally arrived at his battalion head-quarters. "There are ways of doing everything." And indeed there were. Rosa had simply donned her Army uniform, and with the kind and somehow imposing Dedya Petya at her side, made her way from station point to station point to Lugovka, where the 73rd Battalion had taken up snug winter quarters. And there Rosa and Andrei were reunited at last.

Rosa woke first the next morning. They were sleeping on a pine-filled mattress in a wooden bunk built into the side of Andrei's new-cut log hut. It was still dark, but Rosa could see yellow flames dancing in the iron stove that kept the moss-chinked room cozier than any room she had lived in since the start of the war. An orderly must have looked to the fire an hour earlier. Andrei lay beside her sleeping, his warm body touching her own. He was lean and strong and her body still trembled from the joy of their love-making. How long it had been! The thought of it brought on the excitement again.

Actually there had been some shyness, some awkwardnesses about their meeting. It *had* been a long time. She found Andrei older, more mature, more certain of himself. There was about him now a new assurance. At first she had been puzzled. Now she knew. It was the aura of command. He was accustomed to commanding men, to giving orders, to being obeyed. He knew his role in life and was good at it. There was no mistaking the firm jaw, the bright, direct eye. He held his head higher, his shoulders thrown back. His movements were swifter, more functional. Even his lips were thinner, more firm. As Rosa lay beside Andrei, filled with thoughts of him, he quietly awoke, pulled her close to him and they made love again—silent, hard, passionate, swift. When it was over, Andrei lay back, reached his hand to the chair beside him, pulled a cigarette from his pack, lit it, and hunching his back up against the pillow, looked down into Rosa's eyes.

"You didn't think this was possible, did you?" he asked.

She crinkled her eyes. "No, honestly, Andrei, I didn't. I didn't think we would meet until the war was over. And it seemed so long."

"Everything is possible, Rosa," he said very seriously. "You only must know what you want and then set your mind to work to figure out how it can be done."

"Now you are exaggerating, Andrei," she protested. "Not everything is possible."

"Everything," he said. "You can even turn lead into gold if you apply enough power. Of course, the gold made from lead costs a thousand times the price of the gold taken from the earth."

Rosa smiled cozily. "I won't dispute you, Andrei. You brought me here. That is proof enough for me."

"And there'll be more," Andrei said firmly. "We are going to win this war, as you know. It has been hard. It still is hard. Berlin is distant and the way will not be easy. But you must admit it has worked out much as I thought in those first few days."

Rosa agreed. Andrei's vision of the war had been unusually accurate, while she had lost confidence more than once, particularly in that terrible late autumn of 1941, and then again when the Nazis broke into the Caucasus in 1942.

"And things will change with the end of the war," Andrei continued. "It has nothing to do with me, nothing to do with the Dekabristi. It will change whether we are alive or not. It is in the air. When the men come back from Berlin they will make the change."

He felt Rosa stiffen in his arms when he began to talk about the Dekabristi.

"Don't worry, darling," he said, rubbing his nose around the crevices of her ear. "I'll say nothing that will upset you. You know Vanya was here ten days ago. We talked again. He says that our thinking is not unique, not unusual. There are many men of our mind all through the Army. And you can be sure that the men at the top are affected too. I don't mean the old generals, the Budennys, the Timoshenkos and the Voroshilovs. I mean the new ones. The Rokossovskys, the Zhukovs and the others."

Rosa sighed. "I'm sure you must be right, Andrei. But it does worry me to hear such talk. It is dangerous, you know that."

For answer, Andrei gave Rosa a quick squeeze, then pulled himself up. "What the devil is the matter with that man of mine! Breakfast should be here. I told him we'd sleep a little late. But not this late."

At that very instant there was a light knock at the door and a soldier entered with a large tray, which he put down on the table. He took a kettle off the tray and put it on the hot stove, then quickly turned and left without a word.

Andrei got up, pulled on his boots, threw his greatcoat over his shoulders and stepped outside. He was back in a minute.

"Ummm," he said. "Cold, and it looks like more snow. Maybe we'll just stay here today."

They sat by the stove, drinking hot tea with sugar, and munching good moist black bread and cheese.

*   *   *

The snow did come. It began in the morning and it seemed that it would never stop. Rosa left the hut only twice, once for lunch and once for dinner. Andrei reported for a conference at 9 A.M. and again at 5 P.M., but he had no duties. The battalion was resting, waiting for new orders, new equipment and replacements. The interlude was more like peace than war, though how long it might last no one knew. Rosa was not the only wife who had arrived at the encampment for a brief visit with her husband.

Andrei opened up his trunk and took out some manuscripts. "I want you to hear what I have been writing," he said.

He read her a sketch of life in the Caucasian supply company, describing how the driver whose cart had gone over the cliff had been beaten to death.

This he entitled "The Highest Measure of Punishment Is Forbidden."

He had written another piece about Dedya Petya, whose life he had come to know intimately. He knew now, for example, why the soldier had not lived at home for the last ten years. Petya had discovered that his wife had been unfaithful to him during one of his long absences while shipping on the Siberian river Irtysh. He had arrived back at the village unexpectedly and found his wife in bed with another peasant. He had turned his back, walked away and swore he would never return. The only reason he had recently gone back to Simbirsk was that his wife had written him she was very ill and that Ludmilla, his favorite daughter, the oldest girl in the family, had married and he had a granddaughter. He was now in fact what he had so long been called—Dedya Petya, Grandfather Peter. And so, breaking his resolution, he had gone to Simbirsk to see his dying wife for the last time and his new grandchild for the first time.

The story about Dedya Petya, telling of his return to the village and discovery of his wife's unfaithfulness, Andrei called "The Story of a Man." He had done another peasant story, this one about the peasant woman who had been killed by the Red Guards on the train on the way to Armavir in the days of his childhood.

"You understand, don't you, Rosa?" Andrei said. "I'm a writer. I have become a writer in these years of war. And when it ends I will devote the rest of my life to writing."

"I do understand, Andrei," Rosa said. As he read his stories to her, she had felt the power behind his words, his sparse style, the exactness of his phrases. Andrei had not only matured as a man, he had matured as a writer. It frightened her a bit. Andrei was no longer the naïve, bubbling schoolboy she had married. He was now a man with an iron will. She could feel the throbbing strength of his mind.

Most of all, Andrei said, he wanted to write the story of his father's life, and through the story of that life, the history of Russia and the Revolution.

"I want to tell the story of the Revolution as it actually happened," he said with gleaming eyes. "No legends, no lies. The real taste of the people, the color of their blood, the horror, the terror, the sacrifices, the heroism. The good and the evil. The whole story."

The storm had turned into a *burya*, a blizzard, and hardly any light penetrated through the small window of the cabin. They had been sitting all afternoon by the light of a kerosene lamp, Andrei reading and talking and Rosa listening, trying to draw together the picture of this new man who was her husband.

"This will be my lifework," Andrei said. "I want to feel Russia and live Russia and put it all down on paper so that we will know what Russia really is, so that we will know what we have been experiencing these last fifty years."

"That, Andrei, will take you a very long time," Rosa said gently. "And there are going to be problems. Not everyone wants to hear what has truly happened during the last half-century."

"Exactly, Rosa, darling. They don't. But they will hear it whether they want to or not. And after the victory march in Red Square it is going to be very hard to go on stopping up our ears, gagging our mouths and blindfolding our eyes. All this is going to come to an end."

That evening Andrei introduced Rosa to Lieutenant Colonel Smirnov, who kissed her hand like an old Spanish cavalier and said, "Madame, this meeting has long been delayed. For years I have been hearing of the paragon of virtues, the Helen of our day, the divine Minerva. It is my honor to salute you."

Rosa burst out laughing. "That is quite a mouthful."

Smirnov smiled. "Well, it happens to be true. Forgive me if I cast my thought in the language of the classics. I have no natural gift for eloquence."

Rosa liked Smirnov immediately. "But you have the gift of the tongues," she said. "Thank you."

From some secret reservoir Andrei produced a bottle of champagne. "I was going to save it for tomorrow," he said. "But tomorrow is everyone's New Year's Eve. Let's make this our own."

They drank a toast to Rosa. Then Smirnov raised his glass to Andrei. "I raise my glass," he said, "to a fine officer, a sound mathematician, a brilliant social critic and a remarkably fortunate husband."

Rosa's eyes sparkled as she drank off her glass of champagne. Andrei looked sheepish. "That's going a little far," he said.

"Not far enough, dearest," Rosa rejoined. Then, to Smirnov: "Do you really think he is a brilliant social critic?"

"No doubt of it," said Smirnov. "A fine mind, a keen eye and a daring grasp of what is needed to correct our situation. He has no peer."

Rosa smiled warmly. "Andrei," she said. "I think he has gotten to know you better than I have."

"The truth is," Andrei said, "we share many of the same ideas. Perhaps the fact that I think the same as the Lieutenant Colonel causes him to overvalue the clarity and precision of my social analysis."

"Rubbish," said Smirnov. "I raise my glass to the great tradition of the Dekabristi, to Pushkin, to Herzen and his Bell, to the Narodnaya Volya, to the true exegesis of Marxism, to Lenin."

"To Lenin!" Andrei repeated, drinking his champagne.

"To Lenin!" Rosa said. Was it with just a touch of uncertainty? Reflecting later, Smirnov thought he had noticed a fractional hesitation. Andrei, floating on clouds of champagne, radiant in the presence of his wise and beautiful wife, noticed nothing.

With the champagne gone, Andrei and Rosa retreated to the hut. It was a five minutes' walk through the still falling snow, now more than knee-deep and beginning to pile up in drifts. They raced down the company street, hardly touching the ground, Andrei's arm around Rosa, holding her close, lifting her over the drifts. The snow splashed onto their cheeks, into their eyes, they breathed it into their nostrils and they could feel it silting into their boots. It was heaven.

When Andrei pulled open the door of his hut a gust of heat met them. The iron stove was cherry-red. A teakettle sang gently on one corner. He picked Rosa up and whirled her over the doorstep. In a minute they were in the bunk, in each other's arms. Never had Andrei felt so warm, so happy, so thrilled. He closed himself around Rosa as she murmured, "Andrei, Andrei, Andrei, Andrei."

*   *   *

New Year's Eve in the officers' mess there was vodka, port wine, a great sturgeon in aspic, two chocolate cakes, pickled mushrooms, a roast goose, a bowl of mandarins, a huge tin of caviar, cheese, three loaves of white bread, fresh cucumbers . . . It was a stunning feast. All of the officers of the battalion were there and two other wives besides Rosa and the "front wives" of the officers. Colonel Stromlin was with the very blond adjutant. A small orchestra of enlisted men played a *bayan*, a guitar and a violin. "I tried to get a piano, but the division staff laid hands on the only one in the vicinity," Smirnov apologized.

Everyone roared out the songs together. Army songs, Russian songs, Gypsy songs. "Stenka Razin" . . . "Stary Baikal" . . . "Polyushko Pole" . . . Toasts—to Comrade Stalin . . . to the Soviet Union . . . to the Armed Forces . . . to Victory . . . to our glorious allies . . . to the Central Front . . . to General Rokossovsky . . . Toast after toast, all in vodka, all *do adna*, to the bottom. The officers' mess hung with pine boughs, the heavy scent of the pine filling the air. Dancing . . . Rosa whirling in Andrei's arms, spinning like a *snegurichka*, a snow maiden in the ballet. In Andrei's arms, in Smirnov's arms, in the colonel's arms, in the arms of Captain Petroshenko, who tried to pull her close to him. Afterwards Andrei cursed under his breath, "*Swolich*! What a *swolich*! What a bastard! Never dance with him again." More toasts. More songs.

At midnight everyone went outside. There was a tattoo of shots.

Very shells were fired high into the air, the lights candling the whole sky. Artillery shells filled with bright-colored powder exploded, and the sky was crisscrossed with golden tracer bullets. Every one sang the national anthem, and from the distance came the sound of other voices singing. The night was cold and the stars ice-hard in the infinite sky.

Then it was over, and again Andrei and Rosa raced through the snow of the company street, sped to the hut, burst into its snug warmth and lay in each other's arms.

Presently Rosa spoke. "Andrei, do you remember our first New Year's?"

Andrei had one arm around her, his hand covering her breast. "I remember it," he said. "I was very ashamed of the orange I brought you and then you acted as though it was the most wonderful gift in the world and I was in seventh heaven."

"And I was so ashamed when you walked into the room and found me sitting at the mirror," Rosa laughed. "I wanted you to walk in and I wanted to see you in the glass. But I knew that you were too serious for that kind of romantic girls' play."

Andrei's fingers began to play with her nipple.

"You know, Rosa," he said, suddenly, "when your cousin Galya told my fortune with the tea leaves—I always thought she saw something in the leaves that was not pleasant and kept it to herself. What do you think?"

Rosa was sinking into a state of sensual contentment. "Oh, darling, I don't know," she said. "Wasn't that something about your going into the Army—and you did go into the Army."

She kissed the lobe of his ear and turned herself fully toward him.

Andrei was still musing. "Perhaps," he said. "Perhaps. But it didn't sound that way to me. It sounded like something different—as though I was going to leave the country or be sent into exile or something like that."

"Andrei," Rosa whispered hoarsely. "You are a romantic. An incurable romantic."

Their bodies were fusing together, and it was not until hours later, very early in the morning when Rosa awoke, the fire not yet going in the stove, the room cold as frost and Andrei turned away from her that the fortune-telling came back into her mind. Andrei was right. She knew he was. She had felt the same when Galya had spoken, had felt it so strongly she had never asked Galya what it was she saw in the leaves.

What could it have been? Pray God it didn't mean Andrei would be taken prisoner. That was the worst fate of all. The Germans simply let the Russians starve to death, or freeze, or they shot them. It was another way of death. Please God it wasn't that. But the thought left an ugly impression on her mind as she went back to sleep, and in the morning when she awoke she looked long and steadily at Andrei. No, she told herself. It could not be. He had been brought safe thus far through the war. No one, not the Germans, not anyone else, would take him away from her now.

*　　*　　*

Crisp, snowy, clear days followed. It was an island of heaven in a sea of hell. One afternoon Andrei and Rosa went for a long walk, out of the village and along a little road into the pine forest. It had snowed during the night, but now the sun was shining and the snow on the pine branches sparkled like crystal stars. Finally they rested on a stump and looked down the long corridors of the forest, the green pines, branches heavy with snow, and the sun slanting through the tall trees in endless corridors of diamond-faceted white.

"What I would like, Rosa," Andrei began, "after the war is to return to Mineralnye Vody. Not for long, but for two years, or at a minimum one year."

"Do you really want that, Andrei?" Rosa said. The idea did not appeal to her. She had spent long enough in Mineralnye Vody to last a lifetime.

"Well," Andrei said, "I can guess that you don't like the idea very much. But it doesn't have to be Mineralnye Vody. I simply want to go to some quiet provincial town where I can teach school, where the classes are not too demanding, so I can spend my time writing. Get myself started."

"But, Andrei," Rosa protested. "You would be much better off in Moscow. Or even in Leningrad than in Mineralnye Vody. Nobody cares about literature in the provinces."

"That's just it. They don't. I will have plenty of time to do what I please and none of the distractions of the capital."

"But you must have friends to get recognition. I don't think you should bury yourself in the provinces. It would be a waste of time."

Andrei was firm, even grim. He had made up his mind. He would not go to Moscow until he had something worthwhile to show. He had spent four years in the Army. He had to steal time for writing. He must write steadily. Write without interruption. Only then would he come to Moscow.

"I know I must be recognized," he said. "But already a few people know of me. I've sent some manuscripts around; I've had a few letters. Granted, I don't think they yet understand what I am trying to do, but they'll learn."

Rosa dropped her protest. Andrei was hard, unyielding. Perhaps, she thought, he might change by the end of the war.

"And," resumed Andrei, "we can start our family. We must have two children, a boy and a girl. Possibly three, two boys and a girl."

He said this with such certainty that Rosa laughed and put her arms around him.

"Oh, Andrei, Andrei," she cried. "Do you really think you can command everything? Even the sex and number of your children? Really?"

Andrei smiled. "Why not?" he said. "If we put our minds to it we can do anything."

* * *

They rose and walked slowly back to the village and the company street. Rosa's mind was busy turning over Andrei's remarks. She did not want to go back to a provincial town. Certainly not Mineralnye Vody. It would be much better to live in the city. Moscow was the only place to live. And as for children? Did she want to start a family? It was all right for Andrei to speak so positively. Two or three children? Not exactly a blessing. In fact, she didn't want any children. There were, she could feel, problems ahead for Andrei and herself.

Then all thoughts were whipped out of her mind when Andrei bent down, scooped up a handful of snow and tossed it at her head. She made a snowball and threw it at him. They stopped and tusseled, falling down in the snow, covering themselves from head to toe with its white powder, then raced to Andrei's hut, red-cheeked and laughing, and threw themselves on his bunk.

This, Rosa said to herself, is happiness. As for the future, let time care for it. So it went for a week. Then Andrei returned from the morning conference with a serious face.

"What is it, dearest?" Rosa asked. "Bad news?"

Andrei took her into his arms and put her head against his. "Our honeymoon is over," he said at last. "You'll have to leave tomorrow. Our replacements are coming in and we are going to be inspected. So—all visitors must go."

Rosa was to leave soon after daylight the next day. This time Dedya Petya was to accompany her only to the divisional railhead. She and Andrei rose early. Andrei unlocked his iron-cornered trunk and took out a small pile of manuscripts.

"You must keep these for me," he said. "I've made copies so that I can continue to work on them, but I want you to have them in case anything happens to mine."

He asked her to send the story of Dedya Petya to the magazine *Znamya*. "Address it to Feodor Rezinsky," he said. "He is one of the editors and he wrote me a nice letter when I sent him a short story a year ago. He couldn't publish it, but he said it had real merit."

They sat silently at the table for a minute or two before Rosa had to leave. She was filled with premonitions of danger, of death, of fear that she might never see Andrei again.

It was as if he read her mind. "Never fear, Rosa darling," he said. "I will survive the war. My mother was right about that. I know that I shall. And I know that you too will survive. I don't know how long it will take to finish the Germans, but maybe this year will do it, particularly if the Americans and British finally get to the Continent. But it won't be much longer."

Andrei rose and drew Rosa to him again.

"Take care, darling," she said. "Be careful—be careful of everything."

He winced a bit. He knew that she was not only speaking of the war but of his political views, and he made no response.

They walked slowly down the company street. Dedya Petya was waiting with the jeep. He stood almost a head taller than Andrei—very tall and straight and very handsome in his long gray Army coat.

Andrei flung his arms around Rosa. "*Tishe, tishe, dorogoya,*" he said. "Quiet, quiet, dear one. It won't be much longer. The war will end. We'll march in Red Square and I'll come home to sit beside you, writing, night after night, and keeping you awake with the scratching of my pen."

Rosa could say nothing. Tears slowly rolled down her cheeks. She took off her heavy mittens and ran her hands softly over Andrei's cool cheeks. Then she closed her eyes, silently kissed him and got into the jeep.

Andrei stood in the street, watching as the jeep whirled away, sending up little puffs of snow in its wake. He drew off his gloves and put his hands to his cheeks. They seemed still warm with the touch of Rosa's hands. He sighed, put on his gloves, turned abruptly and strode briskly to the headquarters hut. This would be a busy day receiving the new replacements, assigning them to the vacancies and fitting them into the organization. There was much to be done.

Chapter 34

ANDREI could not describe even to himself the feeling that possessed him as—riding in a jeep at the head of his company, just behind the battalion headquarters convoy—the grayish concrete highway came to an end and beside the road he saw the sign: *Achtung! Deutsche Grenze 100 Meter*. The sign was painted in black and white. A wooden sign beside the highway warned the traveler that he was approaching the border of East Prussia. The date was January 21, 1945. Andrei's jeep moved quietly across the frontier, past the still-standing zebra-striped guard's post, past the *Schlagbaum*, the frontier barrier, intact but now tied back from the road with a piece of wire, past the circular concrete pillboxes with their narrow machine-gun slits, past the smashed customs house, onto German soil.

The highway changed here from concrete to black asphalt. It was, Andrei supposed, one of Hitler's famous autobahns. He looked across the landscape—flat, featureless, snow-covered, forests just ahead, here and there peasant huts, some villages that had been badly hit by shelling. There were no people, no people at all, only a gray countryside on this January day, sunless, with heavy clouds that must hold snow. Andrei hoped the snow did not fall until they arrived at their new position. They moved steadily forward. There was little sign of war. The Germans had fallen back too fast. They must have broken off physical contact with the Russians.

Andrei's mind took in these details, but it was filled with other thoughts. His column was headed straight for the Masurian Lakes. The Germans had fallen back to the lakes. He was riding across the very ground that his father had fought over with Samsonov in August of 1914. In his mind Andrei could even see the column in which his father rode. There was no paved road in that time. The Russian forces, moving forward in vast clouds of dust, regimental banners flying; the men all marching, the artillery horse-drawn, with the great teams of eight heavy Belgian horses pulling the big guns, teams of six and four horses for the lesser weapons. The biggest guns had gone forward by rail, mounted on railroad flatcars.

What had they done, he wondered, when they came to the frontier and the wide Russian gauge ended and the narrower European rail gauge began? Did they have to wait for new lines to be laid? That was what was happening here at this very moment. The rail crews had rushed forward, hastily tearing up the German rails and widening them to take the Russian engines and freight cars. Was it possible, he wondered, that his father might have ridden down this very road on some long-ago August day? The Russians had simply poured over the border in 1914. The Germans offered no opposition, falling back and back and Samsonov had plowed ahead, sending the Czar enthusiastic reports of his progress. The crowds stood outside the newspaper offices in St. Petersburg every night and cheered as each new communiqué was chalked up on the great blackboards and artists quickly fixed the new Russian positions on the illuminated maps.

His father would have been mounted on a fine black charger, riding at the head of his battery. More picturesque than Andrei in his jeep. Yet, he smiled to himself, he preferred the jeep. He no longer had any fear of horses after his hostler's experience, but he had no love for them either.

* * *

The battery moved two days into East Prussia. The sun came out and the snow melted a bit, but they were moving on Germany's good roads now and the thaw made little difference. The battle forces, ahead of the artillery, reported no opposition, no sign of enemy units. Andrei could not help remembering the reports of Samsonov's scouts. "Can find no enemy" . . . "No sign of German defenses" . . . "The villages are empty."

These villages were empty, too. So precise, so orderly, compared to the poor Belorussian and Polish villages. The cottages were all of excellent yellow brick or, sometimes, plaster, in careful rows, with shops in the center of each village. The shops stood empty and barren now, a litter of goods scattered in front of them, looted by the advancing Red Army troops. But no one had time nor inclination to bother with the peasant houses. They stood in their rows, neat as toys, no smoke from their chimneys, no women in the kitchens, nor men, nor children.

On the third day the battalion received sudden orders to deploy. There was firing up ahead. The Germans had finally turned at bay. The Russian assault troops were heavily engaged. German tanks appeared in their midst. Andrei quickly positioned his audio unit in a forest not far from the highway, beyond a rather extensive farm and outbuildings in good cover. The cables were run out to the batteries, and with the professional skill that comes from long practice, within

an hour Andrei's men were feeding back the correlations and the batteries were offering supporting fire for the hard-pressed Russian
columns.

It was midafternoon when the battalion went into action and, with
the short January day, dusk was upon them within an hour. The
batteries were occasionally engaged during the night, but the firing
petered out and calls for assistance from the division ceased. At dawn,
Andrei heard heavy firing rather deep in his rear and considerably
south of his position. He was instantly concerned. Possibly the Germans
had successfully enfiladed the position during the night. It seemed
unlikely—they had been steadily retreating. Yet there clung in his
mind the example of what had happened to Samsonov in 1914, when
Rennenkampf failed to move forward swiftly enough on his flank,
opening up a gaping hole which the Germans took advantage of and
proceeded to encircle and then to crush Samsonov. Perhaps something
similar was happening now.

He was on to battalion headquarters in an instant. They had no
information but were urgently querying Division. It was noon before
Andrei got a response from Battalion. It was true. The Germans were
attacking hard at the junction point of the division to the south. The
battalion was ordered to pull back immediately. Its fire power was
needed on the site of the breakthrough, and there was a possibility
of being cut off, even though it seemed unlikely that the Germans had
the power to sustain an enduring counterthrust.

*   *   *

To Andrei it was almost as though he was living over again his father's
life. He well knew the Germans had no reserves sufficient to seriously
impede the Russian advance. But locally and tactically it was a different question. He ordered his men to assemble quickly, calling in
the triangulating points and beginning immediately to pack up the
monitoring equipment. Without a moment's hesitation he determined
that the cable to Battalion must be jettisoned. As fast as the trucks
could be loaded they must be on their way to join the other companies.
His men moved rapidly. There was no waste motion in packing the
equipment. Andrei disliked abandoning the cable, but he had a plenti-
ful reserve supply. Time was more important than material.

Well within the hour they were ready to head back. The battalion
had already pulled out, as Andrei knew from his radio communications.
No problem. He would catch up with the heavy guns quite swiftly.

He was about to order his column into movement, back to the
asphalt highway when one of his outpost men came running up.
"Comrade Captain," he said, swiftly saluting. "There are Nazi tanks
approaching on the highway."

Andrei's company was lightly armed with machine guns and two
light anti-tank weapons, but it was not equipped to do battle with

Nazi panzers. There was only one thing Andrei could do. Halt his movement in the hope that the tank column would pass by without spotting their position in the forest a kilometer off the highway. He ordered all motors silenced and passed word to his men. Utter quiet. If the tanks passed by—well and good. If the company was spotted they would make a fight for it. But in that case he knew the odds gave them little chance.

Andrei could not see the highway, but he heard the approach of the panzers as they clanked down the road. They were, he could tell by the sound, medium or light tanks. This made them more dangerous. They could maneuver off the road and their guns were heavy enough to wipe out his small band. He listened as the machines came nearer and nearer. There was no break in the rhythm of their engines. He could hear the clank of the heavy treads as the tanks moved down the road. Still no pause. Still no firing. Still the same rhythmic movement. Andrei tried to guess how many tanks were in the column. Not too many. Four, possibly, five. Were they carrying infantry? He heard no trucks, but the sound of truck engines could be blotted out by the heavier rumble of the armored vehicles. The sound went on. Suddenly Andrei realized that it was steadily diminishing. The column had passed! They had not been spotted.

They had avoided one peril. What would be the next? So much depended on the strength of the Nazi attack. Andrei could not believe that it would be more than a glancing blow, the thrashing of a dying beast—dangerous but limited. He called his men around him and told them they would remain in position until nightfall. Outposts would observe the highway. At dusk they would make their decision—whether to wait longer or make a move toward rejoining the battalion.

Since the tank group had passed without spotting the company, Andrei felt it unlikely that follow-up units would pause to investigate. The task of the Germans, undoubtedly, was to strike back, impede the Russians, disorganize the advance, then fall back once more on the Masurian Lake defenses.

After posting his lookouts, Andrei drew out his map case. Were there any alternate roads to the east, that is, back toward Russia? There were no turnoff points whatever on the main highway going to the east for nearly fifteen kilometers. At that point there was a village and a crossroads, a secondary road moving north and south. It was probable, Andrei thought, that this north and south road would be temporarily in the hands of the Germans, who would use it as an axis for lateral communications. If he attempted to go east on the main highway he would inevitably fall into German hands.

But he had few choices. To try to make his way east through the forest off the road seemed equally impossible. He would have to abandon all gear and probably would wind up lost in a bog. There was a secondary road, probably not a very good one, that ran east and west about five kilometers north of his position. But to reach it they would have to strike off through the forest. The more Andrei looked at the map the more hopeless it seemed. Then a dim line on the map caught his eye. About six kilometers to the west a small village was indicated. An unimproved road led from this village to the secondary road to the north.

Andrei had an idea. Why not wait until dusk, then pull out and head west, deeper into Germany, until he came to the small village, swing up and around on the secondary road and see if he could reach the Russian lines? Probably a small Nazi detachment was stationed in the village but it would not expect a Russian column so deep in the rear. At dusk no one could tell who or what was moving on the road. It should not be too difficult to overwhelm the Germans.

There was little traffic on the highway. An occasional German command car or jeep passed but there were no more tanks, troops, or air activity. At dusk Andrei moved his column out to the road. He put his machine gunners and his light anti-tank guns at the head of the column, two jeeps with Tommy gunners serving as outriders. He placed himself with the guns. They ran without lights. Orders were to halt for nothing. If a control force was stationed in the village, it was to be dealt with by the machine-gun detachment with the assistance of the anti-tank guns. If any delay occurred the column was to move on through, leaving the gunners to cope with the Germans.

*   *   *

They moved rapidly down the empty highway. There were no lights in the countryside. The sky was leaden and reflected nothing. Andrei watched the odometer closely. It was precisely 6.2 kilometers from the spot where they had got onto the highway to the village. They were moving along the road at forty kilometers an hour. They should reach the village in approximately eight minutes. He reached for his big silver watch, then withdrew his hand. He could not see the watch even if he put it up to his face. The scouting jeeps were about two hundred meters ahead of the column. As they came up to the village, Andrei heard a shout, then a quick burst of machine-gun fire. He was almost certain it came from his men, and a moment later, as he closed the distance, he saw that he was correct. The jeeps had halted, and beside them with his hands high over his head was a German soldier. Andrei came up quickly.

"Is there a garrison in this village?" he asked, speaking German.

"*Nein, Herr Hauptmann,*" the frightened soldier said. "Only our outpost, my comrade Franz and myself."

Andrei then noticed the body of a German soldier face down on the highway.

"All right, men," Andrei said. "Tie his hands and take him along."

He did not stop to investigate the truth of the soldier's word, but pushed into the village to the small road. It was a country dirt road, filled with ruts and ice but easy to follow because farm carts had broken a well-marked trail. Andrei waited in his jeep until his column had made the turn, then hurried up to take the lead again.

So far so good. There was no further incident as the colunm followed the farm road north to the secondary road. Here Andrei again halted and reinforced his orders. They would move east as rapidly as possible until they reached the area in which they might expect to find either German positions or their own advanced outposts. Then they would pause and reconnoiter before deciding on further action.

Andrei's hope was that the German counterthrust might not have extended this far north and, therefore, he might be able to establish contact with the Russians without running the German lines. The column moved slowly, at about twenty-five kilometers an hour, down the secondary road, scouting jeeps in front—Andrei did not want to run into something unexpected. After half an hour he called a halt. There were vague sounds of firing in the distance.

He conferred with the scouts. They had seen nothing, heard nothing. The map indicated they must be close to the north-south crossroad. Andrei ordered his reconnaissance patrol to dismount and move forward on foot for a kilometer or two, proceeding very cautiously. He wanted a report on the crossroads before bringing up his company. The men went off, leaving the column huddled in the dark. Andrei calculated the men should be back within the hour at the most, possibly considerably sooner. Meantime, he checked his column. Gasoline running a bit low, but they had a reserve tank. He did not think it would be a problem.

Sooner than he anticipated the patrol was back. The crossroads was only a few hundred meters ahead. There seemed to be a small checkpoint there. They could not be certain, however, without moving up closer and exposing their presence.

Andrei pondered. It must be just a detail. He decided to try a variation of the tactics he had employed at the village. He formed a small fire party, placed himself at its head. He put Dedya Petya in charge of the vehicles. As soon as the column heard an outburst of fire it was to move forward. If the fire party was still engaged, the column was to move on as rapidly as possible. If the way was blocked, the column would support the fire party.

Andrei ordered his men to tie white handkerchiefs to their arms: "It will be hard enough to recognize each other even so."

*　　*　　*

They went forward on foot carefully, noiselessly, Andrei in the vanguard, with two scouts and the others following. As they drew up to the crossroads Andrei felt his pulse racing. The next five minutes would determine their fate. The checkpoint. It was, in fact, a concrete pillbox, located in the center of the crossroads. Detaching a grenade from his belt, Andrei hunched himself forward with the utmost care. He could see the dark machine-gun slit. Crawling on his belly to within six feet of the pillbox, he slipped the pin from the grenade, lobbed the grenade through the slit and rolled instantly and as fast as possible away from the concrete blockhouse. There was an almost immediate explosion, a flash of flame from the pillbox and the agonized cry of a human voice.

Andrei sprang to his feet, shouting to his men: "Fire. Shout. Raise your voices. Throw grenades."

Pandemonium broke loose. Andrei and his men had seen in the explosion that just beyond the road lay a succession of huts—a cantonment. They faced not just a squad of men mounting a firepoint but at least a company, possibly more. The only hope we have, Andrei said to himself as he ran forward at a crouch and hurled a grenade at the first of the buildings, is surprise. His men followed after him, machine guns spraying the huts, shouting at the top of their hoarse voices. It sounds, Andrei thought, like an attack of regimental strength.

Behind him in the distance Andrei heard his column. The roar of the starting jeeps, the cough of the trucks. It shattered the silent night. Now he was up to the cantonment. He could see men rushing about; one had thrown a grenade in their direction but it landed short. With two men at his side he dashed to the largest cottage. Here, hopefully, the commander of the unit must be sleeping. His men fired a burst from a machine gun and Andrei shouted at the top of his voice in German: "Surrender! *Hände hoch!* You are surrounded! Come out in ten seconds or you are dead men."

He raised his hand to his troopers to hold their fire. Behind him he could hear the solid roar of the approaching column. It sounded like an armored detachment or motorized infantry. As he waited breathless the shattered door of the hut swung open and a German major, his tunic unbuttoned and one hand holding his still-unbelted trousers stepped across the threshold, his other hand in the air.

"Don't shoot," the officer begged. "Don't shoot. We surrender."

"Tell your men," Andrei barked, "or I'll put a bullet through your head."

The major raised his voice shouting, "Men! German soldiers! Surrender. This is your Major Oberhauser speaking."

An orderly appeared beside the major.

"Tell him to pass the word to the others," Andrei said.

The shivering orderly ran down the company street, shouting "Arms down. Arms down. We have surrendered. The major's orders."

Andrei could hear doors slamming, the sound of guns clattering to the ground. At this moment his column with Dedya Petya in the lead jeep arrived at the crossroads.

"Dedya Petya," Andrei shouted. "All hands out. We are taking the surrender of a German battalion."

The men poured from jeeps and trucks, Tommy guns in hand.

Andrei, his gun still pointed at the head of the unfortunate major, said, "Round up your men. Here. In five minutes. No guns." He sent a squad of his Tommy gunners to follow the orderly.

This, he thought, is going to be a close thing. Thank God, the night and the darkness keep them from seeing how greatly they outnumber us.

The surrendering men quickly stumbled up to the road in front of the major's cottage.

"What is your roster?" he asked the major, who had finally managed to get his belt fastened and stood trembling with his hands in the air.

"One hundred and sixty, Colonel," the major said. Andrei smiled to himself. Not much of a major if he could not even tell a Russian captain from a colonel. Not until all of the Germans had been rounded up and counted—there were 148 men; Andrei assumed the others had escaped in the night or had been killed in the attack—and formed into a column surrounded by a hollow square of Russian Tommy gunners did Andrei ask the major the key question.

"How long have you occupied this position?" he began.

Since early morning, the major said.

"And how far are you from the Russian lines?" Andrei asked. He could see the major's eyes start at this. He had obviously assumed that the Soviet column had come from the east, not the west.

"I don't know . . ."

Andrei raised his pistol and took the safety off.

"Answer my question," he said quietly, "or you are dead."

The major hung his head. "Please, Comrade Colonel," he said, "I think the Russians hold the next road. It is about six kilometers from here. I cannot be sure because they may have withdrawn. Or advanced. But at dusk our scouts reported them there."

"Are there any German formations between this point and the Russian lines?"

"No," said the major.

Andrei hoped he was telling the truth. "Very well," he said. "We will march east. You and your detachment will march ahead. If any German fire is encountered, you and your men will feel it first."

It was a tricky situation. A night march. Twice as many prisoners as he had men. The German might be lying. The distance was not too great, but he did not want to approach the Russian lines until daylight. Too easy for mistakes in identity. He had seen that before.

Now he formed up his column. He again put his scouts ahead, and rode just behind them. Then he placed the column of German prisoners with the surrounding Tommy gunners. Their orders were, in case of attack, to open up on the prisoners. He repeated this order in German and asked the major to so inform his men.

The slow progress began, limited to the the pace of the German foot-sloggers. Andrei ordered a halt each hour. At 3 A.M. they had covered almost six kilometers and he ordered a halt until dawn. When the first rays of light began to streak the sky, he sent scouts ahead with orders to report any sign of the Russian lines. He then got the long column of prisoners and his own men under way once more. They had been moving only half an hour when he heard a single burst of machine-gun fire ahead and immediately halted the column. They waited a few minutes when a jeep appeared flying a red flag, a Soviet flag. It was from the Soviet command. The jeep had intercepted Andrei's scouts and had proceeded on westward to verify their story.

*   *   *

Two days later, weary but proud, Andrei led his company back to battalion headquarters. He had lost not a man from his command and not a single piece of equipment except for the cable he had deliberately abandoned. And he and his men had captured 149 German prisoners—the batallion of 148 and the one soldier taken at the village. History had not repeated itself. His father had barely escaped with his life from East Prussia, his battery lost, his guns lost, his men lost, the High Command of the Army lost, Samsonov a suicide in a birch forest.

Andrei was elated. He knew that his father, were he alive, would be proud of him. He could not wait to write to Rosa and to Vanya. Nothing like this had happened in Vanya's career in the infantry. And he was eager, too, to tell his story to Colonel Stromlin. Stromlin, he thought, was the very model of a military man. He always kept his officers at arm's length, no fraternizing, but had keen appreciation of their abilities and achievements. This was an exploit Stromlin would appreciate

Andrei saw to the billeting of his men, the stowing of the equipment, located the new command hut, and found his own billet, a small shack. Here he had Dedya Petya deposit his iron-bound suitcase and the new neat wooden case that he had one of the men construct for his manuscripts. He had decided to carry his papers separately from his clothing; then, if necessary, he could jettison his clothing and preserve his manuscripts. It was after midnight. Andrei tossed his map case on the table, threw himself on the bed and was asleep before his eyes were closed.

He awoke at six and immediately picked up one of the small notebooks he used for his diary. He was busy writing in it at seven when his orderly brought his tea, black bread and cheese. At eight an orderly from Colonel Stromlin appeared. Could he come to the Headquarters hut immediately? Andrei slipped on his greatcoat, his sheep-skin hat, his heavy leather gloves, picked up his map case and hurried out. The orderly had waited at the door and now walked by his side. A little unnecessary formality, Andrei thought. To be sure, the colonel wanted to hear at firsthand the story of their escape from be-hind the German lines. The thought of the adventure and the co-incidence of his moving in his father's footsteps once more filled his mind. What fateful ground was this East Prussian soil! Not only for Russia, but for his father and himself.

He pushed open the door of the Headquarters hut. As always, Colonel Stromlin sat behind his desk. There were three or four other officers in the room. One, Andrei was surprised to note, was the hated Captain Petroshenko. Two others were unknown to him. Lieutenant Colonel Smirnov stood at one side.

Andrei saluted as he entered and Colonel Stromlin rose.

"Captain Sokolov," he said, and his tone seemed even more formal and dry than usual. "Would you be kind enough to hand me your revolver."

Andrei took a step forward, pulling the gun from its leather case on his left hip and carefully placing it on the desk before the colonel.

Hardly had his hand touched the desk than the two men who were unknown to him leaped at him, one from either side, shouting, "You're under arrest!" And with a simultaneous movement, a rip and a tear of the cloth, they wrenched from his shoulders the boards and stars that were the insignia of his captain's rank.

Chapter 35

THE Rossiya Insurance Company was the second largest insurance company in Russia at the time of the Revolution. It was owned by a consortium of "white-stone" Moscow bourgeoisie, as they were called —well-to-do merchants and bankers who grew to wealth in the later half of the nineteenth century.

In 1889 the Rossiya's annual profits for the first time passed the mark of two million gold rubles, and the white-stone burghers decided to move out of their cramped and sprawling quarters in an old palace on Varvarskaya Street in the heart of the Moscow financial district and into a new and imposing edifice more consistent with the grandeur of the Rossiya's capital assets and net profits.

By a stroke of good fortune and some undisclosed but profitable double-dealing among the directors, a handsome site was acquired, not far away, at the head of Lubyanka Square, commanding not only the busy square itself but the park and esplanade leading to the financial district. It was a strategic location looking down the hill to Theater Square, across to the Vladimir Gates of the ancient Kitai *gorod*, or Chinese City, and east to Myasnitskaya Street, which was rapidly becoming one of Moscow's busiest streets and, most important, a place of smart shops and new government buildings.

The directors of the Rossiya Company engaged an excellent, suitably conservative architect named Moronov and erected what was, for its time, the richest and most imposing building in Moscow, a massive structure of eight stories with great plate-glass windows, rich marble columns, fine balconies, peristyles, porticoes and a vast interior courtyard, guarded by huge gates of decorated iron, fully thirty feet high. The opening of the building in 1897 was a Moscow event, attended not only by the mayor and the governor-general but by the high officers of the government. Count Witte, the Czar's remarkable finance minister and later-to-be Prime Minister, graced the occasion with his presence, and the weekly magazine *Niva* ran an article about the building. It published drawings showing the boardroom with its magnificent mahogany carvings and its fireplace of Carrara marble, and sketches of the entrance hall with its spectacular ceiling, decorated in pseudo-Russian style with gold inlay and brilliant tourmaline and crimson accents.

Niva called the building the "pride of Moscow" and suggested, somewhat grandiloquently, that its construction had opened "an entire new vista" in Russian architecture. At long last, in the Lubyanka, as everyone called it, Russia had created an edifice whose renown would carry to all corners of the world. As a tailpiece to its article, *Niva* published an engraving of the remarkable Lubyanka gates, their handsome ironwork embellished with the special emblem of the Rossiya Insurance Company, a heroic R, worked in gold against a shield of black.

* * *

None of this history was known to Andrei as he stumbled out of a taxi and through those gates. He was accompanied by the two Smersh (counterintelligence) men, who had torn from his shoulders his symbol of rank, five days before, and he was worn out, bewildered and badly frightened.

Had Andrei been familiar with the earlier description of these gates, as he became many years later, he would have noticed that the great iron gates now were backed by sheet steel welded to their bars so that no one passing along the street could catch a glimpse of the inner courtyard; there was a fur-capped Security soldier, carrying a Tommy gun, stationed in a small wooden shelter hut at the gate, and a smaller entrance door had been cut in the great gate so that foot traffic could enter without the gates themselves being opened.

The Smersh men had a word with the guard who communicated by telephone with the duty officer within, and a moment later the smaller door clicked open and Andrei, the Security men on either side, his wrists handcuffed but nonetheless carrying his heavy suitcase, walked through the gates of the inner reception room of the most famous prison of the world. *Niva*'s prediction of March 1897 had long since come true. Russia had indeed created an edifice whose renown echoed around the world, and the very gates which had formed the tailpiece of *Niva*'s article had themselves won fame.

They were known, simply, to those who passed through them as "The Gates of Hell." For with the coming of the Revolution, Felix Dzerzhinsky, the fierce Polish fanatic whom Lenin appointed as guardian of the Revolution, made the lavish premises of the Rossiya Company the headquarters of his new and terror-haunted secret police, the G.P.U. From that day forward, the word "Lubyanka" had become a synonym around the world for prison, for horror, for oppression.

Andrei passed through the gates ignorant of the nature of the charges against him. But he had one clue, and it was really all he needed. As he had sat dozing in one of the railroad cars that brought him to Moscow he overheard a remark by one of the Smersh men to the other concerning "the one on the Ukrainian front." From this he deduced that not only had he been arrested but, it seemed probable, his friend Vanya had been seized as well. He could only conclude that somehow, somewhere, his remarks about the Dekabristi must have been read and interpreted—correctly—as dealing with his hostility to Stalin. If this was true, he must assume his future now appeared likely to be neither bright nor lengthy.

*   *   *

In that first moment of his arrest he had leaped back in protest. How dare they touch him? What kind of mistake was this? He had cried out and his eyes had met those of Colonel Stromlin, and he saw there a look of deep compassion and sorrow, a look that told him that Stromlin had not abandoned him. Indeed, he saw Stromlin's lips actually forming the words "I'm sorry." Did he speak them? Andrei could not now say.

And his eyes then had moved to Petroshenko, and there he saw the savage, unrestrained glee of a bully who has at long last tripped his most hated rival and stands over him, boot poised to drive into his victim's crotch. Andrei had not looked at Smirnov. Instinctively he knew that it was best that no flash of recognition, no outward sign of their close relationship, be given in that moment.

The train journey had been a nightmare. The two Smersh men were neither friendly nor unfriendly, neither human nor unhuman. They were two mechanics, doing their job. They had been sent out to reclaim a bit of damaged machinery. They would bring it back to the Center for repairs or the junk heap. They neither knew nor cared for any particular detail of what Andrei might be involved in. They made no attempt to interrogate him. They made no conversation, nor would they respond to Andrei. Their only talk was of petty detail. Sometimes they took off his handcuffs so all three could go together to the buffet car. Sometimes he was unhandcuffed so he could more easily carry his bag. (To Andrei in those first days this was the greatest indignity. He had not realized how much the officer he had become, how much above such menial chores as carrying a suitcase he held himself.)

And here a question burned into his mind and he returned to it again and again. He had gone under the escort of the two Smersh men to his hut to pick up his suitcase. He had already turned over to them his map case, which, as luck would have it, held nothing but military papers, his last letter from Rosa, two or perhaps three letters from Vanya whose exact contents he could not recall and the rough draft of a story or two which he felt certain contained nothing particularly dangerous. But as he approached his hut he literally felt his knees tremble because there on his table they would find the diary in which he had been writing when suddenly summoned by the Colonel, and under the cot was the wooden box which had just been made to hold his manuscripts and papers.

How was he to explain these writings? He knew he could not. He was fully aware of the fatal danger of his many references to Mustache, to the coming changes, his frank and open remarks about the defects of the government, about the Army. Indeed, even the quality and content of his short stories and articles must go against him. One Smersh man went ahead and one at his heels as he entered the hut. Andrei's eyes swept the scene instantly and he could hardly repress a gasp of surprise. The manuscript box was gone from its repository under his bed and his diary no longer lay open where he had left it on the table. Could they already have searched the room and taken them away?

The Smersh men began banging about, turning up the bedclothes, tapping the floor, rapping on the walls, peering into the woodpile, opening the stove, looking into the cranny below the roof, examining the room for any place where materials might be secreted. Indeed, they turned on him and demanded to know whether he had anything hidden. Taking a bold gamble, Andrei shrugged his shoulders and pointed to his suitcase. "There are my things," he said.

The Smersh men seemed to take him at his word. They ordered him to pick up his suitcase and come with them. Nothing that followed exceeded in anguish Andrei's progress through the camp, his emblems of rank torn off, the Smersh men at his right and left. He was not yet in handcuffs, but even the handcuffs did not test his *amour propre* as did this five-minute walk. From every hutment window, he felt the eyes of his comrades watching him. He saw groups of common soldiers staring at him with open hostility, and as he was half shoved into the command car by the Smersh men he heard a voice behind him snarl, "*Naplevat!* Spit on him!" And, turning, saw a common soldier spitting in his direction, a look of cold anger on his face. He saw that same look more than once on the journey to Moscow as some military man would spot his handcuffs and recognize him for what he appeared to be—a traitor to his country.

*   *   *

Now, as he walked through the great iron gates, that humiliation still burned within him, but his mind was on his coming confrontation. He felt fairly sure that the Smersh men did not have his papers.

They carried no luggage and had no place to conceal the papers, Nor had he been able to make out that anyone else was involved in his case with the obvious exception of Petroshenko, whom he blamed for the whole thing.

What could have happened to his things? Who was his guardian angel? It could not be Lieutenant Colonel Smirnov because he had been present in the command hut when Andrei was arrested. Could it have been another officer? Unlikely. Andrei was not close to any of the other officers. Between his duties and his writing he rarely sat around with the junior men reminiscing about the beauty of the girls on the Kreshchatik in Kiev or the Nevsky Prospekt in Leningrad. Andrei could think of only one candidate—Dedya Petya. But how could Dedya Petya have known of the danger? Of this there was no way of being certain. In fact, it all might have been a clever police device to trap Andrei into contradictions. His mind raced around and around the problem. It was not only for himself that he must fear. Vanya, he could understand, must have been arrested as well. And he had others to protect—Rosa, for example. And Lieutenant Colonel Smirnov. And two other close friends from Rostov University, the brothers Voronov, Sergei and Alexei, whom he had met last month at the front and who, in a joyful reunion over a bottle of vodka, had been initiated into his "five."

Echoes of these thoughts turned Andrei's mind into a maze as his heels and those of the Smersh men rang hard against the great granite blocks of the courtyard, which was swept clean with not a flake of snow nor a sliver of ice on its surface, although beyond the courtyard the streets were covered with hard-packed snow. They entered a dimly lit reception room. An orderly sat at a desk. The Smersh men approached him and there was a whispered conversation. The handcuffs were removed from Andrei's wrists, the orderly pressed a button and a khaki-clad guard ordered him: "Go ahead. Look lively. Head down. Eyes to the floor." Andrei muffled a protest, then found himself walking down a long corridor with a dark-brown-linoleum-covered floor, over which lay a russet runner of heavily woven cotton with a broad stripe of green edged in red down its center.

They walked straight down the corridor to a brown-painted steel door. The guard made some signal or pressed a button and the door opened into a common room with an iron-screened barrier at one side and a long counter at another. Here Andrei surrendered his suitcase and was given a scribbled receipt. Here, he was searched from head to toe, and all his valuables, everything in his pockets, were taken. For these, too, he was given a receipt.

Then he was marched by another guard through a tangle of corridors. He tried to count steps and to observe directions, but he lost track. After interminable windings, up and down and around corners he arrived at a cell block. Another warder appeared, clanking keys. He thrust a key into a door which was half wood, half bars, and shoved Andrei in.

"Here you are," said the guard. "Observe the rules."

Before Andrei could catch his breath the door swung shut and he heard the key twist in the lock. He turned to see seven men lying on double-decker bunks. The eighth place, the upper mattress of the bunk furthest from the door, was his.

One of the men cocked an eye toward Andrei. "What are you in for?" he asked lazily.

"I don't know," Andrei answered in confusion. "I think it must be some mistake."

A ripple of laughter came from the bunks. There was a deep stentorian laugh, a light whisper of a laugh, a laugh that quickly turned into a hacking cough.

Then one man, invisible in the murk, said with heavy sarcasm, "He doesn't know why he's here."

Another imitating Andrei's voice precisely said, "I think it must be some mistake."

And another round of laughter shook the seven bunks.

*   *   *

Andrei lay flat on his back on the upper bunk, his hands outside the blanket (the prison rule), his eyes wide open, his ears remarkably sensitive, listening to the breathing of his seven companions. Beyond the cell, from the corridor outside, he heard the pacing of a guard with a squeaking shoe, approaching from afar, first very faint, then growing stronger, pausing at the cell doors. He heard no other sound: nothing from within the building, nothing from the outside.

Andrei thought back over the past five days and there echoed again in his ears the sarcastic chuckles of his cellmates when he announced that he did not know why he was in the Lubyanka and that it must be some kind of mistake. He understood instantly from their sarcasm that his response was a cliché; that he was the ten-thousandth, the one-hundred-thousandth, the millionth prisoner to use those words.

And yet, and yet . . . He had asked the Smersh men the same question: Why was he arrested? What was the charge? And they had replied with what he realized was sheer boredom: "You know very well what you're in for." And he could even believe that these two dolts with the blue cap and red stripe of the Security service knew nothing whatever about why he was being arrested and very honestly assumed that he, Andrei, must know the nature of his crime.

This, then, was the way it happened. This was how one was arrested in this victory year of 1945. Would he get to march in the victory parade in Red Square? Not much likelihood. It would be lucky if he was still among the living by that day. He thought of his last conversation with Rosa and his confidence that it made no difference whether he lived or not, whether there was such a thing as the new Dekabristi or not, that the sheer mass of common opinion of the men returning from the front would turn the country away from Stalin's tyranny and back to the true humanism of Lenin.

Did he still believe that now, lying on this steel cot in the Lubyanka prison in the heart of sleeping Moscow? Part of him, that civic part of him which still was functioning in the time and space of "out there," beyond the walls of the prison, answered yes. But the part that was already beginning to feel like a man behind bars was whispering insistently: You were wrong. You underestimated them. Tonight you are in prison. And how many others? And tomorrow and the day after tomorrow and the day after that, how many more?

As he struggled with these thoughts, Andrei heard the squeak of the sentry's shoes coming nearer. It advanced directly to the door of his cell and he heard the metallic click of a key in the lock, and the voice of the guard: "Sokolov, Andrei Ilych. You are wanted."

Andrei slipped down from his bunk, put on his trousers, shirt and boots as the guard said "Hurry up there. Look lively." Andrei had heard the others in the cell move in their bunks when his name was called. Now he heard them settling back.

He stepped out of the cell. The turnkey locked it, then set him in motion: once again Andrei ahead, again admonished not to raise his eyes from the floor, directed by the guard from the rear who laconically said "Left," "Right," "Up" or "Down" at each turning point or staircase. This time Andrei noticed something he had been too excited to observe when he was led to the cell the first time. As they walked down the long corridor the turnkey behind him kept snapping his fingers, not loudly, but loudly enough so that the sound followed down the corridor. A curious habit, he thought, but later he realized it was a simple prison signal. It enabled the other convoys and turnkeys to note that a prisoner was in transit through the corridor.

Again Andrei tried to count steps and detect directions, and again he became hopelessly confused. All he knew was that it took longer to reach his cell from the reception room than it did to reach the room of his inquisitor. They arrived at the door.

The turnkey rapped twice, stuck his head in, spoke a word, then shoved Andrei through the door. He found himself in a small office, rather smaller than his cell, distinguished by absolutely nothing. There was a dark-haired, rather pale man sitting behind a plain birch desk with a plain wooden top. There was no chair in the room, only a birch cupboard to the right of the desk with glass doors masked by dull-green curtains. A window to the left of the desk seemed to be smeared over with brown paint—at any rate, one could not see out of it. A picture of Stalin hung over the desk. The only incongruous note was a rather large crystal chandelier which hung from the high ceiling. Andrei realized that originally this had been a much larger room, now subdivided, the only remaining evidence of its earlier and happier life being the chandelier.

* * *

Andrei was able to make these observations at leisure, since the man with the tired white face and black hair was busily reading from a liver-colored *papka*, or file, presumably familiarizing himself with Andrei's case. It was difficult to see him clearly, since he had tilted his desk lamp in such a fashion that it illuminated the papers on his desk and then shot its gleam into Andrei's eyes while leaving the interrogator's face in the shadows.

After nearly ten minutes in which Andrei stood silently, not *quite* at attention, the man ceased his reading, scribbled something on a sheet of paper and looked up saying, "Name?"

"Captain Sokolov, Andrei Ilych," Andrei started to reply but was interrupted with an angry snarl: "Shut up! How dare you call yourself Captain! You have been discharged from the ranks of the Red Army for traitorous conduct. You have no rank! I ask you again: Name?"

Andrei responded appropriately. He was asked his birthplace, his father's name, his mother's name, his place of residence "before you entered the ranks of the Soviet armed forces with the intention of betraying your country to its enemies."

"But I never had any such intention," Andrei blurted out.

Again a mountainous wave of rage. "Answer my question!"

Andrei mechanically went through his curriculum vitae. At the end the interrogator paused. "Tell me about your crimes against the state."

"What crimes?" asked Andrei.

"You know very well what crimes!" snapped the interrogator. "The crimes for which you were arrested."

"But—"

"Don't 'but' me," the interrogator raged. "You are a grown man. Don't pretend to be a child."

Andrei stood silent.

"Come on," the interrogator continued. "Speak up. I don't have all night to deal with the likes of you."

Andrei blurted out: "But what am I accused of?"

This time the interrogator did not explode. He regarded Andrei with a weary, care-worn face as though the ordeal was too much for him after a long and busy day.

"We don't play games," the interrogator resumed. "You know your crimes as well as we do. Are you ready to confess?"

He shoved a sheet of paper toward Andrei. "Here," he said. "Let's get this over with. You know you are guilty. We know you are guilty.

You know we can beat the truth out of you. And we will if that's the way you want it. Or you can simply sign this acknowledgment, take your medicine and everything will go much easier."

Andrei picked up the paper and started to read. The interrogator snatched it away from him. "I said, 'Sign,' not 'Read.' Don't you trust the Soviet authority? Do you think we have done something wrong? Here—sign it and get this thing over with."

The man kept one hand down on the paper while he offered a pen to Andrei with the other. Andrei took the pen, held it and started to read the document. It was a confession to conspiracy against the state, to organization of a counterrevolutionary group "with the intention of overthrowing the Soviet government."

"But this is ridiculous!" he exploded. "I've nothing to do with counterrevolutionary activity. I'm a member of the Communist Youth League. I believe in Lenin."

Before he had finished his second sentence the interrogator was shouting at him.

"Silence!" the man thundered. "Here your denials will do you no good. The state knows what you are and who you are. You are not a member of the Komsomols. It was an error to let you into membership and those who did it will be suitably punished. And do not let the name of Lenin cross your filthy lips. The state knows you. The state knows all about your dirty anti-Communist activity. When were you recruited by British intelligence? Answer me that!"

Andrei stood silent. What could he say? He dropped the pen on the "confession," noticing that it spattered ink over two or three lines and stepped back a pace.

The interrogator finally stopped shouting and slumped down in his chair. "Very well, Sokolov, you will regret this night's action for the rest of your life, which I prophesy will not be a long one. I was trying to make it easier for you. You don't want to cooperate—very well. We will change your mind for you and very soon."

As he spoke these words the interrogator's shoulders seemed to sink down and he almost disappeared into his chair, or such was Andrei's impression. He had the feeling that he had won the first contest of wills and that the interrogator was a tired, worn-out man who had hoped with his initial bombast to terrorize Andrei into doing whatever he was told to do. That gambit had not worked.

"We have our ways, Sokolov," the interrogator was saying. "Remember that the Soviet security services are never defeated. The moment will come when you will cry on your bended knees for permission to sign this confession, any confession. But those who defy us must take the consequences."

The interrogator pressed a button on his desk and a turnkey entered the room immediately. Apparently, Andrei thought, the man must stand just outside the door throughout the inquiry.

"Take this *swolich*, this *govno*, this bastard, this shit, back to his cell," the interrogator snapped. "We'll deal with him later."

As Andrei turned to leave the room the interrogator slumped further down behind his desk. Andrei had the sensation that if he waited much longer the man would be completely under the table.

He walked back to his cell, head down, eyes on the floor, following precisely the guard's direction, now to the right, now up, now down, now to the left. He counted the steps more exactly this time. He went up three staircases and down four. There were five turns to the right, seven to the left. He did not have the total number of paces as yet. But if, as he supposed, he was brought back tomorrow, he should be able to get the distances and directions clear in his head.

He walked slowly down the long corridors, hearing only an occasional muffled noise, listening to the strange *snap, snap, snap* of the guard's fingers as he walked through the halls of what was once the Rossiya Company building, the "pride of Moscow."

In the cell only one man awakened when he entered, looked up at him, and apparently reassured by Andrei's appearance, slumped back in his bunk saying: "*Khorosho*, all right." But what it might be that was all right Andrei had not the slightest notion.

Chapter 36

THERE were seven men in what Andrei quickly learned was cell No. 41a of the Lubyanka, and twenty years later he could recite their given names and patronymics, their ages, fully describe each face and person and even imitate the voice. He inhabited cell No. 41a for thirteen days. In the course of these days three men left the cell and three replaced them.

Two decades later, Andrei knew the names of these three as well as the original seven and could still relate their life stories so far as they had been willing to tell them. For in those first days a new sense of purpose began to possess Andrei. He did not know how long he would be confined to prison, he did not know how long he would live, he did not know whether he would ever emerge from the Lubyanka. But, somehow, just as he had known that he would not die in the war, so he now began to feel confident that he would survive the nightmare of arrest, interrogation and imprisonment. And if he did, he would be armed—armed with every crumb of knowledge of this netherworld he could cram into his mind. What he might do with this knowledge he did not at this moment have any idea. But he had the conviction that all he could retain in memory or in notes would serve him in some remarkable way and, through him, serve the cause to which he had always been, and still was, dedicated—the cause of Russia and the Russian people.

Whatever else he might learn through his arrest and imprisonment, it had already taught him one thing with the most rude bluntness— his assessment of Stalin and the regime had been mistaken in one respect. He had underestimated the evil of the man and his rule; he had not comprehended the enormity of Stalin's crimes; he had not been able, with his provincial mind, to imagine the universality of the corruption that Stalin had imposed upon Lenin's Revolution.

In the dim light of the first morning Andrei did not find his cell-mates as cruel and sarcastic as he had imagined from their laughter at his initial words. In fact, he found them, in large measure, warm, interested, helpful, intelligent and filled with knowledge and judgment not only about life behind the bars of prison but about the life of Russia itself.

First, they were eager to hear what news he could bring them from the outer world. "To be sure, we are not entirely cut off," said Professor Derzhavin, until recently a professor of biology at the Agricultural Institute named for Lenin and now charged with "subversive intent" to wreck Soviet agriculture. "We are usually able to determine whether it is raining or snowing or cold or hot on the Moscow streets. And we do hear the salutes each evening—the cannonade in honor of the great cities captured by the Red Army—but it is only by chance that we hear the names of the cities or what may be going on not only within the boundaries of our own country but in the other lands of the world."

Andrei was able to bring them up-to-date on the progress of the Red Army, the push into East Prussia, the long halt before Warsaw, the outbreak of the Ardennes offensive by the Nazis against the Western Allies and his own conviction that the war would be over by early spring.

But Andrei could not answer specific questions put to him by Colonel Alkimov, an articulate and rather fussy little man accustomed, as he said, to wearing a pince-nez (not permitted in his Lubyanka cell), who had been a colonel in artillery supply until three months ago. Andrei was unable to enlighten him as to the present fate or position of a whole series of general officers who, for reasons which the colonel did not make clear, seemed to be of great importance to him.

*　　*　　*

There was only one cellmate who was of Andrei's age and background, he too having been an artillery captain. His name was Vladimirov, and Andrei quickly understood from gestures and winks on the part of a hard-faced muscular engineer named Martov that former Captain Vladimirov was one to be avoided—thought by his cellmates to be a stool pigeon. The oldest man in the cell was, to Andrei's delight, a fellow mathematician, although he had for many years worked as an economist. He proudly announced that he was sixty-three years old, soon would be sixty-four, and had been continuously in one prison or another since 1931, when he had been arrested as a putative member of the so-called Industrial, or Prom, Party. His name was Tyomkin, and he was delighted when Andrei told him that as a schoolboy he had read every word that was printed about the Prom Party trial in *Izvestia* and had been certain from that day that the case was not real but a cooked-up plot, the nature of which he had never been able to understand.

"Imagine!" Tyomkin exclaimed. "Imagine! That a Russian schoolboy could read those accounts and understand the real truth. How amazing! And how encouraging! I have been saying for twenty years that come what may, sooner or later, we will struggle out of the terrible bog into which we have been led. And now you give me new hope, my dear Andrei Ilych. You have brought warmth to an old man's faltering heart."

And his heart was indeed faltering. Tyomkin had not a hair on his head—he had lost it all, he said, in a terrible winter he had spent in the Solovetsky Islands in 1933. His face looked like vellum. You could see through the luminous parchment to the veins and bones, and he seemed so brittle that if he fell he might smash into a thousand pieces like a Meissen doll. Yet somehow he had survived.

"But I'll not live through this," he told Andrei with a queer grin. "This is the last time around for an old professional. I know what I can take and I know what is too much. They want too much of me. I'll simply let them do me in this time. Why not? And you have given me the confidence and courage to let them do it. So long as young men like you are coming along—who will miss an old veteran like myself?"

*   *   *

Andrei was like a child. He could not hear enough from Tyomkin. What was the basis of the Prom Party case? What had happened to him?

It was all quite different in those days, the old man explained with a sigh. Certainly there had been the trial. Some had stood up to it, some had not. It made no difference. They were all convicted except for two stool pigeons—well, you could not even call them stool pigeons because they had never had anything to do with the rest of the group. They were just two paid witnesses. The rest were convicted. Five had been sentenced to death, but the sentences were commuted to life imprisonment. They had all been sent to the islands, and there had been terrible times, especially the winter of 1933. There were thirty-nine of them there. Ten died that winter. In the spring most of the others were brought back to Moscow and set to work on engineering problems. Individual assignments. They were held at the start right here in the Lubyanka. Later they were taken outside Moscow to an old estate, which housed the first of the *sharashkas*, the prison scientific institutes, although that name wasn't then used.

But in 1937 they were packed off to different camps in Siberia. He went to a camp just east of Novosibirsk. He was fortunate—his mathematics got him a job as camp bookkeeper.

"That's why I'm still alive," Tyomkin said with a chuckle. "I've a head for figures—and they needed someone like me."

He had managed to survive three camp administrations and the worst of the war years ("We died like flies in 1942. No food. I don't think any of my comrades from 1931 are still alive.") He was, he said, an anachronism, a link back to times long since gone.

"That's why I'm back here in the Lubyanka," he said, shaking his head. "Lord. It's nearly fifteen years since I've been inside this building. But it's not changed much. The guards still snap their fingers. The food is the best of any of the prisons, but the interrogators—they are worse than ever. They've always been cruel. Now they are ignorant as well."

"But why are you here in the Lubyanka again after all these years?" Andrei asked in curiosity.

"A very good question—a capital question," Tyomkin said, again chuckling noiselessly. "I have asked it of myself countless times. And now I think I have an answer. I am, as I told you, a relic of the past —of the days when there actually were opposing opinions in the Party—not plots, mind you, but honest and deep differences of opinion. The Prom Party—well, it wasn't a party, that's certain—but it did represent a different point of view. So did the Workers Opposition. So did the Right Opposition and the Left Opposition or even"—here he lowered his voice—"the Trotskyites, if it comes to that."

Tyomkin fell silent and stayed silent for a long time. Andrei could almost see the long journey he was taking back into those early days when the Revolution was still a Revolution, when argument still raged, when passionate debate flamed at the Party meetings.

Finally Tyomkin resumed. He could not be certain why he was back again in the Lubyanka. The interrogation had gone so far back, had concerned itself with so many forgotten matters, so many names of men long since dead, causes long since lost. But it was his impression that possibly some surviving Menshevik exiles had fallen into the hands of the police, and that an attempt was going to be made to link these forgotten bits of political debris—these habitués of back-street cafés in Bucharest or Sofia or Belgrade—to certain living, breathing individuals in the Soviet Union, possibly high-ranking individuals.

"You can see for yourself the range of possibilities, my dear Andrei Ilych," he said. "And you can see, of course, how useful I can be as a link between the forgotten past and the soon-to-be-invented present."

Tyomkin was perfectly agreeable to taking whatever role the police thrust upon him. "What difference does it make now?" he said with a shrug of his shoulders. "If not me—someone else. They know what they want. I am an old man. I can't stand up to them as I did ten years ago."

Yet, even so, he was brought back the next day from interrogation a crumpled body, hardly able to walk. His face was bloody and one arm hung useless at his side. He breathed with difficulty.

"It won't be long," he said to Andrei. "I'll not last long. My heart is no good. It will give out at any moment."

"But why . . . how can they do this to you?" Andrei asked in helpless rage.

Tyomkin shrugged his shoulders. "It's the interrogator. He won't take yes for an answer. He has to behave as though there was something to be squeezed out of me. And so he squeezes me. What can I do? I tell him I'll sign anything he wants. But that's not good enough, I have to make up plots for him to expose. I'm sorry. I'm too old. My imagination is no good any more."

On the fifth day after Andrei's arrival at the Lubyanka, Tyomkin did not return from interrogation. "That's the end," Professor Derzhavin said. "His heart gave out. There can be no doubt."

He had taken Tyomkin's pulse and listened to his heart. "The pulse was extremely weak," he said. "And most irregular. It was obvious that there was a critical malfunction."

And so, it appeared, there was. At least in the ensuing years, although Andrei often inquired about Tyomkin and the Prom Party, he heard of no one who had seen him after that winter of 1945. He once or twice encountered persons who knew of Tyomkin and who knew of the Prom Party men, had even stumbled upon one or two in the late thirties. But with Tyomkin, Andrei concluded, the line ran out. Unless a widow survived tucked away in some backwater town, in some thankless clerical job, all living links to a group which had once played a vital role in the debate over the Revolution's course had vanished from Russia, and all that remained were a few foul-mouthed references in yellowed newspapers, and perhaps in some locked-away libraries (or maybe abroad in exile) there were copies of pamphlets and speeches which had been made by them in the 1920's before the great iron barrier came down.

* * *

Andrei did not arrive at this solemn conclusion all at once or, indeed, during his sojourn in Lubyanka. He was, during those thirteen days, a quivering mass absorbing multiple impressions, half paralyzed with fear and so disoriented that he sometimes stood for five minutes before his interrogator, literally unable to apprehend what he was being asked. He had made himself only one rule: to respond slowly and briefly and not to say a word until he understood what it was that he was being asked and the implications of his answer.

The interrogator, Andrei had learned, was named Mikhail Mikhailovich Kharlamov. He had gained this intelligence from two conversations, one which Kharlamov conducted with some unknown person on the telephone, the other a brief interruption when an interrogator entered Kharlamov's office to ask whether they might switch duty shifts the following weekend.

Kharlamov's questioning of Andrei was designed to establish him as a member, if not the center, of a counterrevolutionary organization within the armed forces which had the objective of overthrowing the Soviet regime. This organization, in the interrogator's mind, was directed by British intelligence.

Again and again he pressed Andrei to name the members of the group and the name of his director in British intelligence. In fact, he provided a name for the contact—a "Major Anderson." Once when Andrei had for the twentieth time declared he knew no "Major Anderson," Kharlamov struck him on the mouth. Not a terribly hard blow, but it drew blood. Other than that, he had used no physical violence, but night after night he kept Andrei standing before him without rest, without water, the light constantly glaring in his eyes from 10 P.M. to 4 A.M. At 6 A.M. Andrei was compelled with the rest of the prisoners to arise. He was not permitted to lie in bed during the day.

With such a schedule, it was fortunate, his cellmates agreed, that he was sturdy and in good health. He was able to endure what most of them could not.

* * *

But if Andrei had not yet been subjected to physical torture there was no end to the threats that Kharlamov leveled at him. He would be shipped off to Butyrka, "where they know how to take care of stubborn cases like you," or to Lefortovo, "where they break a punk like yourself as easily as a stick of wood." Andrei was told that his confession was not needed. They had the word of all the other members of the band. It was when Andrei said, "What band?" that Kharlamov had hit him again with his clenched fist.

What gave Andrei some confidence was that no other names were mentioned except for that of his friend Vanya. He took this to mean that, in reality, only the two of them had been arrested and that so long as this was true they could not "prove" any conspiracy. When he tried to offer this as an arguing point one night when Kharlamov seemed more relaxed and less edgy than usual, it drew nothing but a sneer: "A conspiracy need have no more than two persons," Kharlamov said loftily. "In fact it needs only one person and the intent. The intent is all we need. And we know you had the intent. And we know with whom you worked."

This proved to Andrei that they did not, in fact, have any names to add to the conspiracy, and he was confirmed in his judgment by the engineer Martov, with whom he had developed a close friendship. Martov had fallen into the prison system in 1938, as the great purge was coming to an end. He had been an engineer in the cotton textile mills at Ivanovo-Voznesensk, the greatest textile complex in Russia.

"They just cleaned the top management out," he said simply. "All of us—the director, the deputy director, the controller, the chief engineer—that is, myself—and the Party representative. I don't know what became of the others. I think they were all shot. I don't know why I wasn't shot, too. Possibly because they needed engineers."

He was sent to Central Asia to work as an engineer in a textile plant operated by prison labor in Uzbekistan. "Not a bad mill," he said.

"In fact, it had first-class British machinery imported from Manchester. I could have turned it into an excellent operation. But, of course, the director was no good. Part of Gulagprom, the industrial division of the police."

He did not know what he had been brought back for, but he suspected that some kind of action was being put together against the Uzbek Party organization and, possibly, the Uzbek branch of the Gulagprom as well.

Martov was not only a good engineer but also a keen observer of the prison system, and he counseled Andrei to hold fast, admit to no conspiracies, and if hard pressed, to confine any admissions solely to his relationship with his friend Vanya.

"They have you two chickens," Martov said. "Frankly you aren't worth much. There's nothing they really can use you for. Just small fry. Sure, if you admit to having relations with half a dozen others they will sweep them up as well. But if you just hang on and say you've done nothing wrong, just exchanged letters with your friend—well, my guess is they will settle for the two of you."

Was there no way, Andrei asked, in which the truth might not prevail? Was there no way of establishing the actual facts? Martov thought seriously over the question. "I don't really think so," he said. "I've heard now and then of cases—a letter to Stalin, it usually is—and somehow the man is released. But I've never known such a case myself, nor have I met anyone who did. I think that those 'cases' are just camp gossip."

"The best thing you have going for you," he said, "is that your case is so trivial. There's no pay dirt there. And the war is coming to an end sometime soon, you say. And when the war ends—who knows? Possibly there will be an amnesty, and we will all get out."

The amnesty, Andrei found, was the rag doll with which the prisoner went to bed each night. It was the dream that kept him alive. It had even been in the mind of poor Tyomkin—but it had not proved strong enough to keep his damaged heart from stopping.

*   *   *

The former captain and putative stool pigeon, Vladimirov, tried on the second day to scratch an acquaintance with Andrei. By this time Andrei had been relieved of the remnants of his uniform and put into prison dress, bulky fatigues and an ill-fitting tunic. He had neither cigarettes nor money, and Vladimirov offered to tide him over. Effort though it was, Andrei insisted that he preferred to go without; that it would be a test of his character and good for his lungs. Vladimirov then regaled him with stories of his front experiences, choosing anecdotes critical of his commanders and stressing the bungling that befell his unit. Andrei broke off the conversation in anger.

"In my unit," he said, not without pride, "we sometimes had difficulties. But we overcame them. We were never defeated, and I was serving last week under the same command with which I served when I completed officers training."

One of his cellmates was a Baltic baron, or so he insisted. His name was Ukskull and he had been captured in the Red Army's sweep through Latvia. "I am not a Russian," he said in German, drawing himself up proudly. "I am a citizen of the Third Reich. I do not recognize the Soviet authority." He was, Andrei felt certain, the only man in the cell who might be considered a real criminal. He had been installed by the Germans as the lord mayor of Riga, and Andrei had no doubt that his hands were as red with blood as those of any guard in the Lubyanka. He vanished the day after Andrei arrived—shot, rumor had it, in the basement execution chambers of the former insurance company. Another cellmate contended that he was not Russian but French. This was a boy of sixteen, named André Lefarzh, or Lefarge, as the youngster insisted it should be spelled. His father, he said, was a French Communist who happened to be vacationing with his wife and son—André—in Russia at the outbreak of war. What had happened to his parents André had no idea. They had vanished a few days after the Nazi attack on Russia and he had been placed in a children's home. Now he had been spirited away from the home and thrust into the Lubyanka. He kept pleading with his interrogator to let him communicate with the French embassy. The interrogator simply laughed.

The man who took Ukskull's place was a chauffeur named Ivanov who had been working for the British ambassador. He had taken the job because it was wartime, because he had been ordered to take it by the secret police and because he was a heavy drinker and it was possible to procure vodka on ration through the embassy. Now he was in terror, and deprived of alcohol, subject to such trauma that he constantly wheedled his companions, and even the guards, for something to drink. It was impossible to imagine his being guilty of anything more serious than drunkenness or a petty crime to get the money for boozing.

Yuri Feodorovich Kramov, who joined the cell after Tyomkin disappeared, was Ivanov's opposite. He was a tall, serious-looking, long-faced railroad man, a division chief, and on his first night he still wore his greasy railroadman's coveralls. He had been hauled straight from his station on the Moscow-Kazan railroad to the Lubyanka, taken directly from the roundhouse, where he was directing the teenage boys who worked for him in repairing an engine. He had a bad bruise over his eye and one sleeve of his coveralls was torn, and he had, he readily admitted, given "these sons of bitches" a hot five minutes before they forcibly subdued him. "If I'd had my wrench in my hand," he said gloomily, "they would never have taken me or, you can be sure, half a dozen of them would have been laid out in the process."

He knew exactly why he had been hauled in. There had been a wreck on the line five days earlier, a bad one. The braking system on an ammunition train had failed and the train slammed into a terminal. In the explosion the terminal was wrecked and half a dozen people were killed. "They had to have a scapegoat," he said grimly, "and so they picked me. But I'll show them a thing or two." The responsibility, he said—and no one in the cell was inclined to disagree with him—lay with the supervisor who had been warned personally by Kramov that the brakes were not in working order and who had dispatched the train nonetheless. Kramov paced the cell like a lion. "Goddamn bastards!" he kept saying. "Who the hell is going to keep the engines running without me? The bastards! I'll show them! Sabotage—shit!" And he would spit in the middle of the cell.

The last man among Andrei's first cellmates was a priest, Father Feofan, a serene man of forty with a gentle smile and a certainty about the goodness of man and the justice of God's judgment, which Andrei found more moving, more disturbing, than anything in his brief prison experience. He was himself too confused to analyze his own feelings, but as time went by he found himself returning to his conversations with Father Feofan again and again.

When Andrei confided to Professor Derzhavin his ambitions as a writer, the professor warmly congratulated him: "You do not yet know your good fortune, young man. It is only here in the Lubyanka, in the great prisons which you will come to know, that you can learn the real life of Russia. This is the heart of the heart of Russia as it has been for so many generations. Here you can learn. You can talk. You can meet the most eminent people of our age. You can begin to understand the true nature of Russia. All of this is at your command. You should bless your good fortune."

"There are some negative points, however," Andrei observed dryly.

"Quite true, young man. First, you must be able to survive your experience," said the professor. "That is not always easy. I doubt that I shall survive because my age is not very favorable. I am fifty-three, and eight or ten years of life in the camps or the prisons will do me in. But you are young and strong. You can still emerge with your health and your vigor."

The professor fell silent, and then continued. "And there is one other thing. You must be able to write and to publish your observations. There's the rub. I am sure you will survive. But will you publish? By the time you emerge we must suppose that our great leader will have passed on to his just reward. But what of his successor? Will he be any more able to tolerate the words which are burning in the heart and dripping from the pen of Andrei Ilych Sokolov? I wonder."

*   *   *

Andrei could not long ponder the question because that very night, earlier than the usual hour for his inquisition, he heard the approach of the squeaky shoe. Once more the guard demanded his presence. "Bring your things," he said gruffly.

Andrei collected his few possessions and was taken to the reception room. There he turned in his receipts and reclaimed his suitcase, his personal clothing, his possessions. He was led into a courtyard where a small van was waiting, its motor running. Propelled into the rear of the van, into pitch blackness, he realized by the jostling of their bodies that several prisoners were already crowded on the narrow benches. A moment later the van started. He heard a creaking sound, a kind of squeal, which he took to be the opening of the vast iron gate through which he had entered Lubyanka, and then the wheels of the van pounding over the Moscow pavements.

It was still early enough in the evening to hear the sound of other vehicles in the streets, but within the van the darkness was complete. There were turns to the right and to the left, but even had Andrei a map of Moscow imprinted on his brain he would not have known which way the van was going. They rode for nearly an hour, and then suddenly the van took a right-hand turn, could be felt to be moving up an incline; there was the sound of gates opening and the van came to a halt.

A rough hand unlocked the rear door, a rough voice shouted, "Look lively there!" Andrei and half a dozen other prisoners, clutching their few possessions, tumbled out into a snowy courtyard and were swiftly led into a reception room not unlike the one at Lubyanka. Here they deposited their belongings, were given the familiar scribbled receipt, and then, one by one, were marched off to cells. This time the orderlies did not snap their fingers. Butyrka or Lefortovo—which was it? Andrei wondered. Suddenly the guard halted, unlocked an iron door and thrust Andrei inside what seemed to him a cave made of human beings. It was impossible to determine how many men had been crowded into the cell. They were stacked like pinewood almost to the ceiling.

One prisoner, evidently the cell boss, glared at Andrei and pointed to the floor, to a narrow space, not a foot high, beneath the lowest bunk. "There," he said. That, Andrei understood, was his living space. As he scrambled down to worm himself into the clammy ledge, hardly deep enough to hold his body, he murmured to the prisoner, "Lefortovo?" The man nodded. It was, indeed, Lefortovo, the worst prison in Moscow, the hell-hole of the world, as Andrei's interrogator Mikhail Kharlamov had called it.

Chapter 37

LEFORTOVO . . . Butyrka . . . Lubyanka . . For more than six months Andrei shuttled from one to another, each time in a plain blue van, unmarked, bumping through the streets of Moscow, sometimes hearing the sounds of the city, the cry of children, the clang of a streetcar bell, the rumble of trucks, even a shouted exclamation from a pedestrian almost run down by the van. But he never saw the city. Not a glimpse. Occasionally at Lubyanka, he and his cellmates were permitted fifteen minutes of exercise on the roof, walking about a narrow quadrant of cindered rooftop surrounding the great chimneys. They saw the sky, but tall fences blinded them to the city. In 1941, one of his cellmates told him, the roof had been closed. All prisoners were confined to cells. The chimneys were kept burning day and night destroying documents, in fear the Germans would break into the city. The roof was knee-deep in ashes and, it was said, more than one citizen walking near Lubyanka Square had suddenly seen a bit of paper fluttering ahead of him, half-burnt, had picked it up to find it was his own dossier. "A good many citizens of Moscow have slept more soundly of nights since these days in October 1941 when the great burning took place," a tight-lipped, hard-faced one-time deputy commissar of heavy industry told Andrei. "They know that their *papka* went up in the conflagration. The devil of it is, no one knows for certain how much was burned and what was left."

Back and forth. From one interrogator to another, then periods without interrogation. A two-week "siesta," as he came to call it, in Butyrka in the spring, right after the war's end. No one told Andrei the war had ended, but he counted the cannon firings and when it totaled thirty he knew it could mean only one thing—the fall of Berlin, the end of the war. Not long after that, for two weeks Andrei remained in his Butyrka cell, apparently forgotten by the authorities. He was not called for interrogation and could sleep all through the night—restlessly, to be sure, but all through the night. And there was a further blessing. He was confined in a very large cell, really a ward rather than a cell. Not like the sardine quarters at Lefortovo where there was hardly room to turn around, this was a veritable ballroom, with only twenty-eight prisoners in it. There was space to walk in during the day and to gather in at night. During this period the jailers, possibly still drunk from celebrating the end of the war, paid little heed to what the prisoners did. It was here for the first time that Andrei participated in a prison seminar—in higher mathematics. And for the first time since leaving Rostov University, he felt himself challenged intellectually and learned something from his betters. (There were no less than two full professors and one aspirant in mathematics in the cell, all victims of some witch's tale at a mathematical institute in Sverdlovsk.)

And here, too, Andrei met the single most remarkable prisoner he was ever to meet in his long years in the system: Sergei Adamovich Bogdanov, a white-haired man, very thin, with paper-white skin and a high forehead. He wore iron-rimmed spectacles (for some reason they were then permitted in Butyrka). Looking at his face one might suppose he was a long-retired professor, possibly of classical languages, Latin or Greek. There was just the hint of something wrong with his face. When he spoke, it became apparent that his features were slightly out of proportion, the muscles did not fit the movement of his jaws. (In fact, his teeth had been knocked out and his jaws, both lower and upper, had been broken by the blow of an iron pipe wielded by a G.P.U. man in 1923.)

What made Bogdanov remarkable was that he was a genuine survivor of the left Social Revolutionary Party, which joined the Bolsheviks in making the Revolution and participated in the government until, after Kaplan's unsuccessful attempt to assassinate Lenin and the successful assassination of the German Ambassador Mirbach, the party was ruthlessly suppressed. It members were thrown into prison, transported to the islands or, in many cases, simply shot out of hand. And this process, of course, had been repeated again and again over the years every time some supposed threat emerged in the mind of Stalin—any surviving SR's who could be put in hand, in prison or out, went to the wall.

Bogdanov was still alive, still unbroken. His veins seemed to be filled with acid. Of course, he had not a good word to say for Stalin or the regime but openly and, to Andrei, shockingly declined to put all blame on Stalin. "It was Lenin," he hissed at Andrei. "Don't try to put a halo around his head. We SR's knew him for what he was— a dictator. A terrorist. He is the one who devoured the Revolution. From the first day, Stalin simply plodded in his footsteps."

Andrei was shaken to his roots; he reacted with wild and incoherent anger; he defended Lenin and privately he concluded Bogdanov was simply mad, driven out of his mind by long years of prison and torture. But Andrei's rage and indignation did not stir Bogdanov.

"Young man," he said, "you know nothing of history. Go back and look at the decrees. When was censorship imposed? The second day of the Revolution. By whom? By Lenin. When was the Cheka created? In the first month of the Revolution. By whom? By Lenin. When was it ordered to use torture, terror, any means to get results? In the winter of 1918. By whom? By Lenin. When were the first prisoners sent to camps? In 1918. By whom? By Lenin. Who were the first prisoners? SR's, Mensheviks, Anarchists, revolutionaries. Do you hear? *Revolutionaries.* Those were the first to feel the lash of Lenin's state. Go back and read your history. Don't praise Lenin to an old SR."

Andrei broke off the conversation and he did not sleep all night, pondering Bogdanov's words. They could not be true. They were a bitter old man's distortion. Stalin was evil—that, Andrei had long known. But Lenin was good. He was the pure force which had toppled the evil powers that had held Russia in bondage for so long.

The next day Andrei again sought out Bogdanov. The old man was twisted as a crab. He was subject to terrible seizures of fever from the malaria he had contracted when sent to work on the White Sea Canal. How he had escaped death on that occasion neither he nor anyone listening to his tales of hunger, torture and suffering could imagine.

Once again, Andrei tried to state his thesis of Lenin the pure revolutionary, the idealist who dedicated himself to ending Russia's centuries of darkness, who brought forth the Revolution in order that justice and freedom should prevail in the bitter Russian land.

This time Bogdanov was less fierce, perhaps because he felt so ill, perhaps because the sight of Andrei's anguish awakened some last morsel of pity in him.

"Listen," he said. "I cannot convince you about Lenin. I can only tell you where to find the evidence. Look at his works. Look at his writings. Look at his polemics. Who were his enemies? The Czar? Rasputin? The decaying nobility? Only peripherally. His real enemies were the other revolutionaries. When did he spare any weapon at his command against them—slander, libel, intrigue, deceit—any tactic that came to his hand? Name me one time. Do you really think his character changed when the Revolution came? Use your own logic and intuition. True, he fought the capitalists. True, he fought the Whites. But violence against his fellow revolutionaries began before the civil war, at a time when there was really no opposition, in the very first days. Everyone was with Lenin. Even so, he smashed away at any revolutionary who differed with him, who might in some sense be his rival or his competitor. He crushed us. He crushed the SR's without remorse. And the weapons he used against us Stalin simply picked up and used against the Party. Of course, Stalin crushed the Party. But first Lenin had crushed the Revolution."

The old man vanished from the cell after three days. How he had survived, why he was there, what became of him—Andrei was never to learn. But the words he spoke burned in Andrei's mind like letters of fire. He fought with all his strength against them. His life had been fashioned around his faith in Lenin. Even here in prison as he thought of the day, doubtless far distant, when he would emerge, he thought of Lenin. He thought of the overthrow of Stalin, the removal of Stalin, the death of Stalin as being the moment when the principles of Lenin at long last would triumph. Indeed, he even thought again in these late spring days, with the war won and Berlin captured, of the victory parade which must be coming in Red Square. While by now he was less confident than once he had been, there still persisted in his mind the ghost of the dream of the momentous day when the Red Army would march past Lenin's tomb. He could still imagine that—not unlike the famous day in 1825 in Senate Square in St. Petersburg when the Decembrist officers cried out for Konstantin and a Constitution— there would rise from the steel-helmeted regiments that had fought from Stalingrad to Berlin the cry of 1945—Peace and Freedom! And an end to tyranny!

The Carousel was what the prisoners called the practice of moving a man from one prison to another, subjecting him in one to threats and abuse, in the next to physical torture, in the next to the "conveyer," that is, to interrogation by relays of examiners for endless hours, possibly thirty-six, possibly forty-eight, possibly more.

It was powerfully disorienting. Andrei rode the Carousel and lost track of time, of place, of what he had told one interrogator and what another was asking. He lost weight rapidly. No longer did he find it possible to jot down his impressions on the tiny bits of cigarette paper he had concealed in the lining of his trousers. With the constant searches that attended his removal from one prison to another, he was not always able to preserve his notes. Repeatedly he found that he had to destroy them for lack of a secure place in which to hide them. But each time before he destroyed them, he committed the main points to memory so that when he next had an opportunity he could reproduce them in writing. It was after the fourth destruction of his notes that a solution for his problem occurred to him, one which was to serve him well during his prison years. He had no more trouble in committing his prison notes to memory—indeed, less—than in the distant university days in Rostov when he memorized whole pages of trigonometry or advanced mathematical formulae. Why not, instead of constantly scribbling tiny notes and having to destroy them, simply commit the main facts to memory each day. And each day refresh that memory by going over his knowledge in his mind. There would be no paper to worry about and it would occupy his mind in the endless hours of inquisition when the questions were hurled at him like bullets from a machine gun, punctuated with sudden blows, sometimes to the face, sometimes to the stomach, sometimes to the kidneys.

In later years Andrei was not proud of how he had behaved during the last weeks of interrogation. He grew disoriented, battered, confused and less and less able to keep himself from falling into the traps laid by the questioners. He had lost his boots to a couple of criminals in one of the Butyrka cells who had simply taken them from under his head while he was sleeping, exhausted, after a forty-eight-hour session on the conveyor. When he tried to get the shoes back they threatened him with a knife. Finally, acting on God knows what impulse, the chief of the criminal gang in the cell tossed Andrei a pair of wornout *valenki,* or felt boots.

Andrei had no notion whether anyone in the outer world was aware of what had happened to him. He had been permitted to send one postcard, and hoping in some way to protect Rosa, sent it not to her, but to her cousin Galya who was living in Moscow. But were such postcards actually dispatched? No one knew. Sometimes they were, other times not. And he had received no mail, no package, no indication that anyone knew of his plight.

He was in a dismal state of mind and failing in physical stamina when he found himself back once more in Lubyanka, back once more for questioning by his first interrogator, Mikhail Mikhailovich Kharlamov, paler than ever, more dour than ever, pouncing more fiercely on every response, more given than ever to endless silences while Andrei stood immobile before him, sometimes for three hours without a question as Kharlamov busied himself with endless work, reading *papka* after *papka* and sometimes writing during the entire time of Andrei's interrogation period, not directing a single word to him.

One night after Andrei had stood without moving and without a word or a question for three hours, Kharlamov spoke. "You know your buddy Vanya has confessed all. I have his confession here. Would you like to read it?" He motioned Andrei to approach his desk and handed him a long sheet of foolscap covered with writing on both sides. At a glance Andrei knew it was Vanya's writing and his heart fell.

"Take your time," Kharlamov said. "You know your friend's handwriting? You can verify that he has written this."

As Andrei read he knew that not only was it Vanya's handwriting but he recognized his turns of phrase. What had Vanya "confessed"? To being a member of an organization which had as its purpose the overthrow of the Soviet government. To this end he—and this gave Andrei a start—had recruited Andrei Ilych Sokolov and two others, Ivan Denisovich Popkov and Fedya Osipenko. The two names were utterly unknown to Andrei. Vanya said that he had communicated by mail with Andrei concerning his plans and had hoped to recruit other members of the armed forces to assist in the furtherance of his anti-Soviet aims. There was more. References to two or three letters exchanged by Andrei and Vanya on specific dates, references to meetings with Popkov and Osipenko on specific dates. Apparently Popkov and Osipenko were members of Vanya's regiment, but at least one of them, Popkov, had recently been killed in battle. It was not clear whether Osipenko was living.

"You see, Sokolov," Kharlamov said lazily. "We've got it all there. What's the point of your resisting any longer? We know what you've done. I'll get you a chair and table. Write out your protocol and let's end this business tonight."

Andrei sighed deeply. There could be no doubt of the genuineness of Vanya's confession. He knew the handwriting. He recognized the signature. The references to letters were correct. Perhaps he should sign a confession. In fact, there was much to recommend it. He need not expose anyone. He could settle as Vanya had done for the minimum. What would it cost? Eight or ten years in the camps. He should be able to survive that. Besides, the time for amnesty had come and gone. Perhaps it would take place next January when the first meeting of the new Supreme Soviet was held. What was the good of resisting further? In the end they would bend him or break him just the same.

"Give me a pen and paper," he said huskily to Kharlamov. Magically, the pen was in his hand. A table and chair had appeared. Paper was before him.

"Just take your time," said Kharlamov. "Put it all down, the more fully the better."

This Andrei understood. Detail. That was what was wanted, to make it look good. And he also understood something else. Whatever he wrote now would not be sufficient. There would have to be additions, corrections, more details. This was the way the interrogator showed his skill.

He wrote slowly and with many circumlocutions. He drew out his sentences. He filled both sides of a long piece of paper—as much as Vanya had done. But he said nothing Vanya had not already said and, in fact, he left out several details. He made no mention of Popkov and Osipenko. What could he say about them? He had never heard the names before.

At length he turned it over to Kharlamov, who scanned it swiftly.

"You *swolich*! You bastard!" the white-faced man shouted, rising from his desk and striking Andrei across the face. "Do you think you can get by with this cheap piece of fiction? Where is the reference to Major Anderson? Where are the names of your co-conspirators? For this kind of paper I should put you in the isolator. Permanently."

Kharlamov crumpled the paper and threw it into the waste basket. He put a fresh sheet before Anderi. "Here. Write the truth this time."

Andrei painfully wrote his story again. He added a flourish here. A touch there. He mentioned Popkov but not Osipenko. He again omitted the famous "Major Anderson." This earned him another slap

on the face and he was sent back to his cell, this time a single cell so
small that he could not lie down and he was not permitted to sit down.
He finally fell asleep propping himself against the wall.

The next night the procedure was the same. Kharlamov started
out quietly and ended in a mad fury. Andrei gradually fleshed out
his story. He admitted Osipenko. But he stood his ground on Major
Anderson.

On the third night the comedy ended. It was, Andrei thought, a
victory of sorts. He did not admit Major Anderson. But he did admit
listening to BBC and being "affected" by "BBC diversionary propaganda," whatever that might mean. This version did not satisfy
Kharlamov, but he, too, seemed to be tired of the long game. He
accepted the confession and put another paper before Andrei. This
was a "non-disclosure" oath, that Andrei would never disclose any
details of the proceedings against him under penalty of execution.

Kharlamov permitted himself the luxury of offering a cigarette to
Andrei and a glass of tea. To his shame—and the memory still burned
twenty-five years later—Andrei accepted both cigarette and tea.

"You see," said Kharlamov relaxing and putting his head back,
"how simple it all is. Had you had a grain of common sense you would
have done this the first evening. Think what expenses it would have
saved the state. And it would have gone much easier for you, too. Now,
you've done nothing but blacken your record from that day to this."

Then Andrei was sent to a new and different cell, where he had
five cellmates. Each, Andrei quickly discovered, was in his situation.
They had "confessed." What their punishment was to be they did
not yet know. All were gloomy except for one youngster of seventeen,
a machinist in a tool plant near Moscow. He had been arrested for
stealing copper and selling it on the black market. "Of course I did,"
the youngster said indignantly. "Who didn't? How the hell were we
supposed to eat?" For some reason, he had been picked up and had
been charged not with theft but with anti-state activity. When he was
advised of his sentence he found that he had drawn seven years. "So
what," he said with an angry grin. "I'll find a machine shop out there."
[He meant Siberia.] "It shouldn't be any harder to nab a bit of copper
there than it is here in Moscow." Andrei got nine years. He had hoped
to get five. He had feared he would get fifteen.

Two days later, he was once again in the Lubyanka reception room.
Once again he collected his dwindling stock of possessions. Once
again he was led into the courtyard. Once more he stood for a moment
looking at the gigantic gates before he was hustled into a van, this one
somewhat larger than those in which he was accustomed to being transported around Moscow. With twenty or twenty-five other prisoners he
climbed into a large truck with paneled sides and roof and began the
bumpy trip through the Moscow streets. As the minutes passed, Andrei
knew that their destination was not Lefortovo. He had learned those

turns and the timing. Presently he also knew it was not Butyrka. Where could they be going? The journey continued. Soon they were no longer bumping over pavement. They were on a dirt road, a poor dirt road, apparently somewhere in the Moscow suburbs. It was a dusty road, and the dust filtered through the floorboards and the sagging sides of the truck and filled the nostrils of the riders.

Presently the truck halted. There was the sound of the unlocking of a gate. The van proceeded a short distance and again halted. The prisoners jumped down from the truck and Andrei found himself within the inner compound of a construction site.

This was Construction Site 345. For three years it was to be Andrei's life. He was to live there, work there, suffer there, think there, and be educated in his special way of life. As he stooped to pick up his suitcase and his roll of clothing he looked up toward the sky. All around him were high wooden walls, a continuous fence and, atop that, four strands of rusty barbed wire. At two corners of the fence were watchtowers on wooden trestles, and he could see in each a Tommy gunner, his gun in his hands pointing toward the just unloaded prisoners. Beside the watchtowers were great searchlights, and at one end of the courtyard Andrei saw a guard with two large police dogs on a leash.

"Sit down," a guard barked. "Hands between your legs."

The prisoners squatted on the dusty ground and waited for the next order.

Chapter **38**

IT was almost eleven o'clock, Andropov noted by the hands of his Strela watch. He kept the watch two minutes fast—no more, no less. He did not wish to be early for an appointment. Nor did he care to be late, although in dealing with other ministers he consciously permitted his fellow officials to wait for him on a sliding scale of time values— seven or eight minutes for a Minister of Foreign Trade, Heavy Industry or Railroads; no delay whatever for the Minister of Defense or the Minister of Foreign Affairs; no delay for his fellow Politburo members, except that alternate members might occasionally be delayed two or three minutes, just as a reminder.

So . . . another hour, and the Politburo would assemble in the Kremlin, and he still had quite a few loose ends to tidy up. Grechko and the military, for example. This point had become much more important with Andropov's discovery of Suslov's intense interest in the affair. In a sense, this tipped Suslov's hand. He must be playing for big stakes, and his only potential partner had to be the military.

Andropov described his own relations with the military as arm's-length relations. This had nothing to do with Andropov in person. Not only had he tried to cultivate friendship among the senior marshals, he had made every effort at collaboration with them. He had ended the historic rivalry—insofar as bureaucratic rivalry can ever be ended—between the KGB and KRG, the military security and intelligence agency. He understood and sympathized with the deep hostility which so much of the military still had toward the Security service— rooted, of course, in Stalin's use of Security to purge the Army before World War II and his postwar use of Beria as a watchdog over the generals. So deep were the wounds left by that savage tragedy that even today Andropov could clearly feel the military holding back from any intimate association with him.

Thus, Andropov was under no illusion as to the attitude of the military toward himself or toward the KGB. It was hostile, aloof, suspicious.

If Suslov should be able to make a case against the Security services, he was certain of a sympathetic hearing from the military. But there was not enough in the Sokolov affair, any way Andropov examined it, to provide the major case that would be needed to persuade the military to transfer confidence from Brezhnev to Suslov or Suslov's nominee.

Andropov knew without asking what would be Marshal Grechko's reaction to the author Sokolov and the question of, once and for all, getting him off the world's front pages. Grechko had been critical enough of the state's failure to act decisively, and he hardly needed any encouragement from Suslov to take the strongest kind of position. Grechko was a no-nonsense man when it came to intellectuals and the arts.

But was Grechko prepared to follow through with further steps? Was he ready to put the blame on Andropov for mishandling the Sokolov affair? Had he, Andropov, in fact put himself in a no-win position in which he would be blamed first for permitting the situation to fester to the danger point and then for taking action that stirred a storm of international criticism and weakened the Soviet's prestige abroad?

That, Andropov had to admit to himself, was entirely possible, and it would be consistent with Grechko's character. Andropov actually despised Grechko, although he had employed the utmost care to disguise his feelings.

*   *   *

The military—and Grechko understood this perfectly—had called the turn in each of the great crises since Stalin's death. Led by Zhukov, they had stood by Stalin's civilian successors and removed and shot Beria and the other police chiefs in 1953. Zhukov had stood by Khrushchev in 1957 at the time of the anti-Party crisis and thus enabled him to defeat Malenkov, Molotov and all the others. Malinovsky and Grechko, acting for the military, had stood by Khrushchev's enemies in 1964 and enabled Brezhnev and company to oust him. And when, in due course, Brezhnev was ultimately removed, Andropov had no doubt that the military would play the critical role by giving their support to Brezhnev's successor.

The question Andropov had to decide was whether the military had now arrived at the point of withdrawing support of Brezhnev and swinging behind another candidate.

He was aware that the military was unhappy over Brezhnev's policy of détente. They had no more love for stabilization of relations with the United States than the Pentagon had for stabilization of relations with the Soviet Union. The Soviet military, like their American counterpart, well understood that détente meant less spending on armaments and, in the end, that meant a reduced role and influence for the military, as well as a loss of personnel and perquisites. The marshals had never gotten over Khrushchev's savage reductions in the officers' roster and the forced retirements carried out in the late fifties. In fact, it had been precisely these policies of Khrushchev that led the military to put their weight behind the coup to oust him and bring Brezhnev into power. And, to be sure, the big industrial chiefs had made common cause with the military. They had a mutual stake in seeing that the budget remained profoundly tilted toward military spending and toward its sturdy partner, steel and heavy machinery.

It was this alliance of marshals and industrial chiefs which was the target of Suslov's machinations. The industrial chiefs were among Brezhnev's strongest supporters but if they could be persuaded that Brezhnev's policies threatened their well-being, that détente in fact meant more consumer goods, a diversion of funds away from armaments and steel and into housing and agriculture—well, that could provide a very strong political motivation.

If Grechko were making his own judgment, thought Andropov, a swing away from Brezhnev might be entirely possible. Grechko was a pretentious, puffy little man, who had always thought of himself as a greater commander than the heroes of World War II—Zhukov, Konev, Malinovsky, Rokossovsky and the rest. He had enjoyed his role in moving against Khrushchev and in acting as a "partner" of Brezhnev's (although in fact, Brezhnev was far too clever to permit a military man to be his real partner). Grechko would enjoy once again playing the role of kingmaker, but he no longer spoke only for himself. Actually, he was of an aging generation. The new technological generals were knocking at his door already—the missile men, the nuclear men, the supersonic men, the new armored-forces men, and the powerful new Navy chiefs.

Would they support what, actually, was a coup d'état? Not yet, Andropov firmly concluded. He knew the new generals, although not well. They simply regarded him as a part of the scenery, a part of a system long since outmoded. But they were not quite ready yet, he believed, for a big change. If this part of Andropov's logic was correct, the Suslov move would fail—unless . . .

Unless two things. Unless Brezhnev badly misplayed his cards— and he had seldom been guilty of that—or Andropov misplayed his. And if either of those things happened—well, the situation would be ad hoc, free-wheeling. Anything could happen. While the Politburo was made up of the world's most cautious poker players, they were also the best poker players in the world; once a weakness had been exposed, they were quick as lightning to take advantage of it.

Thus, actually, Andropov thought, the greatest danger, if his analysis was right, was that he himself might fall victim, either sacrificed by Brezhnev because it was politically expedient or because, in his rather convoluted handling of the Sokolov matter, Andropov had simply lost touch with the political realities as seen by his comrades on the Politburo.

The situation was every bit as dangerous for him as he had originally suspected, and the Suslov call, while giving him the advantage of advance intelligence and an ability to divine the nature of the game, also put him on notice that play-and-win was not going to be an easy matter. He would need all the cards he could hold and as much game-planning as he could devise. And, a bit of luck. That never hurt.

In a situation as difficult as the one he now faced, he concluded, he must analyze the position of each Politburo man, although he well knew that there were several who carried no real weight, representing, in fact, mere pocket votes to the account of Brezhnev or Suslov.

*   *   *

The buzzer on Andropov's desk sounded, and his secretary entered with a small sheaf of yellowed documents.

"Ah, yes," Andropov said." Thank you so much. Those are the колокола—yes, the copies of Herzen's *Bell*."

"Indeed, they are, Comrade Andropov," the secretary said. She was an intelligent-looking woman in her mid-thirties, wearing horn-rimmed glasses, her hair in a bun, a dark-blue cloth suit with a white shirtwaist and plain, rather well-made, clearly non-Russian oxfords.

She put the faded magazines on his desk. "You'll be interested to notice the notation on the magazines," she said.

Andropov picked one up. It bore the inscription in careful steel penmanship: "Okhrana. Secret. No. 3346. St. Petersburg, June 20, 1851." He smiled. "We have excellent archives." The fact that he, the Soviet chief of Security services, should now be making use of a document intercepted more than a hundred years ago and dispatched to the archives of the Czar's secret police, the Okhrana, tickled his fancy.

He was looking, he saw, at a copy of Herzen's *Bell*, published in London, the issue for June 1851. Prompt work, he thought, on the part of the Czar's police agents. He looked at the cover. Yes, as he had supposed. There was Herzen's motto: **Звенѣть, колокола!** Ring out the Bell!"

He hurriedly glanced at the other copies of *The Bell*. Yes, of course. Each bore Herzen's slogan. He smiled again to himself. There was no doubt that he would have at least one hole card when the discussion of Sokolov began.

Now if he could only put himself in possession of a few more. First, perhaps, he should run through the remaining Politburo men. It would not take him long. He knew their positions so well. Gromyko, for example . . .

Chapter 39

THEY were pouring concrete for the floors of the new hydroelectric energy institute. It was November in Moscow and the temperature was either ten below zero or twenty below zero depending on whether you were sheltered from the wind. Great canvas baffles had been put up along the sides of the building, since the windows had not yet been installed, and salamanders were pouring forth an oily smoke every twenty or thirty feet to keep the temperature high enough so that they could continue to lay the floors.

Andrei was no longer hauling the concrete in yoked pails over his shoulders as he had had to do at the start of his assignment. He had been promoted to the job of laying cement, and he was busily tamping it down when the accident happened. One of the prisoner workers, a young boy of not more than seventeen, was wheeling a load of concrete from the mixing slab in a wooden barrow. He was a slim lad, and was weakened, as they all were, by the thin gruel that was their ration, except for an occasional salt herring and very poor black bread. As the boy wheeled his concrete past one of the salamanders the barrow swerved and overturned the fire, spreading oily flames over the wooden fretwork. Instantly the flames leaped up into the staging of the building.

Andrei saw what had happened. So did the other workers and the two Tommy gunners who were guarding the detail. One guard ran for the fire signal. The other grabbed the youngster and dealt him a dazzling blow on the temple with the butt of his Tommy gun. The boy fell to the floor unconscious. No one did anything about the fire, but in a few seconds other guards appeared. One dragged the unfortunate youth away. The others shouted to the prisoners to attack the fire. But the prisoners had little to attack it with—no hoses, no axes, no fire-fighting equipment. Two threw buckets of water from the concrete mixing platform. Several hit at the base of the fire with their shovels.

Andrei did nothing. There was nothing he could do. He had, moreover, noticed that the fire in the fretwork was already dying out because it had reached a gap in the construction and was not able to spread to the remainder of the building. It was ten minutes before a fire-fighting company reached the site. By that time there was little to do except to quench the dying embers. The fire had, however, disorganized the construction site and the prisoners were returned to their barracks—simple frame shacks, heated by small iron stoves, that kept the temperature of the rooms barely above freezing.

The youngster whose exhaustion had caused the fire was, the prisoners quickly discovered, confined to a punishment cell—a wooden hut about the size and shape of a telephone booth, unheated, too small for a man to lie down, with nothing to sit on. Confinement to the puishment cell in subzero weather was almost equivalent to the death penalty. Unless a man could keep himself in movement—and how long could he do that?—he was bound to freeze to death. The youngster did not survive the night. This the barracks knew because two prisoners were compelled to carry his frozen body to the dump truck in the morning.

* * *

Construction Site No. 345 lay close to one of the principal *chaussées* leading from Moscow to the Vnukovo airfield only a few miles away. The prisoners could orient themselves by the planes flying overhead, and as the floors of the building rose up, they could see out over the environs of the city.

Andrei knew precisely where his world was located—on a large open stretch of ground, almost like the steppe, close to the Moscow city line, not too far from the bluffs overlooking the Moscow River, known as Sparrow Hills in Lenin's day but now, since his death, called Lenin Hills. The site was surrounded by a high wooden fence, dotted with wooden watchtowers, and no prisoner was permitted to approach within twenty feet of the wall. If a prisoner crossed into the "zone," the guards opened fire automatically, as they had one afternoon when the wind snatched a letter from the hands of one of the older prisoners and without thinking, the man, a rather heavily built Ukrainian, lunged after the precious paper. He happened to be standing close to the invisible line of the zone. He took a step or two across the line and was bending over to pick up the bit of paper when a single shot from the nearest watchtower splintered his skull, sending bits of bone and blood in all directions. The body lay on the ground for two hours before a work party of convicts was ordered to cart it away.

* * *

Andrei had seen Rosa twice—from a distance—and for this he blessed his good fortune in being assigned to construction work in the Moscow outskirts, no matter how grueling the labor. Rosa had come to Moscow as soon as she heard from her cousin Galya of Andrei's arrest. In one of his letters Andrei mentioned a walk they had once taken in the Lenin Hills near the new construction site. "I remember you met me that day at noon on the *chaussée* wearing your lovely blue *platok* over your head. "

Rosa took the hint. Two weeks later at noon on Saturday, as he looked out from the unfinished second floor of the building he saw two young women, one of them wearing a blue kerchief over her head, slowly walking down the *chaussée* past the building site. They were so close he could see them glance toward the second floor, and risking the anger of the guards, he swiftly drew a handkerchief from his pocket and waved. Rosa, with a single motion, pulled the scarf from her head and waved back. Andrei stood entranced, eating her with his eyes. It was really too far away to see the expression on her face—but he imagined that she was smiling. Suddenly he heard the guard's voice at his shoulder: "Get along with you. What do you mean standing here daydreaming?" Andrei hastily moved on, his shoulder pails swinging, toward the cement-mixing platform. When he came back to the window the girls were gone.

On the next Saturday he caught another glimpse of her, again with a friend. This time as they approached the high board fence he saw two plainclothesmen move out of the gate and engage the women in conversation. He was unable to remain longer at the window, and the next time he had a chance to look, the girls were nowhere to be seen. Nor did they appear in the weeks that followed. Eventually, he understood what had happened from hints in a letter from Rosa. "I enjoyed so much resuming my old walks in the Lenin Hills," she wrote. "But after one or two I got the feeling that I might come down with a bad cold. So for the present I am not going to be walking that way." Obviously, the plainclothesmen had warned the girls that they would be arrested if they continued to walk in the vicinity of the construction site.

The prisoners worked a ten-hour day, starting at seven, with an hour's rest at midday, and continuing until six. On this afternoon, because of the fire, they had been returned to their icy hutment two hours before mess time. Most of them immediately crawled, fully clothed, under their thin blankets and went to sleep. Andrei did not. He lounged on his upper bunk and drew out his favorite reading matter, the precious Dal dictionary he had carried all through the war. Of his wartime library he had three volumes remaining—Dal, the collection of Yesenin's poems which Rosa had given him, and the Dante, his mother's gift. Clausewitz had been taken from him by the prison authorities. He could not imagine why, unless they thought that with the aid of Clausewitz's military strategy he would be able to break out of prison. He had argued the point stubbornly but to no avail. His contention that he had been permitted to keep Clausewitz in the Lubyanka, Butyrka and Lefortovo carried no weight. He had, however, written a formal appeal of this decision to the Ministry in line with his conviction that unless he fought for his rights, he had no grounds to complain when they were violated. So far he had had no response to his appeal.

*   *   *

Andrei had begun to "read" his dictionary while still in military service. The deeper his conviction grew that writing was his career, the stronger grew his belief that the Russian language had been perverted and cheapened, first by the freedom with which it had absorbed the technical terminology of other languages, particularly German and French, and secondly by the uninhibited infusion of acronyms and bureaucratic jargon under the Soviet regime.

The strength of Russia, he now firmly believed, lay in its deep Russianness. This was true of the Russian people, whom he saw as the real bearers of nationhood. He had argued the question vigorously and inconclusively with one of his fellow prisoners, a brilliant engineer named Rozen. Rozen was, or had been, a strong Party member. He still devoutly believed in internationalism and the antinationalist principles of the early Bolsheviks.

"There is no such thing as a national characteristic," he told Andrei as they lay on their top bunks, across a narrow aisle from each other, the air growing heavy with the scent of *makhorka* and smoke from the kerosene lamp. "This was shown conclusively by Darwin's studies. There are *social* differences among men and *environmental* differences. But the idea of *Russianness* is a contradiction of scientific Marxism."

"That's not true," Sokolov insisted. "Russianness is tangible, even decisive. It grows out of the soil, out of history, out of the folkways of the people, out of centuries of living and striving together, out of a common language, a common religion. It is physical as well as spiritual." Rozen did not respond and Andrei continued: "Russianness is integral. It includes not only the blond-haired, blue-eyed Russian physique, it is also a set of mind, a way of looking at the world that is born of centuries of dwelling on the steppe. Russians are hostile to other peoples because experience has shown them that other peoples are enemies. The Mongols, the Germans, the Balts invaded Russia to seize its patrimony. They killed the Russian men, raped the women and dragged them off to slavery."

Rozen looked at Andrei quizzically. "That doesn't sound like Lenin," he said. "That sounds like Pobyedonostsev. Or Stalin."

Andrei was furious. "That's all very well," he replied. "I understand perfectly the connection between Pobyedonostsev, the arch-reactionary ideologist of Czarism, and Stalin. But Lenin never denied the

Russianness of Russia. He attacked Russian chauvinism—Russian hatred for other nationalities. That in itself shows that he accepted the concept of nationalism."

Rozen was smoking a cigarette of *makhorka*. Now he took a short puff, carefully tapped it out and returned the butt of the cigarette to his pocket for later use. He pulled open the sleeve of his *telogreika*, his warm padded jacket, and began carefully to inspect it for lice.

"It's funny," he said. "I don't see any. I wonder if the weather is so cold that they have frozen to death. I wish we had in our camp collective an entomologist who could enlighten us on the life cycle of the body louse."

Andrei laughed. He was very fond of Rozen in spite of their fierce arguments. In fact, their arguments were one of his few joys in the camp. Rozen was a lean dark man in his early thirties. He had been a hydroelectric engineer and a leading Party worker at the Volkhov power plant, famous because it was the first to be built to carry out Lenin's well-known adage that "Communism is Socialism plus electricity."

Exactly what Lenin meant by this remark the two men had often argued. Andrei, still dedicated to Lenin, took it literally to mean that when Russia was electrified and all enterprises had been socialized, Communism would prevail. Rozen was cynical about the famous aphorism, as well as about its author. "Frankly," he said, "I think it was just a political catch phrase. What does it mean? Nothing, really. It *sounds* as though it had meaning, but it doesn't. Remember the terrible shape of the country in 1921? Devastation and ruin everywhere. Everyone starving. We had won the civil war. We had defeated the Whites and the Interventionists. But could we survive victory? That was the question. Lenin had to say something optimistic. So he did."

Privately, the more he thought about it the more Andrei thought that Rozen might be right. Rozen had found his way into the prison system because of the most common of failings. He had carried out his orders to the letter. When the Germans blockaded Leningrad in the autumn of 1941 one Nazi column drove straight for the Volkhov station. Rozen was ordered to dismantle the power plant, ship out as much of the machinery as he could and prepare to blow up the remainder. He carried out his orders, got the turbines and generators away and set explosive charges at the base of the dam and in the powerhouse. When the Nazis were driven away in December, he went back to his beloved plant and started on the difficult task of restoring the station and repairing the damage he had been ordered to inflict. It was not easy. About a year later he and several of his assistants, as well as the Party Secretary, were arrested. The charge: blowing up the power plant; cowardice and treason in the face of the enemy. The Party Secretary who had given the order was shot. Rozen was lucky enough to escape with a ten-year term. His assistants got seven years.

Out of this experience he had formulated what he called Rozen's law of Soviet bureaucracy. "If you carry out your orders faithfully, one of two things may follow: You may be decorated as a Hero of Socialist Labor or you may be shot."

He agreed with Andrei's view of Stalin as the great betrayer, but he was uncomfortable with Andrei's hero worship of Lenin. In fact, Andrei was becoming somewhat uncomfortable himself. There were questions in his mind that had not existed before he entered the prison system. He had been, he admitted to himself, shaken by his encounter with the old Socialist Revolutionary survivor. From childhood he had had a romantic attachment to the Socialist Revolutionaries. This had existed, almost dormant, alongside his hero worship of Lenin.

Andrei had idealized the Narodnovoltsi, with their dedication to terror, their assassination of Czar Alexander II and the others. And he viewed the SR's as the legitimate heirs to that romantic tradition. At the same time he felt Lenin was right in turning against terrorism. In what he now understood had been his wild romanticism in dreaming of a World War II Dekabristi that would follow in this great Russian revolutionary tradition, he had drawn on his attachment to the SR's and their predecessors. Naturally, nothing of this entered into his arguments with Rozen. He knew now that Vanya had been arrested at the same time as himself, that he was serving somewhere in the vast prison system a sentence similar to his own. He knew that both Rosa and Galya had been questioned by the secret police but apparently without consequences. So far as he knew, none of his other friends or associates had fallen into the hands of the police. This was a blessing, but he understood enough of prison life to realize that, within the narrowest circle, there was always at least one informer, keeping his ears open for some tidbit, such as a reference by Andrei to earlier talks he might have had when he was "out there," as they called the world beyond the prison gates.

Having himself passed through the Gates of Hell, Andrei was determined to drag no others with him. And although he took no pride in having put his signature to the confession of his complicity in what he privately admitted were not entirely groundless charges, nonetheless he did give himself a good mark for not having brought any others down.

His argument with Rozen went on lazily. Neither of them wanted to finish it before they heard the stroke of a hammer on an iron bar that summoned them to mess. The heat of the prisoners' bodies had gradually lifted the temperature in the hutment by a few degrees. It was not entirely uncomfortable, stretched out on the upper bunk. The day had been unusual. It was most uncommon to have any excitement within the camp, and the fire had provided that. It was even stimulating. And being dismissed early, two hours early, was something that

had not happened since Andrei had entered the work site. Two hours
out of the cold. Two hours resting on your side instead of standing
humped over a tamp pounding down the concrete. Two hours when
your hands were not blue and freezing. Two hours when the wind was
not tunneling under your *telogreika*. Well, it was almost a holiday.

*   *   *

Andrei looked about the barracks. His neighbor underneath him, a
machinist who had been charged with sabotaging his machine when
the boring mechanism broke because of a defective part, was lying in
his bunk smoking a goat's leg and looking at the pictures in *Ogonek*,
one of the few magazines that found their way into the camp, although mutilated by the deletion of some articles or pictures. One
never knew whether the censor had simply cut out a picture to pin on
the wall or eliminated something he thought might have a subversive
effect on the prisoners.

Across the aisle, under Rozen, old man Naumov lay flat on his
back, fast asleep, his mouth open, snoring lightly. Andrei doubted
that Naumov would make it through the winter. He was in his late
fifties, a former bureaucrat of some kind. It was as hard to believe he
had ever done anything negative in his life as it was that he had ever
done anything positive.

In the next tier, two men, each square-jawed and hardy in appearance, each a former Army captain and both arrested immediately
on their escape (with great bravery) from behind the German lines,
were sitting silently, their eyes glued to a small chessboard that one of
them had made of cardboard. The pieces were a miscellaneous collection of small objects—a red-headed match was a king, a white-headed
one a queen, the rooks were buttons, the knights were pebbles, the
bishops wedges of bread, the pawns dried beans.

Beyond them a towheaded youngster of eighteen or nineteen
named Sasha was scribbling with a stub of pencil. He was, Andrei knew,
virtually illiterate, and most of the time the pencil was in his mouth,
where he sucked it, apparently hoping that this would impart some
skill to his spelling. Soon, Andrei knew, Sasha would come wandering
up to him, handing over his pencil and the postcard and ask him to
finish it for him. It would be either a request to his mother to send
him food or a crudely lascivious card to one of his girls—Sonya or
Valya or Natashenka, or Marusiya, the list of names seemed unending—
assuring her how much he missed her and suggesting the specific
things he missed most. Sasha had been arrested for a genuine crime—
robbery. He had grabbed an old woman's *sumka*, or shopping bag,
running off with her purse, which contained a couple of hundred
rubles, her ration card and a loaf of bread. He talked freely about his
past, and made no secret of the fact that he was guilty of the theft and
that he had committed a score of similar offenses without being caught.

For this reason everyone in the barracks, Andrei included, kept a close eye on him lest he steal something from their small stock of personal possessions.

On the bunk beneath Sasha lay another *blatnoy*, or genuine criminal, as distinguished from "politicals" like Andrei and Rozen. This man was a murderer. He spoke little, holding himself aloof, but everyone knew he had a knife hidden away, kept their distance from him and quite freely gave him the tributes of tobacco and meat from food parcels which he demanded. He had lost an eye in some past fight—"The other guy gouged it out," Sasha reported breathlessly, "but he cut off the fellow's balls before killing him." The murderer was a Caucasian of some kind, dark, swarthy; he was coughing his way to death from tuberculosis and each morning Andrei expected to see him stiffened in his bunk. He seldom went to the construction site. No one paid heed to this. The guards steered as clear of him as the prisoners. Only Sasha claimed his confidence.

Farther on, Andrei saw the wiry figure of Sergei Morozov sitting on his bunk, carefully sewing a patch on his trousers. He sat cross-legged like a genuine tailor, in his long underwear topped by his padded coat and hat. Morozov was probably the most interesting man in the barracks. He had been arrested before the war, the only one in the group whose imprisonment went back that far. He had been in the State Planning Commission and was arrested as a Right-Oppositionist —a Bukharinite. And, in fact, he actually was a Bukharinite. He had, of course, committed no crime, but at one time he was close to Bukharin, one of the hundreds of young protégés attracted to the brilliant colleague of Lenin and Stalin. Morozov was a stocky man whose camp diet was supplemented by ample food parcels from his wife, who had, of course, divorced him in order to keep her very good job in the Finance Commissariat.

Andrei loved to talk with Morozov because, through Morozov's eyes, he got a picture of the Russia in which he grew up. Morozov had been deeply involved in the first and subsequent five-year plans; he had participated in all the debates which revolved around electrification, around the Kuzbas development and the rest.

Andrei's discussion with Rozen now died away. Rozen was reading for the twentieth time Stalin's *Short Course History of the Party*. He insisted it was the most revealing book of the age, that he never went through it without making yet another discovery of Stalin's megalomania, his manipulation of history, and, Rozen insisted, the inadvertent evidence Stalin gave of his corruption of Communism.

Andrei wished he had his uncle's watch. He would have liked to know how much time there was left until six o'clock and the iron clangor, which meant supper. Thus far, he had managed to preserve the watch by depositing it with his possessions in the reception lockbox, but he could not help wondering when the box was opened—as it would be when he needed something from it—whether the watch would still be there. The custodians, of course, held the keys.

How long he might remain in camp Andrei did not know. The dream of an amnesty still echoed in all prisoners' minds. Maybe May first. Maybe November seventh. Who could say? Meantime, he must prepare himself in every way to turn his pen into the sword of knowledge. Well, that was a contrived way of thinking, he said to himself. What he meant was that when he emerged from camp he must be a fully prepared writer; prepared in technique, prepared in purpose, and in thesis, with the schedule of his writing stretching out ahead. He would be losing several years in imprisonment, but those years would not really be lost. Every day, every hour, every minute he was observing Russian life. He was learning, as Professor Derzhavin had said, the essence of Russia. And Dal would teach him how to write in Russian words that had not lost the pungency of dough rising in the tile oven, of the earth new-turned by the plow, of the milky smell of the breasts of a Russian woman, of the poetry of the white Russian birch, the strength of a great Russian pine.

He lay back and found his place in Dal, but as he did so he heard the iron clang of the blow on the steel bar. Mess time. He slipped swiftly from his bunk, clutching his tin bowl and spoon. It did not do to be last in line. Last in line got the dregs of the dregs. First in line got the best of the dregs.

Chapter 40

IN the end it was mathematics that saved his life, Andrei concluded in later years. It had saved him first when he managed to get transferred from the horse transport company into artillery officers' training. He realized the truth of this when he learned of the fate of the transport company. It had been overrun in the German breakthrough into the Caucasus in the summer of 1942, surrounded and taken prisoner. What had happened to the men? Andrei did not know specifically, but he knew enough of what happened to Red Army men who became German prisoners to guess. Some probably were pressed into service immediately as drovers, some sent back in the miserable foot columns of prisoners of war. They probably did not survive to see Rostov. Some may have simply been shot out of hand. But more likely they were doomed to a lingering fate, worked to death, fed even worse slop than he was getting on the construction site. And if some chanced to survive all this—and here he thought of Prohar Ivanovich as an example—if they survived all this and won liberation from the prisoner camps at the end of the war, well, then, today they existed like Andrei, behind high fences and barbed wire, sent straight from Hitler's camps to Stalin's. So that, he thought, would have been his fate if mathematics had not enabled him to become an artillerist.

Once he had fallen into the prison system it was mathematics that must save him again. It had not taken Andrei long to perceive that if he had to serve his full nine years the odds on survival were not good.

He was young enough and his body was strong enough to endure the labor, at least the kind of labor he was carrying on at this construction task. It was heavy work, but he could feel his muscles filling out, his shoulders getting stronger, his biceps lifting the loads more easily, his back broadening. He could take nine years of this labor and probably benefit by it—except for the atrophy of his mind. As for the cold, this, too, was supportable so long as his body was strong and healthy. The exposure was dangerous for older prisoners who caught pneumonia and influenza and quickly died off.

It would be different if he were sent to Siberia and compelled to fell timber at forty and fifty degrees below zero. He had heard enough about conditions in the East to realize how fortunate he was to be in the Moscow area. He could even stand the bullying of the guards and, he hoped, the dangerous practices of the *blatnoy*, the criminal prisoners who spared nothing in their harassment of the politicals. He had lost his boots and a few other articles of clothing to them. He paid a tribute of his cigarettes and meat to the *blatnoy*, but he could survive that. What was really dangerous was the constant shortage of food. The ration was not sufficient to support even a bedridden invalid, let alone a robust adult engaged in the heaviest kind of labor in conditions of wind and cold. The packages Rosa sent him made the difference between life and death. He had lost, in his first year in prison, about fifteen pounds. This was supportable, but he was hungry all the time, as were all the prisoners. Those who did not receive parcels lost strength, and, within a few months, turned into borderline cases, barely able to fulfill their duties, receiving more than the customary number of blows from the guards, not strong enough to fight their way to the head of the queues at mess time, each day getting less food, until finally they collapsed and died.

The greatest hazard, Andrei calculated, was being compelled to engage in heavy physical labor on so inadequate a diet. The remedy, the only possible safeguard, in fact, was to get a job that did not expose one to the elements. A clerical job, a hospital job, or, best of all, a job in the kitchen with access to food (this was the exclusive prerogative of the *blatnoy*—not a chance for a "political" like himself to break in there). But he could be a bookkeeper, or a storekeeper or clerk. Most of these jobs went through graft. If you could slip a few hundred rubles, or, better yet, a few kilos of bacon fat to one of the lower administrative personnel, you might find yourself in an office job where the temperature was always bearable, where you did not have to queue for rations (there was a separate line for such trusted prisoners) and where you might get other perquisites—more frequent visits of your wife, days off, easy access to the hospital—all of which could spell the difference between life and death.

Andrei hadn't a chance of scraping together the money and goods needed to pay a bribe for such a job. The only thing he could do was call attention to his mathematical abilities.

He laid his campaign carefully. He began to write to Rosa about mathematics. He recalled his university work and the high marks he received. He reminded her how he had been pulled out of an ordinary transport company and sent to artillery school because he was so good at figures. And, finally, he pressed her to send him some new mathematical textbooks. This was calculated to draw attention of the camp authorities to his skills. His letters, like all prisoners' letters, had to be read by the commandant. The mathematics texts, if Rosa sent them, would have to be approved by the commandant. Only an idiot would fail to recognize that he had on the camp rolls a first-class mathematician.

Andrei's campaign bore no fruit. Most of the winter he was kept at pouring cement and tamping it down, and when this was finished he worked as a carpenter, setting in window and door frames. Andrei found that he enjoyed carpentry, even in the cold that numbed his hands, so that again and again he smashed the hammer on his fingers instead of the nail. But gradually he improved and by the time the spring sun began to warm up the icy building he thought of himself as quite skilled.

*   *   *

Spring brought his first visit with Rosa. Again and again they had petitioned without result. Suddenly one Sunday morning, the guard summoned Andrei after the usual breakfast gruel. He was led to the reception office. There he was ordered to draw his civilian clothes from his old suitcase in the locker and escorted with a dozen other men to the baths. The water was actually hot, and each prisoner was given a sliver of hard yellow soap. Then a barber shaved off their rough beards. They dressed in their civilian clothes and were bundled into a transport van. Nothing was said as to the reason for this, but Andrei knew it almost certainly meant a meeting with relatives. The van bumped out of the construction yard, and Andrei could feel the turn onto the *chaussée*, still potholed by winter ice and spring thaw. Then the wheels hit the Moscow pavements. After half an hour the van slowed. There was the creaky sound of gates being unlocked, and a moment later the prisoner found themselves in the Butyrka courtyard.

They were led to the reception room, made to wait a while and then harangued by a prison attendant. They were, indeed, going to meet their relatives. The visit would last half an hour. No messages were to be passed. No articles were to be passed. There was to be no talk about where they worked or what they did. They would be seated across a wooden table from the relative. No physical contact was permitted. No kisses. No embraces. A guard would be at hand at all times. Any violation would be punished—severely.

Andrei's heart began to beat rapidly. It had been three years since he had seen Rosa. Had he changed beyond recognition? What would he feel when he saw her? What would she feel? Suddenly he felt ashamed of his shaven head. He did not feel like a prisoner. At least he hoped he did not. But he *looked* like one. He ran his hand over his face. It was rough and nicked by the heavy-handed prison barber. But there was not time to think of these things. He was being pushed forward by the guard into a room that was cut in half by a long table, the table itself being divided into tiny compartments by partitions that reached up four or five feet. Each prisoner, as his name was called, was directed to a particular seat. Once there he could not see to either side but only straight ahead to where his wife, mother or sweetheart would be seated. Behind the prisoners and behind the visitors patrolled guards who kept everyone in view.

Andrei's name was called and he took his place at the wooden bench. No one was sitting opposite him. Apparently all of the prisoners were first seated, then the visitors. In a moment he heard the visitors begin to be ushered to their seats across the barrier. Then suddenly Rosa appeared and slipped into her chair, her mouth fixed firmly, her eyes just a little frightened, her face set, Andrei could sense, for any kind of surprise, and in that fleeting moment before they spoke he wondered if his face, too, was not a kind of a mask, on guard against shock.

"Dearest," he said, involuntarily reaching his hand out to hers, which lay on the table covered with heavy wool mittens. But he pulled it back just before touching hers, the warning of the guards still sounding in his ears.

Rosa smiled gently. "We aren't allowed to touch, I'm afraid."

Hearing her voice, Andrei felt tears swelling in his eyes and hastily said, "You look very well."

She did too, he thought. She had probably had to wait outside in the drafty entrance hall, he imagined, and the cold had brought a flush of pink to her cheeks. She looked thinner than he had ever seen her.

"Oh, Andrei," she said. "I wish I did look well. But you look strong and healthy. I've been so worried."

"That's because of all the nice parcels you've been sending me, darling," he replied. "Without them I would be just a ghost or a grease spot. But I'm afraid you have been starving yourself to feed me."

"Not true at all, Andrushka," she said firmly. (Actually, it *was* true. It took every ruble she and her mother could scrape together to send Andrei the small packages of sugar and lard and cigarettes.)

"I think it is true, *dorogoya*," Andrei said. "I can see you aren't getting enough to eat, but I'm glad you have a good warm coat."

"Oh, I'm just fine, Andrushka. It's just that I miss you so much."

Actually, she did not have a good warm coat. The sheepskin *shuba* she wore to visit Andrei was her cousin's. She had sold her own to buy food and now was wearing a very old coat of her mother's. In fact, they had to trade off because between them they had only one coat warm enough for Moscow's zero temperatures.

"Are you still at the same work?" Rosa asked.

"Yes, Rosa dear. And I'm getting quite good at it. Still, I'd rather be working with figures. Have you managed to get those mathematics books I asked for?"

She had; she had left them at the reception desk just before coming to see him. He should have them in a few days—if the commandant didn't find something subversive about calculus.

"You never know about that," Andrei said wryly. "You remember Czar Nicholas the First was afraid that sheet music from Germany might contain coded messages to the revolutionaries. The authorities wouldn't let Bach and Beethoven into the country."

"Well," Rosa said, "I guess there's a lesson for us in that."

Andrei smiled nostalgically at the familiar words. "You still find lessons for us out of thin air," he said. "How is your mother?"

She was well, Rosa said. So was her cousin Galya. She herself was working at a small clerical job. (Actually, she had no job but had been promised one.) But she was thinking of enrolling in the university. She wanted to get her aspirant's degree in history.

"We have to think about the future," she said. "When you come out you will be writing. Maybe it will take a little time to get established. If I have my aspirant's degree we will be able to live on my salary."

Andrei approved of that. He was working even now, he told her. Time was not sliding through his fingers. He did not say he was "writing now." The guard might have heard and reported it. If there was one thing the prison authorities worried about, it was "writing." It must, he thought, be a tradition handed down unbroken from Czarist days. Nothing so alarmed Russian authorities as the written word. He realized that his mind was wandering away from Rosa. She was looking at him now with that quizzical expression he knew so well, as though she could read his very thoughts.

"You haven't changed, my darling," he said.

"Nor you," she quickly replied. Too quickly, Andrei noted. So— he had changed, and she had difficulty in concealing the thought.

"Well, darling," he said. "That's not true. I have changed. I am thinner and harder and tougher, less soft and easy. I know you can see that. But that is the only way to survive these years."

Suddenly the guard said: "Time's up! Get moving. Hurry up there."

There was a sound of chairs scraping, of sobbing. Andrei quickly leaned across the table, kissed Rosa on the lips and stepped back so swiftly that the guard did not see him. Or perhaps, he thought later, the guard did not complain because it was over so quickly and because there was still in him some tiny spark of humanity that refused to be brutalized. Rosa blushed and tears flowed from her eyes. "Oh, Andrei, when will I see you again?" she cried.

Andrei formed the words on his lips as he turned from Rosa, the guard prodding him along: "*Skora*, Rosa, *skora—skora byudet*—soon, Rosa, soon, soon it will be."

He moved along in what became a line of prisoners. The men shuffled slowly, their feet lagging, their heads down as though they already were back in their prison garb, mustered out for the morning's work on the construction site. They did not look at each other. Each held within himself his own impression of his meeting. Each wanted to be alone with it. Andrei let his tongue run lightly over his lips. He felt there the warmth of Rosa's lips, warm, soft, velvet, just as they had always been. A feeling ran through his veins, and just for a moment he felt alive again, alive with Rosa in his arms and his body feeling hers, the softness of her skin, the warmth of her breasts, the excitement of her thighs. He let the feeling rush over him, and then, almost with a physical gesture, putting his feet down more strongly on the cold stone of the prison courtyard, drove it out of his mind and out of his body. He could not let such emotions sweep him. He could not bear it. He must remain strong, stern, immune to such tenderness. Otherwise he could not survive.

Andrei clambered into the van, still burning from the meeting, but more than anything else he felt a wave of nostalgia. Rosa's words: "There is a lesson in that"—how many times he had heard her say it and always with a kind of sweet tartness, a wisdom that went beyond the words. But he must not think of this either. To survive he must look ahead, defying ice, hunger, exhaustion, and pit the strength of his body and his determination and his wits against the forces aligned against him.

He sat silently in the van. Deliberately he compelled his mind and his emotions to leave Rosa and focus on the present. The mathematics question. It was good that two books were now at the reception desk. They would be carefully scrutinized—page by page—by the commandant, who would scan the pages for hidden messages, tiny dots or pinpricks beside letters or words, testing an occasional page for secret writing, quite possibly simply tearing out a few pages at random just to scramble any coded message that might have escaped him.

But those mathematical works should have some impact on the commandant's mind in another way. Somewhere in the vast prison system Andrei knew there would be coded into his dossier proficiency in mathematics.

*   *   *

They were back now at the construction site. The men rose heavily and stepped down from the van with fatigue and resignation. Andrei thought they could already feel the fetters around their minds, if not their bodies. They went into the reception room and turned in their clothes. Andrei managed to look into his box for one second. His uncle's watch, by some miracle, was still there. He quickly thrust it down into a pocket of his civilian jacket in the box so that at least it would not so obviously catch the eye of some seeker after the paltry wealth of the prisoners.

In half an hour the men were back at the barracks. Since it was Sunday, most of them lounged in the hut, although a handful stood outside in the thin April sunshine. The courtyard around the barracks was muddy. In fact, the whole site was rapidly turning into a mire.

Andrei threw himself on his bunk. Across from him Rozen was lying with a book on his chest. He had fallen asleep while reading. It was, Andrei saw, Gorky's *Mat'* (Mother)—not one of his favorite authors or favorite works. Not Rozen's either, he knew. But anything was better than nothing. He lay down and deliberately turned his head to the wall. He did not want to sleep, nor did he want to talk. He wanted to think, to analyze his meeting with Rosa. What had he learned? That she was thin and worn. Obviously, she was having difficulty feeding herself and her mother while sending parcels to him. Should he suggest that she cut down on the parcels? It was a touchy question. Finally he decided against this. The plain fact was that over the long run he could not live without the parcels, and difficult as it was for her, he knew that Rosa would be able to survive. He would not ask her to stop sending things to him until or unless he got a job in the office where he would have access to sufficient food and some protection against exhausting labor and exposure.

It was not a gallant decision on his part, but there was no room in the camp system for gallantry. Survival was all that counted. He was glad Rosa was still dressed warmly and comfortably. He could only approve her entering Moscow University. She was a brilliant woman and he could not see her spending her days as a clerk or teaching in secondary school. She had said she was working as a clerk. Did this mean she had not been able to get a teaching job because of being married to a political prisoner? Or was it just that she could not get a teaching job in Moscow and did not want to leave because he was here? From what he knew—and the prisoners often enough talked about the situation of their wives and families—he understood that the stain of a prisoner-relation was enough to bar wives and relatives from many jobs. Would this bar her also from admission to Moscow University? If she was admitted as an aspirant, she would receive a monthly government stipend or scholarship as well as free tuition. But in her *anketa* she would have to fill out the blank under "Single, Married, Divorced." So she would write, "Married." Then she would have to answer the next questions: Husband's name, birthplace, origins, age, *occupation*. Would not that automatically bar her? Andrei thought a long time. No doubt of it. He had never heard of a prisoner's relative being permitted freely to enter the university or receive a stipend. He remembered his own childhood in Rostov and the black mark his mother always found against herself when she tried to get a job. No. There was no way for Rosa to enter the university while married to a political prisoner.

There was only one solution. Rosa must divorce him. It need not have any real meaning. They could continue to see each other, to write. She could send him parcels.

And when he got out of camp they could remarry. Actually, the problem would never have arisen if Rosa had not insisted on their registering their marriage in Rostov. Had they simply followed the ordinary practice—or at least the practice of so many young men and women of his generation—and "declared" their marriage to their friends but not bothered to visit the registry office, Rosa would have no problem with the *anketa*.

Andrei thought a bit more, then reached to a wooden shelf he had built above his bed. He took down a letter form, his nibbed pen and ink bottle. Carefully he began to write in a small hand:

My beloved Rosa,

I cannot tell you how wonderful it was to see you again, to hear you talk, to sit beside you and look into your eyes. I will live now for a long time in the glow of our meeting. I say this so that you will not misunderstand what I am about to write. I believe the time has come for you to get a divorce. I think this is the only practical solution of the problems that lie ahead. I strongly support your plan to enter the University and study for an aspirancy. As you know I will still be here for some years to come, even in the best of circumstances. A divorce will free you from many burdens. You know that I love you and will love you always. When once again we are together, we can decide what is best to do. But for now and in the immediate future I am certain that a divorce is essential for your well-being. Do consider this seriously and practically. My endless love to you and my greetings to your mother.

Your Andrei

He read it over carefully, folded the letter, wrote out the address and thrust it into his jacket pocket. Then he looked across the aisle. Rozen was awake now and looking at him questioningly.

"Well," said Andrei, "what shall we argue about today?"

Chapter 41

THE crisis began in the most trivial way. Andrei was still trying to recover his Clausewitz. When six months had passed without reply, he wrote another letter to the Ministry demanding an answer to his earlier inquiry and requesting to know on what grounds the book was being withheld from him. He pointed out that he had been permitted to keep his Clausewitz in the other prisons in which he had been held, all except the Construction Site No. 345.

"It is not," he explained to Rozen, "that I particularly want the Clausewitz. I've read it all the way through several times. I know Clausewitz's philosophy and I know many of his aphorisms by heart."

"Then," said Rozen, "why bother about the book?"

"Simple enough," Andrei said. "I've two grounds for complaint. First, the book is my private property and I can see no statute under which I can be barred from owning it. Second, the other prisons made no complaint against its remaining in my possession and, moreover, the commandant has cited no authority or reason for forbidding the book."

All of this he put down in his precise handwriting and turned in the letter for forwarding to the Ministry. Two or three days later, sometime after he had eaten the usual swill for supper and gone back with his comrades to barracks, he was summoned by a prison guard who moved him along with unusual roughness. To his surprise he was shoved into the office of the commandant himself, a heavyset man in his fifties with a head as close-shaven as those of the prisoners and a fist as big as a ham. This fist he now brought down on his desk with a resounding bang.

"So, Sokolov," the commandant said, "so—you want to challenge the authority of the camp administration. So you want your Clausewitz back? Very well. You can have it back and I hope you enjoy it in your new location because here and now you are being transferred out of Construction Site No. 345. For obstructionism. For failure to cooperate with the camp administration. For a negative attitude. And maybe for a few other characteristics as well." The commandant called in the

guard. "Take the prisoner away," he commanded, then turning to
Andrei, added: "I just wanted the pleasure of telling this to you myself.
From now on you are rat meat."

The guard led Andrei back to the reception office. He was given
his possessions from his locker, Clausewitz among them. Another guard
had already collected Andrei's small store of belongings from the
barracks. Without further ado he was shoved into a van that rumbled
off into the Moscow night. It was full summer, a hot night. The van
was stifling, but as it passed through the Moscow streets Andrei could
hear music—youngsters were on the streets singing to *bayans* and
guitars. He could imagine the sight. How long it had been since the
evening of his first *gulyanye* in Rostov! The van bumped along, and
Andrei wondered as always what his destination might be. What had
so aroused the anger of the commandant? He must have received a
reprimand or, more likely, been overruled on Clausewitz. Nothing else
could have done it. He had been overruled, and for punishment
Andrei was going to be transferred to another site.

Presently the van halted. There was the familiar fumbling with
locks, and Andrei emerged once again into the Butyrka courtyard.

*   *   *

And so began a further descent into hell. For two months Andrei
was kept in a common cell with common criminals in Butyrka. And
here he came closer to death than he had ever been.

One of the *blatnoy*, a young tough with a gap where his front teeth
had been, demanded that Andrei turn over his money. The demand,
Andrei admitted to himself later, was due to his own carelessness. He
had 141 rubles which he had sewn into the seam of his trousers. He
never touched the money when anyone was in sight. But one evening
when he thought himself unobserved he had slit the seam and extracted
ten rubles. What he had not noticed was the young tough lying in the
darkness of his bunk a few feet away.

As Andrei started to sew up the seam the tough confronted him
and demanded the money. Andrei, dangerous though he knew this
to be, refused. The tough pulled out a knife and started to pick his
fingernails with it, running over in words what he proposed to do to
Andrei. First, he would slice off an ear. Then he would make Andrei
eat the ear. Then he would cut off the tip of his nose. Then he would
proceed down his anatomy cutting off bits and pieces. Finally, he would
sever Andrei's penis and testicles and jam them down his throat.

Andrei knew that he was in deadly peril. This young street fighter
was quite capable of doing exactly as he said. But Andrei could not
imagine bowing to the demand. He had one asset the tough did not
know about. Alarmed by the violence of the *blatnoy* who terrorized
the common cell, Andrei had quietly and secretly filed down the end

of his aluminum spoon on a brick until he now possessed a deadly dagger. It was not as good a weapon as the tough's, but the tough did not know he possessed it. Moreover, Andrei was strong and muscular. He had the advantage of height. The tough was a runt of a man. Slipping his spoon-dagger into the sleeve of his shirt, Andrei moved off his bunk into the aisle. The drowsing prisoners were awake now, alive to the drama taking place before them. In fact, they were scrambling over bunks to occupy ringside seats. Andrei stood quietly, his left hand outstretched, his right with the concealed dagger still at his side.

The tough moved forward slowly and deliberately, his knife blade gleaming. As he advanced, Andrei had a premonition. The man, smaller than he, would thrust upward in a blow toward his abdomen. A split second before the tough made his move, Andrei flung himself forward, his dagger outstretched and jammed it through the *blatnoy's* forearm, literally pinning the arm against the framework of the bunk. The tough screamed in pain, but Andrei did not withdraw the dagger until his opponent's hand unclenched and dropped the knife. With a quick grab Andrei seized the knife and yanked his dagger from the criminal's arm. It was spurting with blood.

Now, Andrei knew, looking at the cruel and greedy faces around him, came the critical moment—the moment when the other *blatnoy*, the other members of the blood brotherhood of the underworld, might throw themselves upon him. He saw the preparatory moves, the swaying of bodies, held back a bit, it was true, by the savage demonstration he had given of his ability to protect himself and by the gleaming weapons now poised in both his hands.

The situation hung at razor's edge when a huge man, six feet tall and built like a circus wrestler, pushed himself forward. He was Stenka the Wolf, king of the *blatnoy*, the tribal chief of the criminals in this cell. He put up his hand in a careless gesture that was designed to restrain his pack.

"*Minutochku*," he said. "Just a minute. Now, young fellow, give me your money."

Still holding the tough's knife forward like a bayonet, Andrei with a single movement, ripped open his lining and flicked the money from its hiding place onto the floor between himself and Stenka. The huge man reached down with an easy grace. He unrolled the fold of money, peeled off twenty rubles, pocketed them, and with a gesture that was almost a bow, handed the remainder back to Andrei.

"Fair enough," said Stenka. Then turning to the young tough: "Next time figure out what you're doing before you do it."

The tough, his face twisted with pain, vanished into the shadows. The remainder of the prisoners moved back to their bunks. Andrei climbed up to his and found himself shaking so violently he could hardly keep the bunk from quivering. He stared down at his hands. The blood still dripped from his dagger, dripping over the roll of rubles that was clutched in the same hand. The other hand held the deadly Finnish knife he had taken from the tough.

Why had Stenka the Wolf come to his aid? Possibly because Andrei had proved his mastery over the tough, or, perhaps a week before, Andrei had penciled out a card for Stenka, a note ostensibly to Stenka's "wife" but more likely to one of his criminal lieutenants in the Moscow slums. Perhaps it was merely the whim of a powerful chief, designed to show that he alone was the arbiter of life and death in this cell.

Whatever the cause, that gesture of Stenka the Wolf was like magic. From that day no *blatnoy* bothered Andrei. He received his food parcels intact. No one stole from him. No one demanded his cigarettes or sugar. And each day Stenka greeted him formally, bidding him good morning and good evening. As time went forward Andrei found that the magic of Stenka's word even followed him to some other camps and more than once in transit camps he found that his name was known.

Stenka the Wolf made only one direct comment on the event. "Next time," he said, "don't bother with the arm. Aim for here." And he thumped his chest over the heart.

*   *   *

Once again, on a cold autumn night, Andrei was on the move. Once again he had withdrawn his tawdry possessions from the locker room and was loaded into a large van together with twenty other prisoners. They rumbled through the Moscow streets, but the destination was one Andrei had not known before, a railroad siding some distance from any station on a line with which he was not familiar. There was a long wait at the siding. Each prisoner sat on the ground with his hands in front of him. Around them was a circle of armed guards. Finally a freight train drew up to which had been attached a prison car—a Stolypin wagon, as they were still called in the name of Czar Nicholas II's Premier, in whose pre-World I regime they were introduced. The prisoners were jammed into the car, each herded into a wooden bunk, without bedding, in a tier of four that reached from floor to ceiling. The windows were barred and hung with heavy wooden shutters. There was no ventilation and the car was lighted only by two or three dim electric bulbs. A bucket in the corner served for a toilet.

The train started its slow progress. Andrei slept little. The train stopped and started, stopped and started, apparently on a local freight service. He could hear men shouting and sometimes what they were saying, but he could not make out in what direction the train was moving. When morning arrived, the prisoners tried to move about a bit, but this was almost impossible in the narrow aisle. There was no sign of breakfast. At midmorning the train rumbled to a halt, and the guards ordered the prisoners to get their luggage. Another long wait. The car was being uncoupled. Finally the train could be heard chuffing away.

Another wait. Then the door opened, the prisoners emerged one by one, and were promptly ordered to sit on the ground with their hands in front of them. Andrei stole a quick glance around. They were on a deserted freight platform in a small goods yard. No one was in sight. They went through the ritual of the calling of the roll. To no one's surprise, all were present. There was another long wait. Finally, a small blue van appeared, and the men were crowded into it. There was room neither to sit or to stand. They were simply tumbled in, and the van set off over a bumpy road. They had not gone far when the van halted, the door was unlocked, and once again they found themselves within a prison courtyard. But which prison? The building looked old and dilapidated. The entrance hall was musty and cold. Could it be? Andrei held his breath. Yes, it was the infamous Vladimir isolator, reserved for the most dangerous prisoners, those of great importance to the state. It was one of the seven hells of the camp system, renowned for the cruelty of its guards, the cramped dimensions of the damp cells, the severity of its discipline, the scantiness of its rations. Andrei repressed a shudder. This would not be easy to survive. Why had he landed here? What could the construction commandant have reported to send him into this hell?

The prisoners waited quietly as, one by one, they were processed. First they delivered their luggage to the reception room. Andrei had a sudden qualm. He still had the Finnish knife he had taken from the young tough at Butyrka. He had managed to fashion a double bottom to a small wooden box in which he had kept odds and ends. The knife was inside the double bottom, carefully packed in grass which he had picked in the Butyrka exercise yard so that it would not move or rattle. The hiding place had passed the Butyrka inspections. Would it pass at Vladimir? And he still had his dagger-handled spoon. He had managed to pass inspection with this, also, by the simple device of whittling a wooden handle for the spoon in which he imbedded the daggerlike point. He shrugged. There was nothing to do now. The attendant perfunctorily checked the list of his possessions in his suitcase, then stuck his hand into the suitcase and gave a toss which disarranged the contents. The knife, at least, had passed inspection.

The prisoners were pushed on through. Their clothing was taken from them and thrown into a boiler to kill any lice. The men were put under a hot shower, but given no soap. Their clothing was handed back steaming hot and wet. They put it on. What else was there to do? Andrei's books were closely examined. He left his Clausewitz and Dante in his suitcase. He hadn't the taste for either. His mathematics books were passed. His pens, his ink, his paper, his bowl, his spoon. Now he was herded into the prison proper. The cells remained as they had been when the prison was a monastery—narrow and stone-walled.

Andrei was thrust into one occupied by six other men. There were bunks for only four, and two slept on the floor under the bunks. Andrei was given a corner next to the slop bucket.

Twice a day, morning and evening, the guard came around with a bucket of swill—sometimes called gruel, sometimes soup, though both tasted much the same. The gruel was made of buckwheat grits, but it was as thin as coffee. Sometimes there was a little sunflower oil in it, usually not. Sometimes there was a hunk of black bread in the morning, eight hundred grams for seven men, about a slice per man. They broke it into bits and used it to mop up the gruel. The ration was not quite as much as at Leningrad in the worst days of the siege, Andrei thought to himself. In the evening the meal was cabbage soup. Occasionally there was a moldy potato in it, rarely an onion, never meat. Sometimes, there was salt fish with the cabbage soup, but it was almost too salty to eat. Andrei took his piece but kept it, chewing only a small morsel at a time, a little piece one day, a little piece the next. That way, he thought, he got what nourishment there was without badly dehydrating his body with excess salt.

The work at Vladimir was of the simplest kind. One detail was assigned daily to break up stones into small pieces that could be used for road surfaces. Another detail hauled the stone to the prison from a quarry within the prison compound. The stone was placed on wooden sledges—whether it was summer or winter, whether there was snow or not and hauled by hand, four men to a sledge. Why the stones were not loaded onto trucks or even carts no one knew. The prison was heated— insofar as it was heated at all—by wood-fired stoves and a wood-burning central heating apparatus. All of this wood was cut and hauled by the prisoners.

Andrei could figure out no reason for these primitive occupations except one. When the Vladimir isolator had been a monastery the monks must have engaged in precisely these activities as their way of doing penance before God. The system had been continued unchanged so that modern atheistic Russia might do similar penance before its own god.

*   *   *

It was at Vladimir that Andrei received Rosa's letter—the one in which she told him that she would, after all, get a divorce. Her first response to Andrei's proposal had been hysterical. She would not think of it. Anything rather than divorce. If she could not get along without a divorce, it was better to end everything. But Andrei had written back a letter that he had calculated carefully. It was soothing, calm, loving and persistent. "You must be practical, dearest," he wrote. "These are practical times. Divorce will be better not only for you but for me. I will be relieved of worrying so much about you. You will be better able to help me. It is nothing but a formality anyway, just a scribbling on a piece of paper. So long as we love each other, what difference does the scribbling make?" Rosa was not moved by this letter. But her response was less hysterical, more calm. "Divorce just isn't necessary," she wrote. "You must put it out of your mind."

Now she had agreed, not only agreed, but, as she said in the letter, actually given the necessary notice to the registry office. All that remained was for the court to act. The court was slow, but approval should be forthcoming within the next two or three months. In fact, Andrei thought, looking at the letter and calculating the date, she might already have gotten the divorce, for the letter had been delayed more than usual in reaching him because of his transfer from the construction site to Butyrka and then to Vladimir.

Now it was November and the letter had been written in July. While Andrei had written Rosa proposing the divorce, while he had steadfastly urged it, the thought that she had actually taken the action, that Rosa was no longer his wife, struck him like a blow. For almost the first time since the fateful day when he was arrested, he had a queasy feeling in his stomach. For just one moment the thought passed through his mind—Perhaps this won't come out all right after all, perhaps I won't get out and return to Rosa. But the next moment he swept that thought away. It was nonsense. Nothing had changed. It was just as he had said: a simple piece of paper. And now Rosa would be able to enter the university and study for her aspirancy. She would be protected from the evil effects of having a prisoner-husband. Yes, it was for the best.

*   *   *

At Vladimir Andrei had another brush with death. Of course there was an informer in his cell—a blond, busy little man named Gusev. He was once a petty official, if his story was to be believed, a provincial man from the Urals—Sverdlovsk, perhaps. Everyone knew he was an informer. He openly listened to conversations and often called the prison guard and said he had to go to the "clinic." And each time, he was promptly taken to the "clinic," although when Andrei had a stomach ache he could not even get the guard to bother to ask the clinic for an aspirin.

Exactly how it happened Andrei never did know, but once, when he returned to the cell and went to his bunk (he now had one, having moved up three places in the cell's hierarchy) he checked his possessions as always. Everything seemed to be in its place, but he had the feeling that his spoon, which he normally carried in his belt, had been tampered with. Nothing happened immediately, but the next day the cell was inspected, as it was periodically, by the guards. They went over the room carefully, then the prisoners were lined up and personally inspected. A guard pulled Andrei's spoon from his waist, held it in his hand briefly, then tugged at the wooden handle—out came the sharpened end. Instantly Andrei was seized and led from the cell to one of the prison chiefs. This was, Andrei knew, a serious offense. He made the best of it, insisting that he had gotten the spoon from another prisoner at Butyrka. Had never known the end came out of the wooden handle. Had never seen the sharpened end until this moment. He had the feeling that the warden, for some reason, believed him, possibly because Andrei was not the type of common criminal who customarily went around with concealed weapons. Nonetheless, the spoon was a dagger. The rule was the rule. There was a moment of hesitation by the warden, then he said gruffly, "Three days in solitary."

Solitary at Vladimir was legendary. All the prisoner's clothing was taken from him and he was thrust into a circular stone-walled pit, not much larger than he could stand in. It was located in the subcellar of the prison, and probably had been a cell in which the monks did penance for the greatest sins. There was an iron grating over the cylindrical chamber. Once every twenty-four hours a dipper of water was passed to the prisoner. No food. It was autumn. The cell was not heated. Naked as he was, Andrei wondered how he could possibly survive. Already he was shivering uncomfortably. Andrei took strong command of himself. He *would* survive. He *would* do it by sheer will power. After all, a Hindu fakir could walk on fire. Cold was no more terrible than fire. For fifteen minutes in each hour he would run in place to warm his body. He then would rest for fifteen minutes, concentrating his thoughts on his past life. He would reconstruct every single episode of his childhood, remember every detail, actually relive those days. After fifteen minutes of rest, he would move his arms for five minutes to keep them limber. He would rest for five minutes. He would breathe strongly for the next five minutes. He would rest for ten minutes, thinking of heat—and the thought would warm him. He would flex his muscles for five minutes, first his legs and then his arms. Then the same thing all over again. When he grew exhausted, he would permit himself to sleep for not more than ten minutes. He would regulate this by leaning against the wall with his elbow protruding in such a fashion that the weight of his body would create sufficient pain to rouse him. He thought of how Rakhmatev in Chernyshevsky's *What Is to Be Done* had trained his body to withstand cold and fatigue. He could do the same.

How would he keep track of time? Well, it did not need to be precise. He would know twenty-four hours had passed when the guard arrived with the dipper of water. If he lost track of time, he need only begin counting his pulse to start a new time sequence. The temperature was well above freezing. He could not freeze to death. He would suffer from exposure—badly, no doubt—but he had the physical strength to endure three days. He would hold in his bowels. Thus, he would retain heat within his body and not foul his chamber. Urination was another matter. He feared that the urine would collect on the floor of the cell and chill his feet, but he discovered there was a drain in the floor and with great care he managed to urinate without wetting himself.

*   *   *

As it turned out, Andrei did endure the three days, but barely, and not exactly as he had planned. He was able to keep to his schedule fairly well during the first twenty-four hours. He dozed off occasionally, but his twisted elbow did indeed awaken him. He was able to take the dipper from the guard's hands and drink the water down, stiff as he was at the end of the first day.

The second twenty-four hours went less well. He lost track of time and had difficulty maintaining his exercises. He was so stiff that his joints pained him. One thing surprised him. He was not as conscious of the cold during the second twenty-four hours. Whether this was because he was gradually becoming numb he could not say.

Andrei found himself remarkably able to concentrate on the details of his life. He went back to his earliest childhood and year by year came forward in time. Again he relived the event he had never known —his father's death; again he relived the train ride to Armavir, and saw once again the soldiers lugging the body of the great peasant woman out of the train and dumping it on the ground. And not only did he remember these episodes, he participated in them and recalled details he had long forgotten: the crack on the wall of their room in Rostov over which they had pasted old copies of *Pravda*; even the news headlines.

He must have sunk into a kind of trance because he felt neither cold nor hunger, nor any other physical discomfort. His mind seemed clear, and he went on reliving his early life. The remembered experiences were more vivid than reality—the colors, the words, the sensations. He was in a state of heightened consciousness. He wondered later if he had not seen the kind of visions the saints had seen. In fact, he wondered if the monks who had dwelt at Vladimir had not immured themselves in the hole for the purpose of cleansing their minds and looking into the past—or the future.

Andrei's mother came to him, not as she had been in later years, tired and hopeless, but as she had been when they still lived in Kislovodsk—young, beautiful and sad. She spoke to him, and it seemed to Andrei that her words were golden balls and that they fell like music on his ears. But what she said he was never able to remember. His state of hallucination became so intense that he was unaware of what surrounded him—he no longer noticed the slime under his feet (or the rats, which he had noticed on the first day), nor the foul mold on the walls of his cell, nor even the nauseous gases that filled the chamber.

Andrei was so unaware of his surroundings that when the guard finally came to drag him out of the pit, he complained bitterly, saying,

"What are you doing to me? Why are you taking me away?" He knew nothing as he stumbled into his cell and was picked up from the floor by his cellmates and put into his bunk. His good friend Vasily Kuznetsov, a sturdy former mining engineer, put him under blankets, and with hands as gentle as a woman's, began to massage his back, his swollen legs and his trembling arms. It was only then that he began to come to his senses, to realize how near he had been to walking through the door which Death had opened for him. It was, he told Kuznetsov later, something like the experience of a person freezing to death in a *burya*, a blizzard. The world of his vision was so complete, so real, so comfortable that he actually *was* once again a schoolboy of eleven running down the Rostov streets to see the latest bulletins in *Izvestia*.

"You don't know how tempting it was," he told Vasily. "And what an effort it was to come back to this life."

Chapter 42

"SO you see," Andrei was telling Rozen, "why I consider mathematics not only the queen of sciences but the queen of my life. Without it I would be rat meat, in the eloquent words of our former commandant."

The men were sitting on their bunks in a clean, well-heated, well-lighted dormitory, located on the fourth floor of the newly completed Hydroelectric Institute just off the *chaussée* leading to Vnukovo Airport, the very building which both men had labored to complete, the very construction site from which Andrei had been cast out into the hell of the Vladimir isolator.

Once again mathematics had indeed saved Andrei's life. He had contracted pneumonia the day he emerged from the Vladimir punishment cell. For a week he lay at the edge of death in a dirty bed in the dismal "clinic" of the prison. But the clinic was warm, he was given liquids, and soup made with meat, and a tired, thin, tall nurse of middle age had brought him tea with sugar several times a day. She felt pity for Andrei, it was clear, and her attentions enabled him to survive. Ravaged by fever, Andrei imagined he was again in the punishment cell. Again he returned to the days of his childhood.

After ten days in the clinic he was returned to his cell, pale, thin and shaky. He was too weak to work, but this did not keep the guards from turning him out into the courtyard, where he sat huddled in his *telogreika* smashing at the stones with a heavy hammer, trying vainly to meet his quota of paving material.

How this might have ended, Andrei told Rozen, he had no idea. Probably with another bout of pneumonia.

"That would have finished me off, I'm sure," he said.

But one morning, instead of being taken to the courtyard, he was escorted to the office of the prison commandant. Here an officer of the police, a uniformed colonel, was waiting to interview him. He questioned Andrei about his background in mathematics, led him through his academic record, his experience in the artillery and his current knowledge. At the end of the catechism, apparently satisfied, he turned to the prison director and said, "*Khorosho.* Okay. We'll take him."

Andrei had no idea what this meant. But two days later he was again collecting his possessions, saying farewell to his companions, particularly to his good friend Kuznetsov, whom he was never to see again. But this time there was a change in the usual routine. He was instructed to put on the remnants of his Army uniform. He was then escorted by a plainclothes officer in a jeep to the Vladimir station. Here he and the officer boarded an ordinary train, sat in ordinary seats in an ordinary coach and made the trip to Moscow.

Once again Andrei was escorted to the Lubyanka and put into a decent cell with only one other prisoner, a silent young man of about Andrei's age. Andrei did not trust his companion, and obviously his companion did not trust him. They exchanged hardly a word. The next morning he was escorted into one of the familiar blue vans and driven off. Andrei had the curious feeling that the van was on its way to Construction Site No. 345. This seemed ridiculous, but, in fact, that was exactly where he was taken. It was no longer a construction site; it was the completed Hydroelectric Institute—the building on which he and his friends had labored, now surrounded by a high wooden wall with a great brick entranceway.

Andrei was taken directly to the office of the deputy director of the Institute, Leonid Rodanov. Here he experienced one surprise after another. It turned out that the Hydroelectric Institute was an institute of the Ministry of Internal Affairs—in other words, of the police apparatus itself. It had been created because the Ministry was about to embark upon a great program of hydroelectric installations. Andrei did not learn then, but soon found out, that enormous water power and irrigation projects were being contemplated all over Siberia, on the Volga, the Kama, the Irtysh and even the Lena. These great streams and many others were to be dammed and the enterprises from start to finish would be carried out by the Ministry. Ministry engineers would design the dams and the canals. Ministry officials would direct the construction. Ministry prisoners would provide the labor. And specialist Ministry prisoners, like Andrei himself, would provide most of the technical cadre.

Andrei, the deputy director declared, had been assigned to the designing department on the basis of his background in mathematics. He would work here in this institute. He was a prisoner. Nothing had been changed. But the conditions of work were different. Some institute employees were prisoners, some were not. There was a lengthy explanation of Andrei's status and a long and deadly warning of what would happen to him if he violated any rule. At the end, the deputy director said, "Do you agree to your conditions of work?"

Andrei, his head ringing, feeling a bit dizzy, unable to make the transition so swiftly from the frigid cells of Vladimir to this comfortably heated, bureaucratic milieu, stuttered his answer, "Yes-s-s-."

*   *   *

And now Andrei was seated with Rozen. They had just finished a decent meal: a plate of good borscht with a piece of meat at the bottom; a dish of kasha; bread—not white, to be sure, but not black either; tea with sugar. Not a meal—a feast. Andrei had not had such food since his arrest in January 1945, and now the year was 1947. His stomach was full. He belched comfortably. He felt drowsy and relaxed. It was as though he had reached home after a long and stormy journey.

There were three of the old construction crew now included in the "black" personnel of the institute—four, if you counted young Sasha, the illiterate youngster for whom Andrei had once written letters.

"God knows why they kept him on," Rozen said. "Possibly as an informer. Not that he isn't perfectly useful to run errands and do chores. After all, someone has to do them."

The other prisoners were Rozen, who, like Andrei, had been selected for the design bureau, and Morozov, the Bukharinite planner, who was assigned to make economic analyses.

"Well," Rozen said, "I don't expect this is going to be an ideal scientific society, but I do think it will be better for your health than spending the nights in an upright stone coffin."

Andrei nodded. What with the warmth, the food and the quiet of the dormitory, he could hardly keep awake. He roused himself for one last remark. "One thing I did conclude in that long solitary experience at Vladimir," he said. "I decided that I must have been wrong about Lenin."

"What led you to that decision?" Rozen asked. "Did you ponder over my brilliant remarks and feel compelled to accept my iron logic?"

"No," Andrei said, grinning and sighing at the same time. "No. It was not the clarity of your thinking. It was one little fact. The Vladimir monastery became the Vladimir isolator in 1918. I don't know who all of the prisoners were at that time. I suppose no one will ever know. But I do know that some of them were Socialist Revolutionaries and some of them were Anarchists. Vladimir served as an isolator for the last six years of Lenin's life."

"I'd never heard that," Rozen said.

"Well," Andrei responded. "I'd never even heard of the Vladimir isolator until my arrest. But one of my cellmates at Vladimir was on good terms with a guard who liked to gossip. He had served at Vladimir for many years and knew its history."

The men sat silently for a while.

Andrei rose. "I can't stay awake any longer," he said, "but one thing is clear to me. It's hard to blame the whole system on Stalin if it was started by Lenin in the first years of the Revolution."

*   *   *

May Day was a holiday for the "black" workers at the Institute—just as it was for all the ordinary workers of the Soviet Union. In fact, it had to be a holiday at the Institute because the peculiar mixture of prisoner workers and free workers made it impossible for one group to work in the absence of the other. When the "white" workers left at five the prisoners had another hour at their drafting boards, but rarely did they work. They gossiped, read, occupied themselves with personal problems. The civilian workers finished at one on Saturdays. The prisoners were supposed to go on until six, but in fact they told stories and amused themselves. Sunday was completely free.

And now they had a holiday on May Day—the only prisoners in the whole vast system, Andrei thought, who celebrated the traditional holiday of the workers except, perhaps, others in similar institutions. He had been told that some of the most important scientific work in Russia was being carried on in these curious places, particularly in electronics and nuclear weaponry. In fact, he had heard that Tupelov, one of the greatest of Soviet aircraft designers, had spent many years in prison, designing planes used in World War II. Only after the start of the war was he released from prison. Ironically, this made virtually no change in his life, since the institute Tupelov headed was the identical one he had worked in as a prisoner; and even after his own sentence was lifted and he became "free," the institute was still closed because of its high security classification.

"Of course we must have a concert to celebrate May Day," Rozen had said. To this there was general agreement among the prisoners, and to Andrei's surprise the administration offered no objection. Morozov, it turned out, was a violinist, and actually had a violin packed away in the baggage room. It had followed him for ten years from one prison to another and somehow was still intact. He had never, of course, been permitted to play it. Now a request was made to Rodanov and, after much hemming and hawing, it was decreed that the violin could be taken from the baggage room for one day only. On the morning of May 2 it had to be returned.

Morozov was philosophical. "Lord knows what my playing will be like. I only hope the strings aren't broken."

Rozen offered to give Chekhov's famous dissertation on the evils of tobacco, and Andrei (shades of his ill-fated acting career!) proposed Hamlet's soliloquy. Young Sasha volunteered to sing village *chastushki*, street songs made up by the singer as he goes along. Galkin and Chaikin, very talented young engineers from Siberia who had been arrested for refusal to submit falsely exaggerated estimates of a newly discovered coal basin, agreed to dance the *gopak*, the Ukrainian national dance. Old Lev Vasilevsky, a soils specialist who had been in prison since the mid-thirties, offered to read some of Pushkin's verses.

*   *   *

May Day was warm and sunny. Early in the morning Andrei heard the sound of bands, and peering from his fourth-floor window, was able to catch sight of some of the columns assembling for the march through Red Square. He had asked Rosa to send him a volume of Shakespeare in English, together with a Russian-English dictionary, but she had not yet been able to find one; or perhaps it was too expensive. But he had run back through his *Hamlet* and found he remembered it perfectly. He also remembered Rosa's remark that there was no way in which so positive a person as himself could capture the spirit of Hamlet's indecision. Well, he would try his best. Perhaps the years had given him deeper understanding of not only his own emotions but those of others.

The program, the "concert," as it was called in Russian terms, was given in one of the workrooms. The drawing boards and desks had been pushed to one side to create a small stage. Somewhere a Soviet flag had been found to provide the conventional décor, and a lectern had been improvised.

The program began after supper. Perhaps that was what was wrong —the timing. The prisoners had all day at leisure. Andrei spent his time writing, busily reconstructing his impressions of the prison system, jotting down all that he had learned in the endless conversations about it. This, he had concluded, must be the basis of his great work on the life of Russia. Rozen spent the day reading. He had managed to get hold of a copy of Heine in German and was reading it not only for the enjoyment of the poetry but to revive his badly deteriorated German.

There was a good deal of loud talk in the dormitory during the afternoon, so much that Andrei quietly slipped away to a storeroom behind one of the laboratories and sat there writing busily until it was time for the evening meal. Had he stayed in the dormitory, he later realized, the events of the evening would not have caught him by surprise. He ate his supper hastily, hardly heeding his companions. He did notice that some continued to chatter away in tones more excited than usual, but he put it down to the holiday mood. He hurried away because he wanted to costume himself in some fashion that would suggest the melancholy prince. Finally, he decided there was little he could do. He would throw his blanket over his shoulders like a cloak. He would take a towel and wrap it around his neck for a scarf and from old Foma, the janitor, he got a piece of broomstick which he thrust through his belt to make do for the noble prince's sword.

Andrei gathered up his stage props and went down the corridor to the laboratory where the stage had been improvised. The room was already filled with the prisoner workers and, he saw that many of the nonprisoner custodial workers—the kitchen help, porters and the like

—had taken seats along the back. To his surprise, he saw the Deputy Director Rodanov in the front row. Not only Rodanov, but also one of his assistants and one of the security officers. Several guards, to be sure, were lolling along the sides of the room.

Rozen had agreed to be master of ceremonies. Andrei and the other participants assembled in a room to the rear of the improvised stage. It was in this room that Andrei had his first premonition that all was not going well. Several performers had flushed faces. When he caught the odor of alcohol, he suddenly realized the reason. Any doubt was dispelled by Sasha, the young street ruffian, who sidled up to Andrei and, with a wink, showed him a bottle of colorless liquid. "Wanna drink?" Sasha said, already slurring his words. Andrei declined. "Better keep that out of sight," he warned. Liquor was forbidden in the institute. "*Nichevo*, Never mind," Sasha said and wandered off. Looking at his companions, Andrei decided that most of them had had something to drink, even Rozen, but they were adult men and he thought they could take care of themselves. As for Sasha, he was not sure.

*   *   *

The program got under way. Rozen's introduction was graceful. The prisoners enjoyed the opportunity of celebrating the holiday that all workers throughout the world, and especially those of the Soviet Union, celebrated to honor their common toil. He even managed the customary reference to the great Stalin who had transformed the Soviet Union from its feudal backwardness and led the Fatherland to victory in the great war. Without even seeing it, Andrei was certain that a smile of self-satisfaction had come over Rodanov's jowls. The first number was the violin solo. Morozov had found his strings intact, but he said, "God knows every hour is a gamble. Let me go on first and get it over with."

He played Brahms' violin concerto. His technique was rusty, he made an occasional error of fingering, and he had found no resin for his bow. But the strings did hold out. The people in the room listened in awed silence, and at the end there was a chant of "*Bis, bis, bis.* More, more, more." Morozov smiled in pleasure. "I wish that I could play more," he finally said, tucking his violin under his arm. "But I don't dare. The strings would never take another composition." There was more cheering, and he bowed off to take a seat in the audience.

Andrei was next. He flung the blanket over his shoulder and strode onto the stage to the applause of the audience. When they quieted, he broke into his soliloquy. The audience listened in rapt pleasure, and when he finished there was an ovation. Andrei smiled, slipped off his "costume" and sat down to watch the rest of the program. Perhaps, he thought, it will not be too bad.

He could not have been more mistaken. The next number was Sasha and his *chastushki*. He accompanied himself on the mouth organ, playing a bar or two and then singing a four-line verse in the typical singsong whine of the street urchin. But the liquor was too much for him. He started with flushed face and slightly muffled voice to sing a typical *chastushka*, the lament of a village maiden for the swains who had forsaken her. His voice was not unpleasant and his style was as Russian as *kvas*. Despite a little tittering in the audience, he got through his number all right. But the art of the *chastushka* is to invent on the spot. They are impromptu verses made up of whatever odd elements the singer puts together. Now Sasha tried to make up a *chastushka* about the institute and its workers. He floundered hopelessly, finally got embarrassed, stamped his foot and shouted "Phooey!" There were scattered boos from the audience, and Andrei saw a look of pain come over Rodanov's face. But it was mild pain, the kind produced by a fleabite. Sasha fell back on another village song, this one about a village swain who had been deserted by all his maidens. He finished it in fair order, and Rozen quickly thanked him before worse damage could be done. With some muttering and bad grace, Sasha backed off the stage.

Rozen, hoping to divert attention from Sasha's fiasco, called on Galkin and Chaikin to do their *gopak*. This they accomplished with great gusto, the audience providing a chorus, clapping hands and singing the old Ukrainian song, *Sinai Platok*, Blue Kerchief. There were cheers for the dancers. Andrei saw that Rodanov was once more relaxed. Perhaps the concert would come off without disaster.

And so it might have if the applause had not been so generous for Lev Vasilevsky's recitations from Pushkin. It was quite evident to Andrei, if not to Rodanov, that the old man had consumed a substantial quantity of drink. Not only were his cheeks flaming, his eyes sparkling and his speech unusually free, but he swayed slightly as he spoke the beautiful and familiar verses from *Eugene Onegin*. He spoke with feeling, with emotion in the over-accented chant of Russian poetic discourse. There was a torrent of applause in which Rodanov joined and cries of "*Bis, bis,* more, more."

Vasilevsky bowed. Bowed again. He was smiling. The applause of the motley audience had deeply moved him. The cheering went on. He raised his hand: "*Spasibo.* Thank you. Let me close by giving you one more verse from Pushkin—his anathema on the hated Czarist regime."

The audience quieted and shifted forward in expectation. Rodanov smiled benignly. Vasilevsky began. With the first two words Andrei sank lower in his seat. Vasilevsky had not given the name of the Pushkin work which he would read. But Andrei knew it by heart. It was the poet's famous "Ode to Freedom." Pushkin called on the "fallen slaves" to arise, and addressing the Czar, declared, "Despotic villain, I despise you and your throne and with a cruel joy look forward to your destruction and the death of your children." Andrei tried to close his ears. Vasilevsky's voice rang out resoundingly.

Narrowly, shading his eyes, Andrei stole a glance at Rodanov. His face was set in a grim mask. The old man went on: "Upon your brow I read the people's curse; you are the horror of the world, the shame of nature, a reproach to God and to earth." Andrei examined the rest of the audience. They were listening now in dead silence, hardly breathing. Only the prison guards sat slumped in their places, unconscious of what was going on, unaware of the meaning of the words. He saw Foma, the janitor, silently slip out of the back of the room. Finally the reading came to an end. There was a scattering of applause that ended almost as swiftly as it began. Before Rozen could step forward and speak the accustomed words: "*Konsert zakonchilsa*—the concert is ended," Rodanov was out of his seat, and with a nod to his assistants, strode from the room, his face a storm cloud.

Vasilevsky was still bowing, apparently unaware of the effect he had created. He bowed, stepped backward and almost fell down. Rozen looked wildly around him, nodded at the audience, and then for some reason clapped his hands a few times. Andrei was inescapably reminded of the manner in which Stalin, standing on the podium, listening to the thundering ovation around him, would join after a moment in the applause himself, looking around innocently all the while as though the ovation were for someone else.

*   *   *

Retribution came swiftly. The room had hardly emptied when Lev Vasilevsky was summoned away. An hour later he stumbled back to the dormitory, his face ashen, his hands trembling, tears in his eyes.

"They're sending me away in the morning," he said helplessly. "To common labor."

He put his head in his hands and wept without restraint. Simultaneously a guard summoned Rozen. What was going to happen? Andrei asked himself. What could he do to comfort the old man? Nothing. Vasilevsky was doomed. He would not live a month in a common labor camp. Nonetheless, Andrei went to Vasilevsky's bunk and put an arm around him. "Never mind," he said. "Never mind. Who knows? It may not be so bad. Fate can take a strange turn."

He did not believe a word of it. Vasilevsky was—in the terrible words of the construction boss—rat meat. There wasn't a chance for him. Gradually the old man quieted. To Andrei's surprise, he had fallen asleep. The old man had simply had too much to drink. Who had given it to him? He looked around the room. Sasha was curled up in his bunk looking idly at the ceiling. Andrei strode over to him. "You rascal! You gave the old man the vodka. And you did him in as surely as if you put a knife in his ribs."

Sasha turned lazily to face Andrei. "So what? So I gave him something to drink. He didn't have to take it, did he? He didn't have to make a fool of himself, did he? I didn't get up on the platform and recite subversive poetry, did I?"

What was the use, Andrei thought. Berating a stupid village boy would not increase Vasilevsky's life expectation. And when all was said and done (and he admitted it was a cruel, cynical way of looking at it), Vasilevsky was serving a twenty-year term. There were ten years to go on it. How old was he? Sixty, perhaps. He was never going to see the outside of the prison system regardless of where he served. Andrei was deep in this gloomy and pessimistic thought when Rozen returned to the room. He looked worn and shaken.

"What happened?" Andrei asked.

"*Nichevo,*" Rozen said. "Nothing, really. I got an awful tongue lashing. Loss of all privileges, whatever the hell that means. Work every weekend. No mail. No packages. I guess I convinced him nothing negative was planned. Either that, or they value my precious talents more than those of poor old Vasilevsky. Oh, yes. It is going to be a stern regime for everyone now. No one is to get the idea that they can get away with anything around here just because they have the comfort and privilege of working in the institute."

Andrei sighed. "Did he mention rat meat?" he asked.

"No," Rozen said. "No rat meat this time."

Chapter 43

THE rain fell steadily over Moscow, turning the still-unsodded, untended fields around the institute into a churning reddish clay. It fell on the red painted roofs of the Kremlin and ran into the silvered gutter pipes and across the asphalt of the Kremlin streets. It rattled down on the carved gables of the dachas at Serebrinaya Bor and the dismal slums of Marina Roshcha. It fell over the whole city like a curtain, shutting people into their rooms, sweeping them off the streets. The city turned inward on itself. Even Stalin in his dacha outside the city looked at the rain pelting in his orchard, drew off his soft calfskin Georgian boots, slipped his feet into his old worn carpet slippers and dozed away the hours, a volume of his favorite nineteenth-century satirist, Saltykov (Shchedrin), open in his lap—the story of the "Town of Gloops" which he admired so much because, as he was fond of saying to himself, Russia was, after all, a nation of gloops, as he and Saltykov knew so well.

Looking out the fourth-floor dormitory window, Andrei could see nothing but gray clouds and fog. He could not even see as far as the Lenin Hills, where the big new Moscow University skyscraper was going up. Outside, it was raw, and in late August the chill of Moscow's short autumn had already begun to deepen. It was a good day to be inside, a day for thought, for laziness. As it was Sunday, there was nothing to do in the institute except to relax, to mend one's clothing, to write letters, to read, to study, to listen a bit to the radio. (One of the blessings of the institute was that they were permitted to listen to the radio, although occasionally without warning and for no good reason it was turned off.)

Andrei had been writing most of the day. In his first months he had taken great precautions to conceal the fact that he wrote anything but letters, but for the last year or so he had grown rather careless, or, perhaps merely conditioned to institute life. There were many things the prisoners did that really were violations of standard prison regime, and there were enough stool pigeons so that all these things were known to the authorities. What Andrei did was to make certain that nothing he wrote was ever left lying about where one of the stool pigeons— Sasha for example, or perhaps Galkin, one of the *gopak*-dancing engineers—could read it. No one was quite sure that Galkin was a stool pigeon, but suspicion was enough to make one take precautions.

Andrei wrote as always on the thinnest cigarette paper in his tiny precise hand, which grew tinier and more precise with each passing prison year. Actually, he had managed to smuggle out one packet of the papers through Rosa during the visits they now had every few months. The institute reception room was not so sternly guarded as in their first tense meeting at Butyrka. The divorce had not, so far as Andrei could see, had any effect on their relations. Rosa was as warm and tender as ever, and, thank God, not strained and drawn as she had been in 1946. Her aspirancy had gone well. She would soon be finished, and there seemed every chance that she would work with her director of studies, the well-known historian Petrushkin, in the Department of History at the university.

In a strange way, seldom in his life had Andrei been so content. His work was interesting, even challenging. He had harnessed mathematical theory to the problems of the great construction works and found a creative satisfaction in solving them. His own purpose in life had been refined and clarified by his years in prison. He knew what he would do when he emerged. The shape of his writing had taken form in his mind, and more than that, he was actually putting his thoughts down on paper.

Andrei understood perfectly well that publishing his work was another question. Yet, even here, he had a hope. Stalin was not immortal. He, Andrei, had been naïve in expecting great changes at the end of the war. The system—Stalin himself—was far too strong to permit that. But when he died? Ah, that would be another matter. And· that moment could not be delayed indefinitely. How old was Stalin now? Almost seventy. The day he died, change would surely begin. As for himself—Andrei was incredibly lucky. He could not complain of life in the institute. Of course, the restrictions were petty and tiresome. The chiefs were stupid extortionists in their work assignments, always demanding twice as much as they expected to get. Still, was it so much better "out there"? He wondered.

Of course, "out there" was Rosa, waiting for him. He had several times offered her full freedom, had urged her, in fact, to marry again. After all, she was a full-blooded woman. The years were passing, He would not be released for six or seven years. It was not easy to urge her in this manner, but he felt it was only fair. She had rejected the idea, had even become indignant, and that, he had to admit, gave him a good feeling. It was not that he *wanted* her to marry someone else.

*   *   *

In this mood of relaxation and contemplation, Andrei wandered over to Morozov, who was sitting on his cot staring out the window where the rain fell continuously, driven against the panes by a gusty wind.

"It's a lazy day, Pavel Nikolayevich," Andrei said to Morozov.

"True, Andrei Ilych, true," Morozov replied. "Man needs a day like this now and again to catch up with his thinking, to understand where he is standing and where he has been and where he is going."

Andrei smiled. "That's what I've been doing."

"And I," Morozov said, "have been going back a long, long way in history, trying to figure out how we have arrived at where we are today."

"Tell me," Andrei said. "For many years, in fact since I was a small child, I had the feeling that something went wrong with the Revolution because of Stalin. That there was evil in him from the very earliest times—at least since the late 1920's. Even before the big purges I was convinced of this. Did you share that feeling at the time?"

"Not at all," Morozov said. "I don't think too many did. I know that Bukharin, for instance, didn't. Not that early. Certainly as we got into the 1930's he began to see that a terrible tragedy was occurring. But not earlier. I'm certain of that. After all—my friends and I, we saw a great deal of him. We were actually very close to Bukharin, especially in the early 1930's."

"How could a man like Bukharin be so mistaken?" Andrei asked. "There's no doubt of his brilliance. And he had known them all— Lenin, Trotsky, Kamenev, Zinoviev, Radek, Pyatakov—the whole lot. Lenin thought he was the most brilliant of all, didn't he?"

Morozov hesitated. "I think Lenin did, but you know he vacillated. I wouldn't say he was jealous of Bukharin, but Bukharin's brilliance put him off at times, especially when Bukharin differed with him."

"But what about Bukharin and Stalin?"

"I think Bukharin deceived himself. He knew what kind of a man Stalin was, but Bukharin was ambitious. He hoped to climb over the others and get to the top himself. He thought he could play with Stalin, play against the others and come out ahead. But he was like so many of them. He underestimated Stalin and in the end Stalin simply toyed with him. Bukharin knew he was doomed, but he went along as far as he could for the sake of his wife and children."

Andrei returned to what was really his chief concern. "You know," he said, "until a few years ago—in fact, a year or two ago—Lenin was my hero. He had done no wrong. The faults were all Stalin's. If Lenin had lived—everything would have been all right. But I can't believe that anymore. I know too much now about the system. The evils didn't begin with Stalin. They began in the earliest times. I hate to say this, but they began with Lenin."

"I agree with you, in part," Morozov said, "but, in part, I disagree. Faults there were in Lenin. No question of it. He was a remorseless opponent of those he regarded as his enemies. The Mensheviks, the SR's, the capitalist parties in prerevolutionary Russia and, of course, the Czarist regime. But there was a humanity in Lenin that never existed in Stalin."

"I don't see that humanity," Andrei said sharply. "Perhaps I used to see it. But no more. When I know that the Vladimir isolator was established in the first year of Lenin's rule; when I know that Dzerzhinsky used the same methods of force and torture against rival revolutionaries that he employed against the Whites and the open opponents of the regime—he certainly didn't do that without Lenin's sanction. And what about the lies? The censorship? The terror?"

Morozov shook his head sadly.

"I know," he said. "I know that it got started very early. But under Lenin there wasn't anything like what we see today—half the country in prisons, the police running the state, a man who can only be classified as a maniac in the Kremlin. No. You have to go back to the time of the Czar Paul or Ivan the Terrible to find some parallel to the Russia in which we live."

"How could it have gone so wrong?" Andrei asked. There was in his question not merely a simple appeal for information but the agony of an ideal distorted, a vision trampled upon, a dream dishonored. It seemed to him that he personally had been betrayed by the great Revolution; that it was his dream, his vision, his ideal that had been besmirched.

Morozov was silent for a long time. The old man gazed out the window. The rain had not ceased. Darkness was falling. The dim halo of distant lights glowed yellow in the mist.

"I suppose," Morozov said, "it is our own fault—I mean the fault of us intellectuals. Men like us made the Revolution. They had the dream. They believed it. But you cannot say they were very practical men. They had to fight too hard just to stay alive. They had to fight the Czar with the most terrible of weapons, the same as he used against them—terror, suppression, iron will, no mercy.

"And they came into power very suddenly. You know that none of them, not Lenin even, really expected the Revolution. Suddenly it was there. And they took advantage of it. They had not made it, but they would ride the whirlwind. And what a whirlwind it was! Brutal, ignorant Russia, bestial dark Russia. The peasants had been idealized by the intellectuals, but actually they were more like animals than humans. There was turbulence, a fanatic struggle, the whole world was united against Russia.

"And the revolutionaries won. They really did win against all the odds. Lenin won. How? By cruelty. By an absolutism that made the absolutism of Nicholas the Second seem like democracy. Well . . . you couldn't expect a tea party after that, now, could you? And on top of that, Lenin died, and our Georgian friend turned out to be the master of every kind of deviltry and came out on top. Is what we see today so surprising?"

To Andrei these thoughts were not entirely new, but he had never heard them so well expressed. They put into perspective the hypothesis that had gradually taken shape in his mind. What Morozov had done was to explain the *reason* for the sequence of events which Andrei had established bit by bit since entering prison.

Andrei bit his lips, then said to his friend, "There had to be a Revolution, of course, but it did not have to be led on the course Lenin selected."

"Possibly," Morozov agreed. "Possibly. But it is hard to argue with history. Lenin made the Revolution. Not Kerensky, not Chernov, not Martov, not Tsereteli, not Shulgin, not Dan. Not any of the others. There is no good arguing with history. We have to take it as it was made."

"True," Andrei said. "But we do not have to agree with it."

*　　*　　*

The New Year's package which Andrei received from Rosa was extraordinary. There was a piece of goose liver sausage. There was a small tin of beluga caviar. There was a tin of Danish butter (where in Heaven's name she could have gotten that he had no idea). There was the usual packet of sugar and three chocolate bars. And there was a new woolen sweater, quite a heavy sweater, of gray wool with a band of white at each cuff and around the neck.

Never had Andrei gotten such a package in the four years of his imprisonment. But there was no letter. He was puzzled at that and depressed that he had not seen Rosa for more than six months. He could not understand why permission for a visit had not come through. He had requested it as usual after the last visit in June. So, he presumed, had Rosa, but nothing had happened. Nor was there any indication that the regime was becoming more strict. Rozen had had a visit at the time of the November 7 holiday. So had Morozov and many others.

Andrei wrote Rosa an ecstatic letter of thanks. "I cannot tell you," he wrote, "how much I owe to you. How deep is my love! And how rare is your affection. I believe that it can survive anything. Sooner than you imagine we will be back together again. Half my term has been served—well, actually not quite half. But it is not so unusual for sentences to be remitted for good conduct. I missed you at New Year's. Always on that day I think of our first New Year's. This time it seemed so real to me, so present, not a thing of the past.

"I can't understand why we have not got permission for a meeting. It must come soon. I'm asking again about it. Meantime, be of good cheer. My New Year's was not bad—except for your absence. I spent it with my good friends," (he meant Rozen and Morozov, but he was not permitted to mention names). Andrei did not say that they had managed to get a little *samogon* through Foma the janitor—just a few glasses, really, but enough to drink the New Year in, and it went to his head very powerfully, for he had not had a drop to drink for four years. Granted that they were in prison, but it had not been a bad New Year's Eve.

The three of them now were something more than friends. They were comrades—the Three Musketeers, the others prisoners called them. The relationship was not unlike that of Dumas's heroes; certainly they were all for one and one for all—insofar as the limitations of prison made this possible. They had even talked about what they would do when they got out of the camp. They did not want to live in Moscow (and there was every probability they would not be permitted to live there anyway). Instead, they dreamed of going to one of the new Siberian cities, one that was far enough away to be out of the oppressive oversight of the Center and close enough to the forests to enjoy the simple pleasures of hunting and fishing, picking berries and mushrooms and—this was very important to Andrei—living close to the people, the real Russian people, the peasants, particularly those of Siberia, where, he was confident, the spirit of Russia still resided.

*   *   *

On February 1, 1949, Andrei was handed a letter by Foma, who had the duty of distributing mail and parcels every morning to the prisoners. He glanced at it with curiosity. It was not from Rosa, nor from her mother, nor from his old aunt Sofia who occasionally wrote him. It was from Rosa's cousin Galya, and that was a rarity. He tore it open with a sense of apprehension, heightened by the fact that he had had no letter from Rosa since before the November holiday.

His eyes leaped through the lines:

Dear Andrushka:
    For a long time I haven't written you. I wish you the very best greetings for the New Year. I am writing because Rosa asked me to because she found it so very difficult. You know you have told her many times that she must think of herself, that time is passing and that you do not wish her to waste her life just because you cannot be with her. Well, for a long time now, she has been trying to decide what is best to do and now she has finally decided that she must take your advice. In a word, she has decided to marry again. It has nothing to do with you, she says. She loves you as much as ever. But— well, I don't have to explain because she is sure that you will understand how it is. And so that is what I have to tell you, Andrushka. And I want to add something of my own. I hope that this does not hurt you too much because you know that ever since I first saw you on that New Year's Eve so long ago I have had a very special feeling for you and if my cousin had not seen you first—who knows what might have happened. This is not a very good letter

and I am sorry for it, but I just don't know how else to write. I know that Rosa is terribly sorry and that she feels very badly. Otherwise, she would have written herself.

To our meeting again!

Love, Galya

Andrei read the letter through twice. Not that he did not understand the meaning, but because he did not know what else to do. He felt like a child who has suddenly been told he must go to an orphanage for committing some sin which he did not know existed. Of course, he told himself, it was ridiculous to feel like this. He had himself urged Rosa to do this thing. It was the only sensible course. Logically, he believed this. The trouble was his emotions did not follow any logic. All he felt was that Rosa was abandoning him.

He loved Rosa, he did not want her in the arms of another man. She was his woman, he was her man. Their life together was the most precious thing in the world. But reason told him: You are not living together. You have hardly seen this woman—you have been separated not only since 1945 but since 1941, when you went to war. Years are passing. What kind of a martyr do you want to make of her?

Such questions did not ease the pain that burned inside of him. He sat with the letter spread on his lap staring out the window. He was startled to hear Rozen's voice: "What's the matter, Andrei? Are you abandoning the institute? Didn't you hear the bell?"

He looked up in surprise. He had not heard the morning bell. Somehow he managed a wry smile. "No, I guess I'll not abandon it," he said. "What else is there to do?"

"Right you are," Rozen said, deliberately ignoring Andrei's mood. "This is our life and we might as well face up to it."

Chapter 44

NATASHA—would it have happened without her? At the time Andrei blamed Natasha, put the whole fault on her. But later on, even before he was finally released from prison camp, he understood that something much deeper, something within himself, was involved.

Natasha was a peasant girl—eighteen, fair-haired, blue-eyed, snub-nosed, with the large breasts, sturdy arms and legs, and strong hips of the Russian peasant woman. She had an open manner that alternated with the kind of pseudo-shyness that was bred into generation after generation of Russian village girls. Natasha came to work in the institute as an "assistant" not long after Rosa decided to get married. Andrei's spirits were low, and his manner was withdrawn and distant. He had turned his mind away from Rosa, away from the present and had concentrated his thoughts on his own past life, trying to draw from his experience deeper understanding of the Russia that had emerged from the Revolution.

Apparently, Andrei's gloomy figure, his remoteness, the lines of pain that marked his face attracted Natasha's interest. He was, so she told him rather nervously in their first conversation, "different from the others."

"I can see that you have suffered," she said. "It is very moving."

Andrei had hardly been able to resist a grin, her cliché was so apt and so Russian. Nonetheless, he supposed, her interest flattered him. He was amused to watch her making small excuses to come to him. She was new in the workroom, her duties were not well defined. She came to him with questions as to where plans were to be filed, how to fill out various forms, all the trivia of bureaucracy. Her father, she let fall, was a lieutenant colonel of police from Tomsk, and she had been born and brought up there in one of the oldest and most traditionally Russian provincial cities.

Any fraternization between the "white" workers like Natasha and the "black" workers like Andrei was not only frowned upon, it was specifically forbidden. Violations were severely punished—strict reprimand or discharge for the civilian worker and transfer out of the institute for the prisoner worker. Outwardly no one was more ostentatious in her obedience to the rules than Natasha, but she was not a peasant girl for nothing.

There came the inevitable Saturday afternoon when the other workers had left the laboratory except for Andrei who was toiling over a complicated formula that involved the total waterflow of the Volga cascade. He was alone at his drafting table in a corner of the workroom when he became vaguely conscious of the door opening behind him. Before he could give this a thought, a pair of hands was clasped over his eyes and he heard Natasha saying in a little girl's voice, "Surprise!" He turned his head, pulled her to him and they locked in passionate embrace. The obvious happened. They made love there—on the spot without removing their clothes, Natasha half bending against one of the desks—hurried love, blind, greedy, unthinking, electric love. It was over in moments and Natasha was pulling down her skirts, putting her finger to her lips, motioning Andrei to be silent and slipping to the door to see if anyone was outside. No one was.

So it began. The opportunities for love-making were not frequent, but they were more frequent than Andrei could have dreamed of contriving. Natasha was a master of petty intrigue. She seemed to get a special delight in inventing ingenious opportunities for them to be alone. She found a broom closet used by old Foma, the porter. It was just off the workroom and was a remarkably big and airy broom closet with a window and a broken-down couch where Foma took his ease. They made love here, although Andrei was in a torment that the squeaking of the springs (and the not infrequent moans and squeals of Natasha) could be heard through the thin walls. Sometimes, she simply pressed her round bottom up against him, and they made love like animals swiftly and silently in the corner of the staircase.

Once old Foma almost caught them in the broom closet, but Natasha, with what Andrei had to admit was admirable presence, immediately began to shout: "Do keep that door open! How do you expect me to find the broom and the bucket?" She shoved the door open and charged out of the closet, broom and bucket in hand, almost bowling over poor Foma with no explanation or by-your-leave, confusing him so that he kept apologizing and tugging his battered cap as though somehow he was at fault.

*   *   *

In spite of himself Andrei grew fond of the girl, and although largely due to Natasha's wits their relations did not seem to attract the attention of the authorities, what was going on was obvious to Rozen and Morozov. Rozen was amused but Morozov was not. Unable to conceal his concern, he warned Andrei. "Sooner or later this is going to cause trouble." Andrei sought to brush the matter aside, but Morozov would have none of it. "You must know, Andrei Ilych," he said, "this girl is possessive as a witch. You're not going to get out of this easily."

But Andrei found Natasha amusing and comforting, and her warm, vigorous body exhilarated him. Later he admitted to himself that had it not been for Rosa's desertion, he might have reacted differently. But he had been morose, lonely and discouraged. Natasha roused his spirits. There was nothing artificial about her feeling for Andrei. She devoured him with her eyes, teased him with her body and was like a child in her eternal questions about his life, about his work, about his writing. Andrei found himself reading to her some of his stories, telling himself it was his first chance to learn the reaction of a simple person, a real Russian. And so, in a sense it was, although he got little from Natasha but "ah's" and "oh's." Once or twice, when he was very naturalistic in his descriptions, she held her nose and turned away. "Dis-gusting!" she said.

One of Natasha's themes was that Andrei had been imprisoned unjustly. "It's all some kind of a mistake," she said grandly. "I know because Papa often makes mistakes. He gets all mixed up. He has too much to do. All of them do in the organs. They can't possibly keep anything straight."

She was certain that if only the facts were known about Andrei's case, he would be released immediately, and then, as she said with a catlike smile, "we could really begin to live." Her idea of "really beginning to live," Andrei soon found out, was to live in a flat in one of the new Moscow apartment buildings (several had specially been put up for Security personnel just in the last two years), go to Moscow restaurants, particularly the Arogvy and the Grand Hotel, buy what she regarded as the most stylish clothes, shop at the Commission stores for jewelry and take a vacation on the Black Sea.

There could not be a life more banal than the one she yearned for, and yet, thought Andrei, who could blame an ordinary village girl whose almost illiterate but wily peasant father had suddenly shot up to the unprecedented rank of lieutenant colonel of police with all the privileges and prerogatives it brought? Natasha, he concluded, could have been much much worse. She yearned for what she did not have and what she thought her betters had. And she was romantic enough, Andrei had to confess, to think that somehow through this gloomy prisoner on whom she had set her heart she might achieve her goals. And he also had to admit, operating on her own premise and utilizing the influence of her lieutenant colonel father, it was not too wild a dream.

The trouble was that there was no part of Natasha's dream that Andrei wanted to share. He was content to enjoy her healthy body and her hero worship, but he was not willing to pay any real price for these pleasures. Early in his relationship with Natasha he had enlisted her aid in smuggling out a substantial part of his writings. He understood that if he asked her to send the materials either to Rosa or to Galya (which was what he would have preferred), he ran the risk of arousing violent jealousy. So to be on the safe side, he had her mail his writings to his old aunt Sofia. He could only hope and pray that Tetya Sofia would keep them safe until he came out. He had confided in Rozen about this. Rozen frankly thought he had taken leave of his senses. "Perhaps," Rozen said, "this is all right for now, but sooner or later it is going to mean serious trouble. If she gets angry that girl will do you in like a streak of lightning."

And, of course, Rozen was right. There came a moment when Andrei lost his temper at her incessant urging to let her father take up his case. "For the last time," he snapped, "I don't want that kind of help!"

Natasha's blue eyes smoked powder. "I suppose my papa is not good enough for you!" she shouted, regardless of the fact that old Foma was sweeping the back of the room. "He's not good enough for you. And I'm not good enough for you. Well, we'll just see who is good and who is not."

"For God's sake, Natashenka," Andrei said, suddenly realizing his danger.

"For God's sake yourself!" she said. "So—one of our prisoners has been trying to persuade one of the free workers to carry messages outside. Is that it? So—one of our prisoners is writing subversive manuscripts, yes? We'll just see who is good and who is not."

Andrei tried to take her into his arms but she shrugged him off insolently, almost casually. "I think this game has been going on long enough," she said, and deliberately exaggerating the swaying of her hips, she walked out of the room, slamming the door.

The door had hardly closed when Andrei dashed for the dormitory. It was Saturday afternoon. He might have a little time before she denounced him. He knew that she was clever enough to make up a story that would not incriminate herself, and perhaps she would even change her mind out of affection. However, he could take no chance. He found the hiding place he had made by loosing a board under his bed, took out everything there—all of the writing that he had accumulated. He hurried to the toilet, opened a window slightly and as rapidly as he could—the flimsy cigarette paper flamed like tinder—burned every scrap, crumpling the ashes in his hand and tossing them gently out the window. In a few minutes he was back at his desk in the workroom, out of breath, intensively apprehensive, but somehow resigned to what inevitably would follow.

He had been working fifteen minutes when one of the guards lazily entered the room and said, "You're wanted."

* * *

Two weeks later Andrei had once again passed through Butyrka and a common cell. The *blatnoy* were as numerous as ever, but after one pass at him a young tough sheered off, gave him the wink and said, "You remember Senka the Wolf?" Andrei did indeed remember Senka the Wolf. The tough smiled a crooked smile. "He told us about you."

Soon Andrei was on the move again. The usual harsh summons, and then Andrei found himself quickly ensconced not in a Stolypin wagon but in an ordinary freight car with barred windows and a hole in the floor for a toilet, a sealed car with forty prisoners, some men, some women and three youngsters who could not have been more than twelve years old, bound for God knows what point in Siberia.

The year was 1950. The season was late spring. It was not too hot during the day and not too cold at night. The guards were no more brutal than usual, but once, for twenty-four hours, they either forgot or were too lazy to bring any water to the locked car, paying no heed to the shouting of the prisoners nor to the banging on the doors. Two of the prisoners were dead when the car was opened up at the Novosibirsk transit point. One was a young girl who had committed suicide by thrusting a long nail up her vagina, quietly bleeding to death one night with no one aware of what was happening. The other was an old man. Until half an hour of their arrival at Novosibirsk the old man had been sitting quietly in a corner of the car, his back resting against the wall. But when the prisoners were ordered out he did not rise. The guards came to shove him along, but grunted in disgust. He had died of a heart attack. They simply threw his body out onto the ground beside that of the young girl, called the roll of the living prisoners and noted the two non-living as present.

* * *

No prison life in the world was to become better known than that at Taishet, Lager No. 303, where Andrei arrived in the summer of 1950. Life at Taishet was to win more fame than that of Dostoyevsky's prison life as told in *The House of the Dead*. It won more renown than the prison canvases of Victor Hugo or Alexandre Dumas. In every corner of the world there were schoolchildren who could draw a map of the "Zone" of Lager 303. They knew the barracks where Andrei lived, his bunk on the left side of the hall, an upper bunk near the entrance to the room. They knew the kitchen where the old peasant Zakhar had worked, and they knew of the potato peelings he smuggled to Andrei which saved his life when he was starving to death in the terrible winter of '51, when so many of the prisoners of Taishet met their end.

The forest station where Andrei was sent out to cut wood, six versts from the camp, across the muddy Svyagy River—where on one February day in 1951 six convicts in a single afternoon perished of exposure in fifty-degree-below weather—was the subject of essays by critics in Brazil and Italy. Danish economists analyzed the underlying profit-and-loss figures of the KGB timbering operation and demonstrated, conclusively, that per-board-foot the Russian convict operation was four times less efficient than the average Finnish timber cutting.

The beetle-browed subhuman skull of Timur Bolchuk, the villainous camp commandant of Taishet No. 303, was caricatured by London newspapers and satirical French journals as a symbol of the Soviet New Man.

But all of this, of course, came later, came after the astonishing success of Andrei's first book, the one which Khrushchev inexplicably (perhaps not so inexplicably, since he used it as a political bombshell against his Stalinist enemies) permitted to be published.

"I would not be so fatuous," Andrei told Rozen when they were discussing the fate of *Taishet 303* (as he called his novel), "as to tell you that in those days, shivering in my *bushlat,* my heavy parka, I thought Taishet was going to become world-famous. I didn't. But I did know this: if I survived Taishet, and you must know that this was often in doubt, I was going to bring down this prison system with my own hands. I *knew* that then. Maybe I had always known it, but I think that it was Taishet that crystallized my conviction. Taishet and, of course, Father Ivan."

Father Ivan was almost as famous as Taishet. But, as Andrei told Rozen, not quite so famous because it was simply impossible in a novel that was being published in the Soviet Union to draw a full-length portrait of an Orthodox priest. Maybe the day would come when that was possible, but certainly it had not yet arrived.

Put in the simplest terms, Andrei told Rozen, Father Ivan had changed his basic philosophy. "I don't have to tell you," he said, "that I was brought up an atheist. Almost the earliest school memory I have is marching in atheist parades, carrying those obscene figures labeled 'Priest' and shouting at the top of my young lungs, 'There is no God high up in the sky.' "

Rozen smiled. He had grown up in exactly the same way.

Andrei went on. His old aunt had taken him to be christened. This had meant nothing to him. His mother was not religious. She had often told him how she and his father made fun of their parents for their religious ways, though late in life his mother had told him almost bashfully that she had started going to church.

"I thought of religion a few times during the war," Andrei said. "You know how it was. There were times when you'd think of anything if you were in a tight spot and wondered if you were going to get out."

But at the time of his arrest he was an irreligious person, if not an atheist. The first believer whom he met in prison was the saintly

Father Feofan. Andrei was struck by his kindness, his gentleness, his transparent goodness. He had met a few Baptists at Lefortovo and he was impressed by them. They had an honesty, a straightforwardness the other prisoners did not have.

"They were not afraid to do good," Andrei said. " I could see that they were brave people. Simple, perhaps, but clean and honest. I was surprised."

He had thought of this not infrequently. The Baptists had been persecuted along with the other prisoners. They were set upon by the guards and by the *blatnoy*. But there was something remarkable about the way they handled themselves.

"You remember my telling you about the time I was put into the punishment cell at Vladimir?" he asked. "I thought a lot about priests and their faith. And I decided afterward that what had pulled me through Vladimir was faith. But it was not as strong as their faith and not as strong as the Orthodox faith."

This was what had struck him first about Father Ivan. Father Ivan worked like the rest of the prisoners at Taishet No. 303. He went out in the woods in the fifty-degree-below-zero weather. He was no more warmly dressed than anyone else. But if a prisoner fell in the snow from weakness, it was Father Ivan who was first at his side—often the only one who went to his aid. When a prisoner was sick and dying in the barracks—and some prisoners were always at death's edge—he did not shun them, did not let them die curled up in a corner of their wooden bunk. He went to them. There was little he could do, but he gave them bits from his own ration, which was no more sufficient than their own. He brought them water to drink. He sponged their faces. He spoke softly to them, and if they wished, he would say a small prayer. It was not much, Andrei said. "Perhaps it sounds like nothing. But Father Ivan was a saint in a camp of wolves. We were all wolves, set against each other. You know the terrible motto of the camps—One of us is going to die and it won't be me."

Andrei had observed Father Ivan, and as time went on he had talked with him. He was not an educated man, but a peasant who came from the black clergy—the married clergy. His father had been a village priest, and it was natural for him to follow in his father's footsteps. His father had been murdered, cut down in his black robes at the door of the village church by a band of ruffians who were conducting an "anti-religious campaign" in the 1920's. Actually, they had been simple toughs, mad with drink. Nothing was done to them for their crime. Father Ivan had seen his father murdered, and as a boy of fourteen, he had determined to follow in his father's footsteps.

"There is little I can do here in the camp," he said to Andrei. "But I help as I can. And for those who want God's faith—well, I help them to achieve it."

It was not in Father Ivan's words that Andrei found the touch of sainthood, but in his deeds and in the aura that the perfection of his faith created, surrounding him almost like a living sanctuary.

"I don't ever expect to be blessed with that kind of faith," Andrei said, "but there was something about Father Ivan that made him a better man than you or me. And it came to him from his God. Just as the Baptists gained their strength and their purity from their God. I've seen it in Lutherans as well. And in Old Believers. And I have no doubt that it is in Catholics and Jews and Moslems."

It was this, Andrei said, that he had not been able to put into *Taishet 303*. For the rest—yes, he thought he had captured the spirit of the *lager*, the corrective labor camp, the basic unit in the enormous network which had spread like a fungus all across Siberia—to the north, to the east, to the south, to Central Asia, along all the great river courses.

"You know," Andrei said suddenly, "have you ever seen a drawing of a patient who has blood poisoning? The poison spreads along the veins, from the small to the large veins and gradually all over the body and into the arteries. That's what the *lagers* have done to Russia."

"And what about you now?" Rozen asked. "Are you a believer? Do you have faith? Have you come back to the church of your ancestors?"

Andrei looked off into space and his answer did not come for a long time. Finally he spoke: "Yes, I do have faith. Perhaps it is not as strong, as all-embracing as that of my grandparents, nor as pure as that of Father Ivan. But I do have faith. And I thank Lager 303 for that. Before 303 I knew what I was going to do, what I had to do. But Father Ivan gave me the faith to do it. Russia is a hard country—in some ways a terrible country. No Russian can really face his fatherland unless he has true faith."

Chapter 45

GROMYKO . . . Andropov pondered. Possibly the best poker player of them all. New to the Politburo after years of dedicated, intelligent service in foreign affairs. Wise, cautious, unassuming. Never sticks his neck out. Not likely to get involved in cross fire between Brezhnev and Suslov. Perfect instinct for the majority (has probably never cast a losing vote in his life). Personal inclinations? Strongly involved in the détente policy. Views it as a means of low-cost enhancement of Soviet military and industrial power. Believes American technology and economic support can be obtained with a minimum price in military-diplomatic concessions. Embarrassed by the Sokolov affair because it plays into the hands of Russia's enemies in the U.S. Congress and adds to the trouble already stirred up by the Jews. Would favor any non-explosive way of defusing Sokolov. Gromyko's basic convictions, Andropov thought, probably are close to my own. On balance, he is more likely to be supportive than not—unless he sees the majority going the other way.

And actually, Andropov told himself, it did not seem that the majority would be going the other way. It did not, he told himself, look as though this was going to be a showdown unless unknown factors came into play. What was likely was the early positioning for a later showdown. And since the immediate crisis had arisen in Andropov's ministry, what was decided today would almost certainly determine Andropov's fate in the ultimate showdown later on.

Thus, he must play his cards in such a fashion that he was not trapped into a position which foredoomed his own fate.

*　　*　　*

A light showed on his console. He glanced at the buttons. It was Abramov calling. He waited a moment then lifted the receiver: "Yes, Abram Abramovich?"

"The report is negative on the broadcast check," Abramov said.

"No references to Sokolov on BBC, Voice of America—any of the foreign stations in the last week."

"Thank you," Andropov said. "Nothing yet from the Gorky Street apartment, I presume?"

"No, Yuri Vladimirovich, nothing yet," Abramov said. "The fact is that Krasin was late in showing up. But he is there now. I should hear very soon."

Andropov hung up and thoughtfully marked down another name on a small scratch sheet before him, a sheet which no one else would ever see. On it were the names:

Brezhnev

Kosygin

Suslov

Grechko

Now he added the name of Gromyko, and with an expression of distaste: Shelepin.

There were many reasons for his distaste. Shelepin had been one of his predecessors as head of State Security. He was an ambitious man, even an able man, Andropov had to admit. And he was fifteen years younger than Andropov. In fact, there had been a period in the early Khrushchev era when Shelepin was known as the "boy wonder." He had come out of the Communist Youth organization to head State Security when the common objective of the leadership was to get the service into the hands of someone who had no connection with Beria and who could be relied upon to clean up Security and not turn it again into an instrument of personal advancement.

Shelepin had been picked for the job and, Andropov had to admit, had carried out the first part of his assignment faithfully. He had gone through Security like a vacuum cleaner—helped, it had to be noted, by the special committee of the Politburo that was established to examine Security affairs. Shelepin had, indeed, cleaned out the Beria supporters. He had carried through the massive dismantlement of the labor camp structure, had overseen the release of several million prisoners, and with the aid of the Politburo committee and the Special Military Prosecutor, had assisted in the "rehabilitation" of hundreds of thousands of persons who had lost their lives, who either were executed by Stalin or perished in prison camps.

But then there was the obverse side of the coin. Shelepin was young, able, ambitious. When he moved out of Security he had managed to establish a dynasty by putting his own man, his chief aide in the youth organization, Semichastny, into his place. So by this time Shelepin was in the Politburo, in the Party Secretariat, and still had his hand in Security. A very powerful position. Too powerful, of course, for the oligarchy. The inevitable happened. His peers moved in on Shelepin, took Semichastny out and put Andropov in. They whittled away at Shelepin's position, every year dropping his functions down a notch. But Shelepin clung to his Politburo post like flypaper and he had not lost his ambitions.

What was most worrying to Andropov was the fact that a decade after Shelepin had moved out of the Security organs, he still had an influence there. Andropov shuffled people around. He retired some and fired others, but he knew that Shelepin's influence persisted. Every so often he saw Shelepin's fingerprints all over an unexpected action. He could not be certain, for example, that last night's ostentatious performance by Petrov in searching the persons of the Morgans had not actually been inspired by Shelepin. Fighting Shelepin's influence had been, for Andropov, like fighting a ghost. He thought he had cleaned out everyone in a particular department (the department of investigations, for example) and then something like this happened. It was enough to make a man paranoid.

What hand would Shelepin play in the present affair? Shelepin would be against Andropov. He always was. But he was unlikely to express such a view openly. He was against Andropov just as he was against Brezhnev, against Kosygin and probably against Suslov. He was his own man. Everyone felt it, everyone was against him, and yet he was too clever to offer a target. His most dangerous tactic, the one that was most disruptive of Politburo politics, was suddenly to come to the support of a man with whom he basically disagreed. When he did this, the whole Politburo was upset because it was difficult to determine whether Shelepin had really formed an alliance with Member X or not. In such a situation denials and disavowals were without value.

Shelepin would play the present situation in whatever manner he felt to his advantage. He was quite capable of offering most solicitous support to Brezhnev—support Brezhnev did not need and could hardly tolerate. In fact, Andropov thought, the very worst thing the man might do would be to come to Andropov's aid, to offer his advice as a former director of Security, to argue that Andropov's conduct had been perfectly sound and admirably executed. Nothing would be more embarrassing to Andropov, nor more damaging, because Shelepin would make his move in such a fashion that while seemingly supportive he would expose any weaknesses in Andropov's position. The only way to rate Shelepin, Andropov reluctantly decided, was as a wild card, a mischief-maker whose tactics were impossible to predict. The only insurance Andropov had was that Shelepin had played this game before, and some Politburo members were beginning to see what he was up to.

A yellow light flashed on Andropov's console. It was Abramov again. "May I come in, Yuri Vladimirovich? Our friend had some interesting things to report."

"Surely," Andropov replied. "Come right around."

Chapter 46

THE fact of the matter was, as Andrei told Rozen and Morozov at the first reunion of the "three musketeers," that if Stalin had not shuffled off the world's stage on March 5, 1953, he, Andrei, would finally have become that "rat meat" which the commandant of Construction Site No. 345 had so many years before predicted as his fate.

The three were sitting in the sidewalk café of the Metropol Hotel, although it was late fall and the autumn winds flapped strongly at the canvas curtains. There was hardly anyone else in the chilly place, but that they welcomed; as old campaigners they did not want people around to overhear them.

Sitting over a bottle of port, Andrei was telling his friends about his life since their separation ten years ago. "I was mustered out of Taishet 303," he said, "about six months after Stalin's death, a year ahead of completion of my sentence with the stipulation that I must reside in Siberia or Central Asia. I weighed a hundred and twenty-three pounds and was losing almost a pound a week."

Andrei had long since ceased to receive food parcels from Rosa. Occasionally he got one from her cousin Galya, and once or twice a year from his old Aunt Sofia. "I had been in and out of the infirmary at Lager No. 303 more and more often," he told his friends. "The only virtue of going to the infirmary was that this spared me a few days from the open forest, felling and hauling trees. One day away from the forest was a week added to my life—or so I calculated. I was coughing persistently, and the cough was growing worse. But I told myself it was simply due to cold, exhaustion and *makhorka* cigarettes."

He was again in the infirmary in the early days of March 1953, wasted, ill, despondent. More and more he had turned in on himself, spending his days in silent review of the mass of information on the camps, the prisons, the prisoners and the prison system which he had stored away, thanks to his remarkable powers of recall. It took him days, of course, even weeks to go through the material. But one thing gave him hope. No matter how frail his body, his mind seemed to stay crystal clear.

"I was sitting on my cot, half bent over, staring into space, concentrating on a complicated version of the execution of Marshal Tukhachevsky and his associates which I had heard in the Vladimir isolator five years earlier," he said, "when an old nurse came into the ward. She was a former prisoner and not quite as sadistic as the others. Her face had a look of blankness, a little like that of an ox that has just been struck by a sledge-hammer, and she seemed to totter on her feet."

Andrei had no love for the hag, but he could not help saying, "Is something the matter?" She looked at Andrei almost unseeing and said, "He's dead. He's dead." Andrei did not have to ask who was dead. Only one death could affect her so profoundly. "What happened?" he asked. "I don't know," she replied. "One of the guards just told the doctor. He died yesterday."

"I must admit," Andrei said to Rozen and Morozov, "that I was so weak and depressed, I hardly reacted to the news. I was hungry, too. It was almost time for supper, and even though I knew it would just be more slop, my stomach was growling."

Rozen had been sent away from the institute about a year before Stalin's death to work as an assistant engineer in a prisoner-manned copper mine east of Lake Baikal. "We didn't hear it until five days after the announcement," Rozen said. "Radio reception was difficult because of the mountains, and the papers came in very slowly."

"Well," said Morozov, "it was different at the institute. We followed the whole thing. They cut off the radio the day of the first announcement of his stroke, but everybody knew by noon. So we had been waiting breathless. I thought there was no doubt, Stalin must really be dying. Otherwise they wouldn't have announced the illness in the first place. The bosses were very nervous and even the guards began to get the jitters about the outcome."

* * *

Two weeks after Stalin's death Andrei filed a written request for a review of his conviction and sentence, but not until just before the November holiday was he released.

"I had two hundred and sixty-four rubles and ten kopeks sewn into my trouser seam," Andrei said. "The temperature was thirty below zero. I thought that my only hope of survival was to go south to Central Asia. The dry climate might put my lungs in order and I would get back my strength."

He headed for Turkmenistan via the Trans-Siberian and the Turk-Sib railroads. His strength had just been sufficient to get him to Ashkhabad. He was not permitted to live in Ashkhabad, so he went to a rather large *ayul*, the village of Kysel-Khor, only twenty-five miles away. There he found a room in a clay-and-wattle hut owned by an old woman named Praskovaya Ivanovna.

"It was not a bad room at all," Andrei said, "compared to what I was used to. In fact, it was very much like the room my mother and I lived in when we came to Rostov in the early 1920's. And Praskovaya Ivanovna turned out to be a saint."

He had not been in Kysel-Khor two weeks when he had his first hemorrhage.

"Then," Andrei told his friends, "I really thought it was all up. Praskovaya Ivanovna managed to put me on a village truck going to Ashkhabad, and I was taken to the polyclinic. I was so weak I collapsed in the waiting room. They took one look at me and clapped me into the emergency ward. I had tuberculosis. Actually, I had suspected this for the last year in the camp, but I would not admit it, and, of course, the camp doctors weren't going to diagnose anything like that because then I would have had to be taken off the labor rolls. And I didn't want to be diagnosed because if I was off the rolls I would simply starve to death."

Andrei spent three months in the special sanatorium for tuberculosis at Ashkhabad. "They were kind to me," he told his companions. "The nurses were mostly dark-eyed Turkmenian girls. They were gentle and liked to make jokes. Most of the patients were Asians, Turkmenians, Uzbeks, Kazakhs, Kirghiz and Azerbaijani. I was one of the few Russians, so I got special attention."

"I suppose," said Rozen, "that those black-eyed beauties fell in love with the handsome blond Russian."

Andrei laughed. "I wasn't very handsome. I looked as if I had been drawn through a ring—and, of course, I had. But I admit that there was one little girl who was very fond of me and I was fond of her, as well."

To the surprise of the doctors—and of Andrei—his lungs improved rapidly. After four months he was released as an outpatient. He was to return once a month for a checkup. He was not to do any work. He was to rest, eat well, get plenty of sunshine.

"It was good advice," Andrei told his friends, "and I was eager to follow it. I had no objection to rest, good eating and sunshine. The trouble was that I had no way of supporting myself and no money."

Here was where Praskovaya Ivanovna came to his rescue. Like so many Russians living in Central Asia, she, too, had come originally as an exile. That had been before the war when her husband disappeared into the camps, never to emerge. She had been permitted to settle in Turkmenistan with her son and daughter. Both were now married. The son, after serving in the Red Army, had become an architect in one of the Moscow construction bureaus.

"She just took me under her wing," Andrei said. "No one could have been kinder. She said I must not pay rent until I could earn some money, and she insisted on giving me meals. I was better cared for than in the sanatorium."

*　*　*

Andrei had begun to write a little in the sanatorium. Now he rose at six every morning and wrote on a wooden shelf which he put up for himself just outside the door of his room. He wrote four hours a day —from six to eight in the morning and from four to six in the afternoon.

Then he did a very bold thing. "First I talked it over with Praskovaya Ivanovna," he told his friends. "In those day I didn't take a step without discussing it with her. She was perhaps the wisest woman I have ever met."

Morozov smiled. "I think we know her very well," he said. "Isn't she Katerina Ivanovna in the story you read us this afternoon, *The Conscience of the Village?*"

"Of course," Andrei said. "Of course, she is. But she was wiser than I made her out to be in the story. By the time I got to the *ayul*, frankly, I had pretty well lost faith in Russian character. Taishet was so shattering. I had come to know how terror and starvation could turn anyone, myself included, into something worse than an animal. The world calls it bestiality. I would call it human degradation. Animals do not act so badly.

"Once at Taishet 303 a shipment of woman prisoners arrived unexpectedly. They were kept side by side with the men. Four strands of barbed wire separated the men from the women. The women used to line up on one side of the wire and the men on the other side. The women would lift their skirts, and the men would shuffle down their trousers and they would go at it between the wire—and many a ragged ass and a bleeding cock would be pulled away. That was bad, but it wasn't the worst. Not by any means. I'd seen myself shivering outside the kitchen door, willing to do anything, anything, mind you, for a handful of potato peelings. And worse. So bad I don't want to think about it. I was more shattered than I realized when I reached Kysel-Khor. Father Ivan had given me the spark of faith, but my spirit was almost too weak to keep it alive. Then to come upon this woman, so serene, so confident, so strong, so clear-eyed, so generous and so *wise*."

Praskovaya Ivanovna was the daughter of a typographer who worked in the great Sytin printing works in St. Petersburg before the Revolution. The typographers were the first workers in Russia to unionize, and they played a leading role in the 1905 and 1917 revolutions. Her father had known both Lenin and Trotsky, had supported them in 1917, but became disillusioned when the Bolsheviks took over the unions and suppressed the press. "Printers like my father," Praskovaya Ivanovna told Andrei, "thought of themselves as more revolutionary

than the Bolsheviks. They did not trust the Bolsheviks and the way
Lenin dealt with the Kronstadt revolution—the smashing of the revolt
of the Baltic sailors at the Kronstadt naval base—was the last straw for
my father."

"Luckily," Praskovaya Ivanovna told Andrei, "Father died in 1928,
before all the trouble began. Otherwise, he would have ended up where
the others did." By the time her father died, Praskovaya was married
to a quiet man, a bureaucrat, chief of a municipal transport bureau.
Her husband was not a political man, but he had joined the Party
because this was insisted upon if he were to head the bureau.

"It cost him his life," Praskovaya Ivanovna said simply. "In the
1930's, when everyone was arrested, they arrested him too. He hadn't
done anything. But who had? It just depended on the job you held.
If he had been content to be a simple streetcar motorman he would
have escaped."

Her husband's arrest and her own exile had not broken Praskovaya
Ivanovna. "What was I to do? Turn my face to the wall and give up?"
she asked. "Not likely. I had my two children. I went to work and saw
that they got an education."

She had lived in Ashkhabad at first. Then, after the war, with both
children married and in Moscow, she had bought the little cottage in
the *ayul* with its garden and orchard. She had a small pension. Her
son sent her a little money. She lived simply. She liked the Turkmenian
people.

"Of course, the Russian officials despise them," she said, "but they
don't know them. In fact, they despise everyone and know no one. The
only thing they respect is the boss on whom they depend for life or
death. And if he takes a tumble they spit on him too."

The Turkmenian women were shy and afraid of Russians. The
Russian men with whom they had come in contact simply wanted to
bed them, and the Russian women turned up their noses at them.

"My Turkmenian neighbors were afraid of me too," Praskovaya
Ivanovna said. "But after they found out I was just as downtrodden as
they were, then they changed."

"Really," Andrei said, "it was because if anyone in the village
needed help, Praskovaya Ivanovna was there to give it. She took care
of sick children and was always ready with a bit of food if it was needed.
She hadn't forgotten her own simple upbringing. She cooked for the
sick and ran errands for the old and the crippled. She was particularly
good with the blind."

"The blind?" asked Morozov in surprise.

"Yes," Andrei said. "There were an extraordinary number of blind
in the village. Some were victims of syphilis, which was very prevalent.
Some of glaucoma. You could see it in the children. Half of them had
pus coming from their eyes."

*   *   *

Praskovaya Ivanovna, then, had become the center of Andrei's life, and so, naturally, he consulted her before his big decision—the purchase of a typewriter. He had so much to write, he had to work rapidly. It seemed the only sensible thing, except for the money.

"We decided, Praskovaya Ivanovna and myself, that if I was going to be a writer I had better get on with it."

He had not written Rosa since getting out of Taishet 303. Now he decided to. "Actually," he said. "I didn't know where else to turn for money. I thought she could spare a thousand rubles. And if she couldn't, it was no harm done."

He got fifteen hundred rubles from Rosa, along with a Lady Bountiful letter which almost made him send the money back. "Praskovaya Ivanovna talked me out of it," he said, laughing. "She said I should just consider it a loan and repay it from the receipts of my writing. Of course, she had no notion of what I was writing or whether it was any good. But she accepted me on complete faith."

Andrei went to Ashkhabad. "The cheapest typewriter I could get was a cast-iron monstrosity," he said. "I think it must have been as old as the one my mother used when she worked in the State Bank in Rostov. It was very handsome, in perfect running order, weighed nearly a *pood* [40 pounds] and cost twenty-five hundred rubles."

There was only one thing to do. Through thick and thin, through one concentration camp after another, through the transit camps, the Stolypin wagons, the trucks and vans that had hauled him around the prison system from 1945 onwards, Andrei had managed to preserve his uncle's silver watch.

"I didn't sell it," he told his friends who knew the significance Andrei attached to the watch. "No, I didn't do that. But I pawned it for fifteen hundred rubles. That gave me a stake of five hundred. I promised myself that the first money I earned would go to Praskovaya Ivanovna. The second would retrieve my watch. And the third debt was to Rosa."

Andrei pulled out his watch. "I have it back, as you see," he laughed, "the product of my *Provincial Tales*—potboilers they really were, but they were good enough to sell to the Ashkhabad papers, and they paid my debt to Praskovaya Ivanovna—my money debt. The spiritual debt can never be repaid. And they got my watch back. And tomorrow I will repay Rosa."

Andrei raised his glass. "To our comradeship!" he proposed. They drank solemnly. "Now *tovarishchi*," Andrei said, "how about a turn in the square before we break up?"

They rose, paid the solitary waiter and left the empty café. Andrei led them to the corner and then turned up Lubyanka Hill. "It's appropriate," he said, "don't you think?"

*   *   *

They walked slowly—Morozov was not in the best of health—up the street, past the Metropol cinema, past the travel bureau and the old bookstore, along the wall of Kitai *gorod* across from Banya No. 1, the finest bathhouse in Moscow, and on up the hill. The Lubyanka frowned down at them as they made their slow progress. It was ten in the evening. The lower floors were dark, but there were lighted windows on the upper floors. "The interrogators are still busy," Rozen said.

"Perhaps they are at work on rehabilitations," Morozov suggested.

They paused beside the grandiose subway entrance and looked across the square to the great structure. The statue of Felix Dzerzhinsky rose black and forbidding in the center of the little square.

"Have you ever figured out the location of your first cell?" Rozen asked Andrei.

"Not precisely," Andrei said, "but I know a good deal about the building now. There are no cells on the side facing Dzerzhinsky Square. I suppose they wouldn't consider it proper if somehow a prisoner managed to fling himself down onto such a public place. Or maybe the screams might carry too well. This side is all offices. The big ones in the center are, of course, for the chiefs. I suppose Shelepin has the biggest one."

"It doesn't look big enough," Morozov said, "to house so many prisoners."

"Well," Andrei said, "Of course, the turnover has always been very high. Most prisoners aren't kept there very long. But the building is deceptive. If you walk around it you will see that there have been very large additions on the side streets. In fact, it is difficult from the street to understand its dimensions—which I suppose someone must have thought of."

Finally, they turned away from the Lubyanka and strolled down Nikolskaya Street. "I really wanted to tell you my plans," Andrei said as the three moved slowly down the street. "I don't know whether I will have the time or strength to complete them—but God willing, I shall."

Andrei proposed, he told his friends, to write a series of novels which would present a panorama of modern Russian life. "I'm working on the first now," he said. "It will deal with the camps and will be called *Taishet 303*. Of course, it will be about Lager 303, but more than that, it will be the story of *all* the camps and of *all* the prisoners, told through the stories of the prisoners at Taishet. The second novel will be called *Lubyanka* and it will concern itself with the higher elements of the police and the prisoners. It will tell the story of the purges of the 1930's, but the principal characters will be Marshal Tukhachevsky and the generals who were shot with him. I think I've been able to put that whole story together, largely through one of the widows.

"Well, then I will jump back in time and write a novel about my father's life, possibly two, to set the scene of Russia before the 1914 war, before the Revolution. Then I will come forward in time once again. I see possibly a dozen novels in all."

Morozov shook his head. "That is a monumental undertaking. Colossal. Something like Balzac's *Comédie Humaine*."

"Exactly," Andrei said, "but I have learned to economize my time. I write very rapidly, I assure you, on my ancient cast-iron typewriter. And who knows? I may soon be able to afford a new one."

The three had halted, and were idly glancing at a window where fishing tackle was displayed. "But that's not all," Andrei said suddenly. "And this is where I must ask you for help. I am compiling an anthology of Stalin's crimes. Well, let me say—even more than that— of the crimes against humanity committed, beginning in 1917, by the Soviet power."

"Don't you think," Rozen said, "that the process Khrushchev began with his anti-Stalin speech is going to continue? Don't you think the state itself will do much of what you propose?"

Andrei deliberated a moment. "I don't know exactly how to answer that, Lev Natanovich. The simplest thing is to say, No, I don't believe so. You notice there is a cutoff date on the crimes that are being admitted—really around 1938. Kamenev, Zinoviev, Bukharin and the others are hardly touched. And Trotsky, of course, remains the archvillain. And such things as my first cases—the Shakhty affair, the Prom Party, the Mensheviks—not a word of them. As for the SR's and the Anarchists and the others who were arrested and executed in the early days of the Revolution—silence."

"But perhaps they will gradually get around to them," Rozen persisted.

"You may be right, Lev Natanovich. You may be right," Andrei conceded. "But there is no way of being certain. Moreover, not one word has been said about the participation of the present leadership in Stalin's crimes. And I must say I have that story very well detailed."

They walked on a bit in silence, Rozen and Morozov thinking of what Andrei had told them.

"The help I want from you," Andrei finally said, "is this. I cannot conceive of this government—unless it moves much more deeply and in a more principled manner to right past wrongs—permitting this record to be published. The novels—yes. I hope that they will be able to appear. I can believe that they will. But the Black Book of the Soviet Era—no. It is the facts and only the facts which will bring about the change which must occur if Russia is to survive, and I need your help to obtain them."

Morozov took Andrei by the arm. "You've not changed, Andrei Ilych," he said. "You talk today as you did when we first met at the construction site."

"Well," Andrei said, "I'm a bit more experienced, I hope. And I'm not depending on a new Dekabristi, that's certain."

What Andrei wanted was that his two friends quietly and carefully begin to collect the same kind of information he was gathering—particularly information about the specific roles of the leadership, the leadership of the 1930's and the 1940's and that of the present.

"Because," he said, "as you know, many of them are the same persons. I think it is naïve to suppose they will honestly expose their own crimes."

"But," said Rozen, "once you have compiled the Black Book, what will you do with it? Certainly, I don't see it being published here."

"Not immediately, no," said Andrei. "I do not see immediate publication either. But I'm not thinking just of today. I'm thinking in terms of the broad course of Russian history. Perhaps it will not be published for fifty years, but if we can compile and put the information together, it will, sooner or later, as inevitably and remorselessly as a great river, sweep the evil powers out of the Kremlin."

* * *

They were now walking through the narrow archway and twisting passage and steps leading down from the Nikolskaya through the Kitai *gorod* to reemerge on the broad square, where the Metropol Hotel stood. As they came out from under the arch Andrei grabbed the arms of his comrades and pulled them into the shelter of a jutting passageway. They waited there a few moments in complete silence. No one passed. Not a footfall was to be heard. Andrei poked his head out. No one was in sight.

"No angels following us tonight," he said with a smile. "I didn't think there would be, but it's better to be safe."

They made their way around to the October Place subway station and parted. Before they parted, Rozen and Morozov clasped their hands over those of Andrei's and swore they would join him in compiling the Black Book.

"Anything I can do, I will do," Morozov said. "My health isn't very good. But I can think of no better way to spend the strength I still have left."

Chapter 47

ROSA had not wanted to meet Andrei. In fact, she would not have agreed had Galya not been so persistent, telling her that "you owe it to your conscience." Perhaps, she thought, it was her conscience that made her agree, but whatever it might be, she was not going to reopen that long-buried wound again. To her grave she would remember the day when she received the letter from Galya. It was the spring of 1945. Victory was almost at hand. She had been worried beyond endurance about Andrei. Not a word since January. She had written Lieutenant Colonel Smirnov. No answer. Could Andrei have been killed in those last fateful days? The thought was too horrible to contemplate.

And then the letter from Galya. Very cautiously phrased, but Rosa knew what it meant. Andrei had been arrested, and she knew instantly what he had been arrested for: that schoolboy nonsense about the Dekabristi. How many times had she warned him to be careful, not to express those opinions? There had even been a moment in Mineralnye Vody when she wildly thought that she would run away if he did not stop talking as he did about Mustache. Shivers ran down her spine even now as she rode the trolley bus through the Moscow streets to her rendezvous with Andrei. How could he have been so foolish, so childish? She had loved him madly with every part of her being, but from the beginning she had known that there was an adolescent streak in Andrei, a streak of mischievousness. Of nonconformity. He had to be different. He hated to be told what to think. Well, look what it had done to his life. And it had come within a hair's-breadth of destroying her own life as well.

Fortunately, when the State Security man had come to interview her, he seemed uninterested in making serious difficulties. He had asked for letters. Well, she had expected that. She gave him a handful. All she had, she told him. He didn't question this, even though he could have seen from the careful numbers that Andrei placed on each that there must have been many more. She hadn't burned the others, nor Andrei's papers, though perhaps she should have. She had left them all behind with her mother in Rostov when she raced off to Moscow after hearing of Andrei's arrest.

So she had not been implicated, but it had become impossible to carry on her studies, to go forward with her career, as the wife of a state prisoner. She hadn't wanted to divorce Andrei, certainly not at first. But as the years began to pass, it didn't seem to make sense not to. And with the divorce she had been able to get her degree, and the job at Moscow University—and her husband as well, for she had married Professor Petrushkin, the director of her studies. He was nearly twenty years older than she, had grown sons and daughters by his deceased wife. He was a kind, comfortable husband. He had become a candidate Academician during the year of their marriage and was now a full member. Their life was pleasant—an excellent apartment just across the Moskva River from the Kremlin, vacations in Yalta, a car and chauffeur, access to closed stores, an electric refrigerator, a fine automatic record player and special consumer goods.

So, Rosa told herself, she had sacrificed the excitement of living with Andrei. But who needed that kind of excitement when it led to prison? Nothing was easy in Russia, and one had to look after one's self.

* * *

Andrei had asked her to meet him at the Café des Artistes across the street from the Moscow Art Theater. It was not her idea of an appropriate meeting place—more like an assignation than a place for an Academician's wife to have a polite luncheon with an old friend. She had, of course, told her husband about Andrei before they were married —a rather edited version, to be sure, which made it seem like a silly schoolgirl escapade. Well, in a sense, that was what it had been.

When she told him that she was meeting Andrei for lunch, he raised his eyes a bit quizzically and asked, "Do you think that's wise?"

Rosa shook her head. "I think I had better."

"Well," he said, turning back to his *Pravda*, "whatever you think best. But I don't believe you should feel under any obligation."

Petrushkin was not, she told herself, a reactionary man. Not at all. But he was careful, and in this, he had shown wisdom. Not all professors of history had come unscathed through the last Stalin years. But he had. Helped, perhaps, by the fact that his specialty was a sound and relatively safe one—the feudal economy of the medieval Moscow state.

Rosa found herself a bit early for the appointment, so she walked down the street, wandering into the bookshops that lined both sides. It had been a long time since she had been in the Pereulok. Her husband didn't care for the theater, and when they went, it was more likely to see one of the Ostrovsky classics at the Maly than the Chekhovian fare at the Art Theater. In fact, Petrushkin found Stanislavsky's style a little too advanced for his taste.

Rosa went into the antiquarian bookstore. She remembered coming here with Andrei on their first and only trip to Moscow. He had loved Moscow's secondhand bookstores, and spent hours poring over books, though they hardly had any money to spend. He had bought her a small, elegant edition of Pushkin, bound in leather, and she had given him a very thin paperbound Tsvetaeva. It must have been one of Tsvetaeva's first collections of poetry. Andrei had been so excited over it. What, she wondered idly, might ever have happened to the Yesenin which she gave Andrei to take off to war?

It was one-thirty, time to meet Andrei. She went up the street again, walking slowly, in no hurry to reach the café, in no hurry to see Andrei. She could not now understand exactly why she had come. She steeled herself, physically bracing her body, walking more straight, and entered the café. She saw Andrei instantly. He was sitting at a table near the rear of the small room, and it was as if a ray had stabbed out from his eyes and penetrated her. She hesitated, then walked to the table. He rose silently, and when she gave him her hand, he raised it to his lips and kissed it solemnly. They sat down, still without a word spoken, Andrei's eyes staring into hers. She cast her eyes down and finally spoke: "Have I changed so much, Andrei Ilych?" Andrei continued to look at her. "Yes," he said at length, "you have changed. Not so much physically, although you are a bit stout. But, I should say, spiritually. Yes. Spiritually you are not the Rosa I last saw."

Rosa did not raise her eyes. "Nor are you, Andrei, the same Andrei."

There was a silence. Then Andrei broke it. "No," he said, "I'm not the same Andrei. For better or worse I have changed and you have changed and there is no use in pretending that we haven't. As to which of us has changed the most—well, I expect we will each have our own opinion."

*   *   *

A waiter came and asked what they wished to order. "Just a cup of tea for me," Rosa said.

Andrei looked surprised. "You're sure you don't want something to eat? Experience has taught me never to pass up an opportunity to have a bite. You never know when the next time will come."

But Rosa refused. Andrei smiled. "Well, then, I'll have a dish of ice cream and we'll both have tea."

Rosa sat back in her chair. She tried to keep her hands quiet, but they kept tearing at the edge of her napkin. She wished she had not come. There was something frightening about this grim, silent man sitting beside her. He was not the Andrei she had last seen, the Andrei of the hurried heart-wrenching prison interviews. Nor was he the gay and optimistic youngster she had married. This was a powerful man with hidden fire burning inside him. She was almost afraid to touch him. She had the impression his muscles were made of steel cord. His face had a leanness now that emphasized his high temples and the hard line of his jaw. His hair had receded slightly, showing his wide brow, deeply ribbed by furrows of concentration. She felt the magnetism and power flowing from him.

Rosa's fear intensified. He hates me, she said to herself. He hates me and he knows that I know he hates me. He can read every thought in my mind, and there is nothing I can do to stop him.

She managed to pull herself together. "What are you going to do now, Andrei?" she asked. "Write?"

"Yes, Rosa," he replied, and she was surprised at the gentleness of his tone. "Yes, I am going to write. In fact, I am already writing in a small way."

"Have you had anything published?"

"Yes, but nothing that you would be likely to see. Only local things so far."

"Are you still living in Turkmenistan?"

"I have been, Rosa, but now I'm moving closer to Moscow. You remember I had the ambition of teaching school in a quiet country town. Well, I've found the town, and I have a position in the school. In Kostroma. You remember we trained near there in the artillery."

Rosa nodded vaguely and sipped her tea. She realized she had nothing to say to this man, who had once been her husband. Nothing.

But now he was speaking to her. "Are you happy, Rosa?" he asked.

"Oh yes," she said hurriedly, "very happy indeed. I have my husband and my teaching. We have a nice place to live, travel a bit. Last year we went to Prague, and next summer we may go to Helsinki."

"No children?" Andrei asked.

"No."

"Do you miss not having any?"

"Heavens, no. Children are a terrible nuisance."

"Your mother is still living?"

"Yes," Rosa replied. "She lives with us. She is quite well."

"Give her my regards," Andrei said, "I was always fond of her."

"I will."

Both were silent again. Finally, Andrei broke it. "Well, I see that we have nothing to say to each other," he said with a queer smile. "It's interesting, isn't it? There was a time when you would have said to me 'There's a lesson in that for you, Andrei.' Do you still say that?"

Later on, Rosa could never explain to herself why it had happened, but at the sound of those words which she had so often spoken to Andrei she burst into tears and put her head in her hands. It was as if Andrei had touched a hidden spot and unleashed all the emotions she had held in check, all of the life she had left behind her. She felt his arm gently circling her back and his voice saying, "Come now, dear Rosa. Come. There's nothing to cry about."

And there wasn't, she told herself, reaching for a handkerchief and dabbing at her eyes. "It's ridiculous," she said, "simply ridiculous. I don't know why you wanted to see me, Andrei."

"Oh," he said. "There was a reason. A good reason, too."

He reached into his inside pocket and brought out an envelope. "Something for you," he said. "And many thanks."

He handed it over to Rosa and she took it wonderingly: "What is it, Andrei?"

"The money," he said, "the money you loaned me."

"But I didn't want you to pay that back," she said. "This isn't necessary at all."

"No, I suppose it's not. But I thought we ought to square our accounts."

She thrust the envelope into her handbag thinking, I must go now. But suddenly she did not want to leave. She looked at Andrei almost shyly. There was a half-smile on his lips. Not bitter, not mocking, but somewhat melancholy.

"I suppose," she said sadly. "This is the end."

"Yes, Rosa, I think it is," Andrei said. "But actually the end happened a long time ago. It wasn't you and it wasn't me. It was the times we live in."

She rose now and began to move out of the café, Andrei following her. "Can I take you somewhere?" he asked. He was being kind to her, she understood. He was trying to make it easier. "No, Andrei," she said. "It's better to part here."

She gave him her hand. Again he lifted it to his lips and kissed it quietly, again he looked into her eyes. This time she turned hers away. For an instant she saw in them a gleam of something she hoped never to see again, just an impression, but it made her shudder and turn away, almost running the half block up to Gorky Street and the comfort of the slowly moving throngs of people. She did not know what she had seen, but the impression came back to her later on in the form of a nightmare in which again she saw Andrei's eyes fastened on hers. They were the eyes, she finally told herself, of a timber wolf—a timber wolf that had escaped from a trap by gnawing through its own leg.

*   *   *

Andrei had one more call to pay in Moscow—a meeting with Vanya, the friend of his youth, his "co-conspirator" in the case that had sent both of them into the prison camps. He knew little enough of Vanya's life, he reflected, as he walked from the trolley bus to the apartment block in southwest Moscow where his old friend and comrade lived. It was one of the new living complexes that were beginning to be built in the Cheremushki section of the city. All Andrei really knew was that Vanya had married and that he was now working in a new electro-magnetic institute, had a good job and was very enthusiastic about it, to judge by his words on the telephone.

The huge building was constructed in great wings, and Andrei had a little difficulty finding the right entrance. Finally he located Korpus 7 and climbed the chilly staircase to the fourth floor. There was no light in the hall, but by lighting two matches, he found the door. There was a not unpleasant smell of boiling cabbage and frying onions in the corridor. Actually, Andrei thought to himself, there were very few smells of cooking that were not pleasant to his nostrils after the years in the camps.

The door opened almost immediately to Andrei's knock, and Vanya—an older, more sturdy, one might even say a rotund Vanya, with an almost completely bald head—stood before Andrei, his arms outstretched, a broad smile disclosing two gold-capped front teeth. He enveloped Andrei in a bearlike hug. Andrei put his arms around Vanya and the two men embraced, kissing each other on the cheeks, then kissing each other again. Vanya thrust Andrei back, holding him with outstretched arms, saying, "Let my eyes get a look at you, Andrushka. My God! It's really you, isn't it? After all these years."

Andrei smiled. It was pleasant seeing an old friend and comrade—more than pleasant—even though it was a surprise to find him, as it were, in a new body, a fat-padded body in place of the slim muscular youth he had embraced at their last meeting at the Front.

Vanya led him into the flat, shouting to his wife: "Valentina Ivanovna. Come here! Meet my old comrade, Andrei Ilych, of whom you have heard so much."

A red-cheeked, very blond, buxom woman appeared, wiping her hands on a towel, which she quickly discarded and extended her hand, saying, "I am delighted to meet you." Andrei a bit seriously raised her hand to his lips. He noticed that her fingers were amost chubby, smelled of onion, and that on the center finger she wore a handsome diamond. Vanya must be moving up in the world. There were red Turkmenian rugs on the floor, Finnish or imitation Finnish birch bookshelves and table, a comfortable sofa covered in tan-and-brown and, most promi-nently placed at the door to the small kitchen, a gleaming white electric refrigerator—the *sine qua non* of Moscow culture in the late 1950's.

*   *   *

Andrei could not help smiling. His friend was in the Moscow swim, no doubt of it.

"A far cry, Vanya, to what we have been used to," he said, with a gesture toward the comfortable furnishings.

"Don't talk of those days," said Vanya with a shrug, "they are be-hind us. Besides, it upsets Valentina Ivanovna. Let's talk instead about the present and the future. What brings you to Moscow? Are you establishing yourself here—I hope? I've some good ideas for you in that connection, incidentally."

Before Andrei had a chance to reply, Valentina Ivanovna had nudged her husband and whispered in his ear. "Oh, yes, Andrusha," Vanya said. "Valentina is reminding me of my husbandly duties. First, before we talk, a drop to wet our throats for old times' sake, eh?"

He led Andrei to the table placed at the end of the living room. Three places were set. There were plates of *zakuski*, white bread and Moscow's wonderful moist black bread, sliced in small pieces, mushroom pickles, smoked carp, salmon, a half dozen kinds of sausage, pickled tomatoes, fresh small cucumbers, Aleutian crab.

"And here is my battery," Vanya said, pointing to a row of vodka bottles—strong, clear Stolichnaya, ruddy hunter's vodka, a smaller bottle of pepper vodka, a carafe of vodka with bits of dried orange peel floating in it, a bottle of port wine, another of Tsinindali No. 3, one of Tsinindali No. 21, and a small bottle of Armenian brandy.

"Take your choice," Vanya said.

Andrei smiled. Vanya's pride in his possessions was really quite childish. Still, Andrei could understand it. After eight or ten years of doing without, there was an almost sensual satisfaction in such simple things as bottles of vodka and fine smoked carp.

"I'll drink Stolichnaya," Andrei said. "After all, what is better than the best?"

"True," said his companion, pouring for each of them a small glass. The two men raised their glasses solemnly. They were small crystal *rumki*, filled to the brim.

"To the future!" exclaimed Vanya.

"And to the past," said Andrei, his face serious.

The men drank quietly, and then with a single motion reached for pieces of bread which they stuffed in their mouths, not bothering to butter them.

"So many years," Vanya said. "So many lives."

Andrei nodded.

"It's a dozen years," Vanya continued. "But now things go smoothly. The institute, my Valentina Ivanovna, the new apartment, enough money for a little ease. Last summer we went to Sochi. Next year when my new appointment comes through—a car and a chauffeur. Yes. Times have changed."

His wife brought a tray of hot *zakuski*: trout morsels in spiced butter sauce, *pirozhki*, hot light turnovers with meat filling. She joined the men and more toasts were drunk. A toast to her. A toast to Andrei's future. A toast to their comradeship.

"Tell me, Andrei," Vanya said. "What are you doing? What are you going to do?"

Andrei fingered his *rumka*. The planes of the crystal sparkled under the electric light.

"Well," he said. "You know that my ambition is to be a writer. Now I am going to work on something serious, big, something important."

He hesitated. For some reason he did not feel like telling Vanya what he was going to write. Perhaps it was the instinct born of years in prison or perhaps it was just his mood. But the contrast between prison and this bourgeois life, between the savagery of the camps and the pathos of real Russian life, seemed too much to bridge in an evening's pleasant conversation, drinking the best of vodka from crystal glasses and eating salmon which cost as much for a small serving as the ration of a state prisoner for two months.

Vanya smiled at him. "You still have your idealistic aspirations," he said. "I can see that. But, still and all, writing is not a bad profession. There are some writers who live very well, very well indeed. Sholokhov, for instance. I have heard that he earned millions of rubles with *The Quiet Don* and *The Virgin Soil Upturned*. He has his own estate on the Don. And they say that some of the playwrights earn as much as a million on a single play. For instance, Simonov with *The Russian Character*. And they get to travel—even travel abroad."

*   *   *

Andrei smiled inwardly. He was right not to explain the nature of his writing. Vanya had become a full-fledged member of the Russian middle cass.

"I don't think," Andrei said, "that my writing is going to earn millions. In fact, that is not what I have in mind. What I have in mind is telling the truth about Russian life, so far as I am capable."

"That is not going to be so easy to do," Vanya said. "And how are you going to support yourself while you are trying to win acceptance? You do have to live, you know."

"True enough, Vanya," Andrei said. "I must live, and I have gotten a job as a mathematics teacher in Kostroma."

Vanya's wife had seated herself again at the table. At the thought of Kostroma she shrugged comically. "I can't imagine why you would want to do that, Andrushka," she said. "I can't imagine anyone not living in Moscow. What will you do? There is no theater there, no music, no stores, no restaurants, no culture. There is nothing in Kostroma. Nothing at all."

Andrei was amused at the strength of her feeling. "Do you know Kostroma?" he asked curiously.

"Yes," she said, "to my misfortune, I do. At the time of the war when Moscow was threatened, in the autumn of 1941, we were evacuated, my mother and myself and my small brother. To Kostroma. Ugh! I'll never forget it. Muddy streets. Wooden houses. The peasants kept their chickens in the hut with them during the winter."

"You can't go to Kostroma," Vanya said. "It's plain madness. Let me make a suggestion. Come to work in my institute. I shouldn't call it 'my' institute, but it is going to be, one of these days. Old Lebedev who runs it is on his last legs and I am going to take it over from him. Very soon, too."

"Yes," broke in Valentina, "do listen to Vanya. He knows what he is talking about. He's only been there three years, but look how far he has come already. He's going to the top. See how well we live. You can live just as well. Oh, of course, you must get married, and I know just the wife for you, don't I, Vanya?"

Vanya chuckled. "You are an inveterate matchmaker, Valentina."

"No, I'm serious about this," Valentina persisted. Andrei could see that the drink had loosened her tongue. "Really, Andrei," she went on. "My very best friend, Tatyana Alexeyevna. She is a beautiful woman. Blond, very Russian. She works in Vanya's institute, too. She was married once before, but, you know, it didn't work out. She would be just right for you, Andrusha."

Vanya interrupted his wife's flow of argument. "Now, Valentina, that's enough. Andrei will make his own mind up about his wife. And now, I think we might have a bite to eat."

A little grudgingly Valentina rose. "Next year," she said, "when Vanya becomes head of the institute we will have a cook, and I'll not have to interrupt my conversation with our attractive guests."

The two men were left alone again. "Seriously," Vanya said, "think it over. You are a fine mathematician. You are a much better scientist than I am, you know that. There's just no limit to what you can do. Perhaps you could get an institute of your own. Actually, I simply ran into a bit of luck. Lebedev is getting on in years and he thought it wasn't necessary to play politics anymore. Well, I have shown him a thing or two in that line. If there's something you want in this country, playing politics is the way to get it."

"You mean," Andrei said thoughtfully, "that you deliberately set out to get Lebedev's job."

Vanya looked a bit embarrassed. "That's putting it rather bluntly, but I suppose you might say that. I came into the institute, saw the opportunity and have made the best of it. After all, you know as well as I that we have each lost ten years out of our lives. I think we are owed something in exchange, and if no one wants to give it to me— well, as they say, God helps those who help themselves."

* * *

The dinner went on. There was a good borscht, with a fine piece of tender boiled beef at the bottom of the plate, and a heavy spoonful of *smetana*, or sour cream, on top. There were more tasty *pirozhki* to go with the borscht, a fine *kievsky kutlet*, the pure sweet butter spurting up at the cut of the knife and splattering both Vanya's white shirt and Valentina's blue silk dress with its green-and-brown embroidery.

"*Chort vozmi!*" Valentina exclaimed rudely. "The devil take it! All over my nice silk gown."

"Well, that's the trouble with eating well," Vanya said complacently. "There is a price to pay for everything."

That there is, Andrei thought to himself, that there is. And the price his friend Vanya had paid for this comfort and the greater comfort that he envisaged in the near future was simply his abandonment of any moral principle. Andrei found it difficut to place the blame for this upon Vanya. It was the system that did it. And not the camp system. The chances were that if Vanya came through the war he would have returned home, sought out a position on the ladder of success, fought his way up step by step, treasuring each victory and exploiting each success, seeing nothing wrong with improving his status at the cost of a rival, enjoying the privileges that this conduct won for him and never looking back on the idealistic dreams of his youth except occasionally to think, "How silly I was then!"

And, he, Andrei, had been silly and naïve as well. How could he have really imagined that with the dough of the Vanyas of Russia he could have baked the loaf of the new Dekabristi?

They had finished the long meal, sampled all the wines, eaten the fresh pineapple that came, Valentina said, from Mexico. Now the two men were sitting alone. Valentina had retired to let the men have their talk, as she said.

Andrei had tried gently but firmly to discourage Vanya on the question of his joining the institute, but Vanya did not give up easily. "You know," Vanya said, "I'm not being entirely unselfish about this. You are a fine mathematician. You would do brilliant work. It would not hurt my position a bit to bring in a brilliant man like yourself. And it would give me another supporter."

"I don't really think the institute is for me. Not now, Vanya. Mathematics has saved my life twice, but I'm not certain it would do so a third time."

"You think about it, Andrushka," Vanya said in a rosy glow of Armenian cognac. "You think about it."

Andrei turned the conversation. "Let me ask you something else. I know you don't want to talk about the past, but something very curious has been on my mind for many years. Did you ever really tell the interrogators that you had recruited me into the 'organization'?"

Vanya laughed. "Yes, I did," he said. "Wasn't it silly? They kept insisting that I had headed the organization and demanding to know whom I had brought into it. So finally at long last I said I had recruited you. That seemed to be what they wanted. I knew you had been arrested, and I couldn't see how it made any difference."

Andrei frowned a bit. "No," he said, " I don't think it made any difference at all at that point. Did they keep insisting to you that we were directed by British intelligence? In fact, by a Major Anderson?"

Vanya thought deeply. "British intelligence. Yes! They certainly used that line. Major Anderson? I don't think so. Perhaps. But it's been a long time. I don't remember that name."

"What about the Dekabristi?" Andrei asked. "Did they ever ask you about that?"

"No," said Vanya, "they never did. I kept expecting that question. Fearing it. But no one ever asked it. Did they ask you?"

"No," said Andrei, "they didn't. It was queer, too, because we had mentioned it in our correspondence, and our correspondence was what they had to go on."

"It was odd," Vanya said.

"Did they find that manifesto we wrote?" Andrei asked.

"This is odd, too," Vanya said. "It was in my papers. But I was never asked about it."

"Nor was I," Andrei said. "But they didn't get a copy of my papers. What about Popkov and Osipenko? Who were they?"

Vanya put his head in his hands. "That was a bad business, but it could have been worse. They were men in my outfit. We had actually talked, you know, about the plans. One of them had just been killed, the other was killed the next week. So I later found out. So naming them did no real harm."

* * *

Andrei sat silently for a time. Finally he spoke: "It is very curious about the Dekabristi, but I'll tell you what I think. I don't believe they ever thought of looking through our letters for evidence of any conspiracy. It never entered their heads that we had really been talking about any political action. The only reason we were picked up was that *swolich*, Petroshenko, the Smersh man in my outfit, who wanted to do me in. He saw one of my letters referring to 'Mustache,' understood that I meant Stalin, and that gave him a case against me for using the expression and against you for not reporting me. Then, once it got to the higher levels of the KGB, they automatically transformed it into a conspiracy and made up the standard kind of case, never once thinking that any real evidence existed."

Vanya shook his head. "Quite possibly, Andrei, but the truth is I'm not interested in anything about those days—the talks we had, the so-called Dekabristi, the years in the camps. That is a closed chapter. Why look back on it? There is nothing there that relates to the present. I've made myself a new life. It is a good life. It is going to be a better life. All of the other is behind me now. I don't want to be reminded of it, and I don't want others to be reminded of it. What is past is past."

Andrei looked up at his friend. "I can't agree, Vanya," he said. "What is past is not past, and unless we remember it our past will become our future."

Vanya chuckled. "There you go again, Andrushka, your old self again. Forget it, I tell you. Come and join me. We'll put the world at our feet and have a good time doing it. And, well, I tried to discourage Valentina from talking about her friend Tatiana—but, just between us, she is quite a woman. Quite a woman. If I didn't have Valentina, I'd be really tempted myself. You could go far and do much worse."

The two men rose. Vanya poured out a last *rumka*, this time of pepper vodka. "One for the road," he said. "There's a chill in the air. *Do svidanya*—to our next meeting."

"*Do svidanya*," echoed Andrei. He knew that in fact this was their last meeting.

Chapter 48

THIRTY years have passed, thiry years exactly, Andrei thought to himself, since as an excited youngster he had pushed onto the crowded train at Rostov for Armavir. Now once again he was riding the train bound for Armavir and beyond—to Mineralnye Vody. Once again it was summer, and as he sat at the train window, not a hard car this time but a comfortable sleeping compartment, he thought that he could remember every detail of that first train ride out over the broad steppe, the endless plains that stretched to the horizon, the fields of grain, bleached to golden hardness by the iron sun burning down from the curved blue bowl that was the summer sky of the Kuban.

This was old Cossack country. The Kuban Cossacks with their long black cloaks, their black caracul caps with a cross of blue and gold sewn in the crown, their strong swift ponies, their long curved swords that cut the air like a flash of fire—who did not know them? They had ridden the broad steppe, their heads high, their pride like a burnished cuirass, their tempers hot as coals, their black eyes flashing, their white teeth glistening like ivory—brave men who fought their hearts out for the Czar. When the civil war was over they had vanished, some into foreign exile to wind up driving Paris taxicabs or drinking themselves to death in Shanghai.

But more, Andrei thought, had been executed or sent off by the thousands to camps in Siberia or the Far North. He watched the heat waves rise and distort his vision over the Kuban fields, and in the distance saw a whirlwind of dust—horsemen making their way across the steppe. Had the Cossacks vanished? Certainly not when he first rode across this plain as a boy of eleven, certainly not. Their capes may have been torn and tattered, their mounts little more than bags of bones—but, no, the remnants of the Cossacks were still on the land. In fact, he supposed, half of the people on that train to Armavir had been Cossacks.

Andrei's eyes were fixed on the distant horizon. He did not hear the *provodnik* at the door of his compartment until the porter cleared

his throat loudly and said, "Would the *tovarishch* like a glass of tea?" Andrei started from his reverie. "Yes," he said, "I'd like a glass of tea very much. With lemon if you have it."

Then his eyes drifted back to the window. What a terrible summer that had been, the summer of 1929, more terrible, of course, than he had known. With collectivization the kulaks, the richer peasants, as a class had been eliminated.

He drank his tea, after putting one sugar lump in the glass. The second lump he automatically transferred to his pocket. One never knew. The habits of a lifetime of preserving his rations, of always saving a good part for the next time (which might never come) would, he supposed, never leave him. Combines were working in the fields through which the train was passing. He never ceased to marvel at these Martian monsters picking their way through the golden grain, with a sweep of a giant hand, they consumed the vast expanse, transforming it from an unbroken sea of yellow to its component parts—earth and dust, chaff, straw and hard-kerneled wheat.

Yes, he had been an idealistic, patriotic, optimistic child when he boarded the train. But by the time he had arrived at Armavir he had been transformed into a frightened youngster, terrified at what he had seen but still not understanding.

And what, he wondered, had happened to frighten his aunt and uncle so deeply that summer? Perhaps he would find out now, for he was on a trip deep into his past, a journey of rediscovery. He was going once again to see his aunt, for she was still alive, still as cranky and opinionated as ever, living (though not very well, he feared) in Mineralnye Vody. He was going to recover from her the hoard of his manuscripts which she had faithfully preserved and—or so he hoped—he was going to learn about his father, his mother and his family. There was so much he did not know, so much she might tell him, if she were able. One never knew with an old woman of eighty-two. Sometimes their minds were crystal clear for their early years, retaining precise recollections, even of conversations.

*   *   *

When he arrived, what struck Andrei most forcefully was the contrast between what he had perceived as a boy and what had actually been happening all around him. He had now been sitting for the better part of three days on a broken-legged stool in his Aunt Sofia's hovel, listening to her talk about "the old days in the family." He was sitting just outside the shed in which she lived, remarkably like the one in which he and his mother had first lived in Rostov, and she was talking of the famine year of 1932–33. It was early evening, the sun had set and shadows were lengthening, but the air was still and warm; his nostrils caught the smell of onions and roasting lamb—someone was cooking shashlik on a clay stove in the near courtyard—and from

the lane outside he heard the shouts of children playing at *gorodki*. Aunt Sofia was talking on and on. "Once I had millions," she said, "and now look at me. But I do not complain. It is God's will." She was wizened and small and nearly blind but tart as an early Crimean apple and just as sharp-tongued as he remembered her.

The stories she told were of one disaster, one horror, after another. Why was it that the old so savored tragedy? Was it, perhaps, because they still lived and tragedy's victims had perished? Not that her stories told him much that was new or unfamiliar. He had come to know the famine of 1932–33 as well as he knew his own life. For one thing, he had spent six months in the same labor gang at Taishet with Dima Dubchek, who had lived as a "middle peasant" all through those years on a former *stanitsa* in the steppe south of the Don. Night after freezing night he had lain in his bunk and listened to Dima's stories—of the village where road blocks were set up and anyone who emerged, man, woman or child, was cut down by machine-gun fire. "The villagers had a choice," Dima said, "to come out on the road and be killed instantly or to stay in their houses and die more slowly of starvation. In the end they all died (and it was not a small village either—it had eight hundred or nine hundred inhabitants), and when the road blocks were removed and the troops entered the village, it was like Pompeii. You remember the pictures in your history book? Some lay on their doorsteps, skeletons or moldering corpses. Some lay around the well, which had been caved in before the road blocks were set up. They had died trying to dig for water. Some lay on their beds, some on the roadway. No one survived. Nor was anyone buried. They were left as they were."

"A lesson to other villagers," Andrei said.

"Yes," Dima said, "a lesson."

No. It was not the horrors of which his aunt spoke that struck Sokolov. It was the fact that they had happened all around him, virtually in his own life, and except for the faint hum of rumors, the empty food shops, the closed stalls at the market, the whispers of the old women, the grim frown that hardly left his mother's face, he had not really been aware. He realized this when old Dima told him how he and the other peasants of his village had caught a young commissar, a raw youngster from Kharkov who had thrown his weight around. "We bound his hands together," Dima said with a satisfaction he could not conceal. "We tied one end of the long rope around the saddle of a Cossack pony. This, of course, was before all the horses died. Then the rider gave the horse a slap with a lead-weighted whip, and the animal bounded over the steppe. A mile or so out on the range the rider cut the rope with a knife. That was the end of the Kharkov lad. The body lay out there on the steppe for days, the buzzards plucking at his eyes and lean-sided wolves stripping the bones clean."

Andrei Sokolov knew about the horrors, but he felt them starkly as Tetya Sofia talked on and on.

"We were living at Nal'chik then," she said. "Your uncle had gotten a very good job. He was driving a truck for the State Farm and they paid him in kind. We got cabbages and potatoes, whole bags of potatoes, and even buckwheat and grits. It was remarkable. No one around us had anything. They were starving. Every day someone we knew died. I was walking down the main street one morning and I saw a man drop dead in front of my eyes. He just passed out. Then I looked again. His eyelids were quivering. I got two men to help me, and somehow we brought him to our flat. I had a pot of hot soup simmering on the stove. I put some in a tin mug. Just a little. I pushed his head back, opened his mouth and poured it in, bit by bit."

She had, she said, saved the man's life. "He was a strong man," she said. "He worked in the railroad shops. But he could get nothing to eat. There was no food. Oh, there were many such cases."

The things she had seen! There was Elizabeta Sosin, a thin, lanky woman with five children. The oldest was fourteen, the next was thirteen, and there were three little ones—four, three and two. Her husband had been sent away to the East. God knows where. They loaded them into freight cars, locked the doors and sent them down the tracks. Not many survived—of that you could be certain. And now there was the famine and Elizabeta had come into the city with her five children. They lived in a shed beside the market and begged for a living.

"She tried to sell herself," the old woman said, "but no one wanted her. Who wanted such a bag of bones with shriveled-up tits? So she tried to sell her daughter—the fourteen-year-old. But nobody wanted her, the scrawny cross-eyed thing! Truth was there were too many women for sale. What else? They all needed food. We were different. Because your uncle had this job driving the truck, we were all right."

One day his aunt noticed the Sosin woman hunched on her heels at the market. Only four children were with her. The two-year-old was gone. The next day it was the same. Another week or two and there were only three children. A month later, only the woman and her eldest two children were left.

"She butchered them," said Tetya Sofia—and Sokolov heard a smack of satisfaction on the old woman's lips. "She butchered them. One by one. They ate the young ones, one after another—she and the older children. We all knew it. Who could interfere? And, besides, it wasn't that unusual."

She grunted. "Do you remember Vanka the teamster?" she asked. "I fancy not. He was all mixed up in that kind of thing."

Vanka, she said, was a good horseman. He had herded cattle on the steppe. He was very handy with a lasso. Late at night he used to lie in wait for unwary pedestrians. When he found one alone, there was the quick and almost noiseless whirl of the lasso.

"Down they went," said Tetya Sofia. "And in a twinkling he had a knife up their ribs and hauled them off to his place—he lived in a kind of culvert under the road coming up to the marketplace."

There Vanka's victims were butchered to be sold in the market the next day as ground meat for sausage or *pirozhki*, for stew meat or, his aunt insisted, even for roasts.

"But he was one they caught," she said with a grim smile. "They caught him. *Slava Bogu!* But did they hang him there in the market-place? Heavens, no! They put him in one of the cars and shipped him out to Siberia. And there, for all I know, he is still at it."

Tetya Sofia's voice crackled on, broken by frequent chortles. She was a survivor, the only survivor, for that matter, of the Sokolov family in her generation. Of all that generation—his mother, his father, his mother's two sisters, their husbands, her brother—only this wizened hag was still living. Only Tetya Sofia and himself.

The thought hit him as it had so often—the toll in life that had been taken during the years he had been on earth, a random toll that struck at the good, the evil, the old, the young, taking nursing mothers and fourteen-year-old girls with the same greed as it did gouty old men and hard-muscled workers. He had survived and his aunt had survived. She had survived because she had been toughest and most selfish. He had understood that, even as a child watching her pop a sweet into her mouth, watching the bulge in her cheek slowly diminish as she sucked it away, never offering one to him.

*   *   *

"You know, Andrushka," his aunt resumed, "you weren't thinking about your old Auntie in those days. You were all for being a soldier and you wanted to follow in your father's footsteps. That's what you thought."

"And so I did, Auntie," Sokolov remarked.

"So you did, to be sure," she said. "But your father wasn't a soldier. I mean, not a real one. Of course, he went to war in 1914. Every decent Russian man did go to war in that year. But he wasn't really a soldier. He was a *narodnik*."

Sokolov fumbled in his pocket and lit a cigarette. There was something in what the old woman said. Not that his father had been a real *narodnik*, one of those selfless young Russians of the 1870's who threw over their lives to join the going-to-the-people movement, who went deep into the vast Russian countryside to dedicate themselves to the task of lifting the "dark people," the illiterate and ignorant peasants, out of their backward life. No. His father was born nearly half a century too late for that. But certainly he would have been a *narodnik* if he had been born into the right decade. From what Andrei had heard about him, that was his nature—gentle, trusting, idealistic. He believed in the perfectibility of humanity and hoped he could help create a better world.

Create a better world. Sokolov smiled grimly to himself. How naïve that sounded today! To think that young people once lived in Russia who really believed that through the purity of their hearts and the charity of their souls they could right great wrongs and build a new and brighter life for mankind. And what had come about in place of the ideal of their dreams? Disillusion, hatred, fear, death and torture, starvation, physical and moral, cannibalism, prisons and exiles, executions, debasement of morality, defilement of human life, slavery, deification of tyrants, banality, the death of religion, the end of honesty, the rule of hypocrisy, the cult of the strong over the weak, malice, ill-will, the desiccation of the spirit, death and cruelty, death and cruelty.

Did not that long-ago scream of the peasant woman in the railway coach contain it all?

Andrei sighed. His aunt had fallen silent. Perhaps she was dozing. He rose and stretched his legs, stiff from sitting on the three-legged stool. "Time to go to bed, Auntie," he said. "I'll come by tomorrow morning before I leave."

His aunt got to her feet. "Lord be with us poor sinners," she exclaimed. "You'll forget me for another ten years, and I'll be in my grave for certain before you come down to the steppe again. But bless you, Andrei, and I'll light a candle for you if my poor legs will carry me to the church once more."

The church. Yes, thought Sokolov, it is not only toughness and cleverness and luck that saw her through. It was the church. She was a believer, and God had been on her side. Even in unholy Russia, God was the most powerful ally.

He left the old woman in her hovel and walked through the narrow back streets to his hotel, thinking about God and Russia. Over the long dark centuries God had protected Russia. Perhaps the times had been hard, but somehow God had reigned over the Russian land and lent his faith to the Russian people. But now God had been pulled down, his temples destroyed and his faith driven from the souls, or at least the mouths, of the people. And how had they fared? Cruelly, cruelly, cruelly.

Andrei now knew that the task he had set for himself—the complete reconstruction of his own life and, with it, the life of Russia in his era, the revelation of the roots and sources of the evil through the systematic reconstruction of all elements of the past—was beyond his powers or the powers of any man. But he also knew that it was not necessary to put together every fragment of the past in order to illuminate in light of such brilliance that it would burn into the very pupil of the eye the shame of the present and point the true path to the future. For this task he already had enough, more than enough.

In the morning, he went again to the little hut on the outskirts of town. His aunt greeted him as before, dressed in her old woman's decent black gown, tucked in a bit at the waist, gathered below the bosom. On her yellowed white hair she wore a neat widow's cap of white. She was in a querulous mood.

"You'll not see your old aunt again," she said. "I'm not long for this earth, but I don't mind. I welcome it. I expect nothing. I expect nothing from you, Andrei. There's too much of your mother in you. Now that you have the papers I saved for you, you will have no time. Well, that's the way life is. There's nothing to do about it."

Sokolov did not argue with the old woman. He sat down on the stool. "Let's sit for a moment in silence," he said. "We'll follow the old custom. I am embarking on a long journey."

She sat on the bench by the table and he on the stool. She sat silently as he did. God alone knew her thoughts. Presently Sokolov rose and broke the silence.

"I must go now, Auntie," he said. "Thank you for preserving my manuscripts. They mean much to me. God be with you. I'll send you a bit of money from time to time."

He clasped her bony fingers across the table and pressed two hundred-ruble notes in them. "Here's a little something to buy you meat for your soup," he said.

His aunt grasped the crisp notes in her hand. "Farewell, Andrushka," she said. "Perhaps you are more like your father after all. I don't know. I'm an old woman and all alone. The rest are dead and I soon will be, by God's grace."

Sokolov held the old woman by the shoulders and carefully kissed her on both cheeks. She made the sign of the cross.

"Go with God, Andrushka," she muttered. "Go with God."

Chapter 49

ANDREI chose well when he chose Kostroma. It was an old town of stone and whitewashed plaster buildings on the upper Volga, where the river was still not as wide as an ocean. The barges loaded with wood and coal and grain moved past Kostroma day after day, en route to Moscow. Great cargoes of cement and lumber and steel came down the river. Kostroma was, or had been, a trading town.

Red-and-white Kostroma cattle were famous in Czarist Russia as fine milk producers. They still were, although the breed was no longer in much favor. The new specialists in the Agriculture Ministry preferred Holsteins and Jerseys and Guernseys. Why, the Kostroma peasants asked? Weren't their old cows just as good? The truth was, Andrei was convinced, the Kostroma cows were the equals of the foreign imports, but the agricultural specialists, like all specialists in Russia, were certain that the foreign varieties must be better.

Kostroma was a sleepy town. It had not much industry, not even a third-rate provincial theater, and only an occasional mediocre concert. Andrei taught mathematics at the high school. He took the minimum number of classes, refused firmly to accept extra teaching assignments, had little to do with his fellow teachers, arrived at school just in time for his classes, left promptly when they were finished and attended only a few of the "collective" discussions and meetings which the teachers were supposed to attend. His standard excuse was ill health, though actually he was strong as an ox. He formed no close friendships.

Andrei lived in a decent, rather large room in an old wooden house on the outskirts of town on the bluff overlooking the Volga. The house belonged to an elderly couple. The husband had been a petty bureaucrat of some kind, and both were now pensioners. It was actually not much more than a cottage, but the room Andrei occupied had been added on as a kind of separate wing. There was a big window that looked out to the river. In summer the view was obscured by

acacias and thick shrubbery, but in winter Andrei could see across
the frigid river ice and snowdrifts to the rolling country on the other
side. It was a cozy room, well insulated, warm in winter. He set up his
typewriter on a plain wooden table before the window, and here he
worked day after day, night after night, never ceasing, typing until the
ends of his fingers were numb with hitting the heavy keys.

Sometimes after six hours at the typewriter he would suddenly
spring from the table, grab his old *telogreika*—don his fur hat and
heavy gloves and push open the door—he had a separate door to his
room—step across the threshold and make his way to the long avenue
that ran parallel to the river. Here he walked from one end of the
town to the other, deliberately putting out of his mind everything
pertaining to his writing, the problems of composition, the problem
of what he must leave out. For he had a whole world to describe, and
it was not possible to put it all down. He must choose the incidents
that were most telling, the experiences that were universal. And
always, as he told himself, nothing went into his novel that was not
true. While *Taishet 303* was a novel, and while the central character
was a composite of different individuals, he had to confess, to himself
at least, that Pyotr, the hero of the novel, or principal figure as he preferred to call him, was essentially himself.

*   *   *

Kostroma was perfect because it did not impinge upon his writing,
upon his task of life, in any way. There were no distractions. The old
couple in whose house he lived was quite content to leave him to his
own devices. The demands of his mathematics students were not great,
and though he did not tell anyone at school he was a writer, he let it
become known that he was eccentric and solitary in his habits, and
gradually this came to be accepted.

He worked at his novel, corresponded with Rozen and Morozov,
wrote an occasional letter to his old Tetya Sofia and tried to find
some trace of Dedya Petya and Lieutenant Colonel Smirnov. He got a
letter from Smirnov's wife. She did not know where Smirnov was living.
They had been divorced in 1945 after his return, and she had re-
married. It was a familiar wartime story.

So far as Dedya Petya was concerned, Andrei had written to his
address at the collective farm outside Ulyanovsk, but he got no response to three letters. One was returned marked "Addressee unknown." The other two did not come back. Andrei feared that the two
letters were lying in the dusty cubbyhole of some village post office or
a disused drawer in the collective farm office, unopened and forgotten.

Occasionally, when he could arrange it, Andrei made a trip to
Moscow. He had sent copies of his *Provincial Tales* to the famous
editor of the magazine *Novy Zhizn*, Boris Stasov, together with a long

letter, telling him of some of his literary ideas. He had made clear
that he himself regarded *Provincial Tales* as merely practice for the
big work now in progress.

A bit to his surprise, but to his enormous pleasure, Stasov invited
him to visit the next time he came to Moscow, an occasion which
Andrei managed to arrange within the next month or two.

Stasov was encouraging. "I cannot tell from the small samples of
your writing as to your ability to handle so panoramic a vista of
Russian life as you suggest," he said. "The subject is colossal. It can
only be treated in a great novel. It is a cliché to say this, of course, but
only a new Tolstoy can do it justice."

Andrei was embarrassed. "I'm not a Tolstoy," he said, "but I am
determined to write this work. I think it is needed not only by Russian
literature but by the Russian people."

Stasov's eyes twinkled. "That is the kind of spirit I like, the spirit
we need today. These are new times. The horizons are beginning to
open up. The ice is breaking. Who knows what may lie ahead?"

They parted with a promise by Stasov to read Andrei's work when
it was completed and to give him the benefit of his critical advice.

"Don't send it to me until it is finished," the editor said. "I like
to come to a literary subject fresh and new, without pre-impressions."

Andrei returned to Kostroma more determined than ever. He
worked through the next summer without interruption, only leaving
his room for the long solitary walks at twilight, when he tried to move
his thoughts away from the unfolding story, the re-creation of the
horrors of Taishet, the pictures of his fellow camp victims. He
wandered by the river bank, often thinking of the Don in his childhood,
of the wide steppes, the open fields, the spaciousness of unending
lands that flowed like the waters of the sea to the very rim of the earth.

Andrei's work went well. When the winter holidays came, he went
again to Moscow, again met with Stasov. He did not bring his manuscript, much as he wished to do so. It was not finished yet and he respected the editor's injunction. But he did tell him of his progress, and
again he went away with encouragement. "You're on the right track,
Sokolov," Stasov said. "Keep it up. If you produce the book I think
you are capable of—we'll fight together to get it published."

*   *   *

And so it was that Andrei was still living in Kostroma, when one
evening in April, the snow still on the ground and the dirty streets
seas of mud, there was a knock on the door of the cottage. It was the
postgirl, her boots and uniform mud-spattered, little mud specks
freckling her tired face; she asked for Andrei Sokolov, and after Andrei
signed the receipt book, handed over a telegram, a small grayish bit
of paper, pasted over on itself to form its own envelope. Andrei thanked

the girl, slipped into his own room and tried to open the telegram with trembling hands. He had personally taken the completed manuscript of *Taishet 303* to Moscow a fortnight before, and left it in the hands of Stasov's secretary. The editor was ill, so he had no chance of seeing him personally.

Andrei's hands were trembling violently, but he finally succeeded in running his fingernail through the pasted-down flap and opened it. The message said: "My dear Andrei Ilych, you have given me the privilege of reading the finest Russian manuscript of my lifetime. I can say no more. I will struggle with you for its publication. Stasov."

Andrei stood a moment with his eyes fixed on the words. Then he threw himself down on his couch, beating the sagging mattress with his hands, tears flowing from his eyes—words, sounds, sobs issuing from his throat. "I can't help it, I can't help it, I can't help it," he told himself, trying to halt the trembling of his limbs, the pounding of his heart, and the weeping that rocked his body. Gradually he came to himself. There was a light tapping at his door. It was his landlady, the old wife of the bureaucrat. "Excuse me, Andrei Ilych," she said, "but I thought I heard you. Are you all right? I hope nothing bad has happened?"

"Oh, no," Andrei said, his voice bubbling and breaking into what his horrified ears told him was something like a girlish giggle. "Oh, no, Alexandra Kirillevna. Nothing bad has happened. Nothing bad at all. I've just had a bit of good news."

Bit of good news or not, *Taishet 303* did not exactly burst into print. In fact, as Andrei later was to calculate, almost two years elapsed between the day he brought his manuscript into Moscow, and left it with Stasov's secretary until the book was actually published. And there were moments when he was not at all certain that it would see the light of day, but in those times Stasov was admirable. He never lost confidence, and when he encountered a setback he did not become discouraged. Instead, he immediately figured out a new way of getting around the obstacle.

There were no problems so far as *Novy Zhizn* was concerned. The collective board of editors was unanimous in voting for publication. But that was only the first stage. Stasov was a skilled literary politician. He was a member of the Party Central Committee, and he had strong ties within the Politburo and in circles close to the Politburo.

From the beginning he told Sokolov frankly that publication would be a Politburo decision. "It can't be otherwise," he said. "The subject of the novel, the treatment, the realism, the *truth*, the absolute absence of hypocrisy and propaganda—all of this means that only the Politburo can decide. Because it represents new policy, and new policy comes only from the Politburo."

Andrei was dubious that Politburo approval could be obtained.

"Just leave that to me, old fellow," Stasov said with a fatherly mien. "I've been through this time and again. It will take a little time. And maybe a little luck. But we will have *Taishet* in print. Just you be certain of that."

*   *   *

Nonetheless, Andrei sometimes lost hope. Occasionally he became revolted by the moves and countermoves, the small steps forward, the pauses, the sudden maneuvers. Of course, he did not know all that went on, though he came to Moscow frequently in this period. Through Stasov he met many of the editors of *Novy Zhizn* as well as other literary figures. But Stasov was blunt about this. "Be careful, Sokolov. Literary Moscow is, for the most part, a pack of jackals. They will tear you limb from limb. Don't enter it until we have your novel approved. After that—well, the world is yours."

One of the editors whom Sokolov met was an assistant of Stasov's, a young, beautiful, blond woman who wore her hair in a golden crown. Andrei could not see her without thinking of that traditional Russian image of the *devushka*, the young woman, a white birch, supple, graceful, delicate. Anastasia—Stasia, as she was called. Perhaps it was his long monastic years, his concentration on his writing, perhaps it was the natural grace and beauty of the girl—she was nearly twenty years younger than Andrei—but he found her irresistible. Each time he came to Moscow he took her to dinner, and finally she invited him to the small flat where she, a divorcee, lived with her mother and three-year-old son. Each evening Andrei talked by the hour of his life and his aspirations. Stasia listened, only occasionally putting in a word. In fact, it was not possible for her to speak because of the stream of words that poured from him.

Occasionally, Stasia's mother was absent from the apartment. There was no one there but the sleeping child. And on one such evening Andrei made love to Stasia, a tender love that was warmer and more close than he could ever before remember. Stasia looked up at Andrei as he still held her folded in his arms, and said quietly, "What is going to become of us, Andrei?"

Andrei looked into her violet eyes for a long time, at the tiny golden sparks in the violet. "My dearest," he finally said, "I'll tell you what is going to happen. You are going to marry me and we are going to live together and bring up our children together and lead our life together, and whatever may happen I will always protect you and cherish you and you will protect and cherish me as well."

The words, Andrei thought later, might have sounded too formal, too old-fashioned, to this lovely young Russian woman. But they seemed to be what she wanted to hear. She was, he came to learn, as old-fashioned, if that was the proper term, as he in her understanding of human relationships. She had married a young student while both of them were going to Moscow University. It had been a passionate relationship but after the birth of her son, Vladimir, both she and her husband realized that their life paths were heading in different directions—he toward greater and greater preoccupation with his career as a physicist, she wanting a more traditional life as a woman who found her fulfillment in motherhood, in the creation of a strong and firm family life and only incidentally in a career outside the household. Moreover, she was an Orthodox believer, something of an anomaly in present-day Russia. Her husband did not object to Stasia's beliefs but as a scientific atheist he could not share them.

The young couple had decided to part before their life became further entangled. Andrei respected the courage with which Stasia had faced that first difficult life decision. He respected and shared her beliefs in the roles men and women should have in relating to each other and toward life. And he, too, believed in the Orthodox faith.

"But first, before we marry, *Taishet* must be published," Andrei said.

Stasia agreed.

*   *   *

Andrei Sokolov met Nikita Sergeyevich Khrushchev himself a week before the issue of *Novy Zhizn* with the first installment of *Taishet* was due out. The question of publication had been resolved nearly two months earlier with an official decision by the Politburo, but even so, the issuance of a permit for publication by Glavlit, the chief literary censorship, took another month. Though the Politburo had formally authorized publication, Glavlit insisted on receiving a copy of the manuscript, reading it in its entirety and only then issuing the official Glavlit permit—in this case No. 26742.

Now, on this March day, Andrei had come once again to Moscow from Kostroma, to attend a reception which Khrushchev was holding at the Kremlin in the great hall of St. George whose beautiful marble walls were engraved in gold with the names of all Russian holders of the Czarist medal for bravery, the Cross of St. George. Khrushchev was meeting with the representatives of Soviet culture—the writers, the painters, the playwrights, the poets, the editors, and not only the literary writers but also the political writers and the party intelligentsia. There was a great rout of some three hundred people, all talking, all wearing their best foreign finery, all jabbing spoons into the rich beluga caviar, drinking the vodka and champagne, reaching for the rich chocolate cakes, the smiling big oranges, the Antonov apples. They were all jostling for position, trying to get as close to Khrushchev and the other Politburo members as possible, to talk with them if they could manage and, most important of all, to be seen by their colleagues in positions and postures of intimacy with the oligarchy that ran the country—and, of course, the arts.

Andrei felt uncomfortable even before he showed his invitation at the Borovitsky Gate of the Kremlin. He left his coat and fur hat in a big cloakroom and, like all the other male guests, hastily ran his comb through his hair to smooth out the creases left by the fur cap.

Within St. George's Hall it was all chatter and craning necks. Andrei recognized several of the guests. He saw Ehrenburg in a corner, a saturnine smile on his face and a tumble of cigarette ash down the vest of his excellently tailored gray English tweeds; Simonov, looking relaxed and slightly bored, his handsome wife by his side; dreamlike Ulyanova, Andrei's star of stars at the ballet for as many years as he could remember, appearing tired, older than he thought, accompanied by a somewhat younger husband. And there was the poet Yevtushenko, very much like the Siberian schoolboy he was—well, older than a schoolboy, but with a schoolboy's dash and irrepressibility. Andrei did not exactly like Yevtushenko but he admired his vitality. He recognized Kochetov, the reactionary editor of *Oktyabr*, chief enemy of *Novy Zhizn* and the liberal tendency in the arts. Kochetov was a bulky man, with a mop of hair which had once been blond, and he cultivated a demagogue's pose, one hand resting on his chest. Then suddenly there was Stasov, smiling and embracing Andrei and saying: "Congratulations, Andrei Ilych. Now come and meet Comrade Khrushchev."

Stasov quickly escorted Andrei through the throng, apologizing here, greeting a friend there, leaving a noticeable wake in his train—a deliberate one, Andrei thought. Stasov was going to enjoy his hour of victory. He pulled Andrei along, a little like the bashful schoolboy Andrei now felt. They moved into the center of the crowd where Khrushchev stood, small and almost miraculously round with his little potbelly and his quick narrow eyes darting this way and that. Khrushchev was standing with Suslov, tall and melancholic on one side, and Marshal Malinovsky, his breast sagging under the weight of what Andrei guessed must be nearly five kilos of medals and orders on his brilliant green-uniformed chest.

"Nikita Sergeyevich," Stasov said. "May I present—"

Khrushchev did not wait for the sentence to be finished. He grabbed Andrei's hand with a strong, swinging grip, holding it as he talked, his eyes lighting up.

"No need to introduce this man," said Khrushchev. "This is one of Russia's new treasures, as the world is about to discover. I congratulate you, Andrei Ilych. Yours is the talent we need for the new days that lie ahead."

Andrei blushed. He did not know how to hold back the blush. "Thank you, Nikita Sergeyevich," he said.

"No thanks are necessary," said Khrushchev jovially. "But let me ask you one question. You talk about potato peelings and how they saved your life at Taishet. I know something about potato peelings, too. When I was growing up at Kalinovka we were very poor. My mother always cooked the potato peelings. They are rich in vitamins, one of the best sources. That's what our scientists say. Do you mean to tell me that at Taishet they threw the potato peelings away? I can't believe that."

Andrei chuckled inwardly. It was precisely the kind of pragmatic question to be expected from this little man, whose curiosity and energy had changed so much in Russia in so few years.

"No, Nikita Sergeyevich," he said. "They didn't throw away the peelings. They were used for the prisoners' soup. But at the ratio of one potato peel for each liter of soup. When they are so thinned out there is hardly any nourishment left. Whereas the potato peel itself— as I am here to testify—is filled with nourishment and will support human life."

"Hmmm," said Khrushchev. "That's more sensible. Now let me tell you something. *Taishet* is a novel that had to be written so that the Russian people could know what happened, so they would not forget. We are in your debt."

"Thank you, Nikita Sergeyevich," Andrei said.

"But another thing, young man," Khrushchev said, drawing Andrei closer to him and speaking in a hoarse whisper which he may or may not have thought was inaudible to the throng gathered around him, "remember that not everyone agrees with me. Just remember that."

Andrei smiled.

Khrushchev turned to Suslov. "Mikhail Andreyevich, have you met our new Russian author, Andrei Ilych Sokolov?"

Suslov bowed gravely but said nothing, nor did he extend his hand. Khrushchev ignored Suslov's conduct and turned to Malinovsky.

"Rodion Yakovlevich," Khrushchev said. "May I present our new Russian author, Andrei Ilych Sokolov."

Malinovsky's portly figure bowed slightly at the middle. "Pleased, I'm sure," said the marshal.

"You may not know this," Khrushchev said to Malinovsky, "but Andrei Ilych had a distinguished career in the war."

Malinovsky's attention was momentarily aroused. "Indeed?" he said. "In what branch of the service did you participate?"

Andrei smiled. "Nikita Sergeyevich is too kind. I was a captain of artillery on the second Belorussian front."

"Nonetheless," Malinovsky said seriously, "service is service, wherever it occurred. The defense of the fatherland is no small thing."

By this time Khrushchev's attention was diverted. He was engaged in animated conversation with Madame Furtseva, the Minister of Culture. Andrei felt Stasov gently tug his sleeve. The meeting with Khrushchev was over. He slipped out of the inner circle, Stasov at his side.

Andrei's life as a celebrity had begun. As he withdrew from the circle around the Premier there was a surge of guests toward him. They came pushing forward. Some boldly shook his hand, offering their names in introduction, and brazenly complimented him on his "great new novel," which Andrei knew they could not possibly have read. Others were a bit more circumspect. They came to Stasov and asked for an introduction.

*   *   *

For an hour, Andrei submitted to the pulling and hauling. Then, with a quick shake of Stasov's hand, he slipped away into the somewhat raw evening, the lights of Alexandrinsky Park haloed in gold and the traffic in the Moscow streets flowing in its customary pattern. He headed for the subway, and fifteen minutes later was knocking at the door of Stasia's apartment.

She opened the door, her eyes glowing. "How is my literary lion tonight?" she asked.

Andrei drew her close to him. "I cannot believe it," he said. "I can't let myself believe it. I wish that I had not been there, that all the others—the Dedya Petyas, the old Zakhars, the Father Ivans—had been at the Kremlin tonight, greeted on the reception line. The Khrushchevs and the Suslovs and the Malinovskys, yes, and the Simonovs and the Yevtushenkos and the Sokolovs, above all the Sokolovs, should all have prayed their forgiveness, knelt before them to wash their feet and comfort them in their sorrows. That would have meant a new day for Russia."

"But," said Stasia gently, "you know something like that did happen tonight. You are the surrogate of the Ivans and the Petyas."

Andrei put his head in his hands and was silent for a long while. "God help me, but you are right in a way," he finally said. "I am a surrogate, for instance, of my mother, Maria. Someone owes penance for her. And my father. He, too, was a victim and there are all the other victims of their generation. In fact, my dearest Stasia, there are so many victims one wonders how we can ever do penance for them all."

Chapter 50

ANDREI had left Stasia early that morning after the Kremlin reception and caught the first train back to Kostroma. He was still dazed by the reception, by the fact that *Taishet* actually was being published, that after all these years he had achieved the first of the goals he had set for himself. But he was overwhelmed, too, by his feelings about those for whom he spoke, the martyred Russian people. Then he heard again in his ear the husky whisper of Khrushchev: "Remember that not everyone agrees with me." And superimposed on Khrushchev's words in his mind's eye was the tall, sardonic, even stately figure of Suslov, his steel-rimmed spectacles on the bridge of his nose, his unsmiling face, looking like a scholar with the fire of a Savonarola burning within him. Surely Suslov did not agree with Khrushchev, and it was no accident that he neither spoke nor offered his hand.

Andrei had gotten back to Kostroma and plunged frantically into work. He was putting the last touches to his second book, *Lubyanka*. The first draft was already in Stasov's hands. He had read it, slapped his head in talking with Andrei and said simply, "Incredible! Incredible, Andrei Ilych! This may take a miracle to get published. But I swear that I will fight for it." Andrei had also laid the foundations for his Black Book. He had collated the papers he retrieved from his old Aunt Sofia, and he had gotten the smaller cache that Rosa's mother had kept. And he had made the basic outline of the form that the Black Book would take.

* * *

Then the storm hit. The postgirl staggered, literally staggered, under the sacks of mail. Sometimes there was nearly a whole bag for him. The telegrams piled thick as autumn leaves on his desk, almost burying his massive old typewriter. There were telegrams of congratulations from Russian writers, from workers' organizations, from Party actives, from writers abroad (how could they know what he had written?)—from Louis Aragon, from Heinrich Böll, from Yukio Mishima, from Sir

Charles Snow, from Arthur Miller, from the Hungarian Marxist critic, George Lukacs.

Telephone calls kept coming in to the Kostroma Post Office. Until Andrei told the Post Office he was taking no more calls, the postgirl made her way up to the cottage through the mud to tell him to come to the station for the calls. There were cables from foreign publishing firms in London, New York, Paris, Stockholm, Tokyo. Everyone wanted the rights to *Taishet 303.*

Then there were the reporters and photographers. Andrei spent half an hour with a man from *Izvestia.* To a man from the *Literaturnaya Gazeta* he gave ten minutes. He refused to see a correspondent and photographer from the magazine, *Ogonek,* but they waited at the door and took his photograph anyway, and later he read the article, based on talks with his fellow teachers at the Kostroma high school. The Writers Union invited him to join and suggested that he affiliate with the Kostroma local. Anderi was astounded to discover there was a Kostroma local and that there were four other writers in town—a feuilletonist for local newspapers, a remarkably banal lyric poet, a retired critic and a writer of cheap adventure stories for children.

For a month Andrei struggled to keep his head above water, to continue his mathematics classes at the high school, to sit at his desk for six hours a day regardless of interruptions. Then, he came to his senses. He realized that his life had changed irretrievably, that the circle of peace and quiet he had drawn around himself had been shattered. The school year was almost ended, and he submitted his resignation. It was accepted, he thought, with a good deal of alacrity by the stern, gray-haired school principal, Irena Vassilevna. She had never been comfortable with the strange fish named Andrei Ilych Sokolov, and now he had clearly become much too big a fish, much too prominent for the quiet and convenience of a small-town school. Just as Andrei's life had become a problem for him, so it had become a problem for the school. Andrei emptied out his battered suitcase and filled it with the letters and telegrams he had received. There was still an overflow. He put the remainder into a worn knapsack and took the train to Moscow. There he laid his dilemma before Stasia.

"Is there some way that you might help me out?" he asked. "I'm simply snowed under. I can't open the letters, let alone read them. I've not answered the telegrams."

Stasia looked at the jumble of paper in the suitcase. "Of course I can, my poor Andrushka," she said. "What you must have is a secretary, and as it happens, I am an excellent secretary."

"You know this is not going to let up for some time," Andrei said anxiously. "I don't know how long the flow of mail and inquiries will continue."

Stasia laughed lightly. "I'll enlist for the duration," she said. "I'll simply tell them at *Novy Zhizn* that I must have a leave of absence.

And if they don't like that, I will leave my job. This is much more important."

Andrei sat lost in thought. He idly ran his hand through the heaps of letters. "Who knows what's in these letters?" he said. "I have a feeling that there is another *Taishet* written in the simple words of the readers."

He was again silent. Then he turned to Stasia. "You know, my dearest Stasia, I want you as my wife. Why should we wait longer? We will live together and work together."

* * *

The old Voskresenskaya Church lay in a small lane only a stone's throw from Gorky Street. A passerby on the busy shopping street, *Brodvai,* the Moscow street urchins called it, would never have supposed that half a block from this vulgar display of Stalin's architectural taste there still existed a small island of the old Moscow, the Moscow of forty-times-forty churches, the Moscow of golden onion domes, of deep-throated church bells, of candle-cluttered altars, of black-gowned priests and white-scarfed women.

Andrei had known the church since his first excursion to Moscow with Rosa. They had stumbled into it one day in wandering through the Moscow streets, and had been captivated by its simplicity, by this bit of the past preserved almost unchanged.

It was to this church that Stasia and Andrei went for their wedding. They had gotten the civil certificate at the Bureau of Registry, a spruced-up place as compared with the dismal office where Rosa and Andrei had gone long ago in Rostov. Now the regime was trying to put a little festivity back into the marriage ceremony. Stasia and Andrei were asked, as was each couple that appeared, whether they didn't want to celebrate the occasion in the "wedding palace"—complete with white gown for the bride, a plain black suit for the groom and a limousine for the guests. A caterer would provide a wedding feast as well. Andrei refused politely, although the idea made his teeth grate. He had already arranged with Father Ipat for the ceremony. The next Sunday was *Troitsa,* Trinity Sunday, one of the most pleasant of Orthodox holidays. The little chapel would be filled with the scent of fresh birch boughs and field flowers specially brought for the occasion. Andrei and Stasia would attend mass, and when the believers left the church, the Father would marry them before the small altar at the side of the church.

"I only wish that Father Ivan could perform this ceremony," Andrei told Stasia. "It was he who gave me my belief. And when I give credit for what I have been able to do I must give credit to Father Ivan and his faith."

The small church was jammed for the *Troitsa* mass. The women parishioners with their white kerchiefs and drab black coats, a scattering of middle-aged middle-class couples and pleasant young people in their twenties, each carrying a branch of some kind—willows, acacias, ash, birch. The chapel was filled with their fragrance and the fragrance of the incense as acolytes and priests swung the censers, chanting the ancient Orthodox prayers. Andrei and Stasia stood at the rear of the church. With Stasia were her mother and her little son, Vladimir, or Volodya as he was called. He wore a white-and-blue sailor suit and a sailor's hat with a red pompon and the word "Aurora" lettered in gold. Andrei had invited only Rozen and Morozov to come, but Morozov was unable to join them. His health was failing and he was confined to his bed. Rozen was cheerfully curious. "After all," he said, "I've never attended an Orthodox service before. I hope I don't make a fool of myself."

The chanting of the mass went forward. The women in their white kerchiefs, each holding a long lighted taper which cast a glow onto their exalted faces, gave their responses. The monotones of the Orthodox chant and the clear simple voices of the acolytes captured Andrei's senses like a golden web. His eyes sought those of Stasia, who clutched his arm more tightly. Presently the mass was concluded, and slowly the crowd moved out of the church into the quiet sun-filled lane.

Now Andrei and Stasia came forward. First they exchanged rings three times. Now they stood before Father Ipat in his white robes, Andrei taking the first step onto the white altarcloth. The altar candles were golden stars beside the cross and the Bible. Andrei caught a glimpse of Volodya's eyes, clear azure and filled with the glow of the candles. Stasia's golden braids haloed her face. There were no traditional crowns to hold over the bride's and bridegroom's heads, but Andrei and Stasia stood straight and solemn as the Orthodox words were repeated. Andrei's "Da," "I do," rang out in a voice that was firm and almost stern. Stasia's words were spoken with a melody that reminded Andrei of the pure tones of a harpsichord. Father Ipat bound their hands with the white scarf and three times led them around the altar.

Then Father Ipat anointed them and gave his blessing. Andrei kissed Stasia's soft warm lips. He felt his hand trembling as it covered hers and hers trembling within his grasp.

* * *

That summer Andrei saw little of Kostroma, though he kept his room there. It was, after all, his official residence. But he and Stasia rented the two ground floor rooms of a dacha in the little summer village of Saltikovka, on the Ryazan *chaussée*, only half an hour from Moscow on the blue electric suburban train. They shared the tiny kitchen and its clay stove with the old woman who lived upstairs and owned the dacha. The house was set in a small forest of straight tall pines that rose like pillars toward the sky. Andrei built himself a small writing table under one of the pines and worked there eight and ten hours a day. Stasia's mother cooked their meals, and Volodya played all day in the sunny yard.

Never had Andrei felt so happy, nor so fulfilled. Never had he found more sheer joy in life, joy such as he had never hoped to experience. Stasia was pregnant, the child would be born in March. "It will be a boy," Andrei said. "I know that. A man's first child should always be a boy. He will be straight and tall and blond like you, Stasia, and we will call him Ivan, the most Russian of names."

The tidal wave set off by *Taishet* went on shaking their lives. Stasia was able to lift most of the burden of the correspondence from Andrei's shoulders. She sorted the mail, sent endless telegrams, refusing in his name invitations to deliver lectures, to write articles, to take trips abroad ("I could never get permission in any event, even if I wanted to go, which I do not," Andrei told her.) Stasia tried to cope with the importunate foreign publishers, some of whom even flew into Moscow and demanded to meet Sokolov—demands he steadfastly refused. "I will not meet with any foreigners," he told Stasia. "I don't know what they may be up to. It is better just now, at any rate, to have nothing to do with foreigners."

How wise, he thought in retrospect, this decision had proved to be; what protection it had given him when things began to change! He had not made the decision by any law of logic except that basic Russian law: it's better to have nothing to do with foreigners, no matter who they are. Even when Louis Aragon and his almost equally famous wife, Elsa Triolet, came to Moscow to pay a visit to Triolet's sister, Lili Brik, and he was invited to meet them at Lili Brik's apartment, Andrei made Stasia refuse in his name. "Just tell them I am so deeply involved in creative work I can do nothing else," he said.

The system did not work perfectly. Arrangements for foreign publication of *Taishet* were a jumble. Andrei simply threw up his hands. "I can't cope with it, Stasia my dear," he said. "You'll have to sort it out some way or another."

What was really unexpected, what Andrei could not have foreseen, was the flood of letters from former prisoners in the camps. They came by the score. Then by the hundreds and finally by the thousands. These he insisted on examining personally, regardless of the time it required.

As he told Rozen: "Here is the raw material for a dozen Black Books." And this was no exaggeration though many of the stories overlapped. Several writers told of the same incident—the use of tanks, for instance, to crush the revolt of the prisoners in the Pechora camps. But each letter had new and different details. There were scores of letters from prisoners whom Andrei had met in his own long years in camp but none from Father Ivan, who he was convinced must have died. And soon enough, he had a letter from an old Taishet prisoner. It was true. Father Ivan had been released from Taishet but had died soon thereafter of a kidney ailment, his body worn out and crippled by years of camp existence.

Andrei's greatest prize was a letter from Dedya Petya. The old man —for he now was indeed an old man—had not written it himself. It was written for him by his granddaughter, the same child whom he had first seen on the compassionate leave which Andrei arranged so he might go on to Rostov and escort Rosa to their front-line rendezvous.

It was a simple letter. Dedya Petya apologized for writing. Perhaps Captain Sokolov had forgotten his wartime companion, former Sergeant Pyotr Demidov. They had served together in the 73rd Artillery Battalion. He had long hoped for some news of the captain, whom he remembered with deep and warm affection. He had, he said, by chance some articles which belonged to the captain. Perhaps he might have the honor of returning them to him. He was a pensioner now, living with his granddaughter, who was a teacher in the primary school in Ulyanovsk. His wife had long since died. So had his daughter. He hoped that his letter would not trouble the captain.

"I must go and see him," he told Stasia. "I owe my life to this man as much as I owe my faith to Father Ivan. I don't think it's accidental that it has been the simple people of Russia, the ordinary men and women of the Russian soil, who have come to my aid, who have changed the course of my life."

*　　*　　*

Andrei took the night train to Ulyanovsk. He reached the sleepy Volga town the next afternoon. He had dozed all night in the soft car, his thoughts carrying him back to the war, back to the days when he first met Dedya Petya, remembering the straight figure of the man, his simplicity and his dignity. He was surprised at the shabbiness of the Ulyanovsk station and the dusty main square. He almost expected to see a few mangy droshkies tied up and waiting in the late afternoon heat of the hot August day. But there were none, nor were there any taxis outside the station.

Andrei shrugged his shoulders, asked a passerby where he could find the address on Dedya Petya's envelope and learned that a bus would take him there. First, he thought, he had best see about a place for the night. The stuffy mustard-brown lobby of the hotel was buzzing with flies. No one was about. The window of the *kassa*, the office, was shut. A gray piece of cardboard had been stuck into it with the scrawled words "*Mesto Nyet*"—no rooms available. Andrei looked about him. It seemed unlikely that the drowsing hotel was filled with customers. He rapped at the window with no result. He smiled grimly. He would again have to revert to the tried and true Russian custom. Taking a five-ruble note from his pocket, he carefully slipped it under the window. Hardly had he done so than the note disappeared and the window flew open to reveal the face of a bored young woman who rubbed her eyes as though she had just awakened from a nap.

"Perhaps you have a room for tonight, Comrade," Andrei said, muttering something about a *komanderovka*—a business assignment. The girl took one look at Andrei, correctly deducing that he must be from Moscow and not from the provinces, selected a key from the board behind her and said, "Please, Comrade. It's on the second floor."

In the hotel dining room Andrei bought a bottle of Moskovskaya vodka, a piece of fairly good sausage and a loaf of white bread. Wrapping them in a copy of *Pravda* to take to Dedya Petya, he set out to find the old soldier. The bus proved to be an ordinary Zis truck with a canvas roof and covered sides into which wooden benches had been fitted. The streets were unpaved, dusty, potholed; the sun blazed down from the steppe across the Volga.

Andrei got off at the end of the line, walked a quarter-mile along a rutty clay road and found the place he was looking for. It was a small wooden house, quite new, but built in the traditional Volga manner with carved blue shutters and sloping red tin roof. There were fruit trees planted around it—apples, plums and cherries—and a little garden where small cabbages and dusty potato plants could be seen. All were suffering from lack of water. It had been a dry summer along the Volga. The garden was obviously Dedya Petya's work. Andrei opened the gate and strode up to the house. At one side, he saw an old man sitting on a narrow wooden bench projecting from the house. He wore a comfortable countryman's cap with a battered patent-leather visor and was dressed in what Andrei instantly recognized as his old Army fatigues, a clean white undershirt and a pair of *bast* shoes. He was staring out over the countryside and did not hear Andrei's approach until Andrei said, "Dedya Petya—I've come to see you!"

The old man started up from his bench, looking at Andrei for a moment in confusion, then stepped forward, straightening his figure as he did so and lifting his hand to the brim of his cap. "Captain Sokolov. At your service, sir."

Andrei took another step forward and threw his arms around the old man, kissing him on both cheeks, which were almost obscured by the great white mustache that raggedly covered half his face. "Dedya Petya," Andrei exclaimed. "My old comrade!"

*   *   *

Andrei spent the evening with the old man. It was as he had long suspected. Dedya Petya was the man who had gathered up the box of papers from the hut when Andrei had been summoned before the colonel. The camp grapevine had known of the presence of the Security officers. Actually they had come two days before Andrei managed to make his breakthrough and return to the battery.

"If you'll pardon the expression," Dedya Petya said after several toasts of vodka had been drunk, "we all knew that *swolich* Petroshenko was at the bottom of it. He had been seen with the Smersh men and had been heard boasting. The fact of the matter is that I was coming that morning to try to give you a bit of a warning when I saw the orderly at your door. I hope that you'll not think I did wrong, sir, but as soon as you had been escorted away I went into the room."

Dedya Petya sheepishly admitted that he had long observed the captain's habit of writing, and when he entered the room he instantly spotted the box of papers and the diary. "I just couldn't help myself, sir," he said. "I had to take them away. I was certain they would do you no good. You know the old saying—Never put any words on paper or they will return to bite you in the throat."

"Well," said Andrei, "thank God once more for your good sense, Dedya Petya. Had you not done that, I would not be here sitting with you tonight. You saved my life, just as you saved it on several other occasions."

The old man sighed. "Well, it is good to feel that one life has been saved where so many were being lost."

"That is right, Dedya Petya," Andrei said. "Whatever became of Lieutenant Colonel Smirnov?"

"Oh," the old man said, "he came out of the war all right. I don't know what happened after that but he was with us when we got to Berlin—which is more than I can say of most of the others."

"What about Colonel Stromlin?"

"Nothing happened to him," Dedya Petya said. Andrei knew Dedya Petya had never liked Stromlin. "Yes. Nothing happened to him. By the time we got to Berlin he had been made a Lieutenant General. He knew how to take care of himself."

"And what about that pig Petroshenko?" Andrei asked.

"Him," Dedya Petya snorted. "He was one who got his just deserts. He didn't make it to Berlin."

"What happened?" Andrei asked.

The old man was silent. Then he looked about cautiously. He knitted the heavy brows of his eyes and leaned toward Andrei. "He didn't last very long. Matter of fact, he only lasted about a week after your arrest. We were moving up again. Got into a fire fight. I don't know exactly what happened, but he never came back."

Andrei looked at Dedya Petya. The old man's blue eyes glinted sharply, then he turned away and fingered his vodka glass.

"Aye," the old man said. "That's the way it happens sometimes. One lives, another dies. It's God's will, you know."

Andrei sensed it would be well to change the subject. He asked about Dedya Petya's family. He congratulated him on his granddaughter, who bustled about putting a fine supper on the table. She was a quiet girl, dark, and with a hint of the same simple dignity and straight bearing of her grandfather. Her husband was an agronomist on a nearby state farm.

As he talked, Andrei thought about the fate of Petroshenko. No one would ever get Dedya Petya to admit it, he thought, but almost certainly he had put a bullet through Petroshenko's body in that fire fight a week after Andrei's arrest. Not only had this simple, quiet man saved Andrei's life, he had exacted vengeance on his enemy, on the enemy of all the good soldiers of the battery.

It was time to leave. Dedya Petya went to the next room, and Andrei saw him fumbling under the bed. In a moment he returned, Andrei's long-lost box in his hands. "Here it is, Comrade Captain," he said. "I've kept it all in order waiting for the moment when I could give it back to you."

Andrei embraced the old man once more. "God bless you and thank you," he said.

*　　*　　*

"You see," he told Stasia on his return to the dacha outside Moscow. "You see what the Russian people really are, the best of the Russian people. Of course, the rulers have debased many of them. I know that. I know how I myself have been debased. But in spite of everything, the pure gold shows through. Dedya Petya, dear Praskovaya Ivanovna who saved my life in Kysel-Khor—how many, many of them there are!"

"And there are many who are not like that," Stasia said, her violet eyes fixed strongly on Andrei. "Remember what happened to the young people who went to the countryside to try to bring light to the 'dark people,' the peasants, back in the 1870's. Remember how many lost their lives, simply murdered by the dark people who were so suspicious of them."

"Ah, that I know," Andrei said. "And you must, of course, remind me. It does no good to idealize anyone. But look what *Taishet* has done. It has stirred them up like a hurricane. It has given them a truth —not a new truth—but the truth they were born with, which generation after generation of rulers has twisted and distorted."

"And my dearest Andrushka," said Stasia, "how many whirlwinds will it take to blow away all the evil from our great Russian land?"

Chapter 51

AS Abramov sank into the chair across the desk, Andropov's quick eyes detected a few thin beads of perspiration glistening on his upper lip. The man, Andropov realized, must be under more nervous tension than he wanted to reveal. Did Abramov sense how critical the moment might be, or was it excitement engendered by the information he was about to impart? Whatever the cause, Andropov immediately moved to ease any tension.

"I know this has been a boring day," Andropov said, "too nice a Sunday to spend chained to our offices. We'll make it up soon. I believe you like to hunt ducks?"

"That is one of my greatest pleasures, Yuri Vladimirovich," Abramov responded, his eyes sparkling.

"Well," said Andropov, "as soon as they begin their fall migration we'll arrange an expedition. I know a marvelous place in Belorussia—perfect. The birds come in over the marsh so thick they blacken the sky. Well, don't get me started on that. What do you have to report?"

With obvious reluctance, Abramov turned his mind away from the thought of ducks.

"To put it plainly, Yuri Vladimirovich," he said, "I haven't got as much as I'd like, but I have rather more than I might have gotten. Krasin was not entirely cooperative. Or perhaps he just doesn't know as much as I expected. But one of the most interesting things was not what he said about Sokolov's activities but the way he described his own attitude."

"What do you mean, Abram Abramovich?" Andropov asked.

"Just this," Abramov replied. "He said, in effect, that Sokolov was more important to him than we were. To use his exact words, and I wrote them down, just as I heard them on the recording apparatus, 'So far as history is concerned, it will record that I was a friend of Sokolov. Nothing else in my life is as important as that.' "

"Well," Andropov mused. "That is a very sweeping statement. Was he warned that he is not exactly invulnerable to charges which we hold against him?"

"Naturally," said Abramov.

"And his response?"

"He simply repeated what he had said in slightly different form, adding that of course he did not wish to go to prison but that prison was a small matter beside his friendship with Sokolov."

Andropov stared beyond Abramov to the bare back wall of his office. This was, indeed, going pretty far. After all, Krasin was not a man of strong character. He was a well-known critic. His association with Sokolov dated only from the publication of *Taishet 303*. He had written the lengthy and exuberant review which Stasov published in *Novy Zhizn* and had quickly become one of the circle that sprang up around Sokolov—not one of the inner circle but close enough to know, in general, what Sokolov was doing and the broad lines of his thought.

The hold Security had on Krasin was a simple one. He had been entrapped in a fairly sizable currency operation in partnership with an Iranian diplomat, trading rubles for dollars which could be used to buy hard-currency foods, American hosiery, French gloves, liquor, cigarettes and perfume at the so-called *valuta* stores. Rather than prosecute Krasin and send him to prison, the Security Ministry had decided to keep him on tab, calling him in to one of their safe houses, from time to time, for "conversations" about intellectuals who aroused their interest.

"Tell me," Andropov said, "has Krasin ever displayed this kind of intransigence before?"

"Not that I am aware of," Abramov replied. "I am sure I would have been told. Nor was he really uncooperative today. He simply made it very clear that in any quarrel between Sokolov and the government his sympathies would lie on Sokolov's side."

This was, Andropov thought, all the more remarkable, but he did not particularly want to stress the point with Abramov. He shrugged his shoulders.

"Well, Abram Abramovich," he said. "You never know with these intellectuals. They tend to be nervous and hysterical. Who knows what may have inspired Krasin to such bravado. Anyway, that's his business."

"Certainly," Abramov replied. "Well, to go on to what he had to say about Sokolov: he claimed he had not seen as much of him lately as in the past because Sokolov had, as it were, drawn into the narrow circle of his old friends whom he met in the prison camps as the controversy between himself and the government had become more intense."

"He is accurate enough in that respect," Andropov said. "That agrees with our own observations."

"Quite true," Abramov continued, glancing at some notes he held in his hand. "As for communications abroad, Krasin said he knew nothing at firsthand. However, he had the impression that Sokolov employed a variety of methods for communicating with his supporters. 'He is a man with a military mind,' Krasin said. 'He thinks of communications and operations in military terms. He would never rely on only one channel, that would be too precarious. He has many ways of sending messages—or manuscripts, for that matter. And he never trusts anyone too far.' "

Andropov nodded. He was aware of this. In fact, Security two years earlier had penetrated one of the Sokolov channels that ran to West Germany. Almost immediately Sokolov had ceased using the route except for innocuous materials, which, Andropov thought, were deliberately intended to conceal from Security the fact that Sokolov knew the route was no longer reliable.

"No doubt of it," Andropov said, "he is a clever man. He knows our techniques and we know his. But that doesn't make it any easier to trip him up."

"So it seems," Abramov said. "Krasin pointed out what we know perfectly well—that Sokolov has numerous contacts with foreigners and foreign correspondents—although for a long time he shunned them like the plague. These contacts give him a multiplicity of means whereby he can easily send and receive communications anywhere in the world. Moreover, there is, as we well know, the international telephone."

"All this is obvious," Andropov said with a suggestion of disappointment. "We know all of that better than he does. What about specifics of his clandestine communications network?"

"Not a thing," Abramov said. "Nor, Yuri Vladimirovich, do I think Krasin is lying. It does not seem logical to me that a man with Sokolov's sense of security would expose such a secret except by great inadvertence."

"Unfortunately," Andropov said, "I am inclined to agree with you. Did Krasin never get any clues from those around Sokolov? From Rozen, for instance, or Morozov?"

"Not a thing," Abramov said, "or so he insists. Here I would take his word, too. You know there always has been great jealousy on the part of Rozen and Morozov. They never showed any sign of warmth toward Krasin or others whom they considered newcomers."

"Well, Abram Abramovich," Andropov observed with a slight grimace. "This sounds like pretty much of a dry haul."

"Not entirely," Abramov said. "He did give us one nugget. He knows what Sokolov is working on—or so he claims."

"Ah," said Andropov, "now I see why you were somewhat enthusiastic. So what is this magnum opus?"

"It's a compilation of Stalin's crimes," Abramov said. "Exactly how extensive it is, Krasin doesn't know. He has heard it referred to only once or twice as 'the book,' and it is only in the context of other conversations that he has been able to deduce that 'the book' relates to Stalin."

Andropov pondered Abramov's news a moment. This *was* a worthwhile discovery. Possibly a trump.

"Does he have any notion what form the book will take?" Andropov asked.

"He says he cannot be certain," Abramov replied. "All he knows is that Sokolov has been at work on it for a long time. With the collaboration, presumably, of Rozen and possibly Morozov. It may be that the idea took shape in Sokolov's mind while he was still in prison camp."

"How far advanced is Sokolov on the work?" Andropov asked.

"Again, Krasin could not say precisely," Abramov said. "His impression is that the work has gone on for several years at the very least. It should be close to completion in his opinion, possibly even completed."

"And does Sokolov propose to publish this abroad?" Andropov asked.

"Presumably," Abramov said. "It isn't likely that it would be published in the Soviet Union."

"I agree," Andropov said. "Not likely. And yet at one time such a publication might have been contemplated. I mean in the days of the Khrushchev revelations about Stalin at the Twentieth Party Congress. Or even, I suppose, at the time of the Twenty-second Party Congress."

"Those Congresses are a long way in the past, Yuri Vladimirovich," Abramov said tersely.

"Yes, but I'm trying to fit this into perspective. Well, I suppose a book about Stalin's crimes could still be a sensation in the West, although, God knows, they publish two or three works a year on that subject."

"But not by Sokolov," Abramov said.

"No, not by Sokolov," Andropov agreed. "Did Krasin think that publication might be forthcoming soon, or didn't he know about that?"

"He just didn't know," Abramov said, "but he felt certain Sokolov would publish the book when he was ready, and he did not think any action by the Soviet state would halt him."

Andropov blinked his eyes. "Pretty cocky, I'd say," Andropov observed. "But not too unrealistic. Does he think the book has reached the West?"

"He does not know, but thinks it may not have," Abramov said, "and I would guess myself that it has not yet been taken out. If it had, I think we would have picked up some report on it from one of our sources."

"Quite probably we would," Andropov said, "although I would not want to guarantee that. Sokolov knows the rules of conspiratorial secrecy and seldom violates them. Anything else?"

"Not really," Abramov said. "Krasin had heard that the visit between the Morgans and Sokolov did not come off well. The Morgans wanted him to come to the West. He insisted that he was a Russian, this was his country and he did not propose to abandon his native land."

"Very well, Abram Abramovich," Andropov said. "I think in one way or another the Krasin talk was helpful. I doubt that I will need you again today, but you might just stay on call for a while until I am entirely certain."

*   *   *

As Abramov left the room Andropov rose to his feet and walked slowly over to the window looking out on Dzerzhinsky Square. As was his habit, he pulled the curtain back an inch or two and stared out. How little of life we really see, he thought, a little more than a glimpse through an inch or two of a silken curtain.

Nothing in Krasin's recital surprised him. Not even Krasin's biographical loyalty to Sokolov. He was a bit puzzled by the fine beads of perspiration on Abramov's upper lip. Nervousness lest his report did not give Andropov as much information as was expected? A call from someone trying to find out what Abramov knew? Gorbunov, perhaps? A minor puzzle. Hardly worth his time and effort with the clock running so fast. It was almost eleven-thirty.

The truth was, Abramov's report gave Andropov the information he needed. Of course, Sokolov was planning to publish abroad his book about Stalin. What other purpose could he have? It would be embarrassing, to be sure. More of a scandal than the one he, Andropov, had managed to stir up over the Morgans, more in the class of the scandal that broke when *Lubyanka* was published abroad. But the Soviet Union would survive. The book would create special political difficulties at this moment when every effort was being made to get the policy of détente firmly established. Stalin's crimes once again would be used as a stick with which to beat the Kremlin. The American Congress would be aroused. But everyone had been through that before.

From his own standpoint, Andropov reflected, a new compilation of Stalin's crimes was not going to turn the world topsy-turvy. Back in 1956, when Khrushchev gave his famous anti-Stalin speech, or even a few years later, the repercussions within the Kremlin would have been intense because Stalin's crimes were not only Stalin's crimes but were shared by others—by his associates in the Politburo. In those days the Politburo was made up of Stalin's partners in those crimes. But today? Who was left? Brezhnev—a mere underling in the worst Stalinist days. Kosygin—a victim of Stalin. Podgorny—a nothing then and a nothing today, a vague relic of the Khrushchev era. Gromyko—never involved. Shelepin, much too young. Grechko—on the Army side. Who was there, really?

A grim smile came to Andropov's face. Yes. There was one person to whom it made a great difference. A vital difference. There was one true Stalinist still in the Politburo, one man who might even be named by name in Sokolov's book: Mikhail Andreyevich Suslov. What a useful coincidence. Of all the men in the Politburo, only Suslov could have any direct personal involvement in Sokolov's book on Stalin's crimes.

Andropov sat down again at his desk. He looked at the list of names he had made. He put a double check at Suslov's name. He must, he thought, for the sake of security, run through the other members briefly. But he could not conceive of a circumstance in which any of them would be a real threat, and as for Suslov, he now felt he could not only check but mate any move that arose from that quarter. Perhaps this was going to be a not too unpleasant Sunday afternoon after all.

Chapter 52

THERE had been a light fall of snow during the night, and when Andrei awoke at 6 A.M., the fire in the clay stove had gone out and he was cold. He threw his overcoat over his shoulders, got a fire going, dressed and walked down the village street a hundred yards to the well. There were already three sets of footprints in the snow where early rising workers had passed on the way to the railroad station a couple of miles distant. Andrei let the bucket down for water, trudged back to his cottage. Although most of the summer residents had gone, and even though the cottage was cold and difficult to heat, he preferred the peace and quiet which enabled him to work with no interruptions.

Back in the cottage, he turned on his small radio just in time to catch an announcement of the "resignation" of Khrushchev and his replacement by Brezhnev. He listened to the communiqué to its conclusion, and sat down to contemplate what meaning this event was likely to have.

One thing was immediately obvious. No work by Andrei Ilych Sokolov was likely to be published in the Soviet Union for the foreseeable future. All of his plans would have to be rethought.

* * *

The announcement of Khrushchev's fall was broadcast Friday morning, October 15, 1964. On Sunday, a day that wavered between thin sunlight and scudding snow clouds, Sokolov, Rozen and Morozov sat around a dirty table in one corner of an almost deserted café on the edge of Neskuchny Park, long since rechristened the Park of Rest and Culture, drank from bottles of strong Moskovskaya beer and ate *buterbrod*, ham sandwiches on fresh Moscow rolls.

"I haven't talked to Stasov again," Andrei told his companions. "I don't have to. He has made no progress in getting approval to publish *Lubyanka*. Certainly conditions will be worse now."

"Naturally," Morozov agreed. "They undoubtedly regarded publication of *Taishet* as a mistake. It may even have been used against Khrushchev."

"No need to talk," Rozen said. "What do we do next?"

"First, and most important," said Andrei, "is the security of the Black Book. The manuscript must be completed and the data put in a safe place which will make future publication possible. We must be prepared to publish abroad if necessary."

Morozov shook his head. "If it is published abroad, this in itself will give the authorities grounds for challenging its authenticity. They will denounce its authors as traitors to the fatherland."

"Agreed," said Andrei. "But that is the price we must be ready to pay. Is it better to keep the manuscript in Moscow, let it be seized and burned by the KGB and its authors sent once more into the Siberian camps?"

Rozen said grimly, "With Khrushchev there was always the possibility of a turn for the better. Now we must plan for battle under new conditions."

"But," Morozov interjected, "the compilation of the Black Book is far from finished."

"I realize that," Andrei said. "We must make entirely new plans. We must send the manuscript abroad in sections. If we have the chance, we can amplify it later on. The important thing is to get the *corpus* outside the country, into a safe and secure place where it can be published by a simple signal from Moscow. Or even without a signal, say, in the event of our arrest."

"That sounds easy," said Rozen with a wry smile. "But we have no foreign collaborators."

"Not true," Andrei said. "We have good collaborators abroad. They simply do not yet know they are to be our collaborators. There are many friends in foreign countries. In Germany, for example. Certainly in France and America. And even in places like Poland."

Andrei glanced about the deserted café. No one had come in. Two slatternly waitresses sat some distance away, not talking, their elbows resting on a cluttered table.

"I already have one route abroad," he said. "I have met a completely reliable journalist—let's say for convenience that he is from Poland. He has equally reliable contacts in France."

"Ah," said Rozen, "then that problem has already been solved."

"Only in a sense," said Andrei. "This is one man, one route. Who knows how long it will prove reliable? We must have at least three routes of transmission to have security over the long run. One channel can be disrupted too easily—the failure of a single individual. No, we must develop more paths. You must give me your ideas."

Morozov and Rozen sat in thought. Finally Rozen broke it. "Andrei Ilych," he said, "I think of one possibility. It might work to get the materials into West Germany."

Andrei interrupted. "Don't tell me the exact means. I don't want to know, any more than I want you to know the exact details of the route I mentioned. You control your own route. I'll control mine. We will have everything done in four copies. One for my route. One for yours. One for that which our friend Morozov will establish."

Morozov looked puzzled. "I can't imagine how I could be helpful here."

"Possibly not," Andrei said with a smile. "But may I remind you of your long-standing friendship with Ludmilla Feodorovna, who for some years was the personal secretary of our late great physicist Zhakarov?"

Morozov smiled sheepishly. "Very well," he said. "We have agreed on the first step. But once the material has gotten to Germany or France—what then? There must be someone to act at our instructions."

Andrei looked about the room. "Let's have another beer, for the sake of appearances," he said.

He called to the waitress. *"Devushka,"* he said. "Three more beers."

The woman rose heavily, went to the cooler, picked up three brown bottles, set them on the table, then slouched away.

"That is more difficult," Andrei agreed, "but I think I can manage it. Let us assume that this point can be taken care of. What more?"

"Well," Morozov said. "One thing. We must accelerate the collection of material."

"True," Andrei said. "To be honest, I already have more material than I have been able to digest. However, in general, you are right. Another thing I must say—it is more important than ever that only we three know what we are actually doing. Fortunately, my interest in prison conditions, in the crimes of Stalin, is so widely known that it is taken for granted by the authorities. They do not look beyond their noses. They think only in terms of individual cases, such as my petition in the case of the Crimean Tatars. They must go on thinking in such terms."

"Remember," Andrei continued, "once the archive has been deposited abroad we will be, practically speaking, invulnerable. That is —the truth will be invulnerable. Regardless of what is done to us, the truth will become known."

                              *   *   *

Stasia gave birth to Ivan Andreyevich, Andrei's first son, in mid-March, almost nine months to the day after she and Andrei had married. It was a raw Moscow day, with gray skies, a cold wind, patches of snow. Andrei took Stasia to the hospital in a taxi, then paced the floor of the small waiting room for four hours until he was finally permitted to come to his wife's side in the spacious ward. She already had the crinkly-faced, reddish infant at her breast. Andrei rushed to her side, half-knelt beside the bed and said, "Bless you, Stasia, my darling wife."

She smiled wearily at him and Andrei said in awe, "So I have a son. Anastasia Nikolayevna, for many years I wondered whether this could ever happen. I thank you for giving me such great happiness."

* * *

This was the week Andrei got his first important message back through the underground channel he had established with the West. He had decided to test the channel for the first time with the manuscript of *Lubyanka*. It was only too apparent that *Lubyanka* was never going to be published in Moscow. Even Stasov no longer had any hope. He had done his best. He had gotten his own editorial board to approve it. He had taken the bold step of having the manuscript set into type and had circulated the proofs to members of the Politburo even before Khrushchev was ousted. But Khrushchev had been too busy fighting for his own survival. It was not a moment when he could afford to expend his dwindling political influence battling over a manuscript so controversial as *Lubyanka*. Once Khrushchev was gone, Stasov sadly confessed he had no hope of winning approval.

"All I can say, Andrei Ilych," he said, "is that perhaps in a few years the political climate will change. You know how it does change. Then we can go back to the battle."

In the months since Khrushchev's death, stories about *Lubyanka* had bubbled through the circles of the Moscow intelligentsia. And Andrei had inevitably heard the gossip that *Lubyanka* was "anti-Soviet" and that its author was guilty of a lack of patriotic feeling toward the fatherland. In general, there was beginning to be much talk in literary political circles that the "thaw" in literature had gone too far. Men like Kochetov, the reactionary editor of the magazine *Oktyabr*, were openly saying that it was "time to teach these lily-handed intellectuals a lesson."

"It looks like the Pasternak story all over again," Andrei told Stasia. "The next thing will be a demand that we shut up or leave the country."

Thus, the fact that *Lubyanka* had arrived in safe hands in the West gave Andrei enormous satisfaction. He had not yet decided whether to permit its publication, but at least he now had that capability.

He told Rozen and Morozov when he reported the success of the new communications route: "They are beginning deliberately to circulate slanderous reports about *Lubyanka*. It is obvious that they wish to destroy my reputation with the Soviet public. Soon there will be excerpts put into circulation by the Security police, through their agents, carefully edited and distorted to prove their case."

"Perhaps," Rozen said, "it would be better to go ahead immediately with publication abroad."

"I would prefer to wait," Andrei said. "I don't want my work published abroad. I don't write for the foreign reader. I write for Russia, for Russians living in their own Russia. Only in the last resort do I want to publish outside Russia."

"Andrei Ilych," Morozov said, "you are coming to that dilemma which has faced every great Russian writer in one form or another— how to get your word to the people. Pushkin was censored. It was not until after 1917, when the archives were opened, that we came into possession of all of his original texts. Gogol was censored. Turgenev preferred to live in France and publish from there because of the Czar's interference. Tolstoy was suppressed. You know the story of Dostoyevsky, Chekhov, Gorky. Gorky had first the problem of the Czarist censorship, then the Communist censorship. The story is as familiar to you as it is to me."

*   *   *

In telling Stasia of the conversation, Andrei said, "There is another reason why I am not eager to publish abroad which I will not conceal from you. We've talked before. I warned you that when you joined your fate to mine I could not be certain down which path this would lead."

Stasia interrupted, "You need not go over that again, Andrei Ilych. We walk together and I know that our path may lead back to Siberia. That has been before my eyes from the moment I met you. Can you imagine a woman who loves you who does not insist on sharing your fate, particularly if it is a cruel and harsh one?"

Andrei sighed. "I know you think that way, *dorogoya*, but I hope somehow to spare you and our little Ivan the worst."

Stasia put her hands on either side of Andrei's head, and looking directly into his eyes, said, "Andrushka, when the Decembrists were exiled in 1825 by Czar Nicholas to the ends of Siberia, their wives and their children accompanied them to that land of cold and hardship. There was no hesitation. They knew this was their fate. I know my fate as a real Russian wife. It is in your life wherever that may be."

*   *   *

It was not until all three lines of communication had been tested, not until the first sections of the Black Book had reached a reliable repository in Europe, that Andrei, with great reluctance, sent a message to the West that he could no longer in all conscience object to the publication of *Lubyanka*.

He had been watching with concern the growing pressure on Soviet writers which began with the prosecution and conviction of the underground poets and critics, Sinyavsky and Daniel, and was to continue with only occasional interruption from that time forward.

"I cannot see," he told Rozen, "any logical reason why this internal repression is likely to lessen. On the contrary, it is much more likely to intensify."

"In fact," Rozen said, "it may intensify to the point of your arrest. And not only your arrest but mine too, and the arrest of anyone known to be your friend and associate."

"Yes," Andrei agreed. "It can happen that way. But I think there is a protection in being known as a world literary figure."

"But we cannot know how long that will last," Rozen said.

Andrei agreed. What disturbed him particularly was word that a West German emigré magazine had published a chapter from *Lubyanka*. How this came to occur, Andrei had no idea.

"I think it must have been the police," he told Rozen. "Proofs of the work have been available ever since Stasov had it set up in type. God knows into whose hands they may have fallen."

"The publication in West Germany," Rozen said, "is a simple provocation. Now they will say that when you could not get the book published here you turned it over to the most bitter enemies of the fatherland."

"I agree," Andrei said. "And in consequence I have today sent a letter to the Central Committee demanding protection against the unlawful publication of my book. I have laid down the exact circumstances and asked that action be taken. I have cabled this German magazine denouncing them for publishing my material without permission."

"That gives you some protection," Rozen said, "but not much."

"Not much," Andrei agreed. "So I propose—unless you strongly object—to let our associate in the West know that in view of the unauthorized publication of my work abroad and the failure of Soviet authorities to protect it, I can have no principled objection against the publication in Europe and America of my genuine text."

"In fact," added Rozen, "it is the only course you have left. There is nothing to prevent the Security police from fabricating a text and putting it into the hands of Victor Louis, whom they employed to peddle abroad the manuscript of Svetlana Alliluyeva."

"For all I know," said Andrei, "that may already be in progress. How else did that chapter get to West Germany? And how many other chapters may be there already?"

*   *   *

In 1967 the Soviet Union celebrated the fiftieth anniversary of its founding. Simultaneously *Lubyanka* was published in all of the principal Western countries to an outburst of critical and popular enthusiasm which equaled the reception of *Taishet 303*. Not a few commentaries noted the ironic contrast between the ideals of the Bolshevik Revolution and the bitter fruit which had ripened under its aegis.

"When will it end?" asked the reviewer for *The New York Times*.

Le Monde said: "*Plus ça change, plus c'est la même chose.*" And Malcolm Muggeridge wrote in *The Sunday Times*: "At last we know what we have always known. The Riddle of Russia which Churchill sought within the enigma is no riddle. It is just the same old Russia no matter whether Czar or Commissar rules in the Kremlin."

And, inevitably, *Pravda* charged in a savage commentary that "One of our internal emigrés [the paper did not deign to mention Sokolov by name] has tried his best to spoil the great celebration of the Soviet people honoring fifty years of enormous never-before-seen-on-earth achievements. But he has, of course, ingloriously failed. The only person damaged by this vile outpouring of filth is the lickspittle writer himself, vainly spewing out cannibalistic trash to the order of his capitalist masters."

A few days later Andrei received a telegram in Moscow advising him that a meeting of the Kostroma local of the Union of Soviet Writers would be held that evening to discuss the case of the writer Sokolov.

There was no time, of course, for him to get to Kostroma. He tried to telephone the Kostroma local's secretary without success. Finally, he sent a telegram demanding an adjournment until he could arrive. He took the first available train, which jolted through the dark evening, stopping at every village. On departing Moscow the train was filled with peasants, their arms loaded with bags and bundles. They had been shopping in Moscow at GUM, the great department store, and the other Moscow stores, for the items impossible to obtain in the countryside—white bread, decent sausage, dress goods, well-made fur caps, toys for their children, electrical appliances, aluminum saucepans. As the train rumbled on they got off at one station after another and other peasants got on with great bags of potatoes or cabbage or onions slung over their shoulders.

It was a chilly November night. The windows were covered with frost, which turned to golden patterns when the train ground to a halt beside the dim lights of the small stations. To Andrei it seemed an even longer ride than usual. Finally, at eleven in the evening, he arrived at Kostroma. The streets were deserted. Tucking his briefcase under his arm, he walked down Lenin Street to the building which housed the local of the Writers Union. It was dark and locked. He went along the street to the old and familiar cottage where he still kept his room and which was still registered as his residence. The two old pensioners had long since retired. He opened the separate door to his room. It was cold and musty. He had not been there for months. He turned on the dim electric bulb and rubbed his cold hands together. Presently he heard a stirring—he had awakened his elderly landlady. He heard the patter of her feet and then a timid rap and her voice saying, "Is that you, Andrei Ilych?"

"Yes," said Andrei. "Sorry to have awakened you."

"Oh, that's nothing at all," she said. "Are you cold? Would you like a glass of hot tea? The samovar is still going."

He thanked her, took the glass of hot tea and threw himself on his old bed, fully dressed.

*   *   *

So, he thought, of course, the Writers Union had expelled him. There would otherwise be no purpose in meeting. But how banal this Russian bureaucracy was. It had not changed in a hundred years. All it could think of was to suppress, to reprimand, to close the door, to shut the ears of all the people, to put a blindfold over their eyes, and if that did not work, to use chains and fetters. There was always bondage and prison. There was always a way to shackle the spirit. How at home Czar Nicholas I would feel in today's Russia. Stalin must be smiling. And Lenin—Lenin, too, would probably align himself on the side of bureaucratic tyranny.

Chapter 53

THE news of Stasov's death in 1969 was not unexpected. The old man had fought too many fights, his body bore too many scars (he had fought as a common soldier in World War II until he was nearly killed by a shell fragment which tore through his abdomen) as well as the deeper wounds of the spirit. His drinking had become heavier in the years since Khrushchev's fall as he watched the ideological tyrants slowly and inexorably turn back the wheels of creative progress.

Despite all this, Stasov had never lost his inborn optimism. The last time Sokolov had met with him, Stasov had been confined to bed in his huge, cluttered apartment just off Gorky Street.

"You are a young man, Andrei Ilych," Stasov said, his great figure propped up on pillows, wearing a torn gray wool sweater, books and manuscripts piled on the bed around him. "Don't ever lose your confidence in victory. I never have, no matter what they have done to me."

Stasov had, actually, just suffered another blow. He had lost the editorship of *Novy Zhizn*, tricked into offering his resignation. The Central Committee had told him it wished to award him the Order of the Red Banner of Labor on his seventieth birthday. It proposed that he resign his editorship before that day to avoid a certain embarrassment because a rival conservative editor was not going to get the order on his seventieth birthday.

"Perhaps you'll think I'm a fool," Stasov told Sokolov, "but I decided to turn in my resignation. I'd be retiring anyway in another year. My health is poor and it didn't seem to make that much difference. The magazine can't publish anything decent in these times, regardless of who edits it."

It was particularly revealing, Andrei thought, that after Stasov resigned, the Red Banner of Labor never was awarded to him. The award had been delayed on one excuse or another. Now the old man had died, and Sokolov thought the duplicity must have hastened his death.

"I cannot be silent," he told Stasia, "when this wonderful man who did so much for Russian literature and for me personally dies in such dishonorable circumstances. I must say what is in my heart."

Stasia looked at her husband with some concern. She had their second son, Boris, born just three months earlier, at her breast. Andrei looked stern—and especially so because he had recently grown a full beard in the traditional Russian style and it made him look like an Old Testament prophet.

"Of course," she said, "you will do what you think is right. But you must be careful, Andrushka. They probably will take steps to prevent you from being present at the funeral."

"No matter," Andrei said. "I will go. If they stop me—well and good. But I do not think they have the courage."

*　　*　　*

Stasov's body was to lie in state at the House of Writers on Voronsky Street, the very Rostov mansion in Tolstoy's *War and Peace* at which the ball is in progress when news arrives of the battle at Borodino. As on all such official or semiofficial occasions, admission to the funeral was by ticket and in this case only members of the Union of Writers or government officials were permitted to enter the building.

"I had been in the country at my dacha," Sasha Semyonov, a writer of detective stories much in vogue, told one of his friends. "I drove into town but I was a little late. Outside the House of Writers there were militiamen and many plainclothes officers. I parked my car and was hurrying across the street when, to my surprise, I saw Sokolov ahead of me, walking very rapidly with a long-legged stride. He was looking neither to the left or right and his full beard seemed to flow behind him."

Andrei crossed the street diagonally ahead of Semyonov. The great double door to the house was open. Half a dozen men in plain black suits stood at the entrance: functionaries of the Union and Security plainclothesmen.

"There was no doubt," Semyonov said, "that they were expecting him. Some of the men had walkie-talkies, and I saw them speaking into them as Sokolov came up to the entrance."

At the door, Semyonov was immediately behind Sokolov. He had his own Writers Union card in his hand. The men at the door said something to Sokolov. "I think they asked him whether he was a member," Semyonov said, "but whatever it was he simply strode past them and into the hall. As I came up they were nonplused. They didn't seem to know what to do."

Semyonov heard a man at a walkie-talkie just inside the hall say, "He's here!" Semyonov followed Sokolov down the red-carpeted hall with its carved mahogany ceiling and paneling. There were many people in the hall, some checking hats or coats at the cloakroom, others strolling toward the great hall where Stasov's body lay.

Sokolov walked down the corridor, head high, ignoring those around him. He was dressed, Semyonov noticed, in a plain Russian blouse of natural linen with only the simplest embroidery in blue at the neck. The blouse was belted with what Semyonov took to be a worn Army leather belt. He wore dark blue Army breeches tucked into polished black Russian boots and no hat.

Semyonov heard one walkie-talkie after another crackle into action as each plainclothesman relayed his information: "He's here. He's entered the building. He's walking down the central corridor."

In a moment Sokolov reached the wide double door leading into the great hall where Stasov's body lay in an open coffin. The room was filled. Every writer and editor in Moscow was present—old Konstantin Fedin, who had broken with Stasov in the 1940's and gone on shamelessly to persecute his old friend and neighbor Pasternak; Kochetov, the crudely reactionary editor of *Oktyabr*; Andrei Voznesenky, the coolly courageous young poet; the poet, Bella Akhmadulina, her red hair a splash of flame in the gray room; Tvardovsky, Stasov's staunch supporter and the editor of *Novy Mir*; the director of the Taganka theater, Lyubimov; Konstantin Simonov who as the years had passed, had drawn closer and closer to Stasov; Leonid Leonov, the crotchety, fussy author of *The Forest*; Yevtushenko, his face almost too much the stereotype of grief; Furtseva, the chameleonlike Minister of Culture; and even Rada Khrushcheva, the fallen Premier's editor-daughter.

At the broad entrance to the hall stood four men, obviously Security plainclothesmen. Sokolov strode past them without a break. Semyonov saw one Security man reach out an arm to bar Sokolov's way, but the writer simply brushed the man aside, pushed his way thrugh the throng, murmuring apologies, emerged into the small space around the open coffin and walked up to where Stasov lay, in a plain black suit and white shirt with, miraculously, the Order of the Red Banner gleaming on his breast. Sokolov bent over, kissed Stasov lightly on the forehead, then rose, squared his shoulders and took his place at the right hand of Stasov's widow, who stood at the head of the coffin.

There was dead silence, broken almost immediately by the husky voice of a plainclothesman speaking into his walkie-talkie: "Yes, as I told you. He is here. He is now standing beside the widow." There was a screech and the walkie-talkie clicked off.

The mourning throng stood silently a moment longer, heads bowed, then old Fedin pushed his way up to the side of the coffin and began to speak: "Dear comrades and friends," he said, "we gather here to pay tribute to one of Russia's great literary figures, a man who . . ." He droned on and on, reading from a paper on which his remarks had been carefully typed. Occasionally he fumbled with a word, misspoke it, then went back and corrected himself.

"I thought he would never stop," Semyonov told his friend, "but he did. He spoke only fifteen minutes. I thought he had been going on twice that long."

Finally Fedin finished and took a step back. There was a movement in the crowd. The pallbearers, eight heavyset men, started to come forward when Sokolov, whose eyes had been cast down throughout Fedin's remarks, raised his head and spoke in a clear carrying voice: "Friends of Boris Maksimovich Stasov. Dear friends. True friends. We come to pay a tribute which can never rightly be paid. Boris Maksimovich gave us and gave our Russia more than we can ever give back to him. He gave us truth. He believed in truth. He fought for truth, and if he did not always win his battles, it was not the fault of Boris Maksimovich. It was our fault, the fault of those who, like Boris Maksimovich, also loved truth but who did not fight as hard as he did for its victory. Let us at his bier make one simple pledge. Let us go forth and fight for the victory of the word. If we do battle as he did, the victory will be secure and the great Russian people will give us their blessing. If we do not—then they will lay upon us a curse which we will deeply deserve. For the truth is a shining sword which can conquer any tyranny."

Sokolov stepped back a pace and once more stood at the side of the widow, who was now touching her eyes with a white handkerchief.

"Did no one interfere?" Semyonov's friend asked.

"No one," Semyonov said. "No one raised a hand. They were afraid. Even a cynical man like myself was afraid. For here was the voice of the camps, the voice of those millions who died there, the voice of our martyred Russian people speaking from the grave. No. No one stirred. Even the walkie-talkies stopped their chatter."

It was the same at the graveside. Sokolov rode with Stasov's widow and Stasov's son and daughter in a black Chaika car to the Novodevichi cemetery. There in a quiet corner, in the "literary corner," the body of Stasov was laid to rest. Sokolov stood beside the open grave, and when the coffin lid was closed and the coffin slowly lowered into the yellow clay, Sokolov reached down and cast the first handful of earth. As the dry earth rattled against the wooden lid of the coffin, Sokolov's lips moved softly and those close by in the hushed moment later swore that they heard him pronouncing the words of the Orthodox prayer for the dead: "*So svetimi ypokoi christos . . .* with the saints give rest, oh Christ, to the soul of your servant . . ."

* * *

When he arrived home, Andrei walked back and forth in the crowded room talking about Stasov, about the continuance of evil in Russian life.

"I've thought a great deal in recent times," he said to Stasia, "about

my father. I've talked so much about it, you know the story of how
he met his death. I could never accept suicide as an answer, although
I know that for some reason which she never explained, my mother
really feared that—felt that she herself was responsible for Father's
death."

"Perhaps they had quarreled," Stasia said. "Perhaps, there was
something between them which she never told you."

"Quite possibly," Andrei said. "But there are two other possibilities—that he was killed accidentally, stumbling over his gun, or that
he was killed deliberately. I have never been able to accept the accident
theory. He was too experienced with weapons. I learned a great deal
about weapons during the war. Father never stumbled over his gun. He
was shot—shot deliberately."

"But who could have done it?" Stasia asked.

Andrei sighed. "That I will never know, but it must have been
someone whom he knew and probably someone whom he trusted because he was shot with his own gun and left for dead."

"Then, really," Stasia said, "you are no closer to the solution of
the mystery."

"I think I am. Almost certainly my father was killed by one of those
peasants, one of those simple Russian souls whose oppression had so
violently stirred Father's conscience and the conscience of so many fine
young Russian men and women."

Stasia nodded. "Yes, I see," she said. "And that is why you have
told me to remind you that there is evil as well as good in the simple
Russian people."

"Precisely," said Sokolov. "Evil which has grown there. Evil to
which the simple man has been trained by life. I can now see that it
made no real difference exactly which peasant or peasants killed
Father. Perhaps it was a band of Reds who regarded him as an enemy,
a White. Perhaps, they were Whites who believed Father was a Red.
What I have only now come to understand is that among those
peasants there was no real difference—Red or White. They did not
know the meaning of the words. And as life exists in Russia, what
difference did it really make whether the Reds won or the Whites won?
They were equally cruel to each other."

"As they are cruel today," said Anastasia.

"It will take many years," Andrei agreed, "to wash away the centuries of evil and of tyranny. But it's time we made the first step."

"The first step has long since been taken," Stasia said. "And you
have taken it."

Chapter 54

SO . . . Andropov looked again at his wristwatch. Twenty-five minutes to twelve. He must leave his offce at ten minutes of twelve precisely. He had fifteen minutes more to reflect on the situation and to order his thoughts. But, as he told himself, he already knew the essential facts. He had been fortunate. He knew the line he would take and he was clear now on the positions of his Politburo colleagues. There were fifteen full members, seven alternates without voting power. He had already considered the roles of Brezhnev, Kosygin, Suslov, Shelepin, Gromyko and Grechko. He himself made seven.

There were eight others, but they could be scanned very quickly. Podgorny was a lost man. He had been a strong Khrushchev supporter who had gone over to Brezhnev. Brezhnev, it was obvious, had given some personal assurances to Podgorny—to keep him on. Podgorny had doubtless given assurances to Brezhnev to vote his way. So it appeared. Podgorny had not deviated since Andropov had joined the Politburo, although he may have wavered during the 1971 crisis. But there would be no wavering this time. Kirilenko—grooming himself to succeed Brezhnev. A two hundred percent Brezhnev supporter. In a showdown. Andropov decided, Kirilenko would dump Brezhnev, but only to take over Brezhnev's job. Was this the moment for dumping? No. This was still a preliminary struggle.

Kirilenko would be faithful to Brezhnev. Grishin and Kulakov—pocket votes for Brezhnev. Newcomers, they would not be playing high-level politics yet. Mazurov—Andropov wished he could understand this man's mind a little more clearly. Mazurov had an independent air about him. He was a real power, had been ever since he climbed up out of the swamps of Belorussia. But he was too old to make his own bid for leadership. He seemed solidly behind Brezhnev, but something told Andropov that Mazurov was much more complex. Perhaps, today's discussion would tip his hand in some way, but Andropov could not see Mazurov following Suslov's leadership. Instinct told him, however, that on the question of handling Russia's most prominent and spectacular dissident, Mazurov might actually come down hard, might even take an independent line. Carefully he put a question mark after Mazurov's name.

This brought him to another of the possible "independents," Polyansky. A year or two ago Andropov would not have been surprised to see Polyansky as the central figure in an effort by the Young Turks to oust the Old Guard. But not today. Brezhnev had been too clever for Polyansky. He first let him expose himself, deliberately drawing him out. Now the Old Guard had seen the danger, had carefully cut back Polyansky's authority, and Polyansky was fighting to keep his foothold in the Politburo. He was available as a possible supporter for almost any maneuver which might promise him a bit more security. Another question mark, then, for Polyansky.

That left only two members of the Politburo—Shelest, whom Andropov despised—and Voronov, for whom he had a certain sympathy, which he concealed so well that he was certain neither Voronov or any of his colleagues suspected it.

Shelest was, actually, a point man for Suslov. A rather rude one. Perhaps, Shelest did not understand this himself, but with his tough, aggressive, vigilante style he was like putty in the hands of the Machiavellian Suslov. Suslov fed Shelest the lines and Shelest did not even understand he was being used. He thought he was originating the whole strategy of the hard-core Stalinist group. Shelest was totally ambitious. He saw no reason why he should not follow in the footsteps of his distinguished Ukrainian predecessor, Khrushchev, and make the flying leap from provincial Party Secretary to Secretary of the whole Party. Because of his ambition, Shelest was only too easy to entrap. Nonetheless, he was not an opponent to minimize. He was capable of evoking support from the military and he had a following in heavy industry and among the provincial secretaries on the Central Committee who found it difficult to handle their responsibilities except with a heavy hand and the threat of a bully.

Shelest, Andropov felt certain, would be his only open opponent, at least at the start of the debate. Whether others exposed themselves depended entirely on the success of Shelest's line and the success of Andropov in refuting it.

Voronov, on the other hand, was the point man for a nonexistent bloc—the bloc of the progressive Khrushchevites. So long as Khrushchev was in power, Voronov played a major role. Khrushchev balanced him against the reactionaries and this created an artificial "middle" which Khrushchev could occupy. But Voronov actually believed in a comparatively liberal policy. Andropov thought secretly that Voronov believed in precisely the principles he, Andropov, believed in. But Andropov took great care never to expose his real views while Voronov wore his convictions on his sleeve. Month by month and year by year, Voronov came closer and closer to losing his Politburo seat. Perhaps, thought Andropov, Voronov felt that there was no way in which he could reestablish himself and therefore he might as well speak his own mind. Voronov would support Andropov, but it was not the kind of support which made any essential difference. The only thing about it, Andropov thought wryly, was that it was not as injurious as Shelepin's false support because everyone knew that Voronov stood only for himself and was playing no game.

So . . . Andropov put his last little check against the list of members and studied it again. So far as he could determine, there could not be more than five possible votes against him, and of these, only one or two would actually be cast unless it became apparent that there was a major shift in the Politburo as a whole. This Andropov was not able at present to envisage. In fact, he found it hard to believe, on reflection, that Suslov genuinely expected to overturn anyone on this issue.

As Andropov studied the position of the members and looked again at the telltale clues of Suslov's manipulations he became convinced that his hypothesis of a "preliminary engagement" was the correct one. Today's meeting would be a duel of feint and counterfeint. It would be designed to demonstrate to the men on the sidelines—the stolid Brezhnev supporters like Kirilenko, Grishin, Kulakov, as well as the Mazurovs and the Polyanskys—that a vulnerability existed, and that next time around, if all joined forces, Brezhnev could be brought down. In other words, thought Andropov, a rerun in somewhat different form of the 1971 crisis.

* * *

Andropov looked at his wristwatch. Fifteen minutes to twelve. He felt fortunate that events had taken the turn they had. He had no qualms about going into the meeting. He had at least three important pieces of information—secret weapons you might call them—which he could use appropriately. He was not going to be beaten this time.

Andropov rose from his desk and once more lifted the window curtain. The sun was bright. It was a hot day. He saw the flash of women in pink and blue dresses, of men in shirt sleeves strolling up Lubyanka Hill. The traffic around the circle moved steadily. The hum of the cars penetrated the almost soundless sanctuary of his office. For the thousandth time he wondered idly whether the heavy bullet-proof glass really was capable of transmitting the ebb and flow of his conversation through laser detection. He shook his head. It simply didn't seem possible.

He went back to his desk. The little bit of scratch paper with the Politburo members' names and checks after them still lay there. He reached in his pocket, drew out a match, touched the flame to the bit of paper and dusted the ashes carefully into his wastebasket.

Time to go. He looked around the room and back at his desk. The copies of Herzen's *Bell* still lay there. He picked one up and thoughtfully put it in his inner pocket. It might be amusing to produce it at an appropriate moment—if an appropriate moment occurred. He saw lying on his desk the old brown *papka* with the file of Sokolov's case. He hadn't gotten around to looking at it. Well, enough was enough. He didn't have to go back twenty-five years for evidence and arguments.

Andropov touched the button on his desk which alerted the corridor guards and his chauffeur, and at precisely eleven-fifty he strode out of his office. Entering his car at the courtyard entrance, Andropov set off for the Kremlin.

Chapter 55

ANDREI took the early train into Moscow from Peredelkino, where he had been staying with a friend, the composer Aram Aryutinyan. Life had become more and more difficult as Andrei had moved openly into the camp of the dissenters, taking his place outside the courtroom where the poet Yashin was being tried on charges of vagrancy; sending an appeal to the United Nations to consider charges of genocide against the Soviet Union for the oppression of the Crimean Tatars; joining his friend Sakharov in the Movement for Human Rights; and finally sending a cablegram to President Nixon demanding that the United States enter into no policy of détente so long as the Soviet Union adhered to its tyranny over "the Russian and other subject peoples." After this declaration made headlines around the world, Andrei had been summoned to the procurator's office and warned that his acts constituted treason against the Soviet state.

"Why, then," said Andrei, "if you consider that I have committed treason do you not arrest me under Article 58 and condemn me to death or long-term penal servitude?"

The procurator answered coldly, "Everything in due course. I am warning you now officially of the grave nature of your actions. You are an adult man. Think seriously, Andrei Ilych. You are no stranger to us."

"Nor you to me," Andrei retorted. "I first met you in the Lubyanka in 1945, and I have met you under many different names and in many different places. You are the voice of Russian despotism."

"For that remark," said the procurator, his cheeks coloring, "you could be transported for twenty years at hard labor. You have a wife and small children, Andrei Ilych. It is time you gave some thought to them."

"Do you have anything more to say to me?" Andrei asked.

"No," said the procurator, "but bear this in mind. There is a line beyond which the state will not tolerate your conduct."

Andrei told Stasia of his conversation. "They are trying to blackmail me," he said. "This is the first move."

The second move came within the week. Andrei was warned that he had no permission to stay in Moscow. He was legally registered at Kostroma. If he continued to live with his wife in her flat, he would be arrested and she would be evicted from her quarters.

"That is the precise kind of trivial, bureaucratic reprisal which they are capable of carrying out," Andrei said. He issued a statement to the foreign correspondents, telling them of his interview with the procurator and the ban on living with his wife.

The next day Aram Aryutinyan invited him to stay at his house in Peredelkino for as long as Andrei wished.

"Do you realize what you are getting into?" Andrei said to his friend.

"Of course," said Aryutinyan. "I grew up in the Soviet Union. I'm not a kitten whose eyes haven't yet opened. Come and stay with me. The hell with them."

*   *   *

So, for the last month, Andrei had been staying at his friend's house. Now on this beautiful June morning he rose at six, walked through the pleasant tree-lined lanes of Peredelkino, past Pasternak's weathered old cottage, across a gently rolling field, and through the graveyard where Pasternak lay buried, skirting the white church with its blue onion dome. He went to the suburban railroad platform, caught a train, and was with his wife by eight in the morning. It was June eighteenth, Trinity Sunday, the anniversary of their marriage.

At ten, leaving the children with Anastasia's mother, Andrei and Stasia left her flat and walked through the quiet sunshine to the Voskresenskaya Chapel. Once again there was a crowd in the little square, and Orthodox worshipers with fresh boughs in their hands. Andrei had brought two birch branches from the country. Stasia and he made their way into the crowded church, where Andrei put some money in the hands of an old woman dressed in black with a fine Orenburg scarf over her head. Receiving in return three candles—one for his father, one for his mother and one for Stasia's father—he lit them and put them on the altar. Then he and Stasia bowed their heads in prayer and the service began.

They stood quietly, side by side, listening to the worn, melodious words of the Orthodox mass, watching the faces of the worshipers, their eyes clear, their faces illumined not only by the glow of the candles but by an inner spiritual light.

When the service ended, Andrei and Stasia wandered out into the sunshine, holding hands. Andrei noticed that a plainclothesman was following them quite openly. He did not bother to mention this to Stasia. What difference did it make?

They walked down Gorky Street and into Red Square. The square was crowded with Sunday strollers. As they passed through the Spassky bell tower Andrei pulled out his watch.

He smiled to Stasia. "Well, my uncle's old watch still tells the hours, even though, I suppose, it runs on Czarist time. My watch says that it is ten minutes to twelve. The Spassky tower says the same thing. Maybe Czarist watches and Communist clocks speak in the same voice."

* * *

They walked into Cathedral Square and on past the Armory toward the Borovitsky Gate. As they approached the Armory a succession of long black limousines pulled up the hill, one after another. Stasia and Andrei halted—a Kremlin guard was blocking off the roadway.

Andrei smiled at Stasia. "I guess our rulers have found work for their idle hands. Not even Troitsa can halt the labors of the exalted leaders."

Stasia looked at Andrei in some surprise.

"Yes, my dear," Andrei said. "This is the Politburo assembling to debate some vital question. Who knows—possibly even the fate of humble creatures like ourselves."

Stasia smiled and gripped Andrei's hand more firmly. "How do you know, Andrei? I couldn't see anyone in the cars because of those gray silk curtains at the rear and sides," she said.

Andrei laughed. "That's exactly how I know, my darling. Only the Politburo, only our highest officials, insist on such modest anonymity."

The guard permitted the crowd to pass on, and Andrei and Stasia went down through the Borovitsky Gate and entered the Alexandrinsky Gardens, where the red sand of the walks was freshly swept and masses of red canna flamed in the flower beds.

Presently they picked a bench beside a large lilac tree and sat down. Andrei had a glimpse of the "angel" changing pace and going back to find an empty bench for himself.

"I was joking, of course," Andrei said, "when I spoke of the Politburo deciding our fate. But not entirely. One of these days, not necessarily today, but one day before long they will meet and they will decide our fate. Or attempt to."

Stasia looked at him in some surprise.

"Oh, yes, *dorogoya*," Andrei responded. "This is a question that only the Politburo can decide. And I have set something in motion which is going to compel them to act."

"The Black Book?" Stasia asked.

"Yes," Andrei nodded. "The Black Book. I have finally concluded that we can hold back no longer. Every week the pressure grows. Someone else is arrested or deported or exiled. The only thing that has held me back has been the thought of you and the children, but we cannot wait any longer."

Stasia turned to her husband. "Did the visit of the Morgans have anything to do with this?"

Andrei smiled. "Not at all. They are perfectly good people. Somewhat naïve, like all Americans. But they have warm hearts. No, my decision was not connected with them. I had come to it already. Actually, the Morgans tried to persuade me to leave Russia and come to America."

"And that you will never do." Stasia smiled indulgently.

"You know my mind and my heart," Andrei said. "Certainly I will not leave voluntarily and I will not go to America under any circumstances. It may be a suitable country for Americans—although how they survive it I don't know. But it is not a suitable country for Russians—that I do know. I do not intend to take my wife and sons to such a land."

"What will they do when the Black Book is published, Andrei Ilych?"

Andrei put his hand under his chin and remained silent for a considerable time. "I think they will send me back to Siberia," he said. "That is the most likely action. But my impression is that they themselves are uncertain. They know that I command world opinion, and world opinion is very important to them—particularly at this time. American opinion is especially important. They want the United States to side with them against China. They need American factories, American technique, even American food. So what they do to me becomes a choice of evils from their standpoint."

"Perhaps," said Stasia, "they will do nothing. After all they did nothing after *Lubyanka* was published except for minor harassment. They have harassed us as you have grown more active politically. But we can endure it."

"Well, they cannot sit with folded hands after the Black Book is published. They may well send us into exile abroad rather than Siberia. As for myself—I am torn. Siberia, after all, is still Russia, not even a bad part of Russia if you are not confined to a camp. I do not know how I can endure not being in Russia."

"Perhaps," said Stasia, "we can create our own Russia somewhere outside the country. Our needs are not great."

"Dear, dear Anastasia," Andrei said, "I have the greatest treasures a man can possess—a real woman for a wife, two sons of my own and another by inheritance. Those men whom we saw just now going into the Kremlin in their black cars with the curtains drawn to protect them from being seen—and to protect them from seeing the world— those men have nothing. You see, now that the Black Book is safely beyond the Russian frontiers, there is nothing they can do to halt its publication. It is like an avalanche which has started down a mountainside. Yesterday it was resting secure high up in the Alps. The Kremlin village lay safe below. But yesterday I spoke one small word.

Just one word. That word is the boulder that will loose the avalanche. It is still high up in the mountains. Too high for them to see or hear. And when they do see and they do hear, it will be too late. They will be swept away in its course."

Stasia shook her head. "It is frightening."

"Quite true, Stasia, dear, very frightening. And I thought long and hard before I gave that word because, once the word is given, nothing will halt publication. Not even if I cry aloud, not even if I petition them, not even if you, dearest, appeal in my behalf."

Andrei continued: "I did not wish to put myself in a position where pressure could move me. I did not want to bargain my life or yours or the children's against Russia's life."

"So those are the instructions," Stasia said wonderingly.

"They are," Andrei said. "And the word has gone out. Not by one route, not by two, but by several. Even—and this was my silly little joke—even through the Morgans; but they will never be aware of it."

Andrei chuckled. "You know, my dear, there are a few amusing aspects to this affair, and one day perhaps we will live to laugh about them."

"But probably not on any day very soon," Stasia said.

"No," said Andrei. "Not on any day very soon."

Chapter 56

ANDROPOV was delighted with his timing. His car moved up the incline to the Borovitsky Gate in a cavalcade of similar black limousines —three just ahead of him, two behind. He could see by the license plate of the limousine ahead that it was Grechko's. There was a slight pause at the gate as the guards checked each car, and Andropov was pleased to see that the Sunday crowd had been momentarily held up by an officer just at the corner of the Armory where the limousines turned into the Palace courtyard. No barricade, just a militiaman with his raised white-gloved hand. That provided the needed protection, he thought, and just a trace of interference with the free movement of the sightseers. He must remember to drop a pleasant word to General Vasilev, the Kremlin commandant. As his car made the turn at Armory corner he looked at the sightseers through a slit in the gray silk side curtain. For a moment he had a bit of a start. A man with a full beard looking remarkably like Sokolov was staring at him. Andropov shook his head. His nerves must be on edge seeing such things.

There was the usual crowding at the Palace elevator. Suslov was already standing in the rear of the nearly filled lift, towering leanly over his colleagues. Andropov let Podgorny and Mazurov board. "I'll take the next car," he said pleasantly. It was the kind of gesture he liked to make. He waited with Grechko and Grishin. Grishin began to talk about the afternoon's football match. Dynamo was playing Spartak. "Spartak will take them, mind my word," Grechko said gruffly. Like most of the older marshals he prided himself on his knowledge of sports. Gromyko came up as they waited, greeting each man solemnly, then clasped his hands over his stomach in a characteristic gesture. Andropov saw nothing in the conduct of these men that marked the slightest deviation from the norm.

As they rode in the elevator Grishin asked Gromyko his opinion about the afternoon's football match. Gromyko said very seriously, "I can offer no intelligent opinion, Viktor Vasiliyevich. I have not watched a football match in twenty-five years."

In the meeting room just beyond Brezhnev's office the members chatted in idle groups. Brezhnev had not yet appeared. Neither had Kosygin. Neither of them customarily arrived until their secretaries reported that all the other members were present. When they came in, Kosygin, by protocol, always stepped into the room ahead of Brezhnev. Andropov did not separate himself from the accidental group into which he had fallen, but his eyes quickly swept the room. Suslov, Podgorny and Mazurov were talking together. They had gotten off the elevator as a group and had not broken up. Kirilenko and Shelepin had not yet arrived. Shelest was arguing with Polyansky as Kulakov and Voronov listened.

The candidate members, as usual, stood a bit to one side. By tradition they deferred to their seniors. They had the right and even the duty to speak on all questions, but they conducted themselves with extreme rectitude. Not having a vote, there was no reason why they should risk a full member's disfavor by speaking against him. On the rare occasions when this happened, it invariably meant that a cabal was afoot and that a senior member had enlisted a junior to make the preliminary maneuver.

* * *

Kirilenko and Shelepin entered the room together. At this moment Andropov began to move about, greeting those members who hands he had not previously shaken. He deliberately waited until all the members except Kosygin and Brezhnev had arrived. He knew the two seniors would appear in a moment, interrupting him; in this way he made it obvious that he felt no nervousness whether or not he had shaken hands with everyone.

Exactly as Andropov anticipated, Kosygin entered almost immediately. Not by chance, Andropov was the closest man to the door and the first to be greeted by Kosygin. As they stood together, Brezhnev entered and naturally greeted Andropov. Brezhnev glanced quickly over the room. "Everyone here?" he asked (knowing, of course, that everyone must be present or he would not have joined them). It was a worn joke, but the members chuckled perfunctorily.

"So," said Brezhnev working his heavy black eyebrows up and down, "what are we waiting for? Time is money, as the Americans say. Let's get to work."

With a scraping of chairs, the members seated themselves. The room was almost Spartan in its lack of decoration. A large portrait of Lenin looked down from the wall back of Brezhnev, and along one side there were portraits of Marx and Engels. Nothing more. The walls were paneled waist-high in the usual Kremlin Karelian birch, and the long rectangular table was covered with the traditional red baize. At intervals there stood crystal carafes of water surrounded with clusters of glasses decorated with a lightly chased pattern of deer's antlers. Before each member was a white paper pad ruled with thin blue lines and three freshly sharpened hexagonal pencils enameled in Kremlin red and stamped with gold.

Sitting just back of Brezhnev and at either side were two middle-aged women with notebooks in their laps and pencils poised. These were the official stenographers who recorded every word that was spoken and all of the votes. There was, of course, also an electronic recording of the meeting. Andropov occasionally inspected the rolls of tape, but by tradition the stenographers' record was official even when, on rare occasions, as Andropov knew, they mistook a word or mistakenly attributed one member's remarks to another. This was the procedure that had been established in Lenin's time and which had, incredibly enough, been followed throughout the Stalin era (although even Andropov was not certain that the record of Stalin's Politburo meetings had been entirely preserved or whether some documents had been destroyed by Stalin's secretary, Poskrebyshev, or by Beria after the old dictator died, or by Stalin himself before his death).

Brezhnev opened the meeting briskly. This was his style: business-like, no nonsense. He immediately called upon Andropov to make his report on what he called the Affair of the writer Sokolov.

Andropov glanced down the long table. Unlike some of his colleagues, he did not use notes unless dealing with a most complex matter. This was a bit of bravado, perhaps, but he felt he spoke with greater conviction if he did not refer to a piece of paper.

He began by going over the background of the case, facts which everyone knew as well as he. The roots of the affair lay back some years and were connected, as all the members knew, with the mistaken decision insisted upon by the former Secretary General that Sokolov's work *Taishet 303* be published. The publication of *Taishet 303* had generated a hysterical interest in the crimes of the Stalin period, crimes which the government had properly brought to a halt, and which had already been sufficiently exposed by the Twentieth and Twenty-second Party Congresses. Unfortunately, *Taishet 303* had engendered an unhealthy reaction abroad, where it was seen as confirming the worst of the bourgeois anti-Soviet propaganda. At home, it encouraged many less stable elements among the intelligentsia to believe that the Party was abandoning its traditional and principled employment of literature and the arts in the furtherance of the interests of the Soviet state and of Communist society.

It had, unfortunately, been some time before the necessary correctives could be undertaken. Not, in fact, until the resignation of the former Secretary General and his replacement by Comrade Brezhnev.

By this time, however, a certain damage—he would not go so far as to describe it as serious—had been done. If mud flies, someone is splattered. The Party and government course had been corrected. The publication of *Lubyanka*, an even more unprincipled and tendentious work, had been forbidden, but unfortunately the author had smuggled the manuscript abroad and arranged for its publication in the West. It was true that positive evidence of the author's involvement in that publication had never been established because of various mistakes which need not be gone into here. The members were familiar with the situation.

Publication of *Lubyanka* had caused the customary sensation in the West. He would not deny that it had resulted in certain negative propaganda consequences. An active counterpropaganda campaign had been mounted, but speaking realistically, he could not tell the members that this effort had been entirely successful.

That damage was in the past. The problem was to prevent its recurrence in the future. There was no denying that Sokolov had achieved a position of prestige in the West through his writings. In fact, to be realistic, he had become a world figure and had employed his influence in a manner damaging to the Soviet Union.

As the members were well aware, Sokolov had issued many manifestoes, proclamations, protests and the like. These had been circulated by the enemies of the Soviet Union, particularly by the bourgeois press in the United States and Europe. The Sokolov declarations were employed by opponents of Soviet foreign policy. They were second only to the vicious Jewish attacks on Soviet policy that had handicapped Gromyko in his able efforts to carry out the will of the Party in pursuing the policy of détente.

*   *   *

Andropov paused a moment and turned to Gromyko, who was listening with his usual stony face.

"I wish," he said, "at this moment to say publicly, as I have so often privately to Andrei Andreyevich, that his skill in overcoming such obstacles well demonstrates the truth of the old saying that a skilled foreign policy is worth two armies."

Gromyko nodded solemnly at Andropov's remark. Andropov was paraphrasing a famous remark of Stalin's regarding Molotov's wartime foreign policy, and he could not resist the quickest glance to see whether this had registered with Suslov. He thought it had.

Andropov reviewed swiftly the evolution of the so-called dissident movement and the actions the Security forces had taken to disrupt it, to disintegrate its forces, to keep it from becoming a major force.

"I think that on this account," Andropov said, "we can in a certain measure congratulate ourselves. We have contained these unruly and non-Soviet elements. Daily they diminish in numbers and we can look to the future confident that they will disappear. They have in no way infected the general population. In fact, just to the contrary. To take Sokolov as a particular example. His book is no longer to be found in the libraries. The copies of magazines in which his works appeared

have been removed from circulation. Our reports from libraries indicate he is almost never inquired about—outside of some persistent
inquiries in Moscow and to a lesser extent in Leningrad. The Komsomol leaders at the universities and institutes report that his name
is seldom mentioned by students. The report of our own Security representatives agree in full."

Andropov admitted, however, that the problem of Sokolov's declarations was by no means resolved.

"I do not wish to mislead the comrades. These declarations do
cause strong reaction abroad. They are beamed into the Soviet Union
by the foreign propaganda outlets—the Voice of America and the like.
And it is for this reason that we in the Security services feel that
serious consideration should be given to reactivating the jamming of
all foreign transmitters beamed to the Soviet Union instead of limiting
this policy to the Chinese."

"We now come to the very latest developments," Andropov continued, "to the development that specifically caused the calling of this
meeting—that is to say, the open demand by Sokolov to the President
of the United States that he refuse to engage in a policy of détente
unless we agree to certain demands in the name of so-called civil
liberties."

There was a noticeable shifting of chairs at Andropov's words. His
colleagues were familiar with his background exposition, expected it,
regarded it as necessary—but now they were coming to the heart of
the matter.

"Such action," Andropov said, "I hardly need remind the comrades,
can well be categorized as treason. It is a deliberate act by a Soviet
citizen to subvert the official policy of the Soviet state. Let there be no
mistake about this. In a former time there would be no such meeting
as this. There would have been quick and immediate arrest followed
by execution or condemnation to lifelong penal servitude. But, as I
need not remind my colleagues, those days are past. The Soviet government is benign. It not only obeys the letter of the law, it seeks in every
way to observe its spirit. If there is a black sheep in the family, it does
not simply cast him out—it makes every effort to turn the black sheep
away from his mistaken ways. But at the same time we must protect the
rest of the family, the healthy body of the Soviet people, which
remains the apple of our eye."

Andropov was secretly amused to see that this old chestnut had
touched the heart of Grechko. The bullet-headed marshal had nodded
his head seriously and solemnly at Andropov's words. What a fool!
But, Andropov told himself, that is an encouraging response. Perhaps
even Grechko can be brought along.

"We have long since taken protective measures of every kind so
far as Sokolov's activities are concerned," Andropov continued. "It is

not possible to penetrate the mind of a man, and I must warn the comrades that Sokolov is not an ordinary person. But insofar as diligence and vigilance make it possible, we try to do our job."

* * *

Andropov paused and looked up and down the table. His listeners regarded him with rapt attention. He thought he saw a faint sign of anticipation on Shelest's face. But that could have been his imagination.

Now was the time to stir them up a bit. "I must now offer an apology to my comrades on the question of vigilance," he said. There was no doubt of it. Shelest's eyes had begun to sparkle. He even noticed Suslov leaning forward a bit.

"I have been, I admit," Andropov said, "guilty of what might be called an act of overvigilance. But I hope that I may be forgiven. In this case it clearly seemed to me that overvigilance was to be preferred to undervigilance, even though we will be compelled to pay a price."

He sketched out the story of the Morgans' visit. "They came here with the intention of trying to persuade Sokolov to leave the country, to seek refuge in America," he said. "I deliberately permitted this visit because I expected that it would shed light on Sokolov's activities. From our intelligence, it seemed unlikely that Sokolov would yield to the arguments of the Morgans. On the other hand, the visit could give us an insight into Sokolov's plans and communications."

He told of the incident at the National Hotel and the skin search of the famous couple. He gave no hint that he was surprised by the skin search.

"I was determined," Andropov told his colleagues, "to overlook nothing. After our operatives had completed their search, including the examination of the bodies of the Morgans, I myself went to the hotel. I realize that some of the comrades may feel that there was no need to involve myself personally. But as Comrade Shelest remarked at our last meeting, vigilance is my custom. Better too much than too little. If you are going to do a job well, you must do it yourself. And there is no substitute for your own eyes."

Andropov hurried on after referring to "your own eyes." This was a slip. This was what Khrushchev had incessantly dinned into his colleagues: "Get out of your office and see with your own eyes." It would be noticed, he realized. But he went straight on. Nothing had been found at the National. Nothing had been found this morning in another thorough examination at the airport.

"There will be an international scandal," he said frankly, casting down his eyes. "The responsibility for that rests on my shoulders. I am sorry, Andrei Andreyevich," he said, turning to Gromyko, "but you will have a small propaganda storm to quiet. Maybe not so small. But better that than to permit Sokolov to manipulate international public opinion in some other manner. I can assure my comrades that no message, no document, no manuscript, no photograph, no microdot passed out of the country with the Morgans either in their luggage or in their bodies. If Sokolov thought to create some new international sensation, he has been thwarted."

                    *   *   *

Brezhnev interrupted Andropov at this point. "Comrade Andropov," he said, "excess of vigilance has never been regarded as a fault among comrades. I congratulate you on your zeal, and I am certain all of us around this table take the same view."

Brezhnev looked around the table, his bushy black eyebrows raised in a question mark. Every head nodded. Was Andropov wrong in thinking that Suslov's nod was held back just a fraction of a second? He could not be certain, but he saw a bright, eager and patently false smile sweep over Shelest's face.

"Excuse me, Yuri Vladimirovich," Shelest said. "May I join in congratulating you on the zeal which once again you have demonstrated in frustrating the enemies of the great Soviet people. May I ask one question to clarify a point which is a bit confused in my mind? You say that you are certain that no message was taken out by the Morgans. Now you also said, I believe, that our Security comrades had confiscated two articles from the Morgans at the airport—a samovar, I believe, and an old ikon. Now, have these articles been carefully inspected? Can you be certain that there may not have been some message concealed in them which Sokolov attempted to send out of the country?"

His face as impassive as that of a sphinx but pleasure bubbling up inside, Andropov nodded carefully.

Shelest's question had given him more information than he was going to give Shelest. It confirmed his conviction that Gorbunov had been in communication with Suslov, and it told him that Suslov was, as he had been certain, employing Shelest as a point man.

"Ah, Pyotr Ivanovich," said Andropov, "a good question, an excellent question. It was one which immediately occurred to us. We subjected both of these articles, the samovar and the ikon, to instant examination. We even took the handles off the samovar and inspected the silver plating. Not a sign of any communication."

"And what about the ikon," Shelest persisted, a dogged look coming over his face. Yes, Andropov thought, it is certain. Shelest knows about the message in the ikon.

"The ikon?" Andropov said. The interchange had captured the attention of his colleagues. He was not the only one who realized that something lay behind Shelest's questions. No Politburo member subjected another to this kind of cross-examination without a serious purpose. The implication was clear that Andropov was concealing something and that Shelest suspected him of it.

"Yes, the ikon, Yuri Vladimirovich," said Shelest, a thin sneer appearing on his lips. "After all, ikons may be holy objects but they can do the devil's work."

He saw Shelepin lick his lips. Yes, thought Andropov, Shelest has taken the bait. He thinks he has caught me. And Shelepin is expecting the kill.

"The ikon," Andropov repeated. "Yes, of course, we did investigate the ikon."

"And found nothing?" Shelest asked eagerly—much too eagerly. Andropov thanked his good luck in having such an enemy.

"No-o," Andropov said slowly. "No. We did find something."

Now everyone at the table was leaning forward, eager, anticipatory. Something was going to happen. Andropov thought that Suslov was pursing his lips to conceal a smile of pleasure. He saw a light frown on Brezhnev's face. Kosygin shifted a bit in his chair, which Andropov knew was a sign of nervousness. Kirichenko's eyes wandered to Brezhnev's and then back. No one in the Politburo liked surprises.

Andropov fumbled in his pocket, deliberately conveying small signs of embarrassment.

"Yes," he said, like an absent-minded professor. "There was something."

Shelest, darting for the kill, interrupted: "Then why, Yuri Vladimirovich . . ." He let the question dangle.

"I have it here somewhere," Andropov said. Then finally bringing his play-acting to an end, he reached into his breast pocket, drew out the envelope, carefully unfolded the piece of paper and laid before him the bit of faded paper which had been concealed in the ikon with its message.

He put the bit of paper on the pad in front of him.

"Yes," he said, "Comrades, we did find this bit of paper tucked behind the frame of the ikon. I invite you to examine it."

He handed it to Brezhnev, who looked at it closely, then raised his bushy eyebrows to Andropov saying, "Yes?"

"Perhaps, we might pass it around," Andropov said. "You can all see the message:

Звенѣть, колокола!

* * *

There was a moment of silence, then Shelest broke out again.

"Excuse me, Yuri Vladimirovich," he said with more than a trace of sarcasm in his voice. "I thought you said that no message had been found, and yet a message has been found. You must pardon me but I do not understand. And do I understand also that you personally gave orders to permit the Morgans to depart even though they attempted to smuggle this clearly subversive message out of the country?"

Andropov's mind went *click*. More confirmation of his suspicions. Petrov's request that Andropov give him an order to permit the Morgans to depart had not been accidental. It was part of the record someone—Suslov obviously—had been trying to build against him.

Andropov sat silently a moment until the message had gone around the table. "Yes, Comrade Shelest," he said, deliberately not employing the familiar name and patronymic. "Yes, I did instruct the Security personnel to permit the Morgans to depart. I am putting to one side the implication of your remark that due to my lack of vigilance I permitted an attempt at subversive communication to be carried out with my connivance."

Andropov paused again. All eyes were on him. "I wanted all of you, Comrades, to see this bit of paper," he said seriously, "because it, indeed, is a message. But I invite your closer attention to its wording. You will note that it says ' Звенѣть, колокола! ' This could quite clearly be an instruction. It might even, shall we say for purposes of speculation, be an instruction to someone to go ahead and publish a document of some kind. Don't you agree?"

Andropov looked about the room. There was a shaking of heads. "So I would interpret it," he continued. "Perhaps some of you may have noticed that it is printed on very fragile paper. This came to my attention when I first handled it and a small corner broke off. Others among you may have noticed something else. This is a printed message and it is printed in the old orthography, the orthography that was abandoned on Comrade Lenin's orders a few months after the Revolution."

There was a buzz around the table. Andropov saw a faint flush spreading over Suslov's face. Suslov was too clever not to understand what was coming. So was Brezhnev, who now cast his eyes down. Kosygin looked on impassive. So did Gromyko. Grechko's face was puzzled. He obviously understood nothing that was happening. Voronov was openly smiling. When Shelepin's eye caught Andropov's he gave him a wink. He, too, had guessed the denouement. But Shelest was still in the grip of his delusion.

"Very interesting, Comrade Andropov," he said, also dropping the familiar form. "But I can't see what Comrade Lenin's views on the old orthography have to do with a subversive message concealed in an ikon being smuggled out of the Soviet Union by American agents of the CIA."

"Only this, Comrade Shelest," Andropov said. "If you will look at the bit of paper, you will see that the word *svenet* is spelled with the letter *yat*. The letter *yat* was abolished from the Russian alphabet in 1919. It has been fifty years since the letter *yat* could be found in a

Russian printing establishment. You are quite correct in your suspicion that these words constitute a message—but they constitute a message from the past."

Andropov reached again into his pocket and drew out the faded copy of Herzen's *Bell*.

"Let me show you something, Comrade Shelest," he said. "The words Звенѣть, колокола! were published on the cover of *The Bell*. They were, in effect, Herzen's call to his countrymen, to let the bell of truth ring out, to rise against the Czar. If you will look again at the message, you will see quite clearly that Herzen's slogan has been clipped from a copy of *The Bell*. I would estimate that this act occurred about a hundred and twenty years ago, maybe in 1851 or 1852. It's not possible to say exactly.

"Why was the slogan concealed in the ikon? After all these years it is not possible to be certain. My guess is, and I repeat that it is only a guess, that some young Russian revolutionary, one of the predecessors of the Narodnovoltsi, perhaps, brought this ikon back *into* Russia at that time and used this device to escape the search of the Czar's gendarmerie. It was, in all probability, an instruction to one of Herzen's colleagues within Russia—an instruction to *Ring Out the Bell!* To publish or circulate one of Herzen's documents."

* * *

There was a rustling of chairs as Andropov completed his statement.

Brezhnev then spoke. "I must congratulate you, Comrade Andropov," he said, "on a brilliant example of scientific detective work. A work, shall we say, in the category of what was his name—that English detective?"

"Sherlock Holmes," Suslov supplied dryly. "May I join with Comrade Brezhnev in his remarks. This is an excellent example of the work of our Security services at their best."

Shelest sat silently, a stubborn look of disbelief on his face. He started to speak, then obviously thought the better of it, and began to scribble violently on his pad.

Andropov relaxed, but hoped he gave no sign of it. It would be all downhill from here on. He picked up his story, sketching it out succinctly and with no flourishes. There was good reason to believe that Sokolov was preparing another major work. So far as the evidence demonstrated, it would fall into the pseudohistorical category. A book about Stalin's crimes which he suspected might already have been sent abroad, possibly even several years ago. The publication of the work would naturally be embarrassing, and quite probably Sokolov would attempt to get the book published quickly as a propaganda weapon against détente.

"But," said Andropov, "to be quite frank, we have survived the publication of two of his books and a good deal of his polemics. I do not minimize this book. It will cause a stir in the West. But practically speaking, what more is there to say? The Twentieth Party Congress and the Twenty-second Party Congress exposed the worst of the anti-Party excesses, the worst crimes of the Personality Cult. What more is there to make public? So far as the Central Committee is concerned, all of this is in the past. There can be no linking of the present Party leadership with these excesses. The old leaders are gone."

Brezhnev nodded his head. "Very true, Comrade Andropov. There is no one around this table who has any secrets to conceal. The Party and the government have made the record public."

Andropov again smiled to himself. Suslov's face was a mask; Shelest's was fiery red—Shelest was beginning to understand what had happened to him. Andropov went on smoothly. There were two alternatives: to take some action against Sokolov now or to await the publication of his book about Stalin. In either case, there was bound to be a storm of international propaganda. For his own part, he would recommend doing nothing at the present time. Who could say? Maybe the new book would never be published. Maybe it could be seized, although he held out no hopes in that direction. In any event, it seemed to him far better if there were one storm rather than two. "Wouldn't that be better in Comrade Gromyko's view?"

"Better no storm," Gromyko said solemnly. "But better one storm than two storms."

"I appreciate Comrade Gromyko's view," Andropov said. "My recommendation, therefore, is that we continue on the present course: careful surveillance of Sokolov, vigilance against any new and unexpected moves on his part, resolute response to any polemics by him (and here I would seriously recommend a reimposition of the jamming of foreign broadcasts), firm repression of any individuals who seek to join with Sokolov or emulate his conduct in any respect, but no major response until or unless the publication of the Stalin exposé occurs. At that time we can decide on the proper course of action—expulsion from the USSR (which may well be the most effective course) or enforced residence in the East or possibly reincarceration in prison."

*   *   *

There was the customary moment of silence. The members of the Politburo always fell silent when a specific proposal was made to them.

Then Brezhnev spoke: "Does any member have a comment to make?"

More silence. Andropov saw Shelest struggling with himself. Finally he could not contain himself. "One small question, Comrade Andropov," Shelest said. "Is it true, as some have said, that Sokolov, in fact, was a member of an anti-Soviet organization which was active among the military during World War II?"

There was a hush. Andropov thought, This man really is determined to destroy himself. Suddenly Voronov interjected: "Comrade Shelest, you are aware, are you not, that a military tribunal considered the charges which led to Sokolov's imprisonment and formally re-habilitated him in 1956? Are you challenging the verdict of the military tribunal?"

"That was not my question," Shelest snapped. "And I asked my question of Comrade Andropov, not you, Comrade Voronov."

But Voronov was on his high horse as well. "I'm sorry," he said with elaborate sarcasm. "I thought that Comrade Shelest had been present when the verdict of the military collegium was read out at the last meeting. I see that I must have been mistaken."

Shelest glowered at Voronov. Those two, Andropov said to himself, are going to devour each other. There was nothing Brezhnev hated more than this kind of family squabble in which dirty linen was flaunted around the meeting table. Brezhnev, looking more than usually stern, intervened: "Do you have some response to Comrade Shelest's inquiry?"

"As Comrade Shelest well knows," Andropov said, "the case of Sokolov was investigated by the special military collegium and the previous verdict was annulled as being without foundation."

"I think that speaks plainly enough," said Brezhnev. "If there are no further comments, I suggest that we put the question on Comrade Andropov's proposals. All of those in favor signify by saying 'Aye.' "

There was a mumbled chorus of "ayes."

"Those who are opposed to the proposals?"

Silence.

"Those who reserve their votes?"

Silence. Shelest looked as though he was about to burst. Suslov seemed plainly uncomfortable. He is embarrassed, Andropov told himself, by Shelest's stupidity.

"In that case, the recommendation of Comrade Andropov is ap-proved," said Brezhnev. "There being no further business, we will be adjourned until the next regular meeting on Wednesday. "

The members rose slowly from their seats. Brezhnev shook hands with Andropov. "Excellent work," Brezhnev said. "A very sensible recommendation. Don't you agree, Comrade Suslov?"

"I do agree," Suslov said. "Vigilance is important. So is intelligent police work."

Andropov passed through the knots of his fellow members, speak-ing now to one, now to another. Only Shelest sulked and pointedly turned away as Andropov approached with the intention of shaking his hand. Andropov shrugged his shoulders. Shelest would not last out the next crisis, he said to himself. Suslov would never again permit himself to be exposed so shabbily. Voronov would be going soon, too. And Brezhnev clearly had nothing to fear in the immediate future. Nor had he, Andropov. He rode down in the elevator with Gromyko. "I'm sorry, Andrei Andreyevich," he said. "I know that I've made trouble for you." Gromyko shook his head. "It's the kind of trouble I've grown used to over the years," he said. "We simply have to expect it and achieve our goals nonetheless."

*   *   *

Andropov drove back to the Ministry. The afternoon was even warmer, sunnier. All of Moscow appeared to be on the streets. He went up to his office. Nothing urgent had happened. The first bulletins were just coming in of the Morgans' airport press conference in Paris. Bad. But no worse than expected. He sat down at his desk. He had come off much better than he had anticipated. Brilliantly, if he said so himself. Shelest had helped by making a fool of himself.

Well, it was the result of careful preparation and attention to detail. He noticed Sokolov's liver-colored *papka* still lying on his desk. He had to admit, the man was clever. How curious that he had thought he had seen Sokolov's face in the Kremlin crowd. He picked up the file and idly began to thumb through it. Yes, here was the report of the military collegium. The charges were unfounded. The case reversed. He flipped back through the file. Here were some of the famous letters which Sokolov had exchanged with his friend Vanya. Andropov glanced at one. His eye caught the closing: "Your Dek–ist." What the devil did that mean? He glanced at another, letting his eye run rapidly through the letter. Suddenly it halted at a word: *Dekabristi*. Decembrist. This was interesting! He read down the text. It was Andrei writing to Vanya. The date was November 13, 1944. Andrei was writing about the Dekabristi and the impact their courage had made on Russian history. Nothing subversive about that—but there was the signature. "Your Dek–ist." Undoubtedly "Your Dekabrist." And here was something else. Andrei writing about Herzen. "Like Herzen," he wrote, "we will ring out the bell."

Andropov closed the *papka* quickly. He rose and went to the great window, once again pulling back the taupe curtain so that he could watch the movement of traffic in Dzerzhinsky Square. He stood there awhile thinking, then turned back to his desk. How little, he thought, we really know of life. And on what tiny accidents fate turns.

He took the small fragment of yellowed paper from his pocket, deliberately crumpled it into dust, then replaced it in the envelope and put the envelope in his desk drawer. He took the copy of *The Bell* which he had displayed at the Politburo meeting and placed it with the other copies, marking them for return to the archives. He ran quickly through the surviving Sokolov correspondence. No other letters contained references to *The Bell* or the Dekabristi. He pulled the single letter from the file, and taking a match from his pocket, reduced the letter to ashes, which he emptied into his wastebasket.

"My God!" he said to himself. "My God! Those idiot men of

Beria! They never even caught it! And Shelest with all his bombast was closer to the truth than anyone is ever going to know."

He drew out his fine chronometer. The hour was just coming up to three. If he hurried he could get to Dynamo Stadium in time to see the last half of the football game. But he would have to hurry.

Chapter 57

THE climax came with almost breakneck speed, faster than Andrei had expected. And yet he had been preparing for a long time, not only psychologically but physically. For several months he had kept his suitcase from Taishet days packed and ready. He had put into it heavy woolen socks, heavy woolen underwear, heavy woolen shirts, handkerchiefs, a thick gray sweater and a pair of work shoes (how long he would manage to keep them out of the hands of the *blatnoy* he could not guess); sugar, chocolate, soup concentrates, cigarettes, writing materials, medicines, his faithful Dal dictionary, two volumes of Stendhal (he had grown passionately fond of Stendhal in recent years), a volume of Heine and a copy of his own *Taishet*. He had lashed to the suitcase his worn *telogreika*, the very one that had carried him through Taishet. His prison number, S-203, was still sewn on with white cotton patches.

"Do not worry about this," he told Stasia the night he dragged out the suitcase and meticulously began to pack. "I do not expect that I will need it. But if I do, it is better that it be packed and ready to go."

Stasia could hardly keep herself from tears, but Andrei put his arm around her. "I'm just being a good soldier," he told her. "We must be prepared for the worst. That doesn't mean that we must expect the worst. When the Black Book is published, anything can happen. The rulers will be like maddened bulls. They will snort and tear up the earth with their horns. There will be no way in which they can halt the Black Book, and in their first anger they may lose their heads completely. That's why I am packing this bag."

Andrei was convinced that if he was imprisoned or exiled, it would not be for long. The prestige and renown his books had won in the West were too great. The West would explode with outrage.

"The rulers have been reluctant to take too hard a line against my letters and appeals," he told Stasia. "Even when I call on the President of the United States to stand against détente they do not take a really tough position. Stalin would have called them mewling lambs."

Publication of the Black Book, he conceded, would create a different situation. The government would be *compelled* to act. Not to act would mean, in Russian eyes, acquiescence in Sokolov's indictment.

"But will they risk the whole policy of détente in order to execute me?" Andrei asked rhetorically. "They will not. And when they imprison me or exile me to Siberia, such a hurricane will rise that it will blow the very bars off the prison windows."

"I can only hope you are right," Stasia said. "But if they do send you to Siberia, they will find me and our boys at the gates of the prison camp, beating them down to make our way to your side."

* * *

Sokolov instructed his colleagues in the West to publish the Black Book on New Year's Day. "That will be symbolic," he told Rozen and Morozov. "We will begin the New Year with the clear voice of the Russian people. It will sound out over every barrier and ring like a peal of bells in the ears of the leaders still befuddled with New Year's hangovers in their Kremlin apartments."

"Tactically," Rozen observed, "the timing could not be better. It will be several days before they get the cobwebs out of their brains and begin to concentrate on the devastation this bomb has wrought."

Yet with all the careful planning, the calculations in timing, the psychological preparation of himself, of Stasia and even of the boys (who had been told that great changes were coming in their lives, but not to be surprised, not to be frightened by anything which might happen)—with all this, the knock on the apartment door at 10:42 P.M. came as a shock.

It was the evening of January 7. For a week the telephone had not stopped ringing. Calls came from New York and from every capital in the world. There were calls from every foreign correspondent in Moscow, from a dozen old friends who checked every few hours to be certain that Sokolov was still safe. There were strange calls in which the telephone was dead, or in which someone could be heard on the line but did not speak. Three calls came from the procurator's office demanding that Sokolov appear, and he refused unless a warrant for his arrest was issued.

During the day he and his family were seldom alone. Rozen, Morozov or one of their friends stayed with them. But on this evening, the evening of Russian Orthodox Christmas, Andrei had sent them all away. They had gone to midnight mass the night before, the *yalka,* or Christmas tree, glowed in the corner. Only Stasia's mother was with them. Everyone was tired. The children had been put to bed, the babies early and Vladimir, Stasia's first-born, now a sturdy twelve-year-old, only half an hour before.

When the knock came, Andrei and Stasia looked at each other. They *knew* it was the police. How did they know? How does a mother's ear distinguish the child's cry of pain from the random whimper; how does the sparrow sense the presence of the hawk? They *knew* it. The knock. A brief pause. A second knock. And almost immediately the ring of the bell.

Andrei rose, and as he rose Stasia threw her arms around him. "Don't open it, Andrei!" she cried. "Don't. They have come to take you."

Andrei gently disengaged himself. "My darling, my love," he said. "There is no good in not opening. They would simply beat the door down."

Nevertheless, as he approached the door he said in a strong voice, "Who is there?"

There was a mumble and new knocking He waited until the knocking halted. "I repeat," he said. "Who is there? Give your identity."

"We're from the organs," a voice said. "Open the door, Andrei Ilych."

"Do you have a warrant?" Andrei asked carefully.

There was a moment's pause and whispered consultation. Then the first voice spoke again. "Open up, Andrei Ilych," the voice said. "We must speak with you."

Andrei hesitated a moment, then unbolted the door.

Four men literally leaped into the room. Andrei stepped back, shielding Stasia with his arms. The rush of the men caught him off guard. Stasia's mother huddled in the corner.

"Everything is completely in order," said the leader of the detail, a serious-faced man, middle-aged and dressed in civilian clothes—a gray fur-collared overcoat, an almost new gray caracul hat (part of the issue that went to all of the higher police officers at the November holiday). He was, in fact, the very same Petrov who had led the detail that searched the Morgans in their National Hotel suite. He had been personally briefed by Andropov on how to carry out the arrest of Sokolov. Andropov was in no mood to permit any "accidents"; the propaganda and publicity surrounding Sokolov's arrest was going to be damaging enough without compounding it by physical violence. Even if Sokolov offered resistance, the instruction to Petrov was to handle the writer with extreme care.

Now Petrov took from his pocket the warrant of arrest. "We have the warrant for your arrest here," he said. "You may examine it if you like. Everything is in order. You are required to accompany us in connection with very serious charges which have been placed against you."

Andrei took the warrant and read it swiftly. It was, of course, in order insofar as any Soviet police action might be said to be in order. He looked at the paper for a moment and turned to his wife. "The document appears to be in order, my beloved Stasia. I must go." He embraced her and gave his hand to her mother. "Do not be afraid." Stasia threw herself against Andrei violently. "We will not be afraid," she said. "It is for them to be afraid."

"Please tell our friends," he said. He stepped to the corner of the room, picked up his old Zek *telogreika*, donned it and turned to the police detail, his suitcase in hand.

Petrov blanched when he saw the jacket with its telltale cotton stripe and the insignia S-203. "You know, Andrei Ilych," he said, "that's not at all necessary. Certainly you have something more appropriate to wear."

Andrei drew himself up. "There is nothing more appropriate to wear," he said. "This *telogreika* saved my life in the old days. I count on it to save my life again."

Petrov stood in indecision. He was on the verge of ordering his men to remove the jacket from Sokolov's back. Then remembering his instructions from Andropov, he said, "Well, Andrei Ilych, that's your decision. Now you must come with us."

Suddenly Andrei's body stiffened. He was going back to prison. Perhaps he was seeing his wife for the last time. Who knew what fate would bring him? Must he now—like so many millions before him—simply shuffle off, a sheep led to slaughter? Was not such submission the secret of the iron hold the police maintained on the Russian people?

"No," said Andrei. "I will not accompany you voluntarily. I will not conspire with you to strangle the freedom of the Russian people. I do not have the strength to resist four powerful men. But I will not of my own accord take one step beside the praetorians of Russian power."

He spoke these words slowly, piercing Petrov with a glance so powerful that the officer turned down his eyes.

"There's no need to play the child, Andrei Ilych," Petrov muttered. "Why make a fuss? It's *nekulturny*, not cultured."

"It's time," Andrei said, "for someone to play the man. There is no place for culture in a struggle with barbarians."

Petrov clenched his teeth and nodded to his men. They rushed forward, grabbing Andrei's arms, and bodily lifted him. One flung open the door and they crossed the threshold, Andrei bolt upright, his arms crossed across his chest.

Petrov stood as if perplexed as to what to do. Then he noticed that his men had left Andrei's battered suitcase behind. He grabbed it, dashed out the door, slammed it and hurried down the staircase to the street, where he found a small crowd, possibly of twenty people, blocked away from the building by plainclothesmen, who exhorted them to move. They stood silently watching the three officers, now assisted by two more, loading into an unmarked gray Chaika a middle-aged full-bearded man who was wearing an unmistakably marked *telogreika*, worn and ragged, bearing in front and back the legend "S-203."

"My God," one white-shawled woman exclaimed as the door of the Chaika swung shut and the car pulled from the curb. "It was *him*."

*   *   *

The ride from the flat off Gorky Street to the Lubyanka took less than ten minutes. Andrei was crammed into the rear seat of the Chaika, an officer on either side. Petrov sat in front, communicating with someone by the radiotelephone. "Yes," Andrei heard him say. "Yes, we have him. No. No problems. No difficulties. Well, just a small matter. Nothing serious."

Nothing serious, Andrei thought, nothing serious in the arrest of a man. Nothing serious in the violation of human rights. Nothing serious in the rape of civil liberties. No difficulties. All was in order on this Christmas night in the Russian state.

The car moved up the Lubyanka Hill past the Metropol hotel at a smooth rate, neither fast nor slow. It turned left into the Sretenka, and in a moment was at the great courtyard gates of the Lubyanka—they swung open when the headlights of the car flicked onto them. Were the guards inside alert and waiting for this particular car? Andrei wondered. Or was there some new electronic gadgetry that enabled the car itself to activate the opening of the gates? Within, the courtyard was as he remembered it. The car halted at the entrance, where a guard carrying a Tommy gun smartly saluted Petrov. Sokolov did not again insist on being carried. He had made his point. He stepped out of the car and was escorted into the familiar reception room. Some things, he thought to himself, never really change. The reception room seemed a bit cleaner. The lighting was better. They had installed some new fixtures in the ceiling. But everything else was the same. The same blank-faced guards. The same blank-faced clerks. The same blank-faced Tommy gunners.

There was no wait this time. He was not processed through the reception bureau. Instead, he was led swiftly by Petrov and the arrest detail past the security door and into the interior. Andrei felt instantly at home and instantly knew from the direction that he was being taken not to the cell block but toward the interrogation rooms. When they came to the end of a corridor and stepped into an elevator manned by a uniformed and armed guard, he realized that he was not headed for any ordinary interrogation.

The elevator whizzed upward and halted. He was whisked out along a carpeted corridor past well-lighted offices with frosted glass doors. This was, he knew, the very heart of the police authority, the executive suite of the Lubyanka. At the end of the corridor a guard was seated at a desk beside a closed door. The party halted a moment. The guard spoke a word on the telephone, the door was opened and they hurried through a reception room. The walls, Andrei noticed, were paneled halfway up in Finnish birch. There was a portrait of Dzerzhinsky, the first chief of Soviet secret police, and one of Brezhnev. They entered another office. A long green-baize-covered table occupied most of it. There were chairs along both sides, a water carafe of blue Czech crystal on a glass tray. Nothing else.

Here Andrei and his escort stood for a moment. The police officers were uncomfortable. Petrov stood first on one foot, then on another. Suddenly a door at the end of the room opened, and a man of medium height with a rather Slavic face, broad shoulders and graying blond hair entered the room. Andrei instantly recognized him. It was Andropov, the Minister of State Security. Andropov walked to the head of the table, called Petrov to his side and spoke an inaudible word to him. Petrov nodded, and the security detail left the room. Andrei stood alone, halfway down the table from the Security Minister.

Andropov stared at Andrei, started to say something, thought the better of it, moved to sit down at the table, then changing his mind, slowly walked along the table until he was standing across from Andrei on the other side of the green-baize barricade.

"You know why you are here," he said quietly.

"Because your men compelled me to accompany them," Andrei replied.

Andropov narrowed his eyes. "Let's not play games," he said. "You are here because you are guilty of treason to the Soviet state. What do you have to say for yourself?"

"If loyalty to the Russian people is treason to the Soviet state," he said, "then you may count me guilty."

"The Soviet state and the Soviet people are as one."

"Then why has the Soviet state found it necessary to execute Russian people by the millions and sentence tens of millions to forced labor camps and permanent exile?"

"Here we ask questions," said Andropov shortly. "It is for you to answer."

"Perhaps," said Andrei, "that is the root of the problem."

Andropov looked carefully at Andrei. His eyes seemed riveted on the ancient *telogreika* and its telltale legend—S-203. How often, Andrei wondered, has the Minister of State Security actually seen a simple *zek* in his simple costume, one of Russia's most familiar sights?

"I did not bring you here tonight to debate philosophy," Andropov said. "The Soviet state does not need your help in resolving any questions of principle. You have been brought here to answer to the most serious of crimes—the crime of treason. You know the penalty."

"I know the penalty which Soviet law prescribes for the crime of treason," said Andrei. "But do you know whom the Russian people hold guilty of the crime of treason against their nation?"

Color appeared in Andropov's face. "You are here, Citizen Sokolov, to answer to crimes, not to insult the state."

"It is not I who speak," Andrei said. "I am merely the voice of those millions, those tens of millions whose voices are silent because their lives have been forfeit to what you call Soviet justice."

Andropov could restrain himself no longer. "Why do you wear that filthy article of clothing?"

"It is the uniform of the Russian people," Andrei said. "I wear it with pride."

"I can see there is no point in talking with you," Andropov said. "You are a true recidivist. You are beyond rehabilitation. For such as you . . ." Andropov's voice trailed off.

"Why don't you finish the sentence?" Andrei said. "Didn't Stalin always say, 'For such as you the only cure is to shorten you by a head'— wasn't that in your mind?"

Andropov stared at Andrei. To Andrei's surprise he saw in the Security chief's eyes some kind of appeal—what it might be he did not know. And it was gone in a flash.

Andropov did not respond to Andrei's comment. He turned and took a step back toward the door, then turned again. "Your fate is settled, Citizen Sokolov," he said. "Do you understand that? I thought you might have some word to say, some explanation of your conduct, some last sentiment that you wished to express. You fought for your country during the war—"

"Yes," said Andrei cutting in, "I fought for my country. I believed in my country. I still believe in my country. I believe in its great heritage. In the Dekabristi. In Herzen. In the Narodnaya Volya. In the SR's. Yes, and in the early Bolsheviks. I believe in the Russian people."

Andropov stared at Sokolov, his jaw clenched firm. "In the Dekabristi . . . In Herzen. Yes, don't we all . . ." Andropov muttered so vaguely that Andrei somehow thought the thoughts of the minister had drifted far away.

There was a moment's silence. Then Andropov spoke again, in a different voice. "The Soviet state cannot tolerate your behavior, Citizen Sokolov," he said sharply. "You know that, and you know the consequences."

He pressed a button at the end of the table. Petrov and his men immediately entered.

"Take him away," Andropov snapped, turning and walking swiftly from the room.

* * *

Again the escort surrounded Andrei, but this time they moved very swiftly. The open elevator awaited them. In a moment they were back on the ground floor. Andrei was quickly processed into the prison. His pockets were emptied, his suitcase and jacket registered, and he was placed in a cell, a perfectly comfortable cell. It had a small red carpet on the floor. A decent cot. A water basin and a flush, seatless toilet.

Andrei had never occupied so comfortable a cell in the Lubyanka or any other Soviet prison. It must be one usually reserved for foreigners, he thought. They would never put Russians into such pleasant quarters.

Andrei threw himself on the cot. The light burned in the ceiling. It made no difference to him. He was tired, but he was tremendously excited.

What next? Andropov's cryptic remarks could mean anything—execution, exile, imprisonment. Yet there was implicit in the Minister's action some unstated factor. Why had the Minister himself spoken with him? What had the curious look signified?

In Czarist days, not infrequently a Minister of State might engage in philosophical argument with a political prisoner, particularly an important one, but this had not been the habit in the Soviet state. Stalin had never been interested in the philosophy of his opponents, nor had his successors. Not so with Andropov. Andropov had sought something from the conversation, something he did not get, possibly something he was afraid to ask.

Andrei turned his thoughts away from the enigma of Andropov and to his own fate. Suddenly there came into his mind the image of the Caucasian officer in the supply company, the brooding captain who had ordered the drover beaten to death. He thought of Stasia's words about the deep strain of violence in the Russian peasant. And of cruelty. Truly, he told himself, we are the dark people. Light comes to us slowly, very slowly. Logic told him they did not dare take his life. Instinct told him: Don't be too certain. They are afraid, Andrei said, and it is when they are afraid that they are most dangerous.

He must have drowsed off, for the next thing he was aware of was a clang at the cell door and the voice of a turnkey: "Come, you are wanted."

Andrei shook himself awake. He had no idea how long he had been asleep. Once again he walked ahead of the guard, his eyes on the floor. Once again he heard the *snap-snap-snap* of the guard's fingers, warning that a prisoner's convoy was moving down the halls.

He found himself quickly in the big reception room. Miraculously, his old suitcase was again in his hand, and he was put with an escort of four men into a police van that rolled out of the courtyard, through the famous Gates of Hell and into the dark predawn Moscow streets. Where was he bound? He had lost that knack of direction which had been so acute nearly twenty years before. It was a long drive. Not Lefortovo. Not Butyrka. Not one of the railroad stations. What could it be? Finally the car ground to a stop, and Andrei was led into a bare-walled building of cement-block construction. It was windowless. A chill ran down Andrei's back—was it an execution chamber? Common sense drove away that macabre thought. After all, the cellars of Lubyanka were still available for executions. Then he heard a plane warming up not too far away. Of course, an airport. But where was he being flown?

An hour passed in silence, the guards withdrawn in their sheep-skins, Andrei huddled in his old *telogreika*. Then three police officers entered and stepped briskly up to Andrei. One drew out a sheet of paper. It was, Andrei could see, an official document.

"I have been instructed," the officer said, "to inform you of the action of the Supreme Soviet of the Union of Soviet Socialist Republics: 'For acts incompatible with the rights, privileges and obligations of Soviet citizenship and hostile to the order of the Soviet state, you, Andrei Ilych Sokolov, are by decree of the Presidium of the Supreme Soviet deprived of Soviet citizenship. Consequently, and in conformity with the above order, you are to be deported from the USSR without the right of return.' "

Chapter 58

ANDREI sank deep into his seat in the airplane. He had been hustled aboard by a plainclothes detail—apparently at the last minute, since the plane departed almost as soon as he was seated with a burly security guard beside him. He and his guard were alone in a forward compartment, and he saw no other passengers—if there were other passengers. He was not told his destination before boarding, and when he asked the escort guard, he got nothing but a sullen frown.

Where was he bound? The plane had climbed through cloud cover, and he could not judge the direction because higher clouds obscured the sun. He presumed he was flying west but had no assurance of this fact. He was rushing through the air at hundreds of miles an hour, but where he was headed and where he would land he did not know. This flight through the clouds in an unknown plane with a silent beetle-browed companion in a direction he could not guess to a secret destination, thought Andrei, was in fact the very symbol of man's fate and specifically the fate of modern Russian man.

His mind gnawed at the enigma. He could not shake from his mind the fate of Antaeus, his strength ebbing away when his feet were torn from the soil of his native earth. What about himself? Could he survive banishment from the black Russian land? This worry had been in his mind during the long last talks with Stasia, but he had carefully concealed it from her, embracing her confidence that wherever they might find themselves they could, within their own close warmth, kindle the spirit of Russia, set the flame burning so strongly that it would warm the inner glades of their souls, despite the long leagues which separated them from the motherland.

Was he less confident now? Andrei looked about him. His eyes fell on the beefy guard, who sprawled in the seat beside him. He looked at the fraying upholstery of the seats, the functional gray décor. His body throbbed to the steady vibration of the huge engines. He felt detached from any connection with life, severed from the earth of Russia and the global solidity of the world, rushing through nowhere into nowhere. There came back to him the memory of that long night in the early days at the front, the endless ride on the railroad flat car through the darkness, not a light showing, the whole world asleep, the great train roaring through the endless gloom, and his wondering whether even the locomotive engineer could be certain of their destination.

So too it seemed today. The plane droned through the clouds. No sight of land. No sight of sun. Nothing to prove that any other human existed beside himself and the hulk of the guard slumped beside him, giving off the musky odor of many days without a bath.

There came to Andrei's mind Gogol's image of Russia, the troika, madly dashing through the air, harness jangling, horses neighing, coachman's long whip crackling—dashing, dashing toward the horizon—but who knew what its destination might be?

But he asked himself, was this not the eternal Russian excuse for submission to fate? Was he not already sinking into the pathos of the emigré, overwhelmed by strengths beyond his strength? Was not this, in fact, the fallacy which had conditioned Russian life for centuries? Oblomovitis, that fatal disease which Goncharov had diagnosed a century before—the affliction of the complaisant landowner, Oblomov, filled with good intentions but spending the whole day in his dressing gown, reclining on his couch, drinking his tea and thinking about the great feats he would accomplish in the future, someday—someday that never came?

As soon as Andrei asked himself the question he knew the answer. His thoughts on this gloomy plane ride were nothing less than a negation of the whole philosophy of his life. He pulled himself upright in his chair, shaking his head to clear his ears, which throbbed with the unaccustomed air pressure, and by that act, he felt confidence flow back into his being. He was not the first Russian writer to go into exile—Herzen, Turgenev, Gorky, the tradition was as old as Russia. Nor was it only writers who had been compelled to leave their country. All through the nineteenth century the best of Russia's thinkers had been driven from the gray land of Czarist oppression, and so it was today. He was not the first. He would not be the last.

Andrei told himself that he must consider practical matters. Where was he being taken?

He hoped, *all* the way West—not to Warsaw or Berlin. A moment's thought convinced him that he must be en route to some capital beyond Moscow's orbit. It might be Helsinki, but that was really too close. They would have landed in Helsinki already if that was the destination. Perhaps Stockholm. Maybe Paris or London. West Germany? Not very likely. Switzerland? Possible. What of Stasia and the children—would they be permitted to follow him? Yes. That seemed to be almost certain. He would demand their immediate release the moment he touched down. But there was something about the way he had been treated—the correctness of the arrest, the conversation with Andropov, the good lodgings at the Lubyanka, the technical formality of the removal of his Soviet citizenship—all this gave him great confidence.

In a sense, he thought, this was, in fact, a kind of rear-guard action by the rulers. He had wounded them savagely, but they were not prepared to return blow for blow. And he understood their reasons. The international political climate did not favor imposing upon him the reprisals which their rage dictated. If they were unwilling to send him to Siberia, they would not wish an even greater cause célèbre by persecuting his innocent wife and children. He had, in fact, been right in his analysis of the effects of the Black Book. It had been the thunderbolt that he had originally perceived it would be. It had knocked them off their balance.

The plane was beginning to descend. His bulky companion had begun to stir. Andrei hunched himself forward, looking out the window. What country would emerge from the clouds below him? What fate lay still hidden in that occluded mist?

*　　*　　*

The plane had landed and was turning at the end of a long runway. Andrei could not be certain yet what city it was, nor what country. There had been a brief glimpse of trees, limbs barren, of fields dressed in the yellow green of winter and the flash of red tile roofs. Holland? He watched at the window as the plane moved slowly up the long runway and moved into the taxi path leading to the terminal. He saw a Lufthansa plane with its blue markings just ahead. Then an Air France liner, a Pan American plane, another Lufthansa and another. Germany beyond doubt. What city? Frankfurt, perhaps.

He turned to the security man. "Frankfurt?" he asked. The security man looked blindly through him. Andrei shook his head. Some things never changed, could not change. The plane had halted close to the terminal. He heard the bustle of passengers. Voices. He was *not* alone. He had simply been placed alone in the forward compartment. He unbuckled his seat belt. The security man unbuckled his and rose heavily, restraining Andrei with one hand: "Just a moment."

Andrei rose, paying the man no heed. He was in Germany. The realm of the KGB did not extend to Germany. He reached above him and pulled down his old *telogreika*, slowly pulling it over his shoulders. His battered suitcase had been placed beneath the seat. He picked it up and moved into the aisle. The security man had disappeared. Andrei pushed through the curtains. The last passengers had disembarked. Two Aeroflot stewardesses stood talking at the door. Andrei walked forward a bit uncertainly, then braced his shoulders. He approached the young women, both blond and heavily built, and saw them draw in their breaths simultaneously—as if they had seen a ghost. So, he told himself grimly, they actually have. He stepped forward now, head high and almost imperious. When he came to the door, he turned to the young women and said seriously, *"Do svidanya.* Until we meet again." He could almost feel them shrink away. Then he ducked his head and walked out onto the steps.

A cheer arose. He saw below him a small group of men, one of them with his arms full of flowers. A bit further back, in a semicircle firmly maintained by police, stood several hundred people, among them what seemed to be scores of television crews and cameramen, now all shouting to him. He paused at the top of the steps, waving a greeting with one hand, then slowly descended. He had not reached the last step when a tall figure whom he instantly recognized as the writer Hans Koch broke from the group, rushed up and flung his arms, laden with flowers, around Andrei's old windbreaker.

"Welcome!" said Koch. "A thousand times welcome!"

Andrei dropped his suitcase and returned the embrace, kissing Koch on each cheek.

"So," he said, "I am in Germany."

"Didn't you know?" Koch said in surprise.

"Only now, when the plane taxied to its landing," said Andrei. "I was not told. It might have been Siberia or Magadan or the North Pole."

The other officials surrounded him, plied him with questions and suggestions. Andrei, his ears long unaccustomed to German, was confused.

"I will take you to my house," Koch said, "so you can collect your thoughts, decide what to do. But—first, do you have a word for the press?"

"I do," said Andrei. He picked up his suitcase, holding on to it even when one of the officials tried to wrest it from his grasp. He squared his shoulders and walked to the police barricade. There was a new outburst of shouting. Cheers. Instructions. Glares and shoving among the newsmen. Finally Andrei held up his head. He kept it there until the crowd quieted.

"I thank you," Andrei said, "and, through you, all my friends in the West. I stand here a Russian writer forcibly torn from his own soil, an immigrant against my will. But I stand here proudly because I am the spokesmen of those Russian men and women, both living and dead, who are unable to speak for themselves. I am only their voice. Nothing more. I wear their uniform, the uniform of the *lager,* the prison camps, the uniform of the *zek.* Note it well. It is unfamiliar to you in the West, but we in Russia have lived in it, slept in it, died in it for many years. That era is now ending. And my presence in your midst is a token of its end. It is ending not because of myself, but because of a weapon more powerful than the sword, a thousand times more powerful than the atom bomb. The name of that weapon is truth, *pravda* as we say in Russia, the word. Before the power of the word, no tyranny, not even the dark tyranny of Russia, can stand.

"The Russian state is the most powerful tyranny history has known. But there is no praetorian guard which can stand up to a small taste of truth. If at first it seems to have no effect—wait. Be patient. It is more strong than any poison of the Borgias, more potent than any elixir.

"I thank you, my comrades of the West. You have helped to spread the truth and the days of the Moscow tyrants are numbered. They know it. They are afraid. They may think that they have rid themselves of Andrei Ilych Sokolov. So they have, physically. I am beyond the borders of my country. But I have not left Russia in spirit. I stand with those tens of millions of my countrymen who are the great body of Russia.

"I ask but one thing of you. Remind Moscow that the voice of Russia still speaks. And remind Moscow that I expect my wife and my family to join me within the fewest possible days."

Andrei turned to Koch. He reached in his pocket and pulled out his old watch, looking at it with care. "Come, my dear comrade, it is time we left. I think I have said enough. I can rest now. For a few hours. But not more. There is so much to do. So little time. And I must get to work."

About the Author

HARRISON E. SALISBURY is one of America's
most distinguished journalists. He began his writing
career at the University of Minnesota, ·where he
wrote short stories and poetry. For many years he
served as a reporter and correspondent particularly
in the Soviet Union, first during World War II and
later as Moscow correspondent for *The New York
Times* from 1949 to 1952. As associate editor of the
Times, he originated and edited the *Times'* Op-Ed
page. He won a Pulitzer Prize in 1955 for his reporting from Russia and is now serving as president
of the National Institute of Arts and Letters.

Mr. Salisbury is the author of many books. *The
Gates of Hell* is his second novel in a Russian
setting. He has spent almost half of his life in and
out of Russia since the days of World War II, living
in Moscow and in the Russian countryside and
traveling the land from the Arctic tundra and the
wastelands of the prison camps to the subtropical
oases of Central Asia.

Harrison Salisbury lives in New York and Con-
necticut with his wife, Charlotte, who is also a
writer.